THE *Stowaway* SERIES

AWARD-WINNING AUTHOR

ALYSSA MILANI

ALYSSA MILANI

The Stowaway Series

Trigger Warning List:

Motorcycle gang

Violence

Language

Gun use

Abuse (among men and women)

Forced sexual activity

Drug use

Foul language

Multiple partners

Betrayal (family betrayal, cheating, gang related)

Mention of sex trafficking (saving the women)

Kidnapping

Death/Murder (blood and gore)

Mention of suicide

Religious views (talks of God)

Graphic sex scenes

I

Forbidden

Zay

AWARD-WINNING AUTHOR
ALYSSA MILANI
FORBIDDEN
THE STOWAWAY SERIES - PART ONE

Choking on my vomit, I gasp as panic rushes through me and I become aware of my surroundings. Turning on my side just in time as vomit spews out of me. Groaning, I think I overdid it last night.

My situation merits it.

No, my situation merits more than chugging from a bottle of Jack and hoping for the best.

I didn't get the best.

I got dizzy.

I got sick.

I almost choked to death.

And now I'm hungover.

I scramble out of bed and charge for the bathroom. I don't think my insides are done battling with the alcohol.

Throwing up again, I moan, wiping my mouth with the back of my hand.

If death had an image, my face would be the cover. Bags under my hazel eyes, red, and watery. Puke is still caked to my neck and in my brown hair.

I'm a mess.

Stumbling into the shower fully clothed, I turn the knob and wince. The water pours over me in bursts of cold at first to wake me the heck up. Now it's warm, soaking into my chilled skin. I'm watching the shower of water, my mind buzzing a mile a minute.

It's crazy how the past twenty-four hours changed my life.

Snap of a finger.

Flip of a dime.

Everything is different.

Closing my eyes, I groan again, nausea taking over. I haven't drunk like this in months. The raging alcoholic in me begging for more of the juice to tame the beasts battling with my insides.

I don't know how long I've been here but the tiny bathroom is fogged. This is my cue to wash the vomit from my body.

This disturbance lurks over me.

I'm still trying to figure out how in the hell I ended up here.

All my wrongdoings catching up with me.

It's deserved, though. *We reap the consequences we sow.* Someone once told me that. It had no meaning then. It sure does now. It has more meaning than I can even fathom.

I wrap a towel around my chest and make my way into the room, stopping dead in my tracks when I see him leaning on the doorframe, smirking at me. The mysterious giant of a man who scares me half to death.

"Good shower?" he asks, his piercing blue eyes scanning me. Robustly tall. Broad chest. Tattoos and piercings. He looks dangerous. Screams violence. He's the devil walking this plane. Savage. Evil. I wouldn't put it past him to burst into flames and laugh as he tortures me.

I nod, tightening the towel around my torso. The way he's looking at me, I'm sure he wants me to drop it. Just for a peek. Maybe a taste. His eyes travel up and down, lingering on my chest and legs a moment longer than I'd like. Men. All the damn same, aren't they?

He points at the bed. "Clean that up, breakfast is ready."

Breakfast, ugh.

Just the thought of food is turning my stomach.

But I do as I'm told. If I don't, God won't be here to save me.

Taking the sheets off the bed, I toss them in the laundry, and make for the kitchen.

It's so quiet here.

Too quiet.

Last night he had music playing and a fire burning. We arrived at the cabin at half-past eleven and I went straight for the booze, drowning myself in it so the thought of being here wouldn't be so bad. I'd rather be lost in a drunken daze. It didn't work, did it? I'm stuck in this cabin, and now I'm so hungover the thought of alcohol is making me nauseated.

This morning, only the fire crackles in the living room.

Pancakes are at the table. Coffee and orange juice, too.

Coffee won't kill me.

Unless he spiked it.

He shakes the bottle of Jack Daniel's. "Little hair of the dog?"

Ugh. Gosh, thinking of alcohol right now makes me want to gag. I shake my head, slowly sitting in one of the grey fabric chairs. The cabin is beautiful. Rustic, yet modern and bright. So damn bright. The entire back wall is windows and glass. Open kitchen to the living room with the dining table in between. If it wasn't for this predicament I've found myself in, this place could be a fun getaway.

He sits at the head of the table to my left, waggling his eyebrows at me when he passes me some syrup. "Eat up, we got a busy day today."

I sip my coffee. "What're we doing?"

He chuckles, a smug grin spreading to his face. "Nothing."

"Nothing, as in you won't tell me, or nothing, as in literally nothing."

His mouth is full of pancakes, no syrup. "The latter."

I scoff. "Why the fuck am I here? I have nothing to do with this."

He grunts, chewing with his mouth open like a rabid dog. "You think I want to babysit you while your boyfriend—"

"—ex-boyfriend—"

"—is paying us back? This ain't some game he's involved in. This is life or death, Zay. It's not my fault he shoved you in the middle of it."

Growling, I bang my fists on the table. "I didn't want to be dragged into this mess. You fucking assholes broke into my dorm and kidnapped me."

He chuckles, leaning back in his chair. "With good reason, I assure you."

I hate how nonchalant he's being. It's pissing me off and scaring the crap out of me. "What reason could that be, huh? Because as I see it, holding me captive in some cabin in the middle of fucking nowhere isn't reason enough."

He pushes the syrup forward, urging me to eat without saying it. I'm too angry to eat. Too nauseated and hungover to eat. I want answers, I want Adam, and I just want to go home.

"You should feel lucky that *I'm* the one watching you."

I roll my eyes. "Because of your witty charm? Please, save it."

He laughs, pointing his fork at me before taking a savage bite. "If it were any of my other guys, they'd have tried something. If you said no, they'd have tried again and again until you weren't able to say no anymore. Catch my drift?"

"What, like, rape me?"

He shrugs a shoulder. "You said it."

Tears well in my eyes, looking at this man who could probably snap me in half with one hand. "I just wanna go home."

"You'll go home, just not today."

"And if Adam can't get the money?"

He shrugs again. "Let's hope that doesn't happen, yeah?"

My breathing stutters as I stare at this man with dark tattoos on his arms.

I'm going to die here.

In this shitty cabin.

And it's all Adam's fault.

Riggs

Twenty-four hours ago, this brown-haired bombshell with the creamiest, softest skin was dropped onto my lap. Not in the way I would have liked or the way I enjoy. In the way of redemption for my sins. Shit, sins that aren't even mine to begin with.

This isn't my style. I don't babysit women.

I fuck them, use and abuse them until I get what I want.

Not babysit.

Twenty-four hours ago our motorcycle club was told to meet in a barn outside of town.

I'd been there before, a ratty little shack with hay on the floor, and horses in the stalls. The owners owed us big and let us do our bidding there when we needed it.

Well, we needed it.

Adam was on his knees, short blonde hair riddled with sweat, begging Crew to give him more time. Crew gave me a look that said *like this guy's pleading will do any good.*

Always knew the kid was never cut out for this shit.

"Just give me one more week, please, Crew. I'm good for it. You know I am," Adam said, hands clasped together and shaking at Crew. All blue eyes and blonde hair, out of place for this life. Kid deserves better, but all he got was this.

Choking on a laugh, I looked at Banks as he cocked the gun, ready to fire.

Crew put up his hand, silencing everyone. Even the rat on his knees. "You're telling me, in seven days, you can get me my money. Five hundred thousand, cash. Unmarked?"

Adam nodded quickly like a little boy making a vow for the first time. "Seven days. I promise."

Banks cackled. "Good fucking riddance."

Crew snapped his fingers. "Do you want to know what'll happen if you don't?"

"You'll kill me," Adam said, still begging, still praying.

Crew snickered, looking at me. "That'd be too easy." He snapped his fingers again.

Thin legs thrashed in the air. Pink panties flashed us from underneath that little red dress. Sexy little thing. Face was covered in a black bag, probably with a gag in her mouth, too. Cleavage hanging out, giving us boys a tease. The creamiest skin I couldn't wait to slide my tongue all over.

Sex on a stick.

The woman was brought to her knees beside Adam, the bag ripped off her head and the gag spat out as soon as she was able. Beautiful wasn't the word to describe this woman. I felt an arrow puncture my chest as she caught my eye for a split second. Something was pulling me to her, dragging me against my will. It took an instant to know that I would lay my life on the line for her. No matter the cost. And I couldn't understand why.

She frantically looked around until she caught Adam's eyes, then the scared little minx turned savage. "Adam? What the fuck is this?"

Crew clapped his hands. "You have seven days to get my money. You don't—" He made his way to the goddess on her knees. "—I'll send you her head."

"What?" she screamed. "What the fuck did you get yourself into?"

Adam wept, reaching for her hand but she shoved him, knocking him over. "I'm sorry, Zay."

"You're sorry?" She rose to her feet, towering over him. "You're fucking *sorry?*"

She bent down to punch him. Crew laughed, watching it happen before he instructed me to step in. *Don't mind if I do.* I'll have my paws all over the little wildcat in no time. I let her punch him once before I stepped in.

She was light; I got her hooked in one arm as she spat profanities at Adam. "…fucking cock sucker asshole dickbag—"

"Enough," Crew shouted.

She spat again. "Fuck you."

Crew chuckled, studying her in my arms. "Don't tempt me."

"What're the orders, boss?" I asked, a growl rumbling through me as her coconut perfume hit me square in the chest. I was almost brought to my knees.

"Cabin." He cocked his head at my bike. "If you don't hear from me in seven days, come home. Alone."

She whimpered in my arms. The type of whimper I wanted to wrap up and hold on to.

Protect her from.

"I'm gonna fucking kill you, Adam, you worthless piece of shit," she yelled, struggling to get free.

Tossing her over my shoulder, I nodded at Crew, heading for my bike.

My bike's the only thing that keeps me at peace. When I ride her, the air on my skin makes me feel free. Rid of this life. Rid of the sins I made. Rid of everything I ever did.

The little wildcat was pounding on my back, kicking and swearing at me. I liked this little firecracker.

Throwing her off my shoulder, I slammed her onto her feet, towering over her by a mile. "You done?"

Her big hazel eyes filled riddled tears.

Scared.

Fearful.

Love the smell of it. The rush.

It excites me when people look at me this way.

That's why I'm in the business. I love the thrill of the madness.

I stand by the guy who runs the show. The position that should be mine since my daddy's in the slammer. But I didn't earn that title. I lost that right.

She whimpered, folding her arms over her as a breeze blew in. It's cold at night around here. And she barely had anything on. I never sympathize with the people I have to kill. I accept it. Allow this bullshit to happen because this is the only life I know. But as I saw her skin pebble in front of me, this urge to change took over.

More tears fell down her face as she looked off at the vast nothingness. "You're going to kill me, aren't you?"

Her eyes flickered back to mine, and for the first time since joining the MC, I didn't think I'd be able to pull the trigger. The way her eyes connected with mine, diving deep into my soul. Changing me. Invading. Shit, this girl's got my mind going wild.

I shrugged out of my jacket and handed it to her; the thing's like a comforter, but it would keep her warm. "Put it on, we got a long drive ahead of us."

She stared at it, eyebrows pinched together. "What if I refuse?"

I took a breath, rolling my head back. This girl was going to be the death of me. I felt it.

"I'd choose me over those fucks." I pointed behind me at the men beating her boyfriend senseless. He doesn't deserve this, I warned them he was useless. "Now put that jacket on and let's get a move on."

Adam's her boyfriend.

Of course, this bombshell had a boyfriend.

Look at her.

All tits and legs.

Big doe eyes that probably got her whatever she wanted.

Sultry plump lips that would look sexy wrapped around my cock.

The things I would do to this woman.

She took my jacket and put it on. I was right, she disappeared in it. "Well, come on, then. Let's go before you have a hissy fit."

"Me?" I laughed. *This girl is a piece of work.*

She rolled her eyes again and winced when she took a step on the gravel road. She was barefoot. Fuckers couldn't even get her some shoes.

Hoisting her up, I walked to my bike. I barely made it a step and she already wrapped her legs around my waist.

Girl was killing me.

It's been months since I got some.

Tramps we call Snake Biters in the club are getting tiring.

Loose.

I need me a tight little one.

Crew said to bring her to the cabin. He didn't say anything about how to kill some time while there.

I got on my bike and spun her behind me, bringing my rumbling machine to life. "Hold on tight, yeah?"

Her arms slithered around me, squeezing my stomach. "I don't get a helmet?"

I chuckled, tapping her hand. "I'm driving. There's nothing you gotta worry about."

Gravel crunched beneath my tires and I sped off, leaving clouds of dust behind me.

Zay

He guzzles down his coffee and picks up his plate. I don't even know what his name is. I don't think I want to know.

Burly Biker.

Muscled Killer.

Tattooed Manic.

Badass Motherfucker.

Whatever. Today is day one. By Friday, I hope to be back in my own bed with a story that'll haunt my dreams.

"Is there anything I can wear?" I ask as he pours himself another coffee. "My dress is kind of dirty."

He sips from the mug, flinching as the hot liquid touches his lips. "You don't have to wear anything."

I raise my eyebrows and scoff. "You can fuck right off."

He nods his head to the hallway, making for it, and I follow. The room he gave me is right at the end, with double doors and a private bathroom. It's adequate; a king-sized bed, bay windows, and a little fireplace with a loveseat in front of it. It's more than what my dorm has.

His room is right beside it. And that's where he leads me.

Drawers open and slam shut; a t-shirt and boxers are tossed at me. "That's it?"

He nods, leaning his hip on the dresser and folding his arms across his expansive chest. "Tomorrow I'll give you another pair."

I groan and go to my room, slamming the door behind me. No lock on it, of course.

Leaning on the door, I stare at the bay windows, wondering how I can escape through them without him finding out. They're crank windows, so it'd be much harder to cover.

I glance around the room for another exit strategy. The window in the bathroom is too small for me to slide out of, he'll be hot on my tail if I try to make a run for it from the front door. There's nothing but this bay window.

Pinching my eyes together, I let out a breath. I have seven days to plan an escape. Seven miserable days.

After I change, I sit on the unmade bed and fall back, staring at the wood-paneled ceiling for what seems like forever. I'm going to die in this cabin.

In a cabin that's riddled with cobwebs and biker memorabilia. So many posters and metal signs it's like their decorator opened a biker magazine and said *add all to cart*.

I stare at the ceiling until my eyes get heavy and close on their own.

Sleep. I'll sleep off this nightmare and wake up in my dorm room. That's what's going to happen.

It has to.

***

A tap tingles my leg and I jolt, staring up at him. He has his fists pressed into the mattress at the end of the bed. "Lunch."

"I'm not hungry," I say, turning over to face the bay window that overlooks nothing but forestry. The only escape route I can think of.

"Up, now." He pushes off the bed. "Don't make me come in here again."

I chuckle wryly. "You can threaten me all you want, I'm still not getting up."

He takes me by the ankle and drags me off the bed. Kicking and screaming, his grip tightens and he drags me all the way down the hall, ignoring my screams.

As soon as he lets me go in the living room, I scramble to my feet, taking a gander around at two other men in leather vests sitting at the table.

Great.

The blonde one chuckles, eyes scrolling over me. "She is a sexy little one, ain't she?"

I narrow my eyes in disgust. "Fuck you."

The other with long black hair smirks. "Like Crew said, we just might."

The man who brought me here glances at me, nodding at a chair at the table away from the three of them. At least he lets me feel comfortable in his own way by putting me at the other end of the ten-person table. "Sit."

Intimidation at its finest.

Stiffly, I sit. I'm too scared to do anything else as they stare at me.

I watch the men eat their food, looking like lions attacking their prey. Disgusting fuckers. Like they've never been in the presence of a woman before. They probably haven't, who am I kidding? All hookers and prostitutes for this bunch.

"Riggs, tell me. She tight?" The blonde bobs his head at me and chuckles. "She looks tight."

Riggs.

My babysitter's name is Riggs.

"Pig," I tell the blonde.

He laughs, sucking food from his teeth. "Lip." He points at the guy with long hair. "Judas." Then points a thumb at Riggs. "And this hunk of meat is Riggs. He taking good care of you?"

I cross my arms over my chest. "Sure. We have an unspoken agreement. He supplies me booze until he has to kill me, and I don't try to run away." I turn my attention to Riggs. "Right?"

"Sure thing," he says, popping chips in his mouth.

Staring at the three pigs in front of me, I scowl. "Do I seriously need three bodyguards?"

Riggs slides a can of soda to me, cracking one open for himself. "We got a deal going down in the town over." He gulps and belches behind his hand. "They're just staying the night."

Lip sticks his tongue out. "I don't mind keeping your bed warm tonight."

Jesus, this guy is relentless.

"You and Judas take my room. I'll room with Zay." Riggs narrows his eyes as I scrunch my nose and he puts a hand up. "I'll take the couch in the room, relax."

"I didn't say anything," I say, picking up the sandwich.

He drains his soda. "Your face said enough."

Silence falls over us. Only the irritating sound of their chewing fills the gap. I gulp some soda and look out the window. All my life, I've found myself staring out the window wishing I were someplace else. Free. I've been trapped in a life that was laid out for me since I was a kid.

None of the decisions have been mine. It's probably why I drank and did drugs. Probably why I used to fuck anything that moved. Until I met Adam, the life I lived was not something to be proud of. My life was disgusting. And all I wanted was to be free of it. When I met Adam, I was free...then he left me, and I wasn't again.

Today is no different. Because today, I wish I was free.

Lip sucks his teeth. "Zay is an interesting name."

"So is Lip."

"Short for Philip," he corrects, sipping some beer.

I look down at my food, unable to even stomach any of it. "Short for Zaynab. My mom named me after the Arabic nurse who saved my life when I came into this world. Means beauty or something."

When I was born, my mother told me the umbilical cord was wrapped around my neck. I came out blue, gasping for breaths. The nurse untangled it, tapped, and rubbed my back, but when my gasps weren't stopping, she had to act fast. She pumped air into my lungs, oxygen next, and soon I was wailing and giving everyone a run for their money. Her name was Zaynab, just like me.

He hums, glancing at Riggs, then Judas. "She's a beauty all right."

These guys are so full of themselves. Talk about misogynistic. Commenting on how tight I am. My appearance and not how tough or strong I am for putting up with their bullshit. No, my looks. Disgusting fuckers, see?

Judas chuckles nasally as he takes a bite out of his sandwich. "Brought you enough food for the week, brother. You shouldn't need to leave."

"Neighbors home?" Riggs asks, moving some chips around on his plate.

Judas nods, speaking with his mouth full as he moves his long hair behind his shoulder. "They think you're here with your lady."

"Least that's what we told them," Lip corrects.

I roll my eyes. "Great."

"Brought you some clothes, too. So you don't gotta wear Riggs's shit," Judas says. "Fed your fish, too."

"Aren't you considerate?" I crack my knuckles and look out the window again. Freedom is a taste away, but I won't get very far with these men sitting here, that's for sure. I wonder how far I can get, maybe to the edge of the property line before the trees take over? All the way to their bikes in the driveway before I'm slung over one of their shoulders? It's useless even thinking about trying to escape while they're sitting here. Maybe when it's just Riggs and I…I'll distract him and make a break for it. "So, all Adam owes you guys is five hundred grand?"

Lip nods, tonguing his cheek. Riggs threads his ringed fingers together, propping his elbows on the table in front of him. Judas side-glances at me as he eats. I've got their attention. Three sets of eyes on me. Riggs's blue eyes seem to shine brighter when they lock with mine.

I nod, getting up and going for the bottle of Jack Daniel's I was milking last night. "If all he owes you is that, then I can get it for you. No problem. But if he owes more than just money—" I pause, looking at the men as they rake their eyes over me and watch me like sharks. "If I pay you guys what he owes, can you let me go?"

Lip chuckles, standing up and coming to me. I step back until my ass hits the couch. "How do we know you ain't gonna go to the cops?"

I pop the top off the bottle and chug. "Believe me, Lip, I'd be in just as much trouble as you. So trust me. I *ain't* going to call the cops on you."

Riggs sits back, staring at me with this look in his eye. A look that's been driving me wild since I met him. The way it scans me, eats me up, and smothers me…with that tongue that teases me every time he licks his lips.

He's trouble.

Dangerous.

And yet, I wouldn't mind dipping a toe in trouble.

Just for a night.

Lip tilts my chin up and takes the bottle from me, retreating to the table to finish eating. "It's something we can bring up to Crew."

He points at my chair, instructing me to sit back down without saying anything. I roll my neck and hesitantly sit back down. Maybe my offer is a good one? I'll get them five hundred grand, something my parents won't miss—the fuckers have enough of it—and they'll let me go. I pray it works.

I bend my leg up on the chair and look at the food in front of me. I don't even know if I can stomach this. Not with the taste of freedom right on the other side of the glass doors. I'll run without looking back and lose them in the forest. Hide in a bush or find a ditch somewhere. I can do it, they're distracted with eating. I can get up and run right now. Something is holding me back. Maybe it's the thought of these men grabbing hold of me and torturing me into submission. Killing me.

I chose not to run away…yet.

As I'm in my thoughts, I glance up at Riggs who has his eyes all over me. When our eyes lock, the corner of his mouth twitches and he slowly licks his lips.

Fucking tease.

I haven't thought about sleeping with another guy since Adam walked into my life. But he broke up with me three weeks ago. I've been a saint since then. I'm thinking I might bring out the sinner again this week. Just for the duration of my stay, at least.

Yet, I love Adam; that's what hurts the most about all this stupidity. I love the bastard that's putting me through this.

But seeing Riggs look at me like I'm a prize?

Like I'm perfect?

Well, I might have to go back to my old ways for a night.

"Think Crew will agree?" Judas asks, tying his hair in a low-hanging knot.

Riggs shrugs, taking a lavish bite of his sandwich and speaking with his mouth full. Why wouldn't he eat with his mouth full? These guys have no manners. I've known him less than a day and I wouldn't put it past him to eat like a savage. "Doubt it, but any extra cash is worth it."

"We should take her money regardless if Crew agrees to it or not. Club can use it," Judas says, eyeing me.

Riggs nods, taking a toothpick and letting it hang from his mouth. "Club can use a lot."

I sense some resentment in his tone. I wonder if he's sour about being my babysitter. I wouldn't want this job, either. I'm a pain in the ass, and I'll be an even bigger pain the longer I'm held captive. Riggs will get a run for his money.

Lip sucks his teeth again, eyeing me. "Not hungry?"

I bring my knee closer to my chest as the ball of my foot rests on the chair. I have nothing to lose, so I speak my mind as usual. "The sight of you turns my stomach."

Judas bursts out laughing.

Riggs brings a fist to his mouth and stifles his.

Lip sits back in his seat, clenching his fist. "You're gonna get cut if you keep it up, bitch."

I roll my eyes and lean forward, taking the Jack Daniel's from the table. "Ooh, I'm shaking."

Lip scoffs, looking at Riggs and Judas. "This gash for real?"

I pour the soda into the glass in front of me with whatever is left in the can, then fill the rest with whiskey. I'm getting hammered again. It'll be easier to deal with these fucks and the fate that's been sealed for me.

"Leave it alone, it ain't worth your time," Riggs says, looking at Lip as his fists meet the table.

Judas recovers from his chuckling, mouth full. He shakes his sandwich at me with narrowed eyes. "I like you. You got spunk and you ain't afraid of us."

I chug from the glass and grimace, letting out a rush of air from my parted lips. "I don't know if that's a compliment or not."

Judas winks. "Compliment, I guess?"

Lip scoffs, narrowing his eyes at me. "Best be afraid of us, bitch. You have no idea what we can do to you."

I roll my eyes again and gulp the rest of my drink, carbonated bubbles making my nose tingle and my eyes tear up. I'm not a heavy soda drinker, I like sweet drinks with strong liquor. But whiskey and soda will have to do for the duration of my stay.

Riggs smirks, eyeing me up and down for the sixth time this afternoon. He doesn't say anything, but those eyes say enough. I'm sure if it was up to him I'd be sitting here naked with my legs open for them to enjoy an all-you-can-eat buffet.

Though, there's a softness behind that dark exterior. A beauty I'd like to unfold.

There's a need in there.

A need that'll soon match my own.

Riggs

She's still wearing my t-shirt and boxers.

I haven't felt my dick jerk this much around a woman like it does around her.

Mind-blowing.

Gorgeous.

The way her hard nipples make themselves known every time I look at them is a tease all on its own. Like they're ready for me. Waiting for my tongue, my mouth.

She's sitting in front of the fire, cross-legged, and sipping whiskey on the rocks. It's raining outside and there isn't much to do around here, other than yard work.

Lip, Judas, and I are playing a game of cards at the table, and I find myself staring at her. Watching as she pokes the fire every so often. How she brings the glass to her lips and takes the smallest sip. Her tongue touches the rim of the glass before her lips do. I don't think she notices she does this before every sip. It's mesmerizing.

Girl's killing me and doesn't even know it.

Judas taps my arm, drawing my attention away from her. "You coming to the deal tomorrow?"

"No." I bring the beer to my lips. "She's my job for the next seven days. If I leave here, she'd have to come with me. We don't need her compromising the deal with that mouth of hers."

She turns her head to the side. "I heard that."

"Keep copping an attitude and I'll show you what your mouth was made to do." Lip picks up a card and clicks his tongue.

"It was made to make fun of you," she adds.

A growl leaves Lip's mouth and he gets up from his seat, taking two steps before I grab his arm. "Can you believe this gash?"

I chuckle, releasing his arm. "Let it go, brother. Ain't worth it."

She chuckles with her back to us, sipping her whiskey again before she gets up.

Those nipples are teasing me again. She looks damn good in my clothes.

Her elegant stride takes her to the sink, where she downs the rest of her drink before dumping the ice. I like a girl who can knock back a stiff drink. Zay seems like that kind of girl.

I haven't been lucky with the girls in my life. They walked out on me or I walked out on them.

The most recent chick I screwed was for nothing but a hole to put my dick in. One of the whores who works for the club. She's been around, but if I wrap it and close my eyes, her loose little pussy feels good for a few minutes.

I don't do relationships. My last relationship nearly killed me, literally.

I can't get involved with Zay. She's the type of beautiful you want under you, but I'm the type of guy you don't want on top of you. I ruin people. I ruin a lot.

I'll keep my distance from her. No matter what my dick screams, he will not enter her.

Judas eyes her, that shoulder of hers exposed.

The creamiest skin that must taste so sweet.

"Where you off to?" Judas asks.

"Bed." She starts for the hallway and Lip gets up, following her. She glances back before he can even make it two feet, scowling. "Alone."

He smirks. "You'll never scream like you would for me."

She snorts, letting out a laugh. "You can't handle me." She takes a step away and shoos him. "Goodnight." She eyes me and winks, swaying those hips down the hall.

This woman is driving me crazy.

"Oof, that mouth of hers." Lip returns to the table, looking over his shoulder again. "Think Crew would let me tear that up before killing her?"

"*If* we kill her," I correct.

Judas guzzles down his beer and burps. "Think Crew will let them live?"

"Don't see why not, they're giving us money," I say, cracking the bones in my neck.

"Yeah, the money." Lip nods slowly, glancing at Judas before he looks back at the cards on the table. "Money," he whispers, like he's hiding something. Is this not about money?

I hate being in the dark.

I've been in the dark for so long because of my fuck-up. I don't think I'll ever be in the loop anymore. I'm left out of everything. All the important deals. All the decision-making. My daddy was president of this club and my fuck-up got him arrested. My fuck-up will get me killed.

Think it's about time I get out.

I doubt they'll let that happen.

Only way out for me is in a body bag.

Lip runs a hand through his hair. "I'm itching, man."

"Need a fix?" Judas asks. Tapping his pockets. Coke heads, the two of them.

I told Crew not to get involved with drugs. That if he got involved, then our MC would abuse it. My daddy stayed away from drugs. He dealt revenge and guns. Not drugs.

Revenge on those who wronged him. Wrong our charters.

We killed for less than five hundred thousand.

We killed for peanuts.

There's more to this whole thing than they're telling me and it's my own damn fault for being in the dark. My fuck-up bumped me down to being treated like a prospect when I'm Vice President of this club.

Lip laughs, waving away the vial of cocaine. "For some pussy, yes."

"You're not getting anything from her," I say, finishing my drink. "She's off limits."

Judas guffaws. "Called dibs already?"

I roll my eyes and get up for another beer. "She's a job, not someone we fuck."

"She's your responsibility, not mine," Lip says, looking down the hallway. "Ima watch her tonight."

Judas chimes in. "Uh-uh, no you're not. I am—"

"Isn't your old lady pregnant?" I interrupt him and scoff. Judas shrugs it off and looks back at the hallway, too. This pang builds inside me, eating me up, like this girl is mine. "Y'know what, none of you are getting into her room. Crew assigned me to do this stupid job, y'all ain't fucking it."

They stare at each other quickly before Lip cracks a grin and Judas chuckles softly. I can't tell if it's the alcohol getting to them or if they're hiding something.

With my luck, something is likely being kept from me.

Judas elbows me when I sit back down. "Alone with that little hottie for an entire week, betcha your dick will get wet in two days."

I laugh, gulping my beer. "Ain't putting my dick in crazy anymore."

"She's the good kinda crazy, not Natalia crazy," Lip says, dropping his cards in frustration.

He's right.

Zay can be good for a release.

She'll leave me satisfied.

Mesmerized.

The only problem is, it's a release I'm not quite sure I'll be able to let go of.

***

She's curled up in a ball in the middle of the bed. I can hear her teeth chattering from the small-ass couch I'm lying on in the bedroom.

Lip and Judas were adamant about trying to sleep in the room with her. I won, of course.

But I don't win the award for being comfortable because this fucking couch is hard as stone. And she's as cold as a penguin's pecker.

Just my lucky day, isn't it?

I sit up, whipping the tiny-ass blanket off me, and make for the bed. "Hey," I whisper.

Her eyes shoot open and she groans, turning over. "Go away."

I poke her this time and she groans louder, sitting up. "What?"

"It's a king." I wave my hand at the bed. "I'm too damn tall for the couch. You'll have one end of the bed, I'll have the other."

She lies back down and scoots to one side of the bed. "There's a perfectly good couch in the living room."

"You were drunk last night, you're not tonight. I can't risk you running away," I say, getting in bed with her, leaving enough room between us that if I turn over, I'm on the floor.

She scoffs, throwing the covers over her head. "I don't even know where I am. Where the hell am I going to go?"

I chuckle, adjusting the pillow under my head, and grunt as I try to get comfortable. I'm lying as stiff as a board. Not that I haven't slept beside a girl before, but I don't want her to feel uncomfortable. I don't want her to do something she doesn't want to, aside from being in this cabin, of course.

She's different, though. She makes me nervous. Not a lot of girls have done that. Not even Natalia did that.

Zay shivers again, shaking the bed.

"You want a sweater?"

"It's okay," she whispers.

I get up and take the blanket from the couch, laying it on top of the ones she has bunched up. "I'd offer to cuddle you, but that's not an option."

She chuckles, curling the blankets under her chin. "Why are you being nice to me?"

"We're stuck with each other for an entire week. Better to be kind than to live miserably." I tap her side and get back in bed, keeping close to the edge so she doesn't feel uneasy. But fuck, I want to hold her right now and warm that little body up.

I stretch my leg out, feeling her cold feet. She flinches but gives in almost instantly when I don't move my leg. Her feet curl around it, sending shivers through me. But it's helping her. Those teeth aren't chattering as much.

Life is fucked right now. But this is the business I'm in. I'm back to being a prospect in the eyes of the men I call my brothers. Not the VP. A low-life prospect that does everything they're told. As if I haven't paid my dues my entire life.

Gotta work my way back up because of my darling ex.

Bullshit I paid my dues for. Bullshit I'm stuck *paying* for.

I let out a slow grumble, fixing the covers on my torso. Zay stops shivering, her bare neck flashing me.

A neck I want to bite.

Might just use her yet. Use her for a release. For a good screw. For a way to make a new life. It's about time I get out. About time I leave this life behind. Death has a way of following me. Betrayal surrounds me. I need happiness again. Happiness in a new life.

Her heavy breathing resumes.

In minutes, so does mine.

Finally, a good night's sleep.

Zay

The rumble of engines startles me awake. I shoot my eyes open and see Riggs's back facing me, on the verge of falling off the bed.

I appreciated what he did last night. A simple gesture that proves he's not as rancid as the other two men who spent the night.

He's different.

Caring. Concerning. Respectful, to a point.

Not so gentle, though.

Gosh, my ankle still hurts from where he grabbed it and dragged me to the kitchen yesterday. Sadly, if he's done that and tossed me on the couch to have his way with me, I don't think I would have minded.

Regardless, I don't trust these demons.

These snakes.

I don't trust anyone since I let my demons win. I let them win and it's still haunting me.

I get out of bed and stretch, using the bathroom to prepare myself for the day.

He's still asleep when I get out.

His gun is on the side table.

Boots on the floor.

As is his shirt.

For someone covered in tattoos and piercings, he's kind of pretty when he's sleeping.

His stern, stubborn face softens. His brow isn't furrowed. Those long lashes frame his eyes.

He's all muscle and ink. Ink that runs down his chest, arms, and back. Ink that's dark and terrifying. I want to turn him over and study them, trace my fingers over the images.

I don't.

I'm far too frightened at what he'd do if I wake him.

I tiptoe out of the room and see the other room is empty. Lip and Judas are gone.

Their room is a pigsty and reeks of whiskey and cigarettes. I may not have acted like it, but I was scared that as I slept, one of them was going to come into the room and hurt me. Riggs owes me nothing. As protective as he seemed yesterday, his protection is as valid as my expired driver's license.

Taking one more scan of the room, I turn my nose up. As disgusting as this room is, I'm hungry. Food is what I need.

Starting for the kitchen, I'm slammed against Riggs's hard frame. "Jesus," I exclaim, pushing against his chest. *Jesus is right.* His chest is amazing. Chiseled and sculpted to perfection. I don't think I've seen this many muscles formed so intricately before. I don't know him at all, but he sure does take care of his appearance. Every edge and ridge is molded like a marble statue. Even his tattoos. There isn't a single one that is faded or scratched. Who is this guy?

He arches an eyebrow, that softened face is stiff again. "Where were you going?"

"To eat."

He grumbles, running his hand through his hair, and points back to the room. "Sit, I'll be out in a minute."

I roll my eyes. "I'm not leaving, all right? I'm making breakfast."

I start to walk away—wrong idea on my part but what the heck do I know— and he grabs the back of my neck, bringing me to bed.

I'm tossed like I don't weigh more than a plastic bag and he goes to the bathroom to do his business. I'm getting kind of annoyed at his manhandling, but what do I know about bikers? He's the first one I've ever met and I already hate them all.

Gritting my teeth, I'm frustrated, and get off the bed to the bathroom. I don't give a shit what he's doing in there, I refuse to be treated this way. No man will ever lay a hand on me and get away with it. I've proven that point before.

…Riggs is naked. Of course, he is.

"Hey," I snap, taking in that perfectly sculpted masterpiece. Ass so fucking tight I could bounce a nickel off it. "Have you no common decency? I'm not an animal you can toss around when you feel like it."

His chuckle is deep and frightening.

As is his nudity.

My face must be red because my cheeks are hot.

And my mouth is watering.

Dare I say it, I *really* like what I see.

"You're a job, I don't gotta treat you like anything," he says, opening the glass door and stepping into the shower.

This fucking guy!

No respect for anyone but himself. I've dealt with rude people before, but when I'm interrupted or brushed off, it gets under my skin and I fucking hate it.

Don't test me, Mister.

"I wasn't finished talking to you."

He whips his head around, then slowly turns his body. Teasing me with that *thing*.

"You wanna talk, you can join me. If not, sit on the bed where I can see you."

I growl, squeezing my hands into fists. "You are unbelievable."

He chuckles, turning back around to show me his muscular back and that clenched ass the gods must've sculpted themselves. Taking their time, the show-offs.

I'm angry *and* turned on. This is not a good thing.

This week is going to be long, I can feel it.

***

I'm upside down on the couch. My legs are dangling off the back of it and I'm staring at the dying fire. There's pressure in my eyes and it is now starting in my nose.

Blood's rushing to my head and I know as soon as I lift it, I'll get that dizzy feeling I search for when I drink and get high.

I'd like to get drunk right now.

Or at least get high.

Because I'm bored out of my mind.

Riggs doesn't speak. He cleans his guns or cleans the kitchen. Sometimes he does push-ups or sit-ups.

There's no TV.

No internet.

The books are boring as shit.

And the magazines are biker magazines with motorcycle parts and ads for leather everything.

We're at a cabin. There has to be something I can do to kill some time. Maybe even swim in a lake?

I sputter, fixing my head on the couch to stare at the ceiling. "Riggs, I'm bored."

"Good for you," he says, sitting in the armchair beside the couch.

I maneuver myself onto my stomach and look at him. His eyes move over me in a way that makes everything about me feel beautiful.

Disturbing, right?

This big guy right here is the man who's most likely going to kill me in six days, yet I enjoy the way he looks at me because it makes me feel alive. I'm so focused on his gaze that it still hasn't registered that these are the final days of my life.

They very well could be and I'm not thinking about my death; I'm thinking about how he stares at me.

Adam looks at me like this all the time.

At least he did until he left me.

I think we should see other people.

Whoever she is better be worth his time because he'll never find anyone like me.

But goddamn if I don't miss him.

"This is your cabin, there has to be something fun to do." I get on my knees and Riggs stares at my exposed legs. "What do you usually do when you're here?"

He smirks, crossing one leg over the other at the ankle. He doesn't even have to speak, I already know what he's going to say by the way he rakes his teeth over his bottom lip.

I narrow my eyes. "You're disgusting."

"I didn't say anything."

I scoff and wave my hand at him, the sneaky shit. "You didn't have to, it's written all over your face."

I'm up on my feet now, walking to the back door. With the little trust he has in me, if any, he's up on his feet, too, sitting on the armrest of the couch behind me as I'm staring out the window. There isn't much out there but tall trees. A small patio set rests out back, covered in fallen leaves, overlooking a clearing in the forest with a firepit. I barely see any of the sky through the height of the trees. It's cloudy, gloomy. It's going to rain soon, which means we'll be cooped up in here again.

I don't think I can stand it much longer.

My parents have a cabin, but I use the word cabin very loosely. They have a mansion on the water we escape to for the holidays. Six-bedroom house with a hot tub and indoor pool that faces the lake. The last time I went there was my first anniversary with Adam. We spent the entire weekend making love, drinking champagne, and eating chocolate-covered strawberries.

If I could have one more weekend with him, I'd give up everything to do it. Just one more.

"It's really pretty out here." I tap on the glass at the forestry. "Is there a lake nearby?"

Riggs grunts. "Maybe, maybe not."

My fists are on my hips when I turn around to face him. He's sitting on the arm of the couch a few feet away, but the man's so damn tall his giant feet rest beside me in those leather boots he wears.

Beast.

Savage.

Why is this exciting me? It's something forbidden, something I've never had.

"It's not like I could swim away. With your big-ass arms, you'd catch me in one stroke and drown me before I even made it a foot." I scoff. "Is it so hard to try to do something fun around here?" Glancing back out the window, I mumble under my breath. "Or be fucking nice to me like last night."

He grunts when he gets up, muttering as he takes a gun from the kitchen table and tucks it into his jeans. "Get your shoes on."

He's allowing me to do something I want to do? Has hell frozen over?

I clap excitedly. Hey, if I'm dying in a week, I have to take advantage of the little things. Little things involve me thinking out of sight, out of mind. If I don't think about the fright inside me at my fate that's been sealed, I'll be able to live the next few days out with an ounce of my sanity.

If I dwell on my fear and let it consume me, the only sanity I have left will leave just as quickly. I'll be left with nothing but waiting for the ending. Positives. I have to look at the fucked-up positives.

I'm dying in a beautiful forest.

I'm dying for a man I still love.

I'm dying for no reason.

But at least today, I get to go swimming.

Following Riggs out into the woods, we head down a narrow path I don't think has been cleared in years, but as soon as we walk through bushes and branches, we make it to a small dock. The water glistens under the shining sun.

Beautiful.

Like stars sparkling before me.

I can't remember the last time I went swimming. There's a body of water close to campus; Adam and I used to go there often. It's my favorite place to lie and watch the stars. But the last time I went swimming must have been months ago. Adam and I were drunk as sin and making out as we floated in the water with waves crashing into us. Simpler times, happier times.

I don't care that I don't have a swimsuit, I pull my shirt over my head and slip off my shorts, running off the dock and plunging headfirst into the water.

It's fucking cold!

My body stings.

Shock.

I'm shivering before I even breach the surface.

Riggs is chuckling, picking up my clothes and dropping them by his feet at the edge of the dock.

"I wasn't expecting it to be this cold," I say, staring up at him.

He chuckles. "You wanted to go swimming."

My teeth are chattering, but I take this as my opportunity to look around the area.

The walk to the dock was six minutes, give or take. I tried counting to sixty, six times, then lost track at one point when he told me to watch my step.

There are three docks in a triangle formation in this man-made lake.

My guess is these cabins also belong to fellow bikers.

I could be wrong.

I might be wrong.

Neighbors think Riggs is here with his lady. Okay, which neighbors, though?

There's the large modern house with too many windows and one too many floors to my left, and the bungalow with a T-shaped dock to my right. Paddleboat out back, tire swing in the tree. One of these two homes could be trustworthy. Or neither of them. If I try to escape, I have to try my luck with these houses. Hope for the best.

Dunking my head under, I come back up, floating on my back. I feel his eyes watching me.

Stalking.

Roaming.

Dirty big-ass man.

Although, he is scanning the area.

Scouring.

Protecting.

Moving my hands above my head, I kick farther away, staring at the gloomy sky.

The water is cold as shit, but I don't want to be in that house anymore. I'm already going stir-crazy.

Even with my ears underwater, I can hear the thunder rumbling.

I don't care. I stay afloat. Closing my eyes and breathing.

I don't understand how I came to be here. How I ended up the reason for Adam's stupidity. Maybe I am to blame. I did encourage him to get out of his shell a lot. I tend to do that to people I love. It's not my finest advice. Some people took it too seriously, and look a them now.

I think Adam got out of his shell a little *too* much.

Muffled calls puncture the water. I don't want to open my eyes. I just want to lay here, floating. Freezing.

But I open my eyes.

Riggs is crouched down looking at me with widened eyes. "Hey."

"What?"

"C'mon. It's starting to rain," he says, waving me out of the water.

He's holding my clothes. It's cute, he's cute. But I can't trust him.

I can't trust anyone.

He's here babysitting me so that his club gets the money my ex owes.

Money I know for a fact he doesn't have.

Come day seven, Riggs's niceness will be short-lived. He'll put a bullet in my head and I'll probably be tossed in this very lake with weights on my ankles to keep my body in its watery grave.

What did I do to deserve this?

Reluctantly, I swim to the dock and place my palms on the wood, not noticing the nail poking out.

Puncture.

Scream.

I fall back into the water and hold onto my bleeding hand, staring at it with teary eyes.

I will not cry.

I will not cry.

I will not cry.

He takes me by the bicep and pulls me out of the water, dropping me on my feet on the dock like I weigh no more than a beach ball.

"Lemme see."

Shaking my head, I wince as I squeeze my hand shut. "I'm fine." Sniffing, I shove my feet into my shoes. "Let's get inside before it pours."

He grabs my hand and pulls it toward him, staring at me with this intimidating gaze burning deep. "Let. Me. See."

"I-I'm okay, really—"

He pries my fingers open and inspects the perfect circular wound in the middle of my palm. Like Jesus on a cross.

I'm trying to hide how painful it is right now.

He grunts, looking up as the sky starts to cry for me. "Move."

So I do; I take my hand back and hold it against my chest, whimpering softly, and letting a couple of tears slide down my cheeks as we make it back to the cabin.

It's a downpour when we reach the patio, soaking us completely.

If I wasn't freezing then, I surely am now.

As much as I'm shivering, the stinging pain is still poking through.

I just want to jump in the shower.

Drown out my pain with the rest of the Jack Daniel's.

Escape for a little while.

Riggs

She winces when I pour rubbing alcohol on her hand.

Stubborn little shit wouldn't let me look at her wound. I had to force her to let me look at it on the dock. And forced her to let me look after her shower. She insisted she was fine and disappeared to warm up. But as soon as the water shut off, I stormed into the bathroom, missing her wet naked body by seconds, and stared at the punctured wound that still bled. Nail got her good.

Observing her as she watches me clean her wound, I take notice of the wrinkle in her brow and the subtle tremor of her bottom lip. There's an odd feeling in the pit of my stomach that twists, urging me to destroy anything that touches this delicate woman. "You got all your shots?"

She nods, her other hand clenched in a fist on her lap.

"Don't think you need stitches. But I gotta keep an eye on it and make sure you don't get an infection."

She winces again when I dab it with gauze. "Do all bikers have a medical license?"

She's funny.

And sexy.

Piece of shit boyfriend stuck his nose where it didn't belong, now she's in this.

Deeply.

I feel bad.

She seems like a good girl.

Nice girl.

Type of girl you bring home to Mama.

But she has a darkness to her.

A darkness I can't wait to meet.

"Don't get it wet."

My thumb grazes a scar on her wrist, going from one end to the other diagonally.

Tried to kill herself and fucked it up?

No.

She doesn't seem that scarred.

She retracts her hand as soon as I wrap it and holds it to her chest. "Thanks."

She stands, flipping her hair behind her, smelling just like my body wash. For some reason, I like that.

I inhale.

Absorb.

Feels right.

This girl is supposed to smell like me.

Stupid-ass boyfriend.

"Let's get you something to drink, yeah?"

She sighs, licking her lips. "Make it a double."

I will.

I do.

Because this woman will be naked in my bed tonight.

Just wait.

Fuck you, Adam.

***

Washing the rain off me, I step out of the shower and pick up all the dirty clothes she left in the hamper. Take the time to clean the shit that Lip and Judas left behind, too.

Dirty fuckers.

I've been around Judas and Lip long enough to know they leave a mess everywhere they go. When the club has to do a stealthy deal, they're the last duo we ask to go. It's usually Banks and I. We work well together, he's quiet and clean. I'm quiet and clean.

Judas? Don't think the fucker owns a bar of soap.

Lip? He doesn't own a dresser. What aches even more, I lived with the bastard for six goddamn months when we were teenagers. Worst six months of my life. But now, I live on top of the bar—our clubhouse, called *Judas's Hideout*. Alone. The place is clean and I can keep an eye on the bar when it's locked up.

I prefer it that way. Just me, my bed, and all the alcohol I could ask for right at my fingertips.

She's sitting on the bed waiting for me, still holding her fist to her chest. I want to hold her, take away all the pain she's in.

Take away the sadness behind those hazel eyes.

"All good?" I say, causing her to turn around. Her eyes look brown in this lighting.

"I'm kind of hungry."

I nod, swinging my head toward the door. "I'll make spaghetti. You good with that?"

Her mouth twitches, trying to hide her smile. "As long as you have Parmesan cheese."

"I'm sure we do. Judas ain't one to skimp when it comes to cheese."

"I like Judas." She snickers. "Anyone who has a love for cheese is good in my books."

I chuckle, running the towel through my hair. "Monterey Jack is my go-to."

I can't believe I'm talking cheese with a girl. But it's helping. She's grinning and making her way to the kitchen.

First grin I've seen on her since she went swimming three hours ago.

Don't get me started on her swim. Seeing her in those white panties and bra that can barely be called that. Little lace number leaving no mystery to those tits.

Gorgeous fucking tits.

Suck me tits.

Goddammit.

It's like this is the first girl I've ever been around. All flustered and jumbled. Chicks don't make me jumbled. They give me one thing. But she can give me so much more.

Sanity.

Purity.

An out.

She sits at the table watching me the whole time I'm cooking. Her eyes are on me like a weight pressed against my chest.

A weight I want to gobble up and tear apart.

In a good way.

She rests her chin on her hand and smirks, eyeing my hands as I wash them, preparing to strain the spaghetti. My Mama taught us how to cook. Simple things like a quick tomato sauce, roast chicken, and the best grilled cheese in San Jose has to offer.

Club doesn't trust me to cook for them anymore. It has been eighteen months of torture on my end like I'm one of the fucking whores.

Disrespected.

Hated.

Abused.

Stooped down to fetching beers and collecting cash from the scums we lend it to.

Bastards, all of them.

Zay moves her tongue around her mouth before she parts those lips to speak. "You wear a lot of rings."

Looking down at my tatted hand and move the stainless steel rings that decorate my fingers. I like the rings. Skulls, snakes, and thick bands. They're annoying as shit to have on, but they help when someone needs a beating. "Better than brass knuckles."

She looks down at her dainty little hands, not a single ring on any of her fingers. Her thumb touches her ring finger, lips pressed together. She's deep in thought. Maybe thinking about that fuckhead Adam. Lucky bastard. "Seems uncomfortable," she finally says.

I grunt a reply and strain the spaghetti, dropping it in a bowl, then mixing my sauce into it. The last time I made this meal, we sat as a family. Now, they're all distant memories of people they used to be.

She's still staring at her hand, the wounded one now, and sighs softly. I wish I could make it better.

Take away all her sadness and worry.

But that ain't my job.

I'm here to watch her, not protect her.

But goddamn is it ever going to be hard to hear her cry without consoling her.

"How's your hand?" I ask, putting the bowl on the table.

She shrugs, rising from her seat to get us plates.

Two broken hearts eating together alone in a cabin. Love story writes itself.

But Zay and I will never be a love story.

That isn't how it ends for us.

Blood. Our story will definitely end in bloodshed.

"Sting, throbs, and I'm sure will be a gnarly scar when it's healed." She sits back down and takes the bowl, serving herself the smallest spoonful, then giving me a whopping scoop. "Not sure it matters, though."

The corner of my mouth twitches, but that's all I give her. If I give her any more, then I'll feel bad for her.

I already feel bad for her.

If I could trade places with this beautiful face, I would.

I'd take away all her pain.

All that fear.

I'd gobble it up and set her free.

But her fate is not in my hands.

Her fate, unfortunately, is sealed.

Zay

I'm three drinks in.

Maybe four.

And Riggs, bless his stone-cold heart, makes each a double.

I moan happily and rest my chin on my hand. The non-wounded one. I'm smiling at Riggs sitting across from me at the dining table. "Tell me, Mister Riggs, what made you want to be a biker?"

"Family business."

He thumbs the rim of his glass and drains the rest, glancing up at me. The way the light is hitting his face, he looks evil. Every ridge. Every contour is illuminated.

The devil sitting right in front of me.

But when he lifts his gaze, the lights soften his face.

Beauty blooms on it. Angelic.

Little saint and sinner.

I can go for some trouble tonight.

"You got a girlfriend?"

"Nope."

I narrow my eyes. "Boyfriend?"

"Negative."

Biting my bottom lip, I sit back, bringing a knee to my chest. "How old are you?"

"How old are you?" he retorts.

"Old enough."

He rakes his bottom lip, mimicking me. "That doesn't bode well with me feeding you alcohol. Does it?"

"Maybe. Maybe not."

He rolls his eyes and lets out a breath. Sitting back in his chair. "Twenty-five."

"Twenty-one."

He nods, the corner of his mouth curling upward. I don't know what's on his mind, but the way his eyes are eating me up is making me crazy. They're devouring, licking every inch of exposed skin. Having a feeding frenzy at my hard nipples behind this tank top.

A shiver runs through me, wondering what his tongue would feel like all over my body. To have that tingle again. That ache and want. It makes me think of Adam and how much I miss him. How I *hate* to miss him.

"Tell me, Zay, you a bad girl?"

Oh, baby, I can be a bad girl tonight.

I giggle. "Maybe. Maybe not."

He chuckles.

Deep.

Guttural.

Insatiable.

It scares the hell out of me. It's also driving me wild.

He nods at my wounded hand on the table, my index finger tapping on the side of the glass. "What happened to your wrist?"

I slither my hand onto my lap, hiding the scar that caused me to meet Adam a year ago. "Nothing."

Riggs drops his arm on the table and lifts his sleeve to reveal a scar. "Scar for a scar."

Frowning, I study the way his supple lips twist into a smirk. "What do you mean?"

"I'll show you a scar, tell you its story, and you do the same."

It is a great way to get to know someone. See glimpses of their moments of weakness. Just like my hand. A new scar added to my body to tell my story. Will it be a memory of that time I was locked in a cabin with a husky biker? Or will it not even have time to heal by the time I'm in the ground?

His long, thick fingers brush over the sliver that interrupts the wolves on his upper arm. Snarling wolves, howling wolves. Pack of them. Most of his tattoos are dark. Not a single drop of color anywhere on his body. Like he didn't want to get anything beautiful, only evil.

"Bar fight."

Getting on my knees on the chair to get a better look, I have the urge to touch it, but I refrain from doing so. Staring at the snarling wolf with an interruption in its neck. It's a thick scar, one that must've needed stitching. "Let me guess, you won?"

He lowers his sleeve, sitting back with a grin. "That ain't even a question."

I lift my chin, showing him a scar under it. "Bar fight."

He gulps back the rest of his drink and shakes his head. "I bet you've never even been in a bar."

I stick my tongue out and slide my glass to him for a refill. "I snuck into a frat party and slipped on some beer on the floor after someone did a keg stand."

He stands, lifting his shirt to reveal that rock-hard stomach I want to drag my hands across. Sculpted. Six-pack that looks fake, like a dream. He's gorgeous.

But I have to stop gushing over him. He could very well be the man who kills me.

"Stabbed."

He's dangerous. I'm so turned on by his dangerous aura.

Wanting it.

Loathing it.

Craving it.

My hormones are on overdrive and my common sense is losing its mind.

It's not like I haven't done bad things before, been with bad people. I have. I've slept with my drug dealer for a bump, turned to drugs and alcohol when my best friend died, then turned to sex when everything felt meaningless. Losing her was the lowest point in my life. And with my raging bad habits, I just made them worse.

I'm studying the scar, that urge to reach a hand out and touch him again is on fire within me. I don't. Instead, I point at two holes, side by side, on his upper rib cage. "And those?"

"Deal gone wrong."

I widen my eyes. "Are those bullet holes?"

He plops back down, filling our glasses two fingers full. "What happened to your wrist?"

Sipping the whiskey, I take a breath. "I was trying to save my best friend."

He frowns as I bring my hand back onto the table and we stare at my wrist. "What happened?"

Darkest time of my life.

Heartbreaking.

Heart-wrenching.

Maddening.

Lillian Delano. Pretty little blonde with the tiniest waist I've ever seen, and the biggest bluest eyes. We were inseparable since the ripe age of twelve. She knew me better than I knew myself, and I thought I knew her, too.

I didn't.

We attended Stanford University together. Got our acceptance letters the same day in the mail, too. We weren't even there for six months before things went sour. She was reserved and kept to herself. Until I showed up and helped her get out of that shell.

I shouldn't have let her get out of that shell.

For about three days before everything happened, she started becoming distant. Quiet, loner vibes.

She'd go out at all hours without telling me and she never did that. She'd come home reeking of whiskey and bad decisions. She had a boyfriend, so this worried me. But I ignored it, even though he wasn't the best boyfriend. I shouldn't have ignored it, though. I should have pressed and pushed and asked what's up. I ignored all the signs.

I'd call her. No answer.

I'd text her. Nothing.

Snapchat her. Nada.

Instagram. Ignored.

I showed up at her dorm after day two, but no one was home. With finals in my grasp, I had to double down and study, or else I'd be kicked out.

Right now, I'd rather have been kicked out.

So, after three days of solitude without my ride or die, I went to her dorm again to see what the heck was up. The bastards didn't give us a dorm together. We weren't even down the hall from each other we were on different floors altogether.

When I walked in, there she was, cold as ice, blood everywhere, and not a single breath left.

I shook her.

I screamed.

I pleaded.

I didn't see the knife when I went to lift her and cut myself on the same blade she used to cut her wrists.

I didn't mean to. In the frantic attempts to save her corpse, the blade punctured me.

She was gone.

I was broken.

The shock was alive and wild when I stared at her.

I was determined to know who did this.

Who would make her hate herself so much to kill herself?

She was lovely.

Happy.

Full of life.

Until three days before I found her.

With every action, there's a reaction, and my determination came with its faults.

Clearing my throat, Riggs is staring at me for an answer. "You ever kill someone?"

He thumbs the rim of his glass, those monstrous arms resting on the table. "What do you think?"

Resting my chin on my hand, I chuckle. "That this is all a ploy to fit in. I think you're a big ole softie."

He laughs. As scary and intimidating as it is, it's hella sexy right now.

Maybe I need to cool it with the alcohol running through my veins. I'm barely out of a relationship with someone I deemed my soulmate. Someone I loved with every fiber of my being.

I still do. I'd do anything for Adam if I'm being honest.

"You ever kill anyone, Zay?" Riggs asks.

I prefer not to answer that.

I prefer it if he doesn't know my sins.

My regrets.

My fucked-up play for vengeance.

Tonguing my upper molars, I lick my upper lip as I stare him down. No one knows my truth, and I'm not about to admit my truth to this man before me. So I'll give in to my needs one last time before I kick the bucket.

One last release.

One last orgasm.

Because I'm pretty sure this guy knows how to screw and I could go for a good screw right about now.

Sorry, Adam.

Narrowing my eyes, I slowly lick my lips again. "You wanna fuck me?" I bat my eyes a little. Adam used to love it when I did that. "You're killing me in a few days anyway, I'd like to go out satisfied." I smirk. "Can you leave me satisfied, Riggs?"

Satisfied as I left *him* before I killed *him*, too.

Riggs coughs, choking on his drink. "I never said I was killing you."

"You never said you weren't."

He clicks his tongue. "What happens after the seven days are up ain't my decision."

I sit back on my butt, cross one leg over the other at the knees, and gulp the rest of the alcohol. I'm done.

I'm dizzy.

Probably slurring.

I should go to bed before I say something I shouldn't. Something like I just said and already feel like a dumbass for asking.

Who the fuck asks for sex in my position?

"You told Lip you wouldn't call the cops if you got us the money," Riggs says, pouring more Jack Daniel's in my glass.

I won't drink it.

Nope.

And I won't tell him why I'll get in trouble. I'm not good under pressure and just the sight of the cops will reveal my secret.

Defeat.

It's been over a year since the incident happened. I was twenty, high on God only knows what.

What the hell did I know?

I knew better than to hurt someone who deserved it, but did it anyway, all because I was hurt.

Broken.

I'm still broken. When I study Riggs, it seems like we both are. We have a cloud over us. A darkness.

I'm going to hell and I think Riggs will be right down there with me.

He finishes his drink before filling it back up. "So, tell me. Why will you be in trouble? You're a good girl, aren't you?"

I chuckle, shaking my head. "I wish."

He leans forward, raking his eyes over me, and clicks his tongue again. I think he's contemplating my offer. What's one night? Another notch in his belt. I'm good at what I do and I'll leave him begging for more. They always want more.

He stares at my lips, slowly moving his eyes up to meet mine. "I've been with a lot of women, y'know."

"Good for you."

He chuckles, slowly moving his glass from one hand to the next. "I don't think you can handle me."

"Mm," I say. "I know I can. But I don't think it's you who can handle me, baby."

His chest heaves at the sound of me calling him baby. I might actually be getting what I want tonight. A moment in time when I can forget the world.

Thumbing my bottom lip, I smile. "Plus, I've already seen you naked. You're not shy about flopping it about."

"You walked in on me getting in the shower. That ain't my fault." He sips his drink. "And I wasn't ready, that's not what it looks like when I'm ready."

I widen my eyes. I'm no prude or innocent little lady. I've been with my fair share of guys and seen my fair share of dicks. But flaccid, they don't all look as adequate as his. "Wait, it gets bigger?"

He laughs again, its sound moving through the cabin and blending with the clapping thunder outside. As if on cue, lightning strikes as he lets his laugh die down. Menacing but potent.

It's getting hard for me to keep it together.

"You're cute, y'know that."

I roll my eyes. "Well, sorry, I haven't seen many giants in my life."

His tongue drags along his teeth, disappearing to his cheek. "How many have you seen?"

"Enough to know what I like."

A low growl rumbles through his chest, then a sound of pure hunger rattles in his throat. He's staring at me like he wants to do this but can't. I don't blame him. I'm a job he has to watch and make sure nothing stupid happens.

Let's face it, money or not, no one is surviving this.

Deciding for him before I make an even bigger fool of myself tonight, I push myself up, sliding the glass to the middle of the table. "Goodnight, Riggs."

He angles his head, that angelic way he does. "Yeah…night."

Making it halfway down the hallway when I hear his clunky boots follow after me. Maybe he changed his mind? I turn, facing him, and he takes my wounded hand, peeking under the bandage. "I gotta change this."

"Damn, and here I thought you had a change of heart."

He smirks, shaking his head. "I can't, sunshine."

It's crossed his mind by the way he's looking at me.

That flicker.

Wonderment.

Pleasing satisfaction within his grasp.

He's staring at my lips, my cleavage poking through my tank top, and he slides his eyes to mine.

Temptation.

Lust.

Want.

Maybe tomorrow.

He's holding onto my wrist and breaks eye contact with me long enough to pull me into the bathroom. His giant hands slide to my waist and lift me onto the counter. He's only this close to me so he can clean my wound, but holy crap is it ever getting hot in here.

He takes out what he needs to clean and dress my wound again, conveniently standing between my legs.

I wince twice as he cleans it, letting out a slow breath when he bandages it.

Our eyes meet and he grins. Not his playful grin like he usually does. That angelic one I'm beginning to admire. "Doesn't look infected," he says, letting go of my hand.

Clenching and unclenching my fist, I wince at the stinging pain that's surging every time I try to open my hand. I shrug, flickering from one of those blue eyes to the other. "Doesn't matter if it does, right?"

I don't even have the time to look down, away from him, he tilts my chin up to hold my gaze. "I ain't letting them kill you, Zay."

A soft nasal chuckle leaves me right as his thumb grazes my bottom lip. He doesn't break eye contact, but he steps closer, opening my legs wider.

"Thought you couldn't?"

His breathing wavers. Is his heart beating as fast as mine is right now?

It's lodged in my throat, as if we're about to do something we shouldn't.

An affair.

A secret.

He leans forward until our foreheads are touching, our breaths mixing. "I shouldn't."

"Then don't."

"I wanna." His other hand grabs my thigh, squeezing. "I wanted to the second I saw you."

Angling my head so our lips are feathering, I slowly wet my lips. "Then take me, right here."

He lets out a breath that I inhale. He tastes like whiskey. "It ain't that simple."

I chuckle, nibbling his bottom lip and it causes him to groan, gripping my thighs with both hands. One on each. "But it is. I'll pull you out and guide you inside me." His tongue teases my lips. "I'm not wearing any underwear," I confess.

He drops his head on my shoulder, breathing heavily. "Fuck."

Groaning, he lets go of my thighs, his hands in fists on the counter beside me. "Fuck."

Their word is their bond I guess.

Don't fuck the bargaining chip.

I won't make him do something that could mess up his loyalty to the club. Even though we both want it badly.

He lifts his head and lets out a rush of air. His gaze holds mine for a moment, and it's enough to know he's not doing this tonight. "I, uh, I'll see you in the morning, Zay."

I nod, pinching his chin and bringing it forward. I leave a soft kiss on his lips. It's enough to make him smile. "See you in the morning, Riggs."

He helps me off the counter and leans his fists on it again, watching me from the reflection in the mirror as I head for the bedroom.

Well, that's sure going to leave me with a proverbial pair of blue balls. I haven't had any since Adam and I broke up. And that was weeks ago.

Just one night of passion. Is that too much to ask?

Dropping on the bed, I look at the bay window again. My escape route.

I've been staring at these windows the past couple of days, but the thought of escaping through them hasn't dawned on me. Mostly because Riggs has been in this bed with me. And my first night here, I was way too drunk to move. I can't remember how I got to bed. He probably tucked me in.

Of course, he tucked me in. He may look big and tough, but deep down, this life isn't the life he wanted. He has a good heart but wasn't raised by one.

As I'm staring at the window now, I have a plan.

A simple plan this fuckhead won't see coming.

Riggs

I tossed and turned all damn night. I didn't dare sleep in the same room as her because I knew if I did, she'd be riding me until the sun came up. I paced.

I showered.

I drank some more.

All it bought was the thought of her perky breasts in my mouth. Those sexy legs wrapped around me. Kissing those lips.

She's a dream I'll only taint with my nightmares.

Forbidden fruit.

I can't fuck up this time. I can't. I have to focus.

She comes into the kitchen with little jean shorts on, a tight white crop top, and hair in a messy bun on top of her head. Breathtaking.

Fuck.

"Morning," her cheery voice says.

The fuck is wrong with me?

I don't go after women like this.

I don't go after women.

I don't fall for women.

I fuck them.

Use them.

That's it.

But her.

She's different.

She's secretive.

Quiet.

Sexy.

There's something wild hidden inside her.

I know it.

"H-hey." I clear my throat, bringing the coffee to my lips. "Morning."

She pulls herself up on the counter beside me, taking the coffee from my hands and sipping it. "So what're the plans today, big boy?"

Little wild cat.

Spunky.

No woman has ever pushed me to the edge.

Tempted me.

Dangled their body before me and I refused.

How can I refuse this beauty?

This temptress is driving me crazy.

"Don't know yet."

"You need some sugar in this coffee."

We lock eyes and she holds my mug out to me as if expecting me to make my coffee to her taste. To her liking.

Like the animal that I am, I snatch it from her and continue drinking it, staring down at the paper in front of me.

Fucking newspaper. I never read this crap. I'm not into sports or politics or anything worldly. My focus has only been on this club. As I live and breathe. It's only been this club. Yet here I am, reading about the politics that are tainting our country.

But she is right, there's fuck all to do here.

Last night, the way she teased me nearly drove me to the edge. How she nibbled my bottom lip, pushed herself into me. I was hard as a rock trying not to let her touch me. She felt it trying to escape from my jeans.

I'm already at half-staff right now.

She still smells like me. My body wash in the shower.

Possessiveness takes over.

Power.

Territory.

She rakes her teeth over her bottom lip and gets a second mug from the dishrack beside her, pouring herself a cup of coffee and adding three spoonfuls of sugar to it.

I'm staring at her mouth, growing stiffer by the second. If she licks her lips one more time, I'm going to kiss her.

I'll take her right on this counter.

She brings the cup of coffee to her lips, licking them before sipping.

Fuck it.

I drop the coffee, its contents spilling on the counter, and grab her face, kissing her, taking her by surprise.

She moves away. "What're you doing?"

"What you asked for."

She holds my gaze for a moment, her heart beating rapidly under my touch.

She takes control and pulls me to her, slamming her lips on mine.

She kisses better than I do.

Experienced.

Tasteful.

She grabs at my jeans, frantically undoing them. So I do the same.

I lift her and yank off her shorts, shoving her against the fridge behind us, and rip off those panties.

Tiny, fragile little thing wrapping her legs around my waist. I'm going to destroy her.

She angles herself toward me, aching for me to enter that paradise.

I'll take her bare.

I have no other choice.

A gasp leaves her as soon as I pull it out, and she moans with a wince as soon as I slide into her.

Fast.

Hard.

Pounding her against the fridge in broad daylight.

Pounding the woman I'm supposed to babysit until we get our money.

I've known the chick for three days and I'm screwing her with the intent of doing it again.

Pulling her breast out of that tank top.

Perky, ripe, firm.

I tongue her nipple, feeling it pebble under my caress. Perk up even more when I suckle it.

She pulls at my shirt, trying to get it off me. Won't have time to do anything of the sort, I'm gonna finish soon.

I grunt, not even two minutes in, and hold still, letting every last drop of my cum fill her tiny pussy as I hold her tightly.

Her heavy breaths caress my neck, kissing softly before she lifts her head.

"Shit," I grumble. "Fucking shit, we shouldn't have done that."

She breathes heavily, licking those fucking lips again. "No." She giggles. "Probably not."

Roaring engines make their way up the drive, polluting their noise out over the quiet trees. She's a distraction. A stupid distraction that took me away from the world. It can't happen again. It damn well can't.

"Fuck."

I step back and remove her legs from around my waist, putting her down, and stare as she bites her bottom lip. "Get dressed."

She chuckles. "Wham, bam, thank you, ma'am."

I grit my teeth. "Go."

She rolls her eyes and picks up her clothes, making her way to the master bedroom.

That was a bad idea.

I shouldn't have given in so easily. Shouldn't have let her take control. Yet, all I want to do right now is go back there and do her right.

Make her scream.

Make her come.

Goddammit.

Fixing myself in my jeans, I inhale a steady breath and adjust my shirt she tried to yank off me, and start cleaning the coffee I spilled on the counter.

Temptress.

Goddess.

Beauty.

Why did we meet under these circumstances?

Front door bursts open, and Lip, Crew, Judas, and Banks strut in. Their loudness eats up the quiet. Chaos coming to rain their darkness upon us.

"Hey, brother," Lip says, kicking out a chair to fall into. "Where's the little minx?"

I nod at Crew, putting more water on for coffee. "Still asleep."

"Came here 'cause Lip says she offered to pay Adam's cut?" Crew says, pulling out a chair and sitting down.

I grunt. "So she says."

"Where she getting the money?" Crew asks, glancing down the hallway.

"Fuck if I know."

Lip snaps his fingers at me and points at the hallway. "Go get her."

Clenching my fists, I despise this tool for thinking he's a higher rank than me. He's sergeant of arms. Nothing more. I'm the fucking VP. I deserve the goddamn respect I used to have before things fucked-up. "Watch your mouth."

Lip puffs his chest out, fucker thinks he can take me. He can't. No one's man enough to try and take me. Not even when everything went down. No one was able to hold me, no one was able to defeat me. Not until a gun was pressed at my temple did I submit.

Fucking bastards.

"Boys." Crew puts his hand up. "Lip, make us breakfast. Judas, feed the fire. Riggs, get the little lady."

"Yes, boss," Lip says, sucking his teeth as he stands.

Fucking prick better watch himself.

My boots make more noise than they should, only because I wear them loosely. They clunk on the ground, sounding heavier and more intimidating that way.

I knock on the door and open it, excitement filling me to see her face again. "Zay?"

Opening the door, the bedroom is empty.

The bathroom. Empty.

I check my room. Also, empty.

Where did she go?

I walk back into the bedroom and that's when I see it, the window is open just a smidge, enough for her to slip out and attempt to shut it.

Stupid fucking bitch.

If they catch her before I do, she's dead.

Or worse.

Quickly cranking the window open, I poke my head out. Lucky for me, there's enough mud on the ground to tell me she went toward the forest, not the road.

Lucky for me.

Footfalls come behind me and Judas can see the aggravation on my face. "All good, brother?"

No, not all good.

It's not good because if they get ahold of her before I do, I'm just as screwed as she is. This babysitting gig is supposed to be my chance at redemption.

How can I redeem something when all this woman does are find ways to piss me off even more.

I shouldn't have given in. I shouldn't have slept with her.

Why the fuck did I do that? And why the fuck do I want to do it again?

I grit my teeth, gripping the windowsill as I stare back at Judas. "She fucking ran away."

Zay

Well, that was unexpected. But it's perfect.

It's just what I wanted.

A little taste left me somewhat satisfied.

No.

To distract him.

As soon as he asks me to get dressed, I do, then slowly open the window, and slip out. I've been planning my escape for some time.

Every time he showers or chops firewood, I plan.

It's easy.

Open the window, slide out, close the window.

The only problem is, the window is a crank window, I can't close it all the way from outside.

He won't notice.

Not now, at least.

He'll be too busy thinking of us having sex to notice. Good fucking sex at that.

What helps is, his buddies arrived right as we finished.

Perfect timing.

Slipping into the forest, I look back at the cabin with not an ounce of regret that I let this man inside me after knowing he's only keeping me here because my dickbag ex-boyfriend owes him money.

I'm no trollop, but I've been around. Exchanged sex for favors.

It doesn't bother me. I like sex. I like the thrill of it. So having sex with Riggs is nothing but a business transaction, in a way.

I distracted him. He got a taste of me.

Leaves crunch under my feet, causing me to look over my shoulder a few times.

Part of me was tempted to take his gun.

The one he keeps under the mattress.

But I didn't have time.

Charging for the water, I have one of two options of houses to swim to. Either they're home and they help me—or sell me out—or no one's home and I jack their car.

"Zay?" Riggs yells.

"The fuck are you, bitch?" Lip calls.

Shit. Shit. Shit.

I dart to a ditch, crouching down and hiding, breathing heavily as I do.

They're going to kill me.

I just know it.

Heavy pounding comes closer to my right. I have nothing around me to defend myself.

Crew is there with Riggs, stopping by the opening of the path to the dock. "How'd you let her escape?"

Riggs grits his teeth. "I didn't let her escape."

"You had one job."

Riggs growls. "And I'm doing that job, aren't I?"

"I'll check by the water, you check that way," Crew orders, running off again.

Riggs grumbles profanities under his breath and as luck would have it, I sneeze.

Stupid allergies.

Riggs clenches his fists, turning slowly.

Terrifying.

Menacing.

Fuck.

He clenches his jaw, grinding his teeth and he charges for me. Four of my steps are one of his. At least.

Trying to dart away from him was a dumb idea. His arms hook around my waist, and he tumbles to the ground, lying on top of me with one hand on my mouth, the other on my throat.

"Are you fucking stupid?"

Coughing under his hand.

Choke.

Gasp for a breath.

He's a completely different person.

The eyes I'm looking into only show death.

He releases my throat and I inhale sharply, coughing a couple of times before he squeezes my face. "You do that again, there's no telling what they'll do."

My voice is raspy, but I speak anyway. "Can't blame a girl for trying."

He gets to his feet, pulling me up by the shirt, and cleaning off his jeans.

Attempt one at my escape was a failure.

I'll try again tomorrow.

"Why the fuck did you do that?" he asks under his breath.

"I don't want to die."

He scoffs. "So you use me?"

"You came onto me, remember?" I say, then giggle. "Butt-hurt that I disobeyed you after I let you inside me? I knew you were a little softie."

He grabs me by the hair and grinds his teeth. "Shut the fuck up."

Crew and his men come running our way and Riggs waves them over.

I whimper when I hear them coming.

"You were taking a walk to the water, yeah?"

I shake my head.

He's trying to save me.

Protect me.

He grits his teeth and sighs heavily. "You were taking a walk by the water while I was still asleep."

Crew grabs the back of my shirt, snapping my bra strap, and throws me onto my back on a pile of leaves.

I groan, turning over as he goes to kick me.

"Stop," Riggs says, pulling him back. "She went for a walk before I woke up."

Lip takes me by the hair and lifts me to my feet. Treating me like a fucking ragdoll. "That so?"

Wincing, I grab his wrist. "Let go of me."

He tugs harder on my hair, making me squeal and suck my teeth in pain.

"Leave her alone, Lip," Riggs says, stepping forward.

Lip licks his lips, raking his teeth on his bottom one. "Lemme have some fun with this one, boss."

"Not yet," Crew says, snapping his fingers.

Lip lets go, shoving me onto the ground and putting his boot on my back.

Savages.

The lot of them.

"Keep a tighter leash on this one, Riggs. Adam's a no-show the last few days. Can't trust no one lately, can I?" Crew says, taking a phone from his pocket. "Here's a burner. I'll call you in two days with my verdict."

I try to push up but that makes Lip step down harder and lift my arm with him. My whimpers move through the forest.

He's about to snap a rib.

Dislocate my shoulder.

Break my back.

I groan, letting out another wail.

I can't help it. I'm crying softly. Praying for an end. Put me out of this misery.

"I told you I can get you the money," I yell.

Crew snaps his fingers again and Lip steps off, forcing a choked sob out of me. I think he really did snap something.

Crew crouches down and presses a gun to my temple. "How can you do that now, sweetheart?" he asks, moving hair from my face with the gun.

I sniffle, pushing myself to my knees and holding onto my shoulder. "My parents have money. Lots of it. Just name your price."

Crew looks at Riggs, tonguing his cheek. "Cash?"

I nod, wincing as I rub my shoulder. "Whatever you want."

"Something to think about, brother," Judas says, his hair tied in a low ponytail.

Banks nods, holstering his gun. "Two days, yeah? We got a job. Once that's done, we deal with this."

Crew nods, gently nudging my chin, and snaps his fingers at Riggs. "Can you keep a leash on her?"

"Yes," he grunts, taking my arm and pulling me to my feet.

I wince sharply and force my cries back.

Riggs forces me to the cabin, and the rest of the gang gets back on their bikes and takes off. I don't like this anymore. I don't want to be here. I don't want to talk or eat or smile. I just want out.

We're alone.

It's awkward.

Quiet.

And I'm in so much pain I might pass out.

My rib.

My back.

My shoulder.

What the heck did Lip do to me?

Riggs tosses me onto the couch and slams the back door. Letting out a loud growl as he stomps over to the couch. "They could have fucking killed you!"

I'm sobbing now, curling into a ball as I hold onto my shoulder. "I don't care."

His angered breaths die down when he looks at me, sighing softly.

He makes his way to me, those heavy footsteps echoing through this damned place.

The couch shifts when he sits beside me, placing a hand on mine that's rubbing my shoulder. "Lemme see."

I sniff, keeping my eyes closed. "It's fine."

He rises, scooping me in his arms and walking with me to the bathroom. His good ole medical kit is in there.

He puts me on the counter and takes my arm, moving it up and down, hand placed on my shoulder as he does it. "Don't think it's dislocated."

I sniff, rolling my shoulder a couple of times. "Mm'kay"

His hands rest on either side of me, staring at my shoulder, my face, neck, then meeting my eyes. "They ain't playing. They will kill you." The softness in his voice sends chills through me. This is a whole other side to him. A caring side. Something I knew was hidden deep in there.

"I don't doubt that."

His gaze flickers from one eye to the other. "Don't do it again."

I inhale slowly, licking my dry lips as I do it.

This giant bastard cares for me. I can see it in his eyes. Eyes that remind me of someone I used to care for, too. But caring eyes lead to betrayal. And one way or another, he'll choose the motorcycle club over me.

I'm escaping again.

I'm not sure if he knows it; it'll happen again soon.

No doubt about that.

I look down and wince as I try to push myself off the counter. He does it for me and lifts me up, holding me close to him a moment too long, and sets my feet on the floor.

There's nothing I want out of him right now.

Freedom, maybe.

Keys to his bike, perhaps.

A fucking drink. That's what I need.

I move past him, rubbing my shoulder as I do, and make for the kitchen.

My legs feel like rubber as I walk, wanting to buckle under me. There was a gun pressed to my head. A freaking gun! Crew could have shot me, killed me in cold blood for something that doesn't concern me. I'm here because of something Adam did.

I take a fresh mug and grab the coffee, hands shaking frantically as I try to pour a cup.

Riggs's heavy footfalls make their way to the kitchen. It's like he senses my fear and places a soft hand on my upper back, taking the shaking pot from my hands. "I got it, sunshine. Go sit down."

I don't move, I break down instead.

Cry like I've never cried before.

And he just stands there, hand on my back, and sighs.

It's going to be a long week knowing by the end of it I won't be here anymore.

The fun, loving Zaynab everyone knew will be no more.

How can my time come when I haven't done anything with my life? This isn't fair.

Why the fuck did I get dragged into this?

Adam, you fucking asshole. My blood will be on your hands.

I'll make sure of it.

Riggs

We're sitting by the fire. She's curled up in the armchair while I'm sitting on the couch with my legs wide apart and a beer in hand. Itching for another taste of her.

I clear my throat, looking at her watching the fire. There's enough heat radiating that I'm breaking a sweat.

"You want a drink?"

"No."

She's been cold all damn day.

Saddened.

Upset.

Scared.

I live off the fear.

Feed on it.

But with her.

I want to take it away.

All of it.

Bury it deep and see that smile again.

That spunk.

Sass.

Woman's so sassy it cracks me up.

Right now, she's worried.

I don't think she believed we were going to kill her come Friday. She thought we'd let her go.

Crew has other plans for her.

But I'm letting her go.

She's not dying on my watch.

There's this itch in me. This protectiveness.

She's my responsibility and I'll make sure she gets out of this alive.

Satisfied, too.

Although there's a darkness inside her. Just like me. And soon I'm going to let it free.

I clear my throat, fixing myself on the couch and wipe my brow. "You feeling better?"

"Peachy."

"Your shoulder okay?"

Her gaze meets mine, no emotion to it. No smirk or sass wrapped around her words. They've broken her. "Does it matter?"

I want to walk over there and kiss her, take all her pain away.

Inhale it.

Consume it.

Let her smile again. Just for a second.

Inhaling sharply before I reply and I almost regret it as soon as I do. "Matters to me, sunshine."

"It shouldn't. I don't matter to many people."

I want to distract her. Take her away from this sadness.

I just don't know how.

I was never good at relationships. Always used the chicks I was with. Cheated. Lied. Did anything but be that perfect boyfriend.

Shit, I don't even think I've had a real girlfriend before. Just a bunch of women I continued to fuck until I didn't. I used them to relieve the darkness this life brings me. This hatred I have. This vomit I absorb. But a relationship, no, I never really had that.

I might've had one with Natalia, but that was short-lived.

Zay is the type of girl you make love to and stay with forever.

Little bit of good. Little bit of bad.

"You in school?"

She nods, nothing more.

"What're you studying?"

She sighs, rolling her eyes to me. "Does it matter?"

I nod, leaning forward, and tapping her knee. "Tell me."

She grins.

Finally.

And moves onto the couch with me.

"Graphic design."

I smirk because someone I once knew was in the same program. I wished the best for them to be away from this life. I paid their way through school with the dirty money I made. Urged them to study and better themselves. But this life took hold and ruined them.

"You any good?"

She takes my beer and sips it, a single drop leaking down her chin. She wipes it with the back of her hand and shrugs. "I think I was. I even got an internship that's supposed to start in the fall. I'd be doing school part-time and the internship part-time." Her face brightens, a twinkle shining behind that pain. "If they liked me, I'd stay there permanently. They even said they'd hold my position until I get my degree." She shrugs again. "It's whatever now, right?"

Taking the beer from her, I sip it, too. Staring at her breaking before me. "It'll be okay."

She chortles, sniffling. "That's what they all say."

I don't know what happened to her in life.

Whatever it was, it didn't bode well with her.

It broke her down, tore away the laughter and sparkle.

It made her into this girl I'm sure not many people who know her would recognize anymore.

I wish I could have met Zay before all this. Walked into a bar and smiled at her.

Drowning in those hazel eyes before she was ruined.

What doesn't help is, I'm going to ruin her just a little more.

***

We don't talk much more after that. It isn't uncomfortable or awkward. It's calming.

Being in her presence keeps me at peace.

Looking over at her, I notice she fell asleep, curled in a ball in the middle of the couch beside me wearing nothing but my t-shirt.

I stare at her for a little.

Watch how the flames cast shadows on her face. A menacing-looking glow that makes her soft features jagged and frightening.

But still so beautiful.

I wonder if we met under different circumstances, would the stars align for us?

Would she like me? All muscles and tattoos?

Or would she judge me? Think I'm nothing but bad decisions?

If I met her in the real world, I'd still lay my life on the line for her. Give her everything that I can give and scrape the bottom of the barrel to give her more.

She can have all of me. Woman is in my blood, mutating like a parasite.

By the time she consumes me, I'll be lost without a way of getting home.

So, I ignore the what-ifs and continue to study her. Treat her like the Snake Biters and fuck her. Imagining what it would be like to do her right and not against a fridge in a frenzy.

She hums quietly and adjusts her head on the back of the couch. She doesn't look comfortable and that protector in me has to fix that.

Cracking the bones in my neck, I rise, making it my mission to make her comfortable. She's a tiny little thing and looks even smaller in my arms. It feels right, though. So right.

Goddammit.

Carrying her to the master bedroom, I lay her on the bed, that long brown hair covering some of her face. Naturally, I move it away as she turns onto her side, and a low hum leaves her again.

Never moved the hair out of a chick's face before.

Never tucked a chick in.

Never made sure she was warm enough or that the blanket covered her arms.

But here I am, delicately brushing hair from Zay's face and pushing it behind her shoulder before I lift the covers over it.

She's stunning.

It's not a wonder why she's with Adam. He seems right for her. A good boy.

I'm not a good boy. I haven't been a good boy since I was fifteen.

No, I haven't been good since before I was born.

I was bred into this life.

Molded into it because of my father.

Our president.

There's no hope for me.

But this woman sleeping soundly gives me that hope.

That twinkle.

This woman makes me want to be better.

I can do better.

For her.

I'll be the best I can with or without her in the end.

Pressing my lips to her head, I breathe in the faint scent of my shampoo mixed with the smell of her.

Girl's killing me.

It's going to be one hard night to sleep after our encounter this morning.

But I walk out of the room no matter the pull trying to keep me there. I walk into my room next door and let out a breath. Then, I close the door and lean my head back on it, closing my eyes.

They're going to kill her come Friday, with or without my say.

Crew is fucked, there's no questioning that. I have to think of something to keep her safe.

Something that will make sure this woman doesn't suffer at the hands of the Snakes.

No one deserves that, not even me.

Squeezing my eyes shut until I see fireworks of colors, I release one last breath before I make for the bed and fall facefirst into it. I'll remain that way until morning when I'll be able to see that beauty again

The beauty whose spark is fading as each day passes.

Zay

I think reality struck me.

This whole thing I'd been treating like a joke.

Another day in the manically crazy life of Zay.

But having Lip holding me down, Riggs's hand around my neck, and Crew's gun pressed to my head? This shit is real. And I need to take it seriously because soon, I'll be a dead woman.

I woke up last night in bed and couldn't go back to sleep.

Tossing and turning. Thinking about what I'd done in life to come to be here.

I fucked up a lot.

Screwed people over and never thought anything of it.

And it all started when Lillian Delano killed herself.

I was a good girl, a little wild, but tamed.

Before Lillian died, I had one boyfriend. He was cute but dumb as a doorknob. We broke up when I left for university. I vowed to play the field and not tie myself down. Lillian was not inclined to behave that way. She was a virgin when we started at Stanford University. As innocent as they came. She pined for someone. Someone I told her was trouble. And I only knew Peter was trouble because I let him inside me two weeks before they started dating. I didn't know she liked him and he didn't know Lillian and I were friends. It was one night and we never spoke again…until she introduced me to him. I kept my mouth shut about our night, but I warned her that he wasn't the right guy for her. He never bought her gifts or took her on dates, and never made time for her, which let's face it, there's always time to be made for someone you're dating unless the only free time you have, you're screwing someone else. He was screwing someone else.

And just shy of her twentieth birthday, she offed herself and I blamed it all on Peter, that jackass. But Lillian, she loved him.

Gave him everything.

Her innocence, her money, her life.

We were good girls together, she and I. Then she left me alone.

Me and my thoughts aren't ones to be left alone often. And the first time we were, well, shit went down.

I kissed whoever came up to me at parties.

Some I slept with.

Many I stole from.

Lillian and I were the good girls.

Straight A's, enrolled in university, always proper in church.

Then she died.

My grades plummeted.

I never went to church anymore.

And drugs became my everything.

My parents cut me off for a while. Thinking it would help me stop.

It didn't.

I had to find other ways to catch that high. And what way's better than my body?

I'd exchange sex for a dime bag of coke.

They'd get off.

I'd get high.

Nothing helped. I still had that pain and heartache inside me from losing my best friend. My sister.

Peter had to pay.

And he did.

He paid the day I quit snorting coke cold turkey. And I'm haunted by my actions every day that passes.

Things looked up seven weeks after Lillian died. I was finally happy again because I met Adam. He smiled at me as I counted change for my coffee—

twenty-five cents short.

He paid for it. He always did. Then my parents saw a change in me and started helping me again. Life was getting back to normal, all because of Adam. He was my savior.

Now he's nothing but a snake taking everything away from me. Yet, I still love him.

If only I knew why or what he did. Maybe we'd still be together.

A knock strikes my door as I step out of the shower, creaking open right as I fix the towel around my chest.

Riggs nods at me, running his fingers through his hair. He's shirtless.

Scrumptious.

Beautiful.

He sees me eyeing him, that ink etched into his skin, so intimidating and frightening.

Nightmare inducing.

Like fallen angels screaming for a second chance.

The way the snake tattoo slithers up the left side of his body, open mouth hissing on his chest. It's beautifully eerie.

He clears his throat, making my eyes shift to his. "Lunch is ready."

"Okay, be out in a sec," I say, taking the toothbrush and rinsing the sleepless night from my mouth. I didn't get out of bed until my bladder started screaming at me.

There isn't much to do around here, so taking long baths or showers have become my go-to.

It's relaxing.

Stress-relieving.

An escape for a short while.

Throwing on a blue dress they shoved into a bag, I wonder what my dorm room looks like after they broke into it. A disaster, I'm sure.

Gosh, my poor roommate.

Riggs is sitting at the table, looking down at his phone as his thumbs move across the screen. Sending off a text.

He glances up, then back at the phone Crew gave him, and does a double-take. Raking his eyes over me. "Made hotdogs and French fries."

Sitting in front of him, I tongue my cheek as I look at the plain hotdog and fries.

I hate hotdogs, but he doesn't know that.

Taking a gander at his phone turned over beside him, I realize I haven't used my phone in three days. No, has it been four?

Ugh, I suddenly miss my phone.

I miss scrolling aimlessly through Instagram.

Miss taking selfies.

Miss texting my friends.

It's like a drug.

I need my fix.

"Can I call Adam?"

Riggs dips his fries in mayonnaise.

Barf.

And looks up at me. "No."

"Please."

I slide my foot up his leg, tempting him to do what I want.

Praying it works.

It doesn't.

He grunts, chuckling softly and sitting back in his chair. "You got me to fall for it once. It ain't happening again."

I frown, scoffing. "Fall for what? You hit on me, remember?"

He tongues his cheek. "You offered it to me. Why would I turn down sex?"

I chuckle, leaning forward. "And I'm offering it again."

"To use the phone? You're better than that."

I'm not.

But he doesn't know that.

Rolling my eyes, I sit back, pushing my plate out. I'm not hungry and eating right now will turn my stomach.

I look out the large windows, the dense forest taunting me. There's a fog between the trees.

Floating.

Hovering.

Wavering when a breeze pools in.

It's a shitty week weather wise.

Also life wise.

It's been a shitty-ass month life wise—year wise. Just wise.

My life is shit.

When I think back on Adam and how he got me mixed up in this predicament, I realize maybe it was all my fault.

It's the only thing that makes any sense right now.

Rolling my head back, I close my eyes a moment, seeing his face so clearly. The smile that made my stomach flutter, those dimples, and blue eyes. I miss running my fingers through his short hair, pulling at it when his head was between my legs.

I miss Adam. I miss him more than words can describe, and yet, I despise him for everything he put me through the past few weeks.

When I look in front of me, I catch Riggs taking a bite of his hotdog and staring at me. What I wouldn't give for an ounce of relief. Just a small bump, a pill.

Anything to escape this nightmare for a while.

Or forever.

Riggs

Perfection radiates off her.

Trouble.

Conniving.

Bitch.

But I want her.

That tight little thing beneath me.

Consuming it.

Destroying it.

Loving it.

She's giving it to me.

Using me.

I don't want to use her.

She has a dark past but she doesn't need to be taken advantage of, as I'm sure she was before. She deserves so much more.

A life.

Love.

Happiness to keep that smile on her face.

That gorgeous fucking smile.

She's staring out the window, watching the trees.

Bewildered.

Sad.

I hate this look on her. It's the same look she had when we first met. Except no tears. She rolls her head back and closes her eyes with a deep breath.

With a gulp, I start eating. Keeping my focus on her. Her creamy skin is like silk. Soft, and it has just the right amount of shine. I trail my eyes down her jaw, her throat, getting lost in the valley of her cleavage.

It was hard not to wake her when I put her to bed last night.

Fuck our troubles away.

It's the best kind of screw, no messiness, no strings. Just hard thrusts and sloppy kisses.

But Zay kisses like a dream.

I don't notice I'm still staring at her as I'm chewing until she swallows and lowers her head.

I avoid her gaze when she looks at me, keeping my attention on my food rather than her.

No bad decisions.

I always make bad decisions.

That's what almost got me removed from the club. My stupid decisions.

Eighteen months ago, I met Natalia. She was cute, tight the way I like them. But she was innocent. Too innocent for my liking. Yet I still used her for a release. The boys took notice and when they took notice, she started sniffing where she shouldn't. Then, the stupid gash ratted on us. I thought Natalia was a good girl just looking for a little bad. Turns out, she was a bad girl craving more wickedness.

Told the cops we were killers.

Drug dealers.

Gun suppliers.

Sex traffickers.

And kidnappers.

Ninety percent of that is true.

Half of our guys got arrested. Some are still in the slammer. Our guns were confiscated, our club was shut down. Judas's bar was ransacked and bugged.

Worst of all, my daddy went to prison. President of the MC.

Nowhere was safe after what she did.

Crew blamed me. Beat me. Almost killed me. All because I was screwing a skinny bitch who said she loved me. I knew the chick for four months and she fucked me over.

Guys took their turns beating me for six days straight.

My face was unrecognizable. They didn't care, though, all they cared about was making sure I wasn't the rat. That no one else got arrested.

It's been fourteen months since she ratted, thirteen months since I last saw her. They still don't trust me. Think I had a hand in the bust. I didn't even know. Bitch had me fooled.

Natalia came into Judas's bar with a mission. Got me mixed into it. Blinded me with her short skirt. Tight top. And nasty tongue. She seemed out of place. Like the outfit she wore wasn't hers. The words she spoke weren't hers. But I needed a release. She wanted me and my dick needed a hole to burrow into for the night.

For four months she was my go-to. Unless we were out of town. If we were out of town, I had my way with girls in the other charters. Teaching them a thing or two.

But Natalia was my girl.

Then she ghosted me.

Left me clueless.

Left my bed cold.

Eleven days after she left me without a word, cops were banging down our doors.

Warrants waving.

Arrests taking place.

All eyes were on me.

Seeing Zay sitting in front of me, flaunting her precious body like it means nothing, reminds me of what Natalia did. I can't go through a betrayal like that again.

Zay shifts her attention back to the phone. Slumping in her chair without touching her food. Must be why the girl's so skinny. She doesn't eat.

I push her plate forward, sliding the ketchup over, too. "Eat."

"I don't like hotdogs."

Taking it from her plate, I drop it onto mine, savagely biting from the one I was working on. "Better."

She stares at my beer, then the fridge. "Is there anything other than beer to drink?"

I stuff the rest of the hotdog in my mouth and make for the fridge, her eyes on me as I do.

Little lady better watch it, I might let my guard down and eat her up.

Shit, she doesn't have to watch it. It'll happen again real soon.

I have no self-control.

I trust too easily when a pretty lady bats her eyes at me.

I'd say it's a fault of mine, but my father's the same. Gave himself to my mother and had his way with every girl who walked through the doors of the club.

Half of them didn't know what was coming to them.

Now he's in prison, and I was supposed to take over his club.

Instead, I'm babysitting a sexy woman batting her eyes at me.

Zay

D umbass.

As soon as Riggs gets up from his seat, I lunge for the phone and dart outside.

I can hear him growl and yell out for me.

But I don't give a shit. I'm getting the fuck out of here.

I'm trying to call Adam as I'm running, but my fingers are jumping everywhere and I keep messing up the number.

After my third try, I succeed.

Riggs is on my ass, though.

I'm three rings in before he grabs me and we plummet to the ground.

We're scrambling.

Rolling in the dead leaves.

Leaping at the phone.

But the line goes dead as soon as I get hold of it.

Riggs is on top of me, hand around my wrist, and banging it on the ground for me to let go. He's going to break my wrist if I don't comply.

I whimper and open my hand, phone flying away.

His massive body is pressed down on me, towering over me, and crushing me. "I told you *not* to fucking do that!"

Huffing, I struggle under him. "What does it matter anyway? Admit it, I'm a dead woman with or without the money. So who fucking gives a shit what I do? I just want one fucking phone call."

He grabs onto my face and bangs my head on the ground. "If you fuck-up or run off, I'm the one who gets the shit end of the stick, and I ain't here for

"

that. So, follow the fucking rules for once."

I grit my teeth, spittle forming. "Fuck you."

An ensuing smirk spreads to his lips. That smug look I despise. "I already did."

Asshole.

I struggle to get loose again when leaves crunch nearby, and gentle conversing comes our way.

Riggs looks up and immediately panics. It's written all over his face.

Redness forms on his cheeks.

His eyes widen.

He rolls his throat.

I can use this as my escape. I can call out to these people and beg them to help me.

But they could be more bikers, dead set on making their president proud.

They could kill me, for all I know.

I reach down and undo his pants, opening my legs around him.

He lets go of my face and takes my wrist again. "What the fuck are you doing?"

Hiking up my dress, I adjust myself under him, making it look like we're messing around. "Neighbors think you're here with your lady, right? So play along."

He scoffs, looking over his shoulder as the footsteps grow closer. I can already see the fisherman's hat bobbing above the bushes.

"Just kiss me." I pull his face down, pressing my lips on his.

It's easy to fake. Easy to pretend this isn't real.

But as soon as our lips touch, a zap hits us and he jolts back, staring down at me.

We hold our gaze for a split second before we kiss like he just got back from war.

Hungry. We're both so hungry.

If we kiss like this any longer, we might actually have sex out in the open.

His dick pokes me and he reaches down, taking it out of his boxers. I don't even think about it, I'm reaching down, too, moving my underwear to the side when someone clears their throat.

Riggs whips his head over his shoulder and gets to his knees. "Clayton." He stands, zipping up his pants and putting his hand out to me.

A chuckle arises in the older gentleman, and a blush touches the older woman's cheeks.

Smoothing out my dress, I pick a couple of dried leaves from my hair, and slide my hand in Riggs's as he stands there, dumbfounded.

"Didn't mean to bother you and your woman. Crew said you'd be here with someone, just thought we'd bring over some of our catch this morning for your dinner." Clayton holds out a dead fish. "It ain't much but should be enough for you two."

Riggs nods awkwardly and takes the fish. "Thanks, Clayton."

He looks up at the cabin and then back at us, grinning. "Wanted to borrow your extra tarp if you don't mind. There's supposed to be heavy rain and wind the next couple of days."

Riggs squeezes my hand and grunts before letting go, walking toward the shed with Clayton close on his tail.

The woman smiles and follows after them, leaving me alone.

Just what I wanted. It's nice when things fall into place, isn't it?

Getting on my knees, I sift through the leaves for the cell phone, finding it face up with a crack in the screen.

There's a missed call from Adam and a message from Crew.

I try Adam again; one ring and he answers.

"Who is this?" His grumpy voice comes through the receiver.

"It's me."

He sighs, slightly out of breath. "Zay, where the heck have they taken you?"

I glance around to make sure Riggs isn't making his way back. "Some cabin. It's like a hideout or something." I wince, holding my shoulder when I move it a weird way. "Look, I don't have much time. What the fuck did you get me into?" Running my fingers through my hair, I scoff. "Five hundred thousand? What did you do to owe them that much?"

His breathing is erratic on the other end. I don't know what he's doing but it's annoying me that he can't give me his full attention. "It's not what I did, it's what I saw."

"What did you see?"

Riggs is making his way back, chuckling with Clayton and his wife.

"Shit, Adam, I have to go. Here." I take the phone off my ear and send him a pin drop of my location. "Fix your mess before they fucking kill me, please. If you ever cared about me, do me this solid."

His heavy breathing moves through my ear once more. "I'm sorry, babe."

Then the line goes dead.

Dropping the phone, I kick leaves over it before Riggs looks up at me standing awkwardly, a guilty look on my face. "Everything okay?" I ask, running my fingers through my hair again.

Riggs scans me suspiciously, looking at the phone face down in the dirt. "Yeah."

"Tarp will do us good through the storm, they're calling for high winds and hail. So be sure to get some candles out, we might lose power," Clayton says, nodding at me.

I smile, clasping my hands behind my back. "Which house is yours? We went down to the water yesterday and I didn't realize anyone else was out here."

Nope, Riggs doesn't like that I asked this.

His jaw twitches. That scowl in his eyes.

Too fucking bad.

Fight or flight.

"One on the right," the woman says, holding one end of the tarp as her husband holds the other.

Lovely couple. Quiet, too. Although, I don't like how this woman is looking at me.

Narrowed eyes, a sour face, like she got a whiff of dog shit.

No matter. All that matters is they are neighbors I can trust if I escape again, with success, hopefully.

Riggs sees them off and takes my hand. Jesus Christ, he's squeezing so hard my knuckles crack.

Can't blame him. I tried to escape twice on his watch. His motorcycle club would have his head for this.

He snatches his phone off the ground and yanks me along with him back to the cabin, tossing me onto the couch again.

This good old sturdy couch.

I collapse on it with a thud and groan, clenching and unclenching my hand.

He's staring at his phone, furious and annoyed.

Angry.

Yep, he's about to do me in.

I had it coming, anyway. I haven't been the easiest person to get along with.

In life, and captivity at this cabin.

What goes around comes around. This is karma telling me she's back with a vengeance.

Rubbing my eyes, I try to keep my shit together. My failed attempts at escaping are going to make him keep an even better eye on me now. Shit, he might start sleeping in my room with me. Might make me shower or use the toilet with the door open.

I'm breaking his trust with my instinct to survive.

Can you blame me?

I wince as I clench my hand, of course, it had to be the hand that's already injured, right?

Not the best luck for my left hand this week.

Or my shoulder…just my left side in general. It's taken a beating.

But I got through to Adam. I got through to him and I'm hoping the love and connection we shared will be enough to save me.

You'll save me, right, Adam?

Riggs

Zay gets off the couch, massaging her hand, wincing. I squeezed it kind of hard. But this woman is trying to get me killed. She's becoming a fucking pain in my ass.

Not only did she escape again, but she took my phone and spoke with someone. And sent them our location. Oh, and the stupid fucking bitch cracked the screen.

Why do I feel so many mixed emotions toward her? She's done nothing but act up.

Not following the rules.

Putting herself and me at risk.

But then she looks at me with those hazel eyes and I'm like a puppy dog, down on my knees and bowing to anything she needs.

I need to focus. I can't let her beauty win again. She fooled me once. Made me lose sight. No more.

"Who did you speak with?" I say as calmly as I can.

She groans quietly, putting her hands by her sides. "Adam."

I growl, thundering toward her. She gasps and tries to step back but I grab her by the arms. "Why do you have to make things so damn difficult?"

Tears well in her eyes. "Because I'm not just going to sit around and be killed without the knowledge as to why. What the fuck did Adam get himself into for me to end up here, with you, in this cabin on a countdown to the end of my days?" She takes a shuddered breath. "Is that too much to ask?"

I can't help it. This girl is turning me to mush.

I release her but stay close, towering over her by a foot and a half.

Little half-pint.

"What did Adam see?" she whispers.

What does she mean? Adam saw nothing. He owes us money because…well, I don't know why. Since Natalia, I've been left out of a lot of meetings. This being one of them.

I was surprised they asked me to come along the other night. When Crew asked me to join them, I wasn't sure he was talking to me until he kicked my door in and told me to pack a bag and get ready. It's not what I'm used to. Pulling the trigger and beating people is what I'm used to.

Watching her is not something a VP does. This is something Banks or Lip can do. Maybe even Judas.

But I sure am happy it's me.

Because she'd be dead if it were one of them.

Maybe we were meant to meet. Fated because of the ties we have to each other. Adam, he's the only tie we have. And Adam is the reason we're both cooped up in this cabin, mad at each other.

When she whispers the same question again. I frown. What did Adam see to force Zay and me together?

By the flicker in her eyes, she can tell I have no idea what she's talking about.

"Adam said he owes money because of something he saw, not something he did. So what did he see?" she repeats like I didn't hear her the first time.

Our eyes are locked, as if the longer and harder we stare, maybe one of us can think of the answer. But it's not going to work.

I need to make a phone call.

Taking her hand, I yank her to the kitchen, digging in a drawer beside the stove for the handcuffs.

Last time I used these was with Natalia; I tied her up and rode her good. Little did I know it was for her to study our hideouts. Cunt robbed us of our lives. Stole our homes and ruined our names. Now, she's gone and not a single soul misses her.

The handcuffs click into place around the handle of the fridge and Zay groans, trying to get her wrist loose. "Really?"

"I gotta make a phone call." I start walking off, then turn around with a smirk. "Don't go anywhere."

"Ha, ha, very funny."

Stepping outside, the wind's really picked up and the sky is darkening. Clayton wasn't lying about it being bad. We might lose power tonight.

I'll call Crew and ask him about Adam to find out if what she's saying is true. I'll know if he's lying, too. He clicks his tongue every time he lies.

Crew answers, slightly out of breath. "Can I call you back? I'm about to be deep in one of Roaden's whores."

Roaden, my uncle. Butt-hurt that he isn't the president, but he's a nomad. We don't give president patches to nomads. He's asked me to join him. Ride the roads and fuck the sluts in other charters. Living out of a backpack and only going where needed. I'm not needed in my father's MC anymore. VP or not, I'm useless here.

I've been thinking about getting out for a while. It all comes down to a vote, and I doubt the boys will want me gone. They don't trust me. Why would they trust me being a nomad and screwing over other charters? I wouldn't, because I don't rat.

After this shit is done, I'm out.

The road's been calling my name for years, but my father wouldn't let me leave. Now that he's in prison, maybe the club's vote will work in my favor.

A taste of freedom can come my way.

I pinch the bridge of my nose and let out a breath. I don't care if Crew is busy, I got a fucking question. "What did Adam see for us to keep his woman hostage?"

Crew clicks his tongue.

A chuckle leaves him. "He didn't see shit."

My fists clench at my sides as I walk the perimeter of the house. "Don't lie to me, Crew. I paid my dues for Natalia. Don't make me pay more when I had nothing to do with her ratting on us. I ain't a rat. You know that. My daddy ran this club before you. Why the fuck would I tarnish his name?"

He clicks his tongue again.

Bastard.

"I'll call you in the morning. Storm's gonna be bad tonight. Stay dry, stay clean, and don't fuck this up."

The line goes dead.

I call Judas. He wouldn't lie to me.

Two rings before he picks up. By the slur of his words, he's drunk as shit. "Riggsy, what's good, my brother?"

Pinching the bridge of my nose again, these fuckers are giving me a headache. I turn the corner to the patio doors, seeing Zay still handcuffed to the fridge with her head inside it looking for something to eat.

Gorgeous little minx.

"Tell me the reason why I'm out here watching this chick."

Judas's beer bottle clanks on the table and he clears his throat. "Brother, y'know I can't betray Crew like that."

I grunt, turning the corner again as I near the front of the house. "She said Adam saw something, that's why he owes money. What did he see? I'm your fucking VP, man."

Judas clears his throat, sighing his deep, husky sigh. "Brother, y'know I love you, man. Y'know I'd lay down my life for you. But I can't say shit. Any one of us who talks gets the boot. I got a kid on the way, man. I can't—"

"It's okay," I interrupt. "Thanks, man."

"Sorry, brother."

Line goes dead.

Goddammit.

Storming back into the house, I find her eating from a jar of pickles. "And?" she asks with her mouth full.

Grunting, I know I shouldn't tell her anything but I can't help it. "Something's going down."

She scoffs, biting down on a pickle, and some juice trickles down her chin. "Fucking Adam."

If my boys won't tell me shit, then I gotta figure it out myself. Figure out how to dig myself out of this mess. Starting with her. She'll give me answers. If she doesn't, I'll pry them out of her.

Torture. *No.*

Beatings. *No.*

Sex. *Maybe.*

"How long were you guys together?"

She wipes her mouth on the back of her hand. "A year, give or take."

Leaning on the island in front of her, I cross my feet at the ankles. "He in trouble?"

She shrugs. "I don't know."

"You gotta gimme something, Zay."

She scoffs, putting the jar down and shutting the fridge. "Adam Lovett. Born and raised in California, only child, his parents weren't a big part of his life, so he was raised by his extended family. I never met any of them before you ask. He graduated high school top of his class and enrolled at Stanford University—where we met. He's a good boy with good grades. He doesn't party, doesn't smoke. Christ, he doesn't even speed up when a street light turns yellow and *everybody* does that." She shakes her head and finishes the pickle. "I think we only broke up because of me. He hated how much I liked to party. But what did he expect?" She shrugs again. "I tried to be good like him, tried not to attend every sorority or frat party, but after losing—" She pauses and clears her throat. "I don't know why Adam is mixed up in this, sorry."

She shifts, her hand gripping the handle of the fridge, and avoiding eye contact. "After losing what?" I press, studying her throat bob on another gulp.

"Nothing."

Tilting my head, I step closer to her. "Boys don't trust me. We're both fucked. So you can either tell me why I'm getting fucked so we can be in this together, or you can let me get fucked alone and reap the consequences I can't predict."

She takes a breath, reaching her cuffed hand out to me before it catches, opening the fridge slightly. "Uncuff me."

"Tell me and I will."

"Uncuff me first."

"Tell me and I will. I'll even let you call Adam again."

She drops her head back with a groan and sputters. "I met Adam a month-ish after I lost my best friend. She killed herself. Didn't leave a note, didn't tell me why. She was like my sister and didn't even give *me* a reason." She keeps her focus on the ceiling as tears slide down the sides of her face. "She was seeing this guy. Kind of an asshole, but she liked him. And who was I to judge who she should be with when I open my legs to whoever? He was her first and it's like he opened this darkness inside her she never let me see. But I know he's the reason she killed herself." Her gaze shifts to me, her head slowly lowering. Her face has darkened, shame and guilt spread to it. "He *was* the reason, at least." She sniffs. "When you asked if I killed anyone…I have. I killed *him*."

Woah.

I wasn't expecting this answer.

And with the tears shimmering in her eyes, I don't think she expected to tell me.

I don't press, I uncuff her and let her walk to the end of the hallway and back to the bedroom. Her soft sobs moving through the silence.

We never forget our first kill.

Never.

Zay

The storm outside is wild. Trees scrape against the side of the house. Rain hits the windows in savage sprays. And I think it started hailing about an hour ago.

I haven't left the room all afternoon. I hate talking about the past. Especially the past involving Peter.

After Lillian's funeral, I went to see him. Bastard didn't even bother to show up. And the bastard tried to hit on me as we lay in his bed and talked about her. That's probably my fault, though. I gave off the wrong impression by lying beside him, staring at the ceiling. I missed Lillian, and by proxy, I felt that if I lay beside her ex-boyfriend, I'd feel like her ghost was right there with us.

It wasn't. Her ghost was gone before she even slit her wrists.

The funeral ended around three in the afternoon and I was zonked.

A zombie.

I dragged my feet to her dorm room. It still had yellow caution tape on the door. It made her room look like a crime scene. Maybe it was. I only had my suspicions, I didn't have any proof. The yellow tape was cautionary. There was so much blood that poured out of her, they had to lift the linoleum floors to redo them.

Flowers were scattered on the floor and cards were taped to her locker. I'd been by almost every day since she died. Laying fresh flowers and tossing out the dead ones. The day of her funeral was no different.

I was going to place a red rose at her door that I took from her casket, the last piece of her I felt like I had left.

But I wasn't the only one going to her room. Peter was there, too.

"Hey," I said, startling him.

He swallowed hard. "Hey, Zaynab." He sniffed, wiping his cheeks. "Sorry."

I'd been crying for days but seeing him cry didn't sadden me. It angered me.

I knew he was the reason she died.

I just had to prove it.

He cleared his throat and slumped his shoulders. "I can't believe she's gone."

Humming softly, I shook my head. "Me either."

He frowned as he stared at her door. He was hiding something. It was written all over his face. Or maybe I just suspected there was something to hide, so I was looking for clues. Something to prove my theories.

Did he always flare his nostrils when he was deep in thought?

Did the vein in his forehead always bulge maniacally?

And his fists, were they supposed to be clenched at his sides like that? Or was this always how he stood?

No, maybe I was looking too much into my suspicion.

He flicked his eyes to me, running his fingers through his hair. "You busy?"

I shook my head. "No."

He nodded, walking toward his dorm room that was at the end of the hallway. "Come on."

So I did. I followed him into his room and plopped myself on his twin bed, falling back. He did the same, adjusting himself so that his shoulder was up against mine.

Uncomfortable, I remember that.

And for thirty minutes, we didn't say a word. All we did was stare at the ceiling, hoping the pain from mourning would go away.

It didn't.

It never will.

Taking a deep breath, I turned my head to look at him. I had to hand it to Lillian, she found herself a model. Tall as a tree. Sharp jawline, big blue eyes, short brown hair with hints of blonde in it from the sun. Freckles on his cheekbones. He seemed untamed, wild. That's why I wanted to be wild with him when we met during orientation week. It's probably why Lillian stayed with him. That fierceness in those soft eyes. He was a looker, and people noticed.

And right then, I was staring at him. Wondering what it would be like to stab his neck with the pen on my side of the bed that I sometimes used to take notes. Peter, Lillian, and I studied together often. We had a few classes together which made it more fun to study. Half of my books were always left in his room. I don't think he minded it, my dorm room was a mess. And Peter kept his clean for Lillian. She was a stickler for cleanliness.

"Why do you think Lillian killed herself?"

A cough left him from my bluntness. Breaking the silence with the harsh reality of our mutual friend. A friend we cared so much for it hurt us to know she was gone forever.

He shook his head. "I wish I knew. I didn't speak with her for three days before she did it. I tried calling her once, but she ignored it. Ignored my texts, too."

"Did she know that you guys weren't dating anymore?"

He gave me a side glance, then returned his focus to the ceiling. "Yes." He sighed. "No." He turned to face me as well. "I tried telling her a week before she died that we'd be better off as friends. I liked her and all, but I didn't like her the way she loved me." He shrugged, tonguing his cheek as his eyes glossed over. "I didn't wanna break her heart by leading her on."

I wiped the tear from his nose. "So you cheated on her, knowing she'd find out?"

He squeezed his eyes shut, shaking his head, and turning it into the pillow to choke a sob. "No, I didn't expect her to find out."

Placing my hand on his cheek, I flared my nostrils this time. The cold, bitter bitch who wanted revenge came pouring out of me. "You're the reason she killed herself."

He whimpered, sobbing with my hand on his face while his hands bunched up his blanket to his chest. "No."

"Yes."

He gritted his teeth. "Stop."

I didn't care anymore. I wanted him to know how much he hurt the people who cared about her. The people that loved her. He never did. Because if he did, then he wouldn't have slept with some sorority chick three nights before Lillian ended her life.

"Why?"

He rolled onto his back and let out a rush of air, sniffling, and breathing quickly.

Tears were rolling down my cheek as I watched him. Tears for her. My best friend. The only person in this world I ever gave a crap about. "She loved you so much and you didn't even have the decency to break up with her before you fucked someone else…how many people did you fuck, Peter? Hmm?"

A soft growl rumbled through his chest. But I continued, getting a rise out of him so he knew how I felt. Understood it.

"I'm her best friend and she couldn't even tell me what was wrong because I told her from the start you were nothing but a scumbag. She didn't listen and look at her now. She's buried six feet underground in that lilac dress she used to wear all the time." I scoff, turning onto my back as well, knocking his shoulder. "Thanks for coming to the fucking funeral, asshole. It was this morning."

He growled again and turned over, laying half on top of me. He placed his hand on my throat, slithering it to the back of my neck. "I know it was this morning, and I was there. At the back, because I couldn't stand to see them lowering her casket into the ground—" He paused, boring deeply into my eyes. "I couldn't love her because everything she did reminded me of you. The way she smelled was just like you. How she clicked her tongue before telling me something exciting. How she always called you after sleeping with me. It was you, you, you." His thumb brushed my lips. I knew what he was getting at, but I didn't want him to say it. I wanted to forget it as much as I wanted Lillian to come back to me. "You think I'd forget the night we met? The night you came into my life and took hold of it. No, Zaynab. I can't forget that night."

I turned my head away from his thumb. "You have to. Lillian didn't know about that."

He lowered his mouth to mine but didn't kiss me. "Every time I was inside her, I was thinking of you." He growled. "We reap the consequences we can't predict, don't we?"

I licked my lips, feeling the tears well up from yet another mistake I made. "Were you thinking of me when she killed herself?"

Disgruntled.

Angry.

Sad.

He slammed his lips on mine, forcing himself on top of me.

I tried to get out from under him, but the way he pushed down on me, I was trapped.

His kissing became savage, shoving his tongue in my mouth and making me gag.

I was pleading, pushing, gasping. And still, I was helpless under his strength.

He grabbed my hands and held them above my head, squeezing my wrists together without knowing the wound on one of them was opening up.

I tried to scream, but every time I opened my mouth, there he was. Breathing in my air, taking away my dignity.

I heard his zipper, I felt his dick on my leg.

I felt the tear of my stockings, my underwear, and the release of my hands so he could force himself inside me.

Ripping my mouth from his, I spat at him. "You think raping me will make the pain go away, you fucking asshole?!"

His hand met my mouth. "Shut the fuck up!"

I screamed under it as loud as I could, trying to bite down. But the more I moved, the harder he'd push.

Until his door opened and his roommate came in. Startled. Wide-eyed. My savior.

Peter looked down at me and mouthed, *keep your fucking mouth shut.*

Shoving him off of me, I fixed my ripped clothes. "You're gonna pay," I hissed and spat at him again. "Go fuck yourself, Peter."

I stormed out of his dorm room so fast that I didn't take notice of who was in my way when I turned the corner and bodychecked someone I would soon discover was Adam. I looked up at him as shock flooded his face, but I couldn't help it. I started weeping.

And he held onto me as I cried.

We didn't know each other then but he held me for ten whole minutes, letting everything pour out of me. Letting the thought of almost being raped by the man I was positive led to the death of my best friend take hold. The life I once knew was no longer. The savage inside me was loose, and soon, I'd be unrecognizable.

When I finally calmed down and his soothing shushing and back rubs stopped as well, I sniffed and looked up at him. "I'm sorry."

He grinned, smoothing out my hair. "Everyone can use a hug every once in a while." He picked up his books and backpack from the ground. "Are you going to be all right?"

I nodded, wiping my cheeks and slowly walking away. He stood there, watching me with a grin until I pushed open the doors to the stairwell. He waved and his smile grew.

I met Adam that day without knowing what an impact he'd make on my life. But our story didn't start there—no. It started weeks later after my partying, drinking, drugging, and sexing.

I met Adam when I got clean.

***

The storm is picking up, crashing, and smashing things outside. It's nearing dinner hour and I'm getting kind of hungry. Only eating a pickle the entire day will do that.

Riggs is sitting on the couch. One arm draped on the back of it, the other on the armrest, and holding a bottle of beer. He's asleep, his head rolled back and snoring softly.

He's handsome.

That manly kind of handsome you know will destroy you in the bedroom.

Looking back at my open door, I sigh. It would be easy to leave again. Easy to escape, but with the rage happening outside, there is nowhere for me to hide without the chance of getting hurt. This storm is insane. So I choose not to leave and not to find his gun.

I choose to stay and ride out this storm. I have a few days left to escape, and I'll attempt it again when there isn't chaos on the other side of the windows.

Dropping down beside him, I bring my knees up on the couch as he snorts, inhaling sharply. He blinks a couple of times, looking over at me as if he forgot I was in this cabin with him.

But I am. And I'm going to confess every damn thing running through my head. I hope Riggs doesn't mind listening to my ramblings.

"I don't think Adam loved me very much, or even at all." I shrug. "Have you ever been in love before?"

He clears his throat and sits upright. Shaking his beer and draining it. "Loaded question."

I sigh, leaning my head on my hand. "Yeah."

He returns his attention to me. "You all right?"

I nod. "I never told anyone *that* before."

He rests his ankle off his knee. "If it helps I've done bad things in my life, too. Killed lots of people. Fucked lots of people. Hurt many people. A lot of the guys in the club never bat an eye at what we do. But I ain't like them. Every time I held the gun to someone's head, all I thought about was their family. What brought them to this point in their life to be on their knees looking up at the barrel of my gun? But here we are."

I killed one person and I'm still messed up over it. He killed *lots* and it doesn't seem to bother him. How can taking someone's life not eat away at him like a nagging tick?

I poke a scar on his cheek, making him flinch. "What happened here?"

He swallows, putting his arm on the back of the couch again, resting it on mine. "Crew did that. Said it would always be a reminder of my fuck-up that almost cost us the club."

"What happened?"

He inhales sharply. "This girl I was screwing was a rat, sniffed her way in, and bugged the entire place. I didn't fucking know, but that didn't stop the men I call my brothers from beating me senseless. Almost disowned me and threw me out of the club." He shakes his head. "It ain't ancient history yet, though. I gotta feeling this whole thing your boyfriend got you into has something to do with me, too."

I study the scar, a small line on his left cheekbone right under his eyes. A mark to remind those of what he didn't do. We're all marked in some way, aren't we?

"We reap the consequences we can't predict."

His fingers graze my forearm, pebbling my skin. "What's that mean?"

Clearing my throat, I scoot closer to him, leaning my head on his shoulder. His body tenses, but that's fine. I just want to be held right now. "The guy I killed said that to me after Lillian introduced me to him, then said it to me before he tried to rape me." He tenses after I say that; he tenses at a lot of the darkness I reveal from my past.

Taking a breath, Riggs's arm falls onto my back, holding me closer. "Lillian was my best friend. But I hid something from her that no one, not even Adam knows." I'm fiddling with the hem of my dress, Peter's face flashing through my mind. "About two weeks or so before Lillian and the guy I killed started dating, we hooked up at a party. I thought nothing of it. Just a guy I slept with during orientation week. I didn't want to break her heart knowing that this guy she was so madly in love with was nothing but an asshole. I can't even explain why he's an asshole, probably because when she introduced me to him, he acted like I didn't exist. Like what we shared that night meant nothing to him. He was the first guy I slept with when I got to university, only the second guy to make a notch on my bedpost. But he didn't care. Didn't even call me after I left his dorm the next morning. I left him a note on his pillow and everything."

Shaking my head, I remember our night like it was yesterday. I saw him walk into the party before he even came up to me. Those intense blue eyes could never go unnoticed. We hit it off, instantly. Even through his nerves. How we floated naked in the water, watching the stars, how we kissed and there was this instant spark like we knew we were meant to be. We weren't. He was just like the rest of the guys who weren't Adam. Assholes who viewed me as some hole to keep their dick warm for a few minutes.

His wicked ways hurt my best friend. Drove her off the ledge because he was too selfish to understand what he did was wrong. She was fragile. "I believed he was the reason she killed herself. No, I *know* he was the reason."

"So you killed him."

"I did."

Riggs runs his fingers through my hair, relaxing the memories of that horrid night from my mind. A night I wish I could forget.

"My first kill was the scariest thing. Then the next wasn't as bad. And the next was even easier until I didn't feel a thing anymore." He pulls my legs onto his lap, tracing the scars on my knees I got after falling off my bicycle as a kid. "I've killed so many people for this damn club. Maybe all this shit happening is my karma. It's deserved."

My fingers meet his chest, tracing the tattoos in the same delicate fashion as he's tracing my scars. "We only deserve the things we regret."

He chuckles, that deep guttural sound moving through him. "The list is endless for that, sunshine."

Lifting my head off his chest, I meet his gaze. "Do you regret screwing me?"

He takes a deep breath, his focus on the wood-paneled ceiling, then slowly rolls his head to the side to look at me. "Under these circumstances, yes. I do regret screwing you."

I'm not expecting to be upset by his answer. But I am.

A regret.

I don't think I've ever been anyone's regret.

At least, no one ever said I was.

But it's out there now.

This man, who my legs are draped on, regrets being inside me.

I can't really blame him. I've caused nothing but trouble.

I am trouble.

But I don't want to be regretful trouble.

I swing my legs off him and rise. "Goodnight, Riggs."

He frowns, reaching for my hand. "You just got out of your room."

"And now I'm going back in it." I snatch my hand from him, letting his comment hurt me more than it should. "Goodnight."

He doesn't follow me.

He tongues his cheek and sighs, falling back on the couch as I slowly close the door and bask in the craziness that is the storm outside.

99

Riggs

I can't sleep with all the ruckus outside. And not being able to sleep is making me angry.

Shooting up from bed, I strut down the hallway to the kitchen. Her bedroom door is closed; it's been closed almost all damn day.

I miss that smile.

That giggle.

I told her I regretted her when I don't.

I want her again.

And again.

And again.

A little thing to call mine for a while.

Or forever.

Like I said, it's crossed my mind a time or two to get out of this business. Away from the club.

I'm on the verge of being disowned.

On the verge of being killed.

I might as well get out before that happens.

Get out and find me a beauty to love.

To make love to.

Have babies with.

Zay seems like the type of girl you have babies with. Even if it's not with me.

It's dark as fuck in the cabin. Doesn't bother me, though. I can make my way through this house with my eyes closed. It was my father's cabin, and that makes it part of the club's. A place for us to lay low. Not a place to raise some kids.

Even if I wanted it back, there isn't anything I can do about it. Not with Crew as president.

Taking a soda from the fridge, the light blinds me, hurting my eyes. I crack the can open, gulping it, when I hear something creaking.

Shit, my guns are in the bedroom. One under the pillow, the other in my boot.

Putting my soda down quietly, I close the fridge. My eyes haven't adjusted yet, they're burning, stinging from the damn fridge light. Whoever made that light didn't think to have a dimmer for nighttime.

Easing toward the hallway, darkness blankets the night, hiding the moon from giving off its glow. I'm relying on instincts.

Rounding the corner, I see a shadow.

My heart races, knowing this can be my chance to let the aggravation loose.

Acting before thinking, I grab the shadow and shove it into the wall.

Zay yelps, gripping my arms as I have her pinned. "It's just me. It's just me."

A growl seeps from my lips. "Don't sneak up on me—"

"You weren't in your room."

We haven't moved.

More like, I haven't put her down.

Her heart is racing.

Her breath is shaky.

I even think her lip might be quivering.

It's taking all the strength I have not to kiss her right now, to take her against this wall, the island, the couch, and make a mess of the bedrooms.

I can own her.

Destroy her.

Please her in all sorts of ways.

But I won't do that.

I fucked up once. It ain't happening again.

"Go to bed, Zay."

Putting her down, I take my soda from the kitchen. She doesn't move. She's planted against the wall in the darkness.

Her quiet voice wavers as I round the corner again. "Can I use your phone? Please."

"Why?"

Vulnerable.

I don't like this light on her.

"I want to call Adam like, you promised."

Grunting my answer, I go to my room. Her little footfalls follow me as I drop onto the bed, gulping more soda.

She's standing awkwardly at the foot of the bed, in my t-shirt, no less. "You can say no."

I tongue my teeth, take another gulp from the soda, and belch quietly. I *can* say no. I can do whatever the fuck I want. She's under my command until we get our money—if we get our money. I don't know what's going on here, nor do I know if I can trust the men I've laid my life on the line for.

My so-called brothers.

They don't seem like brothers to me now. Just people who share the same serpent tattoo as me. Who wear the same cut as me. Who ride a motorcycle like it's the air we breathe.

I can say no, but I don't. Not to her.

The can hits the side table with a bang as I reach for my cell phone and toss it at her. "Five minutes."

Her face lights up from the brightness of the screen. "Thank you." She turns to leave, but I clear my throat, getting comfortable on the bed.

"Don't go anywhere."

It's tempting to ask her to lie with me, to take my shirt off and just lie there. I don't even have to touch her, staring at her will be enough.

Being in her presence is enough to know getting out of the club is at the top of my to-do list.

She stares at the screen for a moment, her fingers hovering over the keyboard.

I hate this feeling.

That itch that can't be scratched.

She's beautiful.

Just the right amount of trouble to keep me guessing.

To keep it alive.

She's good for me.

Wild but tame.

Sassy but cute.

Tight. She's so tight.

I've been itching for another taste. But I can't.

She knows that and so do I.

I gave in during a moment of weakness.

I've been weak enough in the last fourteen months. I've been crawling my way out of the ditch to be back on top. My entire club doesn't trust their fucking VP. My father sticks his nose up to me and blames all this bullshit on me.

I haven't been to see him yet. I'm too scared of what he might do if I show my face.

Shank me?

Choke me?

He might even pull in a few favors from other charters and have me killed in a drive-by.

My father doesn't have much family. We're all he's got.

And I can't even grow a fucking pair and see him.

Some VP I am. Some son I am.

I need out.

To be rid of the Snakes and all their venom.

Once I'm free, things will be so much easier, won't they?

Zay

The line trills, then goes to voicemail.

I call again and it does the same.

Third time's a charm, no?

After two rings, Adam answers.

His groggy voice hits my ear. "Yeah?"

"Adam, it's me."

He clears his throat, there's shuffling sounds, and a door closes. "You okay?"

Scoffing, I sit at the end of Riggs's bed. "What do you think?"

Pinching the bridge of my nose, I start sobbing quietly.

I may not act it, but I'm scared.

I'm petrified.

This is not my doing. I shouldn't be part of this.

Adam sighs. "Hey, babe. It's okay," he says soothingly. "I'm doing what I can to make sure nothing happens, okay?"

I sniff, shaking my head even though he can't see me. "It's too late for that, Adam. Isn't it?"

The bed shifts and Riggs places his hand on my shoulder, squeezing slightly. He doesn't have to soothe me, but he is. He's not like the rest of his motorcycle club, he's so different than they are.

Little things like this prove it.

"Did you talk with my parents? They'll get you the money. If they want more, give them whatever. Just, please, Adam. They're going to kill me," I say through my weeping. He's never physically met my parents, but they know of him. Heard his voice through calls.

"FaceTime, now." He raises his voice, turning our phone call into a FaceTime. I answer, only because I have to see his face. It's the only thing that will calm me. his face is distorted, voice breaking up. But it's Adam. Gosh, I missed him so much. "Hey, look at me, Zay." More distortion, more breaking up. "Have I ever let anything happen to you since the moment we met?"

I shake my head, wiping my tears as he turns the light on in the bathroom. Our faces freeze, then come back and freeze again. Those blonde locks of his are slicked back, gel soaked into his hair, and his bright blue eyes stare at me so intensely that more tears well in my eyes. I don't care how shit our connection is, it's so good to see his face.

"I'm sorry they involved you in this. If I could switch places with you, babe, I would. But I'm going to get you out of there, okay?"

Turning away from the camera, I blink back more tears because I don't believe a word coming out of his mouth. We were great, so great, until he ended things like what we had meant nothing. There wasn't an explanation, there wasn't a reason. *I think we should see other people.*

Is it because he knows I'm not good enough?

Will I ever be good enough?

"Look at me."

So I do, sniffling.

"I'm doing what I can, babe. Okay? I'm doing everything I can—"

The bathroom door opens and he goes to push it shut. "Adam?" a woman's voice asks.

"Just a sec."

I scoff, staring at the man I thought I once loved. "Priorities, am I right?"

He shakes his head. "Zay, it's not like that—"

A sob escapes, I can't even look at him. "Sure. Whatever. Don't worry about me. Seems like you got better things to take care of than the fucking mess you dragged me into, you son of a bitch."

Hanging up, I growl, dropping the phone on the bed beside me. Adam and I haven't been together for weeks, but it hurts seeing him with someone else. It'll hurt him knowing I was with someone else, too. I'm guilt-ridden. Hurt. A burden. Yet, I want to hurt him even more by sleeping with Riggs again.

Self-harm with drinking, drugs, or sex always makes me feel better.

No, it doesn't. It just silences the thoughts in my head and I want to silence them for a little while.

Adam and I had our life planned out. As soon as we graduated, we'd get ourselves a place. We'd get married a year after that, and when our careers were settled, we'd pop out babies.

People change. I get that.

But he told me he loved me and that I was the first girl he said it to and he meant it.

If he loved me, then why the fuck is there someone else in his bed—yet I'm one to talk, given that I was with Riggs yesterday. I'm one to fucking talk.

The phone vibrates beside me.

Adam.

Once. Twice. Three times.

I don't answer.

Riggs doesn't, either.

I don't say anything.

I get up and go back to my room, hiding under the covers in the hopes that maybe when morning comes, this nightmare will be over.

***

Seven weeks after Lillian died, I sobered up and formally met Adam at the coffee shop.

He became my world for a while.

I thought I was his.

I'll never forget the first time we slept together. It took us a few weeks to get to that point. I don't know if it's because he was nervous or maybe I was. I remember telling him on our first date that I have a five-date rule. I don't. Maybe it was the fear that if I became vulnerable with someone I liked, my truth about what I did to Peter would come out.

I knocked on Adam's dorm room and smiled when he opened it, standing there in nothing but jeans.

"Hey, Zay," he said, giddy and radiant.

I must've fallen in love with him the moment he held me. That sweet cinnamon scent wafted off him, no matter the time of day. Like a freshly baked cinnamon roll.

My forest green strapless dress billowed out around me when I skipped to his bed and jumped onto it, sitting cross-legged. "What're our plans today?"

He locked the door, leaning on it and crossing his bare feet at the ankles. "We're not leaving this room, babe."

Groaning, I dropped back on his bed and placed a pillow on my face. Even his pillow smelled like cinnamon. "I don't want to study. All we do is study."

He removed the pillow and parted my legs, lowering his body on top of me. "It's kinda like studying if you think of it. I'll study you, you study me. We've been on more than five dates, y'know."

I did know and I was excited to get to know more about him. To understand him more than through his words, but through his moans, too. The intimate part of him that would consume me entirely.

I smirked, bopping his nose. "Then let's *study* together."

"Over." He kissed my cheek. "And over." My neck. "And over again." His tongue teased my cleavage. "I think we waited long enough."

"Undress me." I breathed, arching my back as he rose to his knees between my legs.

Being with Adam was always special.

He took his time.

Made sure I finished before he did.

And every moment was like we knew each other a little bit better. We knew our bodies.

Our souls.

Our minds.

He was my better half and I was his queen.

He slid off my underwear, staring down at me as I got out of my dress. Pride oozed from his gaze. He made me feel beautiful and not many people did that.

As soon as we were naked, we lay there staring at each other. His hands gently brushed along my skin, sending goosebump trails wherever his fingers roamed.

We didn't have sex right away.

We explored.

The tips of my fingers brushed down his chest, memorizing the contours of his muscles.

His fingertips traced my nipples, making them pebble.

His heavy breaths lingered on my neck, dancing before they evaporated between us.

"I want to touch you," he breathed.

My fingernails lightly scratched from his thigh, up his ass, and skittered along his back. "You already are."

He turned me onto my back, kissing me softly. "Open your legs."

I did.

"Open your mouth."

I did.

He licked his finger, putting it in my mouth to do the same. It was weird, but I went along with it. I remembered thinking he wanted me to taste him. Drink him in.

And I did.

But first, he touched me.

"Try not to make a sound."

Sliding my tongue along my teeth, I arched an eyebrow. "You either."

Reaching between us to touch him, he took my hand as I wrapped it around his cock and stroked the length of him once. "No, you first."

I didn't know it was possible, but I fell even more in love with him right there.

His eyes traveled down my body, just as his fingers did, watching what he did to me.

He parted my lips and touched my clit, slipping his fingers inside me as I squirmed beneath his touch. Tingles rushed through me, twitching my legs before he stopped and slid his fingers into his mouth.

A smirk spread to his lips as I pooled between my legs. "You taste the best out of all the women I've been with."

I breathed shakily. "How many have you been with?"

He bit down on my nipple, softly, yet just right so that it caused me to let out a moan. "Doesn't matter."

His hand slid between my legs again and he finished me off in quick strokes. My body bucked under him, shaking. Adrenaline coursed through me.

When I finished, he lunged over me, taking a condom from a box on his roommate's desk, and slid it on with a smirk on his face.

I pulled him back and kissed him, tasting myself on his tongue. Mercilessly, he eased into me and took me like it was our last day on earth.

Our lips locked.

Our tongues tangled.

Our breathing was hoarse.

"You feel so good."

A moan left his lips, his pace quickened, and he bit down on my shoulder.

Releasing.

Satisfying.

Rejoicing.

My lips feathered his cheek, holding him as we lay there, shaking still.

This was how it was with Adam.

Always intense.

Always euphoric.

Always beautiful.

"I love you, Zay," he whispered, slowly lifting from on top of me.

I breathed in, smiling. "To the end of time?"

He chuckled, kissing my lips. "Forever and always…"

***

I'm taken out of this memory by a loud bang in the kitchen. I jolt from the bed and rub the sleep from my eyes.

Creeping out of the bedroom, Riggs slowly walks out of his room, too. Gun in hand.

He puts a finger to his mouth and lifts the gun as he moves forward.

Nerves run through me.

All I see is Crew coming back to kill us.

Lip being the one to do me in.

My hands are shaking but I follow Riggs, gulping. Cursing quietly. And on the verge of tears again.

I did wrong in my life. But I don't want to go.

Riggs's large, tattooed back covers most of my view. The bulging muscles ripple as he inches forward.

"Riggs?" I whisper, looking behind me as if eyes are watching.

Lurking.

Touching.

Aching for a chance to strike.

He stops, making me bump into him, and holds the gun steady. "This ain't no house to break into."

The hooded person in the kitchen stops, their back to us. The black hood falls heavy over their face as they raise their hands and slowly turn around.

Riggs tenses, cocking the gun. "I suggest you leave before things get messy."

The hooded figure points to a letter on the kitchen table and slowly backs off.

Not a word leaves their lips.

I know this isn't the life I want. I want peace, not madness. How on earth did I fall into this?

I'm holding onto Riggs, my hand digging into his back and the other holding the forearm that isn't holding the gun. I'm shaking, and I think he can feel it. He growls as soon as a whimper leaves me.

The hooded person begins to ease backward, the front door busted open. Then it hits me. That smell. I'll never forget that smell.

I step forward, recognizing the cinnamon smell. "Adam?"

The hooded figure stops but doesn't say anything still, and leaves through the broken front door. It can't be Adam because this guy has at least four inches on him.

But I charge after them, anyway, pushing Riggs aside as I do. "Adam? Wait."

I'm too late.

The black Mercedes drives off, leaving a cloud of dust behind.

Adam drives a Honda.

I don't know who this was, but that smell…

Running my fingers through my hair, I grit my teeth. "Fuck."

Riggs is hot on my tail, taking me by the wrist and pulling me inside as he scans the area. "I'm gonna have a look around. Go to my room and stay there."

I'm shaking.

Worried.

Terrified.

But most of all I'm hurt that Adam wouldn't come to save me. That my Adam doesn't love me enough to protect me. Instead, he's fucking someone who isn't me. Like I'm doing. *We reap the consequences we can't predict*

I'm walking as if looking through a fish-eye lens. Nothing feels right. I'm weightless.

Thoughtless.

Out of control.

In shock.

Sitting on Riggs's bed, I pick up his phone and hit Adam's number.

Three rings before Adam picks up the FaceTime call. He's in bed, alone. "Zay? Zay!" He shoots up, shaking his head. "Last night. That wasn't what you thought. I swear it. I wouldn't do that to you." His breathing is shaky. "She's watching me. One of the member's wives."

I remember when his nervous breaths used to make me crumble.

Now they make me sick.

"I know we're not together, but everything I've ever said since we split is true. I want you back, babe. I never wanted us to end. You're the one who left before I could fix things." He shakes his head again, eyes getting bluer as tears well in them. "I love you, babe. I didn't want this to end. I don't, ever." He sniffs. "Forever and always, remember?"

I can't even take in what he said. I'm on the defense. "Who did you send to the house?"

Tears fall, rolling down his cheeks. "What are you talking about?"

Choking on a sob, I cover my face. "Adam, please don't fuck with me. You're the only person I know who smells like cinnamon." I wince. "I'm scared. I just want this nightmare to end."

He breaks up while pleading with me.

Telling me it'll be okay.

Most of it is inaudible.

Mainly it's his frozen face.

"Love you."

Is the last thing he says before the call drops.

Stupid service.

Falling back on Riggs's bed, the phone fall from my hands, and I stare at the ceiling.

I try to think back on all of his friends.

Everyone he introduced me to never smelled like him.

Someone must be trying to frame him.

Using his hoodie.

Tricking me with that smell.

But who?

Who would do this to me? To us?

Peter.

Someone knows I killed him.

They have to.

The door opens and Riggs comes in, letter in hand. It's open and he's reading it as he slowly sits beside me with a sigh. "My bike is gone. So is the car in the garage. Someone is fucking with us and I think it has something to do with how we're connected."

Looking over at him, I prop myself up on my elbows. "How are we connected?"

He hands me the letter and grunts. "How do you think?"

I don't take the letter. I stare at it, words pieced together by magazine clippings.

The word death flashes to me.

Death.

Someone wants us dead.

Riggs

You think you're here by chance.
Zay and Riggs, a match made in heaven.
But you're both going to hell for what you did.
Death marks you.
Think about it.
DEATH.
Their deaths are on your hands.
Connecting you forever.
You deserve to suffer.
The end is coming.
Death is coming for you.

"What do you think it means?" she asks, watching me patch up the broken glass panel on the front door.

Grunting, I drop the tools on the ground and get to my feet. "We gotta figure out how our lives connect."

She chuckles, stretching her arms above her head. She's still wearing nothing but my t-shirt. Gotta say, it's getting me going.

Tiny little thing is floating in it.

Shoulder peeking out.

Nipples grazing the fabric.

Teasing me all damn morning.

Devil disguised as an angel.

"I can bet you a million dollars you and I don't run in the same circles."

I'm grinning because she's probably right. "You're in school, aren't you?"

She nods in agreement, fiddling with the paper on the table.

I lean on the edge of the table beside her, staring at those smooth legs that look longer than they are. "See, I barely finished high school. I can damn right guarantee you, we ain't running in the same circles." Licking my lips, she bends a leg up on the chair which raises the shirt up and teases me even more.

I don't know how long I can control this urge.

To touch her.

Kiss her.

Ride her.

I have to ignore it. Someone wants us dead, someone I might know. A club member, maybe? Who else would know that we're here?

Her parents have money, don't they? Probably got mixed in with the wrong crowd, mixed in with us Snakes. We fucked over the club, that's what makes us connect.

Revenge.

I swallow hard, resisting the tingle traveling south. "You and Adam? You're not together anymore?"

She narrows her eyes at me. "It's the second time you've asked me that. Isn't it?"

"Because I want to know."

She scans me, taking in my usual look. Jeans, t-shirt, a metal chain that holds my wallet, my black boots that have seen better days, and rings that I forgot to put on this morning.

"Does it matter?"

Her chest heaves, scanning me again, and I can't help it. I let the urge take over.

Walking toward her, I grip the arms of the chair and lower so we're eye to eye. "I don't want to take advantage of you."

She chuckles in this seductive kind of way that leaves me breathless. "Baby, I assure you, you're the one who has to worry about me taking advantage of you."

Slowly, my fingers trace from her lips to her neck, and I shudder when I feel the intensity of her pulse beneath my fingertips. "I'll taint you."

She breathes, curling her chest toward my touch as my fingers trace her collarbone. "I'll destroy you."

"We're connected somehow."

A soft moan leaves her lips, feathering mine. "Are we? Because right now you're standing there, and I'm sitting here." She pulls the collar of my t-shirt. "If we were connected, I'd be screaming your name right now, wouldn't I?"

A growl leaves my lips almost as quickly as I slam them on hers.

I yank the t-shirt off her, revealing that tiny body beneath. Curves in all the right places.

Hips. Ass. Tits.

Perfection.

She has me naked in seconds.

Gasping.

Aching.

Starving.

I prop her up on the table and shove myself inside her, forcing a moan from those precious lips, and I hold still, letting my cock mold to the tightness of her pussy.

But I can't do it like this. She deserves so much more than a quick screw.

Pulling out of her, I step back to take her in.

Precious.

I bite down on my knuckles staring at her. Supple breasts, perky and alert. Drenching the table because of me.

She has this wit about her that's consuming.

Devouring.

The aura that makes me want to be better. So much better. I will be better with or without her. It's about time I think of myself for once. Not this damn club.

Smirking, I come back and carry her to the bedroom. She's kissing my neck, biting, suckling, licking.

Woman is going to make me come before I'm ready.

I toss her on the bed, climbing on top of her with heavy breaths. She arches her back toward me, pressing her chest to mine.

Little minx wants it badly.

So I give it to her.

Rough, hard.

Got her nails digging into my back with sheer pain that matches her screams.

I'm traveling to heaven while I'm inside her, taking a pit stop in hell when I finish.

Her screams of pleasure pierce my eardrum.

Taking over.

I grab onto the headboard and lift my body, staring down at her.

I'm deep, so deep she winces when I thrust. Whimpers when I go deeper and cries when her legs wrap around my waist.

Her pain is kind of turning me on even more, so I continue thrusting at this angle, using the headboard as support to hold me up as it slaps against the wall.

If anyone can hear us, they'll think we're murdering each other.

I let out my own cry when I finish, biting down on her neck until I taste blood.

Creamiest skin tastes like heaven.

She doesn't wince or cry this time. She lets me hurt her.

Destroy her.

The sounds of our breathing take over the whistling winds outside.

I did it again.

Something I shouldn't have done.

I can't help it. Something about this girl drives me crazy. She makes me want to be better. To protect her. To get out of this mess and go places. To fix me. I want to heal her, too, take away her demons, and keep that smile on her face.

Because when she smiles, my heart stops beating.

I can't remember the last time a woman made me feel like this.

I don't think a woman ever has.

Zay and I are a long shot, but to have her for a moment. Our moment. It's everything I could ever ask for.

Devil dancing with an angel.

Just for a night.

Just for a taste.

Just for a moment to be free.

Zay

Riggs rolls off me, breathing hard.

"Don't say you regret fucking me if this was going to happen again."

He chuckles, licking his lips. "Don't wear my shirt without anything else on."

"Don't bring me to a cabin without enough clothes."

He grunts, getting up from the bed and staring down at me again.

Beastly body towering over me.

But damn, he's sexy.

He has this darkness clouding over him, consuming all the good parts. I can break him out of the badness, sprinkle him with a little bit of me, and we'll be a match made in purgatory.

But my heart wouldn't be in it; it belongs to someone else.

And that wouldn't be fair to him.

His eyes rake over me, stroking me without so much as a single touch. "I'm gonna take a shower." He wipes his sweaty forehead.

I hum, rising with him. "Good, I'll join you."

He takes my wrist, spinning me, and pulls me against him. "Little thing like you is trouble, y'know."

Biting his bottom lip, I pull it toward me. "Big thing like you can handle it."

That guttural chuckle leaves him as he swoops me up and leads us to the shower.

He turns the water on and stands there, smiling at me. This monstrosity of a man can eat me up in one swift lick. But he doesn't. He takes my chin and tilts my head up, kissing me softly.

That enormity between his legs jerks up again as we step into the shower, and he lifts me against the tiled wall, taking me once more.

Again, he's rough.

Fast and loud.

Much like his bike.

It doesn't hurt as much at this angle; I don't get all of him inside me as I did on my back. I'm still screaming out of pain and pleasure, though. It's funny how torturous we sound in the throes of pleasure.

He licks up my neck and groans, biting down on my jaw.

My hands are in his hair, on his chest, groping his arms; they're everywhere. We may not get along, but damn, we get along in the best way possible. Our bodies match perfectly. His robustness and my small figure. Yin and yang coming together in perfect harmony for orgasms that should be illegal.

He doesn't last as long as he did before and grunts into my parted lips, breathing in my air.

"Why do bad things always feel so right?"

He chuckles, kissing me before putting me down. "If it ain't a little fun, then it ain't worth your time. Am I right?"

I slide my arms around his neck and kiss him once more before he makes the water warmer.

It's not the greatest shower; it reminds me of the showers in the dorms.

Small.

Claustrophobic.

Not enough room to do anything in them, yet we find a way.

Adam and I always found a way.

He broke up with me in the showers.

Happened to be the second worst day of my life. The day I found Lillian was the first.

***

Adam broke up with me while plowing me in the showers. We tried to be as quiet as possible, knowing we weren't the only ones in there.

We breathed each other's breaths, consuming one another for the last time.

His tongue slid with mine and he grunted, holding steady before he ruined me. "I think we should see other people."

My heart ripped out of my chest. Flopping onto the floor and beating to the sound of its own drum. We were no longer one anymore.

He stomped on it.

Squishing it into the grate.

My eyes welled with tears, taking in his guilty face. "What did you do?"

He shook his head, still holding my gaze. "I would never cheat on you."

"Then what's wrong?"

He breathed deeply, studying my eyes. "I don't know."

He didn't know.

He didn't stop me when I walked out of the shower.

He didn't follow me to my room.

He didn't call.

Text.

He didn't check on me for days.

Days without him felt like I stopped breathing.

And then, after days of being ghosted, I'm woken up in the middle of the night to him kissing me, sliding into bed beside me, and sobbing. "I'm so sorry."

I wrapped my arms around him, letting him hold me and kiss me until he calmed down. "It's okay, Adam."

He sniffed, resting his head on my shoulder. "I didn't want to leave you. But I thought leaving you would protect you."

"What're you talking about?"

He didn't answer. He cried some more and squeezed me close to him.

I wish I knew then what I know now.

The danger he was in.

How he tried to protect me from it.

But it's too late now, isn't it? We're in this.

Deep.

And I'm fucking up everything by sleeping with Riggs.

What's a girl to do when her life is being dangled in front of her? Have a little fun, that's what. No matter how much it hurts. How guilty I feel. I'll at least go out satisfied.

Riggs

It all happened so fast. One minute I was sitting at the booth having a beer with my father, the next, cops were raiding our club. Breaking down doors, busting windows, and tossing my brothers onto the ground. All the cops did was yell, screaming at us to get down.

My daddy didn't listen.

He pulled his gun out and one cop shot him in the shoulder, two stampeding at him and taking him down right after.

We were all in handcuffs by the time the ruckus died down. Everyone was out of breath and angry, spittle and foam forming at all their mouths when I looked up at them. Judas had his teeth gritting like a snarling dog, readying to attack. Lip was laughing, chest on the ground, and a cop with his boot on his back. Roaden on his knees with his hands locked behind his head, smirking. My father, however, was on his belly beside me, cursing me out. Like he knew I had something to do with this.

I didn't. The club was my life. Why would I fuck it up?

"If you had anything to do with this, it's your head on the platter, fucker," he said, blood pooling around him from the hole in his shoulder.

I looked up and saw her on the other side of the window, crying, and glancing around her like a crackhead out of crack. The fucking cunt, Natalia, ratted us out.

All those months of screwing her and this was what I got for it.

"I fucking knew it!" Banks yelled, struggling on the ground. "That fucking whore!"

Lip cocked his head to the side and saw it, too. "You're in trouble now, VP."

"I didn't fucking know!" I screamed, looking out the window at her. She caught my eye and looked away, the ghost of someone I thought I knew. "Fucking bitch! I didn't know!"

"You're dead," my father said, wincing when a cop lifted him to his feet. "Betraying the club, betraying your brothers! I raised you better." The cop dragged him out as he yelled at me, a daddy was disappointed in his son. "What did I tell you growing up? Never trust no tight pussy. Never trust no pretty face." His voice cracked when they dragged him outside, coming across Natalia. "You're fucking dead, bitch. You hear me? You're fucking dead!"

I screamed, so loud my throat hurt.

I let everything out.

All my anger.

All my sadness.

All the betrayal that this bitch gave me.

I screamed knowing I would pay for what she did. Because as of that moment, the men I called my brothers lost all their trust in me.

My cursing moved through the club until a cop kicked me in the face, knocking a tooth loose but also knocking me out.

I didn't come to until an hour later sitting in a jail cell with the rest of the guys.

They didn't look happy.

They were ready to do me in.

When Crew crouched down in front of me, he smiled. "You ready for this?"

He wiped the corner of his mouth with his thumb and clenched his fist. He was going to beat me until the cops pulled him off.

I wasn't ready because I didn't do anything.

I didn't know.

But they didn't care.

To them, I was a dead man.

Zay

I make a FaceTime call with Adam while Riggs is still in the shower. I just need to hear his voice. To know this guilt riding inside me is merited. That even though it feels like I cheated, I didn't break any part of our unity. That one day I can be his again. One day.

Two rings before he answers.

"Adam?"

"Zay? Babe, oh, God."

Putting my hand on my mouth, I sit down on the bed. "Tell me this is a dream. Tell me I'll wake up and you'll be holding me. Tell me we'll be in the showers making love without a care in the world." I sniff, wiping an escaping tear. "Tell me you never broke up with me. Tell me, Adam. Please."

He sobs—heavy, heaving sobs. He's been drinking. I don't even have to see him to know that. It's in the sound of his voice. "No. I'm sorry."

Tears fall and I wipe them away. I hate how hurt he sounds. How bothered.

I feel guilty for what I did.

And what I still want to do.

Fuck.

I try not to cry, composing myself with deep breaths. "They're going to kill me."

He groans on the other end, sniffling. "I'm doing everything I can. I spoke with your parents, okay? I'm doing what I can. They won't kill you, babe. They won't. They won't."

Letting out a pained chuckle, I smile. "It's okay, y'know. We had our fun."

"No." An angered growl rumbles through him. "No, I'm getting them their fucking money. You're walking out of this." He takes a tremorous breath. "And when you do, I'm going to marry you. Fuck, I'll buy you the ugliest ring the store has and marry you Friday when all this is done."

I laugh, covering my face as I do. He knows me so well. I wouldn't want a beautiful ring. An expensive ring. I'd want something that stands out, and people grimace at because it would be the funniest thing seeing their reaction and how they fake nice at how disturbing the ring is.

He sniffs again, and I'm sure he's running his hand through his hair as he does it. He does that when he's nervous. "What do you say, babe? Will you marry me, huh? When all this is over? Marry me. Be mine forever." He sniffles again. "Forever and always, yeah? To the end of time?"

I laugh softly again. "Yeah, what the hell. I'll marry you."

God, I'm such an idiot.

He chuckles, clicking his tongue. A habit he picked up from me. "Tell me you're mine forever."

"I've always been yours, silly."

He laughs, clearing his throat. "Nothing's going to happen to you, babe. Nothing, you hear me." He groans, sniffling. "Nothing."

Shit, I feel like crap for what I just did with Riggs.

Major crap.

"Zay, you remember when we went to the beach and fooled around in the cove?" He gives me a wry chuckle. "That's where I wanna get married. Right there on that beach so I can take you against the walls of the cove after you say I do."

Covering my face that's filled with tears, I shake my head. "I like that idea."

"I love you," he says, sniffling again.

The shower shuts off and I sit stiffly, nodding. "I...um...love you, too."

"I love you more than words—"

"Adam? Babe, what—oh." A woman's voice comes on the phone, making my stomach turn, and a rage burns inside me. *Babe?*

Now, I have no reason to be upset, given that Riggs was just inside me in this very bed, then in the shower. But man, I'm pissed because of the proposal.

I let out a scoff, rising to my feet. "Take that proposal and shove it up your ass. I hope she's fucking worth it."

Adam's voice is panicked. "No, Zay, no. It's not what you thi—"

I hang up. Too upset to hear him out.

Too upset to even think right now.

I'm a fucking idiot. A whore. A gullible fuckhead.

I need a drink, and I need it fucking bad.

Riggs

I shouldn't have done that. I regretted it again after I finished inside her on my bed.

Then again in the shower.

She's different. I like different.

I want her more than I can explain.

I want to show her I can be different, too. Get out of this business. Away from the guns, the drugs, the women, and the violence.

A new life with someone I love. Maybe have some kids.

Someone who doesn't know this business. Who doesn't want to be a part of this business?

Someone who will make me whole.

I'm not saying Zay is that someone. But she's a start.

She's the push I need to get out of a club I didn't want part of, but my father had other plans for his children. Loads of other plans.

I'll never forget my first kill. All the others blend together, but my first, it's crystal clear.

I was seventeen, dumb, young, and looked at my father like he owned the goddamn world—even though deep down I knew he was rotten. He brought us down to the shitty part of town no cop would ever set foot in. Snakes run them streets. Judas, Crew, and I were at my father's side. I was still a prospect. Still a newbie.

Daddy said I needed to start from the ground and work my way up. Earn my patch, earn my tattoos.

A woman was brought to her knees in tears, holding onto a man. "Whores.

The two of them." That's the only explanation I remember my father saying.

Heavy tears. Wailing.

My ears started ringing.

I couldn't hear them speak. Couldn't hear my father spitting orders at us.

I couldn't breathe.

I didn't want this. I was born into it and told this was what I had to do.

But I didn't want it.

My father grabbed the back of my neck and yanked me forward. "I said, take your fucking gun out."

I whimpered but pulled it from the back of my jeans. "Yes, sir."

He pulled me to the screaming couple and held his gun against the woman's head. "Hold it like this." He jerked his head at the man. "On the count of three, you'll earn your patch."

I didn't want it. But I wouldn't dare disobey him with a gun in his hand.

My hands were shaking. I remember the gun moving around so much I had to press it into the guy's temple to steady it.

"Ready?" Crew asked. "Ready to become a man?"

They had different versions than me of what becoming a man meant. To me, it meant the first time you stick your dick inside someone. I'd been a man since I was fifteen. I'd been a man with more than one woman already.

Killing wasn't becoming a man.

It was torture.

Murder.

Something I didn't want a part of but had no choice.

The woman looked up at me. Her deep brown eyes filled with tears. But she accepted her fate.

She closed her eyes and breathed, letting the smallest grin spread to her lips as if she knew the end wouldn't be that bad.

My father cackled when he saw me staring at her with furrowed brows. "Don't be a softie like your mama. Grow a set and pull the fucking trigger."

He did. He pulled it and the woman collapsed. Blood was leaking from the hole in the side of her head. Her husband yelled frantically. I didn't know what to do.

I panicked and looked up at my father for reason. All he did was hold the gun to his own head and tilt it to the side.

Telling me to blow this fucker's brains out without saying a goddamn thing.

I did.

I shot the man and ended his screaming.

Screams that still haunt my dreams.

Screams no one should have to hear.

But to my daddy, I became a man. I became a man three more times that week.

Four deaths by my hand in a matter of five days.

I was only seventeen.

***

I called Judas. Lip. Crew. Banks. And even Skeet. Not a single one of them is answering me.

And I got a funny fucking feeling the reason I'm here with her is because of the guy she killed.

I don't know who he is, but actions have consequences, and I think we're connected because of her dumbass mistake.

She pokes the fire, tossing a log onto it.

"Can I ask you something?"

She looks back at me and grins. "You've been inside me a handful of times. I think you can ask me anything you want."

Wetting my lips, I think about the right way to phrase this. "The guy you killed, how do you know no one saw you do it?"

She pauses as she reaches for another log and straightens her back. "Because I planned that night for weeks. I knew his schedule, his roommate's schedule. I knew where his friends would be and what time everyone on his floor got home. I killed him knowing I'd never get caught."

I grumble, grabbing the beer from the coffee table. "How'd you do it?"

She stalks over to the couch and sits beside me, facing me with her legs tucked under her. "I'll tell you about my first if you tell me about yours."

A smirk sprouts on my lips and I nod, moving hair off her shoulder to reveal those collarbones that drive me nuts.

"My daddy led the club before Crew. He molded me into who I am. Told me that not everything has to be solved with violence or death. Things can be solved with goodness. Kindness. Everything Crew is not. Everything I found out my daddy isn't, either. Brainwashed me to be part of something I didn't want to be a part of." I clear my throat and guzzle down some beer. "It was cold the night I made my daddy proud. We had a deal downtown, the dingy part. Hookers on street corners, not the classy kind, either. The ones you'd catch something from. Drug addicts shooting up with dirty needles they found on the streets. Disgusting place. But Crew likes it because no cop sets foot in the alleys. They'd get eaten alive. My daddy and Crew had me front and center, I was seventeen years old without a purpose and the wrong direction. I'd held a gun before. But never a gun I was ready to use."

Catching her eye, the corner of my mouth twitches, trailing my gaze to her hands. I take one, threading our fingers together for comfort. I think she likes me telling her about my past.

Makes her feel normal, I guess.

"I aimed right at the poor sap begging for his life, then shot. Killed him like it was nothing," I finish, draining the rest of my beer.

She looks at the fire, taking a memory that flashes through my mind every time I close my eyes. Those big brown eyes of the woman that wailed.

Crew's laughter still echoes in the far depths of my brain.

I pulled the trigger, a single hole between the man's eyes.

Blood leaked from it down his face.

I was scared shitless but pretend to be brave.

But that night, they set the monster free.

"What about yours?"

She sputters, clicking her tongue. "Mine is…well, mine isn't as ruthless. But it was deserved. I think about it a lot, wondering if I regret it, and I do, sometimes. But other times when I miss my best friend, I realize that the bastard deserved it. I killed him and yet I don't feel that redemption I thought I'd feel. The part of me who knew him before they got together totally regrets it. He didn't deserve it, y'know. He was the typical university boy—a troubled one."

She licks his lips slowly, staring at our hands. "I took his life without thinking of the repercussions that would happen. Like what his parents would go through, what his friends and—fuck, I don't even remember if he has siblings. Shit, that first instant after it happened, I realized that I didn't even have proof that he killed her."

"There's a chance he's innocent?"

She nods slowly, eyes bouncing all over my face. "Sadly."

A soft grin spreads to my lips, the mutual understanding passing between us. "Sometimes, people deserve what's coming to them. It's the secrets that they keep that cause the bad things to happen."

"Karma?"

I bring her fingers to my lips. "Yeah, sunshine, karma."

She rests her head on my shoulder, sighing softly as she stares at the fire. "Well, karma can shove it up her ass. I may be paying for my mistake, but I'm sure as shit it's not karma knocking at my door."

A booming laugh leaves me as I press a kiss on her forehead. "No, maybe it's not."

Karma is lurking in the shadows, waiting for the right moment to strike and do me in for all the wrong I've done in life. I'm just waiting for my shot.

Zay

Peter and I planned to meet up the night I killed him. Several weeks after Lillian's funeral.

Peter said he wanted to see me. That he missed me. That he was sorry for how things went down between us the day of Lillian's funeral. How he almost raped me because he was sad.

Sad, my ass.

Asshole.

The only thing he missed was the heat between my legs.

But I gave in. I planned and plotted and met up with him in his dorm room.

There was a power outage that night.

Lucky me, right? So no cameras were on.

No cameras meant I wouldn't have to break into the security room and erase the footage.

I went to great lengths trying to figure out what—I was convinced—he did to my best friend.

What he did to me.

I met up with him to hear him out at first. To hear his apology, to get his statement. I wanted to hear it. I needed the truth about her death to come out. She didn't kill herself. I just had to prove it. And like the dumbass I am, I went to his dorm room alone.

Peter was in his boxers when he answered the door, sliding his arms into a t-shirt. "Hey."

Pushing past him, my phone's flashlight guided my way.

He lit candles and scattered them around the room. I should've been nervous. I didn't have anyone to protect me if he tried to hurt me again. But by the regretful look on his face, I didn't think he was going to try anything. I knew him rather well, and Lillian's death aside, he wasn't a bad person.

I sat on his bed and shut off the flashlight on my phone, basking in the darkness lit only by candlelight. "What am I doing here, Peter?"

His breathing shook as he moved closer to me, hesitantly sitting on his bed, too.

There was this look about him.

Nervous.

Distraught.

He was hiding something.

"They cleaned out Lillian's room and didn't tell anyone. Her parents took most of her things, but whatever was left, they tossed in the garbage." He shook his head. "Someone else is in the room now. Can you fucking believe that shit? It's been seven weeks since she died. Seven! God." He scoffed, shaking his head. *Yeah, and six weeks since they buried her.*

Gasping, I place a hand on my heart and fought the urge to scream. "Where's her stuff? The stuff her parents didn't take?"

A lot of her stuff was in evidence. Most of her room was left as such until they deemed it a suicide and let her parents take things. There were a lot of her things I wanted to keep as a memory. They cleared out her room as if we'd all simply forget about her, like she didn't exist. Like her room was just a space that needed to be filled by paying students.

Peter got up and took a box out from his closet. "I took whatever I could salvage."

He placed the box between us and we stared at it for several seconds before I dove in and took the stuffed animal he bought her from the bookstore on their first date.

"You got this for her."

He nodded, taking it from me. "I remember that night. She was so nervous, she kept calling me Potter."

I laughed, digging through the box. "Yeah, she had a thing for Harry Potter and thought you looked like his hotter older brother."

His laugh spread goosebumps over my skin.

Crawling.

Digging.

Irking.

I had major regrets about my decision to kill him.

I planned out that night to a T knowing I'd get away with it, too. But as we were looking at each other, I couldn't do it. He deserved to know how fucked-up it was to be the cause of her death, but he didn't deserve to die for it. I didn't even know if he was the cause. I had to blame someone.

But I wasn't a killer.

Breaking our eye contact, I pulled out a photo of Lillian and me. I wondered why her parents didn't take this. The glass was cracked, conveniently over her face.

My fingertips moved across the glass, her beautiful smile cracked, like our hearts. "It's weird not having her around."

He took the picture from me and smirked. "Weird not being able to call her when I can't sleep."

"Same."

He touched my face in the picture and slowly rolled his eyes up my body, stopping on my lips before meeting my eyes again. "I'm sorry for the last time. I was in—we both were in a bad spot." He shook his head and put the picture frame down. "I got really high before going to her funeral and I wasn't in control. I'm just...I'm sorry."

I took his hand, squeezing. I was still uncomfortable being around him. Petrified he'd do it again without anyone around to hear me scream. Although, with the look on his face, I knew he wasn't going to do anything. Guilt struck him.

Shame.

Disappointment.

Still, there was that lingering sensation that churned in the pit of my stomach. I knew he was hiding something. And that something had to do with Lillian Delano's suicide.

I nodded, looking at the box between us. "All is forgiven." A chuckle left me when I looked at the picture again. "Drugs make us do stupid shit."

"We hooked up because of them."

I narrowed my eyes in thought. "Was it Molly?"

"MDMA." He rolled his eyes. "Same thing."

"I don't remember a lot about that night, I just remember waking up beside you. And being so thirsty. That's why I left. To get a drink. Then I couldn't remember which dorm was yours…my note said it all but you never called."

He frowned. "You didn't leave a note."

"I did."

He wiped a hand down his face. "Fuck, if I would've known—"

I swatted a hand in the air. "It's fine. The past is the past. But having sex while high is the best." Smoothing out the blanket beside me, I chuckle softly. "In this very bed that Lillian refused to sleep in."

He laughed, putting the picture frame back in the box. "Can you blame her? It's not like you or her were the only people I've brought here."

I gasped sarcastically. "Whore."

He nudged my arm with a chuckle. "You're one to talk, sweetie."

"Shut up." I lay on my side, leaning my head on my fist. "Although I'm a pretty good lay, I'll give myself that."

He chuckled, sticking his tongue between his teeth. "Yeah, you are."

Scrunching my nose, I picked at a loose piece of thread on his comforter. I knew what he was thinking and it crossed my mind before I showed up tonight. To give him one more night of pleasure before I ended his life.

I had to put a stop to it. To all of it.

"I met someone. Someone I think might be my person, but I'm not sure. We're going for pizza tomorrow."

"Oh yeah? Where'd you meet this one?"

"I was missing twenty-five cents for my coffee and he paid for it," I say, smiling. "And we just couldn't stop talking until we looked down at our phones and realized three hours passed."

"Must be someone special, you get bored after ten minutes of conversing with me," he teased.

Biting my bottom lip, I giggled. "That's because you're boring as shit."

His laugh moved through the quiet room. "Fuck off."

He put the box onto the floor and lay down as well, his head touching my elbow. We didn't say anything for a little bit and stared at the walls and ceiling. The flames flickering around the room were casting shadows around us. Shadows that knew what my plan was when I agreed to come here.

Death will always follow me.

Regret and revenge, too.

My eyes shifted to Peter, who was staring at the stuffed bear beside him. He picked it up and smirked. I never noticed before but Lillian used her silver Sharpie to put their initials on the hoodie the bear wore. *L+P.*

Taking the bear from Peter, I got comfortable beside him, our heads touching. "Can I keep him?" I fixed the little sweater so the bear had the hood on. "I've always wanted one."

"Why didn't you ever buy one?"

"Because when you bought Lillian one, I didn't want to copy her." I shrugged. "Plus, I haven't had a boyfriend in university yet, which doesn't help."

He smirked. "That just means all the guys you've been with aren't good enough for you."

"Aw, aren't you a little cutie," I said, chuckling as I rested the bear on my chest.

Silence fell around us again, consuming the candlelight dimness. I realized as hurt as I was, as badly as I wanted him to pay for Lillian's death, Peter was nothing but a good guy. I called him an asshole because he ghosted me. Ignored me when Lillian introduced us and acted like he never met me before. The night Peter and I shared was nothing but magical. He didn't deserve any of what I wanted to do.

I wasn't entirely sure how I was going to kill him that night.

To end it all for her sake.

I learned people's schedules, figured out the route from my dorm to his, and sought out safety after the deed was done.

But how I was going to kill the guy lying beside me, was still a mystery.

A mystery I wouldn't fulfill.

He took a breath, his hand reaching over to take mine. I let him. I was a fool for punishment, it seemed. Still wanted a taste of sex to fulfill the emptiness inside me. The chase of the high. But I ended that yesterday and vowed to be better. I want to be better for Adam.

Shutting my eyes, I listened to the loud wind outside as our breaths moved through Peter's room. His roommate, and nearly everyone in the dorm, were at the frat party of the year, held off campus. We were alone. Like I planned. But not how I wanted it to be.

I wasn't scared of Peter, by any means.

We all do stupid things when we're under the influence, so I didn't blame him for what happened. What I blamed him for were the things he said.

You think I'd forget the night we met? The night you came into my life and took hold of it.

He stayed with Lillian just to be close to me.

That hurts more than knowing he didn't love her as she deserved. She was innocent when she met him, a virgin until she was nineteen. Died when she was a week shy of twenty. She died thinking she was unloved—

His lips pressed to mine, causing me to open my eyes. "Peter, what're you doing?"

"I thought we could try this again while not under the influence."

I couldn't do it. Not with Adam on my mind.

So I held his head in my hands and shook it. "*You and I* isn't a good idea."

He pouted. "*You and I* would be fun. Not like we haven't done it before."

I sighed heavily. "Is that why you asked me to come tonight? So you'd get lucky?"

It had crossed my mind twice since lying on his bed. My plan *was* to kill him that night, but again, at least he'd go out satisfied.

"What? No." He sat up, shaking his head. "I wanted to apologize to your face, first off. And I wanted us to go through her things." He pointed at the box on the floor. "Figured you'd want to keep something from it." I sat up with him, placing the bear on his pillow. "Is that why you came tonight?"

No, I came here to kill you.

I shook my head. "I don't know why I came here after you tried to rape me."

He pinched his eyes shut. "Don't say it like that."

"Is it not the truth?"

"I told you, I was high." He sniffed. "Trent gave me this new stuff, Elevate. It fucks with my head—"

Scoffing, I get off the bed. "That doesn't negate the fact that it was wrong."

"I know." His fingers circled around my wrist and pulled me between his legs. "And I'm sorry—again."

As he looked up at me, it reminded me of the night we met. How easy he was to be around, how comfortable I was with him, and how instant our chemistry and connection formed. I was ready to commit when I met him. Ready to say yes to those blue eyes smiling up at me.

I ran my fingers through his hair, causing him to close his eyes. "I get that. But you have to understand, we can never happen."

"Why not?" he whispered.

Because you're the reason my best friend killed herself.

"Just once more? One more time and I'll never speak of it again. A goodbye." His hands slid up my dress, squeezing my ass. "We started out with a bang. Let's end with one, too."

Don't do it.

He slid his fingers inside my underwear. "We can still be friends. Hang out for coffee, study together." His fingers eased their way inside me. "But we won't do this anymore."

"Peter," I said breathlessly.

He lifted my dress, kissing my navel and pulling down my underwear. "Imagine what we'd be like if we gave us a chance."

I can't.

"Peter," I moaned softly, his tongue licking between my legs. "Oh, God, Peter."

He stopped, looking up at me. "Do I continue?"

I was about to kill the guy. This was wrong on so many levels, yet my twisted mind wanted more.

Pulling my dress and bra off, I answered his question. He didn't hesitate. He tore off his shirt, slipped out of his underwear, and turned me onto the bed.

He buried his face between my legs, licking my pussy until I shook and bucked under him. I couldn't silence my moans, not with a tongue like his.

My hands were in fists, bunching up the sheets as I came. Looking down at him licking my clit and fucking me with his fingers.

My legs squeezed his head, that electric sensation coursing through me. I wanted him. I needed it now.

He pulled him away from me, opening the drawer of his side table for a condom.

As soon as the condom was on, he shoved himself inside me.

Nothing at all like I remembered.

Screwed me like a jackrabbit.

Quick, unfamiliar, and lazy.

He writhed on top of me for a full two minutes while I just lay there and let it happen. Boring was a better word for it. Why Lillian was head over heels for this guy was beyond me.

He slowed, kissing me, and moaned into my parted lips. "I'm almost there," he breathed.

He lifted, watching me, staring at everything below him like this was a reward he had to savor. It didn't take him long to finish. Six pumps later, he grunted in my ear.

Now I realized why I didn't remember sleeping with him until I saw him with Lillian for the first time.

Sex with Peter was forgettable.

I remembered *him*, though. I remembered our swimming, our talking. I remembered watching the stars and lying in the sand. Floating. We did a lot of floating that night.

His heavy breathing caressed my shoulder and he lifted, smiling down at me. "You're incredible."

I wish I could say the same.

Adam flashed through my head, thinking about our date. I felt like a whore knowing I'd probably be kissing him on our date. I made a rule. Five dates before we did anything. At least a month before we slept together. I wanted to be better for him.

Peter rolled off me, cleaning himself as I stretched out on his bed. His eyes scanned me staring at my breasts, my stomach, and smirking when he stopped on my open legs. "Gorgeous."

"That's what they all say."

He got in bed beside me, kissing my cheek softly and pulling me close to him. "I hate that this can't work."

"You're my dead best friend's ex-boyfriend."

"And?"

I sighed. "Peter."

He kissed me, letting his tongue slide into my mouth. "Zaynab."

"Don't call me that."

"I love your name," he said, cupping the side of my face and tracing my bottom lip.

"You're a fool." Shoving him off me, I rose to get dressed but got distracted when I noticed one of Lillian's candles in the box. "Oh, this candle is rank." I laughed, taking it out of the box. "Can I light it?"

He laughed, too. "Yeah, I hated that dang candle."

The smile stayed on his face as I made my way to his desk, rummaging through his drawers.

I wasn't going to kill him anymore.

I would spread rumors about him.

Worst lay in history.

I couldn't live with his death on my conscience.

What the hell was I thinking anyway? Slightly unstable with a hint of depression.

As I opened the top drawer of his desk for a lighter, I noticed something. A dark blue phone case with daisies. The only person who had that case was Lillian. The last time I saw Lillian, she had her phone with her and she was on her way to meet Peter.

Why does Peter have her phone?

The cops couldn't find her phone.

Her parents didn't remember seeing it.

They deemed it lost.

But it wasn't lost, was it? It was right here.

Why was it here?

My breathing shuddered and my hands shook. "Peter, why do you have Lillian's phone?"

All the air sucked out of me when I turned around and he was standing, naked, only inches from me. His eyes darkened as he stepped forward, his arms caging me. "The night Lillian died didn't go as planned."

"What're you talking about?" my voice tremored.

He lowered his head, the scant lighting making him look ferocious.

Dark.

Demonic.

"It was an accident."

My heart stopped.

No.

My breathing sped up, clogging my throat.

I reacted, just as he did.

Grabbing the pen behind me, he lunged for it, too, tossing us onto the ground.

"Let go of me!" I screamed as loud as I could.

I was no match for him.

"She screamed just like this. Begging and pleading. But she wouldn't fucking listen to me. Wouldn't fucking acknowledge she's the reason for her own stupidity."

I gripped the pen so tightly, my nails dug into my palms. "You killed her?"

"She killed herself, Zay. You know that," he said, then a laugh rumbled through him. So manic, I started crying. "You really think she'd kill herself over a boy? Lillian was smarter than that."

Everything was closing in on me.

The walls.

The air.

His face.

"She saw something she wasn't supposed to see. Caught me red-handed."

He licked the side of my face and kissed me. Disgusting fucking bastard. "It was kill or be killed."

"Tell me." I struggled to get loose. "Tell me what she fucking saw."

He laughed at me.

Laughed in my face as I tried to be free of him.

Laughed as I head-butted him and stuck the pen in his neck.

His laughter turned to gasps.

Pure, gurgling gasps.

Until they stopped.

Until his blood leaked onto me and his widened eyes held no more life.

Until there was nothing left.

I can't remember what happened next. I just remember sitting in the showers with my clothes on and the bear clutched to my chest, sobbing. I killed him and I made it look like he killed himself.

I cleaned wherever I touched.

I typed out nothing more than *Lillian, I'm sorry* on his laptop and left the pen in his neck.

My plan was set in motion but I wasn't ready for it.

The water fell on me, washing away the sins I created. And I sobbed until killing him felt deserved.

That night still haunts me.

I thought I would heal as time went on.

I thought I would heal when I moved on.

I didn't.

I ached, cried, and pleaded for redemption.

This is my redemption.

This fucking cabin and all its secrets.

Zay

We barely get through breakfast before all the dishes are shoved out of the way.

I know how wrong this is.

I know we shouldn't be doing this.

But something is drawing us together. An untold force bonding us. Molding us as one.

My back arches, legs wrapped around Riggs's neck, and I'm screaming his name. Calling out to God as well.

His fingers move inside me, hitting that spot that makes me see stars. I've been seeing stars a lot with him lately.

All the stars in the galaxy.

Whole goddamn universe.

The second I come, he growls, making me delirious as he laps my clit once more and shoved himself inside me.

He's rough.

Thumping into me and moving the table with it.

The best damn sex I've ever fucking had and it'll be short-lived.

Ending once Friday comes. One more fucking day and all these glorious orgasms will be done.

He grunts, shoving the table once more, and releases my hips; bruising will surely begin to show this afternoon. "Fuck, Zay."

I prop myself on my elbows and giggle, watching as he slowly eases in and out of me. What is it with the guys I've been with always so turned on by watching themselves go into me as if I'm swallowing them up in a moist cave of pleasure?

Riggs slides out of me and bites his bottom lip, studying my body with intensity. I'm covered in hickies, bite marks, a few scratches, and handprints, too. He doesn't wait to test the waters, he dives right in and treats me like a whore in the bedroom and a darling around the house.

Hopping off the table, I look back at the mess, pushing my lips together. "Well, then."

The scrambled eggs are scattered across the floor, some are sliding down the glass windows. The plate of bacon is salvaged, having slid to the end of the table. Our coffee is still soaking into the slices of toast and dripping onto one of the chairs.

A growl rumbles through him and he slings me over his shoulder, slapping my ass as hard as he can, and saunters down the hallway to the master bedroom. "I ain't finished with you yet."

A sentence I've heard time and time again. Adam's words swim through my brain. His smile flashes over me.

I'm doing this as a big *fuck you*.

An *in your fucking face*.

No, I'm not.

I like this. I like Riggs.

I feel this need with him.

This connection.

Something beautiful brewing.

Something beautiful that's ending as quickly as it started if I ever see Adam again.

Riggs tosses me onto the bed and bites his bottom lip as I get on my knees and crawl to him.

"Get on the bed, Riggs. It's my turn to rock your fucking world." A sultry grin spreads to my lips as he captures them, swirling his tongue in my mouth that tastes just like me.

Pushing him onto his back, I straddle him and lick up the length of him, kissing the tip.

There we go again, screaming and moaning like we're being murdered.

Whole lotta pleasure with a little bit of pain.

Perfection.

His head rolls back, Adam's apple bobbing as a throaty grunt escapes him. "Zay!"

I ride him slowly now, taking in the intensity and the length of this monstrosity inside me. "Tell me, Riggs, tell me you'll come for me."

"Yes!"

Scratching down his muscular tattooed chest, I moan. "Tell me!"

"I'll come for you, sunshine. Only for you," he grunts loudly once more and releases, squeezing my ass as he does.

One more day of this before it's over.

Before we're over.

Before my life is finished.

Rolling off of him, I rest my neck on his curled arm. Our hands find each other and our fingers thread together. "Always a pleasure, Riggs."

He laughs breathlessly. "If only there was a way to make this week endless."

I smile, staring at the ceiling as my thumb grazes his. If only there was a way. A way to ride off into the sunset with him on the back of this bike. Living on the run.

Living a beautiful life filled with multiple orgasms.

Filled with laughter.

Happiness.

"Can I ask you something?" He clears his throat, flexing his bicep so I look over at him.

Being in his arms makes me feel protected. Safe.

His robust upper body is breathtaking. A man who towers over everyone. A demon who aches to be an angel.

If we stayed together, an angel he'd become.

"What's up?" I tilt my head to look up at him. Those blue eyes smiling.

His tongue darts out and licks his parched lips. "You're on birth control, right?"

I laugh, turning into him. "I have all my shots, I told you that before."

"Well, I don't know. I don't usually rawdog it."

Kissing his chest, I push myself up on my knees. "I guess I'm special, aren't I?"

He tucks a lock of hair behind my ear, smiling softly. "You remind me of my mama."

I click my tongue, scrunching my nose. "That's not good."

He laughs, sitting up with me and pinching my chin. "I didn't mean like that. I mean in the way you look at me. Like you see *me* and not the monster I became."

Pressing a kiss on his lips, he grins against them, making me smile, too. "You're more than this club. More than the darkness that hangs onto you."

His head lowers, looking down at his thigh which has part of the snake tattoo. It's so detailed, with scales and stomach movements along his body. It must've taken hours to complete. Hours to set the stencil in place from his ankle, up his leg to his shoulder and chest.

It's breathtaking but dark. Everything is always so dark with him.

"You're the only one who sees that," he whispers; a voice so deep it thunders like the weather outside.

There's a sadness in his eyes. That ache that wants to be cured. Set free.

And he will be. He'll smile like he does when we're not thinking about the club or this confusing dilemma we're in.

The secrets that are hidden from us.

I straddle him again, holding his head in my hands. Those angular features make him fierce, but when he's at his most vulnerable, he shines brighter than ever.

"I'm not. And one day someone so perfect will see that too and she'll keep this handsome smile on this face." My thumb touches the scar on his cheekbone. "Your perfect, disheveled face."

He chuckles softly, kissing the palm of my hand. "Disheveled, huh?"

I smile, nodding quickly. "Scars tell a story. They're little imperfections that make someone so much more interesting."

"If only my scars had interesting stories. They ain't something to be proud of." He tilts his head up, the blue in his eyes growing darker. "Nothing about my scars or my ink tells an interesting story."

I shake his head from side to side. "You're getting the wrong tattoos. Christ, you don't have a lick of color on you." Running my fingers through his hair, he closes his eyes and inhales softly.

The angel in him is shining through right now. Coming to life and making me forget the world for a moment. Forget our troubles. Our dilemmas. This beautiful beast is making me want more out of life.

"Let's leave, Riggs. Get away from this madness."

A slight grin spreads to his lips. "If only it were that easy, sunshine."

Maybe he's right. Running away from problems is not the way to solve things. I ignored all the signs when Lillian broke bad. I turned my nose up when I killed Peter and acted like nothing happened.

Turned a page.

I dismissed Adam for having a woman with him when he explicitly told me she was from the club watching him.

Running away from my problems has been my go-to since I was a kid.

My parents argued. I went to Lillian's.

My parents disowned me. I turned to drugs.

I disappointed them time and time again.

Running away from this mistake would be no different.

"If only it were that easy," I repeat.

I rest my forehead on his, closing my eyes, too.

He's right. Life isn't easy. Life is the most complicated nightmare we're given and supposed to cherish. If life is so good, if life is so short that we have to live it to the fullest, then why the fuck am I so damn miserable that I can't wait for my ending?

Riggs

It's Friday.

Two fucking days passed and not a single word from my brothers. No calls, no returned messages. Radio silence and I'm expected to sit here and wait like a fucking bitch. I'm done waiting. I'm done expecting. I'm done.

Moments like this remind me of my father and how we'd sit at home waiting for him to get back from a job. My mother never explained the business to us until we were older, but my father would tell us horror stories about the club. His bedtime stories gave me chills but excited me to be part of something I didn't understand. He told me I'd be president of the club one day. The head Snake, taking over and running this business to the top.

He'd tell me about the guns and explain how to use them. He always reminded us to remove the safety. *Can't get shit done with the safety on.* My mama hated it, she'd yell at him all the time. She'd yell at us too for pretending to be bikers and wearing cuts when we weren't supposed to. I wore my father's cut all the time when he was home. He didn't mind it. Said it made him proud. If only I knew then what I know now and how much that cut would fuck me over.

I didn't care then, I was obsessed with the life.

My mother wanted better for us. I never understood.

Until I was seventeen, then I understood everything she feared.

Coming up behind Zay as she sips her coffee in the kitchen, I kiss the nape of her neck. "Morning."

I'm an equal with her. She doesn't look down on me. Or judge me.

We're alike.

We both have blood on our hands.

The stench of ex-lovers in our beds.

We're both damaged.

I could get used to being damaged with her.

The last two days we didn't speak of our pasts. After she told me about how she planned to kill someone but then didn't want to and ended up doing it anyway. I knew exactly what she meant.

All the bodies lying in a grave right now because of me weren't meant to be there. I was told to end their lives. And when you're told to do something in the MC, you do it.

You lay your life on the line for your brothers.

No matter how wrong it is.

No matter how much it hurts you.

No matter if the last thing those people see is your face before you kill them, and their faces haunt your nightmares.

It doesn't matter.

The MC is what matters.

Snakes are what matter.

Looking back, none of it fucking mattered.

Zay turns and grins up at me, her teeth gnawing her bottom lip. "It's Friday."

Friday.

Day seven.

She gulps, her eyes glossing over. "If you're going to kill me, just do it fast. Please."

After everything we shared.

All the secrets.

All the kisses.

All the messed-up sheets.

She still thinks I'm going to kill her.

Smoothing out her hair, I cradle the side of her head. "I ain't gonna kill you, Zay. I never was."

A smile touches her lips and she places her hands on my chest. "Thank you."

I leave a gentle kiss on her head and step back, fixing the gun tucked in the back of my jeans. "We are getting outta here today."

"Your bike's gone, where are we supposed to go?" She chortles. "Hitchhike?"

Snaking my arm around her, I lift that tiny body, carrying her as she giggles on the way to the bedroom. "Get dressed, pack your things. We're gonna walk to Clayton's and use his car. I got another bike stashed up here, just can't get to it on foot."

She pulls my shirt over her head and tosses it at me, revealing that delicate body I destroyed last night. "We can hide out at my parents' place. They're away until the end of the month."

I nod without thinking her offer over, distracted by that body. She wasn't lying when she said I'd be the one begging her for more. I'm feeling the repercussions of her. The way she feels. Tastes.

It's unlike anything.

It's no wonder people swoon over her.

Her name in Arabic means beautiful. *Zaynab.*

And that's exactly what she is. Beauty in all its forms.

She's not Arabic, neither are her parents. But according to her, that's the name of the nurse who saved her life when she was born. To her parents, it seemed fitting.

Which it is.

Beauty and the Beast. She and I.

She throws on that dress she wore the first time I saw her and stuffs her feet in her shoes, winking at me. She walks out of the bedroom first, leaving me to bask in the memories. This place will always remind me of her, of the what-ifs. What if we weren't from two different worlds? What if we met at a coffee shop like she and Adam? What if I wasn't a killer? What if she wasn't one, either? What if we were two normal people without secrets, without a dangerous past? What if we had a happy ending?

Would that be too much of a fairytale?

Taking her backpack, I fix it on my shoulders, walking down the hallway toward her as she finishes her coffee and rinses off the mug. I don't want to leave, but we have to.

We have to get out of here before those fuckers come back and do us in when we least expect it. It's better to be one step ahead of them. And one step ahead means I have to find out why we're connected. I have to find out what the fuck that note means.

We walk out the patio doors, sunshine kissing our exposed skin, and I snake my hand in hers.

I could get used to this.

I shouldn't get used to this.

It's a short walk to Clayton's house. The entire time she's quiet. I sense the nerves on her. I don't think she trusts me yet.

Hell, I wouldn't trust me, either.

Tall bastard like me. Covered in tattoos. Not pretty ones, either. Dark, dangerous, seething.

She sees through that, but not all the time.

She sees through it when we're vulnerable. Talking and coming down from the high of just having sex. She likes me then.

Not so much when I'm armed.

I got a bad feeling about this. But we march up the stone steps to Clayton's door and I knock. My heavy knock echoes throughout the area.

She taps my arm as a breeze rolls in, squeezing my hand as she does.

Lifting my hand to knock again, she jolts me back. "Riggs, look. Isn't that your bike?"

I turn in the direction she's pointing. Under the fucking tarp I lent him is my bike.

Crew got to Clayton before I did.

Goddammit.

I growl as the front door opens, Clayton smiling when he sees us.

Backstabbing bastard.

"Good morning to you, what can I do you for?" he asks, flicking his gaze between Zay and me.

Pulling her behind me, I let go of her hand to take my gun. "Why is my bike on your property, Clayton?"

His face goes pale.

All the shit I did for this bastard. We protected him, paid for this house, and bailed his boy out of jail.

Ungrateful bastard.

Clayton puts a hand up as I grip the gun at my side. "Now hold up a second. Hear me out."

"Gimme the keys."

He scrambles to the hooks by the front door, dropping a few keys on the ground, and extends his shaking hand to me. "Crew said he needed you there. That she needed to see."

Zay gasps quietly. "See what?" she whispers. The way her trembling tugs at my heartstrings makes me hate who I am.

I grab Clayton by the collar and yank him toward me, the barrel of the gun pressed to his cheek. "You tell anyone we were here and that I took my bike back, I'll come back and gut your pig of a wife. Got it?"

He nods quickly, fear emanating from him.

The shit I feed off of.

I shove him away and gawk around, making sure there isn't anyone watching.

Zay doesn't like that. She cringes when I look at her and nibbles her lower lip. I scared her. Put that fear inside her. I don't like it. I don't want her to see this side of me.

She takes her backpack from me and puts it on as I snatch the keys from Clayton.

The tarp is covered in twigs and wet leaves, but as for my bike, she's dry, perfect.

Swinging my leg over the bike, I put my hand out to Zay and guide her on it.

I bring the bike to life, her purring echoing through the quiet trees. Her purr usually calms me, it usually takes all my troubled thoughts away.

It isn't right now.

It's making all this shit worse.

I can't stand the MC fucking me over anymore. Bringing me down. All because of a mistake that wasn't my fault. I don't deserve this.

I paid my dues.

The last debt I'll ever pay is saving this woman's life whose arms are wrapped around me, squeezing so tight.

We may not be forever. But I'll make sure she lives. I'll make sure she's safe from anyone the MC has running this game.

Because I'm not going to be a pawn. No matter who I have to kill to be free.

I ain't no one's stowaway.

This ends now.

Zay

I'm shaking as we approach my parents' house. I use the spare key under the mat to get in. They're out of town again. I came here and brought Riggs with me because it's the only safe haven I could think of. My dorm is out of the question. I have no money for a hotel.

I can't trust anyone.

Riggs looks out of place here. Rugged, big fella such as himself in a modern home with white couches, marble floors, and gold scents. He's like a bull in a china shop.

I don't know where he lives, but I'm sure he doesn't have an ottoman and a decorative bowl of potpourri on the coffee table.

He looks around, keeping his mouth shut but his eyes say enough. This proves I wasn't lying when I said my parents have money. Money they'd be more than willing to give to get me out of this mess.

I don't say anything. I don't know what to say. After seeing him holding the gun at Clayton, growling those words, I realize he's not the man I slept with the past few days. He's different.

A monster.

I climb the stairs and he follows, holding onto the gun tucked in the back of his jeans.

My room is as I left it. Beige walls filled with hanging picture frames of all my friends and family. There are pictures of Lillian and me from when we were twelve, up until a week before she died. When Adam and I broke up, I came here for a weekend, to unwind and cry without my roommate asking me what was wrong. Without the chance of bumping into Adam on campus.

I came here and took down the photos of Adam and me. But couldn't get rid of them, they're in a drawer in my closet. We're not officially over. Not after he snuck back into my dorm room days after he spoke those broken words and held me all night crying, apologizing, and making love to me well into the morning when he left.

Not when he told me again that he loved me.

Not when he promised he'd fix this mess.

Not when he proposed.

I glance at a picture of Lillian again, the memories her smile holds will stay with me forever. We first met in elementary school. She sat by the playground alone, poking sand with a stick. I made friends very easily, and it bothered me that not a single one of the friends I had walked up to her and said hi. She was the new girl, she didn't have cooties. I walked right up to her and plopped on the sand at her feet, introducing myself. She smiled, and I told her she was going to be my new best friend. We were attached at the hip since then. Inseparable. Until we hit university. Once that happened, all hell broke loose and we lost each other. Instead of working on what we lost, she died. And now I'll never have my best friend back.

Riggs drops my backpack on the bed and groans when he sits down, shaking his head. "We can't stay here long."

I nod, smiling at a picture of Lillian and me on our sixteenth birthday. She's smiling so elegantly, while I'm licking the side of her face. That was us. The tame one and the wild one. The blonde and the brunette. The sweet and the sassy.

He gets up and squeezes my shoulders, leaving a kiss on the back of my head. His grip tightens before he drops his arms at his sides, removing a picture frame that Lillian gave me right before she died. She said it was a piece of us we'd both have hanging in our dorms. Me and her smiling at the camera as a reminder of who she used to be. "How do you know her?"

"That's Lillian, my best friend."

He looks up from the picture and scoffs quietly. "This is Natalia."

I frown, taking the picture frame from him to hang back on the wall. I hung it there when Adam broke up with me. Replacing his picture with her smiling face. "No." I chuckle awkwardly. "That's Lillian. She was the sweetest woman this world ever saw. She wouldn't get herself messed up with bikers and cops and—" I pause, Peter's words infiltrating me.

She saw something she wasn't supposed to see.

Riggs shakes his head. "*This* is how we're connected. She—fuck." He runs his fingers through his hair. "We gotta leave. Now."

I'm trying to put the pieces together.

Trying to understand how Natalia and Lillian are the same person.

My Lillian was a saint.

Calm. Careful.

Riggs isn't someone she would have gone for.

But I always encouraged her to break out of her shell.

She broke out.

Now, look at her.

He's pulling me out of my room toward the stairs. But I stop, tears streaming down my cheeks. "I don't understand. Why would she do that? Why would she risk her life to bury you guys? Why would he kill her?"

Riggs takes me by the shoulders and lowers his face to my level. "We have to go, okay? Let's just get out of here before they come looking—"

"Just give me a minute. Please."

I storm back into my room and slam the door, sliding down until my butt meets the floor.

I'm hyperventilating.

My heart is beating rapidly.

My palms are clammy.

And all I want to do is scream.

This can't be happening.

I somehow stand and stagger to the picture of Lillian and me.

Natalia?

It's a copy of the picture that Peter salvaged from the trash. The one with the cracked glass on her face.

Why did she insist I have this before she died?

Did she know it was coming?

Did she know she was in trouble?

Goddammit, Lillian, I could have helped you!

Riggs opens my door and sees me standing there with the frame in hand. "We gotta leave."

"Did you know she gave this to me before she died? Exactly a week later I found her in her bed." I shake my head. "How is that possible? Did she know?"

He takes the picture from me, his face pinched when he looks at Natalia. She was a dream to all of us. The perfect little woman that melted our hearts and fluttered them in so many ways.

He smashes the picture frame on my dresser, glass scattering all over the place.

I gasp, bringing a hand to my mouth. "What the fuck are you doing?"

He tears the frame apart and the picture falls out with a folded pink paper getting lost in the mess.

We're staring at the folded paper, breathless.

Speechless.

The last words from a person who meant something to us.

My shaking hand reaches for the paper and glass falls out of it as I unfold it. Her perfect penmanship stares back at me.

Zaynab, my spunky little sister from another mister.

Sorry this is written so poorly, I'm in a rush to get this to you. But please remember how much I love you.

I don't expect you to understand anything that's happening. But stay away from Peter and anyone associated with him. Please trust me when I say this, he's nothing but a SNAKE.

I've gone and done something terrible. Something I'm too ashamed to even admit.

You're my favorite person on this entire planet and all of the galaxies. I strived to be as open and as confident as you. And look where it got me.

The one night I go out without you, I meet someone. Someone all muscles and tattoos. But he's sweet. So handsome, too. And nothing like Peter.

We were dating for a few months. But I wasn't ready to introduce you to him.

Because I knew what he did for a living wasn't right.

And I had to right his wrongs.

I tattled and got him in trouble.

I got a lot of people in trouble.

Including Peter.

We broke up months before I told you. Or he told you. He still has a thing for you from that night you guys shared together. He told me and that's okay that you didn't.

All this madness is because of me.

I saw something I shouldn't have one night, walking into the biker bar where Riggs hangs out—Judas's Hideout. I saw Peter kill someone. Shoot them between the eyes. It killed me to know that sweet boy had gone bad. That he ruined his life all because his father told him to.

There's so much to explain and so little time to do it in. But that's okay because the less you know the better it is for you. Trust me.

I want you to know that you shouldn't mourn me. Seeing what I saw will bring me to my end.

And that's okay.

I loved my life. I loved every moment in it that involved you.

My best friend.

My better half.

The only person to ever make me laugh so hard.

Don't worry about me anymore.

Live your life to the fullest.

Be a good girl.

Don't be a hideaway after it happens.

Love.

Love so much that your heart hurts.

Most importantly, don't get involved in this.

Do not try and figure out what happened to me.

Just know you're safe.

You're loved.

And I'll see you on the flip side, my girl.

Love you,
Lillian.

I'm shaking so much I can barely get through this letter. It's left me more confused than understanding what happened.

Riggs snatches it from me, scanning the words before tossing it on my dresser. *"You* killed Peter?"

I tremble, unable to get the words out but I manage. "I told you I did."

"No." He growls, thundering toward me. "You told me you killed someone. *Someone* and *Peter* are two different *fucking* things."

"It was still an accident."

His nostrils flare. "You planned it."

Shaking my head, I raise my voice. "But I didn't want to do it!" I take a gasping breath, staring at this man towering over me. "You knew him?"

He grunts, turning away from me and tonguing his cheek. There's a darkness in his gaze that softens when he answers. "He was—he was a prospect."

I sniff, wiping my cheeks. "He killed Lillian."

"I know."

"I couldn't let him get away with it."

"I gathered."

"I'm sorry," I weep, covering my face.

He grunts again, shaking his head as if what he's about to say hurts him more than it'll hurt me. "You're on your own, I ain't messing with you or your shit anymore after—"

He's cut short when the front door creaks open and the sound of boots hits the marble floors.

"Fuck," he grumbles under his breath.

He unwillingly takes my hand and creeps to the open door, peering out.

Six men walk in.

Three of them I recognize. Crew, Judas, Lip.

Two of them I don't.

One has a hood on. That black hood I saw a few short days ago.

We step back into my room and Riggs points at the closet, taking his gun out of the back of his jeans.

"They ain't here," Judas says, his deep voice sending shivers through me.

"Riggs's bike is stashed nearby," Lip says. "They're here."

Footsteps sound on the stairs, heading for my room. I barely have enough time to make it to the closet, the hooded biker is already standing at the threshold.

Riggs lifts his gun, pointing it at the man as his hands slowly rise. "Take that hood off."

I whimper, my hand clutched to my chest, the other shaking by my side.

"They're in here," the voice calls.

A voice I'm all too familiar with.

Peter drops the hood, smirking at me as both Riggs and I take a step back.

Shocked.

Frightened.

In utter disbelief.

"How?" I manage through a curtain of tears.

Peter cracks his neck, revealing the mangled scar where the pen lodged into him. "Gave me a pretty gnarly scar, sweetie. Not gonna lie."

Riggs's teeth are gritted, the gun still raised. "You were dead! We buried you in the fucking ground!" The emotions on his face and in his voice are painful to watch. He swallows, eyes blinking rapidly. This is a new side to Riggs I haven't seen before. An emotional side. The caring side.

Crew steps in with Lip and Judas behind him. "You had to pay for that whore you brought into the MC." Riggs raises the gun higher. "You think we'd let you get away with it?"

Riggs scoffs, standing in front of me. Even while mad at me, he's still that protector I met and let inside me. "He's my brother!"

I widen my eyes, staring between Riggs and Peter. I never noticed it before but looking at them now. I see it. The eyes, the hair. Even their smirk is the same. "You're...what?"

They're brothers.

I think I'm going to be sick.

Gagging, I push past Riggs, storming into the adjoining bathroom.

I barely make it to the sink, puking in two separate rounds.

I'm still trying to wrap my head around what's going on.

Peter is alive.

Lillian was Natalia.

What the heck is happening?

Riggs

Zay just ran off to puke. She's as shocked as I am.

I buried my brother six feet underground.

I place roses on his fucking grave every month for almost a fucking year.

I can't believe these bastards kept this from me.

Peter steps forward, lowering the gun and embracing me. "I'm sorry, Riggsy. I had to."

"We all did," Judas adds.

Pushing my brother off me, I growl. My little brother, who I've been protecting all my life. "I fucked-up by shoving my dick in crazy, and this is what I get for it?"

Peter glances at Crew, craning his neck, making that scar stretch. That scar. The woman I've been screwing the past week did this to my brother. She thought she killed him.

I sympathized with her.

I felt bad for her.

I'm fucking falling for her.

No, not anymore.

She betrayed me, like the rest.

I want to hate her, but she's changed me in a short week. Opened my eyes to get out of this business.

"You sent your father to prison. You sent almost the whole damn club to prison." Lip scoffs. "The fuck did you expect?"

My voice cracks. "I just want to know why. Why would you lie to me?"

My brows furrow as I look at Peter, taking him in. He's wearing his cut. My baby brother isn't a prospect anymore. I wanted more for him. To better his life outside the MC. Our father wanted us to follow in his footsteps.

When Peter came home with his acceptance to Stanford University, I knew he'd get out.

I just knew it.

But I was wrong.

So fucking wrong.

Our mother would yell at us when we'd wear our daddy's cut. She expected more from me to set an example for him. And I tried. Since I was fifteen and joined the club, I tried.

But Peter, he's like our daddy. He enjoys the killing, enjoys the thrill of dirty success. He doesn't understand the haunting it gives. He'll never understand because he's just a kid. I was there once, too. I loved it, until I didn't. Now I hate every aspect of it and hope this club burns to the fucking ground.

Growling, I slump on Zay's bed, putting my head in my hands and trying to understand what is happening. "You're alive," I whisper.

Peter kneels in front of me and squeezes my leg. "I never left, brother. I stayed with Roaden and learned everything I could so Daddy would be proud of me. Of us." He slips me a smile. "I'm sorry I lied. We paid our dues, though. We paid and look at us now." He leans in closer, lowering his voice so only I can hear him. "Donnelly brothers will run this club." He taps my chest, then his. "President and VP."

Something our father wanted for us the moment he held his sons. But this will never be the life I would want for my children. I should've tried harder to keep my brother away from this life. I wish I'd done more.

Peter gets to his feet and makes for the bathroom to see Zay, that sympathetic look he gave me washes away as he approaches her.

The woman in there planned on killing him. She divulged how sorry she was, how regretful she was for what she did. She told me about Natalia— Lillian. She told me about a girl that I used because she knew nothing. I liked showing Natalia things, I liked her open mind. Her innocence.

I hate it now.

I hate her. I hate Zay. I hate Peter.

I have this fucking club.

Judas claps me on the shoulder and sits beside me. "It'll be all right, brother."

I sniff, holding in the tears but my eyes and throat are burning. "All right?" I scoff. "Nothing's all right until this shit is over."

He squeezes my shoulder and drops his hand on his lap.

How am I getting out of this? How is Zay getting out of this?

I'm trying to decide whether or not I should save Zay.

She deserves better but she planned on killing my brother and believed she did it.

I don't know what to do.

I don't know what to believe.

I can't catch my breath. I can't be here. I can't do this.

How in the fuck is this happening?

Zay

Before I can dive into this shit show, I'm startled by Peter leaning on the doorframe, watching me brush my teeth.

I spit once more as he comes up behind me, pushing himself so hard into me I wince. The vanity is digging into my abdomen.

He breathes into my ear. "You think you can get away with trying to kill me?"

Groaning, I try to push off the vanity but it only makes him shove me harder. "It was an accident. You're fine, are you not?"

He grabs my jaw, holding it steady and locking eyes with me in the mirror. "Not all ghosts can be put to rest."

"Fuck you."

He chuckles, biting my cheek. "I did." His grip tightens on my face and he grits his teeth. "Just like you fucked my brother."

How the hell does he know that?

I wince, grabbing onto his hand. "Peter, please."

"Please, what? Hmm? That's our daddy's cabin. We got cameras all over the place. One in the living room, aimed right at the kitchen table where we used to share family meals. My brother ate a meal on that table, all right." He cackles softly. "I ate a meal, too, the night you stabbed me in the neck."

"You killed my best friend," I whisper, tears sliding down my cheeks.

"I'd do anything for this club."

"Betraying your brother, too?"

He grits his teeth and squeezes my face harder. "Lillian got our daddy sent to prison. She got loads of our people sent to prison. It might not be Riggs's fault, but he brought her into our club."

Attempting to push off the vanity, needing a moment of relief from the pain in my pelvic bones. "Peter, please, stop this. You don't have to kill anyone—"

"You didn't have to kill anyone but look what happened." He licks the side of my face. "Don't worry, I have plans for you to apologize. And it involves you on all fours."

I whimper, struggling to get loose of his grip but it's a mistake. He grips harder and my molars are digging into my cheek. I can taste blood. I'm sure of it. Something that sounds like "stop" leaves my lips. But my winces and cries make more of a sound than my words.

"Enough," Crew says, standing in the doorway. "Let's get to the club and deal with her there."

Wincing again, Peter takes a step back and grabs onto a wad of my hair, dragging me out of the bathroom.

Riggs is sitting on my bed with his head in his hands, unable to fathom this insanity.

He looks up as his brother is manhandling me, showing no remorse.

Whatever we had is gone.

Riggs is not going to save me anymore.

I'll be long gone, like the woman we each thought we knew.

Peter lifts me and tosses me over his shoulder, making his way through the house, and stops once we reach the front door. Two bikers are sitting on the couches in the living room and he taps my ass, gripping roughly. "Y'know, if you scream once we're outside, I'll stab you in the leg. Got it?"

I sniff, muffling a sob. "Okay."

He swings me off his shoulder and shoves me into the front door. "Okay, what?"

Glancing at the living room as the two men rise to their feet and make for us, I gulp. "Okay, I won't scream," I say softly, my lower lip quivering.

Peter smiles, kissing my forehead. "Good girl."

He grabs onto my arm and opens the front door, leading me into the shining sun. He takes me to the black Mercedes that showed an appearance at the cabin and shoves me into the passenger's seat. It reeks of stale cigarettes and his cheap cologne.

As soon as Peter sits beside me, he lights a cigarette and waits for everyone to join us. That scar is disgusting. It spans from the side of his neck to under his jaw; a scar crawling like spider legs. I did that. I tried to kill him because he killed my best friend.

I was defending her when I should have been protecting her.

Where did I go wrong? How did I not see the signs?

I look out the window and start to cry again.

This feels like I'm waiting on death row. My final hours until the sun sets. My last sunset.

My ending. This is my ending.

Riggs

After a few minutes, I compose myself enough to get off her bed and follow everyone outside. Peter is in the car, his hand gripped around the steering wheel as he speaks to Crew. She's looking out the window, sinking into her seat, and crying.

Defeated.

She knows as well as I do that this is the end.

As upset and disgruntled as I am, knowing she's the reason for the heartache I experienced the past year and a half, I'll always have a soft spot for her.

Those beautiful, luscious lips.

Those big hazel eyes.

Tiny little thing.

I walk up to them and open the door to the car, taking Zay by the hand. She frowns, looking at Peter as I yank her out of the car and pull her toward the end of the driveway so we can walk to where I stashed my bike in the bushes across the street.

"Where do you think you're going?" Crew asks.

"Getting my bike."

Peter gets out of the car and his hand slides down her arm and grips her wrist. "You two are riding with me. Mickey will ride your bike to the club."

I flare my nostrils, staring at this boy I wanted more for.

Didn't get what I wanted.

I don't, usually. I always had the shit end of the stick, but I owned it.

Allowed it.

Because people bow down to me. Worship me.

At least they used to before I was to blame for half of our club going to prison.

Peter gets into the black Mercedes. The same one that was at the cabin a couple of days ago. Zay sits in the back seat, looking as though she's given up.

Don't give up yet, sunshine.

I get in beside her instead of sitting next to my brother. Make it look like I don't want her to do anything stupid. And because I'm not ready to face the reality that this fucker lied to me.

He hid.

Pretended.

And I was played like a fool.

My gaze trails over to Zay. She has her head down, tears rolling down her nose as she stares at her shaking hands.

I hate this.

Hate this moment.

I'm distraught. On the one hand, I'm so happy to have my brother back. On the other, I wish I didn't know her truth. I wish we could go back in time and be the way we were at the cabin.

She liked me at the cabin.

I was falling for her at the cabin.

There was no real life at the cabin.

I don't remove my gaze, even though I feel Peter glancing at me in the rearview mirror. My gaze is locked on her.

"Pretty little thing, isn't she?" he says, and that's when I shift my eyes to him. "Have to say, you never screamed like that for me, sweetie."

She sniffs, wiping her cheek. "You're a shit lay."

His grip on the steering wheel tightens and his foot presses harder on the gas pedal. "Yet you still fucked me the night you tried to kill me."

She doesn't lift her head, nor does she say anything else. She sinks into the seat, clenching and unclenching her hands to stop them from shaking.

It doesn't work.

"How'd you know about Zay and me?" I look away from her; it takes everything in me not to hold her hand and kiss those knuckles. "No one was watching the house."

He adjusts the rearview mirror and winks at me. "Crew installed more cameras. I've been in charge of watching them all week." He curls his lip and shrugs. "Kind of weird seeing my brother have sex with the woman who tried to kill me, but she's one helluva woman." He chuckles. "Kind of a turn on."

Looking at Zay again, she glances at me, holding my gaze for a short minute. We had something. Something that's gone now. I felt it leaving when we discovered that Natalia was Lillian. I felt it leaving when I connected the dots and thought she killed Peter.

When she looks back at her hands, more tears line her lash line.

I grip the handle above the door and adjust myself on the seat, staring at the giant homes passing us by. "I needed a release. That's all it was."

She sniffs, causing me to close my eyes and take back every word that leaves my mouth after we left the cabin.

I want to go back.

Just for one more day.

Another day with her in my arms.

Leaning my head back, I look over at her once more; I can't stop staring at her like this will be the last time I see her. The last time I'll be in her presence.

She's fiddling with the hem of her dress. I think it's an anxious tick of hers. She's done this a few times in the past week.

My eye catches a bite mark on her left thigh. One that I left after feasting on the heaven between them. Staring at that bite mark takes me back to yesterday morning.

***

Yesterday I woke up with the pit of my stomach in knots. I didn't know what to expect when Friday came. I didn't want to let her go, either, not after thinking about a future with her. How easy she made running away seem, as if it were a viable option. Half past ten and we were still in bed. She slept on her back, head facing the wall. I stared at her. Tracing her jawline with my fingers, moving down her neck, and pulling the covers off to reveal those succulent breasts.

Nipples stood at full salute.

I kissed her chest, her stomach, and pulled the covers off to reveal the nirvana between her thighs. That clean-shaven masterpiece.

Gorgeous fucking woman.

I took her breast into my mouth, slowly stirring her awake. Then I took the other and she smiled.

"Morning, Riggs," she whispered.

I kissed down her stomach, tongue licking and teeth nibbling.

She opened her legs, welcoming my face as her fingers dragged through my hair.

Tasting her made me crazy.

How could one woman taste so sweet?

Her moans moved through the cabin. Quiet, then loud. And louder, screaming.

Her back arched under me, legs squeezing my head, hands pulling my hair.

"Oh, God, Riggs!"

I tasted her climax; the sweet nectar.

She pulled me by the hair and forced me onto my back. My dick was so hard it hurt.

She gasped, when I entered her, winced when I started rocking, and screamed when I thrust upward.

Tearing her apart inch by inch.

She threw her head back, scratching my thighs. I stared at her, studying everything she did. Every inch of her skin. I needed this photographed. Needed this woman locked in my head.

Her sounds.

Her tits.

Her tight fucking pussy.

Pulling her close to me, I kissed her as I let out my own moans. Mixing our breaths.

I groaned again, scratching her back before I rolled us over and repositioned myself inside her. I shoved my hips forward, rattling the bed. If I fuck her like that anymore, we were going to break the bed. But my balls tightened when I rolled onto my back and she rode me. Hearing her moans bounce off the walls, her pussy taking my dick into a chokehold, I released, filling her up with everything I wanted to give her.

Wanted her to own.

She rested her head on my chest out of breath, and chuckled. "Wow."

I chuckled as well. "Good morning, sunshine."

She rolled off me, lying on her side as I curled my arm behind my head. "What's our plans today?"

Smirking, I tapped my chest. She didn't hesitate. Her head lay on my shoulder, her hand on my chest, and her legs tangled with mine. "I'd like to do this all day if that's okay?"

Her cheeks grew into a smile and disappeared just as quickly. "If only we'd met under different circumstances."

I grunted, playing with her wavy hair. I liked brushing my fingers through it. Felt normal. Felt even more so when my fingers would snag on a knot.

I liked lying with her.

Being with her.

I wasn't up for president of the Snakes.

She didn't have a dark past.

We were two lost souls who found each other.

Molded together to make this perfect fucked-up being.

I liked that.

I liked this, lying in bed without a care as to what would happen to us if we escaped the world.

If we got away.

Went into hiding.

Two of us against the world.

Wouldn't that be something?

"If only, if only."

She poked my chest. "Let's leave, yeah? Get a car and take off. No destination or anything. Just drive."

I couldn't help it, I smiled so big it made my insides flutter. This was the second time she suggested it. "I'd like that."

"You can be a nomad, isn't that what it's called when you don't have a designated motorcycle club?" She looked up at me for the answer.

Shaking my head, I cleared my throat. "I don't wanna be part of this club no more."

A smile. That was all she gave me. "I told you there's a big ole softie in here." She tapped my chest and resumed her position. "Although I am kind of hungry."

"I can make us pancakes."

She squealed and got on her knees beside me. "Blueberry pancakes are my favorite."

I sat up with her, bringing those lips to mine. "Then I'll make you blueberry pancakes every morning until the day I die."

She bit her bottom lip. "Will you, really?"

Brushing my thumb on her cheek, I sighed. "Under different circumstances, I'd give you the world, Zay."

She nodded, kissing my wrist before slipping from my grip. I wasn't lying. I'd give her everything. But this club has me tied down and I can't give her the world.

I can't give her much.

"Wait," I said, taking her wrist. "Here, I want you to have this."

I took a ring off my finger and held it out to her. She chuckled, looking at it and sliding it onto her thumb. "Are you proposing to me, Riggs?"

The idea wasn't as frightening as it sounded, but she didn't need me. I would ruin her. "Maybe in another life, sunshine."

She smiled at the ring and got off the bed, tiptoeing her way to the kitchen. In another life, I would follow her in there, make pancakes with her, and laugh as we smeared batter on our faces.

In another life, being with Zay would be so much deeper than orgasms. It would be home.

***

Blinking, I'm back in the car, still staring at her fiddling with the hem of her dress. She's not the same girl she was the last few days. She's not as happy.

Loving.

She's frightened.

173

I used to feed off the fear.

That terror people would get in their eyes before I did them in. I loved it.

Seeing the terror in her eyes as she glances at me again, I can't fucking stand it.

I want it gone.

I'll take it away. Anything. Just to see her smile one last time.

For me. One more smile that's all mine.

That's all I ask.

She won't give it to me because her brows furrow and she pushes her lips together, crying softly as she stares out the window.

It's over for her now.

Only a matter of time before it's over for me, too.

"Think we should talk, brother," Peter says, glancing in the rearview mirror again.

I shake my head, tearing my eyes off of Zay. "Not now."

Peter sighs, not letting this go. "It wasn't my idea."

"I said, not now!" I raise my voice, making Zay jump.

Putting my hand on her thigh to apologize, she just stares at it. More tears falling.

"Just…I'm sorry," Peter says, licking his lips and leaning his head back.

Everything I did for this kid, and this is how he treats me? This is what he did to me?

Paid his way through school, and paid for a better life for himself, but no, our father has him wrapped around his finger. Anything he says goes. I'm more like my mother. I question things and see the good in people, not the bad.

I don't seek revenge. But I committed it. I committed horrid crimes for the man I thought was God when I was younger. Man who ruins everything he touches.

Fucking Peter is brainwashed. He doesn't know what this club will do to him.

Eat him whole.

Constrict him.

Harm him.
Destroy him.
I'm torn.
Fucking torn.

Zay

It doesn't take us more than an hour to get to the bar I'm sure Lillian visited many times to meet up with Riggs, maybe even Peter. This isn't her scene. Shit, this isn't even mine. A shitty biker bar that looks like it has seen better days, broken windows patched with plywood. Dirt and gravel road has oil stains, potholes, and broken beer bottles everywhere. Even the sign that's supposed to read "Judas's Hideout" says nothing more than "Judas's Hideout."

I don't belong here. This isn't my scene. This isn't what I do. I don't kill people.

But I attempted to kill Peter. Thought I did.

Maybe I do belong here. Scared, broken.

Riggs keeps staring at me. He's been stealing glances the entire ride. Tried to hold my hand twice. But what's the use of giving in? What's the use of showing him I still care?

It's over.

It was never something, but I did feel things. I won't deny that.

He's not Adam.

He was just a dick I used as my last will and testament.

Riggs holds a place in my heart, but Adam owns it.

When we walk into the bar, Peter shoves me into a booth and tells me to stay put. The place is dark, riddled with black leather and red curtains. Reeks of beer and cigarettes with a hint of piss.

What the heck was she doing here?

Riggs is sitting at the bar, glancing at me every so often as the rest of the guys pace the sitting area, whispering plans, pointing at me, and gritting their teeth.

I don't know what their plan is for me.

I know it isn't good.

Peter lights a cigarette—I didn't even know he smoked. I don't know a lot about him, it seems.

Tears slip free and that's when I feel Riggs's stare. I don't want him to see me like this.

Weak.

Pathetic.

On death row.

His gaze holds for a couple of minutes until I look at him. When we lock eyes, he looks away, taking a swig of his beer.

All hope is lost.

***

Just days ago, we were lying in front of the fire, naked and out of breath. He poked the wood, grinning without even looking at me.

"What's that smile about?" I asked, poking his cheek.

He put the poker down and rested his hand on my stomach. "I hated being here with you. Hated your stubborn ass even more. But now, I don't want it to end."

I chuckled, poking his cheek again. "Yeah, I'm pretty annoying when it comes down to it."

"You were."

"Who'd have thought shoving your dick in me would shut me up?" I said, turning onto my stomach. He nods, fingers delicately tracing the curves of my back to my ass.

He traced the butterfly on my lower back. "You have a tattoo."

"It's for Lillian," I said, looking over my shoulder. "She was obsessed with butterflies." He nodded, brushing his fingers up my back and causing goosebumps to pebble. "Which tattoo was your first?"

He grunted, turning onto his back and touching his left side. "This dagger when I was fifteen. My uncle has a tattoo gun." He folded his arm behind his

177

head. "Doesn't mean anything. None of them do."

Touching the open mouth of the serpent, I move my finger along its tongue. "And this one?"

"I was seventeen, had my first kill and my daddy said it was time I ink my skin since I was officially a member of the Snakes," he replied, turning onto his side again. "I've done bad things for the club, and this snake was the start of it all."

His past is dark, something I wanted to learn about, but knew it was not worth it.

"All the taboo things are the funnest, aren't they?" I smirked, biting my lower lip as he stared right at them.

He nibbled my shoulder, getting on top of me. "What's taboo is fucking you raw. I don't do that often. I don't do that, ever."

"Oh, really?" I said as he parted my legs. "Then why don't you show me one more time what fucking me raw is like?"

He breathed against my cheek, tongued teasing it. "For you, sunshine, I'd do anything."

I gasped feeling him slide inside me, one place he remained until we met our fate two short days later.

***

Riggs gets up, draining his beer, and goes behind the bar for another. The men are distracted, huddled together, and speaking quietly.

If I'm getting out of this alive, I need to make a break for it.

The front door is out of the question. They're close enough to it that I wouldn't make it to the bar without a bullet in me.

The exit sign at the back of the kitchen, the light flickering and catching my attention. There hasn't been a single soul walking around back there since we got here.

Riggs is making himself a drink, ignoring the barmaid offering to do it. He gulps his beer, shaking his head. None of the guys are looking at me.

It's now or never.

Sliding out of the booth, I make a run for it, hearing the sounds of Riggs's beer bottle clank on the bar top.

The kitchen is empty as I thought, and the exit sign is right up ahead. I'm going to make it.

Yelling and cursing move through the bar, and the sound of heavy footfalls follow after.

I shove the backdoor open and stumble out into the bright afternoon, skinning my knee.

Riggs is right behind me, staring down at me.

I wince, scrambling to my feet and charging for the parking lot, but he has me by the hair before I even make it a couple of feet.

Sobs leave me as he grabs hold of me and pulls my back to his chest. "Please."

"What part of *stay put* don't you understand?" he growls, whipping me around.

"Riggs, please," I weep, touching his chest. His heart is beating rapidly.

Is it beating for me? Or is it beating at the thrill of killing me?

Lip comes out with Banks, guns in hand. Riggs tenses and grabs my throat, shoving me into the brick wall. "You can beg for your fucking life all you want. I can't wait to be the one who puts a bullet in that fucking head of yours," he says through gritted teeth.

I'm crying, but he doesn't seem to care anymore.

There's nothing but darkness in those eyes.

The same darkness I saw the night we met.

It's over for me.

It's fucking over.

Riggs

Tossing Zay back in the booth, I slide in beside her, snapping my fingers at the bartender. She brings me my beer and drink, eyeing Zay as she cries quietly beside me.

Fuck. I hate this. I hate being mean to her and pretending like it's not bothering me how scared she is.

I have to act tough. If I don't, they'll lose more trust in me.

Sliding my drink to Zay, I take a swig of beer as Peter sits down in front of us. Smug bastard always thought he was better than me. He's four years younger and always thought he ruled the world. Our father didn't make it any better. He told him he would rule and told him exactly what he said to me in Zay's room.

Donnelly brothers will run this club.

I don't want it. I don't want this for him.

When I thought Peter was dead, all hope was lost. This club meant nothing to me anymore. They guys already hated me because of the Natalia fiasco, then Peter died, and I had no reason to be part of this MC. To devote my life to them was useless. Now look at us.

My kid brother in the flesh.

Lying dick thought he'd get away with deceiving me.

He won't.

Brother or not, we reap the consequences we sow. The consequences we can't predict.

Sooner or later, Peter will get what's coming to him for everything he put me through.

"Trying to pull a fast one on us, Zaynab? Hmm?" He kicks under the table and she yelps, reaching underneath to rub her leg. "Show some respect and look me in the eye when I'm speaking to you."

Her eyes shift to his, lower lip quivering. "I lost all respect for you when you admitted to killing my best friend."

He chuckles, taking the drink I made her and gulping it. "If only you didn't find the cell phone, huh, sweetie?"

She lowers her head, staring at the wooden table separating the two of them. The table has been carved into, stained by every substance I can think of, and is constantly sticky, no matter what we do.

Peter chuckles again, his eyes scanning her in that red dress she wore the first time we met.

Gorgeous then as she is now.

But I gotta act.

I have to pretend.

Just for a little while.

After that, I'll save her.

Take a bullet for her.

She's walking away from this living and breathing.

I, on the other hand, might not.

Peter rakes his bottom lip as he stares at her. I remember him telling me about a girl he met at university. *Pretty brunette who drives me wild*, he said.

Little did I know it was her.

Little did I know that his girlfriend wasn't the girl who drove him crazy, but he stayed with her because she grounded him.

Little did I know that Natalia and his girlfriend were the same person.

When Natalia started coming around the bar to see me, Peter noticed her. He never said anything, and neither did she.

Stupid me continued to fuck Natalia, unknowing that Peter was fucking her, too.

All the while he was in love with another girl.

The broken girl beside me.

The broken girl who thought she killed Peter for killing her best friend.

It started as revenge. Now it's just chaos.

He slides the drink back to Zay and taps the table. "We should talk." His eyes shift to me. "In private."

"You and I?" I ask, gulping some beer.

He shakes his head and nods to her. "Me and this beauty that stole our hearts." His lip quirks up to a grin. "You've stolen the hearts of many, haven't you, sweetie?"

Her sad reddened eyes flicker to his. "I don't know why, I'm no catch."

He winks, letting out a chuckle. "It's that tight little pussy of yours that gets us." He rises, taking my beer. "Now c'mon, we should talk."

I don't like this.

The Peter I know is a follower, that's why our father wanted him under his wing.

That's why Crew allowed him in.

I don't follow so well. I have a mind of my own and see the bad in everything. Even though I cause it. I see the wrong this club does.

Yet I still comply. I still kill. I still beat. I still obey orders.

Like I'm waiting for my chance to be rid of this place.

I slide out of the booth and put my hand out to her. She glances at it, then at me. And scoffs, pushing past me.

Blood is drying up on her leg, dripping down her knee. When Peter kicked her, the blood spread to the side of her shin.

Her leg is so red.

I want to help her, clean her wound, and kiss it better.

But what good would that do?

I've hurt her.

It'll only make it worse.

I watch as they walk away, grinding my teeth. I don't like this. All of it is still fishy to me.

Fucked is more like it.

Judas pats my back, holding a shot of whiskey out to me. "He's done well, your brother. Your daddy would be proud."

Shaking my head, I drop back down in the booth. "I didn't want this for him. You know as well as I do, I tried to get him out. I paid for his schooling. I told him to move far away from the damned Snakes. Look at him now."

Judas squeezes my shoulder. "Donnelly brothers at the top, this club won't know what's coming to them. People will bow down to us, brother. They'll fear us more than the Panthers." He makes a fist and hits his chest twice. "Snakes, that's what we are."

"That's what we are," I repeat, shooting back the whiskey and staring at the hallway Zay and Peter escaped to. Our fate is written in stone. Sealed.

There is no changing what is expected of us from birth. What we're supposed to do because our father expects only the best from his sons.

He got the best in me and molded the best in Peter.

But this is done.

I am done.

Donnelly brothers will not run this town.

Snakes will end with me. I'll make sure of it.

Zay

I'm limping to a room at the back of the bar.

It's quiet back here.

Secluded.

Anything can happen.

Peter closes the door behind him and he leans on it as I limp to the couch beside the bed.

Staring at me.

He always stares at me.

He jerks his head at my leg and lets out a breath. "You all right?"

"Never better."

He nods, licking his lips. "We all have to pay for our sins one way or another."

I meet his gaze and stand, limping toward him. "I think I've paid enough, don't you think?"

He laughs, spinning us around and shoving my back against the door. Forearm at my throat, his other hand gripping my hip. "You tried to kill me, Zay. You haven't paid enough. Not until you feel what it's like to have a fucking pen jabbed into your jugular."

A thick tear leaves my eye, rolling until it meets his sweater at my throat.

There's nothing I can do or say anymore that will get me out of this.

My fate is sealed.

"When you kill me, all I ask is that you make it quick." I'm crying again and his face softens. Taking in the fear leaking out of me. "Just please make it quick."

He releases me and leans his forehead on my shoulder, breathing softly. "I understand why you did it, Zaynab. Lillian meant a lot to me, too."

"Then why did you kill her?" I whisper.

He lifts his head to look at me. "My daddy runs this club; Lillian got him put in the slammer. He and six of our guys are in prison because of her. As next in line for president, Crew took the reins and gave me my first order as a member. Kill or suffer the consequences. So I killed and made it look like a suicide." His lip curls slightly. "Much like you tried to do to me, right?"

"I'm sorry," I whisper.

He grunts, tracing my jawline and tilting my chin up to face him. "Lemme tell you a little story, yeah?"

His lips feather my cheek before he presses a kiss to it and sighs. His breath tickles my shoulder. "Two years ago I met a girl at a party. Pretty little thing that captivated me. Her name literally means beauty and she refused to be mine." His teeth rake my shoulder before he continues. "Fast forward two weeks, I thought I lost her. Thought I'd never see her again. Her best friend happens to be the woman I ask out on a date. I'm back in her life, the only problem is, she wants nothing to do with me because she adores the blonde I'm dating. She's a good time, the blonde. A virgin. But she's not *her*."

I'm trying my hardest not to cry or show any emotion toward his speech. But anytime someone speaks about Lillian, I choke up.

He sucks in a rush of air, brushing my tears away. "Months pass, maybe two or three, and that blonde starts coming around my secret club, flirting with the guys, then starts fucking my brother. I didn't know she had it in her. The blonde starts acting like her friend, making her that much more appealing. But still, she's not *her*...things seem to be ending, I said my goodbyes to the blonde who cheated on me and all the while I slept around on her. We were two hopeless romantics in love with other people. But the blonde stuck her nose in something she shouldn't have. She saw something she shouldn't have. And you know what happens to people who see things they're not supposed to see? Hmm?" He kisses my cheek, licking the tear from it. "You know what happens to those who rat on us because of what they see?"

I shake my head. I don't want to hear it. I've heard enough.

My Lillian isn't a whore.

My Lillian isn't a tattletale.

My Lillian wouldn't put her life at stake for these people.

The pad of his thumb brushes my cheek. "They get killed. And that's okay. It's all part of the job, but again, there's a problem. The blonde's best friend wants revenge, believing the blonde was killed and didn't commit suicide. And for some fucking reason, that beauty knows it was me. So I fuck her. Try to get her off my tail. But it doesn't work, does it? No, it doesn't. And here I am again, in a dilemma. Because the girl I'm head over heels for tried to kill me. Oh, and her boyfriend, who happens to be my best friend, tries to pay me off so I won't kill her." He chuckles softly. "And do you know who *my* best friend is?"

My heart is in my throat, and no matter how hard I swallow, I'm choking. Tears keep streaming and every tear that sheds, he wipes away.

The blue of his eyes darkens as he speaks. Showing the hatred in them.

Hatred for me.

For what I did.

For what I know.

"Does the name Adam Lovett ring any bells?"

I gasp, my knees buckling. "H-how do you know Adam?"

No, the question is, why didn't Adam ever say anything? Why did he pretend like none of it happened? Why did he let me riddle myself with guilt over something I never did?

Peter rests his forearms on either side of my head, leaning forward. "We grew up together." He smirks like he's proud of his reveal. Proud to see me weak beneath his towering body. "The day he visited me at the hospital after you did this to me, he told me about a pretty brunette he met with the weirdest name he'd ever heard. And that happened to be you, sweetie." A grin touches his lips again. "Who'd have thunk it? I'm lying in bed, trying to recover from an injury caused by the woman my friend is telling me about. Yet another heart you stole, sweetie. Isn't it?"

He tilts my chin up so we're nose to nose. "He offered me five hundred thousand to keep you alive. Offered the club an extra five hundred from you." He smirks. "You're worth more than a million dollars, don't you think?"

I shake my head, all my stupidity and mistakes rising to the surface. The time I stole money from church, when I stole candy bars from the corner store, how I slept with whoever approached me, how I lied to my best friend about the guy she was dating. Saying he was a good guy, decent. Nice. That I wouldn't sleep with him. But I did. Then I tried to kill him.

And now look at me.

I should be begging for my life.

Pleading. Hoping and praying.

But I'm not.

I just wish he'd get it over with so I don't have to hear any more of his story.

"Don't prolong this any more than you already are. Just fucking kill me, Peter. Get it over with."

His nose grazes my cheek and traces my jaw until his mouth meets my neck. "I'm not going to kill you, sweetie. I never was." A slow breath leaves him and he steps back, staring at me with furrowed brows. "I understand why you did it. I don't like it, but I get it. Lillian meant a lot to you, she meant a lot to many people, it seems. But she wasn't right in the head." He taps his head. "She fucked my family over and the men I call my brothers gave me an order so that I'd be one of them." He lifts his shirt revealing a fresh snake tattooed on the left side of his ripped stomach. A snake just like the one that takes up almost the entire left side of Riggs's body. "Now I am one, and my word matters. If I say not to kill you, those men will listen." He drops his shirt and extends his hand to me. I don't take it, I stare at it and frown.

I scoff, folding my arms. "Then why play these childish games?"

"We've spent enough time together for me to know what you like and don't like. And I remember your love for mystery novels." He takes my hand, uncrossing my arms. "You toyed with me; I only deemed it fair that I do the same."

"Where's Adam? I want to speak with him."

He nods, lacing our fingers together. "We were supposed to meet you at the barn tonight, so we wait until then. He'll bring us the money and we'll let you go."

That's it? They're just going to let me go like I didn't see or hear anything.

Like I'm not their next ghost.

"Why don't I believe you?"

He tugs me closer and runs his free hand through my hair. "You have to trust me, sweetie. I won't let anything happen to you."

Where have I heard that one before?

My eyes well with tears. But I don't let them escape anymore.

Letting them escape proves I'm weak.

I don't want to be weak anymore.

I'm tired of this.

I just want to go home.

Riggs

They're in the back room for twenty minutes doing God only knows what. I know she won't sleep with him. The way she spoke about her feelings toward Peter, it's clear there's nothing remotely salvageable. I can't say the same for my brother.

He falls hard, harder than most. I remember when his first girlfriend broke up with him, he was sixteen, strong head on his shoulder until then. He's easily brainwashed, and when she told him she wanted to end things, he let it happen. She said he wanted to end things, too. For months after that, he lived with me. Moaning and groaning about the woman he lost. Cursing her name, crying well into the night. I believe Zay is just like that one. Someone he'll never truly be able to let go of, not even if it's Adam's girl. My brother's obsession with being loved came from the lack of love our father gave us. All he cared about was the club. It's the only thing that mattered. Our mama thought differently. She loved us and cared for us until the day she died.

Died for this fucking club.

When they finally come out, Zay looks defeated. More so than she did before.

Whatever he told her ruined her even more.

They're holding hands, much to her dismay.

Getting up from the booth, I point at her leg. She's limping. I don't like that. "I'll take her to the bathroom and clean her up a bit. She's getting blood all over the place."

Peter and Zay look down at her leg, the cut on her knee is still bleeding. He lets go of her hand and nods, heading to the bar for a drink.

I lead Zay to the bathroom, all eyes on me as I go. So I play along, grabbing her arm and forcing her forward. She winces, tripping on her feet as she tries to keep up with my pace.

She's in pain and I'm making it worse.

Releasing her when we get to the bathroom, I rub her arm slightly. "Sorry—"

"Don't. I don't want to hear it."

I lift her onto the counter and rest my hands on either side of her. "Trust me, please."

She scoffs. "Trust you?" She lowers her voice, glancing at the door, then back at me. "You just told me you couldn't wait to put a bullet in my head. How the fuck can I trust you? Huh? Were you not about to leave me at my house before they showed up?" She scoffs again, shaking her head, and sucking her teeth. "Trust you."

I grab her face and hold it, staring into those hazel eyes that haven't stopped crying all day. "I thought you killed my brother. Of course, I was gonna fucking leave you. But you didn't. And I ain't gonna let them kill you over something that didn't happen."

She sniffs, removing my hands from her face. "Why didn't you let me run away?"

I sigh, grumbling slightly. "Because if I let you go, then I'd be up shit's creek. Just trying to get us outta this alive, Zay. I promise."

She looks down at her hands in her lap, curling her fingers in the hem of her dress.

I don't push anymore. I grab the first aid kit and look at her knee.

She must've fallen on a loose rock on the ground because the cut is deep. She winces and groans as I clean it but doesn't move. She might need stitches.

Tears are falling, but she still doesn't move.

She's broken beyond repair.

I have a Band-Aid in hand as the bathroom door opens and Judas walks in. Unzipping his fly. "Don't let me interrupt," he says, chuckling.

She sniffles again, wiping her nose on the back of her hand. "There's nothing to interrupt."

Judas grunts, shaking and coming over to us to wash his hands. "Riggsy here can fool everyone but me."

I grit my teeth, fixing another Band-Aid on her knee. "Shut up."

He swats his hands in the air and wipes them on his jeans. "Everything will be fine, Zay. Your friend just pissed off the wrong people. And you tried to kill one of us, but I'm sure everything will be fine."

"Thanks for the pep talk." She gives him a thumbs up and sniffs again, looking down at her knee. "But my fate is sealed. I'm certain of it."

Judas glances at me with sympathetic eyes, clapping me on the back. "Lunch is soon, brother."

I nod, waiting until he leaves the bathroom. I don't know what to do. I want to set her free but in doing so I end my own life.

What the fuck do I do?

"I find it strange that Peter is part of this motorcycle club when he's a student at Stanford University. Or is that all a front?"

I'm happy she talking to me. I can't even wipe the grin off my face when I respond. "I wanted a life outside of this club for him. Paid my dues just so he could go to university and get a better life than this." I shake my head, leaning my hands on the vanity on either side of her again. "Our daddy had other plans. Plans that Natalia witnessed firsthand. She witnessed a lot while we were together. Or while she was with Peter. I don't even know if we overlapped." We meet each other's gaze and the waterworks start up again. "She ratted on the wrong people, Zay. It wasn't my call to make. And believe me, they might not have killed me, but I suffered. I shoulda suffered worse but I'm the son of the president of this MC. If I'd have known—"

"If you'd have known what? You'd try to save her? You'd never get involved with her?" She pushes me away and hops off the counter with a groan, standing on one leg. "Save it, Riggs. I don't need to hear any more sob stories about how Lillian fucked everything up. She's gone, there's nothing we can do to fucking change this bullshit."

Grabbing her arm, I pull her to me. "No, there ain't. But I can sure as shit change what's gonna happen to you, can't I?"

She wipes her eyes before the tears fall and she snakes her arm out of my grasp. "What good will it do, anyway? Life as I know it is done."

I reach up and touch her face; that spark we had is dying. Slowly dissolving. I can see it in her eyes. She's lost all hope.

That beauty and sass that fascinated me are done.

Soon, it'll be gone.

***

The morning of Peter's eighteenth birthday, we were woken up by gunshots. Two shots were fired inside our house. I lived above the bar at this point, having lived there since I was eighteen, but I made sure to be there for Peter the night before his birthday. Sleeping in bed with him, too. Been doing that since we were babies.

Peter and I jolted into wakefulness, rubbing the sleep from our eyes as I grabbed my gun under the pillow. "What was that?" he whispered.

Putting my finger on my mouth, I got out of bed, inching toward the door. It was quiet, far too quiet. I jerked my head at my boots, and Peter took the spare gun I usually kept holstered around my ankle.

As quietly as we could, we inched our way down the hallway and to the top of the stairs, waiting, listening, praying it wasn't a Panther coming to do us in.

Gurgling and gasping came from the living room. Peter and I crept down the stairs to see what was amok. I remember it being quiet, so quiet it scared me. Nothing scares me.

As soon as we stepped into the living room, there our mother was; on her belly trying to crawl away from our father. He sat on the arm of the couch and cleaned his gun.

"Mama?" Peter's voice shook, breaking up the eerie quiet of the house.

I kept my gun raised, making my way to her. "What happened? What the fuck did you do?" The anger that burned inside me brought me to hold the barrel of the gun at my father's temple. And all he did was laugh.

Laugh at the pettiness he believed I was doing.

Defending my mother.

"Rats get what's coming to them. Remember that, boys."

He stepped over her and walked out. He left us to witness her take her last breath in Peter's arms on his eighteenth birthday with the words slipping off of her tongue. "Life as we know it…is over."

With that pressed on my chest, she died, leaving Peter and me in a state of shock. We didn't leave the living room until more of our guys came in to clean up our father's mess. They took her away. Buried her somewhere in an unmarked grave.

Disposed of her like she meant nothing to us.

She meant the world to me.

Peter believed our father. Believed that our mother was feeding intel to the Panthers.

She wasn't.

She wouldn't.

My mama was a saint. She hated the club. Hated it as much as I do.

But someone had to pay. She was the easiest candidate because our father never loved her.

He used her to birth two sons who would take over the club.

Two sons who are nothing alike.

Life as we know it *is* over.

***

I keep near Zay, even though there's evidence she doesn't want me to. I sit beside her in the booth while we eat lunch with Peter and Judas.

The rest of the guys scatter around the bar, drinking, and eating. Doing whatever they can to kill time until we have to leave for the barn again.

My stomach is in knots just thinking about going out there.

The danger she'll be in.

The paranoia I'll have toward these men. After all this is said and done with, how can I trust them again?

For three hours we sit in the booth in silence. I nurse a couple more beers, and she sips at a soda that's probably gone flat by now.

Peter tries talking to her a bunch, reminiscing about their time in school together. He talks about the parties they went to, the pills they took, and how they studied together while on some pills and realized that with the right dosage, they'd be able to create essays that they never deemed possible. They have a history, a friendship that died so long ago.

She barely gives him answers, just nods, and says *yeah, I remember*.

He can feel it, too. She doesn't have the same spark she used to.

I want that spark back, just one last time.

Crew whistles, getting everyone's attention. "All right, Snakes. Let's go."

Rising, I fix my jeans, putting a hand out so Zay doesn't have to do much walking. She can use me as a crutch.

But she doesn't take my hand. She folds her arms and follows everyone out with her head down.

Peter grips my shoulder, my little brother in the flesh. "You protect her with your life, you understand?" he whispers.

I grunt. "Already two steps ahead of you, kid."

The night grows, hovering over us like a blanket. Her chest is heaving, breathing heavily as she stands in the middle of the parking lot, unsure of where to go.

She shifts her gaze to the night sky. The stars are sprinkled throughout. It's a clear night tonight. I think she likes that because, for the first time since we got here, there's a smile creeping on her face.

I step toward her before Peter does, placing a hand on her lower back, and leading her to my bike. She's not riding with anyone but me. I get on first, waiting for her to get on. She hesitates, looking back at the bar, eyeing Peter as he gets in his car. Poor kid has inner ear issues and can't balance on a bike. Always had trouble with it as kids. Didn't learn how to ride a bike until he was ten years old. Tried skateboarding but ended up breaking his arm. Kid can't even walk a straight line sober without staggering.

Nothing the doctors could do but make sure he kept those ears clean and watched for infections. Well, I watched, I paid so much attention and made sure my little brother was okay.

He was until he wasn't.

He nods at her as I bring my bike to life, her purr combining with everyone else's.

"Get on, Zay," I say, holding out a helmet for her. She doesn't take it and swings a leg over the bike, squeezing me with her thighs and those delicate arms around my waist.

I'm a goner and she's someone I can't have.

195

I'm a goner and she's someone I can't have.

Zay

S hit.
Fuck.
Shit.

Fuck.

Shit.

Repeat.

We approach the barn and I'm already shaking. This is my ending and I never thought I'd go out like this. I envisioned a life for myself.

A happy life with someone to love me.

Adam. I envisioned my life with him. The two of us. Maybe a couple of kids. We'd grow old together. Live in a condo by the water. Just the two of us. My end would come when I'm old and gray. Not now. Not while I'm still so young.

I whimper, keeping my head down as we approach the barn doors and Lip swings them open.

Adam is there with Banks, two duffel bags at his feet. He looks like he's been crying.

"Zay!" he calls, trying to get to me but Crew takes hold of my arm.

"You got the money?" Crew asks, squeezing my arm so tightly I feel my pulse beat against his grip.

Adam tosses the duffle bags forward, pointing at them. "Added a little extra. And if you want more, I can get you more. Just let her go."

Crew snorts, letting out a chuckle and turning to his men behind him. "More, huh?"

Adam nods, staring at me. And I can't help it. I'm crying again, wincing from the hold Crew has on my arm and crying. I'm done with all of this. "Whatever you want, I can get. Just, please." Adam furrows his brow. "Let her go."

With a sigh, Crew tosses me on the ground, missing the bags by inches. I don't look back, I scramble to my feet as Adam lifts me, squeezing me tightly and kissing my face.

"Are you okay? Oh, babe, I'm sorry," he whispers.

I grip his shirt, sobbing into it. I have no words. Nothing to say that can assure him I'm fine.

Because I'm not.

I won't be fine until I know this isn't the end of the road for me.

He winces when I wrap my arms around his waist. "You okay?" I whisper.

"When they took you they kicked me a bunch." He burrows his face in my hair. "I'm okay." He breathes me in. "I'm okay."

Crew looks at his men and smirks.

Riggs and Peter glance at each other, then at the men who start circling around us.

Guns are pulled from the holsters. The back of their jeans. Their ankles.

I knew this was too good to be true.

Adam moves me behind him, frowning at Crew and Peter. "You said you'd let us go!"

"I know." Crew shrugs, chuckling as his men surround us. "I lied."

Riggs grits his teeth, stepping forward and pulling on Crew's shoulder. "Hey. They're innocent in all this. Let them go."

Crew cackles, nudging his head at Peter. "Innocent, huh? She almost killed your brother."

"But she didn't," Peter says, staring at Adam and me. "You promised, Crew. Swore it to me and my daddy." He points at the bags. "We have more than enough money in there to last us the year. If we want more, we'll shake them down for more. But right now, let's go."

Crew stares at me peeking over Adam's shoulder. He clicks his tongue and looks back at Peter and Riggs, Lip smirking beside them. "Well, I guess since

I promised your daddy."

Laughter moves around us, taunting us with their demonic gazes.

"These were Daddy's orders after all."

Adam's grip on me tightens, his body is stiff and his breathing is so shaky that I hold onto him so he has that sense of calm.

I look back and see Judas standing there, tilting his head to the side in a sympathetic, forgiving way.

Nothing is forgiving about this.

Riggs looks at me, his jaw tense, fists clenched. I'd hate to see him sad. Big guy like him is always so angry.

I don't think he has a sympathetic bone in his body.

Maybe one. And I used it for a week.

He grabs Crew by the leather vest, towering over him. I can't make out what he's saying. I don't think anyone can. It's quiet and growled between his gritted teeth.

But it's enough to alarm the people around us.

Banks and Judas make their way over, as do a couple of the other guys nearby.

Adam and I are alone and can make a run for it. I just can't walk well enough to do that. He looks around us and brings me back to his chest, kissing my head and cradling it. "Oh, Zay." My lower lip quivers and I can't even look at him before I begin to sob, dropping my head on his chest. "It's okay, babe. It's okay."

"It's not," I whisper, looking up at him. "This whole thing is so fucked-up."

He smooths out my hair, leaving a soft kiss on my lips. "I know."

"Why didn't you say anything?"

"I tried, but I didn't know how. Peter and I go way back, my mom worked for the club for a while. His mother raised me when mine wasn't able to…we all share the same dad. But I didn't know about Lillian. I didn't know Peter killed her until after I met you. And when I visited him at the hospital, I didn't know if was you who did it. We had just met, you and I." He sniffs. "I'm kept in the dark about the club. Seems like I'm kept in the dark about a lot."

I wince, gripping his shirt. "I loved you."

"Do you still?"

"Do you?"

He kisses me again. "I never stopped. I tried to leave you so you'd be safe. To push you away from this bullshit. But they were coming after you no matter what I did." He uses the pad of his thumb to wipe away my tears. "I love you, Zay. I'll never stop, even if you don't love me."

Gripping his shirt, I pull him closer to me. "I'm sorry I didn't say it enough—"

Shots fire, one, two, three before Adam pushes us to the ground, using his body to protect mine.

But it's too late, I've been shot.

My breathing wavers.

Gasping.

Adam looks down at my chest and pushes his hand onto it.

It hurts so much.

But I'm too in shock to react.

I'm too shocked to move.

I gasp for breaths, keeping my focus on his face.

Trying to memorize its beauty before I close my eyes.

They're getting heavy.

"No, no, no, no, no," Adam sobs. "Zay! Zay! Babe, keep your eyes open, okay? Just look at me—" He turns his head and yells. "Get the fucking car, Peter! We have to get her to the hospital." His raspy breaths send a chill through me. "Riggs, please!"

Adam's bleeding, too. His white t-shirt is covered in blood, leaking down his arm.

I try to reach for it and touch his wound like he is mine. But I can't move my arms. They're heavy at my sides. Weighted.

More shots are fired and Adam collapses on top of me, protecting me from the blow. "It's okay, Zay. I promise." His gaze bores into my eyes. "I love you."

My gasps are shorter now, I feel lighter.

Tired.

So damn tired.

Riggs comes to a running halt at my side, tossing his gun and tapping my face. "Zay? Zay, keep your eyes open, okay?"

Adam whimpers, pushing harder on my chest. "She's going to make it."

Riggs keeps his focus on me. That darkness in his eyes is gone. They're tearing up, turning red. But the darkness.

It's finally gone.

Riggs

I've been pacing the hospital's emergency room for six goddamn hours. Peter keeps trying to get me to sit down. Adam keeps saying *she's a fighter, she'll pull through*. But I've seen death enough to know that she isn't pulling through.

Not with a bullet to the chest.

Sipping yet another coffee, I peek over my shoulder at Peter asleep beside Adam. His head is leaning on Adam's shoulder and Peter's mouth is open. Adam smiles at me, stretching out his legs and leaning his head on Peter's. Moments like this remind me of us as kids.

When Crew brought me to the barn a week ago, and I saw Adam on his knees in front of him, I had to act like everything was fine. But it wasn't. Adam is like a brother to me, my mother damn near raised him. But he's not like us, my father made sure of it. Told us he's not part of the Snakes, he'll never be a Snake. My father said he was just a bastard. Not a true Donnelly. I believed him, but I still cared for the bastard just the same.

So when they shipped off to Stanford University, I made sure Peter and Adam weren't involved in the club. Little did I know, Peter was involved and Adam was just trying to make a life for himself with the woman we're swooning over.

Adam's mother did favors for the guys. Moreso my father. Until one day, both my mother and Adam's were pregnant. My father denied ever sleeping with her, but rumors spread quickly around the club. Truth came out when Adam was born with our signature slanted almond-shaped eyes that were blue like Daddy's.

After the seventh hour and eighth cup of shitty, watered-down coffee, the doctor comes in. He takes off his mask and sighs.

Adam shoots up from his seat, knocking Peter awake. "How is she? Is she okay? Can I see her? Please."

"Slow down there," the doctor says, shifting his gaze between Peter and me. We still have our cuts on. Doesn't look good. Taking it off won't be any better, my arms are covered in tattoos, piercings in my ears, and skull rings on my fingers.

"How is she?" I ask, arms folded across my broad chest.

The doctor nods. "She flatlined—"

"Oh, God." Adam slaps a hand onto his mouth, choking back his cries.

The doctor puts a hand up. "But she's okay. She made it by the skin of her teeth." He nods. "She's a fighter. I'll give her that."

"I need to see her," Adam says, wiping his eyes.

She might be in an induced coma, heavily medicated, even. I doubt we'll get to see her today.

"Which one of you is her partner?" the doctor asks, scanning the three of us.

Adam steps forward before I can say anything. "I am."

Lucky bastard.

"Whoever her partner is, we're all getting in to see her doc." I stand taller, being as intimidating as I can be. It's working. The doctor is gulping and looking between the three of us again. "Ain't nothing you or anyone can do to stop us."

He nods quickly, stammering and stuttering before clearing his throat. "F-follow me."

Adam's like a kid on speed. He's nervous, looking around and trying to push past the doctor like he knows where he's going. The kid has always been jumpy. That's why he was never one of us. Never built like Peter and me, even though my parents raised him, he was never one of us. He's a good kid, nonetheless. He's the right choice for Zay.

The second we get to her room Adam bursts in and charges for her. Kissing her hands, her face, those succulent lips.

"Babe, hey. Hey, it's me." He brings her hand to his lips and sits beside her.

"Hey," she whispers, her voice gravelly.

She looks tired. Bags under her eyes, paleness to her skin.

Waxy.

"You're okay," he whispers, touching her face.

"Said the bullet missed my heart by an inch. Imagine that." She tries to chuckle and winces instead. "Pure dumb luck."

Peter taps her foot, then holds it. "Said you died on the table."

She hums, nods, then looks at Adam. "Told you they'd kill me."

Even in a moment like this, she still tries to tell a joke.

Her gaze shifts to me and she winks, licking her lips the way she does, which makes me go crazy. But she's not mine to lose my head over. Never was. We were a bump in each other's roads; the best bump and I'll have a lot of trouble getting over her.

"Hey," Adam whispers, kissing her head and leaning his forehead on it. "Will you still? Tell me you will."

She scrunches her nose and winces when she tries to adjust on the bed. "Will what?"

"Marry me, silly."

She tries to laugh, whimpering and wincing as she holds a hand to her chest. "You were serious?"

"I was, babe." Adam lowers his voice, thinking we can't hear him. "I even got you a ring. Wait until you see this thing. It's ugly as shit."

Another chuckle leaves her. "I love you," she whispers.

Words I wish she'd said to me.

Her eyes shift, meeting mine, like she can feel me watching her. But I don't say anything.

I watch her as she speaks quietly with Adam. How he leans closer to her, kissing her cheek and lips. She's happy, and that's all that matters.

She's happy and I can move forward knowing this perfect little thing is going to make it.

Tapping Peter's arm, I nod my head toward the door. The two of us have to speak about what happened and why he kept this secret from me for so long.

He squeezes her foot and leans forward, tapping Adam's arm. "We're stepping out a sec."

"Yeah, yeah," Adam says, smiling at us.

She smiles at me, staring at me with apologetic eyes. She doesn't have to say anything.

No apology is necessary.

We knew what we were doing. It was a release, nothing more.

But I made it into more. I think she did, too, because she's spinning the ring I gave her around her thumb and keeping her gaze locked with mine as I head for the door.

Closing it behind me, I break our stare as Peter tousles his hair. "She's okay."

He grunts, staring at the door. "It's crazy. For the past year, all I wished upon her was revenge. I wished something bad would happen to her because of what she did to me. But seeing her shot—the worst day of my fucking life."

I nod, sliding my hands into my back pockets. "I know what you mean." But I'm not here to praise the fact that Zay is alive, I'm here to know why he betrayed me. I'm not beating around the bush. "Why did you fuck me over, kid? I'm your brother. Your fucking family. What the fuck does this club owe you that I haven't already given you?" I scoff pointing at the door. "Did that fuckhead, Adam, know?"

Peter sits in the chair by the door and drops his head in his hands. "It was all Crew's idea. He said that I had to do it to make Daddy proud. Said that if I didn't agree, he'd kill you and Zaynab. I wasn't letting that happen." He sniffs. "Adam knew…said he'd pay us off when he got the money to keep her safe. Took him a year to come up with five hundred grand. But Crew set up the whole fucking thing."

"So you come up with this fucked-up idea?"

He shakes his head. "Like I said, Adam offered me money to keep her safe. Crew overheard and suggested we come up with a plan. *This* plan."

"Why wait so long, huh?"

He wipes his eyes and sniffs.

My brother feels bad.

Good.

"Crew wanted to do it when the time was right."

I drop into the chair beside him. "I was a fucking wreck after you died. First Natalia, then you, and then the club disowns me and nearly kills me." My hands are in fists on my thighs. "I buried you. Put flowers on your grave every fucking first of the month. Do you know what mourning and grief do to a person? Huh? No, you fucking don't because you've always been a shellfish motherfucker."

"I'm sorry."

I scoff, letting my anger take over.

There isn't anything I can do to control this rage.

I will not put a hand on my brother.

I never have.

That was our daddy's job.

"It's gonna take me some time to forgive you for this. A lot of fucking time."

"I know," he whispers.

"Fuck."

Shooting up from the chair, I pace, looking at Peter wiping his eyes again. I need out of this hospital before I kick his face in. "I need to take a walk."

"Cops wanna talk to us, have to explain what happened to Zay—"

"Call Roaden, he's got the Captain in his back pocket. All this shit will be wiped clean," I interrupt him and sigh.

I'd make a great president of this club, own it, rule it, and bring in money. Success.

But I don't want it.

I don't think I ever did.

This was my father's dream for me, not mine.

Peter nods, rubbing his eye. "I was going to head to the club, anyway. We have some explaining to do to the guys. Crew is dead, which makes you president, big brother," he says, rising from his seat and clearing his throat. "We have to deal with this before you take your...walk."

It's like he knows I won't come back once I get on my bike.

He knows I'll take her around the country before I sit in that seat at the head of the table.

This MC ruined me. Tainted him.

I'm going back. Not now.

"Let's go say bye to Zaynab and Adam before we go," he adds.

Zay. Beautiful, perfect Zay.

The woman I want but can't have.

I should say bye before I go.

I knock and open the door to her room as she and Adam separate from a deep, longing kiss.

Supple lips that were kissing me yesterday morning.

Snakes ruin everything.

She groans, pushing onto the bed to try and sit up. Adam helps her, lifting her as delicately as he can. "All good?"

Peter nods, coming up to Adam and squeezing his shoulder. "Yeah, we have to get going. Head to the club to settle some business."

"And you'll leave us alone? Leave her alone?" Adam asks, gritting his teeth. "Promise me nothing happens to Zay."

I fold my arms across my chest. "Nothing will happen to your woman, brother."

"All is forgiven? That easily?" she asks, wiping an escaping tear.

Peter takes a breath but doesn't say anything. He doesn't forgive her, I see it on his face by the twitch of his lips. "Yeah, all is forgiven."

"What can I do to make sure of that?" Adam asks, staring at me instead of Peter.

I can't believe Adam knew about this plan and didn't come to me. Didn't try and fix things through me. Crew, the dead bastard, brainwashed my brothers just like my father did.

"If we ever need a favor, we'll give you a call, shaky hands," Peter teases. Adam's hands shake when he's nervous. He'd never be able to handle the club and all the times a gun is held against someone's head.

Shaking hands isn't something worth having.

Zay releases a breath and gulps loudly. "You kidnapped me, held me hostage for a week, and almost killed me, Peter. Your plan almost killed me. I need your word that I am done. That whatever revenge you wanted is over." She whimpers, touching her chest and whispering softly. "Haven't I suffered enough?"

Peter glances at me and I puff my chest out, nostril flaring. He puts his head down, knowing he won't get his way with me around. "Sorry, Zaynab...all is forgiven."

I don't know if she accepts his forgiveness, she still glances at the door and plays with the end of the blanket; as she did with the hem of her dress. And I don't know if I trust my own damn brother enough to believe him.

But I have to.

I want to hold her, gobble her up, and keep her safe. She'll be her safest with me.

Zay looks at me and wets her lips. "You're leaving, too?"

"I am," I say.

But it's not what I want to say. *I'll be back in the morning*, is what I should have said.

I don't, though, because we have to put distance between us.

A lot of distance.

Peter embraces Adam and nods at me. "Call me when you need a lift home."

Adam nods, glancing at me. "We'll find a lift, no bother."

Peter leaves Zay with a kiss on her cheek. She stares at me as he does it. She doesn't want me to leave. That's what those big hazel eyes scream. But I can't stay. I won't be able to see her with Adam. To see them happy.

No, I'm not dealing with that.

Mixed emotions swim through her gaze.

She tries to say something, but her voice comes out hoarse. She clears it twice, drinks some water, and manages to speak. "Can I speak with Riggs? Alone."

Adam and Peter give each other a look, nodding. "I'll be right outside, babe. Okay?"

Peter cracks his knuckles and rolls his neck. "We're getting something to eat. You want more water?"

She grins, licking her dry lips again. "With ice."

Adam chuckles, unwillingly leaving her bedside with another kiss, and walks out into the hallway with my brother. "Love you."

We're alone now. The air feels thick.

Unwelcoming.

But she taps the bed for me to sit with her.

And I do. Of course, I do.

"Thank you."

I frown, confused by her choice of words. "Why?"

"New outlook on life and all that jazz."

"You gonna be all right?"

She reaches for my hand and takes it. "Are you?"

I chuckle. "There're other gashes I can find to fill my time."

She smirks, closing her eyes. "But I'll always be the best."

"Yeah. Yeah, you will be."

I touch the silver band I used to wear on my pinky that's now on her thumb. This is her memory of me. A piece of me she'll keep forever. My piece of her is that smile that will forever be imprinted in my head.

She clears her throat and winces again, bringing our hands to her bandaged chest. "Promise me you'll get out of this business. Get Peter out, too." She wets her lips again, her voice is so weak, it's hoarse and hard to listen to. "Promise me you'll move far away from this place. And when you think of it, all you'll see is me. Not the darkness that surrounds it. Just me. Because I make everything better, don't I?"

I chuckle, nodding with a smile. "Yeah, you're one little pistol I'll never forget."

"Good."

I kiss her fingers, threading them with mine, and bringing them to my chest. "I like you, Zay. If things were different, I really think we coulda worked."

"Mmm, me too."

The stare she's giving me is too much.

Any longer and I'll be on my knees, begging her to be mine.

But that's not right for Adam.

Reluctantly, I get up, kissing her knuckles and inhaling. Even in a hospital bed, she smells amazing. Like fresh mountain air. My smell. She still has my smell.

I smile at her, squeezing her hand while I stare at her lips.

Lips that make my dick twitch.

Fuck it.

Leaning down, I kiss her once more, tasting that tongue one last time. The things she does to me are going to take me a while to get over.

But I have to.

In no way, shape, or form would we ever work in the real world?

She's a student, and I'm supposed to be the president of a motorcycle club.

She's freeing, alive. I'd just drag her down with my madness.

She's happy with Adam.

Adam is happy with her.

It's best for us if I walk away. She knows it, I know it. It's best.

Resting my forehead on hers, I inhale again, remembering this sweet scent that will kill me whenever I smell it.

Ache.

Cold sweats.

But I gotta do it.

I kiss her hand, and her wrist, then loosen my grip. She squeezes my hand before I let go.

But I do it. I let go and walk away, trying my hardest not to look back at her.

It's damn hard not to.

"Riggs?"

I stop with my hand on the door, glancing at her over my shoulder.

"I'll see you on the flip side."

I chuckle, nodding at her with a wink, and leave.

Letting that attachment I have for her snap.

It tries to spring back but I turn the corner, and I keep going until it hurts.

And then I go some more.

The life of a Snake never allows happiness.

In one short week, she showed me what it's like to broaden my outlook. To let the bad things in my life go and not be a stowaway anymore.

In that short week, she showed me peace.

Epilogue - Peter

Zaynab left me for dead.

Stabbed me in the neck with the pen she used the last time we studied together.

Woman I fell in love with the moment I laid eyes on her tried to kill me.

I don't remember much after it happened. I remember squeezing my neck and dragging myself to my cell phone.

I woke up in the hospital four days later.

Tubes coming out of me. Wires and things.

Crew was by my side, Adam, too. Riggs wasn't there, I couldn't understand why at first.

I couldn't remember what happened—then it hit me when I tried to swallow. Zaynab stabbed me in the neck when she found Lillian's cell phone in my desk drawer.

Like a fucking idiot, I didn't get rid of it. I wanted to keep a piece of Lillian with me—or Natalia as she went by—and back up her pictures. But I never had the time and forgot about it completely. Seven weeks later, I remembered it because Zay found it.

Beautiful Zaynab with her hazel eyes and that wild wavy hair she always kept straight. Gorgeous Zaynab who tried to fucking kill me…but as upset as I am, meeting her for the first time had this effect on me I'll never forget.

I was about a week in at Stanford University, can't remember how many parties me and the guys crashed, but this one, in particular, was the one I remembered best.

She sat at the bar, a towel wrapped around a bag of ice that was held to her chin. I thought, *what happened? Why was she holding that on her chin?* I remembered watching droplets of water roll down her wrist and neck. Like a champ, she still did shots that were offered to her.

She caught my attention the second I walked in. I was hooked. Mesmerized. I wanted her and I'd do anything it took to get her.

I made my way across the dancing lunatics and stole the barstool beside her, grinning.

She smiled back, lighting up those eyes of hers. "I wouldn't sit there if I were you."

Arching an eyebrow, I swiveled in the seat to face her. Our knees grazed as I did. "Yeah? Why's that?"

She pointed behind me to a redhead with bushy hair who was swaying as she stood facing a wall. "She just puked on it."

I shot up, looking at the stool, then the back of my jeans. No mess. Someone must've cleaned it. When I turned around, I was standing directly in front of Zay. Between her legs, no less.

A giggle left her as she removed the bag of ice from under her chin, some blood decorating the towel. "It was cleaned a while ago, don't worry." Her giggle hadn't died down. "You should've seen the look on your face, though."

That smile instantly had me.

I nodded at the ice in her hand, rolling my eyes back to hers. "What happened here?"

She lifted her chin to show me a Captain America Band-Aid and snickered. "It's all they had." She pointed a thumb behind her. "I slipped in some beer by the kegs. Gnarly little cut won't stop bleeding, though."

Someone pushed in behind me, taking a bottle of vodka from the bar. I didn't mind, I was pressed against her. My breath lodged in my throat with my heart beating so fast I thought I might faint.

She closed her legs around me, inching me closer with a grin. "I'm Zay."

I pointed at my chest, wanting to run my fingers in her long brown hair she had in waves that night. "Peter."

"What's your poison, Peter?" she asked, grabbing a shot glass for me.

Shrugging, I stared at her like she was the damned *Mona Lisa*. "Whatever you're having, Zay."

She grinned, eyeing me as she poured tequila into our shot glasses. "To meeting new people."

"Pleasure's all mine, Zay."

I couldn't stop saying her name. It was like a dream.

We shot the drink back and groaned at the same time, chuckling, as if on cue.

I don't get flustered around girls. Being around them comes easy to me. Always has. My hair is brown with blonde highlights from the sun, my eyes are so blue they look like they're sparkling. I'm a textbook hunk. My brother, too. My parents blessed us, that's for sure.

But with Zay, I was speechless.

Breathless, too.

The music was already loud as shit, but someone decided to turn it up even more. I could barely hear myself think. So I leaned in, getting as close as I could and inhaling that coconut smell wafting off her.

"Your name, is it short for something?"

She nodded, moving her mouth to my ear. "Zaynab. I was named after the nurse who saved my life when I was born." She moved away from me and smiled. "It means beauty."

Zaynab is beautiful all right.

She poured us another shot as some guy hung his arm around her, kissing the side of her head. My heart shattered as I watched her smile at him the way she smiled at me. I didn't want her to be with anyone. I was hoping she wasn't. But the way the guy whispered in her ear, they had to be something.

He slipped something in her hand and winked at me before he walked off.

"Boyfriend?"

She pointed to her chest, still smiling. "Single."

I did the same, tapping twice. "Single also."

She held a baggie up to me and waggled her eyebrows. "Trent's someone who gives me pick-me-ups. Wanna do a pick-me-up with me?"

"I smoke pot, that's all I've ever done." I couldn't believe I just admitted that to her.

She giggled, tapping my arm. The feeling of her fingers on my skin sent sparks through me. I needed her, badly. I'd do anything to call her mine.

"It's called Elevate," she says, opening the baggie and handing me one of the pills. "It's like Molly and I've never done Molly before."

I nodded because neither did I. "First time for everything, isn't there?"

She poured us another shot and held it up, placing the pill on her tongue. "To getting fucked-up tonight with my new friend, Peter."

I blushed; a girl had never made me blush before. But Zaynab was different than any other girl I'd ever met and had the pleasure of being with.

I copied her, placing the pill on my tongue and shooting back the shot. I knew it was wrong the second I swallowed it. I have addictive tendencies and doing a drug that will make me feel alive was not something I could deal with.

But I'd do anything for her.

Absolutely anything.

She tossed the ice on the bar and nudged me backward, jumping off the barstool. "Come dance with me."

"What?"

She didn't hear me because her hand was woven with mine and she tugged me to the dance floor.

The way she bobbed her hips, swaying them side to side and letting the music take over had me frozen in place watching her. Even with her chin all bandaged up and who knows how many tequilas in, I was smitten.

She laughed as I stood there looking at her. *I don't dance.* She placed her hands on my hips, moving them side to side. "Let the music flow through you."

"I don't dance," I shouted.

She laughed again, nodding and taking my hand to lead us farther on the dance floor. I gripped her hand tightly, not wanting to lose her in the crowd.

She looked back at me once, clicking her tongue and saying something I couldn't make out. "What?"

She laughed again and led us outside. It was still rowdy out on the lawn and the wraparound porch. But she led us away from the chaos. And it was a perfect time, too. Elevate was starting to take effect.

She pulled us to a couch on the side of the house, still chuckling as she got to her knees beside me and leaned her head on her hand.

I let out a rush of air; the world in front of me was vibrating. This couch was vibrating. Everything felt loose, alive.

I was floating. I liked floating, especially liked it while she held my hand.

"I think the Molly is working."

She nodded, letting go of my hand to poke my chest. "I think so, too."

I reached out for her hand again, threading our fingers and smiling at her. "You're really pretty."

"Right back atcha, stud."

Letting out a nervous laugh, I stared at her and leaned my head back on a couch that probably had more fluids on it than there were in that house. "We should do something crazy."

She nodded, jumping up from the couch and pulling me to my feet. "You read my mind, Peter."

Being with Zay felt like being on speed. Wild. Fast. Crazy. I fucking loved it.

The next fifteen minutes were a blur. I remembered her calling someone to let them know she was leaving the party. I let my boys know by text. That was our rule, if we hooked up with someone, we'd send nothing more than an eggplant emoji to our group chat. I sent a heart that night.

"Where're we going?" I asked, looking back to see we'd walked three blocks from the frat house. The pills were making everything fly by.

"My favorite place."

I didn't ask more. The way her face lit up was enough for me to thank her for showing it to me. She didn't know me, yet we were holding hands, going on an adventure together, and floating so high I could see the campus from here.

We ended up at the water. It was dark as fuck but she lit our way with her phone, our hands never parting.

She stopped suddenly and sat down on the sand, pulling me down beside her. "Look." She pointed at the sky, lying down.

Taking one look at the sky, I knew the pills were in effect. The stars were barely sparkling but they looked morphed, like fireballs moving side to side. I didn't want to look at them. I wanted to look at her.

So I did. I stared at her until she felt my stare. Those plump lips crept into a grin, her long lashes blinking so slowly, and the way her jaw angled, I wanted to run my finger over the contours of her face.

Those eyes flickered to mine and I reached over, tracing her lips. "Perfect."

She blinked again and shot up, biting her bottom lip. "Let's go skinny-dipping."

This girl was all over the place. I hated to love it.

I sat up with her, a nervous chuckle leaving me. "We can't do that." I looked around. Not a single soul in sight.

She got to her feet and peeled the dress over her head. *Wow.* Perfect body. Sculpted with curves in all the right places. She was wearing a black thong and a black bra to match.

I was breathless just watching her.

"You said you wanted to do something crazy." She put her hand out. "Come be crazy with me, Peter."

So I did. I peeled my t-shirt over my head and took off my jeans, leaving our clothes in a pile on the sand.

She jogged toward the water; that ass had me turnt. Tight and round and just big enough to grab. I jogged after her, wanting to get in the water to hide my boner. I didn't want to embarrass myself if she didn't want to do anything, so I held onto my crotch.

But she stopped at the edge of the water and giggled. "On the count of three, we get completely naked, and dive into the water, okay?"

Chuckling, a nervous breath escaped my parted lips. "I have a confession to make."

"You have a girlfriend?"

I shook my head quickly, which didn't help my dazed vision. "No, no. None of that." I let go of my crotch and looked down at the outline of my dick tenting my boxers. "I'm hard as rock right now."

She laughed, covering her face in this cute, shy way. "Is that because of me?"

Nodding, I smirked as I reached behind her and unhooked her bra. "One."

She took her arms out of her bra, holding it against her chest as she looked down at my crotch, then the water. "Two."

"Three."

I dropped my boxers and stepped into the water. I didn't want to look back until she was beside me. And there she was, sticking her tongue out as she dove into a wave. I dove under, too, letting the crisp chill of the water consume me.

She stood up, revealing those beautiful, perky breasts. Our gazes met and I let out a rush of air, swallowing hard.

I couldn't understand why some chick made me nervous. I didn't get nervous.

I never felt a churning in my stomach or a lump in my throat.

Not even when my father brought me on business trips.

Or when Riggs tried to act like my daddy.

Nothing ever scared me until I met Zay.

"You look so scared."

"You make me nervous; I don't know why." I stood, walking closer to her as waves crashed into us. "Girls don't usually make me nervous."

Moving the hair off her shoulder, I cupped the side of her face. "But there's something about you I want to devour."

She tilted her head upward; I towered over her tiny body. "I'm not like most girls."

"I can see that."

Her eyes traveled to my lips, and my chest, then slowly made their way back up again, and met my eyes.

She made the first move and tried to kiss me, but every time she got on the tips of her toes, she sunk lower in the sand. "Well." She chuckled. "Looks like the sand is telling me I'm not allowed to kiss you. Sucks, too." She floated back, kicking away from me. "I'm one helluva kisser."

Diving after her, I swam up and slammed my mouth down on hers. I kept that body close to me, pressed hard against my chest.

Her tongue parted my lips and explored my mouth in a way that made me gasp, breathing in her air. Maybe it was the drugs, but she wasn't lying when she said she was one helluva kisser.

I liked kissing her. Even while kissing her, it didn't feel like enough.

We came up for air, gasping. And she laughed, wrapping her arms around me.

"I like you, Peter."

Four little words just made my fucking night. "I like you, too, Zaynab."

She kissed my nose and let go of me. "Zay. I prefer Zay."

"Zay."

We held hands again as we floated in the water, rocking gently with the waves. She liked watching the stars in that spot because they were the clearest place to see them. I didn't tell her this, but I liked watching the stars in that spot with her, too.

It was weird, I never fell for girls. I learned that from my brother. He said *women around here want nothing more than a dick to sit on.* I sometimes wondered if he only said that because he hadn't found someone like Zay. He's been around, that much I knew, but I never saw him stare at someone the way I stared at Zay.

There was this connection I felt, drawing me in.

The second I laid eyes on her, I knew she was going to be mine.

Now that I had her in my grasp, it felt like she was still out of reach.

I needed to savor every single moment with her before I lost them.

Something was telling me I would lose them.

I didn't know how long we were floating there, but she tugged on my arm, leading us out of the water. "I'm getting cold," she said, picking up her clothes. She held out her bra and thong, grimacing. "They're soaked."

I held my boxers up and chuckled. "Mine, too."

She handed them to me and jogged to our clothes, pulling her dress over her head, remaining completely bare underneath.

I didn't have my shirt on before she dragged me away from the water. "Let's go back to the party and drink a little more. Warm us up a little."

Drinking was the last thing on my mind. The Molly had taken its effects, all I wanted to do was get her naked again and ease myself inside that tight little body.

"I have a better idea." I kissed her again and led her to my dorm. She wasn't the first girl I brought to my dorm room, but she'd be my last if she'd let me.

We were a wave of sloppy kisses, stumbles, and laughter as we walked to my dorm room. My roommate went to the party with me, and lucky for me, he wasn't home yet.

She helped herself into my dorm and looked over her shoulder at me to ask which bed was mine. As soon as I pointed at it, her dress was by her feet and she slowly turned around.

Even in the glow of my bedside lamp, she was perfect. The moonlight gave her no justice like this shitty light.

"Wow."

My clothes were off faster than I put them on and her hands were exploring me before I could get out of my shoes.

I had one condom left, I remembered that because I put it in the back pocket of my jeans before I went to the party. And she had no trouble finding it when I stuttered the words out.

She straddled me as soon as the condom was on, revealing how beautiful she looked when she smiled.

The Molly kicked in double-time when I slid inside her, taking over the euphoric experience I'd never had before. We were a blur of screams and moans and grunts. Lying breathless beside each other after what felt like forever. I'd lie for an eternity with her if I could.

"Goddamn."

She giggled, kissing me softly.

We lay there for the rest of the night staring at each other. I was living a dream. I had to be.

She was my everything and I barely knew her.

"You're all right, Peter."

I chuckled, kissing the top of her head as we cuddled in my twin bed. "I can work with *all right*."

She nuzzled her cheek on my chest and sighed happily. "We should do this more often." She said it like this wasn't the first time we'd experienced this.

"Same time tomorrow?"

She giggled, pulling the covers over us and squeezing me tightly. "G'night, Peter."

"'Night, Zaynab," I whispered, sliding my fingers through her damp hair.

She left after I had fallen asleep but didn't leave a note. I went to three different parties the next day, trying to find her, but I couldn't. It was a dream, it had to be.

Until I saw her again, two weeks later, walking on campus with a blonde girl named Lillian. I'd met the blonde a handful of times in class; she liked me. I knew this because every time I walked into class, she'd wave me over and blush when I sat beside her.

But Zay, she wasn't a dream.

We didn't do anything after that. She avoided me most days, and I think it was because Lillian liked me. Zay put her feelings aside for her best friend.

Much like I did for Adam.

***

Adam held my hand as I slept in the hospital bed. I remember that vividly. Crew wasn't there every day, but he was there as much as he could when the club didn't need him. Riggs still hadn't come to see me. He was on probation for the stunt Natalia pulled that nearly got me killed. They beat my brother senselessly and told me not to call him. Told me they had a plan for him and my survival was to be kept in the dark. I hated it, but what was I to do? I wanted to be a member of this club so badly. For my daddy. For Riggs. I kept my mouth shut, hoping Riggs would find out I was alive some other way.

I groaned, bringing a hand to my head when I felt Adam squeeze my other hand.

"Hey, hey." Adam squeezed tighter when I tried to get my hand loose. "What do you need?"

Blinking rapidly, I rubbed the sleep from my eyes with my free hand. "Water."

He offered me a cup of water and finished it in three gulps, wiping my mouth with the back of my hand. "Thanks."

He nodded, finally letting go of my hand and clearing his throat. "You didn't tell Crew. But can you tell me? What happened? You said you were meeting someone and next thing I know, Judas is calling me in a panic. What happened?"

I shook my head, I didn't want to tell him just yet. I needed a minute. Thinking of Zay brought me back to that night in my room, the night I was able to have her again as we looked through Lillian's things. I couldn't tell him that Zay was the reason I was lying in that hospital bed. "Tell me about your date, the girl you met." I sniffed, trying to clear my throat. My voice was off, hoarse, and gravelly. "I don't want to talk about this now. I want to hear about your date with the pretty girl you met at the coffee shop."

"That's not important now."

"It is to me," I said, tapping his hand. "So, c'mon. Spill."

He hesitated. Staring at me like I was nuts. But he smiled, taking his soda from the side table and cracking it open. "I'm going to marry this girl, I know it."

"Oh, yeah?"

I can't remember a time in my life that it wasn't Adam, Riggs, and I. Sure, Riggs is four years older than us, but it's always been the three of us—my brothers. And when I saw Adam that happy about a girl, it made me happy for him. His mother wasn't the greatest and the prospect that stood in as his father was even worse. His mother would do the guys favors—my father mostly. My mama took Adam in when the truth came out that my father was his, too. Adam was six and he lived with us ever since. His mama came every day to see him until she stopped. Daddy didn't look at him like a son, Adam was an outcast. Mama treated him that way, too. Not me, though. Adam was my brother no matter what. And with a shitty upbringing like his, he deserved the world.

He nodded, gulping his soda. "She has this sass about her that makes me laugh. Such long brown hair and these eyes that look like tiger eyes. It's crazy." He chuckled. "Beautiful, though. Fuck, she's so beautiful." He licked the soda from his lips. "We went for pizza and she told me her entire life story before it was even served to us. And you want to know what's funny?" I nodded, smiling, happy for him. "We fit perfectly together."

He laughed again, shaking his head. "I wanted to kiss her so badly, but she made me work for it. I only got a kiss when I walked her back to her dorm room. Says she doesn't want to do anything just yet. She wants to wait until five dates before we do anything and I think that's just perfect. She's perfect. Gosh, she kisses like a dream."

I couldn't help but laugh. I saw the women Adam had been with, not as many as me, but enough to know he still hadn't found the perfect one. This one seemed like the perfect one. "Like a dream, huh?"

"Nearly creamed my pants." He shook his head with a smile. "She did this thing with her tongue—my God, I don't even know."

He ran a hand through his blonde hair. I was always jealous of that. He has enviable blue eyes and blonde hair. The eyes helped us look like brothers. But that blonde hair; the girls we grew up with liked him more than me because of it. That was, until I brought them to bed and he didn't. I was always better at that. Especially with my head between their legs.

I took the soda from him and sipped it, happy, despite my situation. "What's her name?"

He crinkled his nose. "She has the weirdest fucking name. But it suits her, oddly enough." He sighed, exhilarated. "Zay is what she goes by but her real name is—"

"Zaynab."

Adam frowned, tilting his head in confusion. "Y-yeah. How'd you know that?"

I don't know why I never told him about her. Probably because I liked what Zay and I had to be our little secret. Something only the two of us knew about. That magical night I'll never forget. She was my dream. Mine. And now the friend I thought of as my brother was talking about her like I should have the first day I met her.

I tried to gulp and I winced, touching my neck. "She's the one who did this."

Adam's face fell flat, pale. But I didn't blame her. I never did. I explained to him what happened. I explained to him the secrets and lies that Lillian told. I explained everything.

He just shook his head, that happiness fading.

"Hey." I took his hand. "Don't let that flame die. She didn't mean it. It was self-defense." Then I gulped and it hurt like a son of a bitch. I remembered the fear in her eyes, the hatred she had toward me. The MC would want revenge for what she did. I knew it. Fuck, parts of me wanted it, too.

"Whatever I need to do, I will. I'll pay her debt for what she did to you. Please," Adam pleaded, clasping his hands together in prayer. "Please don't let them hurt her."

I nodded, separating our hands. "I would never let anything happen to her."

***

A year has passed since the incident at the barn, and Zay has recovered, but she's still timid around me. Scared that I might give in and seek that revenge the MC wanted. Shit, I wanted it, too, for a moment until I saw her face again. But she's happy now and that's all that matters.

Sometimes I wonder if I'll ever seek vengeance. It lingers at the back of my brain wanting, aching to be free.

Riggs hasn't seen her, either. I don't know what happened between them at the cabin, but he changed. He's different, happier. He got out.

He packed a bag and drove off into the sunset one afternoon after breaking the news to the guys that he was done. Took off his cut and everything. Left it behind when my brother has been talking about being president of this club since we were babies, to make our daddy proud. Look at him now.

With Crew dead and our father in prison, Riggs was next in line for president. Riggs didn't want it. He gave it to Judas and told him to keep me safe.

I haven't seen my brother in nine months.

I see Zay and Adam often, at school, mostly, and at the occasional dinner we go to together. They got back together at the hospital. He should have never left her. He did it for me. He did it when the MC wanted revenge for what she did. He thought it would protect her, cutting all ties. It didn't. It just made it worse.

So he took her back like he wanted to do from the moment he said it was over.

They're meant for each other, anyone who sees it can tell. No matter if she's the love of my life, I have to let her go. Because she's his. And he's happy. He deserves the world and he found it in Zay. *I have to let her go.*

They're getting married today, as he promised. He's calm and collected, as he always is. Being his best man, I'm shitting bricks. I can't explain why. Could be from the withdrawal of the pain meds he asked me to stop taking. I was abusing them, but they made me feel good. They helped me forget the world for a little.

In reality, I'm sweating bullets because it's hard to see someone I'm crazy about looking at another person the way I want her to look at me.

One day I'll find that person. But that day isn't today. Today is their wedding day, and I'm standing outside of the church wondering what the fuck to do. I have two pills in my hand. My last two. I'll take them and never take them again. Just pop them and let go for a little while.

When I walk into the church, Zay paces in a room by the entrance. Seeing her so frantic, I toss the pills. Adam's right. It's time I better myself, just like they did. Just like Riggs. It's time I fix myself and make something of myself. Out of the club and away from what my daddy wanted his boys to be. Right?

I can't help it, I go to Zay. She's breathtaking all in white. In a strapless dress with sequins all over it. She's gorgeous. She looks like an angel in this church. A beautiful angel who captured my soul.

She stops in her tracks when she sees me. Her eyes grow wide, but relief sweeps through her. And I just smile, taking in the sight of her as if it's the first time I laid eyes on her. "Peter, what're you doing here? You should be standing at the altar."

Stepping into the room, I put my hands in my pockets. "Just needed some fresh air."

She looks behind me, I'm sure expecting Riggs to pop in. He won't. I don't think he'd like seeing her in a wedding dress at a wedding that isn't theirs. She touched so many hearts, it's scary. She's easy to love but doesn't love as easily.

She lets out a shaky breath and swats her hands in the air. "It feels good to see a friendly face who won't just tell me everything will be okay."

She shakes her head and takes another breath, hands on her stomach. "I'm so nervous. What if Adam doesn't like me in five years, or what if we don't get along when we officially move in together, or what if he thinks I'm bad at sex? What if—"

"Hey." I step closer to her, cupping her face. "He loves the shit outta you. You know that."

She nods, furrowing her brows. She looks like she's about to cry. A bride shouldn't cry anything but happy tears on her wedding day.

"Hey," I say again, wiping an errant tear. "What's wrong? You're never nervous."

She sniffs, shrugging. "My parents decided not to show up. I got the call five minutes ago. Said they *forgot* about a trip. Who the fuck calls their daughter minutes before her wedding to tell her they can't make it? Is Greece more important than me?"

Pulling her into a hug, I sigh, letting her breathe. "It's fine, sweetie. You don't need them."

"They're my parents."

I nod, dabbing the tears under her eyes so as not to ruin her makeup. "We're your family now."

She chuckles, sniffling. "I don't want to walk down the aisle alone. My dad promised he'd walk with me. God." She sighs, letting out a breath. "Why did we do this in a church?"

"Adam wanted it on the beach, didn't he?"

She rolls her eyes. "But my mom didn't want to ruin her shoes in the sand."

A knock sounds at the door and one of her bridesmaids comes in with wide eyes. "Are you okay? Adam's worried sick."

Zay nods, taking her white roses from the small couch behind her. "I'm good."

The bridesmaid gives me a once-over. She's cute, I've met her before at school. Looks like I know what I'm taking home tonight.

"Let's go," Zay says, but she doesn't move.

I chuckle softly and put my arm out. "C'mon, I'll walk you."

"What?"

"I'm walking my best friend's sexy-ass fiancée down the aisle and there's nothing you can do to stop me, now c'mon." I step closer and hold my arm out again. "Let's get Adam wifed-up."

She chuckles, sliding her arm through mine and we go. Walking to the "Wedding March" as everyone rises. She lets out another breath and I fix the veil over her face, winking at her as I do.

Breathtaking.

Adam's smiling so much that my cheeks are hurting for him. He looks happy. Christ, he deserves to be happy after everything that happened in his life. He was raised by the club. Molded like he's one of us. But that's something Daddy never wanted for him, which is fine because Adam didn't want to be part of the drugs, women, or money, like us. He wanted to be straight. Like Riggs wanted for me.

As I look down at Zay, the scar on her chest catches my eye. An inch to the left and she wouldn't be here right now.

One fucking inch.

What's crazy is, with all the money that was given to us to turn a blind eye to her attempted murder of me, it was never enough.

Lip wants more.

Judas, too.

Riggs got out, but he secretly missed the wealth she gave us.

I walk her to the altar and shake Adam's hand before removing the veil. A smile spreads to her face as she looks at him. A smile she should be giving to me.

I stroke her cheek and pull her into a hug. "This isn't over," I whisper.

She tenses.

"One way or another, Snakes always get their prey."

A shaky breath leaves her as I flash her a wink and stand behind Adam. She knew she wouldn't be able to get away with what she did. My MC wouldn't let it happen. Paying us bought her time. Time she needed to right her wrongs. But the madness never went away. It lay dormant for the perfect moment to return. And why not on her wedding day?

I got out, but I'll always have a finger in the business.

Fear spreads to that face I love so badly.

A fear that I live for.

A fear that will bring us to the ends of the earth to get what we want. Because we always do.

Even if it means faking it.

Her hands shake as she stands in front of Adam, glancing around the church. She spots them. Snakes sitting in different spots in the pews, smiling at her.

Adam doesn't notice. All he sees is her.

The movement of her throat as she swallows.

The wetness in her eyes.

The redness of her face.

It's not over until the Snakes sink their fangs into what they want.

And what I want is Zay.

Sweet, beautiful Zay.

Soon, my love.

This will be over soon.

Her fate is sealed.

II

Salvation

Peter

AWARD-WINNING AUTHOR
ALYSSA MILANI
SALVATION
THE STOWAWAY SERIES - PART TWO

I guzzle down the rest of my beer and stare at Zaynab as she dresses. She's become my Tuesday afternoons because of the debt she owes to the club. The debt she owes me.

I couldn't kill her. That wouldn't sit right with me. Snakes said she owed more than just money. She tried to kill one of us, and almost succeeded, too. Her best friend, Lillian, sent my father to prison, and someone had to pay for that. With Riggs gone, Zaynab's the only one that seemed fitting.

I do it to keep her safe. If she's my girl, the club won't touch her. She's mine. Been mine since the night we floated high.

And every Tuesday afternoon for the past year, she shows up at the clubhouse and meets me in the back room. Adam, from my understanding, doesn't know about any of this. It's good. He deserves all the happiness he can get, but Zaynab has me wrapped around her finger and I don't know how to get out of her grasp.

So I use her, blaming it on the debt she owes when we both know she can just give the club money and we'll leave her alone again. But I want her. I don't even care about the debt she owes anymore, she's mine, and I want her to be mine forever.

Our little secret.

She sniffs, fixing the strap of her dress as she sits at the edge of my bed.

She cries sometimes when we share our afternoon delights. I know it's because of Adam. They've been married for nearly a year and I've shared a bed with her since their honeymoon.

I tried to let it go. I tried to tell the club her debt was paid. But being VP, and Judas as president, it just didn't sit well with a lot of the guys.

She owes, they said.

Blood or money, they said.

I'll handle it, I said.

And I did. Every Tuesday like clockwork I handle it for twenty minutes. Best twenty minutes of her goddamn life.

Oh, yeah. Have I forgotten to mention that I'm the Snakes' new VP? I got out when Riggs left. I got out for a year. I was out until Zay and Adam's wedding day when Judas came up to me and said he wanted me at his side.

Wanted a Donnelly at the table.

I couldn't say no.

I refused to. My daddy started this club, and Riggs and I were supposed to run it until our sons were ready—if we had sons—but my brother left me. He left with no window as to when he'd come back.

Zay leans forward to get her shoes on and I light a cigarette, sitting beside her still shirtless with my jeans undone and no shoes on. "When is this going to end?" she asks.

I shrug, exhaling some of the smoke from my nostrils. "What if I don't want it to end?"

"It has to end somehow."

"You tried to kill me, Zay," I say, moving some hair off her shoulder.

She looks at me with those hazel eyes, red and wet with tears. "Adam and I are eventually going to try for a baby. We can't very well do that with you—" She groans softly, closing her eyes. I don't wrap it all the time with Zay because she's on birth control. First girl to ever get me raw, she should feel special. "I need this to end, Peter," she whispers.

Staring at her, my nostrils flare. I don't want this to end. She's mine. Always has been mine. I had her first and I don't like fucking sharing. I shared her with Adam, then Riggs, and now she's mine again. *MINE.*

"It's coming on a year that we're married and we haven't been able to *be* a married couple because of you. I can't breathe because of you." She's crying softly, looking away from me. "Sometimes I wish I just died in that barn so none of this would continue to haunt me. So Adam can be happy and not worry about the fact that I disappear every Tuesday afternoon for an hour and a half." She wipes her eyes and puts on her other shoe. "We have to end this."

I flick ashes onto the floor and lean forward with my elbows on my knees. "Does Adam know about us?"

She nods slightly, keeping her focus on the cigarette between my fingers. "I told him as soon as you told me my fate was sealed."

I scoff, looking at her with gritted teeth. "I was under the impression this was our secret."

"Why would I keep this deal we have from my husband a secret?" Her voice deepens when she says this and turns to me with those beautiful eyes I refuse to believe hate me. "I was under the impression it was done when I nearly died that night. But no, you had to be fucking selfish and couldn't leave me alone."

My hands are in fists on my lap, grinding my teeth as I hear the words coming from that perfect mouth. "You see this?" I point at the scar on my neck. "You nearly killed me—"

"You see this?" She points at her chest, a scar I kiss every time I see it. "Your club nearly killed me. I'd say we're pretty even, don't you?"

Growling, I get to my feet, pull my jeans up, and put a t-shirt on. "I'll start wearing protection, that's all."

She scoffs, choking on a sob as she collects the rest of her things and makes for the door. "I hope you get what's coming to you one day. *I* certainly have."

She slams the door behind her and the sound of her clunking footfalls moves through the bar. Woman is driving me fucking wild, both physically and mentally. I wish she'd just submit and allow this to happen. Allow herself to be with me once and for all. Why the fuck won't she be with me?

I follow after her and put my cigarette out in the ashtray at the end of the bartop. "See you next week, sweetie."

She looks over her shoulder, tears still falling, and winces. Judas comes in as she's leaving and smiles at her, but she doesn't reciprocate.

I did that to her. That sadness clouding over her since her wedding day. Maybe she's right. Maybe I am being selfish.

I should let her go and tell my club she paid her dues. But Snakes get what they want. And I refuse to believe I won't get Zaynab.

The light of my life.

The dream that consumes me.

"Hey, Zay," Judas says, fixing his cut. "You stopping by for some grub?"

She shakes her head looks at me and sniffs. "Weekly torture session."

He stifles a chuckle when he catches my gaze and shrugs. "We all do things we don't wanna do."

She grunts and pushes open the door, the sunlight lighting up the natural highlights in her long brown hair. Beautiful beyond belief. And she's mine, every Tuesday I feed her, then seduce her. Best damn day of her week.

Judas kicks out a barstool and falls into it, looking at me as I lean on the bartop beside him. "You gotta end this sooner or later, brother. What you're doing to Adam ain't right."

I chuckle with a scoff. "She tried to kill me. She's paying her debt—"

"She paid that damn debt with a bullet to the chest," he raises his voice. "When're you gonna learn? Christ almighty, sometimes I wish your daddy was here to knock some sense into you. Or at least your damn brother."

I grumble, searching for my keys in my pockets, and make for the door. I need some air and away from everyone's negativity.

Maybe I am overdoing it.

Maybe I am overreacting.

I'm not ready to let her go.

I'm not ready to see her smile for someone who isn't me. I got her back. It doesn't feel the same as our first night together all those years ago, but she's mine again. Mine.

I'm not ready.

"Think about it, brother. Zay's a smoking piece of ass, but there are other gashes out there for you to screw," Judas calls as the door slams shut behind me.

Other gashes.

He doesn't know Zay like I do.

She's perfection.

She's a dream.

I need a drink. A drive. A new life.

I'll go to the cabin for a bit and clear my head.

Maybe then I'll be able to fix this mess.

Maybe, just maybe.

Dorian

The airbag hits me like a punch to the chest. I lose my breath for ten seconds.

Unable to gasp.

Unable to move.

Just nothing. Still.

Until I inhale and the world comes into focus again.

I hit a car. I hit them hard from behind. It's not like I didn't notice them. I did. I just couldn't bring myself to react in time. Today is the worst day of my life.

The guy I hit steps out of the car, running his fingers through his messy dark brown hair, and grits his teeth. Those blue eyes look worried and angry. Bushy eyebrows pinch together before they frown and look at me. Beauty in the eyes of a very angry man.

I'm still in shock sitting there staring out the window with my hands gripping the steering wheel and the airbag deflating in my lap. What did I just do? This isn't good. Not today. Why did this have to happen today?

He bangs on my window and demands I get out of the car. But I still can't move. I don't even look at him. I'm staring at the wreck I caused. Wetness forms in my eyes. It's not the first time I've cried today, at least not in public. It probably won't be the last, either.

He bangs on the window once more, shaking me out of my trance. "Hey, get out of the fucking car."

I let out a shaky breath, my chest aching from the impact of the airbag, and bring my trembling hands to unclip my belt. As soon as I unlock the doors, he yanks my door open and begins yelling profanities at me. I shrink in front of him. This slim robust man holds such power, such intimidation. I'm nothing in front of him.

"I'm sorry, I-I-I didn't mean to," I manage between his screams.

"You didn't—" he groans, pinching the bridge of his freckled nose. When his hand drops he takes me in, giving my curves a once-over as I stand there in a black dress and heels to match.

"I-I'll pay for the damage. I-I'm sorry," I say again, sliding my hand up my arm and gripping my elbow.

He scoffs, fists on his hips. "Damn fucking right you'll pay. What were you even thinking? How could you not see me? The fucking light is red, everyone else is stopped." He grumbles something under his breath and takes his phone from his pocket. "Give me your—"

I can't help it, I break down for the first time in front of someone. Crying like I've cried all week alone in my room. It was an accident, just like this one. Except Erin was wrapped around a pole. Come to think of it, maybe I rammed into this guy so that I could be with Erin again. Just for a second. Just so he knows how much I love him.

The guy sighs, locking his phone and stuffing it back in his pocket. "Look, it's fine. I'm not hurt—you, um, are you hurt?" I shake my head, wiping my round cheeks with my head down. "Let's…just forget it, okay. You have insurance?"

I nod, sniffling. "Yes." But I don't, not anymore. Everything was in Erin's name.

"Okay. Then we'll let insurance pay for this."

He looks at the damage done to his Mercedes, shaking his head again, and runs those long fingers through his hair. "Shit," he mutters. We lock eyes and his stare lingers over my curvaceous body, stopping on my exposed legs before he clears his throat. "Sorry for yelling at you. I'm having an off day."

"Tell me about it."

He pokes his chest, blinking slowly. "Peter."

Sniffing again, I take my business card from the side door and hand it to him. "Dorian." He takes the card and scans it front and back. "Whatever the damage, just send the bill to me."

He taps the card on his hand and nods. "Yeah, okay." After another scan of my thick legs, he points at his car. "We should move out of the way."

I don't hesitate and get back into the car. When I slowly back it up, his back bumper falls on the ground. I wince as he picks it up and tosses it into the back seat. There's this boyish charm about him I can't shake off. He yelled at me, then felt bad for me. And how he looks at me with this mischievous glee is not as alarming as it should me.

He leaves me with one last glance as he opens the door to his car. He felt bad for yelling at me after what I did…then again, anyone who knows how shitty my week has been will feel bad for me. All I've gotten all week was everyone walking on eggshells around me. Afraid to say the wrong thing, afraid to mention Erin, afraid to see how I'm doing.

This week is the week from hell and this just made it a whole lot worse because of those sparkling blue eyes.

Peter waves at me with the curl of his lip and gets into his car, speeding off down the road as if nothing ever happened.

It happened all right.

And I'm still trying to wrap my head around how easy this encounter was.

Why was it so easy?

Zay

I've been sitting in my car staring at the park in front of me for sixteen minutes. Every Tuesday afternoon, I feel empty when I leave that place. Disturbed.

Disgusted.

Every Tuesday afternoon, a little piece of me dies inside.

I understand why Peter is doing it. The motorcycle club wants someone to pay for what Lillian did. Riggs is gone, so I'm left to take on the burden.

It was, either, kill me as a lesson learned.

Or this.

Adam offered my parents' money. He offered to be part of the club, to take over the burden of a mistake my Lillian made.

But no one wanted to budge. So they kidnapped me, then I was shot, and now here we are.

They voted, and Judas and Peter were the only ones who agreed to let me live.

Adam was pissed at the decision. In some ways, I'm sure he still is.

It's been a year and I've been sleeping with Peter more than I've been sleeping with my husband. Adam gets disgusted when he sees me with bite marks. Refuses to look at me until I shower and brush my teeth. Tuesdays have become the days I dread the most.

When Peter revealed to me at the altar that the *Snakes always get their prey*, I thought he was joking. Lying. I thought I was imagining the members sitting in the pews.

I wasn't.

Peter told them that even though I married Adam, I was his "old lady." He says it'll help me stay safe, alive. If the clubs think I'm someone's girlfriend, they won't go after me. So, Peter says I'm his. That he owns me.

And it's destroying me.

No one owns me. Not even Adam. All he owns is my heart. But lately, even that is dwindling. The longer Peter and I keep this up, the harder it's going to be on my marriage. Sooner or later, I'm going to be divorced and become Peter's official "old lady."

Isn't that just grand?

I let out a breath and get out of the car, looking up at the house I have yet to enjoy as a home. Adam and I bought ourselves a three-bedroom bungalow with the money we made after paying off the wedding. My favorite part is the park right out front. Trees span for half a mile with a playground on one side, picnic tables scattered around the other, and a fountain right smack in the middle.

It's beautiful, and I find myself staring at it more and more lately, wondering why my life isn't happy anymore. Wondering what I did so wrong to deserve this.

I paid for the mistake I caused. The horror of it.

I paid with a bullet to my chest.

My hand shakes as I search for the keys in my purse. Adam's car is in the driveway. I hate when he comes home early on Tuesdays. He's disgusted with me the most on Tuesdays.

Walking into the house, I find him at the kitchen table, textbooks open and scattered across it, and a notebook in front of him. He has his head on his hand in frustration as he nibbles on his pen. We're nearing the end of our schooling, and we're already stressed out as it is being interns as well. With Peter on top of me once a week, things can get pretty hectic around here.

So much so that we just avoid each other most days.

I miss the days when Adam worshiped me.

When he ravished me whenever he had the chance.

When he was happy to see me.

He frowns whenever we lock eyes.

Curls his lip in when I try to go in for kisses.

And grunts in response to my questions.

I miss being happy.

As usual, we ignore each other. He doesn't look up from his work and I head straight for the bedroom to toss my clothes into the laundry bin.

As usual, I get in the shower and stare at the black and white tiled walls until the water gets cold.

As usual, I feel empty.

I scrub my body until it's red and lean my forehead on the tiles, letting the water hit the back of my neck.

It's funny how much things can change in a year. Two years ago, I was held captive. Two years ago, I met Riggs and realized how connected we are. A year ago, Adam became my husband. The love of my life.

A year ago, I was lucky to be alive.

I let out a quiet sob, placing my hand on my mouth to muffle my sounds. Maybe one day all of this will be a distant memory of a time that never mattered.

Maybe one day I'll look back on this and see how much I've grown.

Maybe one day I'll be able to understand that actions have consequences. I was never going to get away with what I thought I did to Peter. This is my nightmare, and I'll be living it until he's had enough of me.

The shower curtain opens, sending a draft of cool air onto my legs. I turn around quickly and see Adam standing there with his head down and a frown on his face.

The last time we saw each other naked was three weeks ago when I walked in on him changing. He stood there, naked, and watched as I got undressed and did the same. We held our gaze for twenty-three seconds before he broke it and got into his clothes.

We don't talk much, nor do we have sex like a newly married couple. Instead, we grieve. We mourn. We hope for a better life.

I scan his body, taking notice of bruises on his side. I wouldn't blame him if he chose to cheat on me. What I'm doing is exactly that. But I'm jealous. So damn jealous that he'd hurt me willingly when I don't have a choice.

He lifts his gaze, but he's not frowning. He's crying. His blue eyes are riddled with tears.

But I don't go to him. I watch him cry as he watches me cry. Like two broken people unable to express emotion.

"I'm sorry," I finally say.

He shakes his head. "It's not your fault."

"It is." I swallow hard, sniffling. "We should…" I inhale a shuddered breath. "…we should just call this what it is, shouldn't we? We can't live like this. In this disgust and adultery. We should just end it while we can—"

He thunders toward me and grabs my face, kissing me hard. He wrecks my quivering lips and I groan brokenly as his taste soaks into me once again. "I love you, Zay. Forever and always."

"I can't live like this," I sob, touching his face.

He nods, brushing my wet hair back. "That's why I'm fixing things." I shake my head in confusion. "You don't have to worry about it now, babe. Just know I am fixing everything. You and I will be us again." He rests his forehead on mine. "Just us."

Why did he wait this long? Why couldn't he end this before it started? Before I hated myself and wanted all of it to end.

"What do you have planned?" I whisper.

He kisses my lips softly. "I'll tell you when it's time."

I look up at him, that sad face brightening into a devilish grin. There aren't many days that he looks like Riggs or Peter, but right now, those eyes are unmistakably like theirs.

A devil standing in front of me.

Whatever my husband has planned can't be good.

Adam knew most of the guys in the club, he knew beyond them because of his upbringing. And whatever he has planned has something to do with the bruises on his side.

I'd put money on it.

With a weak breath, I wrap my hands around his waist, pulling his body flush with mine just to be able to hear that beating heart that used to belong to me. "Do you love me?" I whisper.

"Forever and always. Forever and always," he says softly, running his fingers through my wet hair as his heart speeds up like a jackrabbit.

I whimper, holding him tighter. "I'm so sorry I'm putting you through this."

"Oh, babe," he says, tilting my head up. "You're not putting me through anything. Peter is the one putting me through this like you're some pawn o-or some trophy in this fucked-up game he conjured up. But you're not." He reaches over to adjust the water to a warmer temperature. "You're so much more than a trophy or a pawn in a game, Zay, you're my fucking queen. And I shouldn't have let that fucking Snake invade my queen."

I lose it, burying my face in his chest and sobbing. Hearing Adam say those things makes my heart flutter again. For months we acted like the other was a stranger. Someone who shares the space we live in. For months, he ignored me and avoided any glance in my direction.

The last time we had sex was in the middle of the night while the lights were off. He took me from behind as we lay side by side. He didn't kiss me or speak to me. He fucked me like some whore, then rolled over without so much as a goodnight.

I miss my husband. The man I used to ravish where he stood. Now we're lucky if we even remember to say good morning to each other. But something is telling me that all of this is going to change. And if it does, I will stop at nothing to make sure I don't open my legs to another man ever again.

This time, I will fight.

"Will you fight for me?"

"Will you fight for *me*?" he whispers, leaving a kiss on my head.

I look up at him, water falling onto my face. His blue eyes flicker from one of my eyes to the next, trying to read the chaos inside my head.

There's so much chaos. Much more than I'm able to muster or understand myself.

"All I want is you. All I want is for things to be normal again," I say through quivering lips.

"You and Peter are done, babe. Done, do you hear me?" he raises his voice. "I've been scared for too fucking long, but not anymore. If they need to hurt someone for Lillian's fuck up, and for your attempt on taking that jackass's life, then they can inflict their pain on me." He holds my head in his hands, staring intensely into my eyes. "Because you, my wife, are done with that club."

Choking on a sob, I try to look away from him but he holds my head still. "What changed?"

"I went to visit my dad this morning," he says, lowering his mouth to mine.

I don't know what he means by that. He never talks to his father...there's so much I don't know about Adam because of our neglect this past year that I'm too afraid to find out.

"We're safe, right? You're not doing something—"

"Do you trust me?" he interrupts me.

"Yes."

"Good."

He kisses me once more, sweeping my mouth with his tongue before he backs away and gives me a once-over. The way he clicks his tongue makes my knees buckle, but I hold myself up. Waiting for him to make the next move.

Instead, he winks at me and steps out of the shower, leaving me to bask in the silence of what the fuck that was. Something's brewing and I don't think it's going to be any good.

Peter

Dorian Wallis.

Big gray eyes, medium-length brown hair.

Curvy girl with the sexiest legs I've seen in a while.

Cute as a button.

I pull into the club and Lip is outside with Judas and Banks, sharing a joint over a couple of beers. I look down at her card again and tap it on my hand. I shouldn't have exploded on her the way I did, but the rage of Zay came pouring out and I couldn't see straight. All I saw was red. Saw her leaving me, living her life without me in it. And I couldn't accept that. I still can't. Zay is mine, but fuck, how am I supposed to go on without her? There will come a time when I will let her go and see Adam happy. He deserves all the happiness.

But don't I deserve it, too?

Maybe this rage will soften as time passes, but right now all I'm feeling is angst. That red seeps into my vision. Same color as Dorian's lips.

"Woo-wee, what the heck happened here?" Banks asks, coming toward me as I shove the business card into my back pocket.

I smirk, nodding at the guys. "Sexy little gash rammed me."

Judas laughs. "Told you there were more out there."

There might be more, but no one makes me feel like Zay does. This decision I have to make whether to let her go or not is torturous. I want to change, I should. But being a selfish bastard is all I know.

Lip circles the car. "That's some heavy damage."

"Yeah, her car was pretty fucked, too," I say, taking the joint from Banks.

"Said she'd pay for the damages." I smirk, hoping I'd be able to see her again. She's a breath of fresh air I didn't know I needed.

"And by pay, you mean with money or with her mouth?" Lip cackles, belching. "Club needs money."

I plop down on the chair beside him, exhaling the smoke and staring at the sky. "I'm working on it."

Lip, Banks, and Judas share glances, descending an awkward silence among us. I don't like this very much. Matter of fact, I don't like this at all. These fuckers have kept a lot from me lately, and I don't know if it's because they don't think I'm ready for this or if it's because I'm not Riggs or my father and I can't handle the bullshit. But I can fucking handle it and have been for a while.

"Peter," Judas starts. "I want you to promise you're not gonna freak out, that you got your anger under control, yeah?"

My anger, like it's a burden. It's always been my problem. I react first, think second. Not the best thing for this club, but reaction gets us what we want. I've been fine the past year sitting next to Judas. I'm not at the head of the table but these guys trust me more than they trust him. I have Donnelly blood running through my veins. I think like Daddy does. I'm not Riggs. Not *Mister Goodie Two Shoes*. I get shit done. And right now, I don't like being kept in the dark.

Don't get me wrong, seeing Riggs is scary as shit and he's intimidating as fuck. But he never liked this life, tried to keep me away from it. But this is our life, it's the only life we know.

Sitting up, I lean my forearms on my knees. "What is it?"

Lip sputters, handing me the joint again. "Take another toke and we'll talk."

"No, you'll tell me now," I demand, grinding my teeth for the second damn time today.

Judas sits beside me, tapping my back, and clears his throat. "Panthers are sniffing around our business. It ain't good, kid."

Sucking my teeth, I look over at the clank from Banks inspecting the wreck on the car. "Elaborate."

"They got Riggs," Lip spits out.

I jolt upright, looking at Lip. They have my brother. The man who raised me and he's only four years older than I am. He left almost two years ago and I haven't seen or heard from him since. I have no idea where he is. No idea what he's up to. No idea if he's happy. And they took him. Does that make him weak now? Has Riggs turned a new leaf and let go of this business in a way that the fucking Panthers were able to snatch him?

This can't be fucking good.

"Where do they have him?" I ask, fuming.

"Don't know." Judas shakes his head. "Called in other charters to keep an ear out. We gotta think of a plan before we break down some doors."

I scoff, running my hand through my hair. "This is my brother we're talking about."

"I know." Judas tips the beer to his lips. "We gotta act right. Ain't no other way around it."

Grumbling, I kick a pebble on the dirt road. This isn't good. Riggs got out. He was free. How the fuck did he get caught?

I've been out of the game lately. My head's been everywhere but here. Zaynab is the only thing on my mind. When I see her, I can focus. I know what to do when problems arise.

But when I'm not with her, I don't give a shit about the club. Worst VP the Snakes has ever had. Yet the guys trust me. They look at me for answers, not Judas. Me. I can think of something, think of a way to save my brother like he's done for me all my life.

I will protect him if it's the goddamn last thing I do.

Adam and I don't talk as much anymore. He's been my best friend, but because of my selfish needs, I pushed my brother away so I could have his wife.

His beautiful wife.

Lucky dickhead.

"Call a meeting, I want everyone in chapel by three." I look at Judas, rubbing my palm on my chin. "Got it?"

Lip snickers, licking the foaming beer from his lips. "Your daddy would be proud."

Proud of what?

I'm a shitty VP.

My brother is beyond nomad. Now captured.

Club is broke.

No one respects us because Judas is a shit president, his family is his top priority, not us.

What's there to be proud of?

If I'm ever president, shit would definitely be worse.

I grunt, spitting the saliva forming in my mouth and head inside. I need Zaynab once more today. I don't give a shit who says no.

I want her now.

And I always get what I want.

Dorian

I pull up to my house to find my sister and her girlfriend have arrived before me. They've been over for nine days straight. From the moment it happened, she's been by my side. I needed my sister at first. Wanted her here, same with my brother.

Now, I just want to be alone.

Cutting the engine, I bask in silence for ten minutes staring at the dashboard. Everything was perfect. Life was perfect.

Now, my life is in shambles.

My sister, Gray, comes out of the house waving at me with a shrug. "Dorian? What the heck, sis?" She's younger than me by a couple of years, and yet, I look up to her so much more than she does me. She's the carefree wild one, and I've always been the serious sister who has a head on her shoulders and thinks before she acts.

I inhale a shuddered breath and get out of the car, forcing a smile at my sister wearing black like me. "Sorry—"

"Did you hit a moose? Jesus fuck, that's some damage," she says, stepping off the front porch and onto the lawn. "How the heck are you going to pay for this?"

I gulp, looking up at the sky. "I'll think of something."

She puts her hand on my shoulder and squeezes. "Mom and Dad went to pick up some food, Bells and I are staying the night. We need some snacks because I don't think I can eat another casserole."

She tells me every day she's staying the night like it's surprising to me. I don't have the heart to tell her to leave, parts of me don't want her to leave. If she leaves, I'll officially be alone. And I don't know how being alone with my thoughts will be.

Yet, I can't fucking wait to be alone without someone checking in on me every five minutes. She tries to understand me, to see the pain I'm in. But I don't show anyone the pain I'm in. No one needs to know what I'm going through, no one needs to see it, either. I haven't cried once in front of my family or Erin's. I haven't shown more than a single tear running down my cheek.

That's all they deserve, anyway. That's all they need.

I'm in mourning. I can't sleep. I can't do anything other than replay our last night together.

Every replay gets worse and worse…

"I'm going to take a quick shower," I say and move past her. "I just need five minutes."

"Take all the time you need. Bells will have mojitos ready when you're done."

Walking into my house, Bells is unbuttoning her dress shirt. She smiles at me, that annoying sympathetic *I feel bad for you* smile that I've been getting for nine straight days.

I'm done with it.

I'm just done.

Climbing the stairs, I go straight for the bathroom, locking the door behind me as I rest my forehead on it to breathe. I've been suffocating for nine days.

This house has been eating away. Deteriorating. Becoming a decrepit corpse of what it used to be. I hate this house. This house is *him*.

Closing my eyes, I take a breath, the ringing in my ears taking over. It's a constant that won't stop. Hasn't stopped since that night. That fucking night when all hell broke loose.

My phone beeps twice. That godawful chime.

All I've heard the last nine days is that thing go off. People I rarely acquaint with. People I never see. People who think they know me but haven't spoken to me since high school.

People who knew *him*.

I check it regardless, in case it's his parents. They were all he had.

UNKNOWN NUMBER: *Hey, it's Peter. Y'know, the guy you rammed*

There it is, the first chuckle that's left me in nine days. A chuckle from this angry man who chose to yell at me over asking if I'm okay. Then apologized for yelling at me. It's crazy, though, when our eyes first locked, I felt that jolt of energy that I only experienced once in my life. Erin's been gone for nine days but that jolt is back.

What am I getting myself into?

ME: *Hey.*
   PETER: *You get home okay?*
   PETER: *Or wherever you were getting to in such a hurry.*
   ME: *Home.*
   PETER: *Cool*

Putting my phone down, I start the shower and slowly undress as it warms up. I realized, I never owned anything black aside from this dress. And it's the first time I wear it. Erin once told me black doesn't look good on me. Makes me look paler than I am. I believed him. And now all I need to wear is black and it's nowhere to be found in my wardrobe.

My phone chimes again right as my leg is in the shower. I haven't felt that tingle of excitement to get a text in a while. Is this allowed so soon after everything that happened? Am I being honest? Loyal? Would *he* be okay with this?

PETER: *You busy tomorrow?*
   ME: *No.*
   PETER: *Good, I'm taking you for coffee.*
   ME: *Is this a ruse so you can ask me for the money for your car while also taking me on a date? If so, just send me the bill and I'll pay for it.*
   PETER: *I just want to take a pretty girl for coffee, I swear*

I lock my phone and get in the shower. All I've known was life with Erin. I never had guys running after me or asking me about my day. I've had one man my whole life. He appreciated me for who I was. Loved me for what I could be. And lusted over me for what I do.

It's been nine days.

A coffee date is not on the to-do list.

Twenty minutes later, I wrap a towel around my chest and tap my Home Screen. Three missed messages from Peter. Excitement jolts me again, a throbbing between my thighs that Erin used to worship. And the last time it was worshiped was nine days ago on that very night.

PETER: *Sorry if I was too forward.*
PETER: *You don't have to have a coffee with me.*
PETER: *I'll send you the bill when I can.*

Rolling my eyes, I lock my phone. His day was obviously as shitty as mine, but that didn't give him the right to yell at me.

If only he knew the blackout I had.

If only he knew why I didn't hit the brakes.

If only he knew.

***

I'm sitting on the couch watching reruns of Antiques Road Show when Bells comes up to me and holds out another margarita. I've had three and it's only four o'clock in the afternoon. "No, thanks. I should eat something before I have another."

My mother is in the kitchen talking with Gray as my father and my in-laws are sitting in the backyard. They've been out there since I got out of the shower and haven't once stepped inside. I don't blame them. This house is us, it's him. I hate being here, too.

"Dorian, dear, come in the kitchen and help me put all this food away," my mother says, helping herself and opening drawers in search of plastic wrap.

Gray glances back at me as I close my eyes and drop my head back, breathing in through my nose and out through my mouth. I just want to be alone goddammit.

"Don't worry about it, Dorian, I'll do it." Gray takes one of the platters and grabs a container from the dishrack. "Just sit, Bells will make you another margarita."

She just offered me one. *I don't want another margarita!*

I want peace.

Silence.

I want to open my eyes in the morning and smile again, I don't want to open my eyes and wish I didn't wake up.

"It's fine, Gray. I've seen this episode anyway and I should eat something before drinking any more of these," I say and rise from the couch, dragging my feet to the kitchen.

My mother gives me a once-over as she helps Gray empty the trays of food I'm sure will meet the trash in a day or two. "Your brother wanted to be here today—"

"I don't want to hear it," I interrupt her, taking a bread bun from one of the bowls and pulling a tray of cold cuts toward me. Thinking of food right now is turning my stomach, although it might be all the tequila I consumed without any food in my system.

My mother clears her throat, looking between Gray and me. It's a rarity to have us three in the same room together without an argument breaking out. Is it weird I kind of miss the screams?

The backdoor opens and my father walks in and pulls his tie off. Bells smiles and holds out the margarita she offered me. "No, thanks, try Bethany outside. Woman hasn't stopped crying all day."

"She lost her son, Dad," Gray spits out, scoffing.

My dad looks at me and places a hand on my back. "How you holding up?"

Taking a lavish bite of my sandwich, I look at him. "Just fine, thanks for asking."

I'm not, but I don't need people worrying about me more than I'm sure they already are.

My dad tilts his head to the side, staring at me with those sympathetic eyes his mouth is about to connect with by telling me he's "sorry". No. I'm tired of that. Enough with the *sorrys*.

"I have a few calls to make," he starts, taking his phone out. "Mind if I use the office?"

Nodding, I take my sandwich and force myself outside with Bells hot on my tail with another margarita. At least out here, Erin's parents will make it about themselves and their loss rather than my well-being.

And there Bethany is, crying into her handkerchief. She's brought three of them out today, each with Erin's initial on the corner of it, covered in tears and snot.

"Oh, Dorian, sweetheart. Come sit with us," Bethany says, sniffling.

I flash a lazy smile at her as her husband is off staring at the orange tree in our backyard with a cigarette between his lips. We've never been close with his parents, always seeing them only when we had to. His father wasn't too proud of his decision to drop out of college and surf around from job to job.

I didn't mind it as much, fewer people to interact with that I have nothing in common with, either. But they are his parents and they're the only family he has.

His father rarely spoke with him to begin with, and now he's in as much pain as we all are, that oranges have become his focus to distract him.

I prefer silence as a distraction.

"Um, h-how are you doing?" I ask, swallowing the sandwich in my mouth.

Bethany sniffs, wiping her nose on her hankie. "I've certainly been better. But sooner or later, we'll all be strong enough to move on from this and remember what a beautiful human he was who loved so much and deserved so much more than…this."

I frown. "Than this?"

Bells sips the margarita, trying to disappear into the patio chair.

"He would've been someone if he didn't drop out of school," his father chimes in, exhaling smoke from his nostrils.

Biting my tongue until it hurts; today is horrible and all his parents think about are the regrets they think he had. Erin didn't have a single regret and it's what helps me grieve. "He was happy with his life, that's what should matter."

Bells snorts, making herself known. "It is what mattered, Dorian. *You* were all that mattered to him. But his parents don't seem to realize that because he crashed his perfectly fine car into a pole without any note or letter as to why he did it."

Bells forgot to mention Erin wasn't wearing a seatbelt.

His mother sobs softly, looking off at the clear blue sky, then to his father as he squashes the orange in his hand and watches the juices drip onto the grass.

I can't wrap my head around it, either. If Erin was so happy, then why did we argue that night? Why did he try to ruin us? Why did he storm off and forget to buckle himself in? He never did that. He never forgot, but that night he did. He forgot and drove straight into a pole flying out the front window, and broke his neck on impact.

Why would he do that if he was happy and *I* was all that mattered to him?

Taking a shuddered breath, I look at the sandwich in my hand, and the margarita in Bells's, wondering which one to bring to my lips. I opt for the drink, it's the only thing that'll help me cure this madness I'm living.

His father tosses the squashed orange up a couple of times as more tears shimmer in Bethany's eyes, then saunters toward me. "Are you going to finish that?"

I hold out the sandwich to him and sigh, I should've stayed in my room. It's the only place I feel sane lately. The only sanctuary that has kept me hidden from the harsh realities of the world.

The only place I can cry without judgement,

Except today. Today was the first time I broke down in front of someone.

Someone who I can't get out of my head. This isn't good, is it?

I down the drink and set the glass down, pushing my slightly buzzed body into a standing position. "Excuse me a minute."

Bethany sniffs and nods as Bells flashes me a lopsided grin. I haven't been able to face his parents for nine days. Bethany and Erin spoke every day, up until the end. Erin would dodge her calls, and tell me to say he wasn't home if she called me. I wish I knew why.

Everyone ignores me when I come into the house and slowly make my way to my room. It's the only quiet I know. But I barely make it more than four steps before Gray follows me, a worried look on her face.

"Hey," she says, taking my hand. "You good?"

I nod quickly, a stone in my throat. "Just have to pee."

"Call me if you need anything," she adds, smiling, and heading back downstairs.

I barely make it to my room and the tears are already streaming down my face. Erin is gone, the only love I've ever known is gone and all I have left to remember him by are the items in this entire house. A house I can't stand being in is all I have left.

Peter

Fixing my cut, I sputter as the guys start piling in. They're laughing and cussing. Half of them are already in the bag. I can't blame them, we don't have much going on lately. Business is slow, and when business is slow, we rely on the bar to bring in cash. But the guys tend to forget they can't drink all the supplies we're supposed to be making money on.

Yet here I am, bringing a beer to my lips. I need something stronger, but it'll do.

Judas bangs his fist on the table, trying to get everyone's attention. He doesn't command the room like Crew did, but the guys respect him more. Judas is loyal. He'd give you the shirt off his back if he could. But his heart isn't in it as it should be. He has other priorities.

And I get that, but some of the guys don't.

Riggs, though, he'd be the best damn president this club has ever seen.

"Settle down, boys, settle down," Judas yells, banging his fist on the table again.

A few of the guys are still chattering away, clanking their drinks like their president isn't barking orders. The fuckers who don't understand that family is a number one priority over the club. The ones who are devout Snakes. My father started this club. They'll listen to me.

"Quiet!" I yell.

The room falls silent.

Lip clears his throat, nodding a head at me to continue. He was the only one not on board with Judas as president. He wanted me. But we all know it should have been Riggs.

If Riggs and I were head of this table, nothing would get in our way. We wouldn't have Panthers sniffing around, we wouldn't have to look over our shoulders to see if other rival clubs are trying to pull a fast one on us because Daddy's in prison. No, we'd rule this goddamn city.

Riggs as president and me as VP. What a beautiful thought.

Skeet plays with his switchblade that gave him that gnarly scar on his cheek. "Whatcha bring us here for, boss?"

The guys look at me.

Judas leans back in his seat and drums his fingers on the table. "Panthers have been sniffing around our business. Stealing our dealers, ending our ties overseas…they're sending us a message. A nasty one." He glances at me before he continues. "They have Riggs—"

The guys start yelling profanities, half wanting to protect my brother, the other half wanting to sink the Panthers. All I care about is Riggs. But sinking the Panthers is at the top of my list, too. They've been nothing but hellish since my father built this club, worse when my mother was around. Now, they're just as annoying as ticks.

"All right!" I rise, fixing my cut. The guys settle down. I don't think Judas likes the power I ooze over them. But what did he expect? You can't be soft in this business. You go for what you want and kill for what you can't have.

I eye each of the men who would put their lives on the line for me. Grateful for all of them. "We'll figure out a plan, speak with their president and see what he wants and see why the fuck he took my brother—"

"Did you speak to your daddy?" Lip asks, elbows on the table. "He's got something under wraps in prison that none of us know about."

Grumbling out a new fucks, I lick my lips and sit back down. "Yeah? Like what, then?"

Banks sputters, whistling at the end of it. "Thinking of joining both clubs. Riggs in your place, Judas."

"How the fuck do you know?" Judas asks, frowning. Like this fucker deserves to be sitting in that chair. But he's right, how the fuck does Banks know this and I don't? My own fucking father didn't have the balls to tell me this was his plan when he's not even part of this club anymore.

Banks nods at Roaden. "He told me."

I scoff, looking at the guys around me, and stop on Roaden, my father's brother. Everything he said, Roaden has backed him up. Except when my father was taken to jail, fucker claimed he wasn't in town when all the shit Lillian ratted to the cops about. Now, he's the only one who visits Daddy in prison. I haven't even gone to see him. It's no wonder my uncle has all the answers.

Am I the only one kept in the fucking dark here?

I narrow my eyes, scouring the fucker. "And why the fuck wasn't I told about this? Panthers have been nothing but fucking assholes for as long as I can remember—"

"Adam's a Panther," Lip spits out. "A prospect for them."

The room falls silent, so quiet the whores laughing in the front room sound like they're in chapel with us.

Adam? No, he's a wimp. Has fucking shaking hands. He can't hold a gun; Daddy always laughed at him when he tried to teach him to shoot.

Adam? No, he wouldn't be a fucking Panther. They're our rivals. He wouldn't do that to Zay. If he loves her as he says he does, he wouldn't fucking do this. Fuck, if he did this, then why the hell doesn't he grow a pair and fight for her? Fight for the woman he proposed to when he thought we'd kill her. Why the fuck didn't he tell me?

I have to speak with him. I need to get to the fucking bottom of this and find out why the fuck no one brought this to me or Judas.

They better not fuck me like they fucked my brother.

Grinding my palm into my chin, I grit my teeth. "Why the *fuck* did no one fucking say shit to me?" I bang my fists on the table, ready to shoot every damn one of them who knew about this. "What more do you know, Roaden? No...*how* the fuck do you know and I don't? He's my daddy! And Adam's my fucking half-brother!" I step back and toss the chair at the wall. "Fucking bullshit!"

Roaden tongues his cheek, looking at Lip, then Banks, and finally landing on Judas. "Your daddy doesn't know who to trust no more. I've been Sergeant-at-Arms for the club since you were thirteen, Peter. Your daddy trusts me more than he trusted your damn Mama." He sucks his teeth. "Thought he'd trust his eldest with the president title, but that backfired. And everyone paid for that. Your daddy is done with Riggs's mistake. He's finished with it."

If he's finished with it, then that means I'm finished with Zay. I'll never be finished with Zay. No, they made us pay for that bullshit Lillian pulled. Or Natalia, whatever the fuck.

I won't believe a thing out of his mouth until I see my father.

Letting out a scoff, I sigh. "Daddy doesn't trust *me*?"

Lip shakes his head. "Your daddy trusts nobody."

"Then how the fuck does everyone but me know? Huh?" I yell, coming back to the table and shoving it.

Judas stands, puffing out his chest. "You need to relax!" he shouts. "I didn't fucking know, either, and I'm the damn president."

I growl, staring at the men watching me like I'm some circus act. Maybe I am. Maybe all this bullshit is too much for me to fathom anymore. Maybe I should've never gotten in this knowing my rage and thinking isn't strategic. That's why Riggs is the best. He'll always be the best.

Yet these guys still stare at me like I'm some prissy bitch having a moment. It's more than a moment, it's my goddamn brother who was taken, my father has business going down in prison, and now my so-called best friend is a Panther. I have every right to freak the hell out.

Fucking cunts.

"Well, then I guess it's time we pay Daddy a visit, huh?" I say, taking my knocked-over beer bottle a guzzling from it. Only foam clouds my mouth.

I don't like being kept in the dark.

I don't like secrets.

I hate fucking looking like an idiot.

And I will *not* be played like a fool.

Daddy, I'll see you fucking soon.

Dorian

It's Friday. Three more days until I'm expected back at work. Three days since I had the accident with Peter. Three days since the funeral. And the last day my sister and her girlfriend are going to be living with me. I'd say I'm relieved that she's finally leaving, but this will be the first time in three years that I'll be alone in this house.

Something about the number three…

"Dorian?" Gray calls from the living room. "Breakfast!"

I slip into my jeans, the ones with tears fashionably added to the knees. When I fasten them, I realize they're loose. All the stress the past week and a half has stopped me from eating right.

Or eating at all.

Gray noticed, probably why she's been forcing me to have dinner every night. Even though I just move the food around my plate.

I'm too scared to eat.

Too sad to chew.

Depression has become my best friend. And who can blame me, am I right?

Pulling a tank top over my head, it's tight on my body, showing off my curves. Erin always loved my curves. Said it was what he loved most about me. I wasn't a skinny girl like everyone tried to be in this town. I have rolls when I sit down, cellulite on my ass and thighs, and a double chin at certain angles.

He loved me for me and never made me change.

He *loved* me. Not a word I thought I'd use when referring to Erin.

I sniff, touching a picture of the two of us taped to my mirror. We had this unique kind of love. This forever type of love. Like we were destined to be together, and destined to meet the moment we did, as if our timelines picked that specific instant just for us.

✳✳

We first met on a windy night. I remember my hair whipping in front of me, tendrils having a mind of their own. I spotted him at the other end of the park stuffing his phone in his pocket. He was beautiful, the way his golden hair looked like it was glowing in the sunlight. We were headed toward each other, but I knew he wouldn't look in my direction. I wasn't perfect like half the girls I knew. Pretty face, but a body that showed I like to eat.

He walked toward me, his entire face lighting up as soon as we locked eyes, but I looked down, trying to avoid him. He made sure I didn't.

"Hey," he said, stopping me in my tracks. I slowly lifted my head and looked around me, wondering if he was talking to me or not. "You look like someone who needs a drink." He smiled, lowering his head a little. "Come have a drink with me."

I was so stunned by how forward he was, I didn't say no. I nodded, the corner of my mouth twitching, and followed him to the closest bar.

"I'm Erin," he said, holding the door for me.

I looked up at him, fixing my purse on my shoulder. "Dorian."

We stood there staring at each other as the rose gold sky began to transition into hues of blues and purples. "Impossible as it seems to meet my forever, this feels right, doesn't it?"

"It feels like something, Erin. It really does."

We sat for hours talking about our lives, our family, our careers. Everything was so natural with him, so freeing. I hadn't spoken like this with anyone I just met, let alone anyone I'd known for years. He knew things about me I never revealed and learned things about him he was embarrassed to talk about. Somehow, our faults worked in our favor. We clicked instantly, loved strongly, and forgot life for a moment.

We talked until the barmaid told us she was closing up. He stared at me and laughed, taking his wallet out to pay for our drinks and appetizers. "Do you live far from here?"

I shook my head, a lump forming in my throat. "A few blocks over."

He grinned, slapping a few twenties on the bar top, and turned to me; our knees grazing as I turned to him as well. "I guess fate is on our side tonight, isn't it?"

He put his hand out and I hopped off the barstool, taking my purse as he threaded our fingers together. The warmth of his hand on mine sent a shiver through me. Our fingers secured themselves so perfectly like we were destined to be with each other. He was right, this had fate written all over it.

As soon as we stepped outside, he smiled down at me, curling my body into his as his arm slithered to my lower back to secure me in place. "Have I told you how stunning you are?" I shook my head, pushing my lips together. "The moment I saw you walking, I knew that someone made you for my eyes only."

I laughed a little, staring at his lips. I've kissed a couple of guys before, but there was something about his lips that made me nervous. I wanted our first kiss to be perfect. And as amazing as our night was, it wasn't our time to cross that line. "You're just saying that so I'll kiss you."

He lowered his head, resting his forehead with mine. "Darling, I'll wait a thousand years to kiss those lips and tell you everything I feel as I wait."

He stepped back and we started walking, our hands joined together. Every word that left his mouth was music to my ears. He was truly the most perfect man that was dropped on this earth for my eyes only, too.

We didn't stop walking and talking until we stood outside my apartment. I invited him up for a coffee and he said yes as if he already knew this was where he'd end up tonight.

As soon as I unlocked my door, I paused and looked back at him, taking a wavering breath. "I'm…don't expect anything from me tonight."

He smiled, moving a strand of hair from my line of view. "Only if you offer it."

Gulping, I stepping into my apartment which was fairly empty considering I'd only been living in it for the past year. I moved back after graduating from Harvard Law the year prior and never had the time to decorate it.

Regardless, he sauntered in and sat on the couch in the living room, tapping the spot beside him. "Tell me what a gorgeous woman such as yourself is doing with nothing in her apartment."

"I don't know what to buy." I shrugged, sitting beside him.

"Curtains for a start." He laughed, nodding his head at the windows which had a perfect view of the building next door. "I don't like the thought of someone seeing you naked."

I swatted a hand in the air, curling up on the couch beside him. "That's the least of your worries."

"Lemme guess, you have a crazy ex-boyfriend I'm going to have to deal with?" He winked, putting his arm on the back of the couch.

Shaking my head, I nibbled my lower lip. "No, um...I've never...y'know done...*that.*"

He leaned forward, breath fanning my neck. "Just how I like you. Perfect."

Giggles left me as the pad of his thumb brushed my lower lip. I didn't know him from a hole in the wall, but he was my forever. I had this funny feeling.

Before I knew it, the sun was coming up. Our mouths were cramping from smiling, our mouths were dry from talking, and our eyes were heavy from fatigue.

Three days later, he kissed me under the moonlight and asked me to be his forever.

A year later we were married and he bought us a home.

Three years after that, he left me.

I don't know what trouble he had gotten himself into. He'd leave some nights and come home reeking of cigarettes. He never smoked, never wanted to, and yet he stank of stale booze and smoke.

I'd ask him about it, he'd tell me *it's just Jesse from work, his car broke down so I give him lifts.* Jesse's car did break down, but Erin didn't give him lifts.

Then he lost his job and well, he still came home some nights smelling of cigarettes.

I'd say I want to know the secret life he lived when I went to work in the mornings. But what if there wasn't any? What if I'm trying to find something that isn't there? What if he worked a second job just to keep us afloat because I wanted this house we couldn't afford and he went and bought it for me?

Erin is gone and I can't even mourn him correctly.

He's gone without settling our argument.

He's gone and I can't even say I'm sorry.

He's gone way too soon.

***

Making my way to the kitchen, I grin at Bells as she has a red permanent marker between her teeth. She's been job hunting for weeks, trying to figure out a way to support my sister. Gray is planning on going back to school and finishing her degree. She can't keep mooching off our parents, or living with me until it's time to face the real world. But "planning" is her new word for "procrastinating."

Although, I have to give it to her. She's been working at McDonald's to help make ends meet for her and Bells. Their shitty apartment downtown is the size of my living room. If Gray finishes her degree, she can work with me and create a life for them. A life like Erin and I were supposed to have.

"Eggs sunny side up with bacon and brown bread," Gray says, sticking her tongue between her teeth. "Maybe I should go into cooking. Be a chef, huh?"

Bells looks up from the newspaper, glasses at the tip of her nose. "You can't handle the stress of someone yelling at you 24/7."

Gray moves a puff of air around from one cheek to the next before blowing it out slowly. "Yeah, maybe you're right. I just...ugh, sorry sis, but being a paralegal is boring as shit. I don't know how you made it through law school." She shakes her head and takes a bite of toast. "I know you're a fancy schmancy lawyer right now, but I don't think I can do it."

I pick up a piece of bacon. "Changing majors?"

I can't say I'm disappointed in her. We were all disappointed when she decided to drop out of school. It was never something she liked to do, much less something she wanted to do to make it in life. That's what our dad always told us. *Study hard and you'll make it in the real world.* So I did. I found myself a cushy job around the time we bought this house we planned on filling with babies. Seems like a waste of money now.

She groans, dropping her head in her hands as her elbows are on the table. "Ugh, I know. You don't have to say anything I see it written all over your face. And I've heard enough of it from Mom, *you have one semester left, just finish it, blah, blah, blah.* I just…can't."

"You'll think of something," Bells says, taking the toast from Gray and slathering jam on it.

My phone vibrates in my pocket. It hasn't stopped vibrating with *I'm sorry for your loss* for the past two weeks now. At first, it was nice to see how many people cared about him, how loved he was by so many who weren't there for him when he was alive and it mattered. Now, all these messages drive a knife into my heart with the thought that he isn't here anymore. He's gone and there's nothing I can do but try and live on without him.

Glancing at my phone, my heart flutters like it used to once upon a time. Peter's name pops up and I immediately open it, eager to see what he has to say. Why must I want this so much when my fucking husband just died? Testing the waters? Releasing my anger and frustrations? My sick way of grieving?

PETER: *I have the invoice, can you come meet me?*
  ME: *Sure, where?*

He sends me the address to a place twenty minutes from here. A bar, no less.

ME: *What time?*
  PETER: *You free now?*
  ME: *Sure, be there soon.*
  PETER:

Finishing the bacon, I push my plate to Bells. "I'll be back soon, meeting the guy I rear-ended to pay for his damages."

"Want me to come with you?" Bells asks, dipping her toast in the eggs.

Shaking my head, I take the keys to Erin's car. The night he died he crashed mine, and I hit Peter with the rental. All I have left to drive is a car I couldn't bring myself to set foot in. Erin's scent is all over it. "I'll be fine."

"Where you meeting this person?" Gray asks, cracking another egg in the pan. "Insurance covering it? Or are you fronting the bill?"

I gulp, looking at the keys in my hand. Erin's helm keychain we bought on our honeymoon in Maine staring back at me. "I don't have insurance right now. Everything was in Erin's name, I haven't switched it over yet."

Bells gives me a lopsided grin. "Time heals all wounds." She stands taller after she says this, proud of herself in a way. She hasn't said much to me since it happened. Hasn't tried to console me or ask if I'm okay. She goes with the motions of how Gray acts.

And sometimes, Gray gets on my nerves.

I chuckle nasally. "Yeah, of course, it does."

"You didn't answer my question," Gray adds as I open the front door. "Where are you meeting?"

Unlocking my phone, I read out the name of the bar, making both Gray and Bells go pale. I don't think I ever heard of the place before. It's called *Judas's Hideout* and the place shows up in the middle of nowhere on my map app. "What?"

"That's—" Bells looks at Gray. "That's that biker bar. The one that got raided three/four years ago. Was in the news and everything. No, I'm definitely coming with you. This is too dangerous of a place to go alone."

"Bells, I'll be fine. I won't even go inside," I say, trying to reassure her. "I'm just paying him for the damages."

"How are you paying for it when you're meeting at a bar? Why not his mechanic?" Gray asks, sliding the egg onto a plate.

I force a smile. "I have my check book."

"Dorian," Gray says, sighing. "I have a bad feeling about this."

Jerking a shoulder upward, I lift my jeans. "Trust me, Gray. Have I ever done anything stupid in my entire life?"

She sighs, shifting her gaze to Bells. "But they're bikers."

"Yeah, and I'm a damn widow. We both have pent-up anger we don't know what to do with," I spit out, taking in the shock on Gray's face. "I'll...see you soon."

"Call me when you get here," Bells adds as I open the door and shut it behind me.

Closing my eyes, I suck in as much air as I can, shaking this gut-wrenching feeling from the pit of my stomach. *This Too Shall Pass.* Erin had that tattooed on his shoulder and it's something I constantly recite to myself every time I have a funny feeling, just like the one that's having a war in my stomach. Three days after Erin died, I tattooed that on my inner bicep with the birth and death dates underneath it.

Just for him.

Inhaling another breath, I open my eyes when I hear Gray and Bells discussing their worry about me, and how they think they should move in with me permanently until I'm able to smile again. I understand their worry about me, about that place, but I can handle myself.

I have to learn to handle myself.

God help me survive this nightmare I'm living.

Zay

The morning of our wedding day wasn't as special as we wanted.

I barely slept at all that night; I drank myself silly to cope with the stares Peter had been giving me. Drank to cope with the fear crawling up my spine, *one way or another, Snakes always get their prey.*

It wasn't over.

I took a bullet to the chest and I still had to pay for a mistake I made.

Adam rolled over, kissing my cheek and chuckling softly. "Morning, wifey."

I let out a shaky breath, the effect of the hangover taking hold. I tried to smile when my husband looked at me. I tried to be happy that the love of my life was mine to hold.

But I wasn't happy. I was broken without any super glue to repair me. And I couldn't hold it in any longer. I broke down, covering my face and crying. "I'm sorry."

"Babe? Hey, what's wrong?" Adam pulled me close and tilted my head to face his. "Talk to me. You're not regretting this? Oh, Zay, please don't tell me you regret this."

Shaking my head frantically, I spilled everything Peter told me. I told him how scared I was. I told him I didn't want to pay for something that more or less didn't happen. I told him I was done.

"Adam?" I whispered.

Adam flared his nostrils, lying back in bed and shaking his head. He didn't say anything for a good six minutes until he climbed on top of me and kissed me, invading my mouth with his tongue.

He took me rough that morning.

Hurting me.

Devouring me.

He took me as Riggs would have.

"You are mine," Adam growled, biting my neck. "Mine."

"What do I do?" I asked through a strangled breath.

He fucked me harder in response.

Snakes put anger in people.

They destroy people.

And Snakes were slowly destroying us.

***

Adam and I are playing hooky today, deciding we need a day for us. We haven't had a day alone without the lingering thought of Peter in months. And when we woke up this morning, Adam smiled. He finally smiled and I couldn't take it. I wept, telling him how much I loved him.

He kissed me in response and told me we were having a day together.

He's made me breakfast in bed; pancakes from scratch and freshly squeezed orange juice. "For you, my lady." His lady, words that will make my day.

Shaking my shoulders at the tray of food he places on my lap, I giggle. "Thank you, baby."

He leaves a soft kiss on my shoulder and tears off a piece of the pancake. No syrup. Reminds me of Riggs. I think of him sometimes, thumbing the ring I still wear around my finger.

No, I think of him all the time and think about what he would do if he knew what Peter puts me through.

I'm too scared to stop it, too scared to fight it, and definitely too scared to ask Adam to stand up for me. I'm not even sure he ever has. He's calm and collected. Not a bad bone in his body. He's perfect.

And then there's me. A fucking mess. But I guess that's what I get for playing with fire. Sooner or later I was bound to get burned. I just didn't know how badly I'd scar.

Adam, however, always tries to see the good in things. Before we avoided each other completely, he always made our mornings special with kisses, breakfast, lovemaking...mornings I miss so damn much.

Adam takes a strawberry from the tray, popping it in his mouth with the arch of his brow. "I think we should hit up the beach today. What do you think?"

I nod, smiling up at him. "I love that idea."

He grunts as he gets up, naked as the day he was born. Beautiful. "I just have to drop something off real quick, then we'll go."

Staring at him as he pulls boxers, shorts, and a t-shirt from his dresser, I study the bruise on his side, and it isn't the only one. There's another on the back of his arm and his calf.

My eyes well with tears at the thought of him cheating on me. I wouldn't blame him in the slightest, I do it to him every Tuesday afternoon.

Please don't ruin us like I already have.

"Adam," I say, moving the tray onto his side of the bed and walking on my knees to the edge of it. "What happened? Why do you have all these bruises?"

He takes a slow deep breath, keeping his focus on the knick-knacks we have on the dresser. Another breath and he slowly turns to me, furrowing his brow. "I'm sorry...I just...I can't say."

I lick my lips and rise, letting the sheet fall so I'm also standing there completely naked. "Who is she?"

He drops his clothes and shakes his head, reaching for my hand. "I would never do that, babe. Never, no." He kisses my knuckles, staring intensely into my eyes for a moment before he closes them. "I told you I'm fixing things, right? I'm ending all this bullshit so we can live our lives. So I can have my fucking wife to myself, goddammit."

He huffs, opening his eyes again. "I've been visiting the ex-president of the club—my dad. That's where I go when I come home late. I asked for his help. He told me he'd reach out to Peter and put an end to it. But clearly, that didn't happen. So I keep going to visit, thinking maybe he'd do me this solid since neither of his other sons go see him. I do. I go and I beg. But..." He inhales a breath of air. "I'm sorry, I can't tell you yet. But I'm fixing things, babe. Okay? I'm fixing it and we're getting away from anyone who owns a damn motorcycle, okay?"

Sniffing, I wrap my arms around his neck. "Please be careful, please, Adam.

Whatever you're doing to right this wrong isn't worth the risk if you're putting yourself in danger, right?"

He kisses my head and chuckles. "Don't worry about it."

I have a bad feeling about this. A horrible feeling that's making me queasy.

The only reason he would need to visit anyone from the club would be because they're family, right? They raised him. But something is telling me he's seeing them for other reasons.

He slides his hands to my ass and squeezes, kissing me softly. I don't kiss back, I can't. I move away and stare at him. Those eyes, they change. The darkness I feared is spreading into those deep blue eyes like a fog taking over a forest.

He snickers, wiping a thumb under his bottom lip. "It's nothing you have to worry your little head around, babe. I told you I'd take care of us, didn't I? And I'm taking care of us."

"Adam?" I ask breathlessly. "What did you do?"

He pulls me close to him, lifting me onto the dresser.

"Adam?"

He smirks, easing me to the edge. We haven't slept together in weeks, and he decides to do this now while my brain is trying to unfold the dirty laundry he's kept in the dark from me. Has he been bad all along and I've been too stupid to notice? Is Adam just as wicked as Peter? Just as sour as the club members? Am I that damaged I let myself fall in love with the devil?

"Adam!"

He silences me by shoving himself inside me and slamming his lips on mine. He's taking me roughly, power oozing out of him. It's so unlike Adam to be like this. Adam's the good one, he's always been the good one, right?

What the fuck is he hiding?

I'm staring at the man I feel like I don't even know.

He lifts me off the dresser and tosses me on the bed. He doesn't roughhouse in the bedroom. He's the calm lover who makes sure I finish every time.

He parts my legs and devours me, licking my clit until I scream, and shoves fingers inside me until I finish.

I should be pressing for answers.

I should be worried.

I am.

But we haven't been us in weeks.

We haven't fucked in ages.

We need this before the truth is revealed. But holy shit is my mind running a thousand damn laps of thoughts about what the hell is happening.

He licks up my stomach, biting down on my nipples and suckling with a moan. "Yours, babe." He shoves himself inside me again and lifts my backside. "Let's see how deep I can go, yeah?"

"Adam!" I squeal when he pushes roughly, making my head roll back and see stars.

He's hurting me, taking me so rough I'm screaming out in pain. "Stop it, please!"

He slows, lowering me completely on my back and rocking steadily on top of me. "Tell me something." He rakes his bared teeth along my jawline. "Does Peter fuck you like this? Did Riggs?"

"Adam!"

He moans, biting down on my neck and leaving his mark. "Betcha they didn't."

I'm still screaming, both out of pleasure and pain. This is a different side of Adam. A side I've noticed change in the last month. He's been distant, yes, but that distance held darkness to it. And I believe this darkness has nothing to do with me.

A side I'm too frightened to meet again.

He grunts, biting my bottom lip and pulling it toward him. "My wife."

We're out of breath, staring at each other as he thrusts slowly. "Adam?" His name leaves my mouth in a squeal and he smiles, kisses me softly, then hoists my legs up. "Talk to me?" I whisper.

He chuckles, on his knees and still slowly moving in and out of me. His length getting my entirety and making my eyes glaze over. "You're a smart girl. I'm sure you can put the pieces together, can't you?"

I shake my head, trying to understand him, and force this pleasure out of the way. "I don't want to play games, Adam."

He watches as he moves in and out of me, staring at us with a smirk on his face. "You should see how beautiful you look from this angle."

"Adam?" I whisper.

He pushes inside me again, thrusting slowly and staring at us like he's watching a movie. I don't move. I watch him watch our sex take place. Normally, this would turn me on. Normally, I would be touching myself as he does this. But this isn't normally.

Something is wrong.

Adam's gaze trails up my body, stopping on my breasts before meeting my eyes. "Lick your fingers," he says, still thrusting slowly and holding my legs open.

I shake my head. "I don't want to."

He shoves it deeper and I yelp. "Lick. Your. Fingers."

Fear spreads through me. An ache I've never had from him before. He's tame. Loving. He's the reason I calmed down.

This new side of Adam is scaring the living daylights out of me.

But he's my Adam. I have to see this through, don't I?

I lift two fingers to my mouth and lick them, holding our gaze as I do. "Now what?"

"Touch yourself."

Swallowing hard, I try to wrap my head around this entire morning. We're supposed to play hooky today, go to the beach and make sandcastles. Maybe even make out a little before we ease into the bedroom again. He had other plans, plans to fuck me like his whore. Fuck me into submission.

As my eyebrows pinch together, he shoves himself deeply again when I don't touch myself right away, breaking my thoughts.

I lower my hand and feel how wet he's making me. He watches my fingers, biting his bottom lip as I play with my clit, bringing her to life in seconds. My head rolls back and the ecstasy flows through me.

His rocks are quicker, and his breathing is erratic, as is mine.

I touch myself and think of his smile, his gentleness, his—I see Riggs. That brute force of a man watching me do this before, too. The way Adam is fucking me feels like the way that burley biker took me all over the cabin.

Then it dawns on me, Adam is trying to fix things. He's trying to right my wrongs.

He's working for the club.

I can't take it anymore, my body bucks as I massage my clit with one hand and pinch my nipple with the other. I'm screaming, moaning, releasing.

Adam growls, his grunts and groans fill the room; once, twice, on the third thrust he moans, grunting loudly and comes.

We're breathing heavily, staring at each other again. But I've figured it out.

He comes home reeking of booze and cigarettes. He comes home tired, and he's covered in bruises. He's paying off my debt by working for the club.

He drops down on top of me, smiling. "I love the fucking shit out of you, Zay."

I lick my breathless lips. "Are you part of the club?"

He shrugs with a smug grin on his face. "I've always kinda been, babe. Surprised it took you this long to notice." He chuckles, kissing me softly. "But I'm not a Snake, Daddy made sure of that."

Thick tears roll down my cheeks.

There's no running away is there?

We all must pay our dues at some point in life.

Right all our wrongs.

As I've been trying to fix my wrongs, I've been sleeping with it all this time. Married to it now.

He wipes my cheeks and kisses me. "There's nothing you need to worry about. I'm handling it."

"Adam?" I whisper.

"There will never be anything you have to worry about."

I shake my head.

"You can try to run away from me, but you're not leaving. You're mine. Understand?" He frowns, tears welling in his eyes. "You're not leaving me, Zay. Please."

"No."

"No?"

I push him off me and try to get out of bed, but he stops me, gripping my wrist.

"It's still me. All this time you didn't know, you were happy loving me. Don't let him ruin us…don't let *this* ruin us," he says, breathing heavily.

"I'm tired of the lying. The secrets. I hate the fucking secrets." I whimper, looking back at him. "All this time I've been with Peter to protect us from them. You're telling me I didn't have to?"

He sits up, scooting closer to me, then runs his fingers across my bottom lip, tracing my jawline and neck before he stops on the scar on my chest. "I hate secrets, too. That's why I'm telling you now." A beat passes and he kisses my shoulder. "I never stopped it because…if they find out what I'm doing, I'm a dead man."

"Get out. Leave this bullshit, then. Let's just be," I sob, taking his face and holding it steady. "Let's just be."

He traces the scar on my chest so delicately, my skin pebbles underneath the pads of his fingers. "I wish it were that easy."

Taking his hand, I kiss it. "If you're serious about this, about me. End it." I shake my head, more tears rising. "Because I won't be a part of this madness." I choke on another sob. "I hate being part of this madness."

His nostrils flare, I don't think he liked that comment very much. "You're going to leave me?"

I sniff, wiping the tears from my cheeks. "No, but I don't want to live in fear my entire life."

"You won't."

He tucks my hair behind my ear and kisses me. "I'm almost done," Adam says quietly.

"Stop this," I whisper.

He inhales deeply, staring into my wet eyes. "Give me time. Okay? Give me time."

How can I do that?

I can't be part of this.

This almost killed me.

This did kill me for ten seconds before the doctors brought me back.

This is my life now, isn't it?

This madness will never go away.

It lies dormant with Peter every Tuesday afternoon for the right time to come back.

I didn't pay my dues. I still owe it.

I can run away all I want but what good would running do?

My fate is sealed.

***

Stepping out of the shower, I stare at my dripping, naked body in the mirror. I have hickies on my neck from Adam, scratches on my back from Peter, and scars on my outer thigh from that one time Riggs and I fooled around in front of the fire and I got burned. A burn so bad, it scarred me.

"Perfect," Adam says, leaning on the door jam and staring at me.

I roll my eyes, taking the towel from the sink. "You have to say that, you're my husband."

He chuckles, still naked, and stands behind me. He yanks the towel off me and drops it on the wet tiles. We're standing in front of the mirror, looking at my body from head to toe. The fingers of his left hand slowly start tracing my hips, moving up to my stomach as the other hand finds a secured spot on my hip bone.

His left hand travels, leaving trails of goosebumps behind, and ignites excitement once more. "These are mine," he breathes onto my neck, fingers traveling higher and tracing under my breasts. "Do you see how perfect they are?"

I nod, watching his right hand find its way to my sex, opening my folds with two fingers.

"And these." His nail scratches over my nipple, sending a shiver through me. "These will give milk to our children one day." His teeth drag along my shoulder. "Perfect," he rasps.

A moan leaves me as his knee pushes my legs apart. "And this heaven right here." He stops touching me and brings his fingers to his lips, licking at the wetness I left on his fingers. "Tastes like heaven, too." He looks at me in the mirror, leaving me aching for more. "Will you be my heaven, babe?"

"Yes," I say, gripping the wrist that's squeezing my breast.

"Tell me you trust me," he whispers.

Wetness is leaking down my inner thighs, begging him to continue.

I'm not worrying about his secrets or the danger he put himself in. Right now, I'm worried about my sex not being satisfied.

"I trust you."

He grins, stepping back and stroking the length of himself. "I want to watch you as you watch yourself come."

Adam's favorite thing is making me finish. I may have not gotten the answers I wanted and I'm left with the worry that my husband might get himself killed or get me killed in the process, but goddamn if we're not going to go down in a state of fucking nirvana.

A moan slips from his lips and he looks down at his dick, already dripping and ready to burst again. I bite my lip as I watch him but he grunts, jerking his head at the mirror.

My hand slips into my folds, finding my clit instantly and I bring myself home. Watching as my eyes glaze over and I grip the sink as I buck and spray my release everywhere.

He growls, forcing me to touch my toes as he thrusts inside me and yanks my hair up, making me watch again. He finishes inside me, our eyes meeting in the mirror as we attempt to catch our breaths after the intense morning we're having.

Adam and I are back to being us, but what scares me isn't the normality that's coming back, it's what lies ahead that is so mysterious, I'm frightened one of us might lose ourselves if it's unveiled.

Peter

Been cleaning my room like a maniac all morning. Dorian should be here any minute, too. I haven't been this excited to see a girl since Zay, and even then, when I think of Zay all I see is the hatred in her eyes. She deserves better but she'll never get better than me. Dorian, on the other hand, has better. And soon, she'll have the best. Me.

When I toss the comforter on my bed, a pair of Zay's highlighter yellow underwear falls out of its folds. Zay had these on the other day, wore them for me.

Like the sick bastard that I am, I bring it to my nose and inhale that sweet tenderness I'm going to see in a few short days.

The club says she doesn't owe.

Says whatever debt she had is paid.

But she doesn't know that and she never will.

She's my girl. My best girl. My only girl.

My Zaynab.

Skeet knocks on my door and pushes it open, jerking his head at me as I tuck the underwear into my back pocket. "Some chubby chick is here for you. Says you told her to meet you here."

I nod, winking at him. "Bigger girls have more fun."

He snorts, agreeing with me. "Refuses to come in, though, thought I'd let you know."

Of course, she wouldn't come in. What self-respecting girl would enter hell and expect to come out alive?

"Yeah, I'm coming," I say, tossing my pillows on the bed that still smells like

Zay's perfume. Exotic coconut.

Fixing my jeans, I be sure to leave my cut behind. I don't want to scare away this girl I barely know like I did when she hit my car. She's cute and I think I can get a taste of cute until I have my fill of Zay again.

Running five fingers through my hair, I strut out of my room and make my way through the bar. Full house this morning, guys are usually sleeping in until at least noon. It's half past nine and they're scattered around, smoking, drinking, making out with the whores that keep this place running.

"Girl outside for you," Lip says with his mouth full.

The Snake Biters made a big breakfast this morning. Some old ladies helped, too. I can see Zay being here, helping out the ladies when they need it—serving us Snakes because they have to.

But Zay's not like that. She dances to the beat of her own drum and I know for a fact wouldn't serve a single one of these fucks.

She'll only serve me. Preferably, she'll be naked as she does it.

Stepping outside, the sun shines down on Dorian's blackhair as she looks down at her phone, anxiously biting her bottom lip.

Holy hell, my dick twitches at the sight of her in those jeans. The way they hug her curves. Giving no mystery as to what that ass would look like against my dick.

Zaynab who?

Dorian looks up at me and grins. I like her, all of her. She's…holy crap, she's perfect.

"Hey," I say, closing an eye from the sun.

Her grin grows to a smile curling a lock of hair behind her ear. She feels it, too. She has to. "Hi, Peter."

Even the way she says my name, pronouncing every syllable. Where did this woman come from?

Guilt rides through me when I realize that a pair of Zaynab's underwear is in my back pocket. Burning a fucking hole it in as I step closer to Dorian.

My newest obsession.

I stammer, chuckling awkwardly. I'm flustered, scratching the back of my head and licking my lips to try and get something out of my mouth. "Um, th-they just made breakfast if you wanna come in and e-eat with me."

She shakes her head, anxiously looking behind me at the bar before meeting my eyes again. "I'm okay."

Putting my hands in the front pocket of my jeans, I shrug a shoulder. "I left the invoice inside."

She nods, biting her bottom lip in this way I don't think she means to be sexy. But goddammit, am I ever in a trance staring at the way her teeth rake over the soft pink flesh, teasing me with slow movements. "I can just wait here, it's okay."

I smirk, running my fingers through my hair again, yet no matter the number of times I do it, hair still falls in my face. "I don't bite. Plus, you look like someone who can use a drink."

Something in her changes. Her cheeks flush, her eyes glass over, and her breathing shakes. "Uh, um. I, uh—" She scratches at her shoulder, flashing a gold band across her finger.

Of course, she's married.

"I don't mean anything by it, just a friendly thing," I lie through the skin of my teeth. Her demeanor doesn't budge, she's still anxiously staring between me and the bar, tonguing her cheek now.

Lifting an eyebrow, I point at her ring. "You married?"

She stammers now, licking her lips a couple of times and dropping her phone. When she picks it up, I look at her with a grin. "I'm kind of...not... it's—I am, but it's...complicated."

I swat a hand in the air. "Relationships are complicated."

She nods, looking behind me at the bar, then at the ground. *Judas's Hideout* has changed a lot since we got the money from Zay. The road is paved with painted lines for parking. New floors were added inside, a stocked bar, sexy leather bar stools, new booths, and our chapel got a new table with our logo etched into it. The place looks like a fucking dream.

"I just have to call my sister," she says and points at the bar. "I-if I come in."

"Yeah, 'course."

I put my hand in my pockets again and watch as she dials. Her long hair shines a hint of gold in the sun from her highlights. All I can see is that pouty mouth of hers on mine—no, wrapped around my cock. Yeah. As those sleek red nails scratch the back of my thigh, my ass. Fuck, down my back when I'm making love to her.

Innocent little thing.

"Hey, Gray…yeah, no. Everything's fine. I'm just going to be a little longer than I thought," she goes quiet, looking at me with a grin, then back at the ground. "Oh, uh, okay."

When she looks up at me her cheeks blush slightly. "Everything good?" I ask, giving her a once-over.

She removes the phone from her ear and holds it up. "Can you, uh, smile?"

I smirk and chuckle. "What?"

She taps on her phone and brings it back to her ear. "Happy? He's not a scarred and burly biker who's going to rape and kill me, okay…yeah, I'll see you soon…love you, too."

She places the phone in her back pocket and reaches for her purse in the car. "Sorry about that."

I laugh a little, running my fingers through my hair like it's some nervous tick. It's getting long and it's out of place today. But Zay seems to like it at this length, that's the only reason I keep it. "Did you take my picture?"

Dorian nods. "My sister's a worry wart."

I wink, tilting my head downward. "Sorry to disappoint you, but I'm not a burly biker." I point at my neck. "I do have a scar, though."

She reaches up and touches it, then snatches her hand away as if she didn't realize what she did. Her fingers etch into my skin, and all I want to do is have her run them all over me to have a glowing feeling. To experience that release. "H-how did that happen?"

I shrug a shoulder, then point a thumb behind me. "Long story that had nothing to do with this, though. Just so you know." That's kind of a lie, it had everything to do with this place, but she's too innocent to learn the ways of motorcycle mumbo-jumbo. I'll never let her into my madness.

I need to reassure her I'm not a bad guy.

Fucked, maybe. But who isn't nowadays?

I want to prove to her I'm good. Show her all the parts that Zaynab saw during our first night together. Show her I can love and be loved. Show her the real me.

Zaynab deserves the real me, too. But that's never going to happen with Adam around and Riggs still fresh in her mind.

Dorian lifts her hair and shows me the side of her neck, a three-inch scar decorating it. "Thyroid issue."

I chuckle, looking into those gorgeous eyes. "Wouldja look at that, matching scars. It's like we were meant to be."

She chuckles at that, the first chuckle I've gotten out of her that shows me those dimples.

Girl has my dick trapped in the confines of my jeans. God help me, I'm whipped.

Cute as a button and has no idea what she's doing to me. No fucking idea.

I start walking and she follows, looking behind her as Roaden starts up his bike. He salutes me, cigarette in his mouth, and rides off. He's been seeing this girl in another charter. Perky little Mexican, hair so thick and curly, he always has some tangled in the zipper of his cut. But he's happy, and that's all that matters.

We walk into the bar and Judas nods at me, eyeing Dorian with a smirk. Some of the guys start whistling but stop as soon as I snarl at them. She doesn't notice the pit bull in me because she's walking with her head down. Placing my hand on her lower back, she tenses up, but I still lead her to my room at the back of the bar.

Riggs used to live upstairs. I'd stay with him from time to time, felt good to have my brother close to me. Then I moved to the dorms, but when I dropped out of school, I had nowhere to go. Lip lives upstairs with his girlfriend, so I took over the back room and the cabin when I needed it. I can surely use a weekend away, maybe she does, too.

She steps into my room and swallows loudly, looking up at me with fear in her eyes. "T-the i-invoice?"

Snapping my fingers, I close the door behind me, going to the desk at the back of the room that's scattered with order forms for the bar, biker magazines, and bills. "Here it is." I look at it, then back at her, grinning at her perfection.

I wonder if Zay will like her for me.

I wonder if I'll be able to give up Zay for her.

I don't know that I can.

But I should.

"How much do I owe you?" she asks, placing her purse on my bed and moving her hair on one of her shoulders.

She shows me her cleavage, not intentionally. I don't think anything sexual is intentional with her. My eyes trail up from her cleavage to those supple, pouty lips. "I hope you take a check."

I let out a shuddered breath. "Y-yeah. Sure, I can take a check."

The beauty in her appearance makes it really hard to focus on anything. And what I can focus on is getting her in bed with me soon.

Rocking her world will be easier than having a normal conversation about my life.

I hate talking about my past. My family. Me.

I've done nothing important. Nothing remotely prideful. I'm a university dropout, a shitty boyfriend, and an even shittier VP.

Dorian seems like the kind of girl that likes talking. Instead of talking, I'll have her screaming.

Soon, she'll see.

Dorian

I don't like the way he stares at me with those big blue eyes.

I shouldn't like this.

I'm in mourning.

My husband died fifteen days ago.

My soulmate.

But here I am wondering what it would be like to be held by this tall, God-like man. He's probably younger than me. Probably has a girlfriend. Maybe even two.

He can't be single, not with the stench of cigarettes and coconuts in his room.

He's too pretty for the single life.

But who am I to judge?

Erin was my soulmate, right?

No matter how many times I lick my lips, they're still so dry. "Here." I sign my name at the bottom of the check and rip it out. "Just write your name on it—"

"Peter Donnelly," he says, that smirk hasn't left his lips since we saw each other twenty minutes ago. "Two Ns and two Ls."

He runs his fingers through his hair again, pieces falling on either side of his face. I look away quickly, writing his name down, and holding the check out to him. I can't be attracted to this. I can't look at another man after Erin. I refuse.

But Jesus Christ, am I ever attracted to this man.

He takes the check with that smirk still there and cracks his knuckles.

"Correct me if I'm wrong, but did you say your sister's name is Gray?"

I nod, letting a soft grin spread to my lips. "Our father is obsessed with Oscar Wilde."

"It's cute," he says, grinning over his shoulder as he places the check on his desk. "I read *The Picture of Dorian Gray* in school, did an essay on it, and everything." His smile falters slightly, but whatever thought crosses his mind, vanishes and that smirk comes back.

There's a hint of regret in his tone.

I can pry and get to know him. But what good will that do? I'm a widow. A widow from a beautiful man who died not too long ago.

A widow of a man who was my everything.

I can find an everything again, can't I?

"Are you, um…what did you study?" I ask, hanging my purse off my shoulder.

He tucks his hands in the pocket of his jeans and shrugs. "I dropped out. I took time off because of this." He lifts his head and reveals that scar on his neck. "Then that time off ended up becoming two years." He shrugs a shoulder this time. "I got this gig, no use in going back."

Tucking hair behind my ear, the corner of my mouth twitch into a grin. "It's never too late to go back, get out of this…life."

"I like this life," he snaps back.

Taking a shuddered breath, I grip the strap of my purse and fidget with it. "S-sorry—I didn't—"

He puts a hand up and chuckles. "No, I'm sorry. I don't like people judging what they don't know."

I nod quickly, looking behind me at the closed door. "I-I should g-go—"

"What did you study?" he asks me before I can finish my sentence.

Shifting from one leg to the next, I cross my arms as he rakes his eyes over me like some lion stalking its prey. I'd be lying if I said it didn't make me feel pretty. "I studied at Harvard Law."

He raises his eyebrows, a smirk spreading to a smile. "Wow, that's really impressive."

"Thanks." I fix the strap of my bra and look back at the door. "If there isn't anything else you need—"

The bedroom door opens and a man with a handlebar moustache pokes his head in. He's massive, at least close to three hundred pounds of pure muscle. "Hey, VP," he says to Peter. "Unexpected visitor."

Peter sighs, running his hand through his hair *again*. "Yeah, gimme a sec."

VP can only mean one thing, he's the vice-president of this establishment. This is definitely my cue to leave. The last thing I need is to get involved with criminals. A handsome criminal that makes my insides take flight and my knees feel like jelly.

"It's okay, I was just leaving." I clear my throat and nod at Peter. "I'll see you round."

He smiles back and steps forward. "Let me walk you out."

Gigantor moves out of the way, flashing me his gold teeth as he looks at my breasts. I've never been disrespected more than the thirty-five minutes I've spent in this establishment. No, I should say I've never been eye-fucked more in my entire life.

Peter's hand finds my lower back and he leads me through the hungry savages as they scan me, scowling, licking their lips, smirking—every single one of them smirks mischievously like they're up to no good. Thinking bad and dirty thoughts.

I can't wait to get out of here and shower.

But Peter, even though he's checked out my rack more times than I can count, he's oddly different than these savages. He stares at me in ways that make my heart breakdance.

We're outside again, the sun bright as all hell. We head toward my car and he salutes a blonde with matching blue eyes who is parked beside mine. The blonde's arm is around a girl whose gaze is focused on the ground. She looks scared, sad.

"Hey, man," the blonde says, scanning me.

Peter jerks his head at him, eyeing the woman with this intense look in his gaze, and the smallest nibble of his lip when his eyes roll over her.

When he looks back at me, he smiles again and clears his throat. "Where are my manners?" He settles his hand on my lower back again, sending a shiver through me. I can't tell if I like this or not. Maybe I like this, but I'm too scared to admit it.

Fifteen days ago you were married, Dorian, you don't like this.

"This is Dorian, the chick who rear-ended my Mercedes last week," Peter says, his thumb moving slowly back and forth on my lower back. I'm not opposed to it, but I don't know if I like this. No, I do. But I shouldn't. "Dorian, this is my brother, Adam, and his wife, Zaynab."

The girl chuckles softly, narrowing her eyes at Peter. "Really, Peter? You're making her pay off her mistake like you're making me?" She scoffs, shaking her head as she looks at the bar. "You're fucking pathetic," she whispers softly.

I don't think she meant for anyone to hear that.

Peter stiffens, a rumble aggravating his chest. I can see it in the way his breathing is quickening. I wonder what this girl is referring to. What makes her hate Peter so much and what mistake is she paying off?

No, the better question is, how is he making her pay it off?

"Exactly why we're here today, babe," Adam says, kissing her temple.

Giving a toothless grin, I nod. "I should get going."

Zaynab comes forward, pulling me into a hug with a lowered voice. "Stay away from him, whatever you do, stay the fuck away."

She releases me and smiles. But it's evident by the fear painting my face that she said something neither Peter nor Adam would like.

I nod again, gulping the lump in my throat, and make for my car, looking over my shoulder once as Peter smiles at me the genuine way he has been all morning.

What do I believe?

This woman I just met?

Or this man I see myself becoming infatuated with?

There's regret that oozes out of him from a life he loves yet doesn't seem to be chosen by him.

There's more to this story, and my stubborn and curious mind has to find out what.

Zay

Watching as she drives off, the curvy girl with the unusual name.

Peter's an idiot.

A bastard.

A goddamn demon walking on this plane.

He always wants what he can't have.

Now is no different.

Peter runs his fingers through his hair, letting it grow out the last few months. I hate it as much as I hate him. "Sorry about that."

"You sleeping with her, too?" I spit out, crossing my arms.

He shakes his head. "It's not like that at all. She's literally just paying off the damages she did to my car."

"Good," I say, which sounds like I'm jealous.

I'm not.

But to Peter, it does and a smirk spreads to his lips. I said *good* because I didn't want him to taint her like he tainted me.

Adam pushes off the car and glances at the bar. "We should talk."

Peter stuffs his hands in the pockets of his jeans and gives me a once-over. His tongue moves along the front of his teeth. "Yeah? What about?" He takes his pack of cigarettes and lights one, exhaling the smoke from his nostrils.

"*My* wife."

Peter shoots his attention back on Adam, that tongue poking his cheek now. "She owes the club—"

Adam steps forward, nearly as tall as Peter, and puffs his chest out. "Not anymore."

Peter scoffs, staring at me as I frown, trying to keep it together. I don't want them to fight—no, I do. I want Adam to fight for me, to show Peter that I'm no longer his. I'm Adam's. I've always *been* Adam's.

But I don't say any of that. I furrow my brows and look down, shaking my head because it's no use. Like Peter told me on my wedding day, *Snakes always get their prey.*

Peter pulls on the cigarette once more and flicks it, tilting his head back to exhale. *"Not anymore,* he says." He nods, spitting a wad of saliva at the ground, and folds his arms across his chest.

He looks so much like Riggs right now. The way he cocks an eyebrow, the twitch in his eye, that smirk. Gosh, even the way his stance is. It reminds me of the first time I met that monstrous man in the barn. How he tossed me around like a rag doll as if I never mattered.

But I was all that mattered to him.

I showed him peace.

My peace disappeared when he did.

My peace lays dormant in hell.

And I'm looking right at the devil as he stares my husband down with a smile pasted on that fucking face.

"Something I'm missing, Adam? 'Cause how I see things, this isn't up for discussion. She fucked me, fucked the club." He snickers, licking his lips as his gaze rolls up my body. "Someone had to pay for what Lillian did. That bitch put Daddy in jail and fucked over my guys. Something we're still trying to recover from. So, you tell me, *Adam.* Who's supposed to take the blame for that, huh? Lillian is dead. Riggs is gone. The only person left is *her* because she tried to kill me with a fucking pen." He puts his hands up and takes a step back. "Now, if you'd prefer my guys taking turns at her, that suits me fine, too. But—"

"Fuck you," I snap, getting back in the car and slamming the door shut with a sob. The windows are open, so it makes no damn difference.

Peter makes me infuriated. The promises Adam made me were that he'd fix things. Everything would go back to the way things were before our wedding day. Before all of this madness.

But they're not.

Why wouldn't they? It's me we're talking about.

Eyeing the side mirror, I watch Adam and Peter standing chest to chest, huffing and ready to go at each other.

After a year of this agreement, not once did my husband lay a hand on his best friend. He let this shit happen to me as if I deserved it. As if he believed I deserved this shit. Now he decides to defend me? I don't understand the change, but I'll accept it if it puts an end to my misery.

Adam scoffs, shaking his head with a lick of his lips as he glances at me in the car. Our eyes meet in the side mirror. "You were always jealous of me. Of *us*." He points at me. "The second I told you about her, all you did was tell me what a bitch she is for doing what she did to you. And I get it, it's fucked up, but I understand why she did it. Because back then, I'd do that to anyone who hurt you or Riggs." Adam bumps his chest against Peter's, moving him back a step. "Now, I can't fucking stand the sight of you." He grits his teeth, fists clenching at his sides. "You're going to leave my woman alone, do you understand? This bullshit about redemption is over. I paid off her debt. It's done. It's *been* fucking done."

Peter runs his fingers through his hair, chuckling as he does it. That manic chuckle scares the shit out of me. "That measly one million from two years ago? Please, that money is long gone—"

"No, I settled her debt by talking to Daddy," Adam interrupts him.

Peter frowns, a look of pure horror paints his face. "You did what?"

A satisfied sigh escapes Adam, and he glances at me again. "You're crazy to think she wouldn't tell me about this deal you conjured up. She's my wife, Peter. *My* fucking wife!" He scoffs, shaking his head. "You've always been so fucking selfish and self-centered that you couldn't even let someone you had one fucking night with four years ago, go? There are so many other women you can go after, but no. You have to choose MINE!" Adam's screaming at this point, getting the attention of some of the men from the bar. Two of them walk outside, beards as long as their hair. "Grow the fuck up and leave my wife alone."

Adam wipes the spittle at the corner of his mouth with the back of his hand

and turns to leave when Peter grabs the back of his shirt and tugs him, then grabs a fist full of his hair and bangs it on the roof of the car.

I kick the door open and fall to my knees beside Adam. He groans, on the ground as blood leaks from a cut on top of his brow. "Jesus Christ, Peter. What the fuck is your problem?"

The two men run over, one holding Peter's arm and the other on a bent knee beside me to look at Adam. "Let's get him inside," he says. "I'll patch him up good."

Peter chuckles, allowing the man to pull him back to the bar, the door slapping behind him as it does.

Secrets break everything in their path.

They almost broke Adam and me.

They broke Lillian.

They broke Riggs.

Soon, they'll break Peter, too.

No one is stepping away from this in peace.

One of the men helps Adam to his feet and I sniff, taking Adam's hand as we follow, looking up at his flared nostrils and twitching eye. "Let's just leave."

He shakes his head. "I wasn't fucking finished."

"Adam?" I whisper, squeezing his hand.

He side glances at me, lip curling up as we step into the bar. "Please, babe. Just—please."

I don't say anything. I shake my head and make my way behind the bar like I own the place. I need whiskey, good ole whiskey.

Adam sits on a bar stool in front of me and taps it for a drink. One of the women slides a beer over to him, placing a glass in front of me.

I hate coming here. All it reminds me of are the days I thought my life was over. That week at the cabin changed my life.

Maybe I did die and this is my hell. It only makes sense. Someone has to pay for the sins I committed.

Peter comes out of the back room with his leather vest on, *V. President* patched on the left breast. He told me he got out after I was discharged from the hospital.

What went wrong for him to want this life?

Riggs hated it.

I hate it.

Peter…he spoke of the benefits, but he promised he'd stay away from it for Riggs.

He promised.

But his promises are worth shit. This is the only life he knows. His father spoke of his sons sitting at the head of the table, running this establishment. Peter speaks highly of his father, well, highly enough for a father that's in prison. His mother, on the other hand, loves her to pieces. Speaks about her like she's on top of the world. But she died because of this club. Murdered in cold blood. And he still thinks this fucking club is worth it.

I don't know how to open his eyes to prove to him that it isn't.

Peter comes behind the bar as one of the women takes a medical kit from beneath it and brings it to Adam. This is the same woman who watched him while I was at the cabin. Mickey's wife.

Adam groans when she starts to clean it, wiping away the blood above his eye. "Patch it quickly, please," he says, eyeing Peter guzzling a beer and leaning beside me.

Tears well in my eyes but I blink them away, pouring more whiskey in my glass. He knows how much this place puts me in a miserable mood. He knows that every time I come here, I end up beneath Peter, then my husband resents me for days until I'm back here again, and then he just despises me altogether.

Adam's nostrils flare, I can't blame him for being angry. Just the thought of being in the same room as any of his exes will drive me to drink. And here we are, flaunting the fact that Peter and I have this disturbing chemistry that oozes so much lust, Adam senses it. He hates seeing Peter and me in the same room, let alone side by side.

I hate this as much as you do, baby.

Peter grabs my wrist to stop me from pouring a glass, taking the bottle and setting it down. "We need to talk."

I shake my head. "Then talk."

"Alone," he says, looking back at Adam.

Adam scoffs, baring his teeth. "She's not going anywhere with you."

Peter leans his forearms on the bar, looking at Adam with those sparkling blue eyes that have no right to be that blue. Although, at this angle, he looks so much like Riggs that it hurts. "Five minutes, brother. We'll do nothing but talk, promise. After that, our Tuesdays will be over…I just want to talk."

Adam looks at me, licking his lips as Mickey's wife takes out butterfly stitches. "Just talk?"

Peter nods, putting his fingers up. "Scouts honor."

"Fine," I say, taking the whiskey bottle and marching off to his room.

***

This reminds me of the first time Peter asked me to do this "agreement." He asked me to meet him at the bar, alone, and to bring a change of clothes.

I did.

Like an idiot, I did.

He smiled at me, called me sweetie like he always did, then led me to the back room to "talk" like he asked now.

So I went, scared out of my mind, but I knew if I didn't, the rest of the bikers could've had my head for not obeying.

What did I know?

I closed his door and he told me our agreement, *in exchange for sex, I'll make sure you're safe. If they think you're my old lady, they won't touch you.*

I believed him because they didn't touch me. They didn't threaten me. They left me and Adam alone.

But I was wrong, so wrong.

My breathing shuddered, trying to wrap my head around what he asked. "Peter, I can't. I'm married." I placed a hand on my head. "Adam and I just got back from our honeymoon two days ago—"

Peter came toward me, that wanting look in his eyes. "You were mine first." He cradled my head, tilting it up to look at him. My heart was bouncing all kinds of crazy. My stomach was in knots. I didn't know what to expect, nor did I know what to do. If I screamed, those men out there would just laugh. Over a year ago I sat in one of those booths begging for my life and those men didn't give a shit about it.

Peter licked the side of my face, his tongue brushing under my eye to catch a tear that slipped free. "Admit it, I'm the best sex you've ever had."

He wasn't. Far from it. Riggs was the best sex I've ever had, but Adam knows my body. We connected our mind, body, and soul. He will always be that person who tore me apart so he could burrow inside me and remain there for all our remaining days on this planet.

I groaned as Peter slammed his lips on mine and invaded my mouth with his tongue. I pulled away, eyes wet with tears. "Your brother was."

He didn't like that very much.

He grabbed a wad of my hair and shoved my stomach into his dresser. I tried to push him off but I was helpless. I fought. I screamed. I pleaded.

All he did was rip my thong off and part my legs.

"Peter!" I yelled. "What good will this fucking do, huh?"

He gripped my hair tighter, making me yelp. "Well, if you would stop fighting it, it would do me a lot of good. And hey, maybe the club will let their sought for revenge go."

I let that fester a moment.

Let the words sink in.

If I slept with him once, he'd find a way to help let this go. The revenge for my best friend gone wrong would be forgotten.

But I couldn't do it, not to Adam.

"No."

Peter laughed, helping himself to the zipper of his jeans. "No, huh?"

I tried to get loose again, but it was no use. He was winning this fight. And I would comply, because what else was I supposed to do?

Be killed?

Be tortured?

Would something bad happen to Adam if I didn't listen?

Peter entered me without protection, shuddering as he did. "Fuck." He thrust slowly, groaning as he did. "If you got a little wet, this would be a lot easier, sweetie. C'mon now," he said, letting go of my hair and turning me around. "I've never fucked without protection before." He kissed me, holding my head in his hands. "It'll be our little secret, but I need you to want it."

I scoffed, wiping my mouth. "I don't."

He growled softly, raking his teeth along my skin. "If you don't pay for the sins of what you did, they will go after Adam."

I whimpered, shaking my head. "Please, no. Leave him out of this."

"Then let me in," he whispered.

I was at a loss for words.

At a loss for a lot of things. Mainly my sanity.

"Let me give you money, as much as you want—"

He chuckled. "Club has money, sweetie."

"Then how is sleeping with you paying off a debt?" I asked, flicking my gaze from one of his eyes to the next.

He inhaled sharply, stepping back and taking off his clothes. "I'm VP of this club. What I say goes because these men listen to me. If I say your debt is paid off, they'll listen."

Shaking my head, I gave his naked body a once-over. "Then tell them it's paid off without any of this."

He took my shoulders, leading me to the bed and sitting me down, his dick at full salute, staring right at me. "Where's the fun in that?"

"I can't cheat on my husband," I whispered.

"It's not cheating if we already slept together, sweetie," he said, winking down at me.

He wasn't wrong. We had slept together twice before and had been friends longer than Adam and I. But *this* was so wrong. And yet all these thoughts of how to get out of this clouded my mind.

Pay off the rest of the club.

Pay off the old president. Find a way to get his father out of prison.

Speak to Riggs.

What good would it do? I had one choice, and one choice only. Sleep with Peter once more and pray he stopped this madness. It was the only option, right?

"Just once, okay? Once and we're square."

So, I gave in. Believing that if I slept with him again it would be enough, and he'd free me of this hell.

He didn't.

Looking up at him, he smirked, as if reading my mind, and held my head in his hands. Slowly, he inched forward, helping himself into my mouth.

I gagged.

I cried.

I studied him as he moaned and smiled while I pleased him. Foul beast.

He removed himself from my mouth and pulled the dress over my head, tossing it aside. His smile grew when he stared at my bare breasts. They were always his favorite.

He slid the ripped underwear off of me, sniffing them as a sound of pure hunger emanated from within. Then he took me. Rough. Hard. Fast.

I lay there allowing him to ravish me in the hopes I'd never have to do it again.

Just like the night I almost killed him.

He grunted on top of me, licking my neck and groaning in pleasure. "God, you feel amazing."

My lower lip quivered, but I pushed them together to stop. "It's over now, right?"

He grunted once more, pushing deeply inside me and making me wince before he rolled off me and cackled. "Oh, babe, we're just getting started."

Shooting up from the bed, I shoved him. "You said—"

His laugh took over everything as I stood there at my most vulnerable. "Yeah, I know what I said. Doesn't mean I meant it."

"You're a fucking asshole," I growled, shaking my head.

He tilted my chin up and I slapped his hand away, taking my dress from the floor. He grabbed me, pulling me back to his chest and holding my head so I'd look at our reflections in the stand-up mirror. "Every Tuesday, same time as now, you're to come to see me. Ready for me, wet for me. Miss a Tuesday and I'll make sure to find you and finish the fucking job that Crew failed to do at the barn."

His tongue met my cheek and he chuckled, staring at our reflection. "You're so fucking beautiful, Zaynab. So fucking beautiful." He kissed me roughly, then backed away and sat on the bed to take a cigarette from his jeans.

I wept, staring at him until I dropped my head in my hands.

My fate writing itself in blood.

***

Bringing the bottle of whiskey to my lips, I suck my teeth as the sting of alcohol travels down my throat. "What the fuck do you want, Peter?" I hiss, looking back at him as he steps away from the door and leaves it open.

He sits on his bed, elbows on his knees, and shakes his head. "What did you say to Dorian?"

I chuckle with a scoff, looking down at the bottle. "To stay away from you."

He meets my gaze. "Why the fuck would you do that?"

Raising my eyebrows, I widen my eyes. "Do I seriously have to spell it out for you?"

He shrugs a shoulder, clasping his hands. "I kinda like her."

"Yeah, well, I saved her from being another woman you ruined," I spit out and take a swig of whiskey.

He gulps, rising from the bed and thundering toward me. "I didn't want to hurt you. And I had no choice but to hurt Lillian. This is my fucking life, Zaynab. This club, their orders. This is what I do." The look in his eyes is so intimidating, so manic. It's not Peter. It's not the man I once knew and spent so many fun nights studying, and partying with. This isn't Peter.

And it saddens me that the only life he knows has ruined him.

I poke the patch on his chest. "This is not you. You're better than this fucking place. Better than these men. I know you, Peter. I met the real you under those stars." Shaking my head, I wipe the escaping tear. "But I don't know who the hell this Peter is anymore."

His blue eyes gloss over, and he turns away from me quickly. "It's okay, we're over. We don't have to do anything anymore, Zaynab." He sniffs, pinching his eyes shut. "It's done."

Tendrils of relief unfurl, making me smile.

After a year of torture, I'm finally free.

A Tuesday will go by and Peter will leave me be. And the realization that I'll never sleep with him again seeps in and the floodgates open.

I put my head in my hands and sob, letting all the madness I've kept inside,

299

release.

Everything time he was on top of me, I'd cry.

Every time I didn't want to do anything and he forced me to, I'd wail.

Every kiss.

Every touch.

Every stroke.

It's done.

But why does it feel like this was too easy? Too sudden? Why now? Why not when I begged for him to stop? What changed?

Of course, I don't ask because I'm too happy. Too fucking happy to get out of this hellhole. I'll deal with the why later in case he changes his mind.

For now, I just want to hold my husband and embark on our journey of a new life.

I rejoice, wrapping my arms around Peter. "Oh, Peter, thank you."

He sniffs again, inhaling as he hugs me back. "Leave before I change my mind."

I let go of him, catching his gaze for a moment. Sadness paints him, sadness he doesn't know how to express.

It's not my problem anymore.

It was never my problem to begin with.

I'm free.

Jogging out of his room, I smile at Adam as he takes a swig of beer. "Let's go home."

He nods, getting up from the barstool as I put the whiskey back and pull him out of the bar. He waves at a few of the men and tugs me close to him. "What happened?"

I laugh, more tears falling down my cheeks. "I'm free."

He frowns, a smirk seeping on his lips as we stop halfway to our car. He holds my head in his hands, that gorgeous smile of his spreading. "Oh, babe."

He kisses me, his tongue slides around my mouth and makes me lightheaded. It was a kiss much like our first one.

Memorable.

Aching as his taste sinks into me.

This is a first kiss to our new life.

Dorian

I've been pacing my room for the last twenty minutes, Peter clouding any thought. All I keep seeing is that smirk on his face lowering to mine, capturing me in a kiss that sends me to Mars. I'm sure he's good at that. No, he's *definitely* good at that.

But the more I think of Peter in wicked ways, the more I know he's already thought of me wickedly, but I also see that girl. The anger that raged from her, seething as she stared at him. He's trouble, the bad kind of trouble that's dangerous and riddled with secrets.

Stay away from him, whatever you do, stay the fuck away.

Yet here I am pacing my marital bedroom thinking about another man naked.

Lord help me.

Knocks strike my door and Gray steps in, margaritas in hand. I don't have the heart to tell her I can't stand her girlfriend's margaritas anymore. But I put up with them so that Gray doesn't pester me with questions and try to pry into my psyche.

I'm fine dealing with my mourning alone.

"Bells and I made tacos, come eat before they get cold," Gray says, smiling and sipping the margarita. "I even made Mexican rice."

Widening my eyes, I chuckle. "You know tacos are the only way to my heart."

She sticks her tongue out. "Yeah, and what about tequila?"

I shake my head with the wrinkle of my nose. Maybe getting drunk tonight will help heal these sinful thoughts of Peter Donnelly and all the wicked things

I want to do to him.

***

Bells is the first of us to get drunk, snorting every time she laughs. I needed this tonight. Two consecutive hours without thinking of Erin. Living in the moment since the accident. I can't remember the last time I didn't have a worry pinching the muscles in my shoulders or the nerves in my temples. I can't remember the last time I felt like I could breathe.

My phone vibrates as I finish off my drink and I glance at it, seeing a message from Peter.

PETER: *It was nice to see you today. I'd like to do it again sometime outside of the bar. When are you free?*

Locking my phone, I ignore his message, because I know if I were to answer, I'd be in his bed naked in the next hour. And I can't do it. Not yet anyway.

My phone goes off a second time, another message from Peter. But I'm too slow to reach for it, and Bells has it in her hand, reading it out in her drunken state. She slurs the words out like some slutty friend at a bachelorette party. "Who's Peter? He wants to go for drinks with you. Says rum and cokes are his favorite."

I frown, snatching my phone. "He's the guy I had the accident with, I told you that already."

"She's drunk, leave her alone," Gray says, defending her.

Tapping my home screen, I glance over his message, rolling my eyes, but also groaning at the raging throb between my thighs. This isn't good. Nope, not good at all.

PETER: *We can go for drinks at a place of your choosing.*
    PETER: *Rum and cokes are my drink of choice*
    ME: *I don't think it's a good idea.*
    PETER: *Why not? We're meant to be, remember?*
    ME: *Because of our scars? I think that's a long shot to be soulmates, Peter.*
    PETER: *Is it, though?*

PETER: *How about this, why don't you think about it? I have a few things I have to wrap up at the club, once I'm square, I'm taking you out.*
PETER: *Sound like a plan?*
ME: *Sure does.*
PETER: *See you soon, Dorian*

What the hell am I thinking?

"You're smiling like you're up to no good," Gray says, pouring more of the margarita mixture into my glass.

I stammer, staring at the messages from Peter and shaking my head to snap out of this lust trance. "It's nothing."

Oh, but it's something all right. Something that's going to get me into a lot of trouble. One of the reasons I became a lawyer, digging deeper into issues that I have no business digging into.

And this…thing with Peter, is definitely something I have no business digging into.

Curiosity killed the fucking cat, yet here I am, biting my bottom lip as I stare at the messages, knowing I'll be tangled in his sheets very soon.

I'm sorry, Erin.

Peter

I'm off to visit my father in prison.

Something I've been putting off since I found out Riggs was taken. Goddamn Panthers have him. And I have no idea why.

My father will have answers, he has to.

Lip is driving the car, all the other guys are riding their Harley's. He isn't much of a talker and cares more about listening to talk radio than having a conversation with me. I've been scrolling through Instagram for forty minutes trying to keep myself busy. But I'm bored outta my mind! I always hated this drive. I've done it only once before. I don't see the point in visiting a man I've looked up to all my life—the same man who killed my mama in cold blood.

Sputtering, I look out the window. It's hazy today, looks like it's going to rain but it's not like it matters to me. Because of a stupid inner ear problem, I can't ride a bike like these guys. Riggs has tried to show me so many times, but I have no balance. It's easier to just drive while the guys follow. Daddy wasn't happy about that, but he wasn't happy about a lot of things I did in life. He hated it when Riggs paid for my schooling. Told me it was useless to work a day job and slave for the rest of my life when money is easily earned in other ways.

Ways I don't want to admit I'm not proud of. But they're ways regardless.

I never planned on getting out of this. I promised Riggs I would. I promised Zay I would. But this is the only life I know. Even when I was in school, all I'd think about was this. Lillian knew that but never said anything. She followed me countless times thinking I cheated on her. She followed me to this club and ended up cheating on me. Fucking bitch deserved what she got for hurting my family.

But what she gave me instead was a broken heart because of Zaynab.

And I let Zaynab go. Haven't spoken to her since, either. It's fucking killing me, but maybe everyone is right. What I'm doing to her and Adam is selfish. She deserves happiness, just like I promised Adam he deserved it, too. But my dick wanted back into that goddess. She's mine, always will be.

Although, Dorian has been flashing through my mind for days. Taking over many thoughts of Zaynab. I haven't seen Dorian since she left the club that afternoon. Haven't spoken with her, either.

I disconnected from everyone the same afternoon I left Zaynab.

The hardest day of my life.

I can't stop thinking about what she said. How I ruined her life.

How all I do is ruin lives.

It hurt more than I thought it would because she's the last person I'd ever want to ruin.

Figured I'd let her go. In time, she'd realize that she needs me and she'll come back.

She'll need me.

I take my phone out and look at my messages. Zaynab is still pinned at the top of my list. That gorgeous face of hers smiling back at me.

How am I going to go on without her?

Time heals everything, kid, in time you'll find a way to smile again.

Riggs said that to me the day our mother died. All I've been hearing is his voice in my head for the last couple of days, healing my dark thoughts.

Healing everything.

Finding Dorian's name, my thumbs hover over the keyboard. Maybe if I take her on a proper date she'll see I'm not a bad guy.

Maybe she'll love me like Zaynab couldn't? No, she refuses to and I don't understand why.

ME: *Hey, you*

Locking my phone, I lean my head back. All night my stomach was in knots, twisting and turning at the thought of seeing my father. It's been at least four years since I last saw him.

Kind of by choice.

He originally didn't like the fact that I wasn't going to be part of the MC. That Riggs told me not to join. Riggs hated this life for me. Told me I was better than this club.

My father didn't think so. He made me do some odd jobs here and there. My very first job was the one Lillian saw. The killing of two Panthers prospects at the back of the club. He was proud of me that day, all right. So proud of me it made me proud of myself.

"We're nearly there, brother," Lip says, adjusting his long fingers on the steering wheel.

I nod, looking out the window and wondering what the fuck happened to Riggs. And why is he involved in something he left two years ago?

***

Sitting at a table, my leg taps restlessly underneath it as I wait for my father to come out. A few families are waiting to see people, too. But they're all smiling, happy to see their loved ones. Kids with homemade cards. Wives with low-cut tops to give their men a little peek to see what they're missing.

And then there's me, the only miserable one here.

A buzzer sounds and gates are being opened, men pile out with smiles—so many smiles—going to their respective families. I look up and watch, waiting for my father.

He's the last one to come out.

He struts his way over to me, a grin on his face, big and thick. It's where Riggs and I get our height from. He's is almost 6'7", big mitts that can kill anyone with one hit. Riggs took after him more than I did. At certain angles, if it wasn't for the gray hair sprinkled through my father's locks or the wrinkles etched into his skin, they'd be unmistakably the same person.

"Peter, my boy," he says and sits down. "About time you showed up."

I nod, putting my head down much like our mother did when he scolded her. "Sorry, Daddy."

"Haven't seen your brother come 'round at all, either."

Nodding again, I lift my head. "I don't know what's going down, Daddy, but Panthers are honing in. They're…they got Riggs."

He narrows his eyes at me and clasps his hands on the table. "What do you mean they got Riggs?"

"Lip and Judas told me," I say, I feel like a kid again, trying to explain what happened while he was away. "They said Panthers took him, said I should come to you and talk. That's all I know, Daddy. I swear it."

He chuckles, looking at the VP patch on my cut. "My boys." He shakes his head slightly with a smirk. "My boys were supposed to take over the club. You and Riggsy at the head of the table. But he went and fucked crazy. Got me locked in here because I took the fall for all you fuckers. Now look at you. Brother runs off leaving his cut behind. You're VP but don't know your ass from your elbow because you only think with your dick." He taps his finger on the table. "You think I care about the payment for what that cunt Natalia did? Bitch was fucking me on the side, fucking your brother, too. She had no idea what was coming to her when I sent you to kill her, did she? Only reason I sought out revenge was because you couldn't let it go. Fucking bitch's best friend tried to damn near kill you, and you couldn't let it go. So Crew came up with the plan, yeah? It worked. Club got some money. But still, your dick couldn't let her go." He leans forward, seeing the wetness in my eyes. "Tell me, son, where's the bitch now?"

I grit my teeth. "Her name is Zaynab."

He rolls his eyes, crossing those brute arms. "I don't give no fucks. What I wanna know is, why my firstborn was taken by the damn Panthers?"

"I. Don't. Fucking. Know."

He laughs, it's deep and guttural like the demon he is. "You talk to Adam? My half-pint of a bastard?"

I shake my head. "Adam and I don't run in the same circles…anymore."

He lets out a nasal chuckle, narrowing his eyes the way he does when he knows I'm lying. But I'm not lying now. "I ain't got time for games, son. I'm locked in this joint for twenty more years. There ain't nothing I can do in here to help out there. You need to speak to Adam. He's doing the club a favor."

Frowning, I look over at a woman laughing as she holds onto her man's hand. "What kind of favor?"

"Ask him and find out," he says, huffing out a breath. "Panthers sniffing around ain't good, son. That's…bad."

Leaning my elbows on the table, I drag my hands down my face. "I know."

"Have they made contact? Do you know if Riggs is alive?" He uncrosses his arms and folds them onto the table instead.

"I don't know, Daddy."

"Have *you* made contact?"

I shake my head. "Guys wanted me to talk to you first."

He nibbles his bottom lip, a scar outlining it. I was seven years old when that happened. Riggs was eleven and woke me up in the middle of the night as he climbed into bed with me. Our daddy was moaning and groaning downstairs. I thought he and Mama were going at it again. He'd force himself on her when we were sleeping. We'd hear her crying and asking him to stop; he never did.

Riggs and I snuck downstairs when she told our father to hold still or she wouldn't be able to patch him up nicely. We loved hearing his crazy stories and what he did for the club. Well, I did, at least.

And there he was, sitting on a chair in the kitchen with no shirt on, blood decorating his tattooed chest, and my mother standing between his legs trying to sew the cut shut. Found out later this was a Panther trying to cut his lips off for mouthing off to one of their women.

Daddy would come home with injuries often and it was up to my mother to fix him. He'd be shot, sliced, dislocated fingers, and once a shoulder. Sometimes Riggs would be there, too, and she'd patch him up. She always did what she was told. Except for on my eighteenth birthday when she fought back.

We all know how that ended.

"Mmm," Daddy grunts. "Well, I don't know what good I'm gonna do. But might as well tell you something. Adam's a Snake. Made him a member last year when he came to see me. Told me what you were doing to his wife and he didn't like it much. So, I told him if I finally gave him a patch, he'd have to do me favors in order to keep it. Know what favors he's been doing?" I shake my head, nostrils flaring, hands clenched in fists. That lying fucking bastard. "He's been giving us intel on the Panthers. Also pretending to be a prospect for them."

Everything around me shoots into focus.

Like a Mack truck hit me on the side of the head. So it's fucking true. I didn't want to believe it. Thought my brothers had their facts wrong because Adam is the biggest pussy I've ever met. His hands have been shaking since he's been a kid. Can't even hold a pencil straight let alone a gun.

"What the fuck are you talking about, Daddy?" I ask breathlessly.

His lip curls in and he grins. "Your half-pint of a brother is one of us."

I can't breathe.

Trying to calm myself, my heart races as I stare at my hands that can't seem to stay in focus. It's not working, though. And when I look up at my father, his face warps. I feel high.

Drugged up.

What the fuck is happening?

"He's a Panther?"

He nods. "Yep."

Then it hits me. He's the reason Riggs was taken, it makes perfect sense.

"Daddy, you don't think your plan might've backfired? You don't think they know Adam is one of us?"

He shakes his head and chuckles. "Boy is blonde, and everyone knows Daddy Donnelly has two sons, not three." Say that to the way his club runs their mouths. Everyone knows we're all Donnelly brothers.

I grind my fist into an eye socket, still trying to wrap my head around this bullshit. "Daddy, Judas has a big mouth. He talks and talks—fuck, his woman used to be a Panther Eater. You don't think he told her and she told them that Adam is one of us?"

My daddy's face goes pale. He didn't think of that one, did he?

He wipes a hand down his face as the buzzer sounds, informing us that visiting hours are over. "Goddamit." He rises, giving me a look of concern.

"Find your brother, y'hear me, son." He takes the back of my cut and yanks me upright, embracing me tightly. "Donnelly's at the head of the table."

"Hey!" a guard yells, banging his baton on the metal door. "No touching."

My daddy releases me, lowering his voice. "Liam Ignassio."

Frowning as he steps away, he winks at me with one more glance over his shoulder as the inmates pile out in single file. "Daddy, wait. Who's that?" He glances at me again, his blue eyes blinking slowly before the guard shoves him along. "Daddy!"

I came to see my daddy looking for answers and I left here with more questions.

***

I'm standing outside Adam and Zaynab's house, a hand on either side of their front door. Daddy said to talk to Adam, so that's what I'm here to do.

Fuck.

Flicking the cigarette, the remaining smoke trickles from my lips as I knock on the door twice. They live in a cute house in the suburbs, a perfect place to start a family. If it wasn't for my fear of kids turning out as fucked-up as me, I'd have popped one into Zaynab.

But what father would I be to a child who'd see the darkness I create? They'd deserve better than me. So much better.

Laughter comes toward the door, her beautiful laugh filling my ears. I close my eyes and smile, listening to her perfection.

God, I miss her.

When the door opens, so do my eyes and it's Adam smiling on the other side of it, frowning. "Peter? What're you doing here?"

I swallow hard, running my fingers through my hair. Doesn't do any good. It falls in my face right after I brush it away. "I went to see Daddy."

Adam sighs, looking back as Zaynab comes into view and stops short, half-chewed popcorn in her mouth. "Peter?" she mutters, looking at Adam, then me.

I smile at her, flashing my signature wink that makes her knees weak. "Just stealing him for a sec, why don't you get us something to drink?"

She rolls her eyes and continues to the living room. "In your fucking dreams."

Watching her walk away, her hips sway. It makes my dick twitch with excitement. Like she knows I'm watching. Little tease in those jean shorts that show just a hint of her left ass cheek.

Goddamn sexy woman.

Why the fuck did I let her go?

Adam blows a kiss to Zaynab, closing the door slowly. "I won't be long, babe."

The last thing I see before he shuts the door is that look over her shoulder. A grin for Adam, but secretly it's for me. I just know it.

Adam shuts the door and puts his hands in his pockets, leaning on the door jam. "What're you doing here, Peter?"

Taking a breath, I look at the sky. It's almost dusk, the sky's a deep blue with hints of pinks and oranges sparkling through it. About that time I first met Zay.

When I lower my head to look at Adam, he raises his eyebrows for an answer. "Daddy says you're a Panther."

Adam looks away, gulping and shifting his stance. He scratches the back of his head and sighs. "He said it would do us good. The club has a rat, and they don't know I'm a member. But when they find out—" He takes a breath. "Whoever took Riggs is trying to piss you off and whoever tells you that I'm a Panther, aside from Daddy, then you'll know who the rat is. That's the plan." He furrows his brows and sniffs. "But Riggs, I don't know how to get him out. Fuck, I don't know what they're even doing to him. Or why they took him."

I grit my teeth, grabbing his shirt and shoving him into the door. "Why the fuck didn't you tell me?"

He pushes me off, fixing his sleeve. "Because Daddy told me not to."

I run my fingers through my hair and shake my head. "I should have never let Zay go—"

He scoffs. "More concerned about your dick than you are your own brother. Really?"

Shoving him again, I put my face close so that our noses are pressed together. "Don't you fucking dare think I don't care about my brother!" I scream, gripping his shirt. "He's my fucking family. He's all I have fucking left of my mama!"

Adam pushes me off, but I grab hold of him, bringing him down with me. We're rolling around the grass, grunting and straining, trying to get a good punch in.

I can't get him because he has me in a headlock, but gets distracted when Zay comes out of the house, shouting at us. Calling us fools, telling us to knock it off.

I can't.

I'm on top of Adam, he has me by the throat, squeezing tightly that I'm gasping for a breath. But I have the advantage.

I swing, hitting him twice. Square in the jaw.

"Stop it!" Zay yells, but I'm seeing red.

Punching him again, he squeezes tighter, harder, his thumbs pushing against my Adam's apple—it's all cut short when Zaynab sprays us with the jet setting on the hose nozzle, hitting me right in the ear.

I yelp, falling on my side and wincing in pain. "Fuck!" I grab onto my ear as a searing pain jolts through me, ringing following suit.

She goes for him instead of me and holds his bleeding face in her hands. "Jesus fucking Christ!" She scowls at me. "What the fuck, Peter? What the fuck is your problem?"

I can't take it. I'm writhing in agony, I swear she busted my eardrum.

"Riggs was kidnapped! He was fucking kidnapped!" I yell, groaning and moaning as I hold my ear.

She gasps, her hand on her mouth. "Oh, my God!"

Those amber eyes fill with tears staring at me with worry and sorrow. "What happened? How—" She keeps her eyes locked with mine, not Adam. *Me.* "Is he hurt?"

Adam sits up, wiping the blood from his nose on his finger, and shakes his head. "I don't know."

"You're gonna help him, right?" She switches her gaze to Adam. He nods but doesn't hold her. I know Zay, she needs a hug.

She needs me.

So I get up, no matter the pain I'm in, and hold onto her. My bleeding ear getting on her shirt. "Nothing will happen to him, Zay, I promise."

She sobs softly, reluctantly leaning her head on my shoulder, and nodding. "I'm tired of this." Her body begins to shake and I squeeze her tighter, taking away all her pain and worry.

She can give it to me.

"It'll be okay," Adam says, taking her hand and kissing it. I'm not letting go of her. She's mine.

Always will be.

"We'll protect you, sweetie," I whisper, wincing as my throbbing ear surges through me, making me shudder.

She grips me, holding me closer to her and pressing her chest into me. Me, not Adam. Me.

Having her arms wrapped around me.

Her body in my arms.

Soon, sweetie.

Soon.

She tries to loosen her grip but I hold on tighter, reminding her that I'm here.

That it's me.

Still me from the night we floated under the stars.

She liked me then.

She'll like me again.

She gives in and lets out a breath as her face burrows onto my neck. Having her this close, consuming me, it's all I've ever wanted.

And suddenly, that pain throbbing in my ear is gone. With her in my arms, I don't feel any pain at all.

Peter

I'm sitting at the clinic with Adam and Zaynab. Like a fucking child being forced to see a doctor for my ear. The damn thing kills like a son of a bitch and I haven't stopped hearing a goddamn ringing for the past two hours. But I don't want to be here, not after the day I had.

But none of that matters because Zay's here. She's worried about me. I can tell because of how she's nibbling her bottom lip and gnawing at her thumbnail.

The doctor finally comes into the room after a nurse brought us in here half an hour ago. I hate fucking waiting, especially waiting when the fuckers know who I am with this cut on. "Mister Donnelly," he says, looking down at my chart. "Any relation to Richard?"

I scoff, a smirk on my face. "Junior or Senior?"

The doctor looks at Zaynab and Adam, then his gaze falls back on me. "Th-the one in prison."

"He's my daddy."

Riggs got his nickname when I was born. I couldn't pronounce Richard Jr., and there's already an RJ from the club. Mama used to call him Ricky, so I'd call him that, too. But with my hearing problems, I had a speech impediment. So his name came out as Riggsy. It stuck with him, our Mama started calling him that the moment it left my lips. I hope he never goes back to being Richard Jr., he'll always be Riggs in my heart.

"I volunteer at the prison, and your father has been in the infirmary a time or two," the doctor says, putting the clipboard down and looking at the rag I have held on my ear that's stopped bleeding a little while ago. He swallows hard, knowing exactly who I am. I'm Daddy Donnelly's son, not someone he's going to mess with or fuck over. "Care to explain what happened here?"

Jerking my head at Zay, I arch an eyebrow. "She took the hose on us and the pressure got me in the ear."

The doctor looks back at her and nods, eyeing the way she crosses those legs at the ankles. Fucker better not be checking her out right now. But goddamn, I can't blame him. Just days ago my tongue was tracing the inner parts of those thighs.

Fuck, I miss it.

"I believe I'm the patient, doc, not those legs of hers," I say, winking at Zay as she rolls her eyes and Adam slithers his arm on the back of her chair.

The doctor clears his throat, taking the tools he needs to check me out. It's the same old song and dance. I've seen at least three different ENT specialists, all of which kept an eye on me until I was eight years old. I have an inner ear problem, had tubes put in my ears when I was a kid, and had thirteen ear infections from the time I was one until age two or three. Daddy said it was nothing and I was weak. But Mama knew something was wrong. It didn't take doctors long to diagnose me, and once the tubes were put in, the fluid was able to drain from my ears. No more hearing tests, no more ear infections. Only speech therapy. And I had slight hearing loss, but I was cleared.

Here I am again after twenty years.

I wince and suck my teeth as he pokes and prods my ear, looking inside it with a light and I yelp when he tugs on the top of it to look deeper. Zay uncrosses her legs and sits up straighter. By the pinch in her brow and the way she nibbles her bottom lip, she's worried.

With a nod, he clicks his pen and jots something down on that clipboard that will be added to my long list of medical injuries from the time I was a child.

But I don't think this injury is going to be a good one.

"What's the verdict?" Adam asks, lifting his leg and dangling it off his knee by the ankle.

"You have ear barotrauma, Mister Donnelly." The doctor tucks his pen away and places the clipboard under his arm. "There isn't much we can do, but you'll be hearing a slight ringing for a little while. And depending on how severe the rupture is, it could last a week to a few months."

I scoff, getting off the table and shaking my head. "How severe is it?"

He eyes Zaynab again, giving her a once-over. It makes my hands clench into fists and my rage boils. She's stunning, but this is not the time to check out a patient's ex-girlfriend. "Your inner ear is too swollen to inspect. I'll prescribe anti-inflammatories and I'd like to see you in a couple of weeks if possible."

"Cool, we done here?" I ask, running my fingers through my hair.

The doctor shifts on his feet, slightly frightened by my presence. I mean, who wouldn't be? My daddy is as tall as a tree, Riggs is only an inch shorter than him and I'm 6'4". We're a bunch of tall motherfuckers. This doctor is right to be afraid of me.

"Peter," Zaynab growls quietly.

I eye her and sigh, folding my arms across my chest. "What're the side effects, doc?"

He swallows hard, hands shaking as he takes his prescription pad from the pocket of his lab coat. "Take this three times a day with food for fourteen days. When these are finished, come back and I'll give you the verdict about the damage done to your ear."

"I got tubes when I was a kid," I add, standing taller.

The intimidation factor gives me a chubby, and seeing this guy falter before me is doing just that. I'm trying to keep it together because I promised I wouldn't touch Zaynab anymore. But I'd be lying if I said I didn't want to bend her over this table and fuck her silly to show how intimidating I can be.

"D-depending on the severity of the damage, there can be permanent hearing loss, a ruptured eardrum, or absolutely no damage at all. T-the ringing will slowly taper off and your hearing will come back once the swelling comes down," the doctor says, handing me the prescription. "Let me know if you have any other questions."

"Yeah." I take the paper and stuff it in my pocket. "Thanks, doc."

He scans us once more and leaves the room so quickly. I don't think he realizes he forgot his prescription pad on the table. *Don't mind if I do.*

Adam sputters, leaning forward with his hands on his knees. "Well, fuck."

I stuff the prescription pad in my back pocket and scowl at Zay. "Think I might go back on my promise, sweetie, as payback for what you did to my ear."

She grits, baring her teeth. "No, you fucking won't. You deserved this, jackass."

"That isn't fucking happening, Peter. You and my wife are done," Adam says, rising from his seat as if he thinks he can intimidate me.

Fucker is only 6'1", he got the short gene because he's not a true Donnelly like Riggs and I. Yet, seeing those big blue eyes stare up at me trying to act all tough for a woman reminds me of us as kids.

I used to get into a lot of fights at school, Riggs would defend me, but it came to a halt when he left school. All I had was Adam. He had my back, defending me, taking punches for me, and putting a kid in the hospital because he bad-mouthed my mama. He was my best friend, he still is sometimes…until Zaynab came into the picture. Once she entered it, I lost him as my brother.

Adam can fight, I'll give him that, but I'm still trying to wrap my head around him being able to hold a gun with those shaky hands.

Hands that are shaking at his side right now.

"You still haven't explained to me why you saw Daddy without coming to me first," I say, eyeing Zaynab as she fixes her shorts around those legs I miss having wrapped around me.

But maybe it's the right time to let her go. Dorian has been swirling around in my head. I'm craving the way I feel in her presence. Supported? No, powerful.

Zaynab owns my heart, but Dorian is chipping away at it. Moseying her way in.

And as much as it hurts not to be with Zay anymore, my heart's fluttering again. Things will look up and maybe, just maybe, I can get out of this and start a life like Riggs has. He's happy, isn't he? Being away from this life and away from the chaos it comes with.

Maybe one day, I'll have that life. Leaving all my hatred and wicked ways behind me.

Maybe one day, I'll have a woman to call mine like Adam calls Zay his.

Maybe one day.

Adam clears his throat, holding his hand out to Zay. "I've been told to fix things, brother."

"Yeah, and how's that turning out for you, huh?" I cross my arms, tilting my head down. "I'm the VP of this club, you fucking run shit by me before doing anything—"

"Daddy told me not to," Adam interrupts me. "What the hell was I supposed to do, huh? He called me. He reached out to me, and when I told him what happened, he gave me orders. And the last time I checked, Daddy was still in charge."

Sucking my teeth, I shake my head which makes the ringing more intense. Zay got me good.

Groaning, I massage my temple as a blinding migraine finally rises to the surface. I need a goddamn drink. Fuck that, I need a bottle to get me wasted tonight. I'll feel better once I pass the fuck out.

"Bullshit," I say under my breath.

Zay touches my arm and sighs. "Let's just get you home."

"Come with me," I tease with a wink.

"Shut up," she says, narrowing her eyes.

If Adam knows any better, he'll hide who the hell he's with and make sure the Panthers stay the fuck away from her. If anything happens to Zay, I'll burn down everything in my path to find out who hurt her. Everything.

***

Adam stepped away to use the washroom, the fast food joint we stopped at for dinner didn't agree with him very well. So it's just Zay and I sitting in a booth at the clubhouse in front of each other, silently sipping our whiskeys.

"How's your ear?" she asks, swirling her glass on the table.

Lifting the glass, the caramel-colored liquid sloshes about before I smirk. "This plus the pain meds are definitely a gift from God Himself." The doctor didn't prescribe me pain meds, but thanks to his handy-dandy prescription pad, I was able to prescribe the same shit I took when she stabbed me in the neck.

Loved me those painkillers.

She chuckles, looking up at me through those long lashes. "Sorry about that, by the way. I didn't know what else to do when I saw you guys wrestling on the grass." She sits back and clicks her tongue. "I could've just showered you with water and watched as you two slowly undressed each other—"

I start laughing. "What the fuck? We're not part of some sex dream you've conjured up, sweetie. He's my brother."

She wrinkles her nose, giving me that laugh that's put me on my knees since I met her. "Leave me alone, it's my fantasy."

Another laugh leaves me, she was always good at making me laugh. Even when I dated Lillian, half our arguments were because of Zaynab and how much I idolized her, stared at her, laughed with her, and asked about her. She wasn't wrong. Zaynab is the air I breathe. But my air is slipping away, and like the good man I want to become, I'm going to let her go.

I'll wear my oxygen mask until Dorian has the same effect on me. And she will because she's unique like Zay. She'll become the woman to raise my babies. I'll make sure of it.

"I missed this," I tell Zay, watching as she licks the whiskey from her lips. "You, mostly."

She shakes her head, looking over at some of the guys playing pool. "Yeah, as much as I hate you, it's nice to get back to our talks like we used to have. Back when being university students was our biggest worry."

Those hazel eyes appear glazed, shaken. I don't like seeing sadness on her face, but it seems that's the only emotion she knows how to fathom.

Because of me.

"Things will get better, Zaynab, I promise you." I reach my hand out to her, trying to reassure her. She doesn't take it. She just stares at it like it's foreign to her. "I...I fucked-up."

Yep, so those words left my mouth and were directed at her.

I knew what I was doing when I forced myself on her. I knew what I was doing when I made the initial threat. But I never realized how torturous it was until now. Until I stopped.

Seeing the hatred in her eyes in a new light, the pain I put her through, the constant disappointment when she didn't love me back. She'll never love me as I love her.

Never.

"You did," she whispered.

I groan, closing my eyes and thinking about Riggs and what he would do. Would he make this better? Or worse?

Better, like our mother would do.

"Please tell me you can forgive me one day and that we can go back to being the friends we used to be. I miss being your friend, Zay. I just…miss you—"

"Like the study sessions that would keep us up all night until we stumbled into some party we shouldn't have been at just to get away from our work," she interrupts me with a smirk. "Gosh, the hours on end we spent sitting on your bed cramming last minute because we chose to party instead of study…I won't lie, university isn't the same without you."

Downing the rest of my whiskey, I lean forward. "Well, I'm not the same man anymore, Zay. And you're not the same woman, I assure you that. But I—"

I snap my mouth shut, stopping words from leaving my lips and spewing all over the table. Zay, however, wants more. I can read it on her face. That hopeful gaze that maybe we can rekindle an amazing friendship. I'm not the same man I once was. I'm tainted, ruined. I'm a fucking snake like the rest of the fucks in this bar.

We sure did have fun. And maybe we can have it again, as friends this time.

"We're still the same, Peter. We'll never change."

We hold each other's gaze for a few seconds before that tongue darts out of her mouth and licks her bottom lip, catching my attention. She brings the glass is brought to her lips, tilting it to me.

"Would we still be floating?"

A smile tries to make itself known. But she stops it, why does she do that?

"If this past year didn't happen. If I never met Adam, then yes. We'd be floating so high Peter, I'd never want to come down without you," she says, putting her hand out.

I catch it immediately and thread our fingers. Closure. The perfect kind of closure for my story with Zaynab. The woman who captured my heart and left it floating in that water, never to return. "I'm sorry, sweetie. Truly."

Adam walks out of the washroom, rubbing his stomach. He nods at Roaden before heading our way. In some lights, we look so much alike. And right now is one of those times. His hair is in disarray, his mouth agape, and his eyes are locked on the prettiest woman I've ever had the opportunity to be with.

"Hey, babe, ready to go?" Adam asks, belching quietly behind his hand.

She nods, looking at me, and slips her hand from mine. Our closure. We needed this talk, and who knows, maybe we'll have more in the future. "Ready when you are."

I slide out of the booth and put my hand out to her.

She takes it again and it makes all the bells and whistles inside me jump with joy.

"I'll talk to you soon, okay?" I say and pull her into a hug, inhaling that exotic coconut perfume that sends tingles to my dick, twitching it to stone. Goddamn, I'm going to relieve this in the shower as soon as she leaves.

She squeezes, arms wrapped around my neck. "Promise me you'll move on and find someone so perfect for you it feels like your heart will explode."

I chuckle, winking at Adam and burying my face into her neck. "I already have her."

"Not me," she whispers.

"I know."

She releases me and it feels like weights have fallen onto me, restricting my breaths. "We'll see you around."

Adam holds his hand out, giving me props as Zay threads their fingers together.

It's time, isn't it?

Time to give myself to someone new.

To release this hold she has on me.

This love reminds me of Mama. How open she is with me. How truthful. How she laughs with me when it matters most.

Now all that matters is her happiness.

I cut that tie I have with Zay because I know deep down, as much as I love this woman and want her in my life, she'll never be more than a girl I floated high with all those years ago.

I have to open my eyes to new adventures.

Maybe adventures away from this club. Giving up my VP patch will be hard, but if I can make a woman smile and love me for me, then maybe getting out of this business is the way to go.

Taking my phone out, I walk to my room and send another quick message to Dorian.

Maybe I'll slide into her life, I'm a hoot to have around.

And Dorian doesn't know anything about my past.

Promise me you'll move on and find someone so perfect for you it feels like your heart will explode.

I will, sweetie, and I'm starting tonight.

Zay

Six months ago, I came to see Peter on our usual Tuesday afternoon. He didn't look particularly happy when I showed up, but he didn't look particularly mad, either.

There was something on his mind, something that distracted him from tearing my clothes off and taking me where I stood. Usually, I barely made it to the bed and he was already inside me. A couple of times, when no one was in the bar area, he'd bend me over the pool table or throw me on one of the leather couches. And only once, he had his way with me on the motorcycle club's table with the large snake etched into it.

But this time, something was off.

I opened his door and knocked softly, letting myself in as he sat on his bed in nothing but his jeans, unbuttoned at the waist. A cigarette dangled from his mouth, but he wasn't smoking it. It's like he forgot it was there.

"Hey," I said, closing the door behind me. For the first time in months, I felt like maybe he'd forgotten about our deal. That maybe he'd finally agree to let me go.

But forgetting was never the case with him…

He slowly turned his head, cigarette falling from his mouth and onto the floor. His eyes were red, but no tears were present.

For a good twenty seconds, he just stared at me. No blinking, not even a twitch of his mouth. The way he stared was frightening. Maybe I did something wrong? Maybe he was on drugs again and I would reap the tail end of that…maybe something happened to Riggs?

Tucking my hair behind my ear nervously, I tongued my cheek and shifted my gaze away from his to the cigarette on the floor. "Y-you okay?"

He sniffed, finally blinking, and dropped his light blue lighter on the floor as well. I always liked that lighter. It was a gift from Lillian. I remember that because he laughed when she gave it to him and told her he didn't smoke. But she wanted him to keep it anyway because it had a daisy on it, and daisies were her favorite.

"You ever wonder what will happen to you once you die?" he said, his voice hoarse and scratchy.

I took a step back, hitting the door, my left side taking the blow from the doorknob. "What're you talking about?"

He cleared his throat and sniffed again. "When all is said and done, do you think everything we do in life will matter? When our hearts stop beating, does it matter if we're good or bad?" He let out a shaky breath. "Where do we go?" he whispered.

Shrugging, I gripped the doorknob behind my back. "It all depends on what you believe."

He glanced at me again, eyebrows furrowing, and that's when tears welled in his eyes. "What if I don't believe in anything?"

I followed that single, thick tear that rolled down his freckled cheek and winced when I felt the emotion he oozed, as if I knew exactly how he felt. Broken.

When in reality, I had no idea what he was talking about. In reality, I hated this man for what he did to me and now I sympathized with him.

The Peter I knew before everything happened began to shine through. I saw it in the quiver of his bottom lip and the way his thick eyebrows pinched together.

The psychotic bitch in me stepped over to him with the intent to comfort him. Everything this man put me through had been uplifted by the sight of his tears. Something was wrong. Peter never cries.

The last time I saw him cry was after Lillian's funeral.

Standing in front of him, I was unsure of what to do. But he pulled me in by the waist and sobbed onto my dress, hugging me tightly. I let him sob and rid whatever demons were eating at him. Had all the disturbing thoughts in his head finally caught up with him?

For the first time, I pitied the man I tried to kill.

He held me, his arms wrapped around my hips and face buried into my stomach, and wept for a good five minutes, relaxing after a couple of them and recovering when he inhaled me.

Running my fingers through his hair a few times, I wondered when would be a good time for me to leave, but I couldn't do that to him.

Not now anyway.

He winced, then whimpered and looked up at me, those blue eyes so damn blue they sparkled like the sea. "I'm in love with you, Zaynab."

Everything crashed into me.

The air was gone.

Reality snapped.

The earth fell off its axis.

Parts of me knew this was the case. What self-respecting man would allow himself to sleep with his best friend's wife over something she had nothing to do with? *Someone has to pay for her mistakes.* Lillian was the reason for all of this and yet I paid her dues.

I never wanted to believe it.

"You shouldn't," I whispered, trying to back away from him but his hold on me only tightened.

His lower lip quivered again. "I'm trying not to."

Looking away from him to a poster that always intrigued me. A woman in a leopard print leotard stood beside a bike. Her eyes were black, staring over her shoulder at the camera. A gun in one hand and a cigarette in the other as smoke billowed at her feet. Her expression was emotionless, but something about it spoke volumes. She was on her own, protecting herself from whatever was to come.

It was her against the world. She reminded me of myself.

No one helped me escape my fate, everyone allowed it to happen. My husband, Riggs, and even Peter had to have known this deal we were doing was wrong, yet he still did it. Still slept with me every Tuesday like I was some lowlife whore.

Every day I held my head high knowing that one day life would throw me a bone and all this would be behind me. A story of that one time a motorcycle club took over my life.

Peter released me, sniffling again as I stepped back and he rested his elbows on his knees. "Did you know today would've been my mama's birthday?" I shook my head, tucking hair behind my ear again. "You remind me of her sometimes. Little quirks, y'know." He smirked, rubbing one of his eyes. "Way you click your tongue when something's funny. How you roll your eyes at my stupidity. And just the kindness—you've always been so kind to me. Saw potential in me when no one else did. Guess it doesn't matter now, though. Guess it never really mattered."

Opening my mouth to speak, yet nothing but air left my lips. There was nothing to say to him, nothing to pity. Yet parts of me wanted to sympathize with his pain. But how could I have done that when all he did was hurt me?

He put his head in his hands again and a quiet sob left him, his shoulders shaking. The air in the room was heavy. Mourning blessed us this afternoon with painful memories that were spread across the bed. I hadn't noticed them before but there were pictures of Peter and Riggs as kids. Their mother was there, too. Adam as well. They looked so happy.

Free.

My eyes jumped from photo to photo, seeing the beautiful woman with long brown hair and freckles, just like Peter. Things must've been different back then because there's a photo of Riggs with her and he was smiling. I don't think I've ever seen Riggs smile that wide. He looked genuinely happy. They all looked happy.

Her death ruined them, it was evident in the way Peter's shoulders were slumped and by the tears running down his nose. Her death broke them, it was the only explanation as to why they are the way they are.

I took another step back, readying to leave when he whimpered, making me ache for him. I was never close to my parents. Wealth and travel were more important than me. I don't think I'd ever act like this if they died and their birthday rolled around.

I wouldn't mourn. I'd rejoice.

Seeing his pain, the misery he deserves, made me get on my knees and leave a soft kiss on his arm. "Look at me," I whispered.

All he did was shake his head.

So I sat there and waited until he relaxed. Waited for over twenty minutes until he finally dropped his hands and found mine, kissing my knuckles a couple of times.

"You didn't have to stay, Zaynab." He sniffed. "You *don't* have to stay, it's fine."

That sympathetic bone aching for him rose significantly and I kissed his knee. "I want to."

A smile touched my lips as I reached over for a photo of Riggs and Peter when they were kids wrapping their arms around their mother. Riggs was always tall and always had that smirk that would let him get away with murder, maybe even death if he flashed it at the devil.

"Tell me about her," I said, putting the picture back.

It was the first time since we met that I'd ever seen Peter truly happy. He beamed when he spoke about his mother, her beauty was unable to be matched, and her kindness was heartwarming.

All she wanted was a better life for her boys. Life outside this club and this madness.

Instead, what she got were her two sons running this club and killing all the demons that came in their path. Ruling the roads was a tough game, but Riggs and Peter knew how to do it.

If only they knew how to sprinkle good on this world like their mother.

Dorian

Looking down at my phone, a text message from Peter pops up. I haven't seen him since Friday and we're Monday evening. I've been avoiding my cell phone all day because I chose to take another day off. Just one more day in my house, but I don't get to be alone.

Gray and Bells haven't left yet. They were supposed to be out on Saturday, but they're still here. Still invading. Still consuming. Still worrying like I'm an invalid.

I wanted one day alone where no one asks me how I'm doing or what I need.

Sleep. That's what I need. Hours on end of sleep.

I received Peter's text around eleven in the morning, but I ignored it, Zaynab's words circling my head.

Stay away from him, whatever you do, stay the fuck away.

But why?

Who the heck knows why? The only way to know is to pry for answers, and do I really want to do that? Peter's a criminal biker, Zaynab is presumably his ex-girlfriend—it was obvious from how he stared at her. I don't need that drama in my life. I just need a release.

Sinking deeper in the tub, maybe if I get off, I might be able to feel a little better. That release I need to rid the tension in my neck and the disturbing thoughts from my head since Peter crashed into my life.

Slithering my hand between my legs, I touch myself and close my eyes, feeling Erin's lips on my neck, his shaft poking me from behind as he watches me over my shoulder touching his favorite thing to snack on.

Yet I feel Peter's hand gripping my hips, biting on my neck as my back arches. Then my legs twitch, and it's a sign that I'm close—so close, thanks to Peter.

This isn't good.

Then, I hear Gray's heavy footfalls clanking up the steps. She has no sense of personal space. All I want is to be alone.

To do this until I feel better.

To watch TV.

To eat chocolate and cry.

To sit in my bedroom and stare at Erin's things and wonder what to do with them.

Do I toss them? Donate them? Be a pack rat and hold onto everything he's ever touched?

Our love story is my favorite. We happened fast and ended fast like it never existed.

And thinking back, maybe it didn't.

***

Erin's hands were covering my eyes, my hands out in front of me, and he chuckled as I walked so carefully, scared to trip. "I got you, babes," he said, kissing my cheek. "All right, keep your eyes closed after I move my hands, yeah?"

I giggled, nodding my head and squeezing my eyes shut when he removed his hands. "Erin?"

"I'm right here," he said, his voice traveling away from me. "Okay, ready? Open those gorgeous eyes."

So I did. He stood there with his arms fanned out and a bottle of champagne in hand standing in from of a house. He bought us a house.

"Oh, my God! W-what?" I stammered and chuckled while holding in my tears. "You—is this ours?"

He took my hand and led us to the front door. "It's all ours, babes. It needs a little work and a paint job—the bathroom is pink with turquoise tiles." He chuckled, tucking the champagne under his arm and getting the keys from his pocket. "But see beyond that, yeah?"

He opened the front door to a dark green kitchen, wood countertops, and oak wood floors. The ceilings featured beams that spanned the entire open concept into the living room and dining room. I had a hand on my mouth as he showed me around, telling me which room was what.

He told me about his ideas for the rooms, how he'd paint them, and his vision for the place. I barely absorbed his words. All I saw was us in the future. The house filled with kids.

Happiness beyond despair.

He pulled me upstairs, taking me to the bathroom first. "See, pink and turquoise tiles."

Pushing my lips together, I wrapped my arms around his waist. "Is it weird I kinda like it?"

He smirked, that dimple poking through. "Then we'll leave this tacky bathroom untouched."

I scrunched my nose as he kissed the tip of it. "It's *our* tacky bathroom, though."

"You and me, babes." He smiled leading me to the master bedroom and spun in a circle.

He was beautiful. A smile that brightened up his face, teeth that sparkled, a symmetrical jawline, and those brown eyes. They were mine. All mine.

"I love you," I said, chuckling as he shook the champagne.

He held the bottle at me and smirked. "How much?"

I put my hand up, laughing. "Erin, wait a second."

He laughed, stepping closer to me as he loosened the cork. "How much, babes?"

He popped it, spraying champagne all over me and laughing as he held onto me and drenched us in champagne.

The house was empty, but pouring champagne all over the wood floors couldn't be good for it. Although, I'd give anything to have that moment back.

Laughing, I wiped champagne from my chest. "We have to clean this up."

He kissed me and dropped the champagne bottle, his hands traveling up my skirt. "Later. We have a lot of christening to do in this house first."

I smiled, biting his bottom lip. "Like right now?"

He spun me, pushing me against the salmon-colored walls of our future bedroom, and lifted the back of my skirt. "Wore this thong for me, didn't you?" He slapped my ass and unzipped his jeans.

I pulled my underwear down to my knees and waited for him to take me. "Only for you."

He gripped my ass and parted my legs, putting two fingers inside me. "Gosh, you're so wet."

I moaned when he pulled his fingers out and eased his shaft into me. "Only for you. Always for you."

He thrust quickly, lifting my backside higher so he could go deeper. Sex with Erin was always spontaneous. It was my favorite thing about him. We never planned sex, never questioned if we didn't do it or why we didn't.

The first time we made love was in the backseat of his car after he picked me up for a movie date. We never made it to the movie. He also didn't know it was my first time until we were done. I didn't care, Erin was supposed to be my one and only.

I moaned loudly and he slapped my ass again, grunting and groaning. "Harder!"

He slapped me again and pulled out of me, forcing me onto the floor. I kicked the underwear off of me and opened my legs for him and he stood above me, staring down at what was his. "Perfect."

"Come back," I said, propping myself up on my elbows.

He started touching himself, just staring at me, so I opened my legs wider. "I want to come inside you."

Reaching down, I circled my sex with my fingers, emitting a gasp from him. "I'm not on birth control anymore."

He got on his knees, still touching himself as champagne dripped from his face, and he watched as I slid my fingers inside me. "I'm coming inside you." He took my hand, putting my fingers in his mouth to taste me. "We're starting a family. Me and you, babes."

Biting my lip, I sat up, taking his face and kissing him. He smiled against them, pushing me back and finishing me off with his tongue. A tongue that always felt so good.

He entered me again, taking me hard and rough on the floors of our new house.

Our moans moved through the emptiness.

Our moans escalated when we neared our climax.

He finished inside me, grunting loudly in my ear. "Always for you."

Wrapping my arms around his neck, I sighed. "We're trying for a baby?"

He lifted his head and smiled. "It's a three-bedroom. We gotta fill this house, don't we?"

Our laughter moved through the home, remaining there for three years until it stopped.

The laughter just stopped.

***

"Dorian?" Gray's voice sounds on the other side of the door. "You okay in there?"

Groaning out of frustration, I remove my hand from between my legs. "Yeah, just getting off—out."

Wrapping myself in a towel, I stare at myself in the mirror. There are bags under my eyes so apparent that I look like a new mom just trying to catch a break.

Erin and I tried to have a baby for three years, giving up about a year and six months before he died. It didn't get us down, though. My doctor said it might be related to my weight. I'm fifty-five pounds overweight. If I have to redesign myself, then maybe I wasn't meant to have a baby naturally. Yes, it was upsetting, but we had plans. We were going to adopt or find a surrogate.

There were options.

But he died and our options died with him.

Opening the door to Gray smiling on the other side of it, I forced a grin. "Hey, sis, down for a board game with Bells and me?" she asks, shimmying her shoulders.

I let out a pained chuckle and shake my head. "It's almost nine and I have work tomorrow."

Gray taps the doorframe, pushing her lips together. "Right. Okay, then. Well, um, Bells and I are going job hunting tomorrow. So we won't be here most of the day."

Shit, why couldn't that be today?

"No problem, see you for dinner, then," I say, looking at my bedroom door, then back at her.

Gray nibbles her bottom lip and sighs. "Fuck, sorry, I can't hold it in anymore. Why won't you talk to me, Dorian?" She sighs, shaking her head. "Erin died and you haven't cried once."

Yes, I have.

She raises her hands and drops them at her sides. "I'm worried about you. You used to talk to me and tell me everything that went on in that head of yours, and now…talk to me."

I clear my throat and adjust the towel. "Well, my husband died, Gray. It's not something easy to talk about. Some people are overcome with emotion in death. I am not. I cry when I need to. I'm strong when I need to. But I'm…okay. I'll be okay."

No, I won't.

"Do you want me and Bells to stay with you?" she asks, eyebrows raised and pinched together. "I'm scared to leave you alone."

Scared of what? That I'll kill myself? Clearly, my sister doesn't know me at all.

Letting out a rush of air, I force another lopsided grin. "You and Bells are welcome to stay as long as you like."

Shit.

She smiles, wrapping her arms around me. "When you're ready, I'm here, okay? I'm here and willing to listen to you rant about how cruel the world is and how everyone shouldn't have died instead of him because he was an amazing person, sis. He was your person."

He was, and now he's dead. And I can mourn in my own way.

"I know." I pat her back and step away from her, needing my moment alone.

I'm starting work tomorrow. That means a day filled with sympathetic gazes from the people who don't know me from a hole in the wall.

Flowers and cards will be scattered all over my desk.

Voicemails and emails will be in my inbox.

I won't get any peace other than my moments in the bathroom.
Tomorrow has become my nightmare.

335

Dorian

I did it.

I made it through a workday.

It's almost three and I'm ready to call it quits when I look up at see Peter talking to the secretary; a sultry grin on his face.

What is he doing here? Better yet, how did he know to find me here?

I don't mind it, he's been on my mind for days and I've only known him for a little over a week. This isn't good. Being infatuated with someone so soon after Erin is making me feel like I never really loved him at all. But I did, I still do. How can I live with the thought of wanting someone new when he'll always be tangled in my soul?

Shit, Peter looks so good right now...*I wonder what he tastes like*—stop.

Sitting down again, I stare at the fifteen unread emails I haven't gotten to yet. I had a total of one hundred and eighty-five when I walked in this morning. None of them were important. Mostly reminders for upcoming deadlines, the staff lunch next week, and the multiple ads from Macy's and Ralph Laurent. Useless garbage that makes me regret coming to work at all.

Taking my water bottle, I gulp from it until it's finished, staring at Peter as he runs his fingers through his hair again, using that charm on the secretary.

She's easy to impress, even the partner of this firm turns her on, and he's seventy-one, overweight, bald, and has a lisp.

I glance at the candy dish I've been attacking all day, then open and close my mouth so my teeth hit each other. *What the hell is he doing here?*

Am I happy he's here? Annoyed?

No, I want him here because the sick part of me wants people to see that

I'm not lonely. I can be happy again. *What the hell is wrong with me?*

Instead, I open the newest email from someone named Liam Ignassio, but I don't get to read it because the secretary knocks on my door, smiling on the other side of it. The partner likes everything to be made of glass. There is no privacy in this office, no blinds to separate the office beside mine. Just glass as far as the eye can see.

Peter smirks when he sees me, tonguing his cheek to hide his smile. "Hey, Dorian."

The secretary giggles quietly, looking back at Peter. "Says you have a meeting. I didn't see him on your calendar."

I look him up and down. Dark wash jeans, grey v-neck t-shirt, and low top Converse that have seen better days. I could turn him away and tell him to leave me alone. I could tell him to shove it. I can call security.

Probably the smarter of the choices.

But that itch only he can scratch comes to life inside me.

Rising from my seat, I lean on my desk. "My head has been a little fuzzy lately. Yes, we did have a, uh, meeting."

She nods, stepping aside so Peter can walk in. He winks at her and comes right up to me, sitting on the side of my desk and looking over his shoulder at the secretary to close the door. "Okay, Mrs. Wallis. Don't forget, you have a nine o'clock with the boss tomorrow."

I nod, forcing a grin. "In my calendar."

There it is. That look everyone has been giving me all day. Soft smile. Eyebrows raised slightly. Sympathetic gaze.

Sorry for your loss.

If there's anything you need, I'm just a phone call away.

Such a tragedy.

I'm here for you.

Died before his time, it isn't right.

No, what's not right is people thinking they know how I'm feeling. I understand the sympathy, it's normal to do when someone dies. But enough.

Just stop!

"It's good to have you back," she adds before closing the door.

Taking a breath, I slowly flicker my gaze to Peter, swallowing slowly as that smirk is still on his face. "What're you doing here?"

He slips my business card from his pocket and taps it on his hand. "You gave me one of these, remember?" He looks down at it with a smile. "You also ignored my texts. I don't like being ignored."

I roll my eyes and sit down. "I'm sure you're rarely ignored, Peter."

He laughs, slipping my business card back into his pocket. "Believe me, Dorian, a pretty face like mine gets ignored, too."

The arrogance he oozes is annoying.

But also a turn-on.

Why can't I shy away from him?

Why is this doing it for me?

Shit, I miss Erin.

I'm sorry.

"What do you want from me? Did I not pay for the damages already?" I ask, standing on my feet again and packing my things.

He takes my wrist as I go to grab my phone, his thumb grazing the veins on my inner part. "You did, I just wanted to see you again."

I wanted to see him again, too, but I can never admit to that.

If I know what's good for me I'll leave him alone.

Just tell him to leave, Dorian, tell him to stay out of your life.

That itch is back again, and he's the only one who can scratch it.

My breathing shudders when he looks down at our hands. He threads our fingers together and chuckles softly, clicking his tongue. "Wouldja look at that? We fit perfectly together, don't we?"

I wince and snatch my hand away from his, packing the rest of my things and walking out of the office before I break down in tears. I don't need this.

Not today.

Today marks the twenty-first day I lost Erin.

Twenty-one days without him holding me.

Kissing me.

Being with me.

Twenty-one fucking days and I'm already thinking of being with another man.

Peter follows after me but doesn't say anything. He follows me to the elevator and catches my reflection in the stainless steel doors. That's when I let go, I put my head down and sob softly. Muffling the sounds with the back of my hand.

The doors open and he places his hand on my lower back to guide me inside so no one else can see me. And as soon as the doors close I lose it.

Sobbing harder than I ever have.

I barely cried when Erin died. I was in shock. I was angry. Most of all, I wished I had the chance to tell him *I'm sorry*.

Sorry for the arguments before the end.

Sorry for not loving him enough.

For not cherishing him.

I'm just sorry.

Peter presses the lobby button, then embraces me, forcing my forehead on his chest. "It's okay, I got you."

He holds me tightly, smoothing out my hair as I weep. Kindness, that's what he oozes now. Not the hatred I suspected because of Zaynab.

Thoughtful kindness.

The elevator dings, opening the doors to the lobby. But neither of us moves. I keep my face buried on his chest and he keeps holding me, lowering his cheek to rest it on my head.

He presses the button for the parking garage as people pile in, and he inhales me, leaving a kiss on my head. "I got you," he whispers.

I'm happy he does because if he lets me go, I might fall to my knees.

The pressure of everyone sympathizing with me today got the better of me. I wasn't ready to come back. I don't think I'm ready to start life again without Erin. I want to stay in limbo for a little while. Play with Peter in limbo until I feel better.

A couple of people whisper, probably staring. But I don't move. I don't look up. I keep my eyes closed and focus on the shaky breaths Peter's taking. Is he nervous because of me?

It's only a fraction of a second before the elevator doors open again and I sniff as he walks us out of the elevator and into the parking garage. The scent of tires and mildew swarm us, and that stagnant heat from outside lingers in the air making everything sticky.

I feel better now, relieved, even.

I break down in private. Away from everyone because they don't need to see me sad. Or see the guilt riding through me.

I should have stayed home today. Taken one more week of solitude before I ventured out into the real world. But I couldn't last another day in the presence of my sister and her girlfriend. I love them, don't get me wrong, but this is too much for me. And I'm too nice to tell them no.

Peter stops when we reach the first cement pillar and moves my face away from his chest.

"I'm okay," I spit out, sniffling and wiping my eyes.

He holds my face and brushes his thumbs under my eyes, assuming to clean my makeup. "No, you're not. This is the second time you've broken down in front of me. What's up?"

I don't know why I feel so comfortable around him to do that.

I've cried for weeks on end, but alone.

No one has seen me cry. Not even Gray.

At Erin's funeral, I was strong. Composed.

Didn't break down in front of anyone.

Instead, I screamed into my pillow the night before we buried him. Cried my eyes out locked in the washroom before they closed his casket, and broke down in front of Peter on my way home.

No one but Peter has seen me cry. And it bothers me to my core.

Maybe there's something about him. Something trustworthy that Zaynab doesn't know about. Or doesn't see.

Maybe I need to see it more, too.

Maybe, just maybe.

Swallowing hard, I move away from his grip. My lower lip trembles along with my voice. My breathing shakes, but I manage to take a few deep breaths and let it out. "My, um, husband died twenty-one days ago."

He blows out a rush of air and runs his fingers through his hair. Speechless, much like everyone else is when they find out.

I don't need his sympathy.

I don't want it.

I think I want one thing from him. A release to set me free.

"That's...fucked." He shakes his head. "I lost my mama when I was eighteen, it sucks to lose someone close to you." He shrugs a shoulder. "But you go through it, eventually you get over it. Of course, it still hurts when you think about them and it makes you sad when you look at pictures, but it was their time, right? Everyone has an expiry date. Your husband's was twenty-one days ago and my mama's was almost six years ago." He brushes a tear from my cheek and slides his hands into his pockets.

He doesn't tell me *I'm sorry for your loss*.

He doesn't tell me *if there's anything you need, I'm here for you*.

He doesn't say *he died before his time*.

He says *that's fucked*, and for some reason that means a lot more than any, *I'm sorry for your loss*.

I sniff again, exhaling a shaky breath, and chuckle. "Yeah, it is pretty fucked."

He grins, lowering his head with his gaze still locked with mine. "You need a drink? I think we should go for a drink."

I shake my head, fixing my purse on my shoulder. "I think I should head home."

"C'mon, everyone's gotta eat, right? Let me buy you a burger. I know this great place—"

"Peter," I interrupt him. "I'm not ready to do this."

He raises his head, shoulders slouching. "It's just food. Don't think anything of it."

Slowly licking my lips, I stare at him. His blue eyes smile, giving me hope that this might not be the end for me.

But what am I going to do with a biker?

Stereotypically, they're dangerous.

Killers.

He can be the most handsome and charming man, but that won't change a thing when it comes to my well-being.

What am I getting myself into?

***

Peter sips his beer, licking the foam from his lips, and places his forearms on the table. "Figure out what you're getting?"

I close the menu and bite the inner part of my cheek with a nod. "Do you?"

He smiles, sitting back. "Can't go wrong with a bacon burger."

Forcing myself to look away from the intense look in his eyes, I spot faded scratches on his neck. Was he with someone recently or are those scars?

My eyes trail up to his face again as he brushes his hair back, revealing his ears, one redder than the other. I point at my ear curious to know why it's so red. "What happened?"

He touches his ear and flinches slightly. "Long story. But now I got something called ear barotrauma." He opens his mouth to unblock his ear. "Can't hear shit out of it other than this pestering ringing."

"Is there anything to make it better?"

He smirks, tongue darting out and dragging along his bottom lip. "Sound of your voice helps."

Clenching my thighs together, I take my wine, letting it slide down my throat in two gulps. I haven't had the intensity of someone's stare like this since Erin. It pains me day in and out that our last conversation, ended with him storming out of the house and driving off. A drive that became his final—

"So, tell me, what kind of lawyer are you?" Peter asks, watching my lips as I lick the wine residue from them.

"I started doing family law, but now I mainly deal with environmental issues." I set the wine glass down and clear my throat. "But I don't want to talk about work right now."

He hums, nods his head, and leans forward again. Those long fingers clasp together. "All right, what do you wanna talk about?" He smirks. "Tell me something crazy about you, and I'll tell you something crazy about me."

I chuckle, looking around the restaurant. It's a rustic burger joint that I've been to numerous times. Erin was a vegetarian and liked the way they made the black bean burger here. Maybe this could be the place Peter and I come to for an escape from our lives. That would be something, wouldn't it? "I don't have any crazy stories like I'm sure you do."

He swats a hand in the air. "Nonsense, lay one on me, Dorian."

Biting my lip, I laugh and cover my face. Gosh, it feels good to laugh again. "I once stole perfume because my mother wouldn't let me have it. Is that crazy?"

He scrunches his nose with a laugh, as if it's the cutest thing compared to what his stories might be. "That's adorable."

"I told you I don't do crazy," I say, moving the wine glass on the table. "But I still wear the same brand of perfume today."

He nods, narrowing his eyes. "That floral I smelled on you?"

Thunder claps in the distance, making me look out the window as the sky becomes a darker gray. It hasn't rained in a few weeks, so it seems fitting for a storm to come in when my wedding vows shot out the window the second Peter walked into my office. "Do you have any siblings?" I ask, blinking slowly.

He's staring at me, eyes scanning my torso. His face goes pale for a slip second and he looks down. Something must have happened to him. I can pry, but what use will that do?

How Peter stares at me, studying every feature of my face, and how he held me while I cried. There's something inexplainable connecting us. It's going to be hard to stay away from him.

His foot touches mine, easing up my leg before he grins and gulps some beer. "Yeah, I got an older brother and a half-brother—Adam, you met him a few days ago." I frown, tilting my head to the side. He rolls his eyes at the annoyance of his response. "My daddy cheated on my mama a lot. I think he cheated on her their entire relationship, but my half-brother was the only proof that he cheated."

He smiles slightly. "Like the angel that she was, my mama raised Adam like he were hers." He gulps his beer, then sets the glass down, staring into it. There he goes again, that worrying look on his face. "Riggs was like my daddy. He's only four years older, but he took care of me my whole life. Made sure I was safe, fed, and paid my way through school. My mama tried her best, I remember that, but with a father like mine, it was hard for her...to, um...she didn't like what he did. But Riggs, he did everything he could to keep me from walking in our father's shoes." Peter takes a breath, scrolling his eyes from the table to my torso, and then meets my gaze. "Then my brother left and just stopped caring. So I followed in my daddy's footsteps only to—"

He pauses when the waitress approaches, smiling at us as she takes our order. He doesn't give her that charm he gives me. As she speaks, he keeps his eyes locked with mine, a hint of a grin on his lips.

His life doesn't seem the easiest, something I can't compare to. Something I want to embrace.

I don't want to brag about my upbringing, but it was easy. Parents cared too much and gave us what we wanted. There wasn't a curfew or allowance. If we went out, we were handed money. If we wanted to buy something, we had to do a chore around the house and we were rewarded. Life was easy. Easier for me than Gray. My parents didn't take too well with her being a lesbian, they kept quiet when she came out. Didn't ask her questions, but they also didn't allow her to have friends over anymore. It was tough for a time, probably why Gray dropped out of school. She didn't see the need to make our parents happy when they couldn't see how happy she was coming out.

She felt free and it was the happiest day of my life when she finally told them. I remember her smiles and the big breath she released.

It's taken them a while, but they accept her. They accept Bells.

Everything was back on track. Then Erin died and we derailed once again.

I grin at Peter, a sense of safety with him. That girl, Zaynab, is wrong. Peter is not someone I should stay away from. He's someone I need to be around, I'll help remove him from this chaos. If I remove him from this life and show him that there is more out there than violence, maybe he wouldn't feel abandoned by the only person he loves.

As soon as the waitress leaves, he reaches over and grabs my hand, sliding his thumbs on my knuckles. "Sorry to unload some of my shitty life on you."

I shake my head. "Thank you for trusting me enough to tell me about those parts of your life."

He chuckles dryly, looking down at our hands. I haven't moved mine away yet. *Why aren't I moving my hand away?* "Is your sister the only sibling you have?"

Cracking my thumb knuckles, I gaze out the window as the sky becomes darker and starts drizzling. The clouds yawn, rain pouring from their gaping mouths. "My sister Gray is younger than me by about three years, she and her girlfriend live with me now. We're so entirely different that when people see us together, they don't think we are related."

"How so?" He finishes off his beer and sits back, placing his feet on either side of me under the table. "She as pretty as you."

Heat rushes to my cheeks and I remove my hand before looking down, moving the fork an inch. "She's taller than me, weighs as much as a bag of flour, and cuts her hair short and spiky. She's also more outspoken."

He smirks. "But she's not as pretty as you, huh?"

Laughing softly, I move my hair off my shoulder, then take out my phone. A picture of Erin and I comes to life on the lock screen before I punch in my code and find a picture of Gray. "This is from last year." I hold the phone out to him and he arches an eyebrow, staring at Gray and Bells smiling at the camera, Erin and I are in it, too. "She's got nothing on you."

Taking my phone back, I smile as I stare at Erin. He was picture-perfect. I can't believe he's gone and I'm here on a date with someone. It's that unresolved guilt causing me to do this, I know it. "We also have a brother. Much older than us from my dad's first marriage. He lives in Australia and rarely comes home to visit."

"By that upsetting look on your face, I take it he didn't come to the funeral?" Peter leans forward again and bites his bottom lip. "If that's the case, that's a dick move on his behalf."

I shrug a shoulder. "Wilde's a dick, so it's expected."

A chuckle leaves Peter and he holds my gaze again. Seventeen seconds go by before I blink and the heat rises up my neck, blooming on my cheeks. "Y'know, people walk in and out of our lives. Some we hold onto, others we let go of, and then we meet that one person who changes everything. Every outlook, every thought…everything becomes them. And you, Dorian, have become that person." He takes a shuddered breath, as if that was hard for him to express. Like maybe he doesn't admit his feelings often.

Maybe that's a good thing, but am I ready to jump into something after my husband just died? This is too much, I should get up and leave. Get away from him if I know what's good for me.

But that's the thing, I don't know what's good for me.

"I don't know what to say," I whisper as the waitress returns with our meals and fresh drinks.

He thanks her and nods at my wine as he lifts his beer. "To meeting new and beautiful people."

I raise my glass and flash a hesitant smile. "To meeting new and beautiful people."

He clinks our glasses and takes a swig, winking when he sets his beer down. "I feel like I can float with you. I haven't felt the need to float in years."

Frowning, I smile with wonderment. "What does that even mean?"

He doesn't say anything in response. Instead, he brings the beer to his lips again and gulps, revealing the tiny scars that line his forearm.

He's mysterious, broken, and easy to speak to.

This spells trouble with a capital T, and yet here I am smitten like a moth to a flame.

Peter

We're wet from the rain, shivering, too, as we run into *Judas's Hideout*. The bar is crowded as shit tonight. We had to park at the other end of the parking lot. It's like everyone had the same idea of coming out and drinking to watch this shitty punk band on this rainy night.

But fuck, there isn't anything shitty about this night. Sharing a meal with Dorian has been the most eye-opening experience of my life. We clicked instantly, speaking about everything from our lives to the sun and the stars. We even like the same movies and have read the same books. She's my equal, soon to be my better half. I can feel it.

Zaynab is my world, but that world is tainted with lies and betrayal. And it's never going to gain salvation.

Dorian will be my savior.

We enter the bar and warmth touches our skin. I look back at her and grin, her exposed skin pebbling with goosebumps. Having her by my side sends this undying joy through me. So much more than anything I've ever felt.

I grip her hand tighter and bring her straight to my room. She doesn't need a drink, she needs me. All of me.

There's resistance in our woven hands.

Hesitation.

But I think she wants this as badly as I do. A release to rid that tension in her shoulders because of her dead husband. If she didn't want this, she wouldn't be here, would she?

I wasn't lying when I said there was a reason she walked into my life by ramming the back of my car. We were meant to meet in tragedy.

Dorian walks into my room first and crosses her arms as she looks back at me.

Gorgeous.

Exquisite.

There aren't enough words to describe how happy I am that she gave me a chance. It's my moment to finally move on from the only woman who captured my heart.

I have to let my Zaynab go.

Closing the door, I smirk and let out a soft chuckle. "Thank you for meeting with me." I wave my hand around. "I didn't think you'd want to see me again because of all this."

She jerks one of her shoulders, running her fingers through her wet hair. "Curiosity killed the cat," she says, a soft chuckle leaving her. "You also came to my place of work unannounced."

I bite my lip and stare at her, her dress is soaked and stuck to her body showing me every curve, every edge, every piece of her that I can't wait to unwrap. She's beyond anything I've ever experienced.

"Tell me something," I say, scanning her shivering body. "If I were to kiss you right now, would you let me?"

She swallows hard, eyeing my lips, then meets my eyes. "My husband just died."

I suck in a sharp breath, releasing it slowly. "And if he didn't? If you never met him and I was the only one in the picture, would you then?"

Her lips part to speak, words captured at the tip of her tongue. But she closes her mouth, her head nodding slightly. It's enough for the flutter in my stomach to activate. She stares at my lips as they quirk up into a grin, taking in her delicious beauty.

Her breathing rattles as her hands shake at her sides; she fidgets with each finger, cracking her knuckles one by one. "Nervous?"

"I've only ever been with Erin," she whispers, holding my gaze.

I grin, breaking our gaze as heat rushes up my neck, and stare at the dirty carpet, kicking at an invisible pebble. "Does it bother you that I've been with a lot of women?"

She shakes her head, still staring at me. I'm dying to kiss those pouty lips, they were painted pink today. I wonder what she'd look like with lipstick smeared all over her mouth because of me.

Her breathing shakes when I step closer to her. And the rise and fall of her chest quickens when I touch her face. "You're so beautiful, Dorian."

Those eyes look up at me, desperate, pleading, and wanting. She places a shaking hand on my chest, feeling the rapid beating of my heart. A heart that's been dead for so long.

I drag my finger under her chin and lift her mouth to mine, meeting it in a soft and gentle kiss. She only deserves the best.

She kisses back, her lips cold and quivering.

She kisses me with desperation.

So much desperation.

I invade her mouth with my tongue, sliding it against hers in a starved and needy way. She gave up her mouth to me, allowing me to wreck it in frantic lapses of my tongue. My hands cup her face, getting tangled in her wet hair before they explore and slide down her back to cup that fucking ass I've been aching to bite.

She gasps in response, breathing in my air as my needy hands roam this succulent figure.

Gosh, where has she been all my life?

She backs away from me, licking her lips softly until the back of her thighs hit the bed. I smirk, raking my eyes over her. The tightness in my jeans hasn't left since I walked into her office. Seeing her stare at me with a hint of fright and so much curiosity made me want to bend her over her desk and take her for everyone to see.

Perfection.

Slowly, and I mean slowly, she unbuttons her sleeveless blazer dress, letting it drop to the floor to reveal a black bra and panties to match.

Fuck.

I drop to my knees, staring at her. This beautiful woman in front of me deserves so much more, but she wants me.

God, what did I do to deserve this?

After everything she went through, she chose me. A man who deserves to be chosen by women is chosen by the best of them all.

Taking her by the hips, I bring her closer to me, kissing her navel and inhaling her pussy that must be desperate for my touch.

My dick hasn't throbbed like this in ages. I feel like I'm in high school again.

I look up at her, a mountain of breasts blocking my view. "May I?"

She runs her fingers through my hair. Its feeling causes me to close my eyes and truly be in the moment. Wanted by someone, loved.

She gives me the power I never knew I had, rising me from the ashes like a phoenix, brought here to change my wicked ways just to see her smile.

Because when she smiles, heaven beams light on all of us.

She takes me out of the moment as soon as her bra unclasps, dropping it on my face. I haven't seen mounds so damn brilliant in all my life. Again, what the hell did I do to deserve this angel?

Her panties are next, revealing that perfect pussy I've been aching to enter all fucking day.

I get on my feet, towering over this wet, naked woman, and peel my shirt off. Her eyes travel from my face to my chest, landing on my Snake tattoo. I'm VP, of course, I'm inked with their logo. Riggs has the same one taking up the left side of his body and he's not even one of us anymore.

Grabbing her face, I kiss her again, bathing her neck in my tongue and bite marks. Woman is moaning in my ear and I'm about to go mental if I don't enter her immediately.

Getting out of my wet jeans, I tear off my underwear with it, revealing myself to her. She stares right at it, scrolling her eyes up my body until she furrows her brows when she meets my eyes.

Vulnerability oozes from us. Taking in each other as naked as the day we were born.

She stares down at me again, swallowing raggedly. She's cute when she's scared.

"Is this okay?" I whisper, curling her hair behind her ear.

She nods, stepping closer until our bodies are flush and she rises on the tips of her toes to kiss me. I savor the taste of her, anticipating what's to come next.

I attack her parted, waiting lips, stroking my tongue with hers until she moans a breath into me, and I lift her, placing her on the bed. Fuck, I'm about to unload all over her, about to make a mess of my sheets. But I'm going to make her see heaven before I come.

Leaving those lips, I kiss her neck, suckle her pebbled nipples, and leave a trail of kisses down her body until I look up at her whimpering and squirming when I reach the river between her legs.

I'll devour her, all right.

My tongue teases her clit, tasting her goodness before I feast.

Her moans fill my room, sultry cold tasty moans that cause me to find her underwear on the floor and touch myself with it.

Her fists clench the sheets around her, lifting her sex onto my face. Fuck, this woman is driving me wild.

She's close, squirming and writhing under my mouth. I stop touching myself and shove two fingers inside her, making her scream louder than expected. Tight as fuck, just like my Zaynab—no, she will not be part of this.

Get out of my head, Zaynab.

I fuck Dorian with my fingers and aggressively attack her clit with my tongue.

Her fingers run through my hair and grab onto fists full, tugging at it. A growl rumbles through my chest, releasing as I bite down and make her groan in pleasure.

She's close.

A knock strikes the door but I ignore it.

A knocks a second time and I suck my teeth. "Knock again and it'll be the last fucking thing you do."

"Phone call—"

"Leave!" I yell at Judas on the other side of the door and bury my face between her thighs again.

It doesn't take me long to finish her off. With a couple more strokes of my tongue and a wiggle of my fingers, her gasps and screams release a flow into my mouth.

God, she tastes so good.

When she has my head in a death grip with her thick thighs, pulling at my hair. I come up for air, licking my lips and smirking at her.

I drag my tongue up her stomach. I'll do her raw, the only person I've done raw has been—

Fuck, get out of my head, Zaynab!

As soon as I part Dorian's legs and ease into her, she squeals, scratching down my back. I take her as I usually take women under me; hard and fast. I cup her ass and bring her closer, diving in as deep as I can go.

But Dorian deserves more than that.

She deserves more than I can ever give her.

I slow my thrusts, kissing her tenderly as I make love to her.

Our shivering bodies are full of ecstasy.

Her heavy breaths caress my neck, kissing and biting. Then she winces, turning her head away from me as I thrust deeply and lift her legs onto my shoulders.

She's not looking at me anymore. Her lower lip is quivering and she's stiff as a board.

I don't stop, instead, I lower myself on top of her again and bathe her neck in kisses. I have to show her I'm here. I won't leave like her husband.

I won't leave.

Biting down on her shoulder, I suckle intensely and leave a hickie. She winces again, and I release, stilling on top of her as I close my eyes and see Zaynab.

Fucking Zaynab, the goddess who stole my being. I shouldn't think of her, I should be here in the now with Dorian. But when I see her teary eyes and quivering lip, it reminds me of Zay and every time we make love.

Fuck.

"You're incredible," I say breathlessly to Dorian.

She doesn't say anything.

I remain on top of her until I catch my breath and shrink out of that masterpiece she allowed me to enter before I roll off her to clean myself with an old t-shirt on the floor. I'm happy. I'm giddy. I can't wait to lie next to Dorian and bask in the after-sex glow.

By the time I look back, Dorian is already getting dressed and sliding her feet into her shoes.

I shoot up from the bed and take her hand. "Wait, where are you going?"

Tears roll down her cheeks and she shakes her head. "I'm sorry, I have to—this was a mistake."

"Dorian?"

She pulls her hand free and leaves, throwing the door open and running into the crowded bar.

"Fuck," I grumble, jumping into my boxers.

I charge after her, bare feet slapping the sticky floor as I roam.

"Hey, man, you gotta phone call—"

I growl and continue to the main door. "Not now, Judas."

Dorian's already out the door, rain pouring over her. I charge after her and am instantly shivering. But I don't care. I wrap my arms around her, stopping her from leaving. Our heavy breaths cloud in front of us through the curtain of rain.

"Talk to me," I say, squeezing her to my chest. "Please, talk to me."

She shakes her head, turning in my arms to face me. "Me and you, this is never going to work. We're from two different worlds." She waves her hand at the bar and the bikes. "This is normal to you. It's not to me. None of this is normal." She stares at my neck and winces; shaking her head again as she searches for her keys. "This was a mistake, Peter. A huge mistake. I'm…sorry."

"Dorian, wait, please." I follow her, teeth chattering as I do. "What happened? What changed? What's different between now and when we were making love?" I grit my teeth. "What fucking changed?"

She pokes at my shoulder, pokes at my neck, pokes at my chest. "Whoever she is…I can't do this. I can't just be a bump in your road…I've been with one person my whole life, but you—I won't be scared of who you've been with before me, but I'll be petrified of the women you'll be with after me—"

"I want to be with you! Only you."

She rips her car door open and gets inside, crying as she does. I reach for the handle, yanking and pulling at it. "Open the door, Dorian. Please." She starts to reverse, looking behind her as she does. I hit the car window, once, twice, and on the third time, I'm running to keep up with the car. "Dorian! Dorian!"

Too late.

She turns onto the road, headlights shining brightly. I'm standing in front of the car with my hands on the hood. "Baby, please," I say, furrowing my brow as we lock eyes.

She shakes her head and honks, holding it steady. I wince, tears filling my eyes as I step away watching her drive off with my fingers running through my hair.

I stand there until I don't see her taillights anymore.

I stand there until my toes go numb.

I stand there knowing I lost the best thing that ever happened to me because of who I am.

With one more huff, I stomp back to the bar and shove the front door open, shaking as I go back to my room. Like the tick that he is, Judas follows me and leans on the doorframe.

"What?" I bark, grabbing a towel from the floor.

He holds the phone out to me. "Like I said, phone call."

I snatch the phone from his hands and place it on my good ear. "What?"

"Peter?" Riggs's voice sounds on the other end. "That you?"

My knees shake and I sit down, sliding my fingers through my hair. "Jesus fuck, are you okay?"

"I ain't got long—"

Grunts and strains move in the background, hissing sounds next, then a voice I don't recognize comes to life. "In three days, you and your president will meet us at the peak. All will be explained then."

I grit my teeth, shaking still. "You hurt him, I'll make sure to kill every single one of you fucks."

Laughter moves on the other end. "Three days or I'll start sending your brother home in pieces."

The line goes dead.

I toss the phone at the mirror, cracking and shattering it. "Fuck!"

"We need to take this more seriously, VP. If they kill him, that sends a huge message through town. Everyone will look at us like fucking pansies." Judas pushes off the doorframe and uncrosses his arms. "Chapel, nine o'clock tomorrow."

He leaves as I collapse on the bed and stare at my ceiling. This day is fucked.

My brother might die.

The woman I'm starting to fall for is gone.

Zaynab is clouding my head.

What's the use anymore?

I close my eyes, inhaling deeply.

It'll get better soon.

Life will fall right back into place and I'll have Zaynab on one arm and Dorian in the other.

My wild girl and my wife.

Yeah.

I like that thought.

But for now, I'm going to wallow in self-pity and drink myself to sleep.

Tomorrow is a new day.

Dorian

I couldn't help it. I was so drawn to him, as if I'd known him all my life. But I just met the guy a few weeks ago.

My husband died and I'm already in bed with another man.

This isn't like me.

Peter took hold of my being and connected with my soul in ways that Erin never did.

He has a way of getting people to do what he wants with that smirk. And he had me naked in a matter of moments. I knew it was wrong, but holy shit did I ever want it.

Truthfully, I was stricken by those blue eyes the second I connected to them, as if I'd known him for generations. But I was too blinded by the wreck to pay any attention.

Erin died and I've carried guilt and heartache with me. But when I met Peter, something about the way he transformed from an angered beast to a caring man gained all of my trust.

I pull up to my house, the wipers scraping the windshield as I stare at the lights leaking from the partially closed curtains where Gray and Bells are sitting at the dining room table, sharing a glass of wine and playing a board game.

The tears come as soon as I look at the front door with the metal knocker. Erin bought that our first night at the house, cursing in frustration as he tried to install it quickly whereas it took him three hours.

The memories of this house ooze him. He's smeared all over the walls, the garden, and this damn car, too.

Tonight was a slip of my normality.

An error in my normal ways because my normal ways are no longer. My ways were destroyed when Erin was.

This version of Dorian is the version that didn't exist in the world where Erin lived. In Erin's world, the old Dorian was faithful, careful, calm, and collected.

In this new world without Erin, Dorian is careless, emotionless, and daring. So daring that she slept with a guy she barely knows all because he makes her feel alive again.

I like feeling alive.

Pushing the door open, I take my purse, sniffling once more with a sharp breath to eliminate any trace of sadness on my face. Gray doesn't need to see me like this. Although I can't blame her for being worried when I'm not like this in front of her. I don't think she's ever seen me depressed. Broken. Again she doesn't need to see me like this. That's why I hide it. It's better if I slap on a mask than bare my truths to people.

The rain showers on my shivering skin, shaking my scattered brain that can't stop thinking about Peter and that look on his face.

I hurt him by leading him on. I let him touch me. I let him hold my hand and kiss me.

I let him do all those things knowing I wouldn't be able to live with myself if I continued.

Yet I still did it. I still want it.

I allowed it because subconsciously maybe I want to move on. Maybe I always have.

Erin and I were constantly arguing by the end of it. Arguing so much that it came to a point where we swallowed our feelings and pretended everything was okay.

But it wasn't.

I carried us because he couldn't hold down a job. He held it against me when he said he never did.

For three years we tried to have a baby and nothing worked. I buried my feelings because I loved him. But I really wanted a baby.

There were faults in our relationship. Faults we plastered, sanded, and painted over to make it seem like we were picture-perfect.

My subconscious mind knows me better than I know myself. She let me open up to Peter, and be with Peter in the most vulnerable way I've only ever been with Erin.

And now, the look of confusion and hurt on Peter's face will forever be ingrained in my head until I dare to accept this new world I live in.

What happened? What changed? What's different between now and when we were making love? What fucking changed?

His words cloud my mind, making more tears rise to the surface because I want all of that, too, and it's scaring the hell out of me. My husband just died and I want…a fresh start.

I want to be with you! Only you.

Taking a huge breath, I release it slowly to rid the tears from my eyes. There's time to cry, and right now is not that time.

As I enter the home, Gray smiles at me over her shoulder and snickers. "Come join us, I'm wrecking her at *Scategories.*"

I shake my head. "Maybe after. I, uh, I need a shower and I have to, um, run an errand for work when I'm done."

She nods, taking her pen and sticking her tongue out at Bells. What I should do is join them, forget this error code in my life and just live on with the people who love me.

I just can't.

Peter's lips are still pressed on my neck, tasting me into an orgasm. It's so damn wrong.

I'm so damn stupid.

Quickly, I make my way to the washroom upstairs and lock myself in. I'm about to break down and Gray will never see me like that.

My phone buzzes in my purse, and I know it's him. Who the hell else would it be?

PETER: *Dorian, baby, please talk to me. What happened?*

PETER: *You said it was okay, I'm sorry if I did something wrong. But we can make this work. We will make this work.*

PETER: *Just talk to me, please.*

Locking my phone, I drop my clothes in the hamper and the urge to clean his hands from me takes hold of anything else. But I don't want to rid his hands from me, do I?

I stand under the shower, eyes closed as I warm up the shivers running through me.

My lower lip quivers and a silent sob escapes, shaking my whole body. I slept with another man. I ruined the wedding vows I took to someone who was my soulmate.

...who *was* my soulmate...

Sometimes in life, you have to let go.

I need to understand that Erin is never coming back. There will never be his smiling face walking through the front door again. There will never be the warmth from the pad of his fingers caressing my cheek.

There will never be love to give.

There will never...be.

I release a shaky breath and look up as the water rains over me. Maybe I need the truth. Answers to who Peter is. The man with the secrets.

Maybe I need something more. Something concrete to make this disturbed feeling flowing through me feel okay...maybe I need closure.

Zay

Adam and are lying in bed staring at the ceiling as we try to catch our breath. It's been raining all day, we have no class because it's exam period, and our internships are on pause so we can study. But all Adam and I have been doing is relishing in our glory of finally being able to be us again. Sure, I should tell him to fuck right off for how he treated me a few days ago, but he's upset. After everything Peter put me through, Adam has full right to be angry.

But something else has been on my mind.

Riggs.

I turn on my side to look at Adam, his chest rising and falling quickly. "Did you know they took Riggs?"

His breathing stops for a fraction of a second and continues with a deep inhale. "No."

He's lying. I know Adam better than myself and he's been lying to me about a lot.

Finding out he was part of the club shocked me more than anything. Riggs and Peter both told me he wasn't cut out for that life because of his shaky hands. Because he's not a true Donnelly.

Maybe that was a lie, too?

"Why won't you look at me when you answer?" I ask, frowning as my eyes well with tears. "You knew, didn't you? You knew and did nothing."

Adam sits up, chuckles softly, and gets dressed. He says nothing as he slides his underwear on. Nothing as he gets into his jeans. And nothing when he turns to look at me and buttons up his flannel shirt.

I get off the bed, remaining as I am, and grit my teeth. "I'm your fucking wife! I will not be kept in the dark by whatever it is you do when I'm not around. I will not be a pawn in your fucking game anymore. I'm done, Adam. Do you hear me? I'm fucking done—" I yelp as Adam grabs my face and squeezes my cheeks together.

"Done, hey? You're done?" he yells. "You'll be done when I fucking say it, do you understand me?" He tosses me on the bed and looks down at me as I cry. "You are *my* wife, so be a fucking wife. Your nose does not need to be in the business and it doesn't need to know what I do when I'm not home."

Where the hell did that come from?

This isn't Adam, this is not the man I've known for so long.

Who the fuck is this monster?

Tears are pouring out of me, shaking my body into showing him my fear. He doesn't need to see how scared I am of him. But I'm fucking petrified of my husband right now.

He grabs me by the hair on the back of my head and pulls my face to his. "I'm loyal to you, babe."

I whimper, shaky breaths leave my parted lips.

He takes my hand, kisses my knuckles, and smirks as he puts it in his pants. "This is yours. Forever and always." I nod quickly, afraid if I don't agree with everything he says, he'll hurt me. But why the fuck would he do this when he loves me?

He loves me, right?

He gropes my breasts, then travels lower and shoves two fingers inside me with so much force I let out a cry. "This is all mine from now on." He pushes his fingers deeper, making me wince. "And you will obey me, do I make myself clear?"

I let out a sob, gripping his wrist to stop, but he pushes deeper regardless. "Adam—"

"Yes or no, babe?"

There it is again, that look only the devil gifts his minions.

Wincing, I nod and lick my dry lips. "I'm yours, Adam. Yours."

He removes his fingers from inside me and kisses me. "Don't you ever question me again, understood?"

I whimper as he releases me, and I push myself up from the bed.

No man will ever lay a hand on me and get away with it. Adam will not, either.

I'm determined to get to the bottom of this, one way or another, I will find my peace.

He stuffs his feet into his shoes and looks back as I pull a dress over my head. "I'll be back in two hours. Be here when I get back…please?"

I grunt at him, taking a fresh pair of underwear to slide into. I will not give him a definite answer, but truthfully, I have nowhere to go.

Come tomorrow, I'm packing my shit and heading home. My parents' guest house is vacant and they wouldn't mind if I squatted there for a little while.

I can't believe it's come to this, that I'm thinking this way about Adam.

My Adam. The only man I've ever loved.

But he isn't Adam anymore. This fucking club ruined him.

It ruins everything.

Jolting forward when he comes up behind me and wraps his arms around my chest. "Don't leave me," he whispers, kissing my neck. "I'm sorry, please don't leave."

"Sure, whatever."

He groans, leaning his forehead on my shoulder. "I'll tell you everything tonight, okay? I'm sorry. I'll tell you everything." He sniffs, whimpering softly. "I'm sorry," he whispers. "So sorry."

With that, he presses his lips on my shoulder and leaves. His heavy stomps move through the house until they're silenced by the front door slamming shut.

I look back at my reflection in our stand-up mirror and sob. I sob because everything we built was a lie.

Our entire life is a lie.

My life just continues to unravel sadness.

Where is my happy ending?

***

It's almost seven when there's a knock at the front door. Adam hasn't come home yet, and he left at ten this morning.

I'll be back in two hours. Be here when I get back...please?

I left the house to go for a run, expecting him to be back when I got there.

He wasn't.

Everything imaginable is running through my head as I stare at the door. The club is here to get me as they did all those years ago, breaking into my dorm and taking me to the barn in the middle of nowhere. If it happens again, there's no telling if I'll walk out of it alive this time.

I know too much. I've fucked too much.

Now my husband is one of the rivals. This can't be a good sign.

I gulp, rising from the couch and inching my way toward the rapping on the door. I have no idea what to expect on the other side of it.

Adam covered in blood.

Peter here to fuck me against my kitchen counter.

Or Riggs here to swoop me away from my nightmares?

With a deep breath, I open the door and Dorian stands there, a pink umbrella with a daisy pattern on it hovering over her head.

Frowning, I peer over her shoulder expecting to see Peter. "Hey?"

"I'm sorry to barge in like this. I, um, Peter told me you guys went to school together...I found your name on the Stanford University website and did some digging." She licks her lips and gulps. "Can I come in?"

I'm a little perplexed by her being here, but nod and open the door because my fate isn't here to kill me yet. "Would you like something to drink?"

I can sure use a stiff one.

She gives me a wry grin. "Coffee?"

Tipping my head to her, I put a kettle on, looking back as she hangs her dripping umbrella on the doorknob, slowly getting out of her booties. Everything is so calculated, and done with such careful precision. I see what Peter likes about her. Her soft, round face has a natural glow to it. Big plump lips I'm sure he's kissed a million times over. And she's tall, which helps since he's freaking 6'4". Beauty emanates from her and I hope she knows the trouble she's getting herself into. Trouble I desperately wish I never dipped my toes in.

"So, it's Dorian, right?" I lean on the movable island that's always locked in place. "What can I do you for?"

She comes into the kitchen and looks around quickly before meeting my gaze. Our kitchen has dark, midnight-blue walls with wood floors and cabinets to match. Adam liked it like this, and being from a home that was bright as shit, I was okay with it. Now, I feel like I'm living in Dracula's lair.

"Um…I have no idea why I'm here. If I'm being completely honest, I got in my car and just came here when I found your address but…I don't know why I'm here."

"Peter?" I ask, standing upright. "You're here about him, aren't you?"

A breath leaves her, heavy and relieving. "Why did you tell me to stay away from him?"

I rub my nose and look down at the island, drumming my fingers on it. "Well, where would you like me to begin? From the beginning? Or from the point in time when my life became a fucking mess that they control?"

Her lower lip quivers, folding her arms across her chest as the kettle on the stove starts to whistle. Perfect timing.

Removing the kettle, I fix us instant coffees. Two sugars and milk for her.

"I didn't mean for it to happen," she says quietly, stirring the sugar. "I'm so stupid." She covers her face and shakes her head.

I take a sip and flinch. "What happened?"

She releases a breath from those plump, parted lips and shakes her head. "He just showed up at my work and we connected because of our losses—we connected instantly like we've been together for ages. Next thing I know we're having dinner together, and I'm driving him back to that biker bar." She frowns, staring at the sugar bowl between us. "He held my hand and everything I lost just went away. All the tears and heartache were gone…we knew each other in a way that my late husband and I never did. We just…shit, it was a mistake."

I smirk, leaning my elbows on the island. She slept with him. That didn't take her long. Didn't take me long, either, when I first met him.

Eyes like icebergs.

Smile that shines like the sun.

Lucifer walking in disguise.

I sniff, looking into my coffee. "Peter and I first met at a party when I got this scar." I lift my chin and show it to her. "We did shots, took some drugs, and danced a bit. Gosh, I was instantly hooked. Something about him that just attracts the right people to the wrong person." Smiling at her, I sip my coffee again. "We walked to the water and watched the stars for a bit until the drugs kicked in. Then we got naked and floated for a while. I liked floating with him." She frowns, listening intently to what I have to say. She connects to him on another level. Much like I did. She's woven deeply into his soul, the same soul I'm escaping from.

"It was different with him, though. So different from anyone I've ever been with. Like you did, Peter and I connected instantly and made love like the sky was fucking falling. But what he told me that night and what I felt for him, wasn't at all what I expected. He ghosted me and pretended I didn't exist when my best friend started dating him. He'd cheat on her and act like it was fine." A shuddered breath leaves me when I meet her gaze and I sniff, looking out the window above the sink. "Then she died and I knew he had something to do with it…long story short, he did."

She gasps, shaking her head. "H-how?"

I tilt my head to the side and sputter. "Well, he killed her and made it look like a suicide." I wipe my nose with the back of my hand taking in the tears shimmering in her eyes. "I didn't know it then, but he was part of the motorcycle club, and she ratted them out. So he killed her as vengeance and I…" I pause, standing upright. "That scar on his neck, I did that when we were going through her things."

She doesn't need to know I plotted to kill him. I'll keep that part to myself.

"Holy shit." She puts her hand on her mouth. "This is…insanity."

I nod in agreement. "But the Peter I first met is not the Peter we see today. Something changed. I don't know if being in too deep with the club ruined him, but deep down, I'm sure there's a good guy still inside him."

"If he's so bad, why do you still associate with him?" She sips her coffee, stirring it again when she sets it down.

"Someone had to take the fall for what Lillian did. And I was the easiest choice." I frown, wiping an escaping tear. "A year ago next week, will be the first anniversary of my wedding with Adam." A soft grin spreads to my lips as I think of the simpler times before all this madness. "Peter walked me down the aisle. But what he failed to mention was the reason he stayed around was because the club had other ideas in mind for me." Moving my shirt down, I reveal the scar on my chest. "I took a bullet for the club and still, it wasn't enough. I had one of two options, they kill me and the debt I owed the club would be wiped clean…or…" I wince, turning away from her at the thought of it.

"Or what?" she asks, touching my shoulder as I quiet sob leaves me.

"Or I become *his* woman and pay off the debt every Tuesday afternoon by opening my legs to him. Which I did for ten months and ten days until he finally set me free." A pained smile touches my lips. "You should stay as far away from him as possible before he ruins you like he ruined me."

She takes a shaky breath and wipes the tear from her cheek. "I'm so sorry, Zaynab."

"Don't be. If you're as smart as you seem, you'll stay away from him."

She pulls in a deep breath, releasing it slowly as she lifts the mug to her lips. Dorian and I are in for a long night of living in my memories, my stories. The truth deserves to leave my lips and penetrate her ears.

She has no idea what she's in for.

None whatsoever.

Zay

Dorian left after I told her about my connection to the club and what happened to me two years ago. I told her about Peter and what we do together. I told her about Adam and how he changed because of this. All the while, the two of us were in tears sitting on my couch and dumping our coffees for vodka sodas. It was eye-opening for her to hear my stories, but I don't think it changed much.

There was still that love in her eyes at any mention of his name.

Much like it is for Adam and me, he's not the man I married anymore, but I'm also not the same woman anymore. I'm tainted by this club, much as he is. Maybe it's better if we put our ruined, tainted selves away, and move on from each other. Everyone deserves happiness, and mine isn't going to be dropped in my lap. I have to find it. And I will, outside of this life.

Dorian left around ten and I decided to head to bed around eleven when Adam didn't come home and ignored my fifty phone calls all afternoon. Saying I'm worried is an understatement, I don't think I've had anxiety like I've had in the past twenty-four hours in my entire life. My heart is in my throat, lodged there with the stone that won't seem to subside. Something bad happened, I just know it.

It's almost eight in the morning when I wake up to pee. I tiptoe to the washroom and do what I have to do, preparing myself for the day while I'm at it. Adam's side of the bed is cold again.

Maybe he slept on the couch not to wake me? Or he slept on the couch because he knows I want this to end?

But no, as soon as I step out of the bedroom, he's not there.

His car isn't there, either.

Not his shoes.

Not his keys.

I call him again but his phone is off.

I'm starting to panic a little.

I don't know where he went or what he had to do.

I'll be back in two hours. Be here when I get back...please?

It's going to be twenty-four hours real soon.

I throw on a dress and stuff my feet into a pair of shoes, then jog out of the house and to my car without a second thought as to where I'm going. He's not going to like it, but I don't care.

Peter will help me find him.

The drive to *Judas's Hideout* isn't far, but it feels like an eternity knowing anything can happen.

Peter owes me nothing.

Those men owe me nothing.

I could walk into the bar and they kill me.

I could walk into the bar and Peter will have his way with me.

I have no idea what awaits me on the other side of that wooden door.

Letting out a breath, I park up front beside a bike that looks like Riggs's. It's not his bike, though, because he had a stainless steel skull welded underneath the license plate. And the reality of it not being his, weighs on me. I'd give anything to see his face again, to hear his husky voice, to watch him be my protector. I'd do anything to have him back.

Closing the door to my car, I stare up at the bar and sigh. It's 8:52 AM, someone better be awake.

My feet feel heavy, working their way up to the door. I hate this place with such a passion, but it's part of my life. And I have a feeling it'll always be part of it.

Lucky for me, the door is unlocked.

It creaks open, but no one is awake to greet me. There are two women, and a man with a long thick beard, sleeping naked on the pool table. Empty beer bottles and the stench of stale cigarettes and pot float in the air. Someone is face-first in the booth, drool leaking from his mouth.

I grimace and quietly step over beer bottles, heading to Peter's room.

The mess continues this way, vomit on the floor by the washroom, and women's underwear are floating in it.

Disgusting.

His door is slightly ajar and I knock, pushing it open. He's naked, alone, with an empty bottle of gin beside him and an overflowing ashtray next to that.

He's hard as rock right now, and it's the first thing I notice when I walk into the room and shut the door behind me. Not as well endowed as his brother is, but still something nice to look at. His dick reminds me of Adam's. Perfect mushroom head, curved slightly to the left, and veiny. Nothing like that monstrosity that tore me up for a week in that paradise at the hellish cabin.

Peter looks peaceful when he's asleep. Stress-free and happy.

The Peter I remember.

"Peter?" I whisper, making my way to him.

He snorts but doesn't wake up.

"Peter?" I say a little louder and shake his leg.

He groans, bringing a hand to his eye. "Fuck off."

"Peter," I say loudly and put my hands on my hips.

His eyes shoot open and he takes notice of me, sitting up quickly. "Zay? What're you doing here?"

I point at his package. "Get dressed, then we'll talk."

He rises, stepping closer to me with a sleepy smirk. "You missed me, huh?"

I roll my eyes. "Get dressed, Peter."

Like I walked into some porno movie, he touches himself, looking me up and down. "Get *undressed*, Zaynab."

I step back. "Knock it off, Peter."

He brings his face close to mine, and his breath stinks. Stale gin, vomit, and cigarettes. "Let me finish. Just watch me." He leans his head on my shoulder, his arm jerking between us.

"Peter." I stare down at his movements, watching him start to leak. "Adam's missing."

"What?" He lifts his head, looking at me with a frown and out of breath. "What do you mean he's missing?" His thick eyebrows are pinched together, eyes studying me with a tired gaze.

"He left around 10:30 yesterday morning and said he'd be home in a couple of hours. He never came home and isn't answering his calls." I cross my arms. "I'm getting worried something happened to him."

He sits on the bed, still naked, and finds his pack of cigarettes. He pulls one out, looks up at me, and lights it. "So you came to me for what? Thinking I can help you?" He chuckles, laying back on the bed with the cigarettes between his teeth. "You did, huh? Well, how about you help me blow a load I've held in for three days? Then I'll help you?"

Scoffing, I kick his foot in frustration. "Just forget it." I turn to walk away but he takes my wrist, tilting his head to the side with a smirk. "I'm serious, Peter. They took Riggs and what if they took Adam, too." I sniff, tears welling in my eyes. "He's way more involved in this bullshit than you think."

Peter flicks ashes on the floor. "What do you mean?"

Shaking my head, I release a breath and tell him everything I know, everything that Adam did to me yesterday that nearly sent me over the edge. I stop once to let my cries out and sit on the bed. Peter drops his head as the cigarette burns between his fingers. "He said he'd tell me everything when he got home but he never came home."

He runs his fingers through his hair and puts the cigarette out in the ashtray. "Fuck."

I sniff. "You can say that again."

"Judas and I are meeting the president today about Riggs," he divulges. "I'll talk to Roaden, he'll protect you in case they come for you."

The room starts to vibrate and closes in on me, capturing my breath as I put my head in my hands. "Me? Why would they come for me?"

Peter tongues his cheek. "People think you're my old lady. And if Adam is a Panther, he'd tell them that he's fucking the Snakes VP's girl just to be on the president's good side."

I fall back on the bed and sob into my hands, covering my face as I do.

Peter lies back with me, taking my hand from my face and holding it.

We lie side by side holding hands and stare at the stucco ceiling until I calm down.

I'm back to being scared for my life.

Back to wondering when my last day will come.

I married a man, knowing his involvement with the Snakes was messy.

Why didn't I run when I had the chance?

Peter squeezes my hand when I calm down and releases a breath. "I'm going to fix this. Okay? I fucked-up but I'll fix it."

"That's what Adam said," I say, looking over at him.

He grunts, meeting my gaze. "I mean it."

A nod leaves me and for the first time in a long time, I actually believe him. "What's the plan then?"

Peter smirks, leaning over to wipe a tear from my cheek. "Just gonna have to wait and find out."

Great, another fucking plan that could save my life or tear me down even more.

And all I can do is sit back and watch.

Riggs

I've been stuck in this fucking dungeon for a while.

Days float into one at this point.

But there's a clock on the wall and an old TV I can watch.

At 8:00 AM they come and give me breakfast.

At noon they come and bring lunch.

Around 6:00 PM they bring me dinner.

And at 11:30 PM I get a water bottle, beer, and a bag of chips.

I don't know what the fuck they want with me. I've been out for almost two years. Hit the road as soon as I knew Zay was okay.

As soon as she was discharged from the hospital, I gave in my patch and set off on my bike.

For about a year I roamed the open road, staying at hotels, getting drunk at bars, and fucking random broads when I needed a bed to sleep in.

Then I stopped at the charter in Texas, and I met Shyanne. Beautiful blonde who has no ties to any club or any charter. She owns a jewelry shop in Houston and offered me a place to stay when she saw me eating on a park bench.

Cute little thing with the biggest blue eyes that match mine.

It didn't take me long to make her mine, and now, she's my wife, pregnant with my son.

Yet here I am stuck in the fucking cell underneath the Panther's clubhouse.

I don't know what the fuck Judas is up to.

Or my father for that matter.

But if anything happens to my family, I'll rip the throat out of every single one of these fucking men just to find out who hurt her and that baby.

I've been using my rings to slowly unscrew the bars around the window. It's working but it's taking a fucking while. But it's me. I'll get out of this and break a couple of noses on my way out the door.

The basement door opens, the squeaking and creaking hinges vibrating my eardrums. I grunt, stepping off the bed, and stand with my arms folded, broad chest expanded, and stance strong in case these fuckers come in and try to beat me again.

Nearly killed two of them last time until more came and held me down.

Fuckers broke my nose.

Two men come in dragging someone down the stairs with a bag draped over their head. "Got you company, big guy."

I scoff, uncrossing my arms. "I don't want company. I want fucking outta here."

The short one chuckles, tossing the guy inside. "We'll be back soon. Got a meeting with the Snakes that you're coming to. Get to see some familiar faces, too, big guy."

I grit and bare my teeth. "Call me *big guy* one more time and I'll rip your fucking throat out."

He lets out a shaky breath and looks at the other guy beside him. "S-sorry." The two of them stare at each other, as if they know I can break the bars on this cage they have me trapped in.

Charging forward, I grunt as they slam the gate shut and lock it in place. "Fuckers."

Looking back at the guy on the ground taking the bag off his head, shock fills me as those blonde locks are unmistakably my half-brother's. "Adam? What the fuck are you doing here?"

He grunts, pushes himself up and sits back against the cement wall. "Could ask you the same thing." His eye is swollen, probably a bum rib, too, since he's holding onto his side. He looks worse for wear.

Not a scrawny kid anymore.

Guess being with Zay has changed him.

Made him a man.

He was the runt of the litter with me as their leader.

I look back at the stairs as the door to the basement creaks shut and we're left here in silence. As unhappy as I am to see him, it's good to have someone familiar to talk to.

"Fuckers took me outta nowhere." I drop on the bed and lean my elbows on my knees. "I got out of this mess, what the fuck am I doing back in it?"

He groans as he sits up straighter, hand still pressed on his side. "No one's heard from you in almost two years, Riggs, a lot of shit's changed around here."

I scoff, looking at the stairwell. "Yeah, I can see that."

He looks over at me, smirking with a chuckle. "Have you spoken to Daddy at all?"

I shake my head. "Haven't seen the bastard since we got raided."

Adam nods slowly, wiping the blood from his mouth. "Daddy's got some plans in place, brother."

"Care to elaborate?"

He smirks again, pushing himself up and hopping on one leg before he steadies himself. "Fuck." He lifts his shirt revealing redness and bruising. "Son of a bitch."

I'm getting annoyed now.

Something's up and I don't take lightly being kept in the dark about a club I used to run for fuck's sake.

"I ain't playing games, Adam. What's going on?"

He leans back on the wall, looking up at the fluorescent lighting. "Peter's VP, did you know that? Doing a bang-up job at it, too. Judas is, well, he cares more about his wife and kid than he does the club, but the guys like him so they haven't kicked him out yet."

I grind my teeth.

Scoffing softly.

My brother is VP? Taking my place.

What the fuck is he doing?

This isn't the life I wanted for him.

This isn't the life he needs.

My daddy brainwashed him. He fucking got him.

Goddammit.

I grunt, shaking my head as my hands clench into fists. "He got out. Why the fuck is my brother back in?"

"Someone had to take the fall for Lillian's screw-up." He flares his nostrils, cheeks reddening. "Peter became VP and the guys wanted Zay to take the fall for everything that happened. Someone had to." He shakes his head with a scoff. "Peter made her his old lady and has been fucking *my* wife every Tuesday for almost a year." He sniffs, jaw clenching. "You should have never left, Riggs. Everything went belly up as soon as you did."

I grind my teeth again.

The Zay that saved me didn't deserve that.

The Zay that took a bullet for the club didn't deserve to continue to pay for it.

What the fuck has this club come to without me?

Getting to my feet, I pace, shaking my head and gritting my teeth.

Fuckers.

"What do I have to do with this, huh?"

Adam winces and pushes off the wall. "They don't trust Judas. They trust you."

I got out.

Wiped my hands of the blood and the violence.

Met my angel.

My savior.

Now I'm back and I don't think I'm going anywhere anytime soon.

My angel could be in danger.

My unborn son could be, too.

This is not good.

I stand in front of Adam, an arm folded above his head, and stare down at him. Intimidation at its finest. "Tell me everything. Now."

Adam's breathing shakes as he stares up at me, like a kid scared of his own shadow.

He'll tell me everything.

If he doesn't, I'll beat it out of him.
End game is, I'm going home to my woman.
I'm going to see the birth of my son.
And no one will get in my way of that.
If they do, there's no telling what these hands will do to them.
Riggs Donnelly is back.

Dorian

I've barely slept the last three days.

Every time I close my eyes I see Peter.

I see Zay and him together.

I see Peter hurting her.

Raping her.

Taking advantage of her.

What he did was savage.

Ungodly.

And yet, every time I'm alone I have the urge to reach out. To answer his messages.

To comfort this sad, broken man.

I can't.

I've lost enough.

I'm hurt enough.

It's finished, but that doesn't mean I don't miss him.

Rolling out of bed, Gray is already occupying the washroom, singing quietly as she showers. I walk in and sit on the toilet, sniffling softly.

The shower curtain whips open. "Hey, you got a package last night, but you were asleep."

I frown, looking at her with confusion. "What do you mean? What kind of package?"

She smirks. "A bouquet of forty-eight red roses." A giggle leaves her. "Is there a secret admirer you're not telling me about?"

There's a whole person and a whole night I'm not telling her about.

I roll my eyes. "Probably someone from the office. Gosh, they haven't stopped with the sympathy cards and the coffees and the fucking *I'm sorry for you loss* bullshit. I just—" I pinch the bridge of my nose. "I need a break from all of this."

"We can go visit Wilde in Australia, but I think he's coming here," she says, closing the curtain. "And…the card is proof that you're not telling me something."

Card?

The shower shuts off and she opens the curtain showing me all of her. Seeing my sister's bush at seven in the morning is not what I had on my to-do list, ever.

"Who's Peter?"

Choking on saliva, I cough intensely. Gray pats my back but I wave her hand off. "I'm okay."

How the hell did he find me?

Is he following me?

Was he following me all this time?

The check.

Shit, the check has my address on it.

I frown as I stare at Erin's toothbrush. I can't get rid of it. I can't get rid of any of his things and yet I was okay to open my legs to someone else so soon after his death.

Erin was my everything. But he's gone.

I don't know how I'll ever love again.

But clearly, I'm okay to move on.

This isn't like me.

I'm not open or easy.

Something about Peter consumed me.

Took over my thoughts and my being.

And he still does.

I quickly brush my teeth and strut to my room to change for work. It's Friday. One more day and I'll have the weekend to breathe.

As soon as I step out of my room, Gray stands in my way with her arms crossed, hip popping out, and foot tapping. "Speak, Dorian."

I shake my head, trying to walk around her. "I don't have time for this."

"Then make time to talk to me," she urges, taking my wrist.

I sigh, looking at her. Might as well tell her I fucked-up. Might as well tell her I'm spiraling and don't know how to control it.

Just tell her.

"Peter is the guy I rear-ended. Okay? I paid him off and he showed up at my office on Tuesday. That's it." I can't tell her I slept with someone else so soon after my everything left me. "Now can I go to work, please?"

She lets go of my wrist, furrowing her brows. "The biker?"

"I'll see you later, okay?"

Making my way down the steps, I eye the bouquet of roses on the island. I hate keeping things from my sister. We tell each other everything. But since Erin left, I don't want to tell anything to anyone.

Bottle it up and hold it in like they're my secrets to keep.

Taking the card from the island, I head out the door. It's a short message, something only I would understand.

Dorian,

You and I have come from dark pasts, but you have brought me back to the light.

Be that light with me.

Peter.

My lower lip quivers and I shake my head, blinking rapidly as I look up at the sun. I don't need this, but holy crap do I ever want him to hold me and make all the sadness go away.

I get in the car and drive off, knowing my day will not get any better if I don't express my thoughts.

Seeing Peter and telling him about Erin gave me so much relief, it made me happy to sleep with him. Happy that I was able to share my darkness with someone who is just as dark as me.

Now, the thought of seeing him again frightens me more than it was when I kept it together at my husband's funeral. It's going to be a long fucking day.

***

It's almost noon and I've been running around the office fixing mistakes that were made by my replacement. I can't blame them, they weren't briefed on what to do, they were handed my files and told to work on them while I left for weeks without any way of contacting me.

It's loads of fun.

Ugh, it isn't. I've argued with coworkers before about my way of doing things, and the second I tell people I'm taking a leave of absence, all hell breaks loose and everything is upside down.

But I've managed to organize everything in the last four hours and it's finally back to normal.

Normal, something I'll never feel again.

I sit back in my chair and close my eyes, letting out a deep breath. Maybe a weekend alone at a hotel downtown will do me some good. Just me, room service, and cable TV.

My computer chimes notifying me of an incoming email and I sputter, rolling myself closer to my desk.

Seven new emails all from a Liam Ignassio.

I open the newest one.

Do not contact Peter Donnelly. Is all it says.

The next one: *Snakes vs. Panthers.*

The third through sixth all say: *tonight.*

The seventh gives me chills.

Dorian Wallis, we've been trying to contact you for some time. You might not know us, but we know you, and we certainly know your husband, Erin. Death came to him when he ignored us, would you like death to come to you, too? Answer me. These will be the last messages we send.

There's a phone number at the bottom. My hands are shaking and I'm hyperventilating.

This isn't real.

How can this be real?

What the fuck is happening?

I take my phone, barely able to see the screen from the wave of tears, and dial a number I swore I'd never call again.

After two rings, Peter answers. "Yeah?"

"Peter, it's Dorian."

Something falls in the background and his voice cracks. "Dorian, what? What number are you calling me from?"

I huff out a breath. "Work phone."

"Talk to me, please. I don't like how we ended things. I didn't like how you ran off." He sniffs. "I like you, okay? A lot and I want to see where this goes. And it doesn't matter if we're from two different worlds. What we share, our connection goes beyond that—"

"I need your help," I interrupt him, looking at the words on the screen. *Death came to him when he ignored us.*

What the fuck was Erin into?

Peter sniffs again on the other end. "We have to talk about this."

I clear my throat and read him the message I received. All of them. And silence consumes my ear on the other end. "Peter? You there?"

He's breathing heavily like he's running. "Dorian, I need you to leave. Come to the clubhouse now. I can protect you here."

"Peter, you're scaring me," I say softly.

"Something's going down, Dorian, and if you're not here I can't protect you from it." He growls and hits something. "I don't know what the fuck is happening, but please, baby, please come here. Please."

I wince, turning in my chair to face the windows behind me that overlook the city. No one in this office needs to see me cry. "Why me, Peter? What do I have to do with this?"

He grunts, a woman's voice asking what he needs that gun for, moves through the receiver. "What did your husband have to do with this?"

I sob softly, muffing my cries with my hand. "I don't know."

"It should take you twenty-five minutes to get here if you leave now. I'll be outside waiting, okay? Nothing and I mean, *nothing*, will happen to you." He groans as a door slams behind him. "Trust me, just this once."

I don't say anything and hang up.

My brain is scattered, packed with thoughts I don't even know are real.

Erin was involved with something dangerous. He wasn't able to kill a spider let alone a person.

Dark sides of my husband are floating to the surface. And now I'm involved.

How the fuck did I get involved with this?

I take a shuddered breath and pack my things. If Peter is true to his word, he'll do what's right. If he promises I'm safe, I have to believe it.

Yet as I pack my things, I find myself dialing the number of the man who claimed death came to my husband.

Peter

I'm pacing the parking lot, smoking my sixth cigarette as I wait for her. The two women I care most about, I have to protect with my life. Zaynab and Dorian.

What am I going to do if anything happens to them?

After I flick my sixth cigarette aside, Dorian's car comes speeding down the parking lot and I dash for it before she even has the car in a spot.

She's been crying, her lower lip still quivering. "Peter, I—" her voice cracks and she shakes her head.

I whip open the door and take her face, placing a kiss upon those plump lips. "I got you, okay?"

She sniffs, closing her eyes and resting her forehead on mine. "I'm sorry."

"Don't be sorry, okay? I'll do everything I can to make sure you're safe, baby. I'll keep you safe if it kills me," I tell her, kissing her softly.

She slowly opens her eyes and licks her lips. "I called them." She puts a hand on her mouth and sobs. "I'm sorry."

I grunt, shaking my head.

Liam Ignassio is who my father warned me about.

He's the same person that threatened her.

And none of the guys know who he is.

We're fucked.

"Don't worry, okay? Don't worry."

But all I can do is worry. I don't know who this fucking guy is and why he reached out to Dorian? Fuck, does it have something to do with her husband? Who the fuck is her husband?

No. It's impossible. They're simple, good people. They wouldn't be twisted in this shit.

She hangs her purse off her shoulder. Those big puppy dog eyes staring at me and all I want to do is fall on my knees. Worship the ground she walks on. She had me whipped the moment she stared at me. Our souls became one the moment our eyes locked the day she hit my car.

But I can't.

Not until this shit is settled. Whatever this fucking shit is.

So I take her hand and pull her close to me, kissing her under the scorching sun. "Do you trust me?"

She sniffs, her eyebrows pinching together. "I barely know you."

Shaking my head, I smirk and kiss her again. "Dorian, you know everything there is to know about me. I have not once lied to you, and I don't plan on doing so—"

"What's your relationship with Zaynab, then? I want the truth," she interrupts me.

I sigh heavily, looking at the bar, then back at those eyes welling with tears. "Long story short, like I told you, we used to go to school together. Fooled around a little. Then…she tried to kill me." I lift my neck. "Gave me this scar."

"Why did she try to kill you?" she whispers.

Wincing, I close my eyes so I don't have to bear the look on her face. "Because I was ordered to kill her best friend and made it look like a suicide." I squeeze my eyes to stop the tears. "I fucked-up, I know. I still fuck-up because of what I put Zay through, but—" I slowly open my eyes and she's staring at me as tears skim her cheeks. "I should've stayed out of this." I point at the club. "But I stayed thinking this would bring me closer to my brother. Thinking it would save him and spare her. It didn't. And I'm in over my head with this shit. I'm fucked, Dorian. And I'm sorry you had to meet me at my worst."

She touches my face, wiping an escaping tear. I don't deserve this. I deserve to be tossed in prison like my father and have them throw away the fucking key. "Promise me, Peter, that when all this is done, you'll leave her alone."

How can she ask this of me?

Zaynab is my world.

She's everything I've ever loved.

She's…she's not *her*.

She's not the woman in front of me who has stolen my heart with her big doe eyes.

I can do it, can't I? I can let go of Zaynab and open up my heart.

Promise me you'll move on and find someone so perfect for you it feels like your heart will explode.

I have, sweetie, and she's right here in my arms. It was fast, but so was my love for Zay.

The moment we met we clicked, and the moment Dorian and I met, we tangled together. Braided ourselves, molded our hearts as one. And now, I'm whipped.

I sniff, kissing Dorian's hand. "I'm yours."

With that, she takes my hand and leads us inside. If I had time and a clean conscience, I'd show her what being hers means. But I don't.

I'm meeting the Panthers in an hour to save my brother's life.

"Iron Maiden" plays as I lead her to a booth. Zaynab is seated there eating a burger and fries as she sips a soda. Her eyes widen immediately when she spots Dorian and gets out of her seat. "What's going on?"

Taking Zay's hand, I lead both my women to my room, staring at them with a smile. I'm fucked and twisted because if I can have this every day, I'd die a happy man.

And maybe that'll happen to me. Maybe I'll die at the hands of one of them, Zay succeeding this time.

Maybe I'll die saving one of them, which is the more likely case with whatever the fuck is going on.

But having both of them in my room makes me whole. My mistress and my future wife, mothers to my babies. Pride fills me staring at them.

But I can't have them, can I? No, I don't even deserve one.

And for the first time when I flicker my gaze from Zaynab to Dorian, I'm not craving that exotic coconut scent like I normally would. I'm aching to hold my floral-scented goddess and kiss those plump lips for the rest of my days.

Releasing their grips, I shut the door behind me. A cloud of panic washes over them as soon as they lock eyes.

It's okay, I'll protect them.

I'm good at that.

I go to my dresser and take the two guns Zay asked me about before. They're fully loaded, made sure of that.

Tucking one of the guns in my jeans, I go to Zay first, handing her the gun. "You know how to use it?" She shakes her head. "See here, safety is on. Once you flick it off, aim and shoot, yeah?"

She shakes her head again. "I don't want a fucking gun, Peter."

I sigh, putting the safety on and holding the gun in her hands. "I don't know what the fuck is going on so I need you to be safe. There's a reason you came to me, sweetie. So let me do my job and protect you." I look at Dorian. "Both of you." I adjust the gun in Zay's hand and point it forward. "Safety off, finger on the trigger, and shoot. Got it?"

She nods, sniffling. "Is Adam dead?"

I frown, tilting her chin up. "I don't know, Zay. But I promise, you will not go without, okay?"

She moves her head away, wiping her cheeks, and looks at Dorian.

The look of despair they have.

Worry.

Torment.

How can I protect these women when I couldn't even protect my own mother?

***

I'll never forget that morning.

Riggs came over the night before, as he always did when it was my birthday. We'd have a sleepover, two of us big-ass guys in a double bed. But that's Riggs, the best big brother. Always looking out for me.

Before we went to bed, Mama had this look in her eyes.

Worry.

Despair.

Torment.

I ignored it, happy that Riggs was home with us. He was happy, too. He loved seeing Mama. She had this aura of kindness about her. Gentle compared to our father.

Sometimes I wonder why she stayed with him for so long. Maybe it was because of us. Me and Riggs, and Adam, too. Maybe it was the money.

Or maybe she truly loved my father and hoped she could change him. But Daddy isn't someone to change. He's set in his ways.

Much like me.

But Mama saw the good in us. Looked past Riggs's tough exterior and always got him to smile. He smiled the most around her.

She had us laughing that night. Laughing until tears rolled down our cheeks. Like she knew.

Of course, she knew that night would be her last with her boys.

When we went to bed just past midnight, Riggs got comfortable beside me, grunting as he always did when he got comfortable as if moving was such a strain on his body. I think it had to do with the time he was shot in the back and the time he was sliced in the ribs. Phantom pains of those injuries.

"Riggs?" I asked, poking his shoulder.

He grunted, turning his head with one eye open. "Yeah?"

Clearing my throat, I sniffed. "Mama seem off to you at all?"

He turned over, letting out a deep breath. "Probably just tired like the rest of us. Nothing to worry about, kid. Get some sleep, it's your birthday tomorrow and we got some riding we gotta do."

But we never got to that riding, did we?

We were woken up by a scuffle, grunts, strains, and a gunshot. Riggs did as always and protected me when we went downstairs, but there was no protecting me when I saw what Daddy did to Mama.

I ran to her, crying, a scream lodged in my throat.

She died with that worry and that tormented look in her eyes.

Died and I did nothing.

I couldn't protect her.

Couldn't save her.

She's gone and it was all my fault.

That won't happen to my women, I won't fucking let it.

***

Taking the gun from my jeans, I hold it by the barrel out to Dorian. "Same goes for you, okay?"

Dorian takes the gun, flicks the safety off, and cocks it. "My dad, uh, hunts. I've held a gun or two before."

Something else I didn't know.

There's a lot we don't know about each other. A lot I need to learn. And I will, soon.

I take a breath, looking at the gun in her shaking hands. "Point, aim, shoot."

She nods, sniffling and looking at me like she's trying to understand how she's involved in all of this. I'm trying to understand that, too.

Maybe it's time for a change. Like I did before and get away from the club. From the madness.

Take a chapter out of Riggs's story.

Change. Much like Dorian wants for me.

Zay sits on the bed and places the gun beside her, fiddling with the wedding ring on her finger, and Dorian is staring at me. Her eyebrows raised, plump lips pursed, and waiting for answers.

Fuck, I don't know what to do right now. I don't know how to be the man she needs and the man who is VP to his club.

"Okay, I, um, have to leave, but only for a little. I'll be back." I take a breath. "I'll come back with answers. They have my brother and I need to know why. Lip and Roaden will be here. If something happens, they will take you somewhere safe. I promise nothing will happen to you, okay?" Zay looks up at me. That look she's given me a million times over still hurts my heart. "Believe me, sweetie. Now more than ever."

She sniffs, wiping her cheeks. "Just come home, okay?"

Progress.

Slow and steady progress.

I shift my gaze to Dorian as she's releasing a breath. "Hey, it'll be okay, baby."

She shakes her head. "Will it? I'm not supposed to be involved in any of this and yet I'm right in the middle of it getting threatening emails from something I have nothing to do with. So tell me, Peter. Tell me why the fuck I'm here holding this gun in your biker club's bar while I wait for you to go and figure this shit out."

I don't know what to say.

I don't know how to make it better.

All I know how to do is promise her safety.

I can give her that. I have to give her that and redeem the ache that's been eating away at me since Mama died. That torment invading my insides.

Grabbing Dorian's face, I kiss her, resting my forehead on hers when I'm done. "It'll be okay."

She inhales sharply and nods, placing a hand on my heart. "Be safe," she whispers.

Zay looks at us and grins softly, happy maybe?

What's there to be happy about when I might not even come home from this?

I could be walking into a trap.

A fucking free for all shooting.

But I have to put the pieces together and fast.

With one more kiss from Dorian, I leave a kiss on Zay's cheek and leave.

I don't look back I just leave.

Fuck.

Judas puts his cut on and gets on his bike. "Let's go, brother."

I nod, jumping into my car and punching the steering wheel. Riggs was right, I can't handle this bullshit.

I can't handle the mantle.

I should have remained a stowaway.

A nobody.

I was trying to prove something, and now, I'm going to die out there.

I'm certain of it.

Riggs

uckers brought us to a deserted area.

Nothing but trees and sand.

It's getting in my boots and pissing me off.

They force Adam and me to our knees and have guns pointed at our heads. Guess we're waiting for my club to roll in and talk this mystery out like men.

As I remain on my knees I wonder why I ever left. If I stayed, bullshit like whatever this is wouldn't have happened.

Peter would still be in school.

Zay would be safe.

Adam wouldn't be involved.

But Shyanne wouldn't know me. We wouldn't have made my son.

If I stayed, there's no telling what the future would hold. But one thing I know, I better be walking the fuck out of here.

Bikes rumble in the distance, roaring toward us and I know the sounds of those bikes. My brothers are here to help.

Four bikers roll in, Banks, Mickey, Judas, and Skeet. And a black Audi follows behind, Peter at the wheel.

As soon as he gets out of the car, his eyebrows furrow, staring at me worried. I can't help but smirk. He's wearing his cut, VP patch on his chest. I never wanted this life for him.

He deserved better just like our mother.

But seeing him here, I'm proud of the kid.

Very fucking proud.

He nods at me, taking in the likes of my face. "You good?" he calls out.

I jerk my head at him as he runs his fingers through the hair he's let grow out. "Look a lot better than you, brother."

He chuckles, shifting his gaze to Adam who's smiling as he stares at the ground. "Adam?"

The leader of the Panthers snaps his fingers and waves his hand. "Yeah, yeah, everyone's fine."

"What're we doing here?" Judas asks, crossing his arms over his chest. That president patch tearing off already.

Fucker doesn't deserve that.

It's mine.

The Panther's leader chuckles, snapping his fingers as someone walks out of one of the many cars they have parked around us. Half of these guys don't ride bikes. Fuckers are a sad excuse for bikers.

I should gun them down.

All of them.

A smug-looking man makes his way over. Snakeskin boots, black leather pants, and brown overcoat. Who the hell is this guy?

He takes his sunglasses off for some bullshit dramatic effect like it means something to us, and eyes Peter, then me. "Donnelly boys in the flesh." He looks down at me and grins.

Those eyes.

Why do I know those eyes?

Peter puts a hand up to block the sun. "You Liam Ignassio?"

Liam nods, snapping his fingers at one of his men. The leader grips my arm and pulls me to my feet, doing the same to Adam. "Guess you're all wondering what we're doing here today, hmm?"

Peter cracks the bones in his neck and steps forward. "I wanna know why my brother's face looks like that when he's not part of the Snakes anymore." He scoffs. "We don't have beef with you, never have. So care to explain why you're sniffing around our shit all of a sudden? And why you had to go out of your way to kidnap my brothers? They have nothing to do with whatever this is."

Liam nods slowly, licking his lips as he pulls a silver gun with pearl inlays from the back of his ridiculous pants. "You boys have a lot to do with this."

Peter is grinding his teeth. Something he's been doing since he was a kid. Mama used to make him wear a mouth guard to bed because he chipped his two front teeth when he was ten from grinding his teeth. Fucker had always been walking in and out of doctors' offices, then once that died, the dentist was his best friend.

"Look." Judas steps in, hands raised. "Can't we settle this over a few drinks? Help us better understand this situation you've brought us into."

Liam chuckles, and he looks at me again, shaking his head. "Man, you look just like your father. Shame, too. Your mother was a beauty."

I thunder forward. "What the fuck do you know about my mama?"

He laughs softly, looking at Peter, and cackles. "Oh, you boys are in for one helluva ride after I'm finished with you."

The leader grips my bicep, trying to hold me back.

It's laughable at this point.

Shoving him, I grab Adam by the arm and urge him forward so we can join my club on the other side of this sad excuse for a standoff. "You got something to tell us, you can meet us at our clubhouse tonight. Just you and none of these ticks you think will protect you. I'll make sure the club is empty. It'll be just my brother and I."

Liam nods, eyeing Peter who helps Adam into the car. "You're not the president."

I smirk, taking a step toward him as his men surround him and cock their guns. "You can, either, meet us at the clubhouse tonight, or wait until we come up with a plan to kill every single one of you." I flare my nostrils, looking down at Liam whose eyes give me nightmares of a time so beyond the man I am today. "I may not be part of the club, but I will be at the head of the table by the time we meet. I can goddamn guarantee it."

Taking a step back, I spit the saliva from my mouth, watching as Liam slowly nods, snapping his fingers at his men.

"Speak soon, Riggsy," he says, making his way back to his car.

I grunt, flaring my nostrils at Peter, and take the keys from him. "Let's get outta here. I need a shower and a fucking drink."

He doesn't question me.

None of the guys do.

Their bikes roar to life, rumbling in the silence and leaving dust motes behind them.

There's so much I didn't know about during the past two years. What changed, and what hasn't? Who's in our pocket, and who isn't? Most importantly, why the fuck was Adam grinning like a fucking tool the entire time Liam Ignassio was speaking?

It's going to be a long drive home, I can feel it.

Zay

I'm lying on my stomach on Peter's bed, finishing my burger as the TV plays some movie from the nineties in the background. Dorian has been moving around the food that one of the women brought in for her. I think in the past hour and a half, she's said one word to me and eaten a single fry.

I get that this is weird for her, but snap the fuck out of it. She opened her legs to the devil, now she has to reap the consequences of that. *We reap the consequences we can't predict.*

Swallowing loudly, I poke her leg. "So, tell me, what do you do, Dorian?"

She wipes her fingers on a napkin placed so delicately on her lap. "I'm an environmental lawyer."

I cough, widening my eyes. "What the hell are you doing with a guy like Peter?"

"I don't know," she whispers.

Another sigh escapes me and I get on my knees, moving closer to her. "Peter is one fucked-up individual, but it has a lot to do with his mommy issues—I guess daddy issues, too—he lost his mother so suddenly because of this club, and his father has brainwashed him into thinking this club is all he has in life." I take her hand and sandwich it between mine. "But you...there's something about the way he looks at you that makes me believe he'll get out of this one day. That *you* will get him out. And I really hope you do." I smile. "There are sides of Peter that are so amazing, I'm sure you see it. Sides of him that should never have been involved in this bullshit. But it's all he knows, and maybe, just maybe, you can show him that there's a life beyond this hell. Show him what it's like to live again."

Tears are streaming down her cheeks, and fuck, they're streaming down mine, too. I never thought I'd cry for someone like Peter, yet here I am feeling bad for the guy because this life was handed to him without a choice. Much like Riggs.

She inhales a breath and chuckles, sniffling as she dips a fry in mayonnaise. "I met Peter on the day of my late husband's funeral."

I can't help it, I push my lips together to try and stifle a laugh, but it comes out as a snort, which makes Dorian and I break out into a fit of giggles.

I don't know what's so funny about this situation, but in our worst, most hectic moments in life, we tend to find that ounce of happiness we weren't expecting. Like when I ran into Adam and he held me while I broke down. Peter tried to rape me after I accused him of killing Lillian the first time, but Adam was there as if sent by my guardian angel. The same bitch who seems to dangle me over a pit of fire, letting the tips of my toes sizzle.

I sniffle, wiping the laughing tears from my face as Dorian is doing the same. Our situations are comedically tragic. Her husband died and she found Peter in some fucked-up way I'll never fully understand. But I see it, anyone can see it if they look closely enough. The way he stares at her is different than how he stares at me.

He sees a future with Dorian. A family.

He sees orgasms with me. Plenty of them.

But that instant connection she feels with Peter is like the connection Adam and I had. That spark ignited and promised a lifetime of happiness. And we had that, then we didn't.

And now, I don't think we'll obtain it again. He's far too gone to be my Adam again.

I'll move on. I'll find that bliss again.

It sadly will never be the same.

"Sorry, I didn't mean to laugh at that," I say, sniffling again.

She shakes her head, lifting a leg on the bed. "No, it's crazy. All of this is crazy."

Letting out a breath, I roll onto my back, that poster of the woman with black eyes staring down at me. I stare at it often, even when Peter was on top of me I'd stare at her and wonder when my time would come. When would I be free?

I don't think I'll ever be free so long as I'm tied to this club.

"Did you love your husband?" I ask as a tear rolls down the side of my face.

She gasps softly, letting the words sink in.

Several seconds pass before she whimpers and a sob escapes her. "I loved him so much. Anything can happen on a day-to-day basis. Life is short, we knew that and made sure to live every day with smiles. But the last few months have been anything but." She wipes her cheek, lying down beside me. "He was hiding something from me, I don't know exactly what it was, but it was big enough for us to argue about it right before he died." She closes her eyes and inhales a shaky breath.

I don't know what it would feel like if I lost someone I loved. If Adam died right now, I don't think I would care. I'm so angry at him for lying to me about so much bullshit, that if the reason why he hasn't come home yet is because he's lying dead in a ditch somewhere, I wouldn't give a shit.

But if he died when we were at our best, I'd be a basket case and need to be locked in a mental hospital.

And I think Dorian is experiencing the former.

The loss of her husband isn't as impactful as it should be.

Her husband died and she's falling for someone new.

"You feel guilty for not mourning like you should?" I ask, turning my head slightly to look at her. Tears descend the sides of her face, thick tears that get lost in that dark hair of hers.

She nods, covering her eyes and shaking her head. "Erin was my world. We were trying for a baby for almost three years, and even when nothing happened, we still stayed strong enough to hold our heads high. But—" she pauses with a groan. "Whatever he was involved in was big enough for him to forget to buckle his belt and ram head first into a pole, flying out the windshield." She sniffs and jolts when I take her hand.

"It'll be okay," I whisper.

"I hope so."

I sputter, looking at the stucco ceiling. "I feel like I should leave my husband. He's lying to me about so much. Hiding so much from me, too. And he's…he scares me. He doesn't necessarily hurt me, but it's getting there. I have this funny fucking feeling that Adam will inherit all the bad parts of Peter. All the fucking shit I despise. I just want to be happy, is that too much to ask for?"

Dorian squeezes my hand, sniffling. "What does he do?" she asks quietly.

So I tell her everything Adam has done, I tell her everything all over again.

Every single fucking thing that has ever happened to me, like she has to relive it as I do every time I close my eyes. From Lillian to Peter to Adam, then Riggs. I tell her every manic detail and every heart-wrenching moment. And she listens to all of it again, tearing up with me as I cry and tell my fucked-up story.

She sucks in a shaky rush of air and releases it in waves. "We were meant to meet in tragedy."

I hum, nodding, and turn on my side to face her. "That we were, Dorian. That we were."

She sniffles again and shifts her gaze to the poster of the woman, studying her as I do every time I come into this room. "She's beautiful."

"She's free."

A hint of a smile tugs on her lips and continues to study the poster. She understands.

Dorian understands all of this madness and accepts it. She accepts Peter and all his devious ways. Allows him in, allows this life in.

Smiles when things are bad.

She has a head on her shoulders. A better life outside this club.

And yet, she accepts her fate.

Maybe she's just as deranged as I am?

Peter

My hands are shaking as I sit in the passenger seat and Riggs guns it out of here like we just robbed a bank. I don't know what the fuck is going down, but it can't be good. I hate being kept in the dark and it seems like none of us know what's going on. Not even Roaden and he's my father's brother.

And when I glance over at my brother who I haven't seen in almost two years, it's like I just saw him yesterday.

Life is different when he's around. I feel lighter, calmer. I'm not on the verge of breaking shit or thinking of ways to ruin my women. I feel…at peace. As it always should be.

Riggs tried to keep me out of the business. I guess when push came to shove and they planned to fuck him over because of Lillian's stupidity, it was the last straw. He left this place. He left me behind.

If he cared about me the way he always did, why did he leave without me?

But I hide my true emotions, it's the only thing I know how to do. Bury my feelings until I explode. And I'll bury them deep down so no one will see them. Not even Dorian and I've told her plenty.

I gulp, looking over at him. His face is swollen, redness around his nose and under one of his eyes. There are scratches on his neck, dirt under his fingernails, and his clothes have seen better days. My brother and I turn plenty of heads, but right now, he looks like he rolled down a hill and smells like he fell into dog shit at the bottom. "They break your nose or something? Your symmetrical features are off," I tease, hoping to get a chuckle out of him.

He grunts, tapping his thumb on the top of the steering wheel as he adjusts his fingers. "Wanna fill me in on what I missed?"

I shake my head. "Well, I still don't know who the fuck that guy is and why the Panthers are sniffing around. But other than that, there isn't anything unusual." I glance out the window and see Adam's reflection in the side mirror. Everything Zay told me comes rushing in and I turn in my seat, glaring at Adam. "But this fucker is hiding secrets from us."

Adam chuckles, groaning as he holds his stomach. "You guys are fucked," he finally says, wiping his mouth.

I frown, staring at him as I try to piece together what he's saying. "You're just as mysterious as Daddy when it comes to answering questions."

Riggs side glances at me and keeps his focus on the open road. "You went to visit Daddy?"

I nod, still staring at Adam. "He had some questionable things to say about our half-pint of a brother here."

Adam hums, agreeing with me as he stares out the window. "Yeah, there's a lot of stuff you don't know about."

Riggs grunts. "Like how shaky hands has been one of us all this time. That ain't right that I was kept in the dark about this. The fuck is going on, Peter? Who the fuck would spill our shit with the Panthers?"

My focus is kept on Adam. "You gonna tell him or am I?"

"I already know this fuckhead is a prospect for the Panthers because of Daddy. Now, tell me what's going on because the last time I saw you, you were out. Now you're VP and—"

"Liam Ignassio is someone both of you are connected to," Adam interrupts him. "That's all I can say."

I scoff, staring a hole through his skull. His blonde hair is stained with dirt and dried blood. I don't know what they did to him, or maybe whatever Riggs did to get answers, but Adam looks like he was also thrown down the hill.

My anger is getting the better of me. I'm about to rip his smug face off. "The fuck you mean that's all you can say?" I say, narrowing my eyes. "Who the fuck is he, Adam?"

He shakes his head and sighs. "There's a lot you don't know, a lot I don't know, but I know enough to know this has everything to do with Mama

Rosa."

Riggs glances at Adam in the rearview mirror, then looks at me. We exchange a similar look. One of confusion, impatience, and...torment.

That fucking look of torment our mother gave us. That look she died with. Torment.

Fuck you, torment, and all that you come with.

Riggs grips the steering wheel, pushing his foot down on the gas. He's pissed and it's showing. "If I don't get a clear answer out of you by the end of the day, Adam, I'm breaking your fucking legs." He glances in the rearview mirror again. "Got it?"

Adam's smug grin leaves his face. He's always been a little afraid of Riggs. Never gave him shit or pushed his buttons like I did. Adam was a good kid.

What the fuck happened?

He takes a breath and fidgets in his seat, opening the window a crack. "I don't even know where to start."

I scoff, still turned in my seat facing him. "Maybe at the fucking beginning, yeah?"

Riggs pulls onto the shoulders of the highway, shrieking to a stop, and takes the gun from under the seat.

He cocks it.

That evil darkness looming over him.

Everything I've always been jealous of. How he commands a room and takes control of a situation.

How people fear him.

Respect him.

Praise him.

He's everything I strive to be.

He holds the gun with his finger on the trigger and turns to look at Adam. There's a smirk on Riggs's face like he missed this shit. Ached for the chance to hold a gun again.

I'd be lying if I said this is all I wanted my whole life. Me as VP and Riggs as President, the two of us running this club.

Running this town just like our daddy wanted.

He holds the nose of the gun onto Adam's knee and smirks. "Go on."

Adam stiffens, pushing himself up, which only makes Riggs press down harder. "Now hang on a minute, Riggs—"

"I said, go on," Riggs raises his voice.

Commanding the room.

We listen.

We comply.

Give in.

When we were kids, we ruled the playground. No one fucked with the Donnelly kids.

Every time Daddy came home with stories to tell us about the club, Riggs and I would sit in front of him, cross-legged like we were the top students in the class. Adam would stay with Mama, too afraid to hear the stories.

Mama never liked it when Daddy told us the stories because he spared no detail. Maybe it's the reason I'm so fucked in the head? But sitting there, knee to knee with Riggs and listening to the mayhem our father caused had to have been my favorite moments with Riggs.

And right now as we're shoulder to shoulder staring at Adam as a cocked gun is held at his knee, I'm in fucking nirvana.

Riggs is back, baby.

I hope he's fucking back.

Dorian

Erin and I were hitting rock bottom around the time he died. For weeks we barely spoke, barely fucked, and rarely saw each other. It reminds me of Zaynab's relationship with Adam. We're walking in similar shoes on two sides of the same coin.

But Erin and I always spoke about our issues. Then we started trying for a baby and that wasn't going according to plan. So we hid our problems and pretended things were fine. Until they weren't. Things didn't get better and after a while, I dove into work and he turned to pot smoking and drinking.

I don't even have a reason why we didn't play the same song and dance anymore.

But it started exactly six weeks before he died. I'd wake up and go to work.

He'd wake up and sit in his PJs all day looking for work.

A month and a half before his death, he was laid off. The company was downsizing and shutting down his department. I told him it was fine, and I said we'd be able to keep afloat.

He didn't believe me.

From eight to four, there was no telling what he did.

He could have cheated.

He could have worked illegally. Criminally.

He could have just sat at home all day and smoked pot like I believed he did.

But after that email from Liam Ignassio, I didn't think it was the case.

The last time we spoke, Erin and I were finally making amends. He didn't feel intimidated about the fact that I had a job and he didn't.

He was home when I got home.

He didn't reek of booze or pot.

He was fresh and clean and so beautiful I forgot what we argued about all the time. I forgot about the silence that continued to grow between us. It was us again.

That smile that made my knees buckle was alive and well.

He was mine.

I walked into the house on the night he died, and he was waiting at the door with flowers he picked from our garden and two glasses of wine on the island.

"Hey, babes," he said, smiling largely at my shocked reaction. "Have a good day?"

Stammering, I glance at the flowers, then at him. "I-I'm okay." I nodded, putting my bag down and getting out of my jacket, which he took from me and hung in the closet. "What're y-you doing home?"

He shrugged, taking my hand and kissing it. "I missed you. I missed seeing you smile. I'm sorry I've been distant. I'm sorry I can't find a job...I'm...I just...I missed you."

I smiled, biting my bottom lip, and chuckled. The stress of not getting pregnant. The stress of me holding down the fort. All of it was gone immediately. He was back. I had my husband back. "I missed you, too."

He smiled, brushing my hair behind me. "We'll be okay." He nodded. "I was scared we wouldn't be. That's all this was. My ego got in the way of our happiness. And it shouldn't have. My insecurity didn't want you supporting us. *I'm* supposed to support us, make a name for us. But...I did good, okay. We'll be okay."

I had nothing to add to that. All I wanted was for him to kiss me again. To love me and tell me we'll be fine over and over. I just wanted him. I didn't care about our arguments or the distance between us. I just wanted him.

I've always wanted him.

At least I thought I did.

"You're my everything, baby. I mean that. No amount of money or job or lifestyle will make me happy. Only you will. Know that. You're enough for me. Always have been and always will be." I chuckled, rising on the tips of my toes. "'Til death do us part."

His breathing shuddered like he wanted to tell me something. But I didn't press. I should've, but I didn't.

Why didn't I?

"'Til death do us part." He lifted me onto the island and cocked an eyebrow, staring at my chest in the tight navy blue pantsuit I wore. "We have weeks to catch up on tonight."

We kissed like the world was ending and undressed like we were on a time limit. Our moans turned to grunts and screams as we tore apart the kitchen, breaking plates, knocking over chairs, and finishing on the cool tiles. Out of breath and laughing.

I turned onto my stomach, fixing my breasts under me. "What made you snap out of it and smile at me for once?"

He rolled his eyes and sat up, slapping my ass. "I've been an ass because I was jealous of your success. Y'know my parents never had the means to put me through school, they never gave me the drive or motivated me and I hated that. So when I got that job and made my way up the ladder, I thought this would be my big win. Then they were audited and lost a shitload. Laid me off and…I lost my pride with it." He kissed my shoulder, inhaling. That same look shot through his gaze. What was he hiding that he couldn't tell me? "I'm sorry, babes. I am."

I loved when he opened up to me. I loved when he spoke about everything and anything all at once. It took guts to admit he was wrong, but something was still off…I simply didn't bother to press because I was smiling with him again. "I love you."

"I love you, too, babes." He bit down on my shoulder, making me shudder.

As I opened my mouth to ask what he'd been doing all day, he bit down harder, making me wince. "Now get up so I can bend you over the dining room table and destroy that pussy again," he growled, kneading my ass and squeezing roughly.

I giggled and did what I was told, numerous times that night. We laughed hard and caught each other up on the gossip, on the shows we watched, and he told me about the job interviews he had. We took pictures, so many selfies.

We drank wine and ate dinner, then licked whipped cream and chocolate sauce from each other. It was the perfect evening.

So fucking perfect.

When it was time for bed, we went upstairs, still naked, and brushed our teeth. During the past six weeks, we'd brush our teeth alone and go to bed alone. I don't recall a single moment when we didn't grunt a good night at each other like it was some animalistic duty to say goodnight.

Watching as he bared his teeth in the mirror and moved the toothbrush over them, I couldn't remember what caused us to stop being like this. What was the turning point that gave way to our downfall?

"Can I tell you something?" He spat the minty foam in the sink and rinsed his mouth twice. "I've been holding it in and I'm about to explode if I don't tell you." He let out a rush of air. "I got…um, a job of sorts."

I spat the foam from my mouth, too, gargling mouthwash. "Of sorts? What does that mean?"

He let out another breath and pinched his eyes shut before dropping his hand. "You trust me?" He looked at me in the reflection of the mirror, that bewildered gaze eating away at him and seeping into me. Filling me with worry.

"Of course, I do."

I couldn't turn around to look at him. If I watched him through the mirror, then maybe what he had to say wouldn't be true.

Maybe it wouldn't be that bad.

I wouldn't be mad.

I wouldn't be scared.

But I was riddled with fear and I didn't know what he had to tell me yet.

He wrapped his arms around my neck, kissing the side of my head and pressing his lips there as he inhaled. As if memorizing my smell, my touch. Memorizing me.

He cleared his throat, lips still pressed on the side of my head. "I found a way to make us money. Don't worry about how…just that we'll be fine. We're protected. I helped us."

"H-how?" I asked, the fear eminent in my voice.

He gulped, moved away from me, and sighed. "You remember when our car broke down on the side of the road a couple of years back and we walked to that biker bar? They helped us out and offered us a lift," he said, turning me to face him.

I nodded but shook my head right after. "What did you do?"

He took my hand and led us to the guest room; the room that was supposed to be our baby's room. But nothing ever changed in there aside from the pale yellow walls.

Opening the closet, a few baby clothes hung from the rods as did a leather vest. A vest that still haunts me.

A large purple panther roared on the back of it as patches lined the top and bottom. "I'm a prospect. President says I have potential to—"

"Are you fucking insane?" I raised my voice, heat climbing up the cords in my neck. "A biker club? They kill people! What the fuck, Erin?!"

He scoffed, tossed the leather vest on the bed, and gritted his teeth. "I have nothing! No job, no fucking savings, everything I have is *yours*!"

"No, it's *ours*. That's what marriage is, Erin!" I bellowed.

"I wanted something that was *mine*!" he shrieked. "Something I could do that would give us everything—"

"No!" I shook my head and roughly wiped away the tears. "We're trying for a baby. You think it's right bringing a baby into this world with this shit?"

He rolled his eyes with a scoff. "We've been trying for a baby for three years, if we were having one it would've happened by now." He wiped down his face as he stared at me. "We need money for adoption, money for surrogacy. We don't have that. None of that. So I chose to do this for us. For *that*."

"This is a stupid fucking decision you should have spoken to me about."

"It's not stupid!" he screamed so loudly, spittle forming at the corners of his mouth. The cords in his neck could be strummed like a violin, and his pale face was a beat red.

I winced, shaking my head and sobbing. "Leave this. If you love me you'll quit."

He shook his head and held onto my face. "I can't leave."

"Yes, you can," I whispered.

"I won't."

I touched his face and gave him a delicate kiss. "If you love me you can."

He growled, anger bursting at the seams. He was hiding more. A reason why he couldn't quit.

But it didn't matter. He stomped out of the room and down the stairs. I could hear his jeans followed by the sound of the door slamming.

That was the last time I saw him.

***

Sitting on Peter's bed, I sniff and look down at my phone. Gray texted me about an hour ago. I didn't answer. Another text comes in from Gray, but I ignore that, too. I don't know what to say.

I don't know what I want for dinner.

I don't know if I'll be home tonight.

I don't know if I'm okay.

I don't know what's going to happen to me.

I just don't know.

Zaynab comes back into his room with two drinks in hand and that sympathetic look I'm accustomed to. We've bonded in the last little while that we've spent holed up in this bar. I feel like a prisoner, but I know we're both here because Peter cares for us. Much more than he'll ever be able to voice.

And as much as I don't think she should leave her husband without attempting to try and make things work, maybe cutting ties with anything that has to do with this motorcycle club will do her justice.

She'll have that peace she's craving.

The corner of her mouth twitches. "You look like you need a drink."

It's funny how one line means so much to me but hurts so much more. I wonder when someone asking if I need a drink won't remind me of Erin. "What's in it?"

"Whiskey."

I hate whiskey. The smoky smell reminds one of Erin. All he did on rainy nights was sit with me by the fire with a glass of whiskey on the rocks in hand. I used to like that smell, then when things started to spiral downward, that smell did nothing but remind me of all the bad things in our relationship. The silence. The secrets. The infertility.

But I need something to ease my nerves.

So I take the drink and shoot it back in one gulp, grimacing and coughing when I finish.

Zaynab chuckles, that sultry grin on her makes me understand why Peter is so obsessed with her. She's angular, symmetrical, and defined. Every feature of her face appears like it's thought out. She knows it, too, because she's always moving her face so the light hits it just right.

"If you want another, don't be shy to make yourself something at the bar," she says and sits on the bed with her back to the headboard. "If you're hungry, I can get them to whip something else up."

Shaking my head, I stand and place my glass on the desk. We've been watching back-to-back nineties movies, more like they've been background noise as she pours her heart out to me again. Every time she talks about her life, I can't help but wonder why she even bothers staying in this city. She should get out of here, and find a new life on the other side of the country. She deserves happiness, more so than a lot of us.

My heart goes out to her and I'll do everything in my power to make sure she achieves that.

I sputter, looking around the room again. Peter doesn't have much in his room, mostly motorcycle posters I'm not even sure are his, to begin with. But there are a few pictures on his desk in fancy silver frames that stand out against the dark room.

Picking up one of the frames, a picture of Zaynab licking the face of a blonde girl with a crack in the glass that hides most of her face. Scratch that, the blonde's face is illegible.

"That was my best friend." Zaynab sucks in a breath as she sips her drink. "Peter dated her for a minute before he killed her."

I cough at her bluntness, turning my head to look at her. She stabbed him in the neck yet acted as if what he did was worse than what she did.

I can't believe I'm even standing in the same room as a woman who has the guts to plan on killing someone. Erase that, I can't believe I slept with a man who has killed someone—killed people! What the hell am I doing here?

Why the hell am I falling for a man I barely know?

I clear my throat, putting the picture down. "Why didn't he kill you, then?"

She shrugs, sniffling, then meets my gaze. "He's in love with me."

Of course, he would be. She's perfect.

Skinny but curvy.

Short but not annoyingly short.

Outspoken and with a mouth like hers, I'm sure it comes useful in the bedroom.

She's the definition of a "hot-ass girlfriend" and yet, the more I study her, I don't understand why Peter is in love with someone who deliberately tried to kill him. She's perfection wrapped in a giant red bow with the label *psychotic* taped right on top.

I don't think he's in love with Zaynab in the way that she thinks he is. I think he's in love with the idea of being in love with someone. With having that family, that woman to call his own. He'll never get that with her, though. She's far too damaged to be able to love anything anymore. She wants a new life outside of this club.

I nod slowly, looking away from her as I pick up another one of him, Adam, and some tall tattooed man. They must've all been in their teens here. Their faces are young, round, and not a stand of hair on their chins yet.

She takes another sip and sucks her teeth. "I don't know why he would be. I have nothing going for me. Mind you, I don't think he's in love with me. He doesn't look at me the way he looks at you."

Opening my mouth to speak, a soft breath of air releases instead. Then I sniff and look down at the picture. "We hardly know each other."

"There's a connection, something inexplainable, right?" she says, swirling her drink. My eyes shift to hers and I push my lips together. "See, it's like you guys are on a different plane. A connection that only the two of you can understand. It's what Adam and I had back in the day. A love that's...forever and always."

"You'll find that again, Zaynab," I say, tears welling in my eyes.

She jerks her head at the picture frame in my hands, wiping her cheek on her shoulder. "Stole the hearts of all three of them and I still can't understand why."

I tap on the picture, my focus on the blonde. "Isn't that your husband?"

She nods, lower lip quivering and she averts my gaze. "He loves me. *Loved* me once upon a time. He was my favorite person in the entire world. And then we got married and this shit with Peter started…my husband and I are two completely different people now. I don't recognize him anymore." She scoffs, swirling the remaining liquid in her glass. "Sometimes I don't even recognize myself anymore."

It's hard hearing Zaynab talk about her life sometimes. She hates it so much but doesn't know what to do about it. She can't leave. She can't run.

She's stuck. Her life dangles in front of her. There's nothing she can do but hope things will look up.

She sniffs, wiping tears from her cheeks. "That's Riggs, the older brother. He looks like a pit bull, but he's a big ole teddy bear."

"Peter speaks highly of him," I say and place the picture frame down, jumping slightly from the slam of the front door opening.

Whimpers, grunts, and strains follow suit. Zaynab quickly gets up from the bed and charges out of the room. It could be anything. It could be the bad guys coming for Zaynab and me. It could be the cops. It could be anything.

Like the curious kitten I am, I follow.

Peter and Riggs are holding Adam, blood is splattered on their faces, and they're putting Adam down on the pool table. His face is pale, teeth gritted, and veins in his neck are bulging as he groans and moans.

Putting a hand on my mouth, Lip comes over and tears off the jeans. There's a hole in Adam's knee, it's spitting blood and none of them are freaking out. This is normal to them.

All of this is just another day.

"What the fuck happened?" Zaynab runs over, taking Adam's hand. "Where the fuck—" she stops when she sees Riggs. He's staring at her, pinched brow, slow roll of his throat. "Riggs," she says breathlessly.

He nods, removing his gaze from hers, and stares at Adam's knee. "He's lucky I didn't kill him."

Shock sweeps through the room and the behemoth with the tattoos takes a step away, crossing the bar and eyeing me for a second before he escapes to the back room. He's the protector. The one people look up to. It explains the shock and awe seeping from their gazes.

Zaynab reaches out and grabs Peter's hand as he starts making his way to me. "Explain why my husband has a bullet in his knee."

Peter grits his teeth, nostrils flaring. "He's a traitor. A fucking asshole who deserves what's coming to him."

The poor girl looks down at Adam who's writhing in pain, groaning and moaning as his whole body shakes on the pool table. "Baby, what's going on?" she says quietly, her voice cracking.

Peter comes to me, blood smeared on his face. "You okay?"

I nod quickly, still registering what's in front of me. My heart is hammering in my ears and I can't even register if this is real life. "Wh-what happened?"

He shakes his head, looking back at Adam with that angered look again. "He fucked-up, and because of that, we're all fucking dead."

I gasp quietly, he doesn't change his expression but it softens slightly.

I didn't want this.

I don't want a life of crime or looking over my shoulder.

I wanted happiness.

Love.

A family.

What did I get myself into?

Peter

I didn't think Riggs would do it.

I thought we'd scare Adam a little, maybe shoot the seat beside him to scare him into telling us what he's been hiding.

But Riggs, he didn't care. After the second time, we asked him for the truth and Adam didn't respond, he shot him.

Adam's screams are still ringing in my ears.

"What the fuck?!" I yelled, looking at Riggs. "You didn't have to shoot him!"

Adam held onto his knee, doubling over in pain as his sobs pierced through. I've never been shot before, but I have been stabbed in the neck and it hurt like a son of a bitch. Riggs has been shot three times from what I remember.

But the knee, fuck, just banging it on something I swear like a trucker.

Riggs glared at me, that same glare he'd give me as a kid when I tried to do something stupid. "I was kidnapped. Taken from my home. My wife is pregnant and she had to come home to a house that looks like a tornado hit it. For a whole damn week I've been locked in a basement, beaten and starved for a club I ain't even a part of." He huffed, tossing the gun in the cup holders. "I ain't supposed to be here no more than you are, you little shit. I want answers to why I was taken and why you're wrapped up in this fuckery." He turned his attention to Adam and grabbed him by the collar. "Now, you're gonna give me answers or I'm gonna shoot your other *fucking* knee, got it?"

Adam nodded quickly, whimpering and wincing. "Okay, okay," he sobbed.

I stared at Riggs. He had this whole life outside of this. A woman. A baby coming. He was probably happy. Free.

I'm going to be an uncle!

And now he's back here again, that same dreary look of sadness clouding over him like a tick burrowing itself inside his skin.

Adam sniffed, squeezing right above his knee. "Daddy called me. He told me to do it."

Riggs scoffed, sitting back in his seat and leaning his elbow on the windowsill, fingers tapping his lips. "Fucking cocksucker," he muttered.

"What did Daddy say?" I wondered aloud.

Adam groaned again, shifting in his seat. "He told me to be a prospect for the Panthers because they've been sniffing around."

Exactly what Zay told me.

"Dumbass thought you'd be the perfect one to do it, huh?" Riggs sucked his teeth. "Goddam shaky hands."

"Why are they sniffing around?" I asked, staring at the blood spitting from the hole in his knee. Bile rose to the surface as I watched it like lava bubbling in a volcano.

Adam whimpered. "He told me that it had to do with Mama Rosa and if I didn't do it, then he'd kill Zay." He punched the back of my seat, nudging my head. "I let you fuck her every fucking Tuesday for a whole year just so she'd be protected and people would think she's your old lady. But a threat like that from Daddy…I couldn't just overlook it."

I chuckled, eyeing Riggs who was grinding his teeth. Jaw clenched, fists ready to attack…probably me. An angry man sat beside me. A man who started a life away from this madness. "Who is Liam Ignassio?"

Adam sniffed again, looking at me with narrow eyes. "Promise me you'll leave Zay alone."

Riggs flinched at the mention of her name, slowly turning to me. "Did you hurt her?"

I shook my head quickly. "It was to keep her safe. Guys were talking about making her take the fall for Lillian and what happened to Daddy and—"

"He won't touch her," Riggs said angrily, those eyes seemingly busting out of their sockets.

"I won't," I whispered, holding Riggs's gaze.

Adam let out a breath, looking heavenward with his eyes closed. "Daddy killed your mother because she was—fuck." He pinched his eyes shut. "She was a mole for the Panthers."

Riggs laughed, that guttural laugh that used to scare me when he'd laugh at my foolishness. "No, she wasn't." He took the gun again, pushing it against the bullet wound. "Wonder what it would feel like if I completely shattered your knee."

Adam screamed, grabbing Riggs's hand. "I'm not lying, I swear it, Riggs! I'm not. I swear on Zay, I'm not! Please!" Riggs removed the gun as soon as her name left Adam's lips. "Liam Ignassio runs the show. He's the one the Panthers take orders from."

"So he's their president?" I asked, staring at the hole in his knee again.

"No, Alphonso is. Liam is the guy they answer to," Adam replied, looking between Riggs and me. "I don't know who he is."

A smile spread on Riggs's lips. "And I'm going to ask one more question before I pull the trigger." The gun resumed its position. "Who is *he?*" The words left his lips so clearly pronounced that I wasn't entirely sure what he would do if Adam didn't tell him the truth.

Adam—the dumbass—shook his head. "I don't know," he sobbed.

Riggs's nostril flared. "Who is he?!" he screamed, making me jump.

Adam shook his head again.

Riggs chuckled and adjusted his grip on the gun. "Describe the pain for me, will ya?"

"No, no, no, no, no!" Adam yelled and knocked the gun away from his knee, the bullet hitting the speaker on the door. "I can't say, I can't!"

Riggs's frustration levels were off the charts, I felt the heat from his red face from when I sat.

He took hold of Adam by the throat and held the gun at his head. "I'm done playing fucking games, kid. You either tell me what I want to know or I will fucking kill you."

Adam sobbed, holding onto Riggs's wrist. He's always been our older brother, the one to protect us. And watching him manhandling Adam, as if he meant nothing, showed me my big brother was done with this business.

"Adam, please," I pleaded, trying to get him to see how stupid he was for keeping it a secret. "Just tell us for fuck's sake. It's *us!*"

Adam whimpered again and let out a sob. "Liam Ignassio is Mama's brother."

Riggs looked back at me, face pale and eyes wide. We never had family other than the club.

When Mama died, we had no one.

Just us, and Daddy.

But Riggs hates Daddy. Tried to get me to hate him, too.

He did kill our mother after all.

And now we know why.

***

Riggs hops in the shower first as I take Dorian's hand and lead her to my room. She looks frightened. Distraught. I don't think I've ever seen this side of her, this fear that this could be her life someday soon. But maybe, just maybe, if I get out of this madness, she won't look like she's about to hurl.

My presence will help her. It'll reassure her that this is not what this life is about.

I have to convince her we're not all entirely bad guys who go around killing and shooting people. *Yes, we are.* Maybe I should take a chapter out of Riggs's book and get the hell outta dodge.

"Hey—"

She grabs her purse and shakes her head. "I don't want to be part of this. This is—you have someone will a bullet that went through their knee out there and no one is doing anything about it. You have to call the fucking cops—"

Taking her shoulders, I slide my hands to her upper arms. "We can't call the cops. They'll investigate where the bullet came from."

She shakes her head. "I'm leaving, I'm fucking—" She covers her face and lets out a sob. "This isn't me."

"I know," I whisper.

She removes her hands from her face. "I can't do this."

"I know."

She sniffs, and I drop my hands, keeping my focus on her face. "I'm sorry."

My bedroom door opens and Riggs steps in, giving us a look over before

415

he brushes past us and takes clothes out of the dresser. "Who're you?" he asks with his back to her.

"I was just leaving." She blinks and steps back.

"All right, *Just Leaving*, do we gotta worry about you talking to people you shouldn't be talking to?" Riggs asks, looking at her over his broad tattooed shoulder.

She shakes her head quickly, shrinking in front of me from the fear my brother inflicts on people. This is one girl he's not allowed to scare.

"This is Dorian Wallis, she rear-ended my car a few weeks back." I let out a breath. "She's my, uh, my girl…friend."

Riggs freezes, frowning slightly, and taking a step toward us. "Wallis? Why does that name ring a bell?"

She shakes her head again, folding her arms. "I don't know," she whispers. Her eyes scan him. All muscles and tattoos. A heart of gold wrapped in a dangerous package.

He folds his arms across his chest, towel tied low on his hips it's barely hanging on, a swath of stomach muscles on display. "What do you do?"

She stammers, looking at me before answering. "I'm a l-lawyer."

His deep voice hums, nodding slowly as he sees the gold band on her shaking hands. "You married?"

"N-not anymore," she replies, bunching her shoulders as tears brim her lash line. Something dawns on her, as her eyes widen and she stands taller. "Before my husband died, he showed me something that he joined. It was vest like that." She points at the cut I'm wearing. "It had a purple panther on the back of it."

My heart skids to a halt, staring at her as she continues to speak. A purple panther? Her husband belonged to a rival gang? What fucking bullshit did I get myself into? Who the fuck is this guy?

A chuckle leaves Riggs. Fuck, I hate when he chuckles like that. Nothing can scare this man. Nothing can bring him down. It's fucking annoying.

He sighs, wrinkling his chin. "Erin Wallis, ya?"

She nods, more tears rolling down her cheeks. "How do you know my husband?"

Riggs turns to me, towering me by only a few inches, but it's enough to scare the living shit out of me. "You really know how to pick 'em, huh?"

"What're you talking about? We met by accident and we're—it's complicated," I say, glancing at her. "I don't know who the fuck her husband is."

Riggs turns again and drops the towel, getting changed and muttering to himself under his breath. Dorian looks at the floor uncomfortably. We're not shy around here. She better get used to it.

As soon as Riggs has on a pair of jeans, he clicks his tongue and sits on the bed. "You like telling stories, little brother, well, here's one for you." He has his hands between his legs, looking up at me and flickering his gaze to Dorian. "See, I used to be VP of this club, then after a crapload of bullshit went down two years ago, I quit. I got out and became a nomad. Was fun for a little, got to meet some people, fuck some women, travel…and then I met *my* old lady. An angel in cowboy boots. Almost a year to the day we met, she tells me she's pregnant." He taps his leg. "I'm happier than I've ever been, a son to call my own. To raise and mold into someone so much better than the life we were given."

He cracks the muscles in his neck and grunts. Tears are blurring my vision imagining how happy he must've been before all this fucked-up mess took place. I can't help thinking it's all my fault.

Riggs shifts his gaze to me, eyeing the scar on my neck, then glances at Dorian, eyeing the scar on hers as well. "But the word around the street is that people want me back. My men aren't handling things like I used to. They're sloppy. People are coming and going. Stealing instead of dealing like we normally do. The whole business is fucked and is fucking up the rest of the charters."

He takes a breath, letting his words soak in. He's not wrong, no one trusts Judas. No one likes him because he doesn't have a backbone. He's someone you tell what to do, not someone who tells you what to do. They listen to me, though. But they'd listen to Riggs even more.

"My wife and I are sitting in our kitchen, I'm kissing her neck and holding onto that belly with my son kicking up a storm." A smile touches his lips, happiness looks the best on him. "Not even ten minutes after she leaves for work, my door is kicked in and six guys knock me out and drag me home. Now, I have no idea if they left a note for her. And I don't know how she's doing. I've been gone for a week." He rises, stepping closer to Dorian. "Before I was taken, I'd receive letters in the mail. Handwritten ones. All of them saying they should contact them, and do you know who sent me those letters, Dorian? Hmm?" He smirks, gaze darkening. "An Erin Wallis. Now, I ain't stupid but I think there's something you're hiding from us that my fuckhead of a brother hasn't noticed because he's thinking with his dick rather than his brain."

She shakes her head, uncontrollable sobs shake her entire body and I take her hand, pulling her close to me. "I swear, I don't know anything about this."

Riggs grunts. "Well, I guess we're going on a field trip."

"Where're we going?" I ask, smoothing out her hair.

Riggs jerks his head at her. "Her house."

He takes a t-shirt and stomps out of the room, anger fuelling inside him from leaving his family and being back in the clubhouse. What is he going to do when all this shit is settled? Leave again so we can be back in this spot in a few years?

"I swear to you, I don't know anything. I just saw the vest the night he died. That's what made him storm out of the house and crash. I yelled at him and told him he was an idiot for being part of a motorcycle club, and then he left and died and fuck—" she sobs, burrowing her face onto my chest. "I'm sorry."

"It's okay." I shush her, trying to soothe her as much as I can. "I got you, baby, I got you."

As we stand there in my room, her muffled sobs wrapping around us, I realize that I'm the one who has to put an end to this so no one else gets hurt, I have to stop it once and for all.

Riggs

I'm fucking fuming as I storm out of Peter's room. I need a fucking drink and then I'm calling Shyanne. She has to know I'm okay.

Fuck it, I need to know she's okay. That the baby's okay. That those fuckers didn't touch her. Heat climbs my neck, sending damning throbs to my ears. I don't think I've ever been this angry in all of my days.

My wife is alone and pregnant.

Probably worried sick.

Probably calling everyone she can to try and find me.

Fuck, what if she thinks I bailed on her? What if she thinks I don't want her or a family?

This fucking club ruins everything it touches.

It ruined me. It killed my mother. It's destroying my brothers. Zay.

I tried to get away from this life, but there is no escaping fate, is there? This life has dragged me back home.

Draping the t-shirt over my shoulder, I stop in my tracks as Zay does the same, her hands bloody and dripping. "H-hey."

She winces, looks away, and continues to the washroom. I don't like that look on her face. That fear. The way her lower lip quivers. She's broken. Still fucking broken because of this place.

Like the dumbass that I am around her, I follow her. The urge to comfort her rises to the surface, as if it never left after all these years. I'm her protector, always will be.

She's sniffling and scrubbing the blood from her hands, cursing quietly under her breath. She hasn't changed much, her hair is a little lighter, clothes are a little less revealing. But she still smells like coconuts. I never noticed how much I missed it.

She senses me coming because she looks up at the reflection in the mirror. As if on cue, fat tears form and fall from those hazel eyes. "Welcome home." Her voice cracks when she speaks.

Closing the door behind me, I take her hands, holding them under the water as the blood washes away naturally. I squeeze lightly as I scrub soap on her fingers. I've done this song and dance a million times over. Getting blood off my skin has become a normal thing. I wonder if this time next year, instead of washing blood I'll be washing paint off my son's hands.

I clear my throat, gently moving from finger to finger on her hands. "Not the welcoming I was expecting."

"Yeah, it's a real shit show of a circus around here." She wipes her cheek on her shoulder, then looks up at me and forces a grin. "H-how've you been?"

I can't help but let a smile tug on my lips. "Helluva lot better than you." She laughs, appreciating my joke. One thing she taught me was to always see the humor in crappy situations. And that's exactly what this is. A really crappy situation we're both sucked into once again. "I'm gonna be a daddy."

Her grin turns to a genuine smile and she leans her head on my shoulder, more tears rolling down her cheeks. "I love that for you. That's the best news I've received in years."

Pressing my lips on her head, I close my eyes as our time together comes crashing in. My feelings join in a moment later.

If Zay chose me, I wouldn't have met Shyanne. I wouldn't be having my son.

If Zay chose me, she wouldn't be in this situation. She'd be with me, messing up sheets, screaming until the sun came up.

If Zay chose me, maybe my life would be the same. I'd be out of this club, we'd be married, and she'd have a big belly with my kid in it.

But she didn't choose me. And I hate that for her.

I hate that I left her behind. That I left Peter behind.

I left thinking of no one but myself. And now that guilt is riding me hard. But I'm going to fix this mess. I'm determined to see that smile that broke me in so many ways reappear on her face.

My feelings for her will always be there, will always have that bond with her. But she didn't choose me and I let her go.

I fucking let her go.

Kissing her temple, I shake my head. "I'm sorry," I whisper. "If I would've known what my brother was doing, what he planned, I would've stopped it."

She lifts her head and looks up at me. "It's okay."

She's so broken that this has become normal for her. This pain and heartache are her life now.

A life I ran away from.

A life she was sucked into.

And I realize I'm partially to blame.

I left and someone had to take the fall.

Someone had to pay.

She paid with a bullet to the chest, then was forced to open her legs to my brother for his own sadistic need to have her and for this fucking bullshit club that deserves to burn to the ground.

She wipes a tear on her shoulder again, shaking her head as if to drown out her thoughts. "Tell me, who's the lucky lady?"

I don't want to talk about Shyanne.

I don't want to think of her while I'm with Zay.

I want to see that smile, the one that broke me.

I want to see it and know that I'll fix everything that broke while I was gone.

I'll make this right again.

Judas kicks the bathroom door open, anger wafting in after him. Saving me from telling the woman who got away all about my wife. It's not a conversation I want to have. "We need to talk."

Looking at Zay, I nod, drying my hands as I kiss her head again. "I'll make this right, I promise," I whisper and leave one more kiss before I walk away.

She still smells as amazing as she did the last time I saw her. Coconuts. She probably tastes just as good as I remember, too. Whiskey and sunshine.

Glancing back at her, I pull the t-shirt over my head and let the corner of my mouth quirk up. She doesn't reciprocate the grin and goes back to her hands. She's even more broken than she was when I left her.

This does not sit well with me, but with the look on Judas's face, it doesn't fucking matter what sits well with me or not.

He looks like he's about to explode.

I cross my arms and cock a brow. "Speak."

He bares his teeth and gets right in my face. "I'm the fucking president of this club, not you. You ain't supposed to make decisions without coming to me—"

I put a hand up and he stops talking immediately. Like the good little puppy dog that he is. "I didn't make any decisions. Those fuckers took me from my home, they're keeping fucked-up secrets that keep unveiling that are even more fucked-up than the last ones." A chuckle leaves me when I look at the president patch on his cut, making Judas take a step back. "We both know you only got that patch because my brother's too much of a fuckhead to lead. But tell me, who do they listen to more? You or a Donnelly?"

Judas flares his nostrils, brushing a hand through his hair and cursing under his breath. "Fucking bullshit."

I grunt, looking down the hallway at Peter and Dorian. He's kissing her, soothing her sorrows. She's fucked. "I want a meeting. Get everyone in chapel."

Judas doesn't say anything, he knows that patch he's wearing is coming off. As soon as it comes off, my cut will be sliding onto my shoulders and one of the whores will be patching me in as president.

I can damn fucking guarantee it.

Cracking the bones in my neck, I make for the phone behind the bar. The one person I have to talk to is probably scared shitless.

I can't have that.

My worries for Zay can take a backseat…for now.

Two rings before that sweet, soothing Southern voice comes on the phone. "Hello?" her voice cracks slightly like she's still crying.

"Babe, hey," I say softly. I tend to soothe my voice when she's sad. Make my tone softer, and keep it rough and nasty when it matters.

A sob chokes her words. "Riggs? Oh, my stars, where have you been? I was so scared you left or saw something in my house that belonged to Denny that I didn't get rid of," she pauses, taking a second to let out a couple of cries as I remove the receiver from my ear and pinch the bridge of my nose. This woman is the only reason I'm not still riding around the country. She's my home, and I can't wait to go home. "Are you okay?"

I groan, sniffling as I try to keep it together. "I'm okay. You don't need to worry about this bullshit, Shyanne. I promised to always keep you safe, yeah?"

"What happened?" she asks, the sound of her blowing her nose moves through my ear.

"Rival gang from the club," I reply, there isn't a single thing I keep a secret from her.

She knows my past. Knows how many women I fucked. She knows that my heart was wrapped around Zay before Shyanne came into my life. Just like I know that Dennis was wrapped around Shyanne's heart before I walked into it. Fucker used to live in the house I moved into.

Used to lie in that bed, too. Disgusting fucker who beat her one night because she went out with her girlfriends. Well, I broke the bastard's arm not even a month into my relationship with Shyanne and told him if he ever set foot in that house or near her, I wouldn't bat an eye at the thought of killing him.

She still finds his things around the house, but it doesn't bother me. She has to know that I wouldn't leave because of him.

She whimpers, sniffling. "Are you coming home?"

"Soon, Shyanne, Soon." I lean my head on the wall by the phone and smile. "How's my boy?"

She releases a pained giggle, and I know she's looking down at her belly as we speak. "He's a kicker. Likes to move a lot and give me heart attacks like his daddy."

Humming, I close my eyes, seeing her face come to life. Those blonde locks dance around her full cheeks, those eyes smile just for me. "I promise I'll be home soon."

Silence spreads between us. A void filling with thoughts neither of us are releasing.

Thoughts of staying here and being the president of the Snakes.

Thoughts of me dying for the club before I get home to my baby boy.

Thoughts of what the fuck all this bullshit is about and why are we going through it almost six years since Mama died.

So many fucking questions and no one to give me the damn answers.

"Tell me," she finally says. "Are you back?"

I groan, hitting my forehead on the wall twice before I open my eyes. "I might be...I might be."

She winces, sniffling again. "Tell me you're coming home to me." A sob crawls its way up her throat and I'm reaping the repercussions as tears well in my eyes. "Promise me my baby will meet his daddy."

I hit my forehead again and grit my teeth, holding in the ache that's burning in my throat. "I'm coming home to my son." A rush of air leaves my lips. "I'm coming home when I get my answers, Shyanne. It ain't right. I need to get my answers."

She sniffs again, a soft moan leaving her. "I love you, Riggs. With all of my being. But yeah, it ain't right. You owe them nothing. Remember what they did to you. How they broke you. Remember that." She releases this breath that causes me to whimper. "Remember that you're choosing to help them. Remember that we're here waiting for you. Me and your unborn son. We're here, Riggs. Right here. If you want to fix things between us, then going back to them isn't the way to do it...because still, you choose them."

The line disconnects and it sends me into a fit of rage. She's not giving up on me, is she? She's upset because I'm choosing the club. Am I choosing this fucking place over my kid?

Don't give up on me, please!

I bare my teeth and growl, banging the phone on the wall, sending shards of it flying all over the place until my fist meets it next.

The whores in the club call out to Lip, he calls out to Peter. But the damage is already done.

My fist is splintered and bleeding. Spittle pools at my lips, saliva dripping from my mouth.

I must look like a feral mutt.

When Peter takes my arm and pulls me away from the broken wall, he sees the tears. He sees them and wraps me in a hug. "Riggs, Riggsy, hey. Hey, cool it, man. Cool it, will you?"

Zay thunders in, eyebrows pinched together and takes me in. Her beauty washes over me and I lose it even more. Tears stream down my cheeks, a growl crawls up my throat. I'm spent.

I've never broken down in front of anyone. Not even when Mama died.

I'm the brute, steel man that people fear.

But if I don't get home to my unborn son, the demons from hell won't be able to stop me from taking down every single one of these fucks.

I'm going home after I burn this place down. I'm going home real fucking soon.

Dorian

y heart is beating so fast, I can barely hear the music playing on the radio. Seeing his brother attacking the wall was just the cherry on the cake. First Adam comes in shot. Then his brother beats a hole in the wall over a phone call. One phone call ruined him.

Unlike me when Erin died. Is this the reaction people are supposed to have when they get devastating news?

God! What am I doing? This life isn't me. I should have stayed away. Said no to seeing Peter. I should have ignored his text and mailed him a check.

I should've left when Erin died. Moved away.

What's that line? You have to move, to move on from loss?

I'm twisted into this madness, connected to things I had no idea I was connected to.

And now, I'm pulling into my driveway with this thickness in my throat. This tightness I have to claw at so I can open up my windpipes.

I close my eyes instead, leaning my head back and tapping my fingers on the steering wheel.

It's okay, I tell myself.

It's okay.

With a shuddered breath that feels like fire and ice are attacking me, Peter taps the window, attempting to open the door. Slowly, I open my eyes, meeting his sympathetic gaze. "Hey," he says. His hair billows in front of his face. He sure is beautiful in that boyish kind of way.

My shaking hand kills the engine and he opens the door, taking my hand as I step out of the car. I haven't said a word to him when we walked through the parking lot. Didn't answer his call when he followed me home.

I have nothing to say other than *what the actual fuck is going on?*

I don't think anyone knows the answer that's why everyone's on edge.

The truth can, either, kill his family, or set them free.

My hands are shaking so much I can't even attempt to unlock the door, even with his hand in mine, I'm still on edge.

Gray whips the door open glaring at me and huffing out her words. "What in the fucking shit, Dorian? Where have you been? I've been calling you for hours."

I nod quickly, then start to sob and she widens her eyes. This is the first time I've broken down in front of her. The first time I've allowed myself to feel anything. I'd cry alone, keeping my tears at bay in front of everyone.

But not anymore.

Now, I've opened the floodgates and they haven't shut for days.

She pulls me into a hug and gives Peter a once-over as Bells comes forward, narrowing her eyes at him, too. "Wait, aren't you the guy who dropped off the flowers?"

He lets go of my hand and I glance back at him, sniffling as I try to compose myself. I'm the strong one. I have to be the strong one. "Peter," he says, tapping at his chest. "Your sister rear-ended my car a few weeks ago."

Bells arches an eyebrow. "So you're the deranged asshole who yelled at her like a lunatic and asked to meet at the biker bar to get paid."

He looks at me with a wry grin. "Deranged asshole, huh?"

I shake my head, wiping my cheeks as he rests a hand on my lower back for a moment. "Her words, not mine."

Gray pulls me into the house and Peter goes to follow but she puts a hand up, pushing against his chest. "I don't know you, so you're not coming in here."

He slowly twists his lips into a sinful grin, sliding his hands into his pockets and tilting his head down to just the right angle. "I'm sure your sister will fill you in."

Gray looks back at me and I take a breath, closing my eyes with the lick of my lips before I spill everything out. And I tell her every single detail down to what just happened at the biker bar we left to come here.

Home. A place that hasn't felt as such in weeks. It's just a building that holds my things and has my bed. Home isn't this house anymore.

But with this weight lifted off me, a lightness flows and I can breath easier. Revealing everything was easy, but unveiling the truth will ruin me.

Bells sputters her lips, shaking her head and running her fingers through her short hair. "This is fucking mental."

Somewhere in the middle of the story, Peter came in and closed the door behind him, leaning on it and staring at me. There's an intensity in his stare and I think he knows it, too. Because every time I glance at him as I'm talking, heat crawls up my neck and burns redness in my cheeks.

I nod slowly, eyeing Peter again. "Um…we'll be upstairs going through Erin's things."

Gray scans Peter, taking a step toward him. "You're probably some tough guy who can snap me like a twig, but if you hurt her, I'll find some way to come back and kill you."

He chuckles softly, smiling at me. "Yeah, I wouldn't dream of it."

Taking a step toward the stairs, Peter follows when Gray clears her throat. "Wilde is coming home to see you." She grimaces. "Just thought you should know."

I close my eyes, wishing she didn't tell me that. "Yeah, thanks."

Wilde and I never got along. He's nine years older than me and made sure to always rub it in my face when he didn't get his way. His mom lives in Australia, moved there when our dad divorced her and she took Wilde to live with her, seeing him occasionally on holidays, and that one time we had a two-week vacation in Byron Bay. I'd like to think that Wilde was jealous of us, but that's a stretch. He has the most beautiful life in Byron, living right by the water. But still, he never tried to be close to us. Even now, a thirty-seven-year-old man can't even send his half-sister a "sorry for your loss" text. And now he's coming here to stay in my house for some godawful reason.

This month just isn't my month.

I look back at Peter and that sultry grin spreads to his lips. I've never brought a man home that wasn't Erin. This was our home. The one he bought for me and promised we'd fill it with babies. Erin was the only person I ever introduced to my parents, too. Gray, on the other hand, brought home countless women. Once she woke up with one woman only to bring someone completely different for dinner.

I'm not like Gray, but here I am leading Peter to my room and wondering what my parents would think of him. Would they even like his cocky attitude? His bluntness? Or the danger that oozes from his freckled pores? I don't think they'd like anything about him, especially his choice of work.

The door to my room is already open, and I walk in, slowly turning around as I fiddle with the single button on my blazer. "I cleared out the guest room for Gray and put all the stuff in a box." I point at my closet. "The vest is on top of it."

He pays no mind to glancing around my room and getting a glimpse into my life like I did his. He goes straight to the box in the middle of the walk-in closet and brings it to my bed. He looks so...right standing in my room. How is that even possible? The way the forest green walls bounce off his skin and make those blue eyes and freckles stand out. I'm spinning, this whole day is making me viably insane.

Your husband just died! Get it together.

My heart's hammering, seizing slightly when he tosses the vest on the floor. It's the last thing Erin showed me before he drove off and crashed into a pole.

As the truth unveils itself, I'm starting to think Erin knew something he wasn't supposed to know. He didn't crash, I'm starting to think he was killed.

Starting to think? No, idiot, he was killed. Admittedly by someone named Liam Ignassio.

Everything is just...crazy.

I huff out a breath without realizing how long I've been in my head, when Peter glances back at me, giving me a smirk that only a demon possesses.

"You okay, baby?" His drawl when he says *baby* sends a tingle through me.

No, not only a tingle, a shiver of fright. Hope also blooms. Hope that I'll be happy again. Hope that he'll escape this life.

Hope.

I've fucking lost it.

I swallow loudly, parting my lips to let out some air. "Why do you call me that?" My eyes shift to meet his. "Do you call Zaynab that?" He shakes his head, tightening his jaw. "Before we slept together, why did you have scratches and bite marks on you?" The words are barely audible as they leave my lips. "Are you in love with her?"

His gaze is molten, but I don't move.

I'm not expecting anything to come of us, but if there happens to be something, then I need to know all the details of his past.

He knows mine, it's Erin and that's it.

He takes a step toward me, his body clashing with mine and he slides his hand to the back of my neck. "Zay is like oxygen to me, I needed her for so long. Needed her even when I didn't have her. I've thought of her while inside other people. Called out her name, too. She's a contagious virus and I'm patient zero." He swallows hard. "The bite marks are gone, they were faded from the day you and I met. The scratches—" He moves his vest over that catches his t-shirt. "—they're scars, see. Zay and I are a relationship that failed. No—" He laughs softly. "A relationship that never happened. She'll always have a place in my heart, I won't lie about that, but you, Dorian." A devious smile spreads to his lips that softens when he lowers his forehead to mine. "I see a future with you and it doesn't scare me. It swells me with happiness I didn't know existed."

The breath catches in my throat, lodged there like a clogged pipe. I have nothing to counter. Nothing to fight. His obsession with Zaynab has to end. She's everywhere for him, and she's nowhere. She's his being. His lifeline. But it's over.

The only problem is, will he be okay with that?

Letting out a shuddered breath, I release my head from his hold and look at the box of things I have no interest in going through. Erin was my husband, but the more of his hidden life is exposed to me, the more secrets were kept. And I don't like the thought of being angry at my husband without any way of confronting him about it.

He's not here and can't fight his battles anymore.

He can't defend his honor, even though I think he lost that a long time ago.

Peter takes a step back, that smirk spreading to his lips and he nods, looking at the box. He kicks the Panthers vest out of his way and rummages through the things. I don't know what's in it, truthfully, I never looked. I just emptied the drawers and placed the vest on top of it. I should go through it. I owe Erin that much.

Peter, moves things aside and examines pieces of paper and knickknacks until he finds a flip phone. "I'll take this, the rest you can keep," he says, sliding the phone into his pocket.

"That's just his old cell phone from high school."

Peter chuckles, arching an eyebrow. "It's a burner phone, baby." His attention is drawn away from my scared and shocked face when Gray steps into view, leaning on the doorframe.

"So, is pretty boy staying for supper?" Her voice is so dry and comedic, it's almost sad how she's not angry with me for moving on from Erin so quickly.

Have I moved on?

He places a hand on my lower back, urging me closer to him. "Love to, but I have some family business to take care of." He looks at me with a smile. "I'll be back soon, I promise." He leaves a gentle kiss on my lips and nods at Gray before his heavy footfalls travel through my home and out the front door.

Gray scoffs, dropping her crossed arms and stepping closer to me. "What the fuck is that, Dorian? He's a criminal and you're—"

Here it comes again. Like a freight train without working breaks. All of my emotions come pouring out of me like a waterfall. I'm heaving and sobbing, letting my heart flop out onto the floor.

Gray's taken aback, shaking her head in shock, wrapping her arms around me and letting me crumble as she strokes my hair.

Showing emotion was always a sign of weakness for me. And yet, all I want to do is weep until my head is ready to explode so I can cry some more about everything and nothing all at the same time.

Maybe I need help.

Maybe I need a new life.

Peter

I sputter nodding my head at Roaden who stands at the entrance of *Judas's Hideout*. There's a line forming around the bar, regulars and newcomers eagerly waiting to come inside and get their drink on, get some food, and listen to one of the local punk rock bands get on the makeshift stage and play a few ballads tonight. We don't have many bands playing, but the drummer's sister is Judas's girlfriend. We kind of had no choice at this point. My mind is racing all over the place. The last thing I need is to hear a bunch of guys screaming stupidity into a microphone for forty-five minutes.

Grumbling, I push the door open, finding Riggs sitting at the bar and scarfing down a burger and fries. Guy eats like a man who's four hundred pounds, but has so many ridges and edges it's a little annoying. Perfectly sculpted body like Daddy.

Lip, Judas, and Mickey are scrubbing the last of the blood from the pool table and floor, cleaning it for the crowd that will be swarming this place soon. The last thing we need is some fuckhead calling the cops on us over a little spilled blood.

Skeet is guzzling from a beer bottle as one of the whores sits on his lap. The Snake Biters are dressed as serves tonight. A black t-shirt and booty shorts with thigh-high boots. I think I'll steal one of these for Dorian. Seeing that ass in shorts like this is already giving me a chubby.

Dorian, not Zay. I'm making progress.

The whore is playing with Skeet's wizard-looking beard when I approach. "Hey, Petey, what can I do you for?" he asks.

I hold out the burner phone, nodding my head at it. "Do what you can with this."

He takes it, pushing the whore off his lap. "Whose is it?"

"Some guy who's connected to us through the Panthers. Might give us some answers to whatever the fuck is going on."

Skeet looks down, keeping his focus on the phone as his exposed cheeks darken a little. "Y-yeah, I'll see what I can do."

I frown, annoyed at how he's avoiding eye contact with me all of a sudden. I think Riggs notices, too, because he glances back at us over his shoulder, slowing his chewing down so he can listen in. "Everything good?" I ask, folding my arms across my chest.

Skeet rises, waving the phone at me, and nods. "Yep, I'll get right to it VP."

Watching as he scurries out of the bar, the front door slaps behind him on the way out, and the noise from the antsy fans wanting in fills in the rest.

Something felt odd about that encounter, but I paid no mind to it. I'm worried sick about Dorian and how she's handling all this.

ME: *Hey, baby. Call me when you can, I need to hear your voice and wish you goodnight.*

As I slide my phone into my pocket, a picture of Zay lights up. She's been the background of my phone for months. A photo I took of her sitting naked on my bed, a sheet covering her chest as she stares at the poster I have above my bed. She's fascinated with that poster and I can't understand why. I found that thing in the trunk of a car that Mickey jacked because the owners owed us money. It's been hanging in my room ever since.

And I love this picture as my background.

But it only reminds me that Zay must be panicking right now. I let her leave with Adam when Lip couldn't fix his knee. I'm sure Roaden made a call to the Captain so they won't ask questions about the bullet. Worry pours out of her and tears stain her cheeks. I'm going to make her feel better. I've always been good at making her feel good. One call and I'll have a smile on her face.

I head for my room to find my cigarettes. Disgusting habit I need to quit, but I need one. Just one more before I toss the damn pack and give it up. Dorian doesn't need a boyfriend who smokes.

She's my, uh, my girl...friend.

Introduced her to Riggs as my girlfriend and she didn't correct me. It gives me hope and upholds my promise that I'll find someone who makes my heart explode. Because she does. She will.

Riggs pushes my door open, two beer bottles in hand and his plate of food in the other. "What'd you give Skeet?"

Exhaling the smoke from my nostrils, I sit on my bed. "Went through a box of Dorian's husband's things and found a burner phone. Figured there could be something on it."

He grunts, making his way to the bed and handing me a beer. "Why didn't you just go through the call list?"

"Because I'm VP of this club," I scoff, taking another pull on my cigarette. "These fuckers can do some grunt work for me."

He chuckles, taking a swig of his beer and placing his food behind him. "Look at you, kid, growing a set of balls, huh?"

I smirk, flicking ashes on the floor and draining some of the beer. "Learn from the best, Riggsy." Although I sure am fucking worried about what could be on that phone. Shit, maybe he's right. Maybe I should've gone through it before handing it off.

He sets his beer down and clasps his hands in front of him. "Tell me, this Dorian chick, she worth it? I ain't lying when I say I've gotten mail from her husband."

I swallow the clog in my throat. What if her husband was involved in something beyond any of this? "What did the letters say?"

He looks heavenward and sighs. "Most of the letters were just his words... venting, I'd say. They started with warnings that something was coming. Then they were threats but by the last couple of letters, it's like he knew he was going to die. He told me about his struggles with his wife, his family, and tried to tell me the reason he became a Panther."

"Why's that?"

He shakes his head. "Said he had no choice, and would explain in the final letter, but the last letter was never sent. Don't know how he found me, but I think there's a rat in the club. And that's the reason Daddy asked Adam to prospect for the Panthers. Whoever this rat is…" he pauses, looking at my open door, and lowers his voice. "I think the rat is one of ours."

Frowning, I shake my head. "You can trust Dorian." I get up from the bed and close the door. If Riggs is right, I don't want any of these fuckers listening in on our conversation.

Turning on my stereo, I raise the volume enough to be annoying and sit beside him again. "How do you know the rat is one of ours?"

Riggs sniffs, taking his burger again. "Only people that knew where I lived were three of the guys." He takes a lavish bite, licking his lips. "Judas, Lip, and Roaden. So explain to me how the Panthers found me when the damn house ain't even in my name?"

I refuse to believe one of us is a rat. We're family, known these men all my life. Some of them took bullets for my father.

Then again, half of these men don't care about anyone but themselves.

One of our men being a rat makes the most fucking sense.

I take some fries from his plate and scarf them down. "What about the Houston charter? Do they know you're still a Snake?"

He holds the burger out to me and I take it, even though he has his burgers are always plain. I take a big bite and glance at him. "I don't have my cut no more, left it here when I rode off. All I have is this tattoo and my bike. But I rarely ride that anymore, the people in town get kinda jittery about me and I don't want Shyanne to lose out on customers because of my love for my bike." He takes a couple of fries. "But no, they don't know about me in that small town."

I'm trying to wrack my brain around how they could have found him without one of our men leaking that information. One of the men being our president.

I can't believe it. I refuse to. Not yet at least. Not until I have some valid proof.

"Shyanne, huh?" I smirk, taking another bite of the burger before handing it back to him. I'm tired of the secrets, the madness. I just want to talk with my brother like old times. "She cute?"

His whole demeanor changes. He brightens up, smiling, and chuckles softly. "Like a goddamn angel." His smile grows as he shakes his head. "I was in a real rough spot when she found me and offered me a place to stay. I made her mine as soon as I could and married her when she got pregnant at her chapel with her family."

I put my arm around him, smiling, too. "I'm so happy for you, Riggs."

He tips his beer to me and takes a swig. "We're having a boy, too, and I'm gonna raise him right, kid. Raise him like Mama tried to raise us without Daddy's darkness."

I lean my head on his shoulder. "He'll be the luckiest little shit this world has ever seen."

A smile touches Riggs's face, his head resting on mine for a second. It feels like we're kids again. Just the two of us hiding away in our room from our father. Sometimes Riggs would distract me with stories and movies, anything so I wouldn't hear the roughness that was on the other side of the door.

That smile disappears from Riggs's face and he slowly licks his lips. "You wanna tell me why you've been forcing yourself on Zay all these months?"

Lifting my head, my shoulders hunch and my head drops between them. "I don't know…I was so angry at her for what she did to me. And the club said someone had to pay for what Lillian did and I came up with the plan of sleeping with her—"

"It wasn't her bed to make," he says, the anger insanely apparent in his tone. But I'm too frightened to look at him. "She looks so fucking horrible, Peter. She used to glow and now she's…burnt. She's not Zaynab anymore. You took away her sparkle."

I wince, my lower lip quivering, and I let out a sob, pinching my eyes together. "I fucked-up. I know. But I'm trying to make it better. I am. I swear it, Riggs. I'm trying."

"Mmm," he grunts. "You leave her be."

"I will."

He puts his arm around me, tapping my back. "And this new girl, do I gotta have this talk with you about her, too? You forcing yourself on this widow?"

Shaking my head, I look over at him with a sniff. "No, I'm not. I really like her."

He chuckles, nodding his head. "Like you really liked Zay?"

A heavy sigh leaves me as I wipe my eyes. I'll tell him the truth, he'll understand. He always does. "I'm in love with Zay, but she's someone who will never love me back." I drain the rest of the beer and sniff again, groaning as I drop my head again. "Dorian is so different than any girl I've ever been with. The first time I saw her, we had this connection. It was soul rendering. Like we were meant to meet the way we did. Which is crazy because we're so connected in ways that I could never imagine. Ways we shouldn't be."

I look over at Riggs, seeing the version of him I looked up to when I was younger. It makes me smile and realize I have my brother back. I never noticed how much I missed him.

The first time we spoke about girls was on my sixteenth birthday. He was over with our mother, setting up the table with chicken cutlets, potato wedges, and green beans; my favorite dish of hers. She kissed my cheeks twice and told me to wash up before dinner.

Riggs followed me to my room and pointed at my neck. *You better cover those hickies before Mama gets a good look at them.* I couldn't help but laugh, they were the first hickies I ever got because it was the first time I fucked a woman and I wanted to show them off with pride. Show Daddy that I wasn't a pansy. But I respected Mama too much to disrespect her like that.

Riggs got me some of her makeup and covered the three hickies on my neck, then laughed, asking how it was. *I loved it, my dick loved it, but she screamed and told me I was too big for her.* He laughed again, tapping my back. *There are other holes in the world that aren't virgins. So plug one of those.* I snorted, shocked that this was his response to losing my virginity, but Riggs and Daddy were close around this time, so it was normal for Riggs to spew Daddy's words instead of his own.

Do you believe in love? I asked.

He shook his head, *love isn't real, kid. You'll realize that one day. Women want the same things from you; safety, money, and babies. Give them those things, and they shut up. You'll see.*

I wonder if he still believes that.

I sniff, wiping my eyes again look at him "Do you love Shyanne?"

He takes a breath, but no smile spreads to his lips. "I never thought I'd love someone. Daddy made it seem like all women want from you is sex and money. But it ain't true. When you find the right one she'll give you so much more than just sex. She'll give you hope. A future. She'll give you laughs and make you feel stupid at times, but it's cute in its own way. Then she'll give you babies, and you fall in love with her all over again. And that's what I feel like I had. That unique kind of love that I never thought I'd find." He looks at me, gently nudging my chin with his fist. "If you feel this way about Dorian, jump headfirst and see what happens. If you fall and hurt yourself, it'll be fine. You'll get right up and walk it off. We're the Donnelly brothers, no woman will ever break us."

I laugh, wiping my nose. "Zaynab almost did."

He nods, finishing his burger. "But she didn't choose us. Maybe if she did, we'd have loved and lost. But she didn't choose us." His voice raises at the end, angered slightly at the fact that beautiful Zay didn't choose him. I guess their connection was more intense than I thought.

"Now," he starts, getting up from the bed. "I'm going wash up, and when I get back, we'll have a sleepover like old times. But I want you to promise me that what you're doing with Zay is over. Give it a go with Dorian, you might fall head first."

He smiles, touseling my hair, and saunters out of the room toward the washroom.

Riggs is right. He's always right.

Now I have to get out of my head and away from this life to smile as brightly as my brother does. And seeing Riggs smile is the best sight I could ask for. It's surely been a long fucking time since I felt at home again.

My phone vibrates and I glance at it, a new message from Dorian comes in.

DORIAN: *Goodnight.*
ME: ♥

Silence.

I try to call her but her phone is off.

I'll see her tomorrow. I'll make sure of it. But for now, as I stare at the background on my phone. Zaynab needs me, she needs someone to shake the negative thoughts in her head. And I know I'll be the right person to do that.

I scribble a quick message for Riggs, letting him know I'll be home soon.

My heart jumps around, knowing Zay will be in my arms again. This time, it's not an urge for sex. It's not an urge to kiss her. It's an urge to calm her and be there as a shoulder to cry on. This time, I'll be there as the Peter she knew back in school.

I'm righting all my wrongs, starting with Zaynab. Her glow will come back. I will not be the reason she lost herself. I refuse to be. *Come back to us, Zay. Please be that sassy woman again.*

Sitting in my car, I sigh with my hands on the steering wheel. The stars are shining brightly tonight, making me smile up at them. "I'm fixing things, Mama. I swear it, I'll make you proud this time."

With that, I start the engine and rev down the dusty road to new beginnings.

***

The burner phone turned out to be shit. Whatever was on it, Dorian's husband was smart enough to sweep it, covering his tracks. Not smart enough, unfortunately, and got himself killed.

Or maybe smart enough since he left his wife alone in a cold bed only for me to warm it up.

Yeah, I'll wife her up and treat her right. Dorian deserves it.

I left her house in the hopes that I'd find something. I didn't. All I saw was a home she lives in with a man she loved. I wouldn't mind moving in with her, living in that beautiful home, and filling it like she wanted. I think she'd be happy if I gave her babies.

Maybe she'd love me. I think I deserved to be loved by someone like her. Someone so perfect, so beautiful, and so effortlessly forgiving. Woman was made for me and doesn't even know it.

When I left the clubhouse, Riggs called and said we didn't have to be in chapel until tomorrow, which gives me loads of time to check in on Zay at the hospital.

As soon as I step off the elevator, I spot Zay yawning and making her way toward the coffee maker in the waiting room. It's almost eleven, I wonder if Adam is still in surgery?

"Hey," I say, walking toward her cautiously.

She sniffs, holding out the coffee cup for me and taking another one. "Hey."

When I take the coffee from her, I sense something is off. Nerves? No, sadness, and not because her husband is in the hospital. Sadness because of this life we dragged her into. A life she didn't choose for herself. And it's all my fault.

"How's he doing?"

She shrugs, sighing heavily. "He's still in surgery. The doctor told me that it might take a while. The bullet shattered his kneecap." She stirs sugar into her coffee and sips it, grimacing at the taste yet going in for another sip. "How's Dorian taking all this?"

I chuckle, adding milk and three sugars to my coffee. "I don't wanna talk about my girl with you."

She hums, nodding. "I don't want to talk about Adam, so I guess we're even."

Sitting down, I take her hand to sit beside me. She keeps her gaze on the shitty coffee in hers, staring into it as if the answers to a better life will just appear.

They won't.

I know everything I did to Zay was wrong. I shouldn't have forced myself on her, I shouldn't have made her my girlfriend, I shouldn't have allowed any of this shit to happen to her. But I was so fucking angry that she didn't choose me. So fucking angry that she tried to kill me and got away with it by being happy with Adam.

She deserved to pay for what she did to me. And she did. She paid enough, I see that now. Getting revenge was not sweet, it was sour and disgusting. My stomach is still in knots about it.

Letting out a rush of air, I reach for her hand, bringing the back of it to my lips. "I'm sorry, Zaynab. I'm sorry for everything I put you through."

A gloom overcomes her and she sobs, her shoulders hunching. "I'm...I think I'm leaving Adam."

I frown, putting our coffee on the floor. "What do you mean?"

"I'm so sick of this life, Peter. Day in and day out, all I do is pray for the end. I pray that one of the Tuesdays I come to see you, the rivals will gun down the club, and it'll be my last day on earth. What's scary is it makes me so fucking happy when that thought goes through my mind. And I shouldn't be thinking that way. I should be living my life with my husband, I should be making friends, going out, and thriving. But I don't do any of that because of that thought." Her eyes line with tears, her head shaking. "If I cut ties to all of you, then maybe, just fucking maybe, I'll be happy again. Don't I deserve some happiness after this fucking life I was given?"

She wants her life to end because of me? Of the life we dragged her into?

I can't accept this. I refuse to believe any of this. No, she never thought this way.

She couldn't have.

I lift her onto my lap and hold her as she cries. "No, Zay, you deserve so much more than just happiness. You deserve the world. And I'm sorry I made you—fuck. I'm sorry, sweetie. But you shouldn't leave Adam, you should talk this through. Move on from this. Live that life you deserve, but don't end it. Please don't end it."

The thought of Zay being single again doesn't even cross my mind. If she left Adam, I'd have the chance to right our relationship. But it's not what I want anymore. No, I've finally moved on from her. How crazy is that?

"I'm tired of this, Peter," she whispers, her voice thick with tears.

My heart is twisted. Afraid to let her go. If I let her go, then she could do something stupid. If I let her go, then she could leave and I won't see her again. I might have started to move on from her, but I need her in my life. *She will always be my oxygen.*

"Do you remember when we first met? You got that scar under your chin?" I ask, forcing her head on my shoulder so I can lean my head on hers. She sniffs and nods, nuzzling into me. God, my heart is skipping all kinds of beats having her this close and she willingly wants to be there. "Well, that scar has a happy memory to it, doesn't it?"

"It's one of my favorite nights at Stanford," she says, her voice heavy with emotion.

I let out a soft chuckle. "Yeah, mine, too. But what I'm trying to say is, not all scars are bad memories. That scar brings you back to our night under the stars. A night that made me believe in fresh starts."

Her fingers trace the beauty marks on my bicep. "Why did it make you believe in a fresh start?"

I inhale her coconut scent as it fills my lungs. "That night was the six-month anniversary of my mother's death. I went out that night intending to get shitfaced and wake up in a pool of vomit, but instead, I met you." I smile, tilting her chin up. "You see, sweetie, all bad things have good things waiting for them around the corner. This is just a bad bump in your road, something good is right around the corner for you, I just know it."

There it is, that smile that can bring anyone to their knees. "Yeah, I guess you're right, Peter."

Kissing her forehead, I hold her like that until we settle into an awkward position and take a quick nap. I need the shut-eye, and I'm sure she does, too.

Things will be better for Zay. I fucked her life up, now it's up to me to fix it.

And I'll do it, Zay, I promise you, sweetie, I will.

Zay

I've been pacing this hospital for thirteen hours and drinking shitty coffee while Adam is in surgery. We left just a few minutes after Peter and Dorian did, knowing that if we didn't get my husband to a hospital, he would die on that pool table.

And Lip wasn't having that since he was the only one who bought the pool table.

I've avoided Riggs like the goddamn plague, knowing if I fall to my knees before him, I'd only beg him to come home from a life he's built without me.

A happy life with a wife and a baby.

Unlike mine.

Lip left about four hours ago, saying he was hungry and needed sleep. Then Peter showed up for a couple of hours, and left, too. So I've been here alone with my thoughts. And my thoughts are not something I should be alone with.

I pinch my eyes shut after my inner voice screams at me to rob the medicine cabinets of Xanax when clunky footfalls make their way down the hallway toward the waiting room.

Adam's been out of surgery and has been in his bed for a few hours now, but I can't sit alone with him. Not after our last encounter. The man I've loved and felt safest with for so many years, I now fear. And what I fear, even more, is the decision I keep going back to. Am I leaving Adam? Am I choosing to end this?

He's not the same person anymore. He's different. Maybe us getting married and Peter and I being…whatever it was that we were, officially ruined our relationship.

This club ruined all of us.

I sniff, elbows on my knees and head in my hands when the clunky footfalls stop and sit in the chair right in front of me. Instinctually, I look up to find Riggs sitting there with fresh coffee and bagels.

"Hey, sunshine."

His deep voice sends shivers through me. It always has. Even when I feared him, his voice brought me to my version of safety.

"What're you doing here?"

He shrugs, holding the coffee out to me, and takes a sip of his. "Can't listen to Judas bitch about his kids anymore."

I nod slowly, knowing exactly what he means Judas is a great father and cares for his kids so deeply, it causes the men who wear the same Snake tattoos and vests to stick their noses up to him. All because the club isn't his priority. Double fucking standard.

Holding the cup in my hands, I ignore the searing heat radiating off it. "I thought you guys had a meeting or something."

Riggs nods, adjusting his stance, which is just opening his legs wider. *Motherfucking tease.* "Guys are coming in from other charters. Chapel's only taking place later."

I sit back and exhale a breath, trying not to look at him and how utterly perfect he looks. His hair is shorter than I remember, and his beard is stubble now. But he's still Riggs. Still has that 'I can kill you with one punch' aura with a sprinkle of genuine niceness. It feels good to know he got away from this life.

Feels good to know there might be hope for me, too.

After a few awkward minutes of his gaze piercing a hole through my skull and me narrowly avoiding it, I finally lift my eyes to meet his again and he smiles. Fuck, why does he have to smile?

"How's life?" I gulp back the rock lodged in my throat. "H-how have you been?"

He slides his foot out, tapping it once and inhaling a breath through his nostrils. "I'm gonna be a daddy soon." The smile that forms on his face brings a line of tears to my eyes. I've never been more happy for anyone in my entire life than I am for Riggs right now.

He made it.

"That's amazing," I manage through the curtain of tears that refuse to break free, and a wavering voice.

His smile falters when he glances up at me and sees my tears finally slip free. "Maybe, but that doesn't excuse the fact that you had to go through so much shit because of me."

I shake my head. I would never blame him. Not in a million years. "We reap the consequences we can't predict."

His nostrils flare and adjusts himself again, sitting up straight. "My mistakes were not yours to pay for."

I sniff, wiping my cheek on my shoulder. "I tried to kill Peter. He was making me pay for that—"

"By forcing himself on you?"

Frowning, I look down at the coffee in my hands that has caused them to go numb from the heat radiating off of it. "It's fine."

"It's not fine."

"I don't need you to protect me, Riggs. You stopped protecting me when you left and didn't try to reach out to see how I was." I look over at a nurse walking past. When I look back I see him staring at the scar on my chest. A scar I got because of the fucking club. Something I am not ashamed to leave out on display. It shows me the error of my ways. The stupidity I caused by trying to kill Peter and thinking it would heal my wounded heart.

I sniff, licking my dry lips, and set the coffee at my feet. "You got out like you wanted, so don't act protective when you come back and see everything in shambles."

He cracks the muscles in his neck and sets his coffee and bagels down, leaning forward on his knees. "I will do everything in my power to see that smile on your face again, Zay. Every-*fucking*-thing."

I chortle and rise, wiping a tear away again. "Don't fucking bother. My smile left a long time ago and it's not coming back."

He sighs. "Zay, please let me protect you—"

"Things would be so different if I chose you, wouldn't it?" I interrupt him, sniffling.

He nods, rubbing his hands together slowly. "But you didn't."

"And I regret it every single fucking day."

Stepping away from him with the intent of checking in on Adam, Riggs grip takes hold of my wrist and he pulls me toward his broad chest, wrapping me in a tight hug. I choke on a sob and release, wrapping my arms around him, too, and weeping into the crevasse of his chest. I missed this much more than I wanted to admit.

"You're never alone, Zay. It ain't right what my dickhead of a brother did to you." He presses a kiss on top of my head. "I plan to right his wrongs, sunshine. And if it means coming back and running this club myself, then I'll do it. But I want you to know, that no matter what the decision is, you are safe. You will always be safe with me around."

My sobs have become unbearable. But that doesn't stop him from holding me tighter, leaving kisses on my head every so often. "Breathe, Zay. I'm here. I'm right here."

The little assurance I needed to guide me through this nightmare I have yet to wake up from. And still, I don't believe a word coming out of his mouth. He left me once before, who's to say he won't give me broken promises just to try and fix something that's beyond repair?

"I can't do this anymore, I'm done." I push off his chest and look up at him. Those blue eyes gloss over. "I'm leaving Adam."

He frowns, a tug of his lip is hidden with a deep breath. "I'm fixing things, Zay. You guys deserve a fresh start. It ain't right what he put you through, what Peter put you through. None of this is justified." He leaves a kiss on my forehead. "Let me fix this."

I sniffle, gulping down the lump in my throat. "Why? Why fix something that's already ruined?"

He smooths out my hair and tucks a lock of it behind my ear. "Because all of this, everything that's happening to you, is because of me. And I can't have that. You're supposed to be happy, Zay. Living in that cute little home Peter told me about. Popping babies that have Adam's eyes and your smart mouth.

I wanted to hear about that internship you were excited to start, I wanted to see pictures of your wedding, the honeymoon, your graduation, and all the memories I know you post on your Instagram. But I saw none of that, sunshine. You don't post anything anymore. This club took over your whole life and that ain't right." He leans his forehead on mine, a big breath of warm air fanning me. "Let me make this right."

Wincing, more tears threatening to break free. "Making it right won't heal my scars."

His thumb brushes my cheek, making me part my lips in the hopes he'll kiss me for closure's sake. "No, but they'll help you move on from this and make a life worth living for yourself."

My lower lip quivers and I grip him, sobbing once again at the thought of smiling. Could that truly be an option for me? Is the Zaynab I was when I met Adam still inside me? Laying dormant and waiting for her time to shine again.

If anyone can bring her back to life, it's Riggs.

If anyone can make me whole again, it's Adam. I have to find my Adam again. The man I loved even when I didn't deserve it.

My life is spiraling and my head is jumbled with a million different thoughts.

I don't know if I'm coming or going.

I just don't fucking know anymore.

Riggs holds me, kissing my temple repeatedly until I stop crying.

But the problem is, I don't think I'll ever stop crying. All of the things I went through for this club will haunt me for all of my days. How can I ever heal from that? How can I ever move on and pretend life is good again?

The dormant Zaynab will never come out to play. She's gone and she'll remain that way. Can I find a new version of happiness with someone I don't recognize? Is Dorian right? Should I give Adam a second chance?

Would he give me one after all of this is said and done?

Taking a shuddered breath, I grip Riggs's t-shirt that's wet with my tears. "I want a life worth living, Riggs."

"I know, and you'll get that life, sunshine."

"Promise?" I whisper.

He lifts my head, tilting it back so I can meet his gaze. "With my life."

There it is, a hint of a grin spreading on my face. Should I believe him? Can I hold that sense of hope that life will be better?

What other choice do I have?

***

Hesitantly, I walk into the hospital room and smile at Adam as he hits the remote to try and get the TV to work. His solution to anything is hitting it a couple of times. I've watched him slam the wireless mouse so many times trying to get it to do what he wants, I never have the heart to tell him he just has to charge the damn thing. It's my favorite quirk about him.

"Hey, babe," he says, smiling at me like he used to. "Where'd you go—" Then he's cut short when he sees Riggs stomping in behind me. "Riggs." He gulps so loud it makes my palms clammy.

"Just thought I'd come to see how you're doing since I'm the one who put a bullet in your knee," Riggs says, making his way around me and kicking out a chair to sit in, jerking his head at the other for me.

"Riggs, please. I told you everything I know," Adam pleads, stiffening before he looks at me with furrowed brows.

A slight nod moves Riggs's head, but his focus is on Adam and the bandage wrapped around his knee. "It's crazy how I had to put a hole in your leg for you to speak. Was I not a good enough brother for you to tell me things?"

Adam shakes his head. "I had no choice."

That evil laugh moves up Riggs's throat, seeping from those full lips. "Everyone has a choice." He leans forward, his fingers teasingly feathering the bandage. "Just like you chose to harm Zay, forcing her into this life."

"I didn't—" Adam's yells pierce through the silence as Riggs flicks the bandage.

"Do not interrupt me, yeah?"

Adam nods quickly, glancing at me as tears slip free from his gaze. I'm a mix of emotions right now. I want to protect my husband, the only man I've ever loved. And then I want to stand behind Riggs and put my hand on his shoulder, supporting him on his climb to glory.

"You will leave the Panthers. And I will see that you and Zay are protected

448

and out of this town. I have a safe house in Texas. You'll pack your shit and when you're outta this hospital, that's where you'll go." He takes a breath, content with his decision for us. "Now, the safe house you're going to is my wife's, and I will not get her involved in any of this bullshit. The two of you will stay there until I come to get you, and when I do, all this madness will be done. Do I make myself clear?"

I nod, even though he isn't talking to me.

Riggs sits back, a gentle smirk spreading to his lips. "One last thing, Adam."

Adam's face reddens, his body so stiff, he's becoming like hardened cement.

"If I find out you hurt Zay or force her to do anything she doesn't want to do, I will personally wrap my hand around your neck and snap it with my bare hands. Do I make myself clear?" His voice raises at the end of that sentence and I jump, tears welling in my eyes. "She is your wife, the woman who chose you when she could have lived her life with someone who would do anything for her. But she chose *you*, and you treat her like she's nothing. Letting Peter fuck her without a fight." That devious smirk seeps onto Riggs's lips as he lifts his leg and lets his foot dangle off his knee. "She told me how you forced yourself on her, how you shoved your fingers inside of her just to get her to submit to you." He eyes the bandage again. "I'm half tempted to shove my finger in the hole I created just to hear you scream and tell her how sorry you are, but she convinced me not to hurt you." He grits and bares his teeth. "Because she fucking loves *you*. So please, look at *your wife* and tell her how sorry you are before I ignore her request and hurt you anyway."

Adam's gaze shoots to mine and I focus on his quivering lip as I roll my lips in and bite down on them. "I'm sorry, babe. You know me. I'd never hurt you, I swear it." His breathing shakes when Riggs shifts again, leaning forward with his elbow on his knees. "I'm sorry, Zay."

Riggs tilts his head side to side and glances at me for approval. I nod slightly, sliding my hand onto Adam's ankle.

With that, Riggs gets up and fixes his jeans. "I'll be back tomorrow, we got a chapel meeting I ain't missing. After that, you'll pack your shit and I'll have you on your way to Texas."

Adam clears his throat, both of us watching the monstrous man walk away.

"Why Texas?"

A smile crests Riggs's lips. "It's home."

The air is thick when he winks at me, heading for the door. I keep quiet even though I'm screaming inside, aching for his arms around me. The door clicks shut between us, and Adam and I are left to bask in the silence that is our new life. All the while, a pang of regret flows through me.

Did I make the wrong decision? Should I have let Adam go for getting me involved in this in the first place and chose Riggs? The only man who makes me scream so loudly, the gates to heaven open up calling out to me to come in.

"Babe?" Adam's voice cracks, reaching a hand out to me as mine is still on his ankle.

I whimper, shaking my head. "I was about to walk in here and tell you I want a divorce. Believe it or not, Riggs talked me out of it. He said that we deserve a fresh start. He promised me things would be better." Tears roll down my cheeks, dripping off my chin. "But will you promise me that things will be better, or is my initial instinct right and should I just walk out this door and never see you again?"

Adam's weeping, the back of his hand on his mouth. "I never wanted to hurt you, babe. I never wanted this life for us. I wanted out, but Daddy said that if I did this one favor to find the rat, he'd promote me to VP once Peter gets his president patch. But I didn't know it was to be a prospect for the Panthers." He shakes his head, whimpering as more tears roll down his cheeks. "I didn't know, Zay, I swear it. I tried to get out, I tried so hard. But they found out I was Daddy's half-pint, and they threatened me, threatened to kill you if I didn't—if I—fuck."

My breathing shakes and I sit on the bed beside him. There are so many secrets hiding inside of him, so many things I don't know it's like I'm staring at a different man. "Didn't, what, Adam?"

He lets out a breath, taking my hand and kissing the tips of my fingers. "About five-ish weeks ago, a Panther tried to kill Daddy in prison." He sniffs, threading our fingers and kissing each knuckle delicately. I wish he'd just spit it out already and tell me what the hell started this war in the first place.

"Daddy ordered a retaliation, he told me to tell Judas. So I did. I told him and he ordered the hit."

"Is that why the Panthers kidnapped Riggs?" I ask, trying to understand what he's getting to. "How could this be the reason you didn't get out?"

Adam sputters, dropping his head back on the pillow and looking at the tiled ceiling. "Judas isn't the best president, everyone knows that, and Peter reacts before he listens. So Roaden is the one who decided how to retaliate. He sent Judas and Skeet out to gun down someone at their home, but they ended up running them off the road instead. The guy died on impact. He was—"

I gasp, interrupting him. "Oh, my God!"

A sob breaks through when I realize that Dorian's late husband is most possibly the man they ran off the road. He's most probably the man who sacrificed himself for this fucking club.

Dorian's life was ruined thanks to this club.

"What?" Adam asks, frowning.

I wipe my cheeks and let a sob break free. "Peter's girlfriend, her husband was a prospect for the Panthers...that's—he died in the same fashion."

Adam shakes his head and groans. "This is fucking—are you sure?"

I nod, taking his water from the side table and gulping it. "I hate this fucking life, Adam. I hate it so much. It ruins everything it touches, everyone who crosses its path. It's ruined me, you, Peter. That poor woman—her husband died for this fucked-up club." I let go of his hand and stand. "Riggs got out and is finally smiling, he's happy. But look at where he is. He's back, and I don't think he's getting out again."

"We're getting out, babe. We are. This life is dead to me because you are all that has ever mattered," he says, reaching for my hand and pulling me toward him. "Tell me that I'm all that matters, too. Tell me we can get away from this life of death and madness."

I'm crying as he forces himself to swing his legs off the bed so I can stand between them, groaning and wincing in pain. "Tell me, babe. Tell me we'll start over," he whispers as he brings my forehead onto his shoulder, beads of sweat trickling down his forehead. He's in pain but trying to comfort me.

"Tell me, let me hear you say we're not done. Let me hear you say we just need a reboot."

I'm incapable of calming down. My wails move through the room, shaking my entire being.

Dorian lost her love for this club.

Peter ruined me for this club.

Adam was shot for this club.

But Riggs, he crawled back to this club. The only life he knows.

"I want to start over," I whisper, feeling Adam squeeze me tighter.

He bathes my neck in kisses, sniffling. "Then let's start over. In Texas."

A pained chuckle leaves me, lifting my head to look at him. "Texas, huh?"

"Me and you, babe," he says, wiping my cheeks. "Can you forgive me?"

I sniffle, leaning into him. "I can try."

And I will.

I'll try, giving him that second chance. Life is so short that he could be taken away from me in the blink of an eye. I don't want to lose him any more than Dorian wanted to lose her husband.

But it happened, and if I can prevent that from happening to me with my second chance at a new life, then so be it.

Texas, here we come.

Peter

I'm pacing the front of the bar, waiting for Riggs to get back with the Audi. I told him I went to visit Zay last night, he didn't seem too pleased with that. When I woke up this morning, he wasn't beside me.

I puff on a cigarette, the smoke circling in front of my face as I see the black car turn into the parking lot. He's talking on the phone with someone, his face smooth and gentle, compared to his usual frown and natural snarl.

Must be his woman back home.

Shit, I'm going to be an uncle. I'll be the best damn uncle for my nephew. I'll spoil him rotten and get him everything that Riggs says no to. He'll hate me for it, but that's what uncles are for.

Or in my case, every time Daddy said no to something, Riggs was the one to bring it to me. When Daddy said no to another cookie, Riggs always gave me his. When Daddy said no to TV, Riggs snuck into my room at night with Mama's tablet so we could watch Batman together. I want to be like that for my nephew. I want to right my wrongs with this little one.

If Riggs will let me.

He pulls into a spot and a smile spreads to his lips before he frowns, and that normal disgruntled look showers over him. Guess the call didn't go well. I watch as he continues to talk, pleading. He wipes a hand down his face and his mouth forms the words *I loved you, babe. I did,* before he hangs up with an aggressive tap on the dashboard. Nope, that didn't end well.

He punches the steering wheel and closes his eyes with his head hanging between his shoulders. I hate seeing him like this. Sad and angry. He's the one who's supposed to support us. The one I look up to all the time.

He's my lifeline. But he changed after all that shit that went down, and this proves it.

The thick fuck gets out of the car, and sighs, tilting his chin up at me when I smash the cigarette under my shoe.

"You good?" I ask, raising my hand to hide the sun from my eyes.

He grunts, lifting his jeans and scanning the area. Typical Riggs always on the lookout for danger. "My wife ain't too happy with me being back. Thinks I'll fall right into the spider's nest and be sucked into the web of bullshit all over again." He crosses his arms over his broad chest. "It ain't right, but I'm not leaving until this shit is settled."

I nod slowly, accepting the fact that my brother wants out of this mess. Whereas I just wanted to rule it. "If Judas steps down, will you take the reins?"

Riggs cracks the bones in his neck and signs, nodding at Lip who opens the front door. "Let's go, brothers, chapel's ready," Lip says, tapping the doorframe.

I grab Riggs's arm before he starts for the bar and frown, wondering what the fuck is going through his head. I need to know if I have my brother back, or if he's just here for a fucked up vacation. "Well?"

"It is what it is, kid. I don't know what I'm doing. The only thing I know is I ain't risking my wife or my unborn son. They're my priority. This shit is secondary," he says, marching past me. Reluctantly, I follow.

Don't know what it is, but I have a bad fucking feeling about all this.

Lip holds the door for us. "Weapons on the pool table."

I scrunch my face in confusion. This is never the case for chapel. It's the one place we can do whatever we want and no one says a thing. "Why?"

"Boss's orders," Lip says, eyeing the two of us like he's some bigshot.

Scoffing, I fix my cut. "I'm not leaving anything—"

"If you don't, then you can't come to chapel," Lip interrupts me, that stupid grin on his face I want so badly to smack off. "Boss has some news I think you two need to be unarmed for."

Riggs scrunches his chin and nods, looking at the closed doors to chapel. "All right." He tosses his knife, and the gun from around his ankle onto the pool table; resuming his tough-guy stance and crossing his arms. "I don't need a weapon to kill a guy, and I can't very well leave my hands behind, now can I?"

Lip snorts, tapping his arm. "Believe me, brother, I know."

Riggs stares at me to do the same. The gun tucked into the back of my jeans makes a clank as I toss it at the pile of guns, knives, and oddly, a pair of nunchucks. But I don't toss my knife. Fuckers can take away my guns, but my mother gave me this knife and I'll be damned if it's not on me in chapel.

Lip pauses at the doors, the laughter and chatter of men on the other side of it sounds carnal. Disturbing. As if we're about to walk through the gates of hell.

As soon as the doors open, Riggs and I step through, then freeze. The air is thinning and I swear a noose wraps around my neck.

One of the whores, a blonde bitch with tiny tits and a big ass, is standing at the head of the table between my father's legs stitching up wounds on his face and chest.

My father.

He's out. How the fuck did that happen?

Riggs's entire body tenses and heat radiates off of him. Angry. He's so fucking angry.

"My boys." Daddy laughs, pointing at the chairs on either side of him. "Sit, we all need to talk."

Riggs growls, taking a step forward. "The fuck you doing here, old man?"

Daddy laughs, demonic. "You fuckheads don't know howta run shit. Figured if I fucked the right people, they'd help me escape. Little slutty nurse helped me escape." That smile, as sinister as I remember. "Slit her throat when I stole the keys to her car. Bitch is rotting in the trunk."

I grimace, looking at Riggs. Our rule is we never kill women unless it's deserved. Daddy doesn't believe in that. He never did. But I'm too shocked to muster up the courage to yell at him. Bile rises in my throat, the fear eating away my insides. I'm suffocating. This place is too fucking hot. Daddy is here. Here's right fucking here and it means shit is about to go down.

"What the fuck is going on?" Riggs yells, shoving one of the chairs outta the way so he can charge at my father. The blonde whore flinches, trying her hardest to fix the damage on Daddy's chest with shaking hands.

"Down, boy." Daddy motions for the chair he tossed, snapping his fingers at me to take the other one. "Sit and I'll explain."

Riggs glares at me over his shoulder, seeing nothing but red while I see nothing but roaring flames around the room.

I've entered hell, and I don't think I'll be able to get out of this one.

Riggs

Everything my father put me through is pouring in as my nails are digging half-moon ridges in my palms. I'm grinding my teeth so damn hard I'm sure pieces of my molars are chipping off.

But it doesn't matter, see. My father does what he wants when he wants. Gets away with it, too.

He killed my mother, he killed innocent people. He busted out of prison and acts like it was no big deal because he took the fall for all of the bullshit Natalia put us through. Put *me* through.

And now I'm back here, on the verge of losing my wife, all because of this giant fucker sitting in my seat at the head of the table.

If someone doesn't shoot him soon, *I* fucking will.

Peter clears his throat, looking up at me, as I slump into the chair to Daddy's left. As he sits at the head of the table, he eyes the guys around him. Fuckers have been known to betray us multiple times, thought they'd changed, but nothing fucking did. This entire MC is a sham. Everyone fucking over everyone just for the power and money in their pockets.

This place deserves to be burned to the ground.

Peter's stuttering, probably as nervous as I am that Daddy's back. "W-when did you g-get here?" He nervously reaches for his cigarettes, taking him three tries before a flame ignites on that girly lighter he won't get rid of.

Daddy shoves the blonde away and rests his elbows on the table. Man looks more evil than I do when he scours. Arms as thick as a normal man's thighs, shoulders broad and defined, and that jawline that can cut like a knife. What I hate the most, I look just like him and it's killing me to see that I'll become the devil if I keep it up.

"Couple hours ago when this fucker was visiting Adam at the hospital." He claps my shoulder and shakes it. "You realize I asked the bastard child to join for a purpose?"

I grit my teeth and shove his hand away.

All it does is make him laugh.

"All right, men, think it's time I tell you what's happening around here, yeah?" Daddy adds, taking Peter's cigarette and pulling on it. "Mmm, smoking looks good on you, boy."

Fucker.

Peter glances at me, I'm sure reading the spite on my face. "Filthy habit."

Daddy grunts, exhaling the smoke in my direction.

Asshole.

"Seems some of you have met Liam Ignassio?" Daddy says, putting the cigarette out on the table and sitting back.

Mickey spits his tobacco in that nasty mason jar he brings around with him. "Yeah, who the fuck is that? I thought Tony Alphonzo was the leader of the Panthers."

Judas grunts. "No, Domino's the leader. Tony's his son."

Roaden sucks his teeth. "You fucks don't know shit. Miguel is the leader—"

"Ignassio is the leader," Daddy chimes in. "And the bastard is out for blood because of me."

I grind my palm into my chin, scratching at the beard that's grown in. "And why the fuck would he be after us when you've been in prison for four years."

That demonic grin spreads to his face.

A smirk from the devil himself.

"Because Ignassio is your Mama's brother. And I killed her for it."

Peter and I share a glance before his fists hit the table and he shoots up. "That's why you fucking killed her? You fucking prick!" He lunges at our father, but Judas has Peter by the arms before he even moves a foot. Lip stands up next, right beside me like he thinks he can stop me. I'll use him as a fucking weapon to beat Daddy with.

Fuckers. All of them. They knew this secret and kept it from me. From us.

I need to speak with Daddy alone, but I don't think I can contain my rage enough to do that.

Peter elbows Judas in the gut, and that's when Mickey steps in to grab onto him, too, as he spits out profanities at Daddy. Calling him every damn name in the book, a few I might have to repeat to him, too.

As the ruckus is going on, I slowly rise, my jaw cracking from the grinding of my teeth. Daddy's laughing, looking at Peter like he's the scum of the earth, but really, he should be looking at me.

Grabbing a wad of Daddy's hair, I tug him toward me, gaze seething with rage. "Why the fuck would you kill Mama for that? She was nothing but a saint, you goddamn bastard!"

The room falls silent.

For the first time in my life, Daddy looks terrified.

No one steps in. No one stops me.

Right now, it's just me and my father, and from where I'm standing, I'm winning.

But I don't have a weapon on me. Only my bare hands.

And if he thinks I wouldn't rip his throat out with them, he's got another thing coming.

Daddy forces a devilish smirk, tapping my arm to release him. But that's the last thing I'm going to do. "Leave me and my sons alone."

Roaden is standing behind me, he knows not to lay a damn finger on me if he want to keep it. "You sure about that, brother?"

That laugh of my father's, so torturous and disturbing. "Yeah, I'm sure."

Judas lets go of Peter and pushes him into his chair. Peter grits his teeth and growls at him. Mickey chuckles, spitting at Peter's feet; that gagworthy tobacco he has in his cheek that soaks into his saliva is leaking down the front of my brother's torn Converse.

It only makes Peter growl again, flaring his nostrils. There's the fire in my brother. The same rage that eats away at me. That demon trying to claw its way out.

For years I tamed mine. Put the demon to rest so I could live.

But the demon's back and he brought his brother with him.

I still have Daddy's hair in a death grip, still seething and staring down at him like it'll make any difference.

It won't.

Peter's gripping the handles of the hair, he doesn't know what to do. His eyes are red and probably burning. On the verge of tears for our mother. She was the best, he knew it as well as I did but she shut her mouth. Daddy let her do whatever she wanted as long as she raised his boys to be like him.

And when she fought back, he'd smack her around, he'd rape her, he'd abuse her, and make her think she was worthless.

Our mother was far from that.

The night I came home from my first kill, Mama snuck into my room after Daddy finished blowing his load inside her against her will, and lay beside me. She didn't say anything, she just held me and let me cry. Daddy would've hit me if he found out I cried, but Mama, she held me and laid kisses on my forehead.

It's okay, she said. *One day you'll be free.*

When I asked her how come she wasn't free. She told me that *not all fallen angels can rid themselves of the devil.*

With that, she held me close to her chest and I eventually fell asleep. But Daddy busted into my room and dragged her out of it with the belief that she babied her children too much.

Things didn't get any better from then on.

I moved out, thinking if I wasn't there, then Daddy wouldn't have to go home as much and he'd stay at the club. It helped for a little while. He'd crash in the spare room that's now Peter's.

But Peter witnessed a lot of the evil our Daddy produces.

And four years later, Daddy killed her.

Now as I stare into the devil's eyes, I want to know why our mother deserved that ending.

The door closes, leaving Peter and I alone with our father. Peter's heavy breathing causes me to glance at him. He let a tear loose. A single tear is rolling down his cheek.

He's showing weakness.

Daddy doesn't like weakness.

He looks up at me, those fucking blue eyes that were handed down to all of his children. "You mind letting go of me, Riggs?"

A growl rumbles through my broad chest, making my hold tighten and emitting a wince from him. "I've about had it with your fucking bullshit."

He laughs, it's pained because I'm sure I'm pulling out every last piece of hair he has on his head. He puts his hands up in surrender. "And I've about had it with your whining. We can't all get what we want now, can we?"

Peter sniffs, slowly rising and looking at Daddy with that glare I've only ever seen on myself. That moment right before I take someone's life. That fear I lived off of. That fear I feed off of.

He has it now.

"Why did you kill Mama?" Peter's clenching his teeth as he speaks, grinding them like I am. A technique our mother told us to do when we wanted to talk back to Daddy.

Bite your tongue if you know what's good for you, she'd say.

So we do.

All the damn time.

Daddy shoves my hand, hurting himself more than he hurts me, and sucks his teeth in. Fucker pulled out a wad of his hair and I can't help but laugh at him for it.

"You boys act like your mama was a saint. She was as bad as the fucking whores we got walking around this club." He rubs his head and narrows his eyes at me before sitting back. "She came to me one night, the year before you were born Riggsy, cold and shivering with nothing but the clothes on her back. Her parents kicked her out for smoking. Religious fucks." He takes Peter's pack of smokes again and lights one, sliding the pack and lighter to Peter. Peter watches it as it slides right off the table, the lighter clanking on the floor.

Mama used to make us go to church on Sundays, I never liked it. I always felt out of place there. My father said, *you boys better watch it, you might burst into flames for having Donnelly blood running through your veins.* I always believed that, but Mama brought Peter and me anyway. Said it would do us some good. We learned about Jesus and his followers. I learned that the money the church collected was left in the top drawer of the pastor's desk until Tuesdays. When I told my father, he'd make me snag some. *Not a lot,* he'd say. *Just a little off the top so no one's suspicious.* Mama stopped bringing me to church when I was thirteen years old, catching me pocketing some change. *Your damn daddy,* she growled, taking my hand and leading Peter and me to the car. *That's the last damn time you're allowed in a church until you beg God for forgiveness.*

I don't think God will ever be in a forgiving mood for me.

Daddy tilts his head to the side and blows smoke from his nostril. "She walked into the club and smiled at me. Always been a pretty little thing." He smirks, brushing his right hand over her name tattooed on his left hand. "I made your mama mine that night and kept her ever since." He smiles sheepishly and lets ash fall onto the table. "But that beautiful selfless woman that you two cherish so much, was a lying cunt. Bitch fucking lied to me about everything. She snaked her way into my life so I'd tell her all the crap our club does."

No, he's the fucking lying cunt!

Peter takes a step forward, his face right up close and personal with Daddy's. "Mama wasn't a rat!"

Daddy shoots up, knocking Peter back a step. I'm big and scary, but Daddy is on a whole other level. He's got muscles as big as mine and scars tearing apart his body, one right down the side of his face. No one wants to square up with him, especially when I'm by his side.

But every time he tried to put Peter in his place, I was right there to defend him, much like I am now.

I grab his wrist, yanking him back a step, away from my little brother.

Daddy laughs, wiping his lip with the pad of his thumb. "You boys are so fucking blinded by that woman, you think she was innocent because she was sweet to you—"

"You used to fuck her against her will when she didn't want to fuck you, old man. So don't come here and tell us we were blinded by her shit when all she wanted was a better life for us. A life that didn't include this fucking club," I yell, shoving him farther away from us. "You better fucking explain why you killed our mama. Because you can spit lies about her all you want, we ain't gonna believe a damn thing you say."

Daddy sucks in his bottom lip, looking between Peter and I. Frightened fuck. I can taste it. "Your mama's brother is Liam Ignassio, the leader of the damn Panthers. I had no idea until I caught them one night talking downtown. He slipped her money, she slipped him a piece of paper. Don't know what was on that paper, but what I do know is, your mama was a rat." His gaze goes feral when he glances at me. "Now you understand why I was so mad at you when your little slut betrayed us?" He chuckles, licking his lips. "Natalia was a tight little thing, wasn't she?"

Rolling my eyes, I glance at Peter. He's shaking but trying his hardest to compose himself. He's going to piss our father off if he sees his weakness. Peter's not cut out for this life, he deserves better. So much fucking better.

"Mama was not a rat," Peter says through gritted teeth.

Daddy tilts his head, letting a shoulder rise and fall. "'Fraid she was, son."

I scoff, sitting back down. I'm trying to wrap my head around this and trying to understand how someone so sweet would risk her life like that.

If she loved us, she wouldn't do something so stupid.

But it's not like we can ask her.

It's not like Daddy saved any of her things for us to go through. Letters she might have left. A diary. Something. There's nothing left of Mama but the memories in our heads and the photo albums Peter has in his closet.

Daddy sighs, sitting forward, and thrumming his fingers on the table. "Don't know why Liam wants revenge now. Your Mama's been dead for ages." He grunts, shaking his head. There's a sadness there. I think he actually loved her, but if he didn't make her pay for what she did, then what kind of example was he setting for the club? He was the president of the Snakes. If he showed mercy, he showed weakness.

The dust is starting to settle, and answers are coming in, slowly, but they're coming.

My brother and I share a glance, speaking without words. We know what we have to do, and that's kill our father. Make him pay for what he did to our mother. There was a reason for everything she did. She shared information with Liam Ignassio for a reason, but what they were, I have no idea.

Peter falls back in the chair and takes the cigarettes from the floor, lighting one quickly. "We need to know what he wants."

Daddy guffaws, looking at the ceiling with a sigh. "He wants me dead, that's why. And if you don't protect me, that's gonna happen."

I let out a laugh, even more disturbing than my father's. "If you think we'll protect you, you got another thing coming." I jerk my head at the door, looking at Peter. "Let's go."

Daddy puts a hand up, keeping his gaze on the groove on the table made by a knife. "He has a few guys looking at that little blonde with the baby in her belly." His fingers trace the groove as mine curl into fists. "Shyanne, is it?" A smile spreads on his face as he looks up at me. "Why didn't you tell me I was gonna be a granddaddy?"

I grab his throat and shove him into the wall behind him. Every nerve ending in me is ready to kill my father. "If anything happens to her or my son, I will rip your throat out with my bare hands."

He laughs.

That's all he does.

He fucking laughs and sends chills through me. Enough chills that cause me to release him and step back. Watching this maniac lose his fucking mind.

And if I'm being honest, I'm close to losing mine, too.

Peter steps around Daddy, places a hand on my shoulder, and pushes me back as he continues to fucking laugh.

He's taking me away from him because he knows I'll kill the son of a bitch.

And if I don't do it, Peter will.

I need air.

I place to lay my head.

I need out.

Dorian

Kisses meet my shoulder, that stubble that used to annoy me follows suit. A smile spreads on my lips and I reach back, welcoming the kisses as they come.

But there's nothing to reach back for.

I turn over and stare at my empty bed. The spot that I used to watch and admire so often is cold. It's almost maddening that Erin isn't here anymore. Yet here I am, moving on from him so quickly. It's as if he never truly mattered to me when he's all that mattered. Our ending soaked me with guilt.

How could he have been so stupid to involve himself in something he never should have been involved with? And why didn't he talk to me about it before it was too late?

Now he's gone and there's no way of ever seeing him again.

I sniff and roll onto my back, staring at the ceiling and remembering the night we ended as if it happened only yesterday.

I got the call two hours after he stormed out. I must've dialed his number so many times, that when my phone rang, I thought I was dreaming.

A stoic voice spoke on the other end asking if I was Dorian Wallis, then proceeding to tell me my husband was dead. Breaking me in ways I never knew I could break.

But it happened.

I broke and then broke some more when I had to identify the body.

He wasn't my husband anymore. His jaw was broken, and gashes and wounds covered his body. His fingers were inverted, legs bent in other directions. His entire corpse was black and blue.

He was as lifeless as they get. Deteriorating already.

I gagged, vomiting everything in my system on the floor beside his corpse. What a way to commemorate his death by showing how disgusted I am to see him at his absolute worst.

I was numb from there on out. Nothing could fix me. Nothing could save me.

Nothing could bring me back to life.

But then, I rear-ended someone. And as scary and disturbing as his life is, my heart skips when he's around.

I'm sorry, Erin.

I'm so fucking sorry.

***

I'm in my backyard, sitting on the porch swing and drinking my coffee. It's beautiful this morning—clear blue skies, the sun is bright and warm. And just the perfect amount of birds tweeting before it gets annoying.

Erin purchased this home for us knowing that the backyard would be perfect for our babies. There is green grass for them to run around in, enough room for a kiddie pool, a sandbox, and maybe even a swing set.

But we never got to that point.

And we never will.

The backdoor opens and Gray pops her head out, smiling. "Hey."

I hold out my coffee mug and she takes it, gulping the rest. "How'd you sleep?"

She shrugs, pointing behind her. "That biker is here for you." A smirk spreads to her lips. "He brought you flowers again."

Heat crawls up my neck as I rise, looking down at Erin's t-shirt that barely covers my backside. I swallow hard, nodding at her and taking back my coffee mug.

"Be careful, please," she whispers.

I touch her shoulder, seeing the worry on her face. "Don't worry about me. I'm always careful."

"I'm serious, Dorian. He's bad news."

I know he is but my conscience doesn't.

All I leave her is a smile and step into the house. He's killed people. He's hurt some and forced himself on many. Yet, none of that bothers me when it should.

My life was always played by the rules.

I slow down at yellow lights.

I give change to the homeless.

I recycle.

I compost.

I drive an electric car for Christ's sake!

I do everything by the book, and when Peter crashed into my life, something felt new.

That little bit of bad sprinkled on all of my goodness.

Gray isn't wrong, Peter is holding a small bouquet of pink roses and nodding at Bells as she makes him a cup of coffee. That leather and cigarette smell eating up the kitchen.

"Hey, Peter," I say, slowly crossing my arms.

He whips his head around and gives me a once-over, a smile spreading to his face as he brushes his hair back when he gets sight of my legs. "Morning."

Licking my lips, I push them together to hide my smile. But I'm failing because he steps forward and holds the flowers out to me. "Thanks, um, what're doing here, Peter?" I sniff the flowers, looking up at him.

The corner of his mouth curls in. "I wanted to see you."

Bells snorts, sliding the mug of fresh coffee to him, and arches an eyebrow. "You know her husband died like six weeks ago, right?"

He nods, keeping his gaze on me. "I know."

Placing my mug on the island, Bells refills it, glancing between Peter and me. The awkward silence drapes over us like a dense fog. But that doesn't stop Peter from keeping his eyes locked with mine, as if we're the only people in the house.

Gray brushes past me, snapping her fingers to stop this. "You staying for breakfast, Peter?"

Glancing at Gray, then Bells as she takes out a loaf of bread. I meet his eyes again, they're smiling at me and taking in my nerves with a soft chuckle.

"Um…d-do you want to?"

He shrugs, taking the milk and pouring some in his coffee, then takes sugar and adds three spoonfuls, sliding the sugar over to me. "I'd love to, but we should talk first," he says as I'm stirring sugar in my coffee.

"O-okay," I say, looking at Gray before heading to the stairs that lead to my room. He follows with his coffee in hand, grinning at my sister and her girlfriend.

His clunky footfalls echo throughout the home. Erin was light on his feet, he'd startle me constantly, and often on purpose just to tease me. I miss how he used to tease me.

Sipping my coffee, I put it on my dresser when I walk into my room, and the sound of my bedroom door closing and locking causes me to turn around to look at Peter.

He makes his way to me, putting his coffee down as well. The subtle parting of his lips when he looks down at me throws my stomach into overdrive like tumbling clothes in a dryer.

"What're you doing here?" I ask breathlessly.

He takes a strand of hair and twirls it around his finger before tucking it behind my ear. "Showing you that this can work if you'll let it."

He lifts my chin and places a soft kiss on my lips, waiting until I deepen it. But I don't.

I step back, leaving his grasp that feels empty without him. "I don't want to be involved in any of your…business."

He shrugs off his leather vest and tosses it aside. The rings on his fingers slowly slide off next and are placed on my dresser. "Then I'm done." He holds his gaze with mine, intense and ferocious. I'm scared if I look away he'll grab me and force himself on me.

No, he'd never do that to *me*.

He's not evil like the people he associates with.

Peter's different. A soul who got lost on the way to salvation, looking for an escape.

"I can't have you do that. Not with everything happening." I take a shuddered breath as his hand touches my face this time, teetering off my chin. "Y-your brother. Isn't something bad going on because of him?"

He shakes his head. "No, baby, nothing my brother does is ever bad. It has everything to do with our daddy. He's the one who's fucking up our lives."

He gets out of his boots and takes my hand, leading us to the bed. I'm hesitant at first, but something about Peter calms my nerves. Something about the way he looks at me, how he worries without saying anything, and his loyalty to a club that ruined him shows how devoted he can be. But devotion has a price, doesn't it? I mean, look at what he put Zaynab through, she didn't deserve that. But he's fixing things, he promised he would.

What the heck is wrong with me that I'm sympathizing with a biker who's killed before?

And what the heck am I doing liking said biker while at it?

He cups the side of my face and smirks before leaning down to kiss me. And I let him. I let him consume all of me.

I know it's wrong.

I knew it was the moment I stepped foot in that club and let him drink me in.

But he's got me now.

Molded me to him.

We're naked in moments, lying on my bed as he parts my legs and eases into me.

I shouldn't be doing this. But I can't help it. He's making the pain go away. He's taking my heartache and gluing my broken pieces back together.

He makes love to me, kissing my neck and holding my hand above my head while the other is gripping my thigh. I've only ever been with Erin. Everything I've learned was from him. Yet being with Peter feels just as new and exhilarating as it was the first time Erin and I made love.

The passion. The excitement. The nerves and fear as my back arches and I let out the softest moan.

Peter's lips meet mine, and for a moment, I remember Erin as the man he used to be. The perfect gentleman who loved me for everything that I am. But he's gone, and I have to accept that.

Peter's thrusts speed up, causing more moans to leave me. "Shh, baby. We don't wanna get in trouble now, do we?"

Just the thought of someone walking in drives me over the edge. My nails dig into his back, scratching deeply. He winces, but that only causes him to thrust harder.

Soon, we're both suppressing our moans and releasing.

He grunts, stilling inside me, and relaxes his body on top of mine. I don't regret it this time.

I welcome it. Encourage it to happen again.

He's a lost puppy looking for a home and guidance. I can try to be his guide. I can try to show him a life outside the motorcycle club. Maybe I can heal him, too.

He exhales sharply and lifts his head. "I like you, Dorian."

Licking my lips, I brush strands of hair off of them. "I'm starting to like you, too." Then I frown when his smile spreads to his lips. "What about Zaynab?"

He shakes his head. "I'm done with that."

"You're in love with her, it's not something you get over so quickly," I say as he rolls off me and puts his hands behind his head.

No, it's not. And here I am opening up to another man when I loved Erin, too.

He scans my room slowly, trailing his eyes to mine. "What about your husband, are you over that?"

I turn on my side to face him, curling a hand under my chin. "No, I'm not over him. He died in the middle of an argument. I never got to say goodbye and I'll always keep that with me." I meet his gaze. "But Zaynab, you forced yourself to be with her for almost a year when you didn't have to. You admire everything she does, and I don't blame you for it. She's breathtaking and has this quirk about her that's addictive. But if this is going to work, you have to let her go."

He turns on his side to face me, moving hair behind my shoulder. "I have let her go, baby. It's you."

"But we barely know each other," I whisper, placing my hand on his that's caressing my face.

The tip of his nose touches mine and he closes his eyes, a grin spreading to his lips. "I know you feel it." He keeps his voice low, and serious. "That instant connection that feels like we're on another plane of existence." He slowly opens his eyes and bores into mine. "You feel it, too. That's why who I am doesn't scare you. That's why you're with me. And that's why I'm here, giving myself to you, and telling you that I'm out. After all this bullshit, I'm out."

Tears blur my vision and I nod. Believing everything he's telling me. Because I feel it, too.

That connection, that urge to be near him.

Two lost souls uniting in the middle.

Finding each other and promising bigger and better things.

"You'll do that for me?"

He nods, kissing me and pulling me on top of him. "I'd do anything for you, Dorian. Anything."

And I'm sure he would. But would I be okay with starting something new so soon after Erin? The only man I've loved, the only man I've been with. Am I okay with this new thing?

Peter folds his arms behind his head, staring at me like I'm the *Mona Lisa* at the Louvre. "What's that look about?"

I frown, stammering slightly. "What look?"

He chuckles, running his fingers through my hair. "You look like you're about to give me shit."

I adjust my hands under my chin, feeling the beating of his heart under my palms. Erin's used to race like this whenever I lay on him. I loved listening to how it would beat quickly, then relax, and as soon as I kissed his chest, it would speed up again. Peter's is the same.

Letting out a breath, Peter's hand resumes its position behind his head and my eyes catch his. "I found a letter last night, something Erin wrote. I think it has something to do with your brother."

Peter closes his eyes and inhales sharply. "Riggs told me about the letters your husband sent him."

"He spoke about me in those letters?" I ask as tears threaten to escape.

"Apparently."

I roll off him, staring at the ceiling as tears roll down the sides of my face. I never understood why Erin joined the biker club. I still don't understand him, even after reading this letter. But he said he did it for me. To save me. I wish I understood why.

Peter turns over, tucking me to his chest and resting his chin on my head. "Hey, talk to me."

Pushing off of him, I get up, pulling Erin's t-shirt over my head as I take the folded letter off the dresser. I stare at it as more tears form, and turn to find Peter on his knees in the middle of the bed, sitting back on his heels, staring at me. "This is the letter."

He stares at it, then at me, thick eyebrows furrowing. "If I read it, will it change how you feel about me?"

I shake my head, having read this letter six times already. My heart still beats irregularly when I look at Peter, and in so many ways it kills me that it has been this easy to move on from Erin. Was he not my true love? Or was he the man to show me that love exists and that even though he's gone, I can love again the same way I loved him?

Coming closer to the bed, I hand Peter the letter, holding my breath as he takes it and opens it. Erin's last words.

Here's the last one. The one that's supposed to tell you we're coming to find you. But frankly, I don't even know why they told me to send these. Each one was supposed to be threatening. Supposed to make you think that you're not safe anymore. But you've always been safe, Riggs. None of us were coming to get you until he's released. And I don't know when that happens.

I joined this motorcycle club for two reasons. The first was for the safety of my wife and the second, was to make sure my wife is set in case something happens to me. We've been a little rocky lately, been trying for three years to give her a piece of us, but nothing's working, and adopting is expensive as shit, so one day I walked into the Panthers' club, offering my services. Next thing I know, I'm delivering stuff late at night. Picking up bloodied men, dirty hookers, and stashing murder weapons. After three weeks, I was given a vest with my prospect patch. I was damn proud of that, it was something I earned after getting laid off.

But my wife, I still have to tell my wife.

Turns out, the club had their eye on her for some time. "Best lawyer in San Jose," Tony told me. But I wouldn't let them anywhere near her. She's too good for this life. And now, because of me, she's part of this life whether she wants to be or not.

I just want to make her proud. Make her happy again.

This is the final letter, and I hope you know that we mean no harm to you or your wife, Riggs. We just need you to come home one last time to settle the dust that's been ruffled.

Once the dust is settled, you'll be able to enjoy your little family, and maybe one day I will, too.

Until we meet in person, Erin Wallis.

I wipe my cheeks as Peter puts the letter down, tonguing his cheek and narrowing his eyes at something beside me. "I don't understand what he's talking about."

He shakes his head, glancing at the letter again. "Liam Ignassio is my uncle. My mama's brother apparently." He sniffs, tears welling in his eyes now. "My daddy killed her because she used to give Liam intel on the Snakes. But I don't know anything more than that." He roughly wipes his cheeks, gets off the bed, and takes his coffee. "We're supposed to plan a meeting with him soon."

"Am I safe?" I whisper as he gulps his coffee.

He nods, tracing his finger down my nose. "You'll always be safe with me."

A smile spreads on my face as tears spill free. Things will be different around him. Less depressing and more chaotic. Once the dust settles, we'll be able to blossom this thing we're trying. We'll be able to laugh and live life like a normal couple. We'll smile. We'll be happy. Things will be normal. But what's normal in my life without Erin?

Maybe one day I will, too.

***

Bells and Gray are sitting in the living room when Peter and I finally leave my bedroom. The beginning of a relationship is my favorite. The infatuation, the touching, and the kissing. The sex that feels like it's never enough.

I want to experience happiness with him, too, but fear still simmers at the back of my mind. When is this going to end? When is he going to be sick of me? Or when is the motorcycle club going to need him again? Is he ready to give up this life of crime for me?

Bells gets off the couch and saunters to the kitchen, taking plates out of the oven. "I kept the heat low so the food wouldn't get cold, thought you guys would be quicker."

Gray smirks over her shoulder, sticking her tongue between her teeth. "Next time, have sex on a bed that doesn't squeak so much."

"Oh, God." I cover my face and shake my head.

Peter laughs, removing one of my hands. That smile that melts my heart is on his face. I blush, putting our coffee mugs down. "A-are you still going to stay for breakfast?" I ask him.

He sets his boots by the front door and salutes Gray and Bells. "No, I can't, baby. This little visit took longer than expected." He smiles at my sister and her girlfriend. "Sorry, I can't stay for breakfast. I'll see you later, ladies."

Bells shrugs a shoulder, taking bacon off one of the plates. "Suits me fine."

He snatches a piece of toast and holds it up to Bells as a thank you, returning his attention to me. "I'll be gone for two days, okay? But I'll come here the minute I can."

"It's okay," I say, staring at his lips. "Be safe."

He cradles my face and kisses me like he's going off to war, paying no mind to my sister and her girlfriend. Erin and I weren't affectionate like this in front of people. We'd kiss now and then in front of family and friends, keeping our hands to ourselves until it mattered.

But with Peter, I have a feeling I'm going to have to get used to his needy hands on me no matter who is in the room with us. Present company included.

He winks at me, stuffs his feet into his boots, and walks out into the sunny morning.

He doesn't ride a motorcycle like everyone else does, his ears have given him trouble since he was a child. Which is enough for me to be okay with us. Some form of safety in a way, knowing he won't be on a motorcycle without a helmet. Just the thought of him being on a motorcycle turns my stomach sour. I don't like this feeling. But I guess it comes with the territory of falling for a dangerous man.

I stand at the door, waving at him as he flashes me a wink before getting in the car. He taps a cigarette out of a pack and places it between his lips. "See you soon, baby," he calls through the open window, then speeds off, the unlit cigarette dangling from his mouth.

Gray cackles, getting on her knees on the couch to face me. "New boy toy coming in handy, huh?"

Bells pushes the plate toward me as I shut the door, eyeing me like my mother did when I said my first cuss word. "You sure about this?"

Shrugging a shoulder, I nibble my bottom lip. "No. I don't know. He's good to me but his 'company' is...dangerous."

"Just be careful, okay?" Gray says, furrowing her brows. There's more she wants to say, it's clear by the way she's tonguing her cheek. But she has nothing else to add.

I don't blame her.

What I'm doing is madness, but it's my madness.

The last few weeks before Erin died weren't the greatest. We were disconnected, we rarely spoke, and the weight of that drifted us apart.

We were over, but none of us had the heart to end it.

Scarfing down the plate of food, I need to run to the store for a munch needed morning after pill, and gulp another cup of coffee. It feels good to be eating again because I'm hungry. Not forcing myself to eat through nausea from crying in private.

I need a shower, but I also need that pill. Peter's cum is pooling in my underwear and I haven't decided if it's a turn-on or if I'm disgusted with myself for opening up to someone so soon.

Sliding my feet into my shoes, I grab my purse. "I'm heading to the store, you guys want anything?"

"Mint ice cream," Bells says, raising the volume on the show.

Gray glances over at me, that look still on her face, but there isn't anything else I can say that will make her feel better. "Cones, too?"

With a nod, I walk out of the house without making things right with her.

Without reassuring her that things will be okay. Seems to be my habit. I brush everything under the rug until it's too late.

Getting to my car, I toss my purse in, looking at the house as I nibble my bottom lip. I have to go back in, I have to make this right. She's my sister and has been nothing but supportive of everything I ever did in life. Staying with me for six goddamn weeks to make sure I don't crack.

Christ, I'm not healed yet, but Peter has helped a lot, she has to see that. She's helped, too, keeping me distracted by cooking and playing board games.

She's been the rock I didn't know I needed.

I groan, about to close the car door when everything goes dark. A bag is draped over my head and sting pricks the side of my neck as a hand is held on my mouth.

Panic sets in and I thrash my arms and legs at whatever is around me.

My screams are masked, my energy is weakening. But I force myself to fight. I just can't move my arms.

The hand slides from my mouth, holding my body up as my legs have given up on me.

I'm barely able to let out a cry when everything around me is no longer visible…

Peter

It's been almost a day and a half since I saw Dorian. I can't fucking stand it. She's like a drug I tried once and now I need my fix every second of the day in order to survive. I think she feels it, too. At least I hope she does. Not a single fucking text has been answered back. I don't know whether to worry or beat myself up for opening up to her.

"What time did he say he'd be here at?" I ask Riggs. He's sitting in the passenger's seat, drumming his fingers on his knee as he scans the area.

"Half past noon," he says, looking in the side mirror at Lip and Judas parked beside us on their bikes and sharing a joint. They should be in their right mind, but I get it. I need a toke, too.

Daddy took his bike out of storage and fixed it up all day yesterday, riding it like a kid who got his first bike on Christmas. He's on my left, smoking a cigar as he speaks with Roaden.

I have nothing to say to that man. Not after finding out he killed Mama on a hunch. He had no real proof that she was a rat. Nothing concrete that would merit killing her.

He slipped her money, she slipped him a piece of paper. Don't know what was on that paper, but what I do know is, your mama was a rat.

He didn't fucking know what the paper was. It could have been anything. Mama and Liam Ignassio were siblings for Christ's sake. Daddy should know the bond of brotherhood better than anyone.

Fucking bastard.

Riggs taps my hand as I reach for a cigarette, shaking his head. Great, I can't even smoke now. "Where'd you go this yesterday morning?" he asks, his gun ready and steady in his other hand.

I shrug, leaning my head back. "To see Dorian."

"The chubby brunette, huh?"

I nod, pushing my lips together to hide my smile. "The one and only."

"Find anything else from her?"

Shaking my head, I brush my hair back. "It's not like that with her. I actually like this one. She's good for me. *Going* to be good for me. I think she'll set me right."

"That's good, kid." He looks over at me and the corner of his mouth quirks up. "That's real good. We'll finally get outta this shit and raise some kiddos. Maybe out in Texas?

"Yeah, that sounds like something we can do." I chuckle, looking over at him. "Texas?" He nods, tapping my knee and sitting up straighter when something takes his attention away from me.

Dust clouds rise in the distance, and I know it's them. All of us are on edge, ready and willing to kill whoever needs to be killed. This bullshit has to end. I want answers. And I want to know why the fuck all this shit was stirred now and not when it mattered.

Where was Liam at Mama's funeral when we needed family the most?

Riggs gets out of the car, and naturally, I follow. Always in his shadow. Always just a shadow around him. But I'll have his back. Through thick and thin, he'll always have me.

Four bikes stop with a white Cadillac in the middle. Liam Ignassio gets out of the car first and laughs when he sees Daddy, a shake of his head and twitch of his jaw proves that he isn't happy to see him.

But I see it now, those eyes. Riggs kept saying there was something about Liam's eyes that he couldn't stop thinking about. And I see it now. Something about them is just like Mama's eyes.

Daddy gets off his bike, arms outstretched. "Liam, my boy, good to see you again."

"I'd like to say the same, Richard." He tilts his head. "You know why I wanted to meet you here?"

Daddy rolls his eyes and swats a hand in the air. "Yeah, yeah, yeah. Revenge for killing your sister."

Liam chuckles, snapping his fingers. "Someone has to pay for your sins. My sister didn't deserve that any more than those boys she raised deserve you as their father." He takes a breath. "If only we could've been in prison at the same time, I would've killed you myself."

"Ahh, no use in dwelling," Daddy says, snickering.

Liam scoffs, staring at us. "You know what your mother did to help us?" I shake my head, seeing Riggs tense at the corner of my eye. "Hundreds of innocent girls were saved because of her. Girls that didn't know anything other than the life of drugs and sex." He glares at Daddy, Mickey, and Roaden. "Something those fucks helped out in! They helped kidnap these girls and sell them to disgusting billionaires for some change. And your mother died for *that*!" He shouts. "She died saving hundreds of girls."

Riggs growls and turns to Daddy. "Are you fucking kidding me? Why the fuck didn't I know about this? Why the fuck would you agree to that?"

Daddy laughs, scoffing at the end of it. "Money's money, boy."

"You're disgusting," I spit out, unable to look at the man I worshipped for so long.

The man I work for.

The club I agreed to run.

This happened under our noses and I let it.

I fucking let it.

Girls? Innocent girls I had no idea were even being kidnapped and sold. How did they do it without us noticing? How the fuck could Riggs and I be kept in the dark for so long?

"Now you see why I need revenge? Why I want my sister's death to have more meaning than your father thinking she was a goddamn rat!" Liam yells, fuming with rage.

Red.

That's all he sees and whatever he has planned, we're in the line of fire.

"Why wait so long?" I call out, but my words go ignored.

"We can come to an agreement," Daddy says, folding his arms across his chest.

Liam shakes his head. Glaring at us. If looks could kill, we'd all be dead before we got here. But he's right. Mama's death will not go unnoticed. She will be avenged.

She was a perfect woman. Reminds me of Dorian. Beautiful and kind. So damn kind.

She died for nothing.

He snaps his fingers again and screams fill the area. Screams of two women being pulled from the car cause Riggs and me to tense up. Dorian, and what I assume to be Shyanne, are pushed onto their knees in front of Liam, gags in their mouths, and their hands tied behind their backs.

I just saw Dorian yesterday. I was just with her.

Those fuckers followed me and waited. They fucking waited to take her when I wasn't there. If something happens to her, every single one of these men will reap the consequences.

"If you fucking hurt her, I will make sure everyone important to you is slaughtered," Riggs screams, eyeing his woman and her growing belly.

Liam laughs, grabbing a wad of Shyanne's golden locks. "Your father killed your mother in cold blood over something he wasn't even sure was true—"

"Well, was it?" I growl, staring at Dorian as she weeps in horror.

"Of course it was true," Liam says, lifting Shyanne to her feet. "Your mother—my sister—was sent to the Snakes' clubhouse as a mole to give me intel on these girls. Instead, she fell in love with the president she was supposed to take down!" Liam grits his teeth. "She betrayed all of us by staying with him and procreating three of you idiots. She didn't deserve to die for this club. And I want someone to pay for her useless death."

Riggs steps forward, hand gripping the gun that's firmly tucked in the back of his jeans. "No one has to pay for shit."

"Your mother sent me to prison for ten goddamn years! I couldn't do anything when *he* killed her," Liam hisses, narrowing his eyes at Daddy. "Now that I'm out, I'm taking back what's mine." He removes a knife strapped to his leg, causing Shyanne to yelp and tremble. "A life for a life."

One of Liam's bikers steps over to Dorian, gun pressed to the side of her head. My entire body seizes, I can't let her die for something she has no involvement in. "Now who will you choose." My heart hammers violently, causing my breathing to quicken and my brain to see the inevitable if I don't do something. *The gun goes off, sending her head flying sideways with that look of torment frozen on her face. Blood sprays onto the ground, bubbling from the hole in her head. Then, the gun is pulled on Shyanne, and she's on the ground in seconds before Riggs or I can react*—NO! I won't let that happen. I refuse to let anything happen to her.

Riggs pulls his gun out but I grip his arm, stopping him from doing something that could get us all killed. He will not die for something Daddy did.

"Take me," I say, keeping my eyes on Riggs as tears well in them. "You need someone to pay, right? Just take me."

Liam's laugh is just as evil as Daddy's, shivers flow through me. "Sacrificing yourself for a person who has done more bad than good? For a man that doesn't give a shit about anyone but himself—"

"Let them go and just take me!" I shout, staring at Dorian. "Just take me."

Liam ponders it a second, looking at Daddy who, for the first time in all his existence, has nothing to say. His mouth opens, sputtering out a grunt and staring at me with those eyes his three sons share.

"You think dying for something that happened ages ago is the right thing to do? Boy, you're as pathetic as your whore of a mama. You ain't no son of mine," Daddy says, scoffing and folding his arms across his chest.

"Fuck you," I mutter, keeping my eyes on Dorian as she sobs, staring at me with such hatred, I'm scared to hold her when all of this is done.

If I make it out of this.

Riggs's gun is at his sides, hands shaking for the first time in his life. "Peter, no."

But my decision will not change. I am not the same person I was when I met Dorian. I want to prove myself. I want to show these fucks I'm not some loser who forces a girl to sleep with him over something that the club doesn't care about anymore. I need to prove my worth.

Dropping my gun, I slide my cut off with it, and step forward with my hands up. "Let them go."

One of the bikers lifts Dorian to her feet and pushes her forward, making her trip before I catch her. Her eyebrows raise and more tears flow, but I smile and kiss her softly before pushing her toward Riggs.

Shyanne is next, that pregnancy glow makes her look angelic. I see what Riggs loves about her. Those blonde locks bounce on her shoulders, and her big hazel eyes shine a soft green from her tears.

"You're okay," I whisper to her and send her off to Riggs, too.

He darts for her as soon as Liam releases her and kisses her face repeatedly, apologizing and holding her belly. He'll be a great father, the best kind. "You're okay, babe. You're safe."

He shoves her into the back seat of the car with Dorian and comes back to the show. Impatiently waiting for something to happen. "Let's end this fucking bullshit, Liam. The past is the past. Daddy will pay for what he did, but my brother has nothing to do with it."

"Oh, c'mon, a life for a life is pretty generous of me, don't you think? Hell, if I wanted, I could have killed those two whores and sent you their body parts. Sent you that unborn child in a box," Liam says, scoffing. "Sing me another song, boyo."

"Fuckin' bastard," Riggs grumbles, adjusting the gun in his hand.

Liam smiles, taking a few steps closer to me, that knife glinting in the air. "You look so much like your mother. Except for your eyes. You have your father's eyes."

He circles me like a shark waiting to attack. My heart is beating so fast, knowing that these are my final moments. My final seconds.

I turn around and see Dorian helping Shyanne out of her restraints. She'll be all right. They both will. Dorian will live a happy life with lots of smiles and love and happiness. A life so beautiful and filled with so many babies. I just hate that they won't be mine.

"Take me!" Daddy screams, charging forward. "You ain't taking my boys."

Liam cackles, lifting his knife, and as soon as Dorian and I lock eyes, hers grow wide and that's when it happens. Liam plunges his knife down on me.

I'm about to close my eyes and accept my fate when I'm jolted and shoved to the ground. I look up to see Daddy's gut being stabbed six times, causing yells to echo in the area and guns to fire.

Liam and Daddy fall to the ground, he fixes the knife deeper, savage eyes staring into Daddy's. "For Rosa."

Daddy coughs, blood seeping out of his mouth as he takes Liam by the throat and spits blood at his face. "Fuck you."

Liam's head goes flying back, blood and brains coating Daddy's face. Riggs pulls me away, grabbing Daddy and holding him like he held Zay. Only this time, no one is making it out alive.

I sob as bullets fly around us. He sacrificed himself for me.

The bastard chose to die to save me.

Riggs is holding Daddy, tapping his face a couple of times. He's going. He's slipping away from us. The fucking asshole doesn't deserve to go down like this. He deserves so much worse after everything he put us through.

He deserves more.

I crawl over to Daddy and Riggs, taking Daddy's big mitts. "Daddy, hey, Daddy. Hey…" I whimper, holding his hand to my chest. In the end, as much as I hate him for what he did to Mama and for all the new bullshit we found out, he's still my father. The man I worshiped for my entire life. "…don't go soft on me now."

Riggs's eyes are red and wet with tears, I've never seen him cry as much as I have the last few days. "Daddy, you fucking bastard, hold on tight, yeah? Don't go yet."

My big brother, the big ole softy.

He presses a hand on Daddy's stomach, pushing as hard as he can, and shouts at Roaden. "Get the fucking car!"

Daddy wheezes, pulling me closer. His voice is gravelly, hoarse. "Roaden… Roaden's the fucking rat."

"Wh-what?"

Daddy's words are muffled. Coughs and wheezes follow suit.

I look at Riggs as he stares at Daddy, then at me. Eyes wide and mouth parted slightly.

All this time, our uncle was the fucker who started this chaos.

My vision blurs.

Betrayal takes hold as Roaden snaps the neck of Tony Alphonzo and glances back at us. Disgusting bastard should be lying on the floor with my father right now.

Daddy gasps, gurgling blood. It's getting hard to breathe for him, like a weight is on his chest, restricting his airways.

Riggs turns to me and taps my face, then returns his attention to Daddy. "C'mon, Daddy. Stay with me okay, stay—Daddy?"

I let out a sob, watching as Daddy takes his last breath. "Hey! Daddy! No! No, no, no!"

It's over now. The devil is finally put to rest.

Redemption is a cold bitch.

Zay

dam is in crutches, moving around the house in attempts to help me pack what we need. I don't know how we're going to survive in Texas, but if Riggs has a plan to keep us safe, then I trust him. Wholeheartedly.

We haven't been home for more than three hours when a knock strikes the front door.

Adam frowns, attempting to get up from the bed, but I beat him to it. "Don't answer it."

"What if it's Peter or Riggs?" I say, helping him to his feet.

He adjusts his crutches when another set of knocks strikes the door. "Lemme answer it."

I chuckle, tilting my head to the side. "What're you gonna do? Hit them with your crutches? Just be ready in case it's something bad."

He hobbles toward the front door, waiting for me to answer it with a pale worried face. "Babe—"

I open the door and Riggs is standing there with a pregnant blonde woman. This must be his wife. Peter stands behind him, his eyes are red and wet with tears. Dorian is nearby, shoulders hundred and eyes cast downward. "H-hey? Is everything okay—"

Riggs lunges forward and embraces me, softly sobbing into the nape of my neck. "He's gone. He's fucking gone."

I stiffen, staring at the blonde who's rubbing her stomach. I've never seen Riggs like this. Never seen a behemoth of a man breakdown and melt before me. But Peter comes forward, too, embracing me and wails, embracing both of us. What the fuck happened?

I wrap my arms around them, rubbing Peter's back slightly and tangling my fingers in Riggs's hair. I'm still at a loss for words as he cries, squeezing me tighter.

"Wh-who is?" I finally say, leaving a gentle kiss on Riggs's neck.

The Donnelly brothers' sobs increase and Riggs drops to his knees, taking me and Peter down with him. "Oh, Zay, I never thought something I was praying for would make me feel this bad," Riggs says through sniffles and muffled sobs. "I don't know whether to smile or grieve."

"Hey, what's going on?" Adam asks, eyeing the women standing at the doorway.

The blonde shakes her head, placing a hand on Riggs's trembling shoulder. "His father," she says in a southern drawl.

Frowning, I lift Riggs's head and hold it in front of me. By some miracle, those intense blue eyes seem to have gotten even more blue. "What happened?"

As if a Mac truck just slammed into Peter, he gasps, shaking his head in disbelief. I gulp back my anxiety, wondering if I'm in danger or not, managing to get the words out. "What happened, Riggs? Where's your dad?"

Riggs sniffles, boring into my eyes with such depth that I feel like I can depict every emotion passing through him. Tears are captured like little waves in those big blue eyes, waiting for the right moment to leave. I thought they hated their father, despised him for what he put them through, for what he forced them into, and for what he did to their mother.

I guess I was wrong. I guess the love for a parent can never be broken, no matter what they put you through,

"He killed him. The fucking bastard killed him." He drops his head between his shoulders, shaking it as tears drip from his eyes.

Looking at the blonde woman, this natural beauty exudes from her. And the way the setting sun is shining behind her appears like a halo glowing around her head. She's the angel Riggs needed to cleanse his soul.

"He saved us, Riggs. Your father's death will not go unnoticed," she says soothingly.

Adam's weeping behind me as one of his crutches collapses on the floor. The Donnelly brothers are breaking. And I should feel for them. I should sympathize.

But everything their father—the founder of this fucking club—put me through over the last few years drives me to become this emotionless pit of emptiness.

He's gone, and yet, I still don't feel free.

I leave a kiss on Riggs's cheek and sit back on my heels, my eyebrows furrowed. "When is this going to end? How many people have to die or get hurt for all of this madness to be put to rest?" I scoff, looking between Riggs, Peter, and Adam. "When can we finally give this life the middle finger?"

Riggs helps me to my feet, reaching for the blonde's hand. "With me at the head of the table, no one else is getting hurt. I promise you, Zay. I'm changing this club and I ain't gonna let it get as bad as it was. It'll be different. So fucking different."

"Does that mean you're back?" Adam asks, voice weak and vibrating.

Riggs stands tall, a scary bastard. "Yep, it means I'm back."

The blonde releases his hand, holding her belly. "We still did promise you a safe place to live. And I stand by that promise—"

"But if it's done, that means we don't have to move, right?" Adam interrupts her.

A thick rush of air leaves Riggs, glancing at Adam. "Roaden is the rat." He frowns, with this fright boiling in his gaze. I don't think I've ever seen him so scared before. "Who knows what shit he's been spilling."

I turn to Adam, tears welling in my eyes. "Is that why you joined the Panthers?"

He nods, sniffling. "He wanted me to find the rat." He looks at Peter, a single tear rolling down his cheek. "How do you know it's Roaden?"

"Was the last thing Daddy said," Riggs answers, staring at me. "We found out a lot of shit from that fucker who calls himself our uncle."

"Like Liam Ignassio?" Adam asks, hobbling to me.

Peter nods, taking my hand. "We found out why Mama died. And what this fucking club has turned into."

Dorian's eyebrows raise, as if her interest has finally peaked. "What do you mean?"

Peter sniffs, interlocking our fingers. "Mama died for saving innocent girls."

I frown, glancing at Riggs. "What?"

Riggs stiffens, eyeing the scar on my chest. "We found out that Daddy had other ways of making money. And that's through sex trafficking."

"Jesus," Adam whispers, reaching for my hand.

These men all use me as their crutch. Their woman who heals their souls.

"We're putting a stop to this before we get out," Peter adds, sniffling, then letting go of my hand to reach for Dorian's. She doesn't look as scared as I imagined her to be. She's become stagnant. Used to this life already.

"But keeping you safe…" Riggs starts, locking his gaze with mine. "…is all that matters."

Taking a breath, I wonder how in the fuck a biker club turns to this insanity to make a quick buck. "I think I'm going to need more of an explanation as to what the fuck is happening, yeah?" I pinch the bridge of my nose. "Maybe over a few drinks."

Riggs turns to the blonde, urging her forward. "You can use the restroom, babe."

Hearing him call someone else *babe* turns my stomach.

Why am I so jealous?

I chose Adam when all was said and done.

I chose to end things with Riggs.

I fucking chose this life.

I would've been protected by Riggs.

Loved by him.

Worshipped.

I love Adam with everything that I am. He's my world. My person.

But Riggs hits differently. And no one understands it as we do. I can still see it in his eyes when it lingers a moment longer than I'm sure his woman would allow.

But it does and it always will.

Adam points behind him. "Down the hall on the right."

She smiles and steps into my home, leaving Riggs to stare at me with such sad eyes, it's breaking my heart to see him like this over a man he's despised all his life. He must feel how I felt when I lost Lillian. A piece of me was missing. But he lost his father before. Sent him to prison for life. Now Daddy Donnelly leaving is permanent.

"You wanna come in, too?" I ask, shrugging a shoulder at Peter and Dorian.

Riggs grunts, stepping past me and brushing his fingers against mine. That spark is back. That urge I had no idea was missing.

But I can't give in to it. I can't allow that to happen.

I'm married. He is, too, and has a baby on the way. Our lives were meant to cross for one week only. Now, our lives are just a jumbled mess. And the person who kept us connected is dead.

How in the fuck did that happen?

Riggs sits at our kitchen table, sniffing as he turns the fruit bowl in the center of it. A brown banana, apples that have seen better days, and two tangerines sit in it just waiting to be tossed out and put out of their misery. Much like me.

Peter follows, pulling a chair out for Dorian before he sits down, eyeing me to join them. I will, as soon as I snap out of this weird fucked-up family we've created. There's no way I would have looked back and thought I'd be here sitting with bikers and their women. When I saw my life, I always saw a family, happiness, and someone to call mine. Not confused feelings for a married man that could snap me in half.

Sitting at the table with Peter, Dorian, Adam, and Riggs is oddly surreal. This is what my life has come to. What all of our lives have come to. We're broken in so many different ways, yet, we're one.

Adam hobbles over and sits beside Riggs, touching his forearm. "Is that your wife?"

Riggs nods, placing his hand on top of Adam's. "Shyanne."

"What're you having?" Adam asks, wiping his cheek on his shoulder.

"Boy."

I sit in front of Riggs, my brows pinched together when it hits me: today is Tuesday. I look over at Peter and take his hand, squeezing it tightly as the tears begin to rise. Tuesdays were always the worst days of my life. This day is now one of theirs. The tables have turned and yet I still feel as horrible as I did then.

I never met their father, never spoke a word to him. Yet here I am about to cry for a man that had everything to do with ruining my life.

He ordered the killing of my best friend. He ordered the insanity that caused me to become intertwined with the Snakes. He birthed three men I've spent nights with, and yet here I am weeping softly at the thought that even though he's gone, none of this will be over. My life will still be shitty, and nothing can change that. Not even the death of Lucifer himself.

Adam wraps his arms around me, kissing my head softly. "It's okay, babe," he whispers.

It's not okay.

None of this is.

When is enough, enough?

"It's over, sweetie," Peter whispers, kissing my shoulder.

Is it, though? It's never fucking over when it comes to this club.

Riggs sniffs about to reach for me when Shyanne makes her way back to us, waddling over to him. He looks so happy when he looks at her. Even through the curtain of sadness, there's pride in his gaze. That peace he always thrived for.

He finally found it.

He puts his arm on the back of her chair when she settles in her seat, and clears his throat, looking up at me as I rise and take a bottle of whiskey and a few glasses. Jealousy will not soar through me. Not today.

Pouring each of us two fingers of whiskey, I sigh, looking at the caramel-colored liquid in the glass. Peter hates whiskey, and so does Adam, it only seems fair to drink something they hate in their father's honor.

Peter clears his throat, lifting the glass. "I worshiped Daddy all my life, wanted to be just like him when I grew up. But opening my eyes over the last few years, I realize that the only person I should have ever looked up to was you, Riggs. You've been like a father to me all my life, and I can't imagine what I put you through when you thought I was dead. Daddy fucked-up with me, but he did the best damn job with you."

The corner of Riggs's mouth twitches, keeping his gaze on his brother. "Mama's the one we should thank. Daddy did nothing but turn me into a monster."

"You're not a monster," I whisper, meeting his eyes.

Adam groans, swirling the liquid in his glass. "For you, Daddy, you crazy bastard."

"I hope you burn in hell," Peter adds, shooting the liquid back.

"Hear, hear," Riggs says, draining his drink.

He nods, adding more whiskey to his glass. "He was an asshole, but he loved us. Loved Mama, too." He keeps his eyes locked with mine as he speaks. "If it wasn't for Daddy, I wouldn't have run away from this place and found peace."

Redemption hasn't tasted so sour.

I gulp down my drink and pour some more. "Why did he do it? Why'd he sacrifice himself when you told me he's been nothing but a selfish asshole all his life?"

"He did it to save me," Peter says, looking over at me. "I was going to sacrifice myself to save Dorian and Shyanne. All Liam wanted was revenge for what Daddy did to Mama. He was going to kill me to get that revenge. But Daddy…he jumped in front of me and took a knife to the gut."

Riggs goes on to tell us about the guns, the kills, all the illegal shit the club does for money, and what little he found out about the trafficking. He spills the beans on his club, giving us information cops would cum for.

He tells us about his mom and what happened to her.

He tells us about his dad and how fucked in the head he is.

Bastard.

He tells us everything.

Adam sits back in his chair, having known all of this beforehand but hearing it from Riggs's mouth makes things so much clearer.

So real.

"What do we do now?" Adam asks, sniffling and focusing his gaze on the empty glass in front of him.

Riggs shakes his head. "Fuck if I know."

This dense fog fills the room. A sour sadness that keeps growing the longer we're basking in the madness. Basking in something I never wanted to be a part of.

But I am. I'll always be. I was dragged into this because of Lillian and what I did to Peter.

Now I'm tied to it because of Peter and his half-brother. Then Riggs slipped into the chaos and now…now I'm stuck. The love I have for them will always be there.

No matter the time that passes or the distance between us.

I'm stuck.

I look at the ceiling and close my eyes, tears rolling down the sides of my face.

My fate isn't sealed anymore and for some reason as I look at Riggs, I don't want to be freed.

Peter

I open the back door to find Zay standing there staring at the stars. Whenever I'm broken, she has this way of making me feel better. But I shouldn't lean on her, I should lean on Dorian. My girl is sitting at the table, drinking a soda, and getting to know my big brother. My saving grace.

Clearing my throat, I slide my hands into my pockets. "Hey, sweetie."

Zay side glances at me, returning her attention to the night sky. "The stars are extra clear tonight, have you noticed?"

I step closer to her, running my fingers through my hair, and look up at the sparkling stars. "Smoke is finally cleared."

She hums, crossing her arms and taking a breath in. "You ever wonder if the reason why we see a bright light when we die and not darkness is because we're being reborn into someone new? A new life...a reboot."

"It's a possibility," I say, sliding my arm around her shoulders.

She leans into me, naturally. After all these months of hating my guts, she's finally letting me in. But the flutters aren't as potent as they used to be. I'm not on the verge of shoving her against the wall and fucking my feelings away. My flutters belong to someone new. The sexy, curvy woman sitting at the dining room table talking to my family.

"How're you holding up?" Zay asks, lifting her head from my shoulder so she can get a better view of the stars. "You lost your father today."

I grunt, sniffling. "Yeah, I did. But the bastard deserved to die. He put us through so much as kids, I don't even know why I looked up to the guy all my life. He didn't have a compassionate bone in his body. Selfish fucking dickhead who would rape my mama whenever she said no to him. And then, he saves my fucking life and dies…a goddamn hero."

"He's not a hero for saving you, doofus," she said, chuckling softly.

"Shut up."

She nudges my side, turning her attention to the full moon. "With death comes life. Your dad had to die for a new life to begin. He sacrificed himself to right all his wrongs, and now, his life is over, giving way to something new."

I nod, pulling her closer to me so I can leave a kiss on her head, inhaling that coconut perfume that still makes my knees weak. "I guess you're right."

"I'd like to think that," she says quietly, looking up at me. Something about the way her eyes darken with worry sends a pang of guilt through my insides. She should never have been involved in any of this. I see that now, I just wish I saw it ages ago."Tell me the truth, Peter, is it finally over? Or is your father dying going to start a war?"

I study the stars that spread out for miles. It's something I don't usually look up to. To be honest, I don't think I've ever stopped to stare at them. The first time I did was with her floating in the water as the Molly was kicking in. It's remarkably beautiful. "I don't have an answer for you, sweetie. All I know is, Riggs and I are taking this shit down. The Snakes are fucking done."

"Promise?" she whispers.

I glance down at her, those hazel eyes look brown in the dark. The furrow of her brow and the slight quiver of her lip reminds me of Mama. The last vivid memory I have of her before she died.

***

On my eighteenth birthday, I got out of the shower, having left the school earlier than usual to come home and see Mama. Riggs was over, doing his laundry. He'd come over in his free time to see her. I think she liked it best when it was just the three of us, no Daddy, no Adam, just her boys.

"Peter? Sweetie?" Mama knocked on the door as I ran a towel through my hair. "Can I come in?"

I fixed the towel around my waist and opened the door, a gust of steam floating around me as if I were a demon stepping onto Earth, burning down its atmosphere. "Everything okay?"

Her eyes were bloodshot, her lower lip quivering and she hugged herself. Something was wrong. I could feel it. "Riggs is downstairs."

Looking behind her at the stairs, I returned my attention to her. "Is Daddy home?"

She shook her head, curling her thumbs in her sleeves. "No, sweetie. It's just us."

I took her by the shoulders, lowering myself to meet her gaze. "Lemme get dressed, Mama, and I'll be right down."

She nodded, opening her mouth to speak but stopped. She snapped her lips shut, turning on a dime to head back downstairs. I could faintly hear the sound of Riggs's clunky boots walking back and forth.

He paces when he's nervous. And we were equally as nervous as to what Mama had to say. She was never anxious around us. She was levelheaded, and calm. But lately, something didn't sit right. And she was about to tell us what.

Barely drying off, I pulled on a pair of boxers, yanked a t-shirt halfway over my head and I jogged down the stairs. Riggs had his hands on the back of a chair, knuckles white as can be. And Mama sat at the head of the table, a set of keys in front of her.

"What's going on?" I asked, fixing the t-shirt around my waist.

Mama forced a grin, putting her hand out to me. "Come sit."

I shot a look at Riggs, frowning. "What is this?"

He jerked his head at the chair beside her, telling me to sit without saying anything. So I did. I sat down and Mama took my hand, squeezing it. I remember her hands being so cold when she always had the warmest touch.

Riggs sat down next, resting his forearms on the table as Mama looked between the two of us. "What do you gotta tell us?"

She smiled, taking Riggs's hand, too. "My boys. My most prized possessions."

"We love you, too, Mama," I muttered, furrowing my brow. I was frightened, a shiver running through me. But I didn't want to show it. I liked being strong in front of Mama, and my strongest in front of Riggs so he'd see I was meant to be at the Snakes' table with him when he was president.

Mama cleared her throat, bringing our hands to her chest. "I know you see what your daddy does to me. How he treats me. But your daddy loves me, I need you to know that. He's always loved me even when he…hurts me." She sniffed, giving me the softest grin. "I've decided after twenty-two years with the bastard, it's time I get out before you, my sweet Peter, get involved in the madness like your brother."

"I'm sorry, Mama," Riggs said, putting his head down.

She shook her head, letting go of his hand to lift his chin. "Don't be sorry. You don't know the half of what this club is involved in, and I prefer it that way. I prefer it if you boys stay clean and innocent. And by God, your daddy will not ruin my boys like he ruined me."

Riggs narrowed his eyes, frowning as she spoke. Her lips twitched into a smile as she held his chin. I have my Mama's mouth and the shape of her eyes, down to the freckles that are splattered on my cheekbones. "What're you talking about?"

"I'm leaving your daddy," she started, letting go of his chin and taking his hand again, then looked at me. "I have someone to help me, someone you've met before, Riggsy, when I was pregnant with your brother. He's someone I trust to protect me—"

"You let us protect you, Mama," I interrupted her, letting a tear slip free.

"No, if your daddy finds out you helped me, you're as good as dead," she snapped, kissing the top of my hand, then Riggs's. "I'm gonna be gone the day after your birthday, sweetie. But I will reach out when I can, I promise you. I want my boys home with me until then. Promise me you'll stay with me until I leave."

"Of course, Mama," I said, squeezing her hand.

"I ain't going nowhere," Riggs added.

Her big eyes blurred with tears. "I promise, I will make a better life for you boys. A life I wish I'd have given you sooner."

I pulled her hand toward me, kissing her knuckles. "I love our life, Mama."

"You'll love your life more when we're safe," she said, as Riggs stood up and planted a kiss on top of her head.

***

I wish I knew now what I didn't know then. Mama was trying to leave the night she told Liam Ignassio about the girls the club helped traffic. Daddy killed her for it. He killed her and now he's dead. Burning in hell as she watches from heaven and laughs.

I nod, pulling Zaynab into a hug. "I promise, Zay. I'll protect you and Dorian with my life if I could."

"Start now," she says, looking over my shoulder. "Keep her away from this life."

"I will."

The back door slides open and Riggs steps out, nodding at us. "We gotta get to chapel."

"Yeah, okay," I say, letting go of Zay. "A promise is a promise, sweetie."

Riggs steps forward, taking Zay's hand and placing his gun in it. "If anything happens—"

"Point and shoot," she interrupts him. "I know."

"Make sure the safety is off," I add, winking.

Zaynab looks down at the gun, her hands shaking as she gets a feel of the weight of it. "Adam can't really do anything because of his bum knee, but he has a couple of guns in our bedroom."

"I taught Shyanne to shoot, she can handle herself with a gun," Riggs says, smoothing out Zay's hair. "Can you?"

She shakes her head. "I've never shot one before."

Riggs glances up at me, worry painting his battered face. Something about Zaynab has all of us tied in a knot. She's taken hold of our hearts in so many ways, even when we move on we can't.

"Dorian's daddy hunts, she knows how to shoot a gun," I add, tilting Zay's chin up like Mama did to Riggs all those years ago. "You're safe, sweetie. I won't let anything happen to you."

"Let's hope you boys can uphold that promise, hmm?" she says, sniffling and dropping the gun at her side.

"We will." Riggs's nostrils flare as he glares at me as if this shit is my fault. Maybe it is for involving her in this madness. But I did it to protect her. As fucked up as it is, I did it for a purpose.

Riggs leaves a kiss on the corner of Zay's mouth, pressing his lips there longer than appropriate, and goes back inside. Nodding at his wife as he snaps his fingers at Adam, probably so he can get the guns Zay spoke of.

"Fuck," she grumbles.

"It'll be okay, sweetie."

She nods, looking at the stars again. "One can only hope."

Zay deserves to smile again, to have that light shining from her like it used to. And I promised her it would. *You'll love your life more when we're safe.*

"You'll love life again, Zay, you'll see," I whisper, curling her hair around my finger.

Dorian clears her throat, tapping her finger on the glass door. "Peter?"

Zay's hair unravels from my finger, falling onto her shoulder. She looks at me, those eyes sparkling like the stars. But I can't be pulled into them. I can't be sucked back into the man I used to be because of that stare. I will keep her safe and I will protect her, but I will not fall to my knees and beg for her love anymore.

I smile, hesitantly stepping away from Zay toward this new beauty in my life. She's capturing my heart, consuming it. But holy shit is it still hard to stay away from Zay. "Hey, baby."

"What're the next steps? Do we run? Are we even safe here?" Dorian asks, her eyes welling with tears.

I glance back at Zay who's sobbing softly, staring off into the darkness. "You stay here. I can't trust anyone anymore. Until we finish this mess, you guys are to stay here, lock all the doors when we leave, and stay armed. Okay?"

Dorian groans, sniffling as I cradle her head. "This is a lot," she whispers.

"I know," I say, pressing my lips on hers. "It'll all be over, soon."

She nods, looking at Zay, then back at me. "Is she okay?'

I sigh, leaning my forehead on hers. "She will be."

With one last kiss, I move past her and into the house, knowing I shouldn't leave Zay in tears, but I have no choice. We have to end this fuckery.

Studying Shyanne, her beauty is unmistakable. High cheekbones, narrow eyes, thin pouty lips, and golden locks that frame her face. It's no question why Riggs was drawn to her. And something about the southern accent that adds a little bit of quirk to her that's soothing, like Mama.

I clap him on the back as he rubs Shyanne's belly. "Ready to go?" he asks.

Looking behind me, Dorian slides her arms around Zaynab and pulls her into a hug, letting her break down the way she wants to without any of us reassuring her things will be okay. Because none of us know if things will be okay. Who the fuck knows anything anymore? Everything is so fucked up, I'm scared of who I should and shouldn't speak to.

I clear my throat, giving Shyanne a grin. "Ready when you are."

Riggs jerks his head at Adam as he hobbles into the kitchen with guns tucked into the front of his jeans. "Anyone comes in here, Adam, you protect them with your life, yeah?"

"I'll do my best," Adam says, putting the guns on the table. "This is all we have in the house. Ammo is in a shoebox in the bedroom."

Shyanne takes one of the guns, places it in front of her, and nods. "Come home to your son, Riggs."

He grunts again, leaning down to kiss the top of her head. "I will."

I squeeze his shoulder and urge him out the door without so much as a look at my women on the back porch. I'll protect them with everything that I have and make sure they don't end up like my Mama.

"Fuck," I mutter as I drop into the passenger seat of Adam's car.

Riggs grips the steering wheel, looking over at me. "You know what we gotta do."

I nod, looking down at my hands in my lap. "Something we should've done to Daddy when he killed Mama."

"Yep," Riggs says and starts the car. "You ready?"

"Ready as I'll ever be, brother."

As he reverses out of the driveway, I close my eyes and see Mama, her beautiful smile brightening my thoughts. She's always been my guiding light, always been the woman to teach me right from wrong. And I lost all of that when she died. I lost myself when she died.

I'm making progress to be the man she wanted me to be. To love like she wanted me to love. I'm changing things with Riggs. Bringing everything back to the days when Mama smiled.

You'll love your life more when we're safe.

Riggs

Peter and I pull up to *Judas's Hideout*. Most of the guys are already at the club. I recognize them by the bikes parked out front. Fuckers. All of them. Are they lying to our faces about what was going down? How many of them were into the trafficking and did it behind my back? How fucking stupid was I not to notice it?

And Roaden? When I get my hands on him there's no telling what I'll do.

Peter's fingers drum on his leg, he's probably itching for a smoke. Daddy must've offered him a toke when I wasn't looking, and now the fucking kid is addicted. I should've been there. I shouldn't have left him alone, thinking if I kept my distance and forced him to focus on his studies, he'd stay out of the club bullshit. But Daddy sunk his claws into him.

I was too late to fix him when he killed Natalia. Too fucking late now to cure him of this sickness that belongs to the club.

Returning my attention to the bar, I like what they did with the place. Put some of the money to good use at least. The place is crowded most nights, too. Local bands play on occasion because beer is cheap and the whores that keep this place running are easy. Snake Biters, we call them.

Tonight is different.

Tonight, the closed sign is glowing a bright fluorescent red.

I don't know what to expect when we go inside. Argument? Relief? A shoot-out? Anything could happen now that Daddy's dead. Daddy's fucking dead, I don't think it's fully hit me yet.

I cried because, in the end, he was my father. The man who supported us when Mama was home doing all the grunt work and raising us. He was still our father. And as much as I hate him, there will always be love there. I know Peter feels it, too.

Skeet's smoking a cigarette, kicking a stone as he speaks to Judas. Whatever they're talking about, can't be good. Judas grits and bares his teeth, shoving Skeet and flicking his joint. Fingers are being pointed. Chests are puffing up, and when the voices start to raise, Judas looks over and notices us sitting in the car, watching these betraying fuckers.

It's about time I get outta the car and show them who's the boss around here. That president title is mine. "Think we gotta go in now," I say, glancing at Peter whose hands are forming into fists.

He grunts, shaking his head. "I left my cut at Zaynab's."

I scoff, killing the engine. "We don't need no cut, kid. We're Donnelly's. This club is ours, with or without a cut on."

He sniffles, eyes cast downward. He doesn't like this any more than I do. But this is the life.

We lose our family.

Our family betrays us.

Betrayal becomes our worst enemy.

And our worst enemy is the person we have to kill.

Peter gets out first, brushing his hair back. He's nervous, I can see it in the way he keeps swallowing hard and wiping his hands on his thighs.

Neither of us knows what to expect, we could walk in there and the club turns on us. Total Donnelly wipeout.

Or we could walk in there and they listen to me. Bow down like they should've when Daddy got arrested and I was supposed to take the mantle.

Now, I'm back and it's mine.

Skeet nods his head at us, opening the door as Judas fixes his cut. That president patch is no longer there. Damn right.

The whores are at the bar, wiping down the bartop and cleaning the nozzles. But the atmosphere seems off. No music is playing, no sound of the pool balls clacking into each other, and there isn't a whiff of cigarettes in the air.

I don't fucking like this.

Peter waits for me to step in first, the kid is scared and I don't blame him. I don't think I've been more afraid of anything in my entire life. I've walked through shootouts, been stabbed, shot, and taken down by men twice my size.

But walking into chapel with all these betraying assholes hits differently.

Or maybe I have more to lose.

My wife and my baby boy…and Zay.

I walk in and see Roaden standing behind the chair my father used to sit in. The president's chair. Motherfucker better move out of the way before I break every bone in his body.

I take Peter by the back of the neck and direct him to his seat. "Sit."

Like the good puppy dog that he is, he obeys.

Everyone slowly sits down, staring at me and Peter with heavy gulps. Except for my good ole uncle. He doesn't move.

"Think you're standing in my spot, Roaden," I say, folding my arms across my brute chest.

He smirks, jerking a shoulder. "Am I? Because how I see it is you left, Riggs. Left this club to be run by a fucking idiot, and your brother. With Daddy Donnelly gone." He taps the top of the chair, smoothing out the sides. "This bad boy is mine."

I growl, narrowing my eyes. "Title goes to next of kin."

Roaden arches an eyebrow. "And that would be me."

I take a thundering step toward him. "Try it and I'll tell everyone what Daddy told me, rat."

He laughs, looking at the men who start to whisper as Peter clenches his fists and stares at us. "What're you gonna do, boy? Who's gonna back you up? You abandoned your club when the title was handed to you. Abandoned it for a woman? Fucking pussy! You and your brother both. There ain't nothing either of you can do that will stop me—"

Peter shoots up from his seat, gun ready and aimed at Roaden. "Just tell me why you did it. Why did you rat out the club that you and Daddy formed together?"

Roaden inhales, fingers twitching at his sides. "Because your daddy was going sideways. Sex trafficking, gun laundering, killing people that owed us pennies compared to the money we needed. And look at what happened to your girlfriend, Peter. Nearly died with a bullet to the chest because of this club." He shakes his head, looking from us to the rest of the gang. "When Rosa's brother came to me and asked to join forces, I agreed but I knew Judas wouldn't be able to do anything about it. He's worthless when it comes to the title. Got one of the Panther's prospects killed over a retaliation gone wrong."

Peter steps forward, gun still steady. "Why do you mean?" Tears well in his eyes and he glances at Judas. "What retaliation?"

I shouldn't have fucking left. Everything has gone to shit without me here. It's time to fix things. Time to make things the way they should be.

Judas takes a shaky breath, lifting the beer to his lips and guzzling half of it before he sets it down. "Daddy was attacked in prison by a Panther. Stabbed in the side. He reached out to me and asked for revenge. Mickey and I went out one night—"

"Planned to go after one of the prospects who lives close by," Mickey adds.

Judas nods at him in agreement. "Ended up driving the guy off the road and he hit a pole. Fucker wasn't wearing a seatbelt and went through the windshield—"

"You killed Dorian's husband?" Peter's voice cracks, shaking as he speaks. "You did—oh, fuck." Tears are streaming down his cheeks when he looks at me. Feeling all the pain his new girl must've gone through. "You killed him?"

Judas shakes his head. "Guy was suffering. What was I supposed to do? Leave him to choke on his own blood? No, I snapped his neck and—"

Peter shoots twice, hitting Judas in the chest, then returns the gun to Roaden.

As soon as shots are fired, everyone is lifting their guns.

Peter isn't fast enough, our uncle has his gun out faster than I can shove my brother out of the way, taking a bullet to the shoulder because our uncle is one fucking bastard who would rather kill his family than admit defeat.

"Fuck!" I scream, using my body as a shield to protect Peter from any shrapnel.

"He fucking killed her husband! He kill—"

I grab Peter's face as the bullets stop firing and squeeze. "Don't you ever pull a trigger on an unarmed man, go it?"

He nods, whimpering. Fucker has gone and done it now.

Roaden grabs me by the hair and pulls me to my knees, gun pressed at my temple. "Big boy ain't so tough, now, huh?"

I laugh, looking at the men frozen as they watch the inevitable. I see is Shyanne, her perfect smile, and the way she glows when she looks down at her belly…I see Zay, her beauty becoming me. "What're you gonna do, uncle? Kill me? Take the title?" I drop my gun and raise my hands. "Tell me, who's gonna trust you if you kill an unarmed Donnelly?"

The men rise, holding their guns out, and point them at Roaden. Peter stays down, staring at me with those wet blue eyes. Glimpses of Peter at four years old move through my mind. Daddy had me by the throat for taking the last of the chicken legs without asking if he wanted more. The fear coming from my brother now is gutwrenching. He's only known fear. Only witnessed what it's like to inflict it on people.

But now is not the time to panic.

No, now is the time to act.

"Tell me, uncle, who's going to trust you now?" I yell as he presses the gun harder.

Mickey and Skeet have their weapons pointed at Roaden. Lip is tending to Judas, and Peter slowly gets to his feet, dropping his gun as well. "Is the president patch worth this much to you?" Peter asks, raising his hands.

Roaden grits his teeth and growls, shoving my head aside. "It's my title! I deserve this fucking club!"

"A club you were planning on doing what with? Huh? You ratted our shit to the Panthers for what?" Lip shouts, pushing against the bullet wounds on Judas's chest to stop the bleeding.

Roaden shrieks, kicking the chair out of the way and aiming the gun at Peter this time. "A brother for a brother—"

Never ignore the man you pointed a gun at, fucker.

I have Peter's gun lifted faster than anyone notices and fire. One shot at the temple.

Roaden falls to his knees and then collapses on the floor with a loud thud.

Fucker got what he deserved.

I grunt and groan, holding my shoulder as I get to my feet. "Anyone else have any-*fucking*-thing to say?"

The guns drop on the table, and the men move to their seats, eyeing me to make a move. I wince, squeezing the hole in my shoulder that spills blood. I've been shot before, but the pain always feels new. Always feels like the first time.

Peter picks up my president chair and rolls it behind me, tapping my side before he sits down as well. "Floor's yours, pres."

With a strained sigh, I sit down, leaning back in the chair, and smile. "Well, it's been an interesting twenty-four hours, hasn't it, boys?"

No one says anything.

They're all scared of what I have planned.

I have nothing planned that's the scary thought.

I wanted the title to change things and now that I have it, I have no idea what to do.

We sit there, breathing heavily, sharing glances, and wondering what the hell this domino effect will do to our club.

Ruin it, that's for fucking sure.

Zay

Shyanne is asleep in my room, Dorian is in one of the guest rooms, and Adam and I take the couches. I don't know how long Peter or Riggs will be, or if they are coming home. All I know is I'm not getting any sleep tonight.

I've gotten to know Dorian over the last few weeks, and she's so completely out of her element, but in some ways, she suits Peter. She'll help him escape this life.

And Shyanne is magical. She's so utterly perfect for Riggs, I sometimes wonder why this pang of jealousy flows through me. I chose to be with Adam. I could have chosen Riggs, I felt things for him during our week together that were different, so beyond love. But I chose Adam.

Now as my life crumbles, I get to see Riggs flourish. And seeing him happy is enough for me to ignore my jealousy, and attempt to work things out with Adam. The only man I've ever truly loved until Riggs stepped into my life bringing chaos with him.

***

Shyanne and I were sitting on the back porch after they left, staring at the stars. I'd been sipping another glass of whiskey and she'd been chugging water bottles like they were going out of style. But seeing her glow the way she does is a beautiful sight to see.

She crumbled the water bottle and placed it at her feet. "Back home, the stars are so clear at night, they look like glitter."

"Must be beautiful," I said, looking over my shoulder as Adam hobbled to the couch with Dorian behind him carrying pillows and blankets.

Shyanne nodded, taking my hand which startled me. "Riggs talks about you all the time. Y'know." She tapped my hand. "You're that one that he'll never let go of."

I grinned, tapping her hand back before she let it go. "Yeah, seems to be a theme with the Donnelly brothers."

"Things will get better, darling," she said, running her fingers over her stomach.

"That's what everyone keeps saying," I whisper, meeting her eyes as tears well and roll down my cheeks. "I'm tired of people telling me things will be better when they aren't. Things just keep getting worse and worse until one day, I'm just going to give up. I'm going to stop trying and let them win." I sniffed, rising to my feet. There was this cloud over me that not even alcohol or the stars help calm.

I tilted my head to the sky and let out a laugh. "It doesn't matter if things will get better, does it? I've already watched the world burn. Watched my life crumble. I've already seen what rock bottom looks like, and Shyanne, I'm living in it."

She stepped over to me, took my hand, and placed it on her stomach. Kicks hit the palm of my hand and I let out another laugh, feeling a part of Riggs inside her kicking my hand to help me snap out of it.

"There's no use in stopping when there's so much ahead of you, darling. Don't give up, not until you've tried everything in your power to survive," she said, moving my hand around her stomach as the baby continued to kick. "I survived an abusive relationship. I came out stronger on the other side. And you can, too. Just don't give up."

"But giving up is so much easier."

She nodded, dropping her hands. "Riggs tried to give up. He tried to kick in the bucket and leave. But sometimes, leaving isn't the answer either. Leaving causes breaks, and tears in the timeline of your life. Don't run away from your problems, face them head first and make sure you've got your middle finger raised as you do it." She looked up at the sky. "When I met Riggs, he was sleeping on a park bench. I brought him food and coffee and offered him a place to rest his head and wash up. He refused, saying he deserved to sleep on the streets, out in the rain. But I still went to see him every day until he gave in and came home with me. I think I fell in love with him in less than a week. He doesn't see his worth like I do, like I'm sure you do, too. All he sees is the darkness his daddy forced on him. He doesn't see the goodness his mama also gave him." She smiled at me. "You know firsthand he has so much more goodness in him than bad."

She chuckled softly, rubbing her stomach, and continued. "Riggs would shake you silly if he knew you were giving up. All he ever told me was how strong of a woman you are. How you fought right to the end of the craziness they involved you in."

I laughed again, wiping the tears from my cheeks. I did fight only because I had fight left in me. I don't know if I do anymore. "Riggs was never someone to open up about his feelings, but he told me a lot about his life."

"It wasn't the greatest, but he is a good man."

"He is." I wiped my cheek on my shoulder. "Thanks."

"No need to thank me. I didn't do anything, darling. Just a shoulder for you to cry on because you mean the world to Riggs. And if you mean something to my husband, then you mean something to me," she said, tapping my arm before retreating into the house.

For so long, all I wanted to do was pray for my ending.

Over the last few weeks, that feeling uplifted, but it was still present. Living in the unknown and wondering when a knock at my door would be my last.

But seeing Shyanne, and knowing how broken Riggs was when he left, made me realize that second chances are worth a shot.

***

Peter left his cigarettes on the dining room table, and I'm holding one between my fingers, wondering what people would think of me if I started smoking. Would they look at me and think *figures*? Or would they slap it out of my mouth and call me an idiot for thinking it?

Peter left his lighter behind, too. The baby blue lighter with daisies on it that Lillian gave him. I remember when she bought it thinking he would like it, but back then, he didn't smoke. *He'll use it for our camping trips, you'll see.* And he did, on the only camping trip we went on together. I'm ashamed to admit that after Lillian fell asleep, Peter and I stayed up by the fire, making out until the alcohol wore off and I came to my senses. I wasn't the best of friends looking back, but Lillian hid so much from me that I don't carry that guilt around anymore.

It's crazy to think that all of this chaos started because of a crush.

If Peter never smiled at me, they would have never met.

If Lillian didn't want him to be her first, she never would have died.

And if she never died, I would have never met Adam the way I did running out of Peter's dorm room.

If only, if only.

Don't get involved in this. Do not try and figure out what happened to me. Just know you're safe. You're loved. And I'll see you on the flip side, my girl.

I'm starting to wonder if I'll ever get to the flip side. Or if my side flipped when this started and I'll never be able to flip back and smile.

I hold the cigarette to my lips when Adam moans softly, wincing as he moves on the couch. "Babe?" he whispers.

I drop the cigarette on the table, inhaling sharply. "Yeah?"

He rubs his eyes and sits up, wincing again when he moves his legs off the couch. I already know I'm going to have to serve him for the next six months because of that cast, or at least until he's out of crutches.

And I'm not even sure I want to anymore. Everything that's happened has desensitized me to life. I don't want to do anything. I don't want to smile, I don't want to laugh. All I want to do is lie down and release. Stare at the stars until they become me.

The stars have always been my saving grace since I was a child. The only time I felt free was watching the moon outside my window, wondering what life would be like if I wasn't me. And I don't like being me any more than I used to. I was just better at hiding it then.

"You okay?" Adam asks, getting up and hopping on one leg over to his crutches leaning against the armchair. "It's like three in the morning."

"Can't sleep," I say with a breath.

He hobbles over, trying to make as little noise as possible. "Hey." He stands beside me, looking at the cigarettes on the table. "C'mere."

"I'm not in the mood, Adam," I say, flicking the lone cigarette to the other end of the table.

He sets his crutches on the back of the chair and takes my hand. "Come here."

I stare up at him, those blue eyes grinning at me like they did the first time he held me and let me break down in his arms without knowing who I was. He's the compassionate one. The one that would do anything for me no matter what it is.

Tears shimmer in my eyes, blurring his beautiful face. "Why?"

"Because I want you to come here." He takes my hand and helps me to my feet. "Now." He cradles my head. "Smile for me."

I sniffle, letting the tears fall. "It's hard to smile when life is fucked."

"It's our new beginning, babe. We're getting out of here, remember?" He wipes the tears from under my eyes, kissing the tip of my nose. "We're not going to think of the logistics of it, we're just going to do it, okay?"

I shake my head, removing his hands from my face. "Adam, how can you think of starting over after the last year we've had? We should've just ended it when you left me, just let things die between us without trying to salvage this shitty excuse of a relationship."

He shakes his head, pulling me in again. "No. No, I won't allow that."

"Why not?" I whisper, intertwining our fingers at our sides.

"Because we've been through hell, you nearly died and have suffered for so long. I got lost trying to save you, losing myself in the process, but now that we're back, babe, there's no stopping us from thriving." He grins, running his fingers through my hair and pulling me closer by the back of my neck. "Tell me we're getting our reboot again. Like you said earlier. Tell me, please."

"I don't know anymore," I whisper.

He shakes his head, weeping as he leans his head on mine. "No, Zay, please."

"I need time—"

"I'll wait for an eternity for you," he interrupts me. "In this life and the next one, I'll wait for you, babe."

We're crying in our kitchen, sobbing because our happiness together lies in my hands.

My happiness crumbled because of his ties to this club.

My happiness died because of him.

How can I ignore any of that?

"Will you be able to leave everything behind?" I ask, looking up at him. "Will you be able to cut ties with Peter? Riggs? And all the guys you've called family for so long?" I whimper. "Will you be able to say goodbye to them for me?"

He nods quickly. "They're done."

He's been my everything for over three years and I know sometimes it's okay to let go of things. To smile and live life without an inkling of fear crawling up my spine.

I keep circling the thought of letting go. Of leaving this life.

But a reboot is what we poke about at the hospital.

A reboot is what I need in life. And cutting ties with my current life is the first thing on my list. Can I trust him enough to care for me? To love me as he had?

Am I in the right mind to make this decision?

"Don't listen to that negative voice in your head, Zay. Listen to me, please. Listen to *me*, the man who has loved you through a thousand lifetimes, who has tried his best to save you from a life you never deserved. Listen to your husband, the man who will walk through fire just to see you smile. I fucked-up and let the power take hold of me." A tear rolls down his nose and falls on my face. "I love you, babe. Please smile for me again. For us in a new life. A life we planned before this chaos. Remember? We'd live in the city, close to a park for our babies." He smiles as he presses his lips on mine. "Give me babies. Be my home, Zay. Flourish in your endeavors, but be my home."

I wrap my arms around his neck, weeping as I do. "I don't like this home you've become."

He winces, squeezing me tighter. "I'm sorry. I'll be the man you fell in love with again. I'll be him, I swear it."

As I let out a shaky breath, lights outside the home catch my eye, and I tense. "Adam?"

"Yes, babe?"

"Someone's outside," I whisper.

He whips his head around and hops to the couch, taking the gun from the back of it. "Stay back."

I nod, my shaking hands reaching for the gun on the table, and freeze when the doorknob jiggles. "Adam?"

He winces as he hops to the front door, poking his head out the side window, and sighs. "It's just Peter." He unlocks the door and uses the door jam as support to stand. "Hey, man, everything good?"

Peter sighs, looking up at me as Riggs walks up behind him like a gigantic shadow. "It's done. It's finally fucking over."

I release this breath that's clogged my throat for months.

Could it be? Are we finally free of this insanity?

Only one way to find out, isn't there?

We have to move on. To do what Riggs planned for us. What Adam is begging of me. We have to get the hell out of dodge and live our lives the way we always wanted. Free.

Peter

I smirk at Zaynab as fresh tears slide down her cheeks, there's a flicker of hope in her gaze. A hope my big brother and I put there by making sure our women are safe. We laid down the law with the club and told the guys the new plan, one that Roaden set in motion. But we don't take kindly to rats in our MC. Roaden died for being sneaky, he died for things I didn't even know he did until Riggs sat down at the table and the men we've called our brothers started spilling their guts out.

Riggs grabbed Judas's beer and drained it, wiping his mouth with his good arm. "Any of you other fucks got anything else to say? We don't have all damn night. This fuck is gonna start bleeding out, and I got a bullet in my shoulder thanks to my trigger-happy brother."

A few of the men shared glances, but none of them said anything.

I slammed my hand on the table, startling a few. "Your president asked you a *fucking* question!"

Mickey spat the tobacco in his mouth into that godawful mason jar. "We ain't been doing the sex trafficking since Daddy went to prison."

"Who're the people involved in that?" Riggs asked, sucking his teeth as he moved his shoulder.

"Only us, original six," Skeet said, clicking his tongue. "Mickey, Roaden, Daddy, me, and Crew." He swallowed slowly. "It's done now, we ended things when—when that girl ratted on us."

"Who'd you bring the girls to?" Riggs went on, I heard him grinding his teeth from where I sat. "I am the president of this fucking club now, there ain't gonna be any secrets, understood? Not a single one of you fucks will try any of this shit on me. What you're all gonna do is tell me every fucking thing that was kept from me *and* my brothers. You're gonna tell me all the contacts we have with guns, drugs, and the contacts for the fucking girls, do I make myself clear?"

Everyone nodded, grunted, clicked their tongue, and tipped their beer to Riggs. No talking back like they did to Daddy, no scoffing or rolling their eyes like they did to Judas. Riggs was right where he belonged.

"Now." He gritted his teeth as he adjusted himself in the chair again. "Wanna tell me who the fuck is the contact for the sex trafficking?"

Mickey spat again, sitting back in his seat. "Why? We're done with that."

Riggs smiled, that satanic fucking smile I used to fear. But now, I've adopted it because of the power it exudes. "I'm gonna finish what my mama started. I'm gonna take every one of those fuckers down. And if you wanna continue being part of this club, you will stand by my side, gun in hand, and fuck some shit up with me."

"You know I'm there, Riggsy," I answered without skipping a beat. "Shower of bullets coming at us, I'll be right at your side 'til the end."

He smirked, tapping my hand and holding it. "Come a long way, kid."

"Grew a pair when he got that scar," Lip commented, then licked his lips. "I'll be right there with you, too, brother."

"Aye." Mikey raised his glass.

"Me, too," Skeet said.

Judas grunted, his face pale and sweaty. "Ya."

Riggs pushed himself up, nodding at the crew. "Let's fix this mess, brothers. Let's get the Snakes back to how they used to be."

Skeet cleared his throat, putting his hand up to stop the guys from cheering, and glanced at Riggs, then Lip. "Your old girl, Natalia. Roaden is the reason she died. He told her to rat on Daddy."

I frowned knowing this couldn't be possible. Roaden and Daddy were the ones who told me to kill her and make it look like a suicide. "What?"

"Daddy Donnelly thought it would show how faithful you are to the club if you could kill your girlfriend. Like he did with your Mama." Lip removed his hand from Judas's chest and swatted his hand. "Just like how Roaden said Zay had to pay for the mistakes Natalia and Riggs made. But they didn't make any mistakes. He was testing your loyalty."

Riggs bared his teeth, punching his fist on the table. "So Zay suffered for nothing?" he yelled, staring back at Roaden bleeding out on the floor. "Fucking bastard."

"It's done now," I said getting to my feet and touching Riggs's shoulder. "She isn't going to suffer anymore. I fixed that, I promise I fixed it."

Riggs growled, glaring at me, then returned his attention to the men. "Anything else anyone wanna say?"

Judas groans, teeth chattering. "There's one other thing. It ain't that important, but there's someone else who leaked our business. Someone knows we were involved in taking girls."

"Who?" Riggs asked, nostrils flaring.

Judas shook his head. "He goes by The Ghost. That's all I know."

I pinch the bridge of my nose, groaning in annoyance. We didn't need this. Not another mystery to fucking unravel in our laps. "How do you know this?"

Judas sniffed, shifting in his seat. "Been sending Daddy letters in prison."

Riggs and I shared a glance, returning our attention to Judas. He was not looking well, but we weren't going to the hospital until all questions were answered. "I've been getting letters," Riggs said, touching his shoulder again. Sweat trickled at his temples, coating his forehead. "But it wasn't from someone named The Ghost. It was that prospect you ran off the road."

"Who is The Ghost? Another rival gang?" I asked, taking the bandana that Roaden always kept in his jeans pocket.

"No idea," Lip said, sighing. "Whoever it is, they know a lot."

Riggs wiped his hand down his face, wincing as I tied the bandana around his shoulder. "Great."

"Look," Skeet said, rising to his feet. "Let's have chapel again tomorrow morning. You and Judas get to the hospital, we'll call the Captain and have the gunshots shorted."

Riggs grumbled, agreeing with him. "All right, 9:00 AM, sharp. And get this shit cleaned up. I don't wanna know what you do with my uncle, but I want his body to be untraceable. Got it?"

"Yes, boss," Mickey said, tapping the table.

"Our new president, boys," I said, that glimmer of pride in me coming through. Something Daddy always wanted for us. Riggs at the head, me by his side. President and VP.

Cheers and whistles came from the men looking at my brother. He won't admit it, but pride oozed out of him right then. Pure and honest pride that he would run this club.

But, will he run it to be like it used to?

Or will he run it into the ground and send it straight to hell?

***

I wink, stepping into Adam's house. "Hey, sweetie."

"Is it really done?" she asks, but she isn't looking at me or Adam. She's staring at Riggs, his shoulder bandaged and arm in a sling. "Tell me it's over," she whispers.

He grunts, moving past me toward her. "Yeah, sunshine, it's done."

She frowns, going to him and inspecting his shoulder. "What happened?" Adam tenses, he doesn't like the two of them being in a room together. Something about their week at the cabin makes him frightened that she'd leave him for Riggs. I'm sure if things were different and Adam wasn't apologizing like a fucking tool at her bedside when she was shot, tables would be turned and the pregnant one would be this beautiful ray of sunshine, not Shyanne.

Riggs shakes his head, reaching for her hand and kissing her knuckles. "Not important. Just another scar to add to my collection."

Touching his face, she smiles. She fucking smiles again, which causes Adam and I to share a glance. We smile, too, knowing the woman we've loved for so long, has released the weight pressing down on her. A weight we put there because of this club we're involved in.

Something that will change. We'll be a motorcycle club. The good guys again who used to ride for charities.

Riggs hesitates, stammering on a couple of words as she looks up at him, eyes glazed over. Their relationship was never defined, *a bump in the road*, as she calls it. But I think it's much more than that. Something their hearts refuse to let go of.

He leans down and kisses Zay's lips softly, grinning as he does. "Get some sleep, sunshine. We got a lotta shit we have to finish up before we move to Texas."

She touches her lips as Riggs steps away, watching that beast head for the bedroom to sleep beside his wife. He looks over his shoulder once when he gets to the door, a grin still on his face. "It's almost the flipside. Smile, sunshine," he whispers, opening the door and disappearing into the darkness.

I don't know what he means, but it's enough for her to let out a chuckle and look at Adam, tears welling in her eyes as that smile grows on her face. Beautiful as ever.

My smirk spreads to a smile as I press my thumb into my palm and jerk my head at Zaynab. "He's right. You got major bags under your eyes, sweetie. Sleep, I'll make pancakes in the morning." I touch her shoulder and nod my head at Adam. "We got chapel in the morning, too. I think you should be there."

Adam hops once, shutting and locking the door. "Yeah, I'll be there. As long as you promise me my wife will never be part of this."

"None of our women will be part of this, I cross my heart, brother," I say, running my fingers through my hair and sighing. "I'll see you in the morning, okay?"

Zay nods, tears finally slipping free. "I expect fluffy pancakes and bacon to wake me up."

I chuckle, heading to the guest room. "Of course, sweetie."

As much as my heart flutters and my stomach is doing backflips when I see her smile, Dorian is the woman I need to hold and kiss goodnight. Zay used to own my heart, but I found someone to bring it back to life. Someone who accepts me as I am. Faults and all. She accepts me.

I stop when I reach the door taking a page out of Riggs's book, and look back at Zay. She's been mine since the night we floated high, but now that everything is said and done with, I can finally set her free.

She releases a breath, a deep heavy breath that has been held for far too long. And wraps her arms around Adam, the pair giddy and laughing softly. They can finally be happy. I ruined them on their wedding day, and now as

I see the pieces coming together, it feels good to fix my wrongs and be the man my mama wanted.

"Peter?" Dorian asks, her phone lit up in front of her face. "You're home late."

I nod, kicking off my boots and peeling my shirt over my head. "It's been a night."

She places her phone on the nightstand and lifts the covers for me as I step out of my jeans and fall onto the bed with a groan. "Tell me about it," she whispers.

"We're changing everything," I say, half of my words are muffled into the pillow. "With Riggs and I running things, it'll go back to how it used to be."

"That's good, isn't it?"

I hum, closing my eyes with another deep sigh. "Will you be at my side while all this is in motion? I don't expect you to be like the women at the club, but will you be mine? Club aside."

She brushes my hair out of my face and grins, those plump lips coming closer to me and placing a kiss on my forehead. "You and I, Peter. We were meant to be, remember?"

I chuckle, taking her hand and holding it curled under my chin. "I do."

"Get some sleep, we'll settle the future in the morning." She kisses the tip of my nose. "G'night—"

I grab her face and kiss her, tongue circling her mouth. Her nails drag down my chest and she pushes me onto my back, straddling me with those thick thighs I squeeze.

She isn't wearing anything but my t-shirt, ready and waiting for me. "Soulmates," she moans quietly as I enter her. Being in her erases all the women I've been with. Every pussy I'd touched, every ass I've dominated. Nothing compares to her tight fortress. My fucking everything.

She rides me, taking my soul and twisting it with hers. We're far too intertwined to ever be apart. Dorian is mine, she accepts me.

Fuck, she loves me.

We make love well into the early morning, the sun cresting the night sky, and fall asleep holding each other.

For the first time in years, I close my eyes and know that this club is changing into something we can be proud of. It's changing and my brothers are changing it with me.

This is for you, Mama. Everything we do is for you.

Epilogue - Adam

It's been six months since the chaos went down. I wouldn't say we're better off, but I haven't stopped seeing the men I call my brothers smiling. Life is different, to say the least. Extremely different that being together today seems surreal.

Zay and I pull up behind Peter's car, he's leaning on the side of it, feet crossed at the ankles, and puffing on a cigarette. His hair is short again, something he had a hard time getting used to. I think we all did, Peter suited long hair. But he looks more pristine and put together now. Happiness does wonders for a person.

When he looks up at me and jerks his head, I kill the engine and glance at Zay. The most gorgeous woman I've ever laid eyes on, and she's mine. We've been working on our relationship for the past few months. A mandatory date night once a week, upping the sex in the bedroom with toys and oils, and for the first month we tried the couples counseling thing. We did one session and laughed as the door shut behind us on the way out. We concluded, not for us.

We were better off talking in our most vulnerable, pillow talk right after sex. We solved a lot of our issues that way, thriving because of it.

She's been my girl through all of my lifetimes.

Taking her hand, I squeeze, grinning at her. "Ready to give this place one more goodbye?"

She hums, nodding and licking her pink lips. "To new beginnings."

I leave a soft kiss on her knuckles. "To new beginnings, babe."

She winks at me and clicks her tongue, getting out of the car as Peter's eyes do their normal roaming. The man has changed drastically over the past six months. But the one thing that's the same, is his endless love for my girl.

Can't blame him, either, she's a fucking smoke-show. Usually, I give him shit, flick him on the neck, punch him on the shoulder, or like last week when he almost fell out of his chair trying to look at her ass while she bent over. I shoved him out of the chair and made sure to cuss him out. But I'll let him have it today.

"Mr. and Mrs. Lovett in the house," Peter calls, sticking his tongue between his teeth. He flicks the cigarette and embraces Zay, then me. That glow about him makes me so happy for him. He truly did grow up.

"Where's Dorian?" Zay asks, looking into the car

He nods at the tree hanging over the headstones. "With Riggs and Shyanne. She wanted to see Carter."

We start walking in their direction, I'm still limping, though. And it's very annoying. But I deserved the bullet to the knee and the endless surgeries. I fucked over my family because I was pissed. Now I reap the consequences and walk with a cane. But not today, I'll tough it out today.

I clap Peter on the back. "When're you going to quit? You have a kid coming in three months."

He chuckles, looking up as Dorian smiles at him. Her hand is on the small of her back as the other smooths out her growing belly. "I haven't smoked in three weeks, but today called for one. I really fucking needed one today."

Zay threads her fingers with mine, looking over at Peter. "You guys ready for the move?"

He nods, smiling as he looks at the grass. "This time tomorrow, we'll be on the road. Her sister is already there with her girlfriend painting the place and setting up the baby's room."

She scrunches her nose. "I can't believe you're going to be a dad."

He laughs, winking at Dorian as we approach. "New beginnings, right, sweetie?"

Zay giggles, her smile growing as Riggs nods his head at us, his son Carter in his arms. "Gimme him," she says, reaching out for my nephew.

The kid is a mixture of Shyanne and Riggs. Hair so blonde it's blinding in the sunlight, and he has those Donnelly eyes all of us inherited. It's weird seeing Riggs as a dad. Big tough guy who looks like he can snap anyone in two, softens so much when he holds Carter. When he was born, the baby practically fit in his hand he was so tiny. The stress of everything that happened wasn't good for Shyanne, going into labor two months early. But the little guy made it, he pushed through and fought until they were able to take him home.

I don't think I've seen Riggs stop smiling since.

His smile grows when he sees my Zay holding his son. A baby looks good in her arms, but I want us to be one hundred percent before we think of kids. It hasn't even been a discussion yet. Although by the look in her eyes when she scrunches her nose at Carter, I know her ovaries are burning up.

She leaves kisses on Carter's cheek as he gnaws on his fist, Riggs hand meeting the small of her back. "You guys ready to get this over with?" she asks, inhaling my nephew. He smells the absolute best.

Riggs grunts in response, looking at me, then Peter. Dorian smiles at me and smooths out her belly again as Peter comes up behind her, kissing her temple, her ear, and then her shoulder, placing his hands on top of hers.

"I'm ready to get out of this town," Peter says, kissing her neck this time.

Shyanne smiles, leaning over and placing flowers on Daddy's grave. "To new beginnings."

Peter inhales sharply, eyes downcast. "To new beginnings."

It has been a wild ride, something I don't even know how half of us survived. And it all started with a smile. Zay smiled at Peter, consuming him. Then Lillian smiled at Peter, catching his attention. And those smiles went downhill from there. The cabin fuckery. Zay getting shot. Peter fucking my wife. Riggs shooting my leg for Daddy's stupid plan to find the mole. And then Daddy dying with a smile on his face.

Now look at us. All six of us smiling because life is good. For once, life is fucking good.

All of us are staring at the headstone, crisp granite with Daddy's name etched into it.

Richard Donnelly Sr.
A light from our lives is gone, but not forgotten.
1975-2023

Riggs grunts, shaking his head. "Which one of you chose that for Daddy's headstone?"

Zay snorts, chuckling as she bobs Carter in her arms. "You didn't choose that, you big ole softie?" she teases, winking.

He smirks, hand still on her fucking lower back, and flips her off with his free hand. "I ain't no wimp, sunshine."

Peter laughs, squeezing Dorian as she leans into him. "Except when it comes to my nephew, huh, big guy?"

Shyanne giggles, staring at Riggs with a frown. Seeing him as a family man still needs some getting used to because we all know this burly tattooed savage is not the same man he used to be. He's soft, loving, and the protecting Riggs I remember when I was a kid.

It's good to have him back.

His arm slides around Zay's shoulders, smiling at her, then his son in her arms. She looks over at me, hand slithering into mine, and puckers her lips. I immediately steal a kiss, showing these men that she will always be mine.

Silence showers over us as we stand there staring down at Daddy Donnelly's headstone, many of us speechless, most of us relieved that the thorn in our side is gone.

I didn't see the darkness as they did growing up. My birth mom tried her hardest to raise me, but Mama Rosa was the woman I called Mom for my entire childhood. She shielded us from that darkness, urged my mom to be better with me, and would give us every Sunday together while she brought Peter and Riggs to church.

Peter and I truly only started seeing the bad parts of the club around the time Riggs joined. Mama Rosa was more protective toward us then, making sure that we were all properly kept and hidden from anything Daddy brought home. That meant, hiding from drugs and abuse. The Sundays I got to share with my birth mother stopped when I was thirteen and Mama Rosa forced me to church. But I still snuck out to see her when I could. Daddy didn't like it that much. He called me a rat, a half-pint, and told me if I disobeyed him by sneaking out, he'd order Riggs to kill me.

Sometimes I'm scared he still might. I was never one of them, I was just a mistake that happened. But lately, I've felt more connected and close to these men than I ever have. We're Mama Rosa's babies through and through.

Zay takes a deep breath, looking around at the men who would do anything for her. "You fucks look like you can use a drink."

Laughter fills in the silence, cackles and sputters take over the gentle breeze and tweeting of birds. Our cue to get the hell out of here and say goodbye to this town that brought us so much heartache.

Peter kisses Dorian's cheeks and steps back. "I know this good burger joint we shared our first date at that'll be the perfect place for our last meal here."

Shyanne nods, puffing out her bottom lip in agreement. "I could go for a burger—"

Zay gasps, moving away from Riggs and Shyanne. "R-Riggs." She points at Shyanne, her voice is wavering and breathless.

Dorian yelps, curling into Peter as we all glance at the red dot on Shyanne's forehead.

But before Riggs can do anything, shots are fired, one after the other.

Peter pushes Dorian to the ground, lying on top of her for protection. Zay hides Carter against her chest as I do the same and lie on top of her, looking back at Riggs. He stands there, staring down at his wife's lifeless body as bullets fly past him. All of them were meant for us.

As soon as Carter's piercing cries meet his ear, he collapses to his knees, eyes wet with tears, and looks off into the distance as three black cars speed past and leave, ending the rain of bullets.

Peter gets off Dorian, her sobs make themselves known as soon as she's away from his chest. "Riggs? Riggs! We gotta go! We gotta get them outta here!"

"Why would they do this?" Riggs whispers, voice choked with sobs and face riddled with tears. "She had nothing to do with any of my bullshit...she had nothing—"

"Riggs!" Peter screams, tires shrieking back around. "Snap the fuck out of it and let's go! We'll come back for her."

I help Zay and Carter, then lift Dorian to her feet pulling the girls with me toward the cars as fast as my limping will let me. And no matter how much pain I'm in, nothing is going to happen to these women and these babies.

I don't know who this could be. We squared all our wrongs when Daddy died.

We got out.

We made amends.

Yet the look in Riggs's eyes as he takes Zay's hand and leads her and his son to his truck tells me that revenge never tasted so fucking sour.

Peter takes his gun from the glove compartment of his car and cocks it, ready for a shootout as soon as the girls and babies are safe. "Adam, get the other one in Riggs's truck."

The cars do another turn and charge for us. A faded logo I can't depict on the hood of the car. It isn't clear enough to make out.

Riggs shoves Dorian into the backseat, lifting Zay in next, and freezes when the car slows down beside him. Peter runs for him, gun in the air. But no one moves. Only the driver's window rolls down and a letter slides out, falling like a leaf to the ground.

Before Peter even skids to a stop next to Riggs, the car speeds off with the other two behind it.

I cock the gun as I make my way to the front seat, looking back at Zay and Dorian, shushing Carter quietly.

Peter's heavy breathing fills in the tension, the silent ringing buzzing through my ears. "What the fuck?"

Riggs groans, putting the back of his hand to his mouth, and stares off at Shyanne's body lying on the ground. "Who the fuck would do this?" he sobs, hands in fists.

Jumping out of the truck, I glance in the direction of the cars, slowing to a stop on the other side of the rows of headstones.

"Guys!" Zay says quietly through a sob. But no one is listening to her, we're far too distraught.

"I don't fucking know," Peter growls, touching Riggs's arms.

I bend down to pick up the letter, Carter's cries haven't subsided and no one is strong enough to soothe him after the loss we endured.

More death for this damn club.

More heartache.

More tears.

When is enough, enough?

"Guys?" Zay calls, shushing Carter.

Opening the letter, my hand shaking try to steady it so I can read. Peter holds Riggs as he sobs, and reads over my shoulder.

You thought things were over?

Oh, Donnelly boys, things are just getting started.

Ever wonder why things turned out the way they did? Why everything was a mystery until now? Things aren't over until you all die by my hand. You'll pay for everything you did. All the women. All the money. All the fucking gut-wrenching pain you put us through.

Remember this name, for it'll be the last name you scream before I slit your throats.

P.S. Thanks for keeping my sister safe. We'll raise the baby right.

The Ghost.

"What?" Peter yells, turning around to see Zay bouncing Carter and sobbing. "Where's Dorian?"

Zay shakes her head, holding Carter close to her as she presses her lips to his head with a cry. "She went—"

"Dorian?" Peter shouts, running to the other side of the truck. He glances up, watching as the three cars stop at the other end of the rows of headstones, and spots Dorian getting into the middle car. She glances back at him, tears rolling down her cheeks before the door closes and the cars drive off.

"Dorian!" Peter howls, charging after them, his screams and cries move through the area.

Zay sobs, slowly getting out of the truck. "Riggs?"

He wraps his arms around her and Carter, sobbing uncontrollably as I watch Peter running in terror. His girlfriend betrayed us and is taking his child with her.

The world is crumbling around us.

Our lives were supposed to be changed. Supposed to be better.

New beginnings.

Now, everything is just...fucked.

III

Redemption

Zay

AWARD-WINNING AUTHOR
ALYSSA MILANI

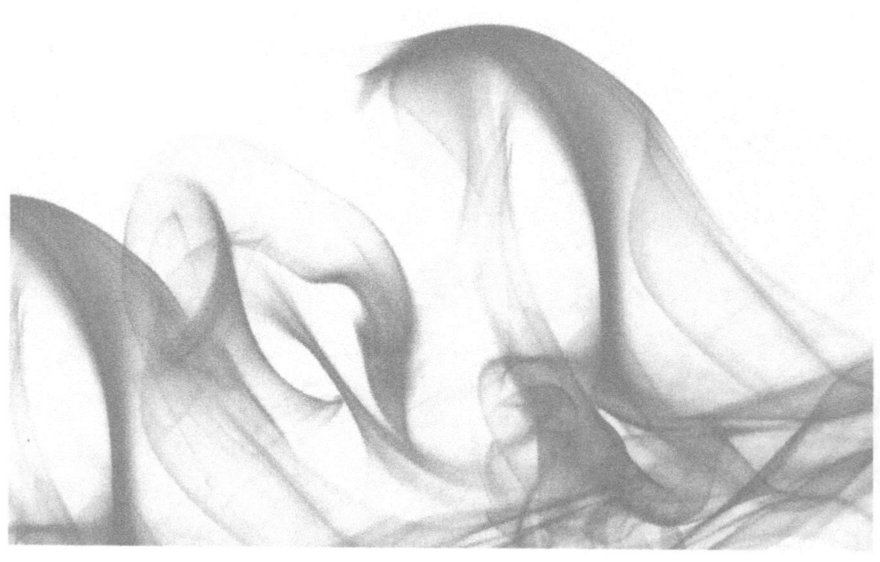

REDEMPTION

THE STOWAWAY SERIES - PART THREE

Oh, God, where do I begin?

It's been six months since Dorian betrayed us and we lost Shyanne. Six freaking months that feel like an eternity.

But the last six months have brought me back to life in so many ways, I'm kind of thankful for what happened.

Does that make me fucked in the head? Maybe. But take away the tragedy, and it's true.

I have purpose again. I can smile without force.

I'm me.

We sold our house and planned to move to Texas before the shit went down at the cemetery, but we discovered that none of Dorian's things were ever sent to Texas and there was no house waiting for us. Her sister, Gray, and girlfriend, Bells, were also nowhere to be found. Peter never met her parents, either. Dorian's disappearance was part of something bigger. A devious plan she conjured up before she met him.

We've reached out to other charters, called all our contacts, and did everything we could. But Dorian was just like her accomplice. A ghost.

Peter's hit rock bottom.

Drinking.

Snorting cocaine.

Sleeping all freaking day.

Adam has stepped in as VP until Peter's in his right mind.

And Riggs? He's dove head first into being the president of the Snakes, changing the club slowly but surely into what he wanted. He's also a drunk.

The problem with that? I'm stuck raising his kid because he's too heartbroken to do it. Which, let's be honest, I love Carter as if he were my own. But the kid needs his father. Not someone who comes around when he needs a shower and a change of clothes.

Riggs bought us a house big enough so we could all live together. I liked it at first because all my favorite people were under one roof, but now, it's the most agonizing thing to be the mother hen of these children who call themselves a God amongst women.

I've been with Riggs and I've been with Peter, one is a God, and the other is a child who needs to grow the fuck up.

Scratch that, they equally need to grow up and smell the fucking flowers. *It's been six months, open your eyes and get shit done instead of moping.*

Cracking the bones in my neck, I look at the time on the stove as I sip my coffee. It's almost eight and Carter is still sleeping. He's been teething lately and wakes up often at night. But for the last two days, he's been sleeping his nights.

I'd say I'm relieved, but I'm not. Waking up often has my body set to an automatic clock.

Yet this morning when I woke up, there was a prospect sitting on the front porch smoking a cigarette, waiting for me.

Though, he's been nothing but nice to me, all of the men treat me like a queen at the club.

Which I fucking deserve.

But this particular prospect lets his eyes wander a little too much for my liking.

When I opened the door to greet him, all he did was stand, stare at my cleavage, and hand me a stack of envelopes from *Judas's Hideout*. "Riggs is passed out in the back of the car," Slade added, pointing at the black Audi sitting in the driveway. "Can I borrow Adam's car until the fucker wakes up?"

I nodded, taking the keys to the Honda off the hook and handing them to Slade. "Fill her up while you're at it."

He smirked, lifted the keys at me, and stepped off the porch. "Yes, ma'am."

I narrowed my eyes with a scoff. "Don't call me *ma'am*. We're the same damn age."

He chuckled, backing away with that award-winning smile that made me want to smack it right off him. "I'll call you whatever you want, princess."

With another eye roll, I closed the door and groaned, sifting through the envelopes in my hand. I paused when I stopped on a beige envelope with Peter's name on it, tears shimmering in my eyes. *This is Dorian's handwriting, isn't it?*

Now, here I am standing in the kitchen, hands shaking as I sip my spiked coffee and debate what to do with this letter addressed to Peter.

Riggs is still asleep in the backseat of the car, I can see his big leather boots sticking out the back window.

Adam stayed at the club last night, something about a shipment coming in that Riggs was too wasted to be a part of.

I have to hand it to my husband, he's been the rock this club has needed for the past six months. Peter is in a downward spiral.

Riggs is all over the place.

Adam is the only stability the club has when Riggs is in one of his stupors.

Like he's been the last three days.

With a gulp, I take the letter and head for the marble staircase with black metal handrails.

Riggs bought us the bougiest house he could find. The entire house has white walls, gold accents, and marble floors spread throughout the majority of it except for the upstairs. It's all hardwood floors. I don't know if he was trying to impress me after seeing the home my parents owned, but this place is not something anyone would guess belongs to a biker family.

Creeping to Carter's room, he's on his stomach still asleep and curled in a ball. Most of Carter's appearance is Riggs. Those blue eyes, his smile, the way he laughs. But now and then, we're gifted with pieces of his mother, Shyanne, we lost too soon.

There's going to come a day when Carter will ask about her, I don't think Riggs is prepared for something like that. He's still a mess right now.

I've been the rock these men have needed, the rock that helps them through their rough days, and the shoulder that helps them through the days that aren't so bad.

Today, as I walk into Peter's room with the envelope in hand, is going to be a bad day.

Tiptoeing to his side of the bed, I set the envelope on the side table. He's on his stomach, one arm draped off the bed, shirtless, drool pooling from his mouth as a vial of cocaine rests open and empty on the floor. *Great.*

Beer bottles and an empty vodka bottle are scattered beside him, their liquid soaking into the sheets. Guess it's laundry day *again.*

I smooth out his hair, he grew it out again. I don't think he meant to, he's too hurt to care.

"Peter," I say, delicately moving a lock of hair from his face. "Hey, Peter? Wake up a sec, yeah?"

He grunts, letting out a rush of air, and sucks his teeth. "Leave me alone, Zaynab."

I slide my hand to his sweaty back, rubbing gently. "I need you to wake up, okay?"

He opens one eye and looks at me, crust holding his eyelashes together. "Why?"

I glance at the beige envelope with Peter's name scrawled on the front and take it off the side table, holding it in front of my mouth. "This came for you."

He lifts his head and frowns, wiping his mouth with his forearm.

Snatching the envelope from my hand, he scoots over in bed and taps the spot beside him. Gross, do I really want to sit in this cesspool?

He taps the spot again, harder this time; his focus stuck on the envelope in his hands. "Please," he mutters. "I can't do this without you."

I sit, mentally reminding myself to do his sheets as soon as we're finished here.

He sniffs, hands shaking as he turns the envelope over, then hands it to me. "I can't open it."

Without hesitation, I tear it open. A letter and three pictures fall out of it. I don't even have to question what these pictures are, it's the baby we lost because of that lying, betraying cunt. "Oh, God, Peter. It's a girl. You have a daughter."

He half laughs, half cries as he picks up the first picture, touching the baby's face softly. "She's beautiful."

Almond-shaped eyes that are strikingly gray-blue look back at us. The baby's face gets rounder in the other pictures, a big pink bow is on top of her head in the second, and she's smiling in the third.

"That's my baby girl." He whimpers, bringing the pictures to his lips and kissing them with his eyes closed. "Why would she do this to me?"

I wipe the tears from my cheeks and open the letter. When did my hands start shaking?

My beloved Peter,

I don't even know where to begin.

Do I start with I'm sorry? Do I tell you that everything I felt was real? That you are and will always be the love of my life?

I doubt you'd believe any of that. But I do, Peter, I do love you and I never wanted any of this to happen. But it did and there's nothing I can do about it.

Let me start from the beginning, maybe that will help explain this hole I drilled through your beautiful heart.

Lenora Thrills. Does she ring any bells? She happens to be someone close to our family, someone the Snakes kidnapped four years ago and sold to the wrong people. She was raped, abused, then after seven months of torture, she was bought by someone powerful. Too powerful for us to save.

She is why I had to do this. She's the only reason I was told to break your heart.

No one knows I sent you this letter. No one knows how hard I've been working to try and screw things up so nothing goes to plan. But please, if you've ever loved me, please don't go looking for me.

The people involved are far worse than anyone you've ever met, and if anything happens to you, I'd never forgive myself. I can't even begin to forgive myself for what I did at the cemetery. Your screams still haunt me.

But it happened. Shyanne died because of this revenge.

No one else has to die, Peter. Remember that.

Don't turn to drugs to cope.

Don't turn to drinking.

Turn to those who love you. There are so many of them right there with you.

But please remember, if you choose to seek me out. Or seek out The Ghost, I can't protect you.

I love you, from now until the end of my days.

Soulmates.

Forever yours, Dorian

P.S. I named her Rosa. She came out looking just like her daddy and is as stubborn as he is, too. She'll always know who you are, I'll make sure of that.

Peter curls onto my lap, wailing, and holding the pictures to his chest. I'm trying to keep it together myself, but it's hard when I'm witnessing the one person I've hated for so long be broken into nothing.

This wimp deserves this.

But he doesn't, does he?

I quietly shush him, petting him gently to soothe his cries. But nothing is working.

I'm starting to sob, too, sliding my arms around him and holding him to my chest. "It's okay, we'll get her back, okay? We'll bring Rosa home."

He squeezes me, his cries dying down. His breathing is erratic, staring at the photos in his hands. "Why would she do this to me? I know I deserve it for everything I've ever done in my life. But this is the worst feeling in the entire world. I wish she'd just have had me killed instead of *this*." He sniffs. "Not this," he whispers.

Kissing the top of his head, I take notice of how greasy his hair is. "Go take a shower, okay? We'll have something to eat and then we'll figure this out. We're getting her back. Whatever it takes."

He sniffs, squeezing me and using my chest to wipe his tears. "Whatever it takes."

I close my eyes and lean my head back, tears escaping the slits. As fucked up as life was a few years ago, it's about to get a lot crazier.

And as much as I wanted out, I'll always be along for the ride.

The sound of birds chirping outside moves through the quiet. "Come, let's get up and look presentable, shall we?"

He grunts a response.

"Shower, wipe those eyes, and come downstairs to me. We'll figure this out, okay?" I touch his face, brushing away a falling tear on his cheek. "Hey, do you trust me?"

He sniffs, sitting up and looking at the pictures again. "With my life."

Warmth blooms inside me, knowing in some sick way that these guys would do anything for me. Am I insane?

Probably.

Do I care?

I haven't cared since I was forced into captivity at that cabin we haven't been to since Dorian announced her pregnancy.

"Good," I reply, pinching his chin. "Take a shower, leave the drugs and alcohol, and meet me downstairs for some breakfast and lots of coffee. Yeah?"

He sighs, closing his eyes and touching my hand. "Sweetie, why are you doing this?"

I shake my head with a frown. "Doing what?"

"Being nice to me." He opens his eyes, red veins crawling around his iris. "You're supposed to hate me. Not support me. Or worry about me." He lowers his head, another tear rolling down his nose. "Care about me," he whispers.

I let out a pained chuckle and get off the bed. "I'm fucked in the head, what do you want me to say?" Pointing at the en suite, I tilt my head to the side. "Don't make me ask again, Peter. Clean up because you smell like literal ball sacks that have been sweating for hours."

He's laughing, whipping the covers off. "You always knew how to make me smile, sweetie. I'll be down in ten, I want a grilled cheese."

Nodding, I put my fists on my hips. "And when you get downstairs you can make it your-damn-self. Hurry up, we have some work to do."

He gets out of his underwear, revealing his flaccid dick that has a bush of hair around it. He hasn't tamed his balls, his face, or his head in six months. He needs a serious overhaul.

As soon as he enters the bathroom and I hear the shower, I take the letter, pictures, and envelope with me and head downstairs to the kitchen.

I don't even have time to glance at the obvious time stamp from the post office on the envelope, I catch a glimpse of Riggs's crossed feet still poking out the back window of the car.

He's had a rough last couple of days. Shyanne's birthday just passed and any mention of her name sends him on a whirlwind of vodka shots. It's not a pretty sight to see.

Leaving the house, I head for Riggs, his snoring rattles through the car. Opening the backdoor beside his head, I leave a soft kiss on his cheek and put my hand on his chest. "Riggs? Hey, wakey-wakey."

He snorts, grunting as he turns his head toward the seats. There are scratches on his neck and bruises on his cheekbones from a bar fight that took place two days ago. One he started in a drunken blur to drown out his mourning.

I touch his face softly, caressing his cheek with my thumb. "Riggs, come on, wake up. We're home." My hand slides down his face to his chest and I tap my hand twice, another kiss to his forehead. "Come on, time to wake up. Carter needs you."

With a groan, he uncrosses his arms and rubs his eyes, blinking rapidly. "I'm up, sunshine." His hoarse voice does so many wrong things to me that I can't help but clench my thighs together and smile down at him.

He grunts a lot lately, sore from all the hell he put his body through. All the hell he continues to put his body through.

The devil incarnate at my fingertips.

"You smell like your brother." I scrunch my nose as he sits up with his legs wide open. He's much too damn tall for the back seat. I don't think Riggs went in here willingly. "Like sweaty balls."

He smirks, tilting his head to the side, and glances up at me. "I remember a time you liked my sweaty balls."

I shove his head and yank his arm to get out of the car. The big son of a bitch doesn't move. "Get up, c'mon."

He squints, putting his hand up to the sun, and staggers when he gets out of the car. He's still drunk, that's probably where the stench of stale beer is coming from. His damn breath.

He hangs an arm off my shoulders, leaning on me as I help him up the steps to the front door. "Have I told you how much you mean to me lately?"

I grunt, helping him into the house and onto a chair in the kitchen. "Nope, and you're not going to. Not until you're sober enough to remember what you say."

He smiles, taking my wrist. "So if I told you I loved you, you don't think I'd remember it when I sobered up?"

Swallowing thickly, I know it's just the alcohol talking, and force a chuckle even though my heart is beating out of my chest and a lump is forming in my throat. I don't know how to break it to Riggs that even though I love him, too, this can never be.

"No, Riggs. You wouldn't remember." He pulls me in, taking me by the hips and kissing my stomach. "Riggs, don't do this," I whisper. He bites down on my shirt and pulls it up, revealing some of my stomach. His teeth rake along my skin, sending shivers through me.

And that's what makes me snap out of it.

"Okay, it's enough." I push his head away and let out a rush of air. "Coffee. You need a coffee."

He shakes his head, gets to his feet, and staggers toward me. "Why didn't you choose me?"

I make him a mug and slide it over, looking at him. I don't think he can see me straight let alone know he's pouring his heart out to me.

As if this broken man can't get any more pathetic, he trips on the rug under the sinks and falls flat on his stomach with a loud thud and a grunt that pains me.

"Jesus Christ, Riggs." I get to my knees beside him as he turns onto his back. "You need to grow the fuck up already. You and Peter are falling apart and I can't handle this anymore. Either you wake up, or I'm taking Carter and I'm leaving this fucked up family dynamic we have going—" I yelp when he grabs my face pulling it right up to his.

"If you leave with my son, I will never forgive you," he growls.

Lowering my face, I grit my teeth as our noses scrunch together. "Then be the Riggs I know. Be a man to me and this family."

He releases me when Carter lets out his morning cry, alerting us to go get him. And I do just that. Leaving Riggs on the floor staring at the ceiling I'm sure is spinning out of control.

What in the fuck was that? I'm conflicted and have been for six months. I wanted out of this life only to be in it fully, raising the president of the Snakes' baby while at it. Yes, I may be happier, but this is not the happy ending I was expecting.

Peter sniffs, wiping his face with the towel as I pass his room, and he glances over at me. "Hey, what's the yelling about?"

I scoff, opening the door to Carter's room, and smile as he sits in his bed looking up at the crib mobile of different colored motorcycles. "Hi, my love."

Carter smiles, his little teeth make me giggle as he reaches out to me. "Mama."

I close my eyes with a sigh, opening them right away and smiling as I pick him up. It's hard hearing him call me his mother.

I'm not. Far from it. Shyanne was an angel and didn't deserve what these fucks did to her.

Just like Carter doesn't deserve to grow up without her as his mom. Life is so unfair.

So fucking unfair.

"He's been calling you that a lot lately," Peter says, leaning on the doorframe with the towel wrapped around his hips in that teasing way that used to make me want to smack him. He tamed that beard on his face, at least.

Leaving a kiss on Carter's temple, I bring him to the changing table. "I don't know what to do about it."

Peter scratches his chin and sighs. "Family meeting. That's the only way to settle it."

I nod, blowing a raspberry on Carter's stomach just to hear that contagious laugh. "After we deal with the letter. I don't know if you noticed, but there's a time stamp on the envelope. Which means location and a date."

Peter stands up straighter, eyes brighten with hope. "I didn't even notice— are you sure?"

I nod, smiling slightly. "I would've started researching, but Riggs was passed out in the Audi. Slade drove him home this morning. And your brother is still piss drunk."

Peter lifts a shoulder lazily. "It was Shyanne's birthday yesterday."

"I know." I inhale a breath. "Doesn't give him the right to act like an asshole and forget about his kid all week."

Peter remains silent. All he does is step into the room and take Carter from me, smothering him in kisses. "Good morning, my man."

I brighten when I see the love he has for his nephew, an ounce of what he would have for his daughter. We'll get her back, and when we do, there's no telling what I'll do to Dorian.

No telling at all.

Loud footfalls thump up the steps, staggering down the hallway and stopping at Carter's room. Riggs smiles, eyes red and beady, and trips on the area rug, muttering under his breath.

Peter acts fast and hands Carter to me, putting a hand on Riggs's chest. "Hey, why don't we clean you up a little before Carter sees you like this." He taps him on the breast. "A son shouldn't see his daddy fucked up."

Riggs keeps his eyes on me, eyebrow cocked. "You were right about the time stamp, baby."

It drives me crazy when he calls me *baby*.

But that tingle can wait.

"What do you mean?" I ask, adjusting Carter on my hip.

Riggs leans his weight on Peter, emitting a grunt out of him. "Bitch is still in California. An hour from here."

Peter's eyes shoot to me, wide and full of hope. "Oh, God."

Riggs chuckles, tapping Peter's face. "Let's bring Rosa home."

Tears slide down Peter's cheeks.

Happy tears. Hopeful.

This family we created will be whole again.

We'll finally get our happy ending.

Our new beginning is just out of reach, isn't it?

Time will tell.

Riggs

I'm sitting in the shower, hot water pelting the tilted walls and sobering me up. I overdid it last night. I've been overdoing it for months.

But Zay's right. I need to snap out of it for my son—the son Shyanne and I made together.

The son she'll never see grow up.

The son she'll never get to love.

I groan, closing my eyes, and sigh. I have to be the best man for him. Raise him right.

Properly.

Raise him like Mama would've wanted.

A knock strikes the door, a cold draft comes in afterward. My eyes are closed, letting the water fall on me, but I get a whiff of coconuts and know in an instant that it's Zay.

She taps her finger on the glass. "Riggs?"

I grin, leaning my head back, my eyes still closed. "I'll be right out, sunshine."

"Lip's on the phone. Something about a trip Judas and Mickey are going on today."

I nod, wiping a hand down my face. "Adam's at the club?"

"Yep, he's been there since yesterday."

With a sigh, I push myself up, grunting and groaning as I do. My shoulder throbs when it's about to rain, and my scar aches when it's cold. I'm twenty-eight and falling apart because of this damn club.

She hands me a towel as soon as I step out of the shower, averting her eyes from me.

"You've seen me naked, y'know. No need to be shy about it now." I take the towel, running it through my hair. "Still impressive, isn't it?"

She narrows her eyes, checking me out with reddened cheeks. "Shut up."

Hanging the towel off my shoulder, I stare down at her. Her chest heaves, her bottom lip curls in and she nibbles on it. "Admit it, sunshine. You miss me."

She lets out a shaky breath, swallowing thickly. "Even if I did, I'm married."

"I was, too." I step closer to her, wet chest directly in front of her. My dick is growing quickly, poking her in the stomach. "Tell me, baby. Tell me you miss me. Because I've missed you for too damn long."

She's backed into the vanity, breathing quickly. Reminds me of the first time she laid eyes on me. She was scared. Nervous.

Woman didn't know if I'd kill her or destroy her.

Instead, she destroyed me.

I loved Shyanne. I always will.

But Zay hits differently. Always has.

Now that I'm available, I won't hold back. I'll have her with or without Adam.

She's *mine*.

I lower my head, tilting it slightly as she leans her head back, parting her lips. "Tell me you miss me, baby."

Because holy fuck I miss you.

Cupping the side of her face, my thumb grazes her bottom lip. "Fuck," I draw out and lower my head. "I need you, Zay. So fucking bad, baby."

"Zaynab?" Peter calls. "Carter shat *everywhere!*"

Her breathing shudders, gulping loudly, and pushes against my chest. "Riggs, we can't."

"Yes, we can."

She stammers, stuttering on a couple of words, and shakes her head. "I have to, um, the baby—"

I grab her face and plant one on her.

Aching for more.

She'll give me more.

Zay and I will be together. Just like we planned.

I'll make you blueberry pancakes every morning until the day I die.
Will you, really?
Under different circumstances, I'd give you the world, Zay.

I step back, wrap the towel around my waist, and chuckle because the world I'm giving her is already in the making. "*Our* baby needs you."

Her eyebrows furrow, studying my gaze as tears well and fall. My son calls her Mama. He calls out for her. Wants only her.

Shyanne may have birthed him but Zay is his mother. It should hurt me more than it has. Shyanne was an angel sent to save me. And she did. She saved me and gave me a son, gave her life for this club. And how do I repay her? Poorly. I'm a fucking shit widower.

But my heart belonged to Zay long before I met Shyanne. Good ole fucked-up Zay.

Two broken souls united under shitty circumstances yet again.

Zay whimpers and pushes past me out of the bathroom as her soft sobs echo through the hallway.

Shit, I didn't mean to make her cry.

Maybe Peter is right. Family meeting tonight.

I brace my hands on the vanity, drop my head and breathe. Usually, I'm like my brother. I wake up "hair of the dog" style most mornings, more alcohol to cure the aching hangover throbbing in my temples.

But not this time.

No, this time when I look at myself in the mirror, I don't see the man I wanted to become. I see the monster I used to be. I changed and became a better man for Shyanne. The angel that brought me back to life.

And when she died, my life died with her.

But for Zay, I'll be reborn again.

Staring at my blue eyes, I sigh. "I'll be the best man I can be for our son, I promise you, Shyanne."

I brush my teeth and head for my room. It's the one right across from Zay and Adam's. They don't fool around as much as I thought. And if they do, they're quiet about it.

Sometimes I sneak into their room just to hold Zay. I need her at night the most. I need her soothing voice, her silky skin, and I need to hear the sound of her heart beating. Its rhythm is quick and slow all at the same time.

I'm broken and only she can repair me.

With basketball shorts on, I jog down the stairs to the kitchen where Zay and Peter are laughing as they hose off Carter in the sink.

Peter looks back at me, bags under his eyes. "He's your son all right, shits just like his daddy."

Zay grimaces, glancing over at me and going straight-faced. Great, now I made it awkward. I didn't want to, but I've been holding in my feelings for years.

Enough is enough.

Maybe I should've done this when I was one hundred percent sober.

Yeah, sober me would've been the better decision.

I wink, taking the coffee from the counter. Sweet and spiked. It's Zay's.

"I gotta go to the club, talk to some of the guys about the charter in Richmond." I gulp some more coffee and suck my teeth at the sweetness. I prefer my coffee black, but Zay has more sugar in this than a damn chocolate bar. "I wanna head out by this time tomorrow."

Peter nods, wrapping Carter in a dishcloth from the waist down. "And what do we do when we get there? I don't want to charge in without a plan."

Stepping forward, I smirk at my son. He's the perfect mixture of Shyanne and I. She'd love him to bits if she were alive right now. Kissing him, tickling his toes, and calling him her little man. I don't know how I'm going to explain to him what happened to her.

I don't know how I'm going to explain a lot.

Like how he calls this woman in front of me with the amber eyes his mama.

Life took us by the balls and squeezed until there was nothing left. But Zay made the best of it.

She always makes the best of it.

I take him, kissing his cheek. "I know. That's why I wanna go to chapel, call the charter nearby. See if anyone can scope out the area for her."

"No bikes, please," Peter says. "The second they hear a bike they'll go into hiding."

Nodding, I adjust Carter in my arms as he reaches out for Zay. "No bikes."

I don't know how we're going to do this but I also don't want Peter to worry if we can't get his daughter back. I will do everything in my power to try. She's family, named after my mama. She's coming home, even if we have to burn the city down to find her. I'll do my fucking best.

Zay clears her throat, taking her coffee from beside me and gulping the rest of it. "When are you heading to the club? I have to get Adam's car back. Think you could drive me since your bike is here?"

Shrugging, I hand Carter over to her; his arms naturally wrap around her neck, and his head leans on her shoulder. It hurts me that my late wife isn't here. She cured me. Saved me.

And now she's dead because of me.

I need a fucking drink.

"Yeah, uh." I pinch my eyes shut, drowning out the image of Shyanne in my head. "Peter, can you stay with Carter today?"

He nods, buttering some bread. "Boy's day, hey, big man?"

He's the best uncle. Stepped right in when I was overwhelmed. Adam, too. These men have been more of a father to my kid than I have.

And it's not fair.

But I'm hurting. I don't want my son to see me sad.

He deserves far more than this life I've given him. That's why I trust Zay to raise him. She had a good head on her shoulders once upon a time.

"Eat something, drink another coffee. I'm getting him changed and then we leave." She starts walking for the stairs and calls out. "Sobriety starts today, Donnellys. If any of you drink or smoke or snort anything, you'll have to answer to me."

Peter smirks, sticking his tongue between his teeth. "You say that like it's a bad thing," he shouts.

"It will be," she shouts back.

I laugh, taking her coffee mug and making myself a fresh cup. She bought this ridiculous coffee machine that uses pods. One pod per cup. I hate it so much. Yet here I am deciding whether I want French vanilla or hazelnut to start my day.

"She's happy," Peter comments, flipping his grilled cheese in the pan. "She's her best when she's happy."

I grunt, waiting for my salted caramel flavored coffee to finish brewing. "We promised her new beginnings."

"That we did."

Taking my mug, I sip it. I hate to love how much I enjoy her stupid coffee choices. "And I'm promising that to you now, brother. We're getting your daughter. And I don't give a fuck who I have to kill to get her. She'll be raised in this house with her family."

Peter's eyes well with tears and he whimpers. "Does it make me fucked in the head that I don't want you to hurt Dorian? Even after what she did to me?"

I shake my head, putting the mug down. "She betrayed us, kid. She technically kidnapped your daughter, had my wife killed, and had been planning this whole thing before you met." I suck my teeth. "Her husband died trying to mosey his way into the secrets this club has. And when she didn't get what she wanted outta that, she opened her legs to you and got fucking pregnant, hearing all our secrets in the process. She fucked you, Peter. Fucked you right up the ass and you took it."

He sniffs, wiping his eyes. He doesn't see the betrayal like I do. He's blinded by everything.

Blinded when he forced Zay to sleep with him.

Blinded when he forgave Daddy for killing Mama.

Blinded when he pretended to be dead just so I'd learn a lesson.

Fucker.

Clapping him on the back, he flips his grilled cheese once more and slides it onto a plate. "All I care about is getting Rosa home."

"I know," he whispers.

"She's coming home."

He nods, taking my coffee and bringing it to the seat at the island, adding sugar to the coffee and dropping in some milk.

I can't even get a decent coffee his morning, can I?

Taking the strongest pod, I put it on and roll my neck as it brews, but wince at the pain in my neck. In my drunken stupor, I've gotten into a few bar fights trying to let out as much anger toward my situation. It's not working. I'm just waking up with bruises, busted knuckles, and disappointed looks from the guys at the club.

I'm fucked, they gotta understand this, don't they?

Our newest prospect, Slade, eggs me on sometimes. He's a pistol whip, eager to get out there and fight. So I give in. I fight with him. Release some of this rage.

I'm not crazy about the guy yet but he's loyal. And loyalty is what we strive for. He's committed to fixing the mess this club has become. But I don't know if I want him around. The way he looks at Zay makes my stomach hurt. I'm surprised Adam hasn't kicked his ass yet. Slade undresses her every time his eyes roam. I'm twitching now just thinking about his eyes soaking up her body.

Fuckers.

The lot of them.

Peter scarfs down the grilled cheese, hunched over his plate with his cell phone in one hand and breathing heavily through the hot sandwich. Even as a kid he never waited for things to cool off. I don't know how many times he complained about a burnt palate throughout his life. Or the number of times he burnt his lips or fingers trying to eat something right off the pan or fresh out of the oven.

He's impatient. And it's funny being on the opposite side of impatience. I can't wait to break down doors and burn down the city to find my niece. Peter can. He doesn't want to destroy the calm.

As soon as I bring the coffee to my lips, Zay is back in the kitchen holding Carter like a football. He laughs the most when he's held like this.

I've been a wreck for the past six months. Diving head first into the club and turning it around. We don't deal with guns anymore. The drugs are dwindling, but a lot of the guys want to keep their toes in with the big guys.

They think it'll be good for business if we ever need them.

I can't argue with that.

And I've beat the crap out of every single one of the men who confessed to being a part of the trafficking. The only problem is I haven't found the source yet. I don't think I ever will. This shit is nasty, dark, and beyond anything I'm capable of.

Even a big bastard like me knows when to surrender. But I'll make sure none of my men will ever be part of it. Our sons, too.

I take in the beauty that is Zay with my son. Happiness bleeds from her now compared to when we reunited seven months ago. She smiles all the time. She loves.

Maybe she'll love me.

We shared something. A unique bond that can never be broken. She feels it, I know she does. The intensity of it sends goosebumps along her skin when she knows I'm staring at her.

And I stare at her a lot when I'm home. *Too much*, Peter says.

I don't care. Adam argues with me all the time. *She's my wife. She married me.*

Woman will be mine again very soon.

She puts my son in the high chair and takes his water bottle from the island, placing it in front of him before preparing his breakfast.

Effortless.

Everything she does flows smoothly.

Naturally.

The Zay I got to know at the cabin has been coming back to life. I just wish I wasn't so heartbroken so I could take her in.

Every time I open up, I think of Shyanne and how she saved me. I see her angelic face and all the love she had. All the patience. The belief that I'd get away from this life.

But that's a load of horse shit, isn't it? I'm right in this life. I'm the fucking president of the club that ruined me.

Killed her.

Killed my mama.

Killed my no-good daddy.

Nearly killed my brother.

And ruined my sunshine.

Zay places a bowl of oatmeal in front of Carter and looks up at me with a gulp. "Get dressed, I've got shit to do today and it doesn't include waiting for you. Let's go."

I chuckle, running my fingers through my hair as her eyes dance over me. "Yes, ma'am."

She narrows her eyes. "Don't call me *ma'am*, I'm younger than you."

Peter smirks, dropping the last bite into his mouth. "You're extra spunky this morning. I like it."

She rolls her eyes and leaves a kiss on Carter's head, whispering goodbyes. It's funny, I never wanted this. A life with a woman and kids.

My life was the club. Women were just holes I shoved my dick in.

But then I met Zay, and she's become so much more than I can imagine. She's taken my heart, squeezed it tightly, and hasn't let it go yet.

But she didn't choose me. So I had to let her go once she gave me peace.

Shyanne was my peace. She still is at times.

But my peace is gone. Lost. My peace will never return but she gave me a part of it. My Carter.

I never wanted kids because I didn't want them to be part of the Snakes. I didn't want to be like Daddy and only see the pride in his kids when they broke bad and did dirty for the club.

Carter will not be part of the club.

I won't allow it.

Zay puts her fists on her hips, arching an eyebrow as I study her. God, it's nice to study her. "Let's go, Riggs."

I nod, jogging off to get ready.

I hear them whispering as I pull a t-shirt over my head and jump into a pair of jeans. They do that a lot. Whisper secrets.

I don't know what they are. Maybe it's just Peter opening his heart like he always does. He wears that on his sleeve, pouring his emotions onto everyone.

One day, Zay will trust me enough to speak to me. For now, I'll continue to watch her until she does. Watch her like I did when I fell for her. I'll watch her for the rest of my days if she'll let me.

"Let's go," I call, getting into my cut.

She winks at Carter and heads out the door. Girl is killing me in that black dress and sandals that make her legs longer than they are.

"She's married, brother," Peter says, sipping his coffee.

I look back at him over my shoulder. "She was married when you forced her in bed, too, kid."

He scrunches his chin with a nod as I snag the keys from the hook.

I can look all I damn want. She lives in this house I bought, raising my son.

No one will stop me from looking unless they gouge my eyes out.

I swing my leg over the bike, kicking the stand off. "You ready, sunshine?"

She gets on behind me, sending my heart into overdrive when her arms wrap around my waist. "No helmet?"

I smirk, looking back at her. "You're safest with me, baby. You know that."

An aggravated sound escapes her as she adjusts her arms when I back us out of the driveway.

She trusts me enough to protect her with my life. And I will.

My family is my priority.

The club is in for some big shit.

So big I don't think we'll be able to walk out of this one with our heads held high.

Adam

Groaning, I turn on my side. It's the third night I've had to sleep at the clubhouse in Peter's old room. He's a wash lately because of what Dorian did. And Riggs is drunk off his ass half the time that the big decisions land on me. The half-pint Donnelly.

It's fucking annoying.

I'm the only one without a snake tattoo, too. Daddy preferred it that way. Said even though I have Donnelly blood running through my veins, I wasn't a true Donnelly. I was a bastard. And bastards don't get Snake tattoos to fulfill his stupid godawful legacy.

Yet here I am running this fucking club because the asshole brothers I have had given up on it. Okay, Riggs lost his wife and Peter lost his woman and unborn child. But still. I can't do this on my own.

It's not my legacy, right?

It's almost seven o'clock and I hear Slade making his way to the room, his loud clunky footfalls send a growl through me. I hate those stupid combat boots he always wears.

He knocks quietly, opening the squeaking door. "Adam?"

I grunt, turning onto my back again. "What?"

"Shipment will be arriving in twenty," he says, then sighs. "Also, Riggs is passed out on the couch. He puked all over the damn floors."

Rubbing my eyes, I sit up. I'm already aggravated, why not add annoyed and fed up to the list of things I woke up with this morning? "God-fucking-dammit." I shake my head and push myself up to my feet, hopping slightly on my good leg before I steady myself. "Get Judas. The two of you can put him in the Audi and drive him home. Zay should be up, ask her for the keys to the Honda."

Slade nods, a stupid smug smirk spreading to his lips. "Will do, boss."

Taking a t-shirt from the floor, I sniff it. Cigarettes and pot, this must be Peter's. "Oh, and Slade," I call as I slip the t-shirt over my head and make my way to him. "Don't hit on my wife."

He laughs, deep and booming, and continues to the bar as he runs his tattooed fingers through his blonde hair. He walked into the clubhouse a few months ago. Lip and Mickey vouched for him. Said he was loyal and good to have. He's as tall as Riggs but thin. He's a cocky guy, yet loyal is the number one trait that I like about him. He'd do anything for the club, that's what matters most.

What I hate about him are his wandering eyes on Zay. She's gorgeous, everyone knows that. But everyone also knows to keep their hands and eyes to themselves when she walks in here. They know she's my wife.

Guys also know that Peter and Riggs would cut off anyone's hand if they touched her. Slade doesn't really care about that. He likes looking at her and says *she's funny*.

I have a funny feeling if I ever left them alone, he'd break that loyalty he has for the club for a taste of her. Shit, who wouldn't?

As soon as I step out of the bathroom and fix my pants, Judas and Slade are carrying Riggs to the car. The guy is mourning, we all know that. But he hasn't left the bar in three days. Wakes up to a drink, and only lets his head hit the pillow when he passes out after a bottle of vodka. That's his newest obsession.

He's been getting into fights, too. Fights that Slade has instigated and separated since his job this month is security for the bar when it's crowded.

Riggs doesn't care. He's hurting but can't seem to snap out of it and realize we all need him. Carter needs him.

This shit has to stop.

We have a shipment coming in today. It's supposed to be alcohol for the bar, but something tells me that Judas is hiding something. Riggs is too out of it to notice, but Skeet warned me that Judas has been skimming off the top of the earnings. Been trying to make a better living since we got out of guns. He thinks we should make the whores be what they are with customers and charge them. But this is a bar, not a brothel.

I've been watching him like a hawk, trying to figure out what the hell he's hiding. But the guy has been cleaner than I've ever seen him.

I don't like it.

Lip nods at me, coming off of a yawn. "Fucker overdid it last night. Getting the prospects to clean up this shit."

I nod, looking out the window as Judas and Slade attempt to fit Riggs in the backseat of the car. They opted for letting his feet stick out the back window. Zay's going to have a field day with this when he gets home.

"Who's delivering today?" I ask, keeping my focus on Judas as he watches Slade adjust Riggs, lighting himself a cigarette.

"Sebastian something. Judas says it's his guy and we can trust him," Lip answers, bringing a coffee mug to his lips.

Figured he'd say that.

Slade drives off, leaving a cloud of dust behind as Judas watches him, this disturbing itch I can't scratch is taking hold. I don't trust him. I know the guys do to an extent—he was the president for almost two years, but no. He's slipped around the end of his reign. And I don't think he bedded with the right people.

I turn to Lip and lower my voice. "Keep an eye on Judas, yeah? Something doesn't sit right with me."

Lip belches softly, looking over my shoulder. "Something hasn't been sitting right since The Ghost killed Riggs's old lady."

Inhaling sharply, the front door opens and slaps shut, Judas's whistling filling the silence. "This stays between us."

Lip nods, arching an eyebrow when the door opens again and Domino steps in. "The fuck you doing here?"

I reach for my gun tucked into my jeans, holding it steady at my side. Panther's president walking in here is not a good sign. I had a funny fucking feeling about this morning.

"Woah, woah, woah," Domino says, putting his hands up. "I'm just here to talk, honest."

I jerk my head at a chair, pressing the barrel of my gun into the table in front of it. "Then talk."

His breathing quickens when Skeet stands up from the bar. "Brave of you to come alone."

"I just wanna talk," Domino says again.

Lip slowly pulls his blade from its holder. "This gutted a cat once." He snickers. "Me-ow."

Domino swallows thickly, sweat trickling at his temples as he sits in the chair and I sit in the other. "S-some of the guys said you were looking for The Ghost."

I frown, sliding the barrel of the gun on the table until it lands on his lap, my finger steady on the trigger. "Who told you that?"

His hand shakes when I move the gun to his forehead. "You know Bo from the LA charter? H-he said that Riggs called them a while back."

"What's this have to do with the Panthers?" Lip asks, turning the blade in the light.

"We got a letter in the mail warning us that The Ghost is coming." Domino shakes his head. "I don't know what that means."

Wiping a hand down my face, I shake my head and I glance back at Lip. This is something Riggs should be coherent for. Something he would be able to process and fix.

Well, I guess I have to fucking deal with more bullshit yet again. Something tells me shit is going to get messy really fast.

"Show me this letter," I say, sitting down in front of Domino.

His hands shake as he takes the letter from the inner pocket of his cut. He was never meant to run his club. Only given the title because a lot of people stepped down when Liam Ignassio was killed.

And a lot of the Panthers fear us after what went down, too. When Daddy died, they thought we'd seek out revenge.

We didn't.

I have a feeling Riggs is planning on joining forces with the Panthers. Getting them to drop their purple cats and wear our red and white snake with pride.

Taking the letter, I unfold it, tucking my gun away in the process.

Snakes are first.
Panthers are next.
I'm coming and I hope you're ready.
When I wipe you out, none of what's left will be able to rebuild.
Be prepared.
- The Ghost.

I take a breath and look back at Lip, handing him the letter. "What do you expect us to do?"

Domino leans forward, tapping the table. "Riggs was in talks with me about us becoming Snakes. Is that still on the table?"

I chuckle nasally and sit back. "My big brother is a little impaired right now, but I'll speak with him and get back to you."

Domino nods quickly. "Please. We got kids living at the clubhouse. If something goes down, they'll be killed."

Skeet sputters, wiping a hand down his face. "The Ghost wouldn't be that ruthless. They're fucking kids."

Scoffing, I glance at him. "Dorian ran away with Peter's baby in her belly. The Ghost doesn't give a fuck about kids."

Rising from my seat, I walk over to the bar and take a glass, pouring myself a shot of tequila. "I'll fix this mess, yeah? I just need a second to breathe."

I don't know what to do. It's not my decision to make. I'm a stand-in VP, not a permanent one.

None of what I say is permanent.

I need my brothers here. I need them to wake the fuck up and smell the damn bullshit that keeps piling up in our club.

Because fucked-up shit is going down and none of us are safe.

Zay

I'm gripping Riggs's waist as we ride his Harley to *Judas's Hideout*. He's placed his hand on mine six times since we left the house, thumb grazing my knuckles. I'm unsure if it's to let me know he's got me, but those butterflies are taking flight again.

This isn't good.

Turning into the parking lot, Adam sits at the picnic table, laughing at something Slade tells him, Lip, and another new guy, Dillon. Adam looks beautiful with all this power in his hands. I've always found Adam attractive, but something about how he's stepped up to the plate the last few months is making it hard for me to keep my hands off him.

I guess this is what I see in Riggs: that beauty and power.

No, I see so much in Riggs it scares me. It makes me believe I chose wrong all this time. Fuck, I hate my second-guessing. My dark thoughts come creeping in when Adam's not around and I don't like it. He's my future. Always and forever.

But sometimes I wonder what it would be like to have Riggs in the same way I have Adam.

Mine. All mine.

Riggs brings the bike to a stop, killing the engine. I don't let go right away, that intense forest scent wafting off him brings back so many feelings I've been bottling up for so long. I missed this more than I like to admit. "You can let go of me now, sunshine."

Immediately, I release him with one last inhale. "S-sorry."

I get off the bike and he takes my hand before I'm able to run off to Adam.

That smoldering look in his eyes when he stares at my lips, makes me part them and naturally tilt my head up. "We have to finish our talk from this morning, y'know."

"No, we don't," I say breathlessly.

He's so damn tall that Adam can't see me from this angle. Hidden behind this behemoth of a man.

Riggs lays his hand against my chest, feeling my heart beating like a jackhammer. "Your heart says otherwise."

I gulp, stepping back. "She's a cold bitch, there's no trusting her."

His laugh booms, spreading goosebumps like wildfire across my skin. "And yet it took hold of me and refuses to let me go."

Our eyes haven't broken their hold on each other for a good thirty seconds. Blue on hazel, getting lost there for a little.

It scares me.

All of him scares me.

***

We moved into the new house not even a month after everything went down. After that betraying cunt broke Peter, and Riggs lost his wife, we needed something to bind us together. To bring forth those new beginnings we promised each other.

I had trouble sleeping most nights because of Adam, his knee throbbed constantly and he refused to take painkillers in case he'd become addicted like Peter—they inherited the addictive personality trait like their father.

Mainly, I didn't sleep at night because I was scared someone would break in and kill us. The person seeking revenge was called The Ghost. He could roam our house without us knowing. He could seep into these walls like a ghost, hidden in the dark corners.

I'll never forget the first time Riggs opened up to me. It started with a simple kiss when we thought he settled things. Then it got worse when Shyanne died. He'd walk into my room and slide into bed with me just to cuddle, even if Adam was in bed. He'd take my hand, pull me into hugs, and purposely leave pecks on my lips whenever he left the house. And every time I rejected his advances, he turned to alcohol.

He loves me. Has since the cabin and only shows it now.

But I didn't choose him.

That first month in the house, I roamed around a lot at night. Too much some would say. But I couldn't rest knowing danger lurked at every corner.

A week or so after we moved in, I tiptoed down the stairs, creeping through the darkness toward the kitchen for something to help me sleep. But nothing worked. And I wasn't turning to sleeping pills.

I opened the fridge, its light casting shadows around me. Orange juice or red wine. Not many options.

As I reached for the bottle of red, hot breath fanned my face and I jumped, seeing Riggs leaning beside me as quiet as a mouse.

"What the fuck, Riggs?" I shoved his chest. He didn't budge an inch. "You don't sneak up on someone like that."

The shadows on his face made him look demonic, a stranger in the glow of the fridge. "Don't walk around in the dark."

I scoffed, slamming the fridge shut, which let the darkness consume us once more. "I didn't want to wake anyone up."

His hand touched me, his fingers trailing up my arm. "I used to remember a time you liked sneaking around in the dark with me."

A squeak escaped me, taking with it a thumping heart that crawled its way up my throat. "I'm married, Riggs. So were you six weeks ago."

He stepped forward, walking with me until my back hit the counter. A sound rumbled through him, pressing his bare chest into me. "I'm broken, baby. Heal me," his deep voice grumbled as his forehead leaned on mine. "Only you can heal me."

I placed a hand on his chest, pushing slightly. "I can't."

He lifted me onto the counter, grunting loudly because of the bullet wound healing on his shoulder. His hands were braced on either side of me, his head bowed forward. "I need you," he whispered.

He groaned again, adjusting his head on my shoulder as his shuddered breath tickled my chest and reeked of whiskey.

I couldn't do it. I refused to give in to him. Adam was my husband. We were going almost nine months without me being with Peter on Tuesday afternoons. Adam and I were going strong. Really strong. We were happy again.

Fuck, I was happy again because I was with all of my loves and my little man all under one roof.

My hatred and resentment for Peter dwindled significantly when he showed me how apologetic he was. I didn't like what he did and I don't think I'd ever forgive him, but I would tolerate him. He was family in the end. His pregnant girlfriend betrayed us.

We would be whole again.

But the way Riggs was looking at me in the glow of the moonlight made me realize that maybe this was a bad idea.

I winced as he started sobbing, resting my lips on his shoulder. We remained like that for a little while. At least until he stopped crying.

I'd never seen him so broken before.

A man so strong. Powerful. Built like a shit brick house, was torn to shreds.

He was nothing more than a man lying in a coffin waiting for someone to nail it shut.

I didn't know how to help him or why he wanted me to help him. I wasn't someone he came to. I wasn't a shoulder to cry on.

I wasn't his.

He sniffed, lifting his head and sighing. "Why didn't you choose me?"

Not this again.

He'd been holding the fact that I chose Adam over him since I was shot. I didn't know Riggs, then. Didn't know I would have these feelings for him grow tremendously. I didn't know. And now I'm being tortured for it.

Constantly.

Day in and day out I see his broken heart resting on his sleeve and know I could've saved him if I chose him.

But I didn't.

"Riggs," I started in a whisper. "I can't do this—"

He winced dropping to his knees with his face between my legs. "Do this." He inhaled, resting his forehead on me. "Please give me a chance."

I lifted his head, smoothing out his face. "Let's get you to bed, okay? We'll talk and think more clearly in the morning."

He got back to his feet and cradled my head in his hands. "It's you."

He pressed his lips on mine, holding them there until I made the move to go further.

I didn't.

Carter let out a cry, interrupting this moment.

I moaned softly against his father's lips, and Riggs released me, dragging his tongue on my bottom lip. "I'm in love with you, Zay."

I shook my head and pushed him back, jumping off the counter. "No, you don't. You're in love with the idea of loving me because it's easy to mend a broken heart with love. But you don't love me, Riggs. That's the alcohol talking."

He grunted, taking the bottle of whiskey from the island and guzzling from it as he staggered to the living room.

Proving my point.

But he's confessed his love for me countless times. And half of those times he wasn't sober.

***

"Babe!" Adam calls, hopping off the picnic table on one foot before he settles on both. "What're you doing here?"

I lick my lips and step away from Riggs, forcing a smile at my husband. "Coming to get the car."

Slade cocks an eyebrow, giving me one devious once-over before he straightens up from Riggs's piercing gaze. "Hey, pres."

Riggs jerks his head at the bar. "Shipment come in?"

Adam kisses my head, handing me the keys to the Honda, and gulps softly. "I gotta talk to you, yeah?"

With a nod, Riggs takes my hand and pulls me into the bar with him, as if this has something to do with me. I just want to get back home to Carter and continue our daily routine. I don't want to be in this place anymore than any of these men want me to know the dirty side of the club.

Adam is two steps behind us, nostrils flaring at Riggs's hand in mine. "H-how's the boy?"

I look back and smile. "He's good. Slept another full night."

"And how'd you sleep?" Adam asks as we walk into Peter's old room, eyeing how Riggs adjusts his fingers with mine even though I show no semblance of holding his back. "Alone, I hope."

I scoff, rolling my eyes. "I was awake every hour on the hour. Alone."

Adam licks his lips, folding his arms across his chest and kicking the door shut. It's taken some getting used to, seeing him in that leather vest like everyone else. He owns it. Something about the power of wearing the vest brings out this attraction.

Maybe it's just that, power. Belonging to something that's against the norm.

"Shipment of liquor came in this morning around 7:30. Something about the shipment didn't add up, there were eight crates of kegs and bottles of alcohol, but one crate was already opened up when we started unpacking. Asked around and Skeet said Judas took off with something when he and Mickey left on their trip. He's been pretty fishy since everything went down."

Riggs frowns, taking in what Adam's saying. All the while gripping my hand like he's scared to let go of me. I try once to pry my hand loose and that just entices him to squeeze harder.

Great, now I can't feel my fingers.

Adam unfolds his arms and slides his hands into his back pockets. "Domino showed up this morning right before shipment came in."

This gets Riggs's attention.

"Panthers' Domino?" he asks, clicking his tongue.

A nod leaves Adam. "The Ghost left him a letter, too. Think we need a sit-down with the Panthers. Sort this shit out once and for all. He was talking about joining forces. You good with that?"

Riggs lets go of my hand and sits on the bed, wiping a hand down his face. "Think we found Dorian."

Adam straightens out his spine. "How?"

"She sent pictures of the baby to Peter and didn't take into account that there's a time stamp on the envelope." I lift a shoulder. "They have a girl named Rosa."

Adam scoffs with a grin, looking at the ground. "That's what Slade tucked into his cut this morning."

Riggs arches an eyebrow with interest. "He knew?"

"I don't think so. Think he was just taking the mail to you guys. But a lot of shit is going down, Riggs. We need you here." Adam takes a breath. "Snakes need their president."

Tension fills the room and I look down at Riggs, sliding my hand to his shoulder. I can hear his teeth grinding from here.

So much shit is going down, shit we knew was coming. But I don't think any of us were prepared for it to happen so quickly.

One thing piling onto the other.

Now, the only thing we have to do is be prepared.

We have to be prepared. I refuse to lose any of these men.

New beginnings. They promised me that.

"Slade didn't know anything. He just said that mail came in for us," I add, glancing at Adam.

Riggs releases an aggravated sigh. "Then let's get to fucking work."

Adam claps his hands, smirking and pulling me toward him. "Go home, babe. Shit's about to get messy."

My heart surges, knowing that death is making its way to San Jose. And soon, it'll be knocking at our door.

Peter

I'm staring at pictures of my daughter. My beautiful baby girl who has my eyes and my smile. Christ, she's all me.

She's perfect. I don't think I've ever seen anything so stunning in all my life. And I had Zaynab.

My little Rosa is coming home. Riggs promised and he's never broken his promises to me.

But something is telling me this will be harder to come by than the stupid TV shows he'd sneak into my room and let me watch on the tablet as kids because Daddy wouldn't let me watch anything childish. But Riggs always kept his promises and let me watch the shows.

I'm craving a drink. No, I'm not. I'm craving cocaine. I've been sniffing the stuff for the past couple of months. Smoking pot like I used to smoke cigarettes, and drinking vodka that still hasn't quenched my thirst.

I'm a fucking mess and the only thing keeping me going is knowing one day I'll see my baby again.

Carter's crawling around, babbling like he usually does, going from one box of toys to the next. He's a car guy like me, all he plays with are the same three cars even though we've filled his playroom with so many things, it's a child's ultimate dream.

Mama tried to have a room like this for us, but Daddy didn't want us to act spoiled. He told her to only give us gifts when it was our birthdays or Christmas that way we'd appreciate what we were given. But Riggs, no matter what, always found a way to make sure I got the toys I wanted even when it wasn't my birthday. I want that for my nephew and my girl.

I smirk as Carter sputters, trying to make the sound of an engine with a car Riggs gave me when I was his age. "Hey, big guy." I smile when he raises those big eyes to meet mine. "Your Daddy gave that to me, did you know that?"

"Car," Carter says, handing it to me and pushing his lips together. "Daddy car."

Laughing, I take the red sports car that has a rattling wheel I'm sure is on the verge of falling off. "Yeah, that's Daddy's car."

He crawls over to his bookshelf that Zay filled with Robert Munch books. She said he was her favorite author as a kid. She reads to him all the time and the funny thing is, the kid is interested. He sits there and listens as she says the words, making silly voices where appropriate. She's the best mother this kid will ever have.

Carter lifts himself and pulls out one of the books, looking back at me with a grin that's just like Riggs's.

"Come, I'll read it to you," I say, putting my arms out.

Moments like these bring a tear to my eye because I'd be reading my daughter stories. Telling her all about her uncles, and of course, Mama. I'd tell her all the made-up stories I can storm up. And she'd listen to all of them.

My baby girl would be excited to hear my voice.

Instead, I have my nephew grinning from ear to ear with a book in his hands as he takes his first step toward me.

"Oh, my God." I push off the floor and get to my knees. "Come on, big guy. Come to Uncle Peter. C'mon." I'm smiling just as big as he is, tears streaming down my cheeks. "C'mon, c'mon." He wobbles, making it to me and I hug him, squeezing and kissing and only imagining the joy I'd feel for my daughter when she does this.

I missed her birth but I will not miss her first steps.

Kissing Carter's cheek, I put him down, crawling back a few feet. "Let's go it again, okay?"

I take my phone and hit record, chuckling as Carter comes to me again, falling after four steps. "Good job, big guy."

Life is better when he's around.

I don't drink.

I don't do drugs.

I'm stone-cold sober whenever I'm with my nephew.

Now that I have pictures of my daughter and some semblance of where she is, I'll sober myself up for her. Zaynab's right, I need to stop this bullshit and snap out of it.

Sending Riggs and Zay the video, I pick Carter up, kiss his cheek, and head downstairs. I'm cleaning my room as soon as someone gets home. I'll toss out all the garbage I sniff and intake. I have to better myself for my daughter and my nephew. We're all they have.

When I pass the front door, I freeze, taking notice of a black sedan sitting across the street. The front window is slightly open and someone's tattooed hand pokes out, flicking a cigarette.

"Fuck," I mutter, looking at Carter.

I can't go out there and handle this. If something happened to me with Carter around, I'd never forgive myself.

Shit, my brother will hate me for all eternity.

A growl rumbles through me. "Fuck."

I get my phone to dial Riggs's number only to see he's calling me instead. A happy phone call about his son taking his first steps is ruined because of this damn club. "Hey, man—"

"He's walking," Riggs interrupts me, laughing on the other end. "Guess we gotta baby-proof the entire house now."

I groan, forcing a chuckle. "Yeah, guess we do."

Riggs's breathing increases, I can hear him grind his teeth through the speaker. "What's wrong?"

I click my tongue, a habit I picked up from Zay, and adjust Carter in my arms. "There's a black sedan parked out front."

He growls, cursing as he stomps on the other end. "I'm coming home, take the boy and go upstairs."

Passing by the front door again, Zay pulls up and looks back at the black sedan. "Shit, Zay just got home—" The driver's door on the black sedan opens and a man in a devil mask steps out, machine gun in hand. "Oh, fuck, no!

Zay!" The phone slides out of my hand and crashes onto the floor.

I whip open the front door eyes wide with fright. "Zay, get in!"

Too late.

Shots are fired and I have a split second to protect my nephew over the woman I've loved for years.

I'm on the ground, body protecting Carter as his cries pierce my ears.

Who the fuck is out there?

How the fuck did they find us?

The house we bought is far from the club, no one is allowed here by motorcycle, either. Only Riggs. The less we attract the neighbors, the better.

Yet here is this man shooting at our house as Zay is crying outside.

"Peter!" she calls through a sob. "Peter, please!"

Grinding my teeth, I act fast and stay low as I head for the laundry room, putting Carter down and closing the door. I don't care how much he's howling, I have to protect my family.

I snag the gun from inside the vase on the decorative piece in the dining room and head for the door.

Zay has her hands on her head, crouched in front of the car as bullets shower around her. Ricocheting off the car. Our windows in the house are being blown out, glass covers the floor. Our once gorgeous home is now in ruin.

"Zay," I call out. "Just stay there, okay?"

She nods quickly, sobbing still.

Fucking bastards.

I poke my head out when the bullets stop firing. Meaning the fucker is reloading.

Charging out of the house, I raise my gun and fire three shots, hitting him on the shoulder on the third.

Gun still raised, I continue to him, calling to Zay over my shoulder. "Baby's in the laundry room."

She sniffs, whimpering, and runs into the house, leaving me to deal with this fucker.

I rip that godawful mask off to find him laughing behind it. "Who the fuck are you?"

His laughter increases, tears sliding down the sides of his face. "A man who'll haunt your dreams, *Peter*."

I grab him by the throat and shove him into the side of the car. "How did you find us?"

He groans, wheezing as I squeeze his throat a little more. That fucking smile spreads to his face again. "You can't hide from The Ghost."

I press the barrel of my gun into his shoulder, emitting a yell out of him. "You come anywhere near my family, I'll make sure to skin you like a fucking deer. Do I make myself clear?"

Laughter.

So much fucking laughter it sends a thrill of panic through me.

Everyone is scared of me, scared of my name and title. But this fucking guy is laughing.

We're not the top dogs anymore, we're nobodies. And I have a funny feeling there won't be anything I can do to save my family.

We're haunted.

All of us are marked by The Ghost.

Riggs

I'm running red lights.

Cutting people off.

My heart is in my throat, beating so roughly it's making me light-headed.

They came to my home where my son sleeps.

Where my brothers live.

Where Zay is.

I keep calling Peter. Must've left him over thirty missed calls. I'm calling Zay, too, but she's not answering, either. My mind is going a mile a minute, trying to figure out what the hell is happening. How these people found us?

Why am I thinking that? It's not that hard. Anyone could have staked out the club and followed one of us home. Our house may be far from the club, but it's in the same damn city we've lived in our whole lives.

Fuck, Adam's instincts could be right and Judas turned on us because he's a sour fuck who had the president title and lost it.

The only men who deserve to wear this patch must have Donnelly blood in their veins. If I die, it goes to Peter, if he dies, he'll give it to Adam. And if Adam dies, it goes to my son. My fucking son who was in the house that was shot at and I wasn't fucking there.

I wasn't there.

I shriek to a halt when I see cops parked in front of my house. There's an ambulance, too. Six cop cars from what I can count. And I'm sure one of the pigs looked up the owners of our house and knows who we are. If they see me, see my cut, they'll disregard us immediately. I have to stay back. I have no fucking choice but to leave my son. No fucking choice.

Fuck.

Turning left instead of going straight, I head for the park nearby. A park Zay and I bring Carter to every Saturday morning. It's crowded today, school must've let out early. I have no choice but to sit here and wait.

Hitting redial on Zay's name, then Peter's, I call and I call and I call. And nothing! Fucking Christ. My heart is beating like a jackrabbit for one of them to pick up the damn phone. For one of them to tell me they're okay.

Motherfuckers.

I dial out Zay's number again and after two rings, she picks up. "Zay? Oh, fuck, are you okay? Is Carter? What happened?"

She sniffs, saying something away from the phone, and clears her throat. "Cops are taking our statement." She lowers her voice. "Please tell me you're safe?"

I grumble, closing my eyes and dropping my head back. "Don't worry about me."

"I'll always worry," she whispers.

Sighing in relief when I hear Carter babbling in the background, I chuckle, pinching my eyes. "What happened, sunshine?"

She sniffs again, exhaling sharply. "Someone shot up the house."

There it is again, my heart seizing. They shot at my family. Some motherfucker shot at my kid and my Zay. "Is Carter okay? Are you okay?" I repeat, my throat burning.

She exhales slowly, voice still low. "He's okay, I gave him some M&Ms and he's acting like nothing's wrong."

"And you?" I ask, looking up as a few kids let out a scream and run through the grass.

"I'll be fine."

I crack the bones in my neck. "Zay."

"I was shot, nothing bad. It just knicked me slightly. Another scar to add to my collection, right?"

I growl, gritting my teeth as I lean forward, running my fingers through my hair. "I'm sorry I wasn't there, baby. I'm so fucking sorry."

She breathes softly, groaning. "Things are changing, Riggs." She whimpers, lowering her voice to a mere whisper. "I'm done with this."

"It's okay," I tell her, but is it really?

She stammers, sighs softly, and clears her throat as someone asks to speak with her. "I have to go, Riggs. I'll call you later. Just know we're okay—"

"Let me talk to Peter," I interrupt her.

"He'll tell you the same damn thing, we're being haunted by The Ghost."

With that, she hangs up and leaves me with my hands shaking.

The Ghost.

The fucking Ghost who doesn't have the balls to come forward and talk to me. He hides in the shadows like a fucking pussy. Wait until I get my hands on this guy. The last thing he'll see as he takes his final breath will be my face, my fucking face.

I don't like this.

Not one bit.

Zay

I hang up the phone as Peter fixes his t-shirt and comes to sit beside me at the dining room table, kissing Carter's temple. My nerves are rattling, dread crawls up my spine. But he's here, and with Peter here, I know I'll be safe.

He takes my hand and kisses my knuckles next, portraying the couple we are pretending to be. The last thing we need is to draw attention that we're three males, one female, and a baby living under the same roof. Oh, and the three males are all members of a biker gang. Yeah, the less attention we give to that garbage, the better. So Peter and I agreed to portray a happy couple with a baby. Innocents, I suppose.

"Who was that?" he asks, threading our fingers and keeping them in front of him. I think he can feel how badly they're still shaking.

Swallowing the saliva build-up, I release a wavering breath. "Riggs, he's waiting nearby."

Peter kisses my hand again, resting his head on it and sighing. "I don't know what the fuck happened, sweetie. I don't know how the fuck we're going to explain this to the cops." He scoffs, shaking his head. "Nosy fucking neighbors."

"They heard gunshots, of course, they're going to call the cops," I whisper sharply.

He glares at me, clicking his jaw. "I don't like this, Zaynab."

"I know," I whisper, touching his face as Carter reaches for him.

He jerks his head at my neck. "It's not that bad, is it?"

I shake my head, touching my neck, and then my chest which has dried blood splattered on it. "Bullet almost got me good, didn't it?"

"Zay," he hisses quietly. The number of times I prayed for my ending when I suffered through his Tuesday afternoons nearly became permanent. Carter saved me from those thoughts, oddly enough, he saved all of us.

A woman in beige slacks and a matching shirt sits in front of Peter and me, taking out her notepad and clearing her throat. "You folks sure know how to wake up the neighborhood, now don't you?"

I force a grin, meeting Peter's eyes. "Who was that man?"

The woman scoots her chair closer, clicking her pen. "Better question is, Mrs. Donnelly, what business do you or you, Mister Donnelly, have with the cartel?"

Peter frowns, stuttering. "We're good people, officer. My wife and I bought this place a few months ago so we can raise our family here—"

"Peter Donnelly, son of motorcycle club leader Richard Donnelly, recently deceased. The youngest brother of Richard Donnelly Jr., known as Riggs to fellow motorcycle members on the streets," she interrupts him, closing her notepad. "You didn't think I'd check the owners of this home? I know who you are Mister Donnelly, so my question still stands, what business do you have with the cartel?"

Peter shakes his head, keeping his gaze on the woman even though Carter is squeezing his cheeks. "We have no association with any cartel. My daddy was a bad man, officer, but I am nothing like him. And my brother is part of a club, but he doesn't deal with any illegals. Last I checked, it wasn't against the law to have a group of men riding around on their Harley's."

She chuckles, eyeing me. "No, it is not."

Carter reaches for me again. "Mama."

"Lemme ask you something," she continues, clicking her pen once more. "Are you three the only residents of this house?"

I speak without thinking, biting my tongue as soon as the words leave my mouth. "His brothers stay with us from time to time."

Peter lets out a quiet aggravated breath, clearing his throat. "Whenever they're in town, yes. My brother, Adam, is attending Stanford and comes home on weekends to do laundry. And Riggs drops by to see his nephew when he's free."

"And where does Riggs live?" she asks, taking notes as we speak.

Peter and I share a glance, I think we're both stumped on how to answer this. If we tell them he stays at the bar, they could head over there and raid it. And if we give some bogus information they can look it up and know we're lying.

So, I speak without giving Peter the chance to formulate a lie. "He's a nomad, right? He doesn't have a designated place to stay."

She regards me with a nod and puts her notepad away. "I'd like you to come to the precinct to take your statement, Mr. and Mrs. Donnelly. Seems like there's more to this shootout than you're letting on."

I scoff, rising from my seat. "We were in the middle of cleaning the house when someone started shooting at us. There's nothing we're hiding from you."

Peter stands up as well, placing a hand on my shoulder. "Baby, it's okay."

I groan, unable to stop these emotions from getting through. "It's not okay." Tears blur my vision, rolling down my cheeks. "They shot up our home where my son lives, where we live. We're good people. This…this is bullshit."

I storm off with Carter in my arms, leaving Peter calling out to me.

I don't need this insanity.

I don't want any of this in my life.

This burden was bestowed upon me like some fucked up version of karma for all the stuff I did after Lillian died.

We're *not* good people.

We're horrible people who deserve everything that comes our way.

Every-fucking-thing.

Peter

Wiping a hand down my face, I sigh and watch Zay charge for the stairs. She hates this as much as I do. I can't blame her, either. We forced her into this life years ago. My stupid urge to seek revenge. *We reap the consequences we can't predict.*

I regret that every day I look into those hazel eyes and know I could've kept her away from this madness. But my selfish needs got in the way.

All of this is my fault.

I return my attention to the officer, swallowing thickly. "Sorry about my, uh, wife. She gets sensitive when people suspect us to be bad people because of who I'm related to."

No, of what I am capable of.

She taps the notepad on her hand and slides it into her back pocket. All of this stupidity will be handled as soon as I call the Captain and explain to him our story. He's settled business for us for years. He was one of Roaden's guys but respects the club enough to continue doing us solids.

She hands me her business card and nods. Detective Marie Johnston. Just what we needed, people investigating our shit. The second I have my hands on this Ghost guy, he's a dead man.

"We can't help who shares a blood type with us, but we can disassociate ourselves from them, Mister Donnelly. And if you care about your wife and that baby of yours, I suggested you do just that," Detective Marie Johnston says, looking at the glass decorating the floor. "Tomorrow, you and your wife can come down to the precinct and one of my men will take your statement."

She doesn't know anything about our life. What we went through or how much we suffered. I would've walked out there unarmed if it wasn't for Carter and Zaynab. I would've killed that man with my bare hands if it wasn't for those nosy neighbors.

There isn't anything I can do about this situation other than pray my family doesn't get hurt. Living at the cabin is looking like a permanent thing once this shit is dealt with. Raising my baby girl to fish and walk in the snow. I think she'd like the snow the most. Or seeing Zay play with Carter in the sand, helping him build sandcastles while Riggs and Adam fix the dock.

Yeah, that'll be the life. My brothers, my nephew, and my girls all under one roof, smiling.

Always smiling.

"Yes, ma'am," I say to the detective and put my hand out to shake hers. "Thank you."

"If you think of anything else, please give me a call. I'll have one of my men parked outside until tomorrow," she adds and jerks her head at another officer to follow her out of the house. "Tomorrow, Mister Donnelly, do not forget."

Great, just great.

The shooter is sitting in the back of an ambulance, handcuffed to the bed, and laughing as he stares at the house. I'm going to fucking lose my shit soon if we don't figure out who the fuck sent him and what this has to do with us.

I take Zay's phone from the table and call Riggs, letting him know he won't be able to come home until the cops leave. The last thing I want is for my brother to get arrested for something he didn't do. He doesn't have priors, but his name is in the system for the raid that Lillian caused. Carter can't lose his daddy to something that's out of our control.

We can fix this. We can control all of this if we figure out some shit.

Getting Zay and Carter to safety is the priority.

Riggs answers after barely one ring. "Zay? Zay, what's happening? I see the cops leaving. Are you—"

"We're fine," I interrupt him and stop in my tracks; Zay sits on the floor of Carter's room, sobbing, as he plays with his toys. "All our front windows are shot out. The damn house looks like a shooting range."

Sitting behind Zay with one leg on either side of her, I force her head back against my chest. "Don't come home, brother."

Riggs growls, I'm sure hearing Zay's cries through the speaker. "What the fuck do you expect me to do? My son is with you and my—" he pauses, taking a breath. "I'll stash my bike, and walk over."

She sniffs, relaxing into me and sending my heart fluttering a million beats per minute.

I can't do this again. I can't go down that road. My daughter, she's who I have to focus on. Not these unsettled feelings that closure did fuck all for.

"They have a patrol car parked out front until tomorrow," I say, leaving a kiss on Zay's head.

Another growl leaves Riggs, causing me to put him on speaker. "I want to come home."

I don't know what to say to him. He can't. If he comes home he'll get taken into custody. I know he will. That detective is onto us. I can feel it.

And the last thing we need is a cop sniffing around.

"I'll call Roaden's guy. The Captain. Have him settle all this bullshit," I say to Riggs, kissing Zay's temple and rocking her in my arms. "Is Adam coming home tonight?"

"No," Riggs answers, bringing his bike to life. "He's staying the night until we have this Domino bullshit settled."

I frown, bringing the phone closer to my mouth. "What Domino bullshit?"

"I'll explain when I get home. Keep them safe."

With that, he hangs up.

"Fuck," I mutter, tossing the phone and running a hand down my face.

Zay sits upright, turning to face me. "I can't do this, Peter. I can't be in this life again. We got out and then it came back with a vengeance. But now...if anything happens to Carter, I will never forgive *any* of you."

I study her tears as they roll down her cheeks, getting lost from her chin to her neck.

The last thing I ever wanted was to hurt her.

And I did. So many different ways and so many different times.

But this ends now.

"Nothing will ever happen to you, sweetie. I promise I'd take a bullet for you, and that goes twice as hard for Carter," I say, wiping her cheek with my thumb.

More tears rise and fall, making this so much harder than it needs to be. But I have to do what's best for my family. "Until all this shit is settled, I think it best if you and Carter head to the cabin."

She doesn't fight back.

No snarky remark.

She pushes herself up and sniffs. "I'll start packing our bags." She looks down at me. "You're coming with me."

I jump to my feet, the rush of blood to my head is making it spin—no, the lack of cocaine in my system is many me nauseated and dizzy. "I have to be here, Zay."

She puffs out her chest. "And what if something happens to us while we're alone out there, huh? Are you going to be able to live with yourself knowing we were in danger and you weren't there to help us?"

Uncontrollable tears are rolling down my cheeks, taking this woman in and listening to the squeals coming from my nephew. She's right, but I have to be here, too, and stand by Riggs's side to deal with this bullshit. *Donnelly brothers at the head of the table.*

She sniffs, about to walk away from me when I take her hand. "Let go of me, Peter."

"Give me a sec, please," I say, squeezing my eyes shut and trying to think.

The cabin was my sanctuary. The place I loved to escape to. The place that helped me heal from the wound she gave me and conjured up a hatred that was never truly there.

Now, the cabin looks nothing like it used to.

It's just an escape. It's not a sanctuary.

But getting out of here is what we have to do. Once and for all.

"Let me find Rosa, and when we do, the four of us will get out of here." I cup the side of her face. "I promise you, sweetie."

She pulls her hand from my grip and leaves the playroom, making me look back at Carter to see what he's doing. He's standing at the bookshelf again, looking at me with a smile.

It's funny how the day started like this and it's not even lunchtime yet and here we are, going full circle.

"What do you say, big guy? Should we start over?" I ask him and get on my knees. "A new life, new beginnings. Happiness, hmm?"

He lets out a giggle and takes a few steps toward me, falling onto my chest with all the love I could ever ask for.

Riggs

I tail it back to the club and barge in like the fucking cops did when they raided us. I need to find Adam, take his keys, and be home where I should fucking be. Not this club, not this life. Shyanne was right, I deserve more than this. More than this heartache. All this club has ever done was ruin me. And it's still doing it with me at the head of the table.

Skeet whistles, taking in the nervous, scattered way I storm in. I'm sweating profusely, my hands are shaking. I must look like a crackhead aching for a fix. "Whatcha doing, pres? You ran outta here like your ass was on fire."

"Where's the half-pint?" I growl, wiping sweat from my forehead. "I need to fucking talk to my brother."

Lip hits a few pool balls and uses the pool cue to lean on. "He's out back, why? What's wrong, brother?"

I don't want to give them the time of day, letting this club slip through my fingers, but I gotta. "Fuckers shot up my house."

"What?" Lip drops the pool cue, snapping his fingers at Dillion. "Where do you need us to go?"

I shake my head, putting my hand up. "Cops are posted at my house. We can't do shit until they leave."

Skeet nods his head at me. "Kid hurt?"

I scratch at my chest nervously, looking at the EXIT sign that leads to the backdoor. "No, he's fine. Peter was there to help them."

"What happened?" Dillion asks, fixing his sunglasses on his forehead.

I scoff, wiping more sweat. "That's what I'm trying to figure out." I charge through the bar, running through the kitchen, and shoving the back door open. The last time I used this door, Zay was trying to run away from me.

Now I'm trying to get her to come back to me.

My, how the tables have turned, huh?

Adam and Slade are laughing as they share a joint. Slade's sitting on the wooden swing set Roaden built when Peter was born. Something for us to do when Daddy brought us to the club. All I wanted was for my son to use this when he got older, now when I look at it, I hope the fucking thing crumbles to the ground.

"Adam," I call, marching over to him. "Gimme your keys, now."

He takes a pull on the joint, holding it before releasing the smoke through his nostrils and handing it off to Slade. "Everything okay?"

I wipe a hand down my face for the millionth time today. "Someone shot up the house with my kid and Zay there."

Adam's face goes pale and his hands begin to shake. "Is she hurt?"

Just thinking about something happening to her makes my heart sink. This is my nightmare. My son and Zay. The only people who matter more than anything in this world, I left alone to deal with MC shit. My priorities are fucking shot.

I release a breath. "Keys, now."

Slade gets up, taking keys from his pocket and handing them to me. "Where's Peter?"

"With them," I say as I'm walking away, but they're following me closely. "I'm going home alone, boys."

Adam scoffs, taking the keys from my hand. "My wife was shot at, you're not going anywhere without me."

"They have a cop posted out front, Adam. We can't just roll in there with our cuts on." I go for the keys but he holds them away from me.

Big fucking mistake.

I bare and grit my teeth. "I don't got time for this, Adam."

"Neither do I, let's go—" I have him by the throat and push him into the side of the bar. My breathing is ragged and short. "Gimme. The. Fucking. Keys."

Slade grips my shoulder, trying to pull me off. Good fucking luck. He may be as tall as me, but I've got a good two hundred pounds of pure muscle on the guy. "Let it go, dude. We're all coming. No one can stop us, all right? Just let him go."

Adam gasps, his wheezing and straining bring back that tickle I used to love when I took someone's life. That fear that made my dick twitch.

Not a good sign.

Releasing him, I step back and shove Slade away from me. "Hide your tattoos." I shimmy out of my cut and toss it at Adam. "Put this inside and get to the fucking car."

I'm so damn angry, I think I cracked a tooth but it doesn't stop me from grinding my teeth even more as a sharp pain blasts through my jaw.

Charging inside, I head for the back room to snag a long sleeve shirt. Slade's on my ass like an agonizing mosquito on a humid summer day.

I peel my shirt off and turn, tossing it at his face. "Back the fuck up."

He puts a hand up, removing the shirt from his face with the other. "You're at your boiling point, pres. We need you to take a chill pill before you do anything rash."

I laugh, that deep demonic laugh that scares people. "Rash, you say?" I stand taller, folding my arms across my brute chest. "Do you know anything about me? About my life? There ain't nothing rash I wouldn't do to protect my kid or my lady, so I suggest you back the fuck up before I do something I regret."

Slade puts both hands up now, that's right, fucker. "Isn't your lady passed?"

I flare my nostrils, my eyes widening with rage.

I'm about to hit this guy right between the eyes.

No, fuck that. I'll shoot him right between those eyes that look at Zay the way only I'm allowed to look at her.

His hands slowly drop and he swallows hard. "That's Adam's wife, pres. I don't know what drama went down between you guys, but we need you to be the president you've been before your wife died. We need you now more than ever."

I inhale sharply, a tinge in my jaw.

We need you now more than ever.

No. No, I don't like that line.

My mama said that to me the night before she died. She said it and it's weighed on me for years. She said it and so did Zay. My Zay who denies her love for me. My Zay who stole my heart so many years ago. My Zay who I keep letting down.

***

We finished eating cake for Peter's eighteenth birthday. I was in the kitchen cleaning the mess and Mama was laughing as Peter told her one of his stories. She loved it when he told her stories. The kid had a knack for it.

I walked back into the dining room as he finished off his story, and handed him a beer. "What's got you all giddy?" I asked, squeezing Mama's shoulder before I sat down.

He smiled, taking Mama's hand. "Just finished telling Mama about my day at school."

I sat on the opposite side of Mama, cracking open a beer as she put her hand on mine, smiling.

"Your brother is going to be famous one day with his words. I can feel it," Mama said, tapping my arm. "You make sure he stays in school, Riggsy."

I nod, bringing the can to my lips. "Of course, Mama."

Peter smirked, rising off the seat to take a paper from his back pocket. "You don't have to worry about me, Mama. Look." He slid the paper over to her, pushing his lips together to hide his grin. "See?"

She unfolded the paper and brought a hand to her mouth, tears welling in her eyes. "My baby boy."

Taking the paper from her, I scanned it. Fucker got into Stanford. "Wouldja look at that."

"I promise I'll visit you every day, Mama," he said, taking her hand again. "I'll try to at least but I will call you every morning when I wake up and every night before I fall asleep. It's not that far of a drive, either."

She nodded, wiping her cheeks. She's been different tonight. Something seemed off but we didn't ask questions. Sometimes she was like that after an argument with Daddy.

I didn't pay attention and I should've.

I let it slip.

I missed the signs.

Peter got up, heading for the bathroom, a smile still on his face. He has freckles like Mama, but hers weren't as pronounced as his. Most gorgeous and selfless woman this world had ever seen and I dare anyone to say otherwise.

Mama told us that she'd be leaving for a little while, taking a trip she said. It's weighed on me since, but I didn't know how to bring it up again. She never spoke of it since that night, but with the look on her face, I knew something was wrong, yet I said nothing. I fucking said nothing.

She rose from her seat and placed her hands on my shoulders, then hugged me. "My boys."

I placed my hand on her arm and smiled. "We love you, too, Mama."

She kissed the side of my head, squeezing me tighter. "We need you now more than ever, Riggs. Promise me you'll keep your brother safe. Promise me."

I didn't know what she meant then.

I didn't know a lot about what Mama did while I was gone and Peter was at school.

I wish she let me in. If she did, maybe she'd be alive right now.

"I'm here, Mama. I ain't going nowhere," I said, looking back at her as she released me. "Is everything all right?"

She sighed heavily, delicately taking my chin. "Handsome, just like your daddy."

The toilet flushed, sending a couple of the old pipes banging. Something I never got the chance to fix.

Something was off. But I didn't fucking push.

I should've pushed.

"I broke the seal," Peter said, scrunching his nose. "I'm going to have to take a piss every five minutes now, watch."

Mama laughed, leaving a kiss on my head. "Enough time to have a drink with your mama before bed, hmm?"

I raised my eyebrows, slumping back in my seat. "You're gonna drink with us?"

She grinned, taking three shot glasses from the hutch and the bottle of whiskey. "I wanna have a memorable night with my boys." Peter hated whiskey but he drank it that night for her.

We had three shots before Mama put her hand on her head, still laughing, and kissed us goodnight.

She held on a moment longer than she usually did, whispering her usual prayer before she headed off to bed.

I missed the signs. That's all I took from that night.

We need you now more than ever.

I know, Mama, and I'm sorry I failed you.

***

I huff, yanking open drawers on the dresser to look for a long-sleeve. Slade does the same, tossing his cut on the bed and pulling a hoodie over his head. Boy has more tattoos than I do. Covered from under his chin down to under his feet. Even his damn balls have tattoos on them. Don't ask how I know, fucker likes to whip it out and show people when they don't believe him.

Adam clears his throat and knocks at the door. "I can't get ahold of Zay."

"Cops are at the house, they're probably questioning them," Slade says, rolling up his sleeves. "You try Peter?"

Adam nods, eyeing me as I pull this godawful shirt on me. "Yeah, twice."

Slade looks back at me, pulling the hood over his head. "You ready, pres?"

I grumble, strutting past them, and head for the car.

This day feels like it's been a lifetime.

A lifetime played out in a matter of a few hours.

Fuck, it's going to be a long ass week if I don't fix this mess.

"Cops are at the house," I say, fixing the shirt on me. "We have to be smart when we pull up."

This shirt is tight as fuck. Probably Adam's, too. He's been sleeping here often. Don't know if it has anything to do with Zay, but I know half of it is because of the club.

All of me hopes it's because of Zay.

Slade throws the back door open, dropping in the seat. Adam hands me the keys and gets in beside him. He knows better than to be near me when I'm like this.

Fucking Christ, I didn't even get to have chapel and discuss how things will go down with getting Rosa back. Or the Domino crap. Or the fucking Ghost shooting up my house.

I'll deal with it tomorrow.

I mumble profanities under my breath and shift into gear as I gun it out of the parking lot.

Home.

I need to get home before I break. And it's coming. Very fucking soon.

Adam

We pull into the driveway and see the cop parked across the street looking down at his damn phone. Some protection they're providing.

The entire ride over, Slade and I shared glances knowing Riggs was going to do something he'd regret if we didn't find a way to calm him down. And knowing my big brother, he'd use my wife for just that. But I have a funny feeling Zay is in no mood for one of his prissy moments, she's probably pissed off and terrified that something bad could've happened to Carter.

I'm still shaking that something happened to her and no one has told me. Eighteen unanswered calls to Peter, and four times that to my wife.

I have no idea what we're going to walk into when we go inside. All I know is that our house looks like an overused pegboard. The shooter didn't miss an ounce of brick when he hit the area around the front door and dining room. All the windows are shot out, the bricks are crumbling off, and our Honda belongs in a junkyard. It's going to cost us a fortune to fix this house.

Peter is in the dining room picking up pieces of glass, and sweeping in some areas. I don't see Zay, she might be upstairs with Carter. She clings to him sometimes when she's anxious or we leave on a trip for the club. Scared something will happen to us.

Zay and I could have left this life when Shyanne was killed and Dorian left us, but we didn't. Zay and I stayed because that's what family does. They protect what's theirs, and help when they need us most.

I think I've been blinded by the idea of us having a family life. I might've missed some things. There's this look she gives me whenever I go on a job.

A disturbed, uncomfortable look. She doesn't like me taking over the club when Riggs and Peter can't, but they don't trust anyone else to do it.

And by God, I'm fucking good at it. *Sorry, babe.*

Riggs gets out of the car and starts for the house, looking back at the patrol car for some stupid reason, then takes a few steps toward it.

Slade and I share one glance because we know shit's about to go down if we don't stop him right now.

He places his hands on Riggs's chest, stopping him on his path to life in prison. "Remove your hands before I do it for you," Riggs growls.

"Don't make things worse, pres," Slade says, nodding at the house. "Let's go see your kid."

Riggs grunts, slapping Slade's hands away, and marches for the house with one last glare over his shoulder. "Fuckers," he mumbles under his breath.

I shoot another look at the cop and he doesn't even glance up at us. Oblivious to the three men coming into the house that was just shot at. If he's oblivious to us, imagine The Ghost who flies under the radar. Fuck, what if this fuck is in The Ghost's back pocket? Roaden has a guy, it only makes sense if this fucker does, too.

Riggs storms in, finding Peter picking up glass from the floor and Zay at the kitchen sink in nothing but her black bra and red lace underwear. My blood boils, I can feel it by the heat rising in my cheeks.

What the fuck is happening here?

I push past Slade as he tilts his head to the side to check out her ass. "Babe?"

When I approach her, that's when I notice the blood. "Holy shit, what happened?"

She picks up some glass from the sink, dropping it in the trash can beside her. "Bullet grazed my neck."

Riggs thunders forward. "Is it bad?" He reaches for the bandage but she takes his hand.

"I'm fine. Looks a lot worse than it is," she says, pointing at the windows. "Board these up, will you?"

Riggs threads his fingers with hers, sending my blood pressure skyrocketing. I'm her fucking husband. I'm the one who asks the questions when it comes to her well-being. But no, not with him around. Nothing compares to him. "Where's the baby?"

"He's playing," she replies, removing her hand from his grip and looking up at Slade. "Why are you here?"

He gives her a once-over and sucks his teeth. "Extra protection."

She hums, nodding. "Don't think my tits need protecting, doofus."

Peter chuckles, emptying the dustpan into the trash, and tilts his head to the side. "She's not wrong." He's one to fucking talk. I'm sure it was his idea for her to walk around in nothing but her underwear.

God, I hate to love these fucking guys.

I nudge my shoulder into Riggs's on purpose as I take Zay's hand. "Come, babe. Let's get you cleaned up."

She sniffs, dropping the cloth wrapped around her hand to reveal another cut probably caused by the glass they're cleaning. "Please clean this up. The last thing we need is a piece of glass in Carter's foot."

Peter jerks his head at Riggs, smiling. "Big man's totally walking now. You should see him go. It's like something just clicked."

"Mmm," Riggs grunts. "Of all fucking days."

Carter's cackles from the living room, the kid is probably in the playpen tossing around his blocks. Or maybe he's jumping up and down for that godawful Baby Shark song he can't get enough of. I never thought I'd hum a kid's song at the club.

Zay peers at Peter over her shoulder, sensing his eyes on her as we walk off. I don't know what's going on between them. But I know Zay, she wouldn't hurt me. She's not that way inclined. With Peter, she had no choice. She hated every second of it and I saw it in her eyes. She pulled away from me, hoping I would leave her. And sadly, there were times I wanted to. When she'd come home on Tuesdays smelling of cigarettes and that cologne Peter used to wear, I wanted to call it quits. Then, she'd look at me with those hazel eyes and I knew things would get better for us. Sooner or later, we'd be okay. Back then, however, she had no choice. I was too stupid to do anything about it because I thought we had no choice.

But there's always a choice, isn't there?

I hope Zay chooses the right one. I hope Zay chooses me.

Leading the way, I take her hand as we step into our room. The number of scars she has on her body because of this club is never-ending. But I'm fucking ending this shit. She will not have to bleed for this club anymore. "Lemme see, babe."

She shakes her head, unhooking her bra. "I just need a shower. I'm fine."

"Hey," I say soothingly, pulling her into me. "Talk to me."

She sniffs, gripping my shirt as her sobs commence. I hate it when she cries. She hasn't cried in months, either. We've been happy, so fucking happy.

We've had a glimpse of what it would be like to have a family. She's stunning as a mother. Seeing how she stepped in and helped raise Carter made me fall in love with her all over again. She wakes up in the middle of the night to care for him. She's the one who stays home and watches him. And she's the one he calls Mama. We created a life here. A good one. One that I wouldn't change; unless there's a way to eliminate my brothers from staring at her like horny savages. Or Riggs constantly trying to win her heart.

This life is something we deal with together.

Because she's my wife and no one will take her away from me.

I hold her until she calms, kissing her head a few times. "I'm here, babe."

She whimpers, gripping me tighter. "What if they shot Carter?" She's trembling, her entire body in shock as if she held it in until I came home. "Whatever these people want, they don't give a shit who gets hurt. That guy came into a family neighborhood and shot up our house. We could've been killed. Oh, God. We could've been killed and you wouldn't have known until it was too late." She's sobbing uncontrollably, shaking like a leaf in a cool breeze. "Did you see our house? It looks like a massacre happened here."

There's nothing I can say to make this any better. Nothing I can do but continue to promise her new beginnings, when in the end, there's no escaping this fucking life, is there?

I kiss the top of her head and lift her, taking her to the shower. She grips me tightly, her sobs dying down with every inhale she takes.

With her legs wrapped around my waist, I turn the shower on and attempt to undress without setting her down.

I hate seeing Zay so helpless, and I know this is how she feels.

Scared.

Speechless.

Worthless.

I'll fix this, my love. I promise I'm trying.

She sniffs when I put her down and hugs herself as I get out of my boots and jeans, tossing my hoodie aside. "Come," I tell her, helping her out of the red lace underwear.

Carefully, I remove the bandage on her neck to reveal a deep gash and a small scratch. One at the nape of her neck, and the small one on her collarbone.

She leans her head back on the tiles, letting the hot water fall upon her closed eyes. "When will this end, Adam?"

I brace myself in front of her, hands above her head, and look down as the dried blood rolls down her curves. "Soon, babe. Very soon."

She blinks, staring up at me as I block her from the water. "As soon as we get Rosa, I'm taking the kids and leaving. They do not need this life. And they will not ever be part of it."

I lower my head, meeting her lips. "We'll be a family, Zay. A fucked up one at that, but a family all the same. I promise you this."

"You'll be able to leave all this behind?"

I don't even think over my answer. I nod, thumbing mascara from her cheek. "Forever and always, remember?"

She nods, licking her lips as the door to the bathroom opens and Riggs walks in with his arms crossed. Her body tenses, head lifting off the tiles. But I don't move, I'm still shielding her from his starving eyes. "Do you mind?" she jeers, arching an eyebrow.

No damn privacy in this fucking house.

I groan and step forward, using my body as a way to cover hers. But Riggs doesn't care. He never fucking did. Whatever he wants, he gets. And he wants my woman.

He leans his forearms on the glass shower, his eyes eating up what he can see of her body. "Family meeting in ten."

I lower my head, blinking from the falling water as I try to look at him.

"Yeah, just give us a sec."

A deep chuckle leaves him, teeth raking his bottom lip. "You doing all right, sunshine?"

"Just peachy, Riggs."

I keep my eyes on him, but he doesn't give me the satisfaction of meeting my gaze when I speak. "Again, give us a second, man. We'll be right out."

I wonder how much of our conversation he heard.

He lowers his head in that intimidating way that scares the living daylights out of people. "I heard what you said, sunshine. Didn't we already discuss how I feel about you taking my son?"

Yep, he heard what we said.

She pushes against my chest, going right up to the glass and tapping her pointed finger on it. "You're telling me you want this life for him? Hmm? You want him to be home and randomly get shot at? Is that what you're trying to tell me? Because if so, then why the fuck am I raising your fucking kid for?"

His nostrils flare, lowering himself even more so he's eye to eye with her, and all that's separating them is a one-inch pane of glass. But I don't care how big and tough he is, one hand on my woman and he's dead. "Whether you like it or not, Zay, you're his mama. But if you remove him from my life, we will have big fucking problems. Do you understand me?"

She growls, banging her hands on the glass, blood from the cut on it smearing. "Fuck you."

I wrap my arm around her waist, moving her away from that satanic look in his eyes. "Babe, take a second, yeah? Breathe, just breathe."

Riggs bangs the glass back, kicking my boots, then knocking over a little shelf before slamming the door behind him. "Big fucking mistake, sunshine."

Great, she poked the bear.

She grits her teeth and hisses as she scratches her chest, winching when she touches her cuts. "I don't give a shit what he says," she starts, then raises her voice. "And I hope he's fucking listening!" An audible growl leaves her as she releases a breath, lowering her voice again. "I'm getting Carter out of this life. And when you guys find Rosa, she'll be out of it, too."

I kiss the back of her head, breathing her in. "Okay, babe. Anything you want to do, I'm in your corner."

She huffs, wincing again as another sob chokes her. Another thing to add to our list of devastations. Another day to circle as a shit day.

Some day soon, her smiles will remain. They were there for months.

They'll be there again.

She and I away from the fucks that live in this house. We'll be a family. Raise those kids the way Mama Rosa wanted to raise us.

Everything will be okay.

Everything will be okay.

Peter

Riggs and Slade are helping me pick up the glass from the windows. Slade is a good guy, he's loyal as hell. He's helped us a time or two around the house when we needed it. Helped us more at the club. He's a yes-man. What we say goes. There's no denying how deep he'd get in the club if Daddy or Crew were running it. He'd get lost. I got lost but now I'm home.

I'm home and soon my baby girl will be home, too. Be it here or at the cabin. Just home.

Riggs grunts as he bends over and picks up the last of the glass on the kitchen floor. Slade found some scrap wood in the garage for when we started finishing the basement and is nailing it to the opening of the window.

Another gruff breath leaves Riggs. It's clear he's upset about the whole situation. Who wouldn't be? This Ghost guy is fucking with us and our family over something that was out of our control. Everyone who was deeply involved in the trafficking was killed off.

How is it still our fault?

Riggs kicks the toolbox as he tries to walk past, mumbling under his breath. He wants to go upstairs, he hasn't stopped looking at the staircase since Zay stormed up there with Adam.

But Zay is not his woman.

Adam has made that perfectly clear for all of us.

***

Riggs and I were sitting in the backyard our first month in the house. Zay fell asleep with Carter a couple of hours ago, leaving the men to bask in the silence as we watched the stars. She's so good with him. So loving and protective. She'll be an exceptional mother one day.

I looked up at the stars. It was fairly clear that night. Riggs kept his eyes on the prowl, protecting and scanning the area while I smiled.

I love watching the stars because of her.

Adam came out to join us, a few beers in hand. "Hey."

Riggs grunted, as usual.

And I nodded at him, still despising him for having a woman who loved him and would do anything for him. Unlike Dorian who ruined me. Took my child from me and escaped the life I promised her. It was a good life, a beautiful one filled with love, happiness, and so many babies.

I never saw any signs. I wish I did. I wish there was a glimpse of something that could point to her betraying me. But there wasn't a single thing. We were so happy.

She worked long hours but she's a lawyer. She'd ask me to join her at office events. But I said no. I always said no. I didn't want her to come off as a whore for moving on from her husband so quickly. I now know that even her husband was as worthless to her as I was.

She betrayed me and I was blinded by it all.

She's a great fucking actress, I'll give her that.

Adam sat on the chair beside me, reaching over to hand Riggs a beer, then unscrewing the cap and handing me one. "Think we can talk?"

Riggs sniffed, draining his beer. "There ain't nothing to talk about. We got chapel in the morning. Whatever business you're thinking about can wait until then."

Adam chuckled softly, shaking his head as he thumbed the corner label. "No, uh, I wanted to talk about my wife."

Both Riggs and I share a glance, slowly easing our gaze on Adam. Zaynab had been our rock those weeks. She'd listen when I broke down, she'd soothe me, and tell me not to worry.

Things will look up, she'd say.

We will find your baby, she'd say.

I'm never leaving your side, Peter, she'd say.

Whatever Adam had to say wasn't going to be good. And if I lost Zay, then there was no telling if I'd lose myself, too.

Riggs finished off the beer and placed it at his feet. "What about her?"

With a deep inhale, Adam peeled the corner of his label and cleared his throat. "I just wanted to remind you that she is *my* wife. I get that you've both been with her, but in the end, she married me." He held my gaze for a moment longer than I liked. "I don't want either of you to try anything. I think she's been through enough because of you two. And I understand some fucked up shit happened at Daddy's grave, and if you need Zay as a crutch to help you heal through that, then fine. But she'll only be a shoulder to cry on or an ear to listen to. She's not going to be a hole you release in." Riggs cracked the bones in his neck, looking at the night sky. "Because again, she's *my* fucking wife and we haven't had the chance to be a couple since this fiasco started because of this damn club. So please, just…leave her alone."

I stood, draining the beer and tossing it at the wall behind him, sending brown glass shattering everywhere. "Yeah, she's your wife. Adam. I get it. Don't need the fucking reminder."

Riggs chuckled, pushing off the chair as well. "I make no promises, shaky hands, because, in the end, it is her decision. Not yours. She may have married you but she ain't a dumbass who ignores her feelings. If Zay wanted me, she'd have me. No paper will stop that."

Adam scoffed, setting his beer down and running his fingers through his hair. "I can never have anything, can I? Growing up you always had to show off what you had versus what I had. Which was *nothing*. You rubbed in my face that Mama Rosa was the best mother in the world, whereas mine was a fucking junkie slinging tricks for a dime bag. I always got your hand-me-downs, always had to share, I never had something that was just mine." He shook his head dropping it between his shoulders. "Even Zay who fucking chose me was tainted by you, Peter, and then when I tried to get her out of my life, you guys brought her back in, and then you ruined her, Riggs." Tears rolled down his nose, his hands shaking in front of him. "Zay chose me and I still can't fucking have her, can I?" He pushed off the chair and started picking up the pieces of glass from the ground. "Fucking bullshit," he mumbled, sniffling.

Riggs stared at me, wiping a hand down his face and going inside. He doesn't give a shit. If he wanted Zay, he'd have her. Much like I used to think, but Dorian changed me. Fucking cunt changed my way of thinking.

I crouched beside Adam and nodded, placing a hand on his back. "I'm sorry, brother. Truly. Zay just hits differently, you know that. Something about her draws us in. She's...fucking incredible. Our nirvana." I smirked. "But you're right, she is your woman. I haven't tried anything on her and I don't plan on it, either. I broke her last year and it was wrong. But she's my friend and I need her now more than ever, Adam. Okay?" My voice cracked by the end of it, wiping my cheek on my shoulder. "I need her," I whispered.

He dropped the glass he picked up, beer dripping off his fingers. "Yeah." He sighed, taking a breath. "Yeah."

I felt the annoyance wafting off him that night. I understood it. And yet, it still angered me. Zaynab became untouchable, even when she always was. Hearing Adam say something made it permanent in a way.

Not watching them get married or seeing them hug and kiss. No, hearing him ask us to leave her alone because she was his made all of this fucked up lifestyle we have break just a little bit more.

***

Slade pulls his hoodie off, fixing his undershirt. "Neighbor is outside talking to the cop."

I drop more glass in the trash and look out the window in the dining room. "Yeah, she's a nosy fucking bitch." I suck my teeth, cracking my neck and crouching to continue sweeping. "Husband works on the oil rigs so he's not here a lot. They don't have kids so she spends her days gossiping with the other housewives on their morning runs."

Slade chuckles, sliding his tongue over his teeth. "She looks tasty."

"I'm sure she'll scold you if you get anywhere near her," I comment, grunting as I reach under the table and pick up more pieces. "She gave me shit once for parking crooked in my own driveway."

Slade's laughter is cut short when Riggs's heavy footfalls barge down the stairs and into the kitchen, heading right for the whiskey in the hutch. "All good, man?"

Handing the dustpan to Slade, lunge at the bottle, taking it away from Riggs's lips. "No, we promised Zaynab we'd sober up."

He scoffs, grumbling as he wipes his mouth. "She's planning on taking our kid away from me."

I frown, shaking my head. "What do you mean?"

He slumps into a chair, rubbing his eyes. "She warned me this morning that if I don't fix myself, she's taking Carter and fleeing." The muscle in his jaw tightens, clicking his tongue. "Said when we find Rosa, she's taking her, too."

I want to be mad at Zay, I want to yell and stomp my feet and tell her she'll never get away with this. But she's right.

Taking the kids out of this life is the way to go. It's what we discussed earlier, too.

I'm not mad at her. I'm happy she took a stand against my gorilla of a brother.

"I know," I tell him, nodding. "I told her this is what she's going to do once we find Rosa. Keep them as far away from this life as possible."

He scoffs, dropping his hand on the table. "You're okay with this?"

I lift a shoulder, leaning on the table beside him. "Zay's been through enough, Riggs. The last thing we need is for our kids to get hurt. Fuck, look what happened today. What if I wasn't home and Zay was here with Carter? What if they were playing in the front yard or—" I pause, pinching the bridge of my nose. "What if that fucker got into the house and held them at gunpoint? What then, hmm?"

Riggs's face is red, teeth grinding as Slade sweeps as quietly as he can. He knows I'm right. He knows this life is never going to work with our kids.

Someday soon, we'll have our happy ending. But today is definitely not that day.

"We'll move them to the cabin as soon as the cops let us leave," I say, wiping my hands together. "Until then, family meeting like we discussed."

He grunts, flicking a piece of glass off the table and watching as it ricochets off the wall and onto the floor. Riggs is my big brother and he's the one I'm supposed to look up to.

The one I've always looked up to. But he's not thinking rationally right now.

He has to start before his anger and revenge get the better of him and we're all lying six feet underground with a bullet between our eyes.

Zay

They're all slumped around the table, while I'm sitting at the island looking at the bootle of alcohol. I'm contemplating taking a glass but I just gave shit to the Donnelly assholes about sobering up so we can get the hell outta dodge.

It's not going well.

I took longer than I should've to come down here because I hate family meetings. At the last family meeting we had, Adam was given the stand-in VP patch, I was asked to sign Carter up for daycare in the fall, and Riggs showed up wasted, he was barely coherent during the decision-making. I had to sit in the bathroom with him as he puked his guts out and confessed his undying love for me yet again.

Drunk Riggs sure likes to admit his feelings, I have yet to hear sober Riggs tell me he loves me. I wonder what that would feel like. I wonder if he even does.

Before coming downstairs, I studied myself in the mirror above the staircase. There's worry on my face, deepening the slight groove between my eyes. I'm tired of this life and I don't know how many times I have to say it. I'm done. Whatever needs to be discussed downstairs, the only thing I'm listening to is Carter and I taking our bags and leaving this place.

Our luggage is already packed and sitting in the garage, waiting for the okay from everyone. I highly doubt they'll be okay with this. Especially Riggs, but I have to do what I have to do. He can hold down the fort with Peter while Adam takes Carter and me to the cabin until this shit is over with. Then, when Rosa is home, I'm taking the kids and getting the hell out of here. I've always loved Maine. My parents had a home out there by the water we'd go to every summer. Maybe we can move out there.

It's decided. I'm finally getting out of this mess. And I have the perfect plan lined up if shit goes sour.

Riggs is scowling at me, enraged that I would remove his son from this life. Can he blame me, though? We were shot at and lucky nothing happened. This shit could've been so much worse than it was. The horror that paints my mind sends tears to my eyes. All I see is Carter, lifeless, blood pooling around him because I wasn't there to protect him.

I swallow thickly and glance at Riggs again. Argh, I want to smack that look off his face and shake him until he understands.

But he won't. He's one stubborn motherfucker.

Slade is in the living room playing with Carter and watching something on TV, I hear his cackle every so often. It's becoming more irritating by the second. I don't even know why he's here. He's not family. Then again, neither am I.

My guess is he's here as an eyewitness in case one of these Donnellys goes on a murder spree. Riggs is one more snarky comment away from slapping me silly and taking the gun on the cop outside. No, that's not right. If I make one more snarky comment, I think he'd bend me over this table and take me from behind while everyone watches just to put me in my place, then take his gun out and kill that cop to prove an even bigger point that we don't need these cops to protect us, he's more than capable of doing it himself.

Evidence states otherwise.

"Babe?" Adam says, tapping the chair beside him. "Come sit."

"Nope. I'm good here." I take the bottle of whiskey and gulp from it, grimacing at the sting in my throat.

Peter jerks his head at me. "Thought you said we're not allowed to drink that shit anymore."

I inhale a breath, narrowing my eyes slightly. "I deserve every fucking drop for being part of this family."

Riggs lets out an exasperated chuckle, still scowling. He didn't like that one bit.

Adam sighs, catches my eye, and holds it for a few seconds before blowing me a kiss. He's the only reason I put up with all of this garbage. Adam and Carter. I like the idea of starting a family with him, it has been something we spoke about while dating. He was secretive at the time about his family life, but always said he wanted a big family. *As many kids as that perfect pussy can give me.* Carter isn't even mine and I'm in love with the thought of raising him away from motorcycles and guns.

I keep seeing us at that cabin. My family running through the grass, swimming in the water, and roasting marshmallows by the fire. I see us happy, so damn happy. Like we were a year ago when all of us went up there with our people. Pure happiness bloomed on that day.

Now, there isn't an ounce of happiness in this room aside from the look my husband is giving me. He's my reason.

The only reason.

Riggs bangs his fist on the table. "Sit your fucking ass down at the table, Zay."

"Hey," Adam hisses.

Peter shoots up from the other side of the table, fists pressed firmly on it. "Relax."

I start laughing, bringing the bottle to my lips as I do. There it is. My breaking point. "I'm fucking done with this bullshit. For years I've suffered because of you fucks. And now that life is finally looking up and I finally feel like I have a purpose, you wanna rip it away? So you know what? Go right a-fucking-head. Because I am done." Scoffing, I gulp another sip. "I don't understand any of this. God, I wish I knew what I have to make you fucking Donnellys obsessed with me like I'm some kind of succubus luring you in."

I'm fuming, I can feel the heat in my cheeks, the twinge in my jaw, and the rumbling in my stomach. That shiver soaks into me and causes an urge to scream. No, cry. I've blown my fuse. I knew it was coming, but oh, man, I'm livid and about to tear some heads off.

Pointing at Peter, then Adam, and stopping on Riggs. "I'm done with all of you. So raise your own fucking kid, clean your own fucking house, and wash your own underwear. I. Am. Done."

I don't realize it, but tears and rolling down my cheeks as I stomp out of the kitchen. I don't even bother using the front door, I head straight for the garage and slam the door behind me.

It smells like motor oil and tires in here.

Fucking Riggs.

I can't take it anymore. I'm tired of the worrying, of the fright.

Gosh, of the fucking thought that something is going to happen to Carter because of the people seeking revenge for something that happened years ago.

Something I had nothing to do with.

Taking off Riggs's ring from my thumb, then my wedding ring, and place it on the shelf. I remove the chain around my neck that Riggs gave me for my birthday, too. I'm *that* fucking done.

I need a breather and if I stay in this house any longer, someone is going to get hurt by my words or by me throwing something at them.

Without thinking twice, I open the garage door and march for the Audi. There are bullet holes in the trunk, but I don't care. The asshole who shot up the house totaled the Honda and barely hit the Audi. Probably saw the "Baby On Board" sign on the back of it.

I reverse out of the driveway like a woman on a mission. I don't know where I'm going, but it's away from the Donnelly men, that's for certain.

I think I'll just head home.

Adam and Peter run out seconds later calling out to me. Adam chases the car, hitting the back of it when I slow down and make a sharp turn at the corner of the street. "Babe! Stop, please! Let's talk about this!"

Riggs stands at the front door, staring at me with furrowed brows.

I don't need this anymore.

I should have left months ago.

I should have never taken Adam back.

I should have died in the barn so none of this would weigh on me.

Life was horrible, then it was good. So good, and then it wasn't.

And now, I'm driving away and praying I never have to shed another tear for the men who have ruined me over and over again.

I press harder on the gas pedal and cry as I see Adam shrink in the rearview mirror.

Carter is playing in the living room. I left and he'll never forgive me when he's older if I don't come back for him.

I've thought of a plan. A good one.

A plan that will save us from this life.

I'm heading to Richmond.

Riggs

She left.

Just like that.

She fucking left us.

My heart is rumbling like the engine on my bike. It's chasing after her like Adam, pleading with her to stop and come home.

But my body is right here, frozen.

Hands gripping the doorframe.

My mouth is dry like sandpaper, as if I was sleeping with my mouth open all night.

But my heart's after her, begging her to come home.

My heart left without saying goodbye.

"What the actual fuck just happened?" Peter asks, coming into the kitchen and searching for something.

It's probably the keys that Slade has tucked into his front pocket.

It's no use.

Running after Zay will only add fuel to the fire.

I drop onto the stool she sat on and take the whiskey. *You and me, baby. I'll give you the world someday, I promise.*

Adam charges upstairs, also looking for the keys. I'm not opening my mouth to let them know Slade has them.

Nope.

I'm sitting right here and getting drunk off my ass until I fall out of this chair and feel a little better.

Yep, that's what's going to happen.

I guzzle down a bit more and hear Peter scoff. "Don't think drinking right now is the best idea, Riggs. Zay just walked out because you don't know how to fucking control your emotions around her. Fuck, we're all hurting, man, hurt with us so we can fix this mess."

"What's there to fix, huh? Shyanne died. Dorian ran off with your kid. Now there's someone who wants us dead for something Daddy did and I don't know how to fucking fix it." I grunt, putting the bottle down. "And Judas is up to something but he's with Mickey, so I don't—" I rub my eyes and groan. "When the fuck did life gets so goddamn complicated? Fuck, we never had shootouts at the house as kids. Never, and fucking now we do. Look at this house. You don't think my biggest fear is something happening to my kid or Zay? Why do you think I taught her how to shoot? For situations like *this*. I can't—" I sniff, looking at the whiskey. "I can't do this," I whisper.

Peter rolls his eyes, tilting his head back. "For situations like this? Where someone shoots up the entire front of the house? How was she supposed to defend herself, huh? With the snubnose I used? No, brother, she's right and you know she's fucking right." He glares at me. "You *can* do this, do you hear me? You're Riggs fucking Donnelly, the big brother I looked up to my entire life. Nothing, and I mean *nothing*, ever stood in your way, man. Don't let this, either."

I scoff, fiddling with the rings on my fingers. I haven't taken my wedding ring off yet. Doesn't feel right. I never had the chance to get a tattoo for Shyanne, either. Now it seems too cliché. The only way I'll ever take off this ring is if Zay tells me she loves me, too. I'll rip this ring off and get on my knees to praise her. She deserves redemption. She deserves a better life.

I exhale a rush of air, looking at the bottle again as Adam comes back into the kitchen out of breath. I know Peter's fucking right but my head and heart haven't had a conversation about it yet. My heart's with Zay, soothing her, consoling her. And my head is telling me to shut her up and make her listen to how things have to be.

But it's wrong.

Slade walks into the kitchen, clearing his throat. "Sorry to interrupt…but if I may." He bows his head and inhales. "Zay doesn't need any of you right now. She's stressed as it is with everything that happened today. She belongs to all three of you and y'all treat her like a housewife. Expecting her to keep your home and your kid, but none of you have asked how she's doing." His eyebrows raise slightly, shifting his gaze between the three of us. "She needs a friend sometimes."

Fucking guy better stop while he's ahead before I cut his fucking tongue out.

"Sometimes a smile hides so much more than anyone notices," Slade adds, fixing his jeans.

He gulps when he looks at me, taking a step toward the island. The thought of Zay hiding her feelings irks me. She never hides anything. Whenever something is bothering her, she's the first to open her mouth about it.

That sass and spunkiness I love about her.

But now, I'm wondering if it was all fake. All a way to hide her true self because we pulled her away from her life. Her dream of being a graphic designer. Of finishing university.

We took that away and handed her a baby.

She's perfect.

Knows it, too.

But we were all blinded by the truth because of the life we gave her. And if that doesn't set a fire under my ass, I don't know what does.

Slade shakes his head, pointing at the phone in Adam's hand. "Call my cell phone, yeah?"

"Why?" Peter asks, his shaking hand scratching his chin.

"Left it in the Audi this morning when I dropped Riggs off." He stalks for the fridge and takes a beer, spinning the cap off and flinging it at the sink. "She took the Audi, didn't she? Honda's fucked."

Adam dials out Slade's number, holding the phone to his ear. Peter takes it from him and taps the speaker button so we can all listen to the agonizing trills.

After three rings, she answers. "Slade's phone." That sass coming through the phone makes me smirk. I'm an asshole to her because I'm sour about her choice and she doesn't deserve that.

"Babe? Jesus, what the hell was that? Come home, okay, we'll talk about this," Adam says, leaning his elbows on the counter.

She scoffs, inhaling a breath. "No."

Peter growls. "Where the fuck are you gonna stay, huh? All your shit is here."

"Don't worry about it," she says, then hangs up.

I wipe my mouth, a smile quirking on my lips. I know exactly where she's going.

She's going home.

And she'll have a smile on her face when she sees me waiting there for her.

I push up from the chair and put my hand out to Slade. "Keys, now."

He hesitates but holds them out to me anyway. Gotta give it to him, he's a loyal fuck. "What're you gonna do, boss?"

I shake my head. "I just need some air. Going to the club to get my bike."

He glances at Adam, then nods. "Cool, I'll drive. You've been drinking."

I scoff, going for the keys but he puts them back in his pocket.

Fucker.

"I had one drink, I ain't drunk. Gimme the keys," I demand, my body tensing.

Slade lifts a shoulder, those colorful tattoos irritating me. He's the only one Skeet had trouble figuring out where to put the Snakes logo. We don't do face tattoos, *sends the wrong message*, Daddy used to say. He hated hand tattoos, then got Mama's name on his hand when she gave birth to Peter. It's the reason I have a rose tattooed on my hand. Slapped that there when she died.

Slade swallows hard, that throat tattoo twitching as he brings a hand to his chest and scratches. Snakes' logo is still fresh on his finger. "No can do, pres. I'm driving."

I grumble, dropping my hand and taking the bottle for another sip. Might as well since the fucker is driving.

Adam tries Zay again, but she declines him after one ring. "Fuck, Zay, c'mon," he hisses under his breath, calling her again.

Peter stares at me with narrowed eyes and chuckles, shaking his head. "Guess I'm watching your kid again, huh?" He proceeds to curse under his breath and goes to the living room as Carter lets out a cry.

I flare my nostrils, knowing I need to be more present in Carter's life but I can't be.

I failed him as a father by not protecting his birth mother.

And now he's being raised by all of us. Raised in a life of crime and danger.

My son deserves so much more.

Fucking Christ I hate it when Zay's right.

Slade

Riggs has been huffing beside me, cracking his knuckles even when there isn't anything to crack. At this rate, he'll snap a freaking finger if he doesn't knock it off.

I get it, Zay's a firecracker. Smoking hot bod with a "go fuck yourself" attitude that makes my cock grow stiff.

The first time I met her, I pulled my signature move. Running my fingers through my hair, biting my lower lip, and finding any excuse to take off my shirt.

Then I found out she was Adam's wife.

Peter's ex-girlfriend.

And Riggs's…well, that's a little messy. I'm still trying to piece together that part. She raises his kid, who isn't even hers. And yet, he calls the kid theirs and calls her his girl.

I'm just as confused as anyone about what on earth happens in that house behind closed doors. I'm all for polygamous relationships, but this one is fucked up. They're all brothers, it would be wrong to fuck someone while your brothers watch, or better yet, participate.

Shivering at the thought of fucking in front of family, I check the navigation system on the dash. We're a minute out. I don't even have to look at the dashboard, Riggs is sitting up straighter and rubbing his hands on his jeans. "We shoulda gone to the club, pres."

He shakes his head and points at one of the houses. "Nope, it's better that I'm here."

"Adam should be here, y'know."

He shakes his head as we pull up to the mansion. "Adam never met her parents."

That's a helpful tidbit of information.

I whistle, looking up at the house. Impressive fucking place. Grey brick and windows are what make up the majority of the front. I can only imagine what the inside looks like. This house is something out of those rich people magazines from the dentist's office.

"All right, pres. Now what?" I ask, putting the car in park in the empty driveway.

He unclips his belt and grunts when he gets out of the car. "Knock on the door and put her in the car."

I chuckle, following him, and taking his elbow. "Let me go in. Don't think she'll be too happy to see you."

He cackles, pulling his arm from my grip. "She has no choice."

"And it's comments like that, that make her want to leave."

He folds his arms, lowering his head slightly. We're almost the same height but this fucking guy is a monster. I'm surprised someone as tiny as Zay didn't get lost in his embrace.

"With the way you look at her you think I'd leave you two alone? That ain't happening," he says as the front door opens to a man whom Zay strikingly resembles. Guy must be on edge because of the frantic way his daughter looked and the way he whipped open the door, as if waiting for someone.

"Can I help you?" he asks, eyeing Riggs, then me.

I smile, clapping Riggs's shoulder and stepping forward. "Yes, sir. We're friends of Zay's. You think we could come in and see her."

The gentleman frowns, scanning me as I approach, then glancing at Riggs. "You're her husband, right? The blonde who she went to school with?"

I smirk, putting my hand out to him. I knew that tidbit of information would be useful. "Adam, sir. This is my brother, Riggs."

He shakes my hand, nodding his head. "Nice to finally meet you."

Guess she's not that close with her family. Been married to Adam for three years and they haven't met the guy yet. Now I know why she clings to the thought of a family life, the thought of her happy ending is always out of reach.

Well, I can be a proper university student and a husband for a night.

"Pleasure's all mine, sir. Would you mind if we came in?" I ask, smiling.

He clears his throat, staring at Riggs. "My daughter came in here crying, bandages all over her neck and hands. I'd like to know why before I invite you into my home."

Clearing my throat, I nod my head and try my best to come up with a lie. I'm good at lying my way into getting what I want.

I put my hand up to ease that intensity in his eyes. "One of our windows broke and she cut herself helping my brother pick up the glass." His shoulders ease back a little as if that bogus lie seemed true enough. "And her tears are probably because she got into an argument with my brother. Our living arrangement has been shaky the past few months and my brothers live with us. Close quarters and all." I jerk a shoulder. "It's been a little stressful lately. If she wants to stay the night, I hope that's okay. All I ask is if it's all right that I check on my wife to say goodnight."

Her father looks back as a woman with dark brown hair cut short and framed around her face comes into view. I can see where Zay gets her beauty.

Her father eyes us again, opening the door wider. "Adam, is it? *You* may go see my daughter." He stares at Riggs. "*You* will wait for her in the den. My wife brewed some tea."

Riggs snorts with a soft chuckle, nodding when we lock eyes. "Yes, sir."

I step in and slip out of my combat boots. Fucking things have seen better days and her father takes notice with the grimace on his face he tries to mask.

Her mother comes closer with a tray of tea, brows pinched together. "Hello?"

I put my hand out, smiling. "Adam, ma'am. Your son-in-law. This here is my brother, Riggs."

A couple of once-overs are enough to sense her judgement. All my life I've been judged. I'm used to the scowling looks. The looks that scream *this guy is a bum, he's dangerous, he's poor.* And her mother is giving me all of those. "Oh, well, my daughter has always been into…eccentric things, hasn't she?" she says, eyeing her husband.

Riggs and I share a glance, stifling a laugh. "Yes, ma'am, she has," Riggs says.

Her father ushers Riggs into the den and points at the stairs. "She's the third door on the left. There's a large letter Z on the front."

Taking the large stairs two at a time, I find Zay's room with ease.

A smirk touches my lips, knowing it would be so easy to get her in bed with me if I wanted.

But I wouldn't do that to Riggs or Peter…or Adam.

Girl gets around, man. But so do I, no judgement.

I open her door and hear her sigh, those long tanned legs bent up on her bed. Goddamn, all I wanna do is run my tongue up her legs and get lost between them.

Yeah, I like the thought of tasting this spunky little sex kitten.

Just for a night.

"I'll be down in a sec," she says, pinching the bridge of her nose.

I close the door and lean on it, crossing my feet at the ankles. "I'm not one of your parents, sweet thing."

She gasps, kicking her legs and moving up her bed. "What the fuck, Slade? What're you doing here?" She scoffs, frowning. "Better yet, who the fuck would let you in?"

I look around her room. Tons of pictures are pinned to a corkboard on her wall. Pictures of her and Adam at school. There's a couple of her and some blonde girl, and one picture of her, the blonde girl, and Peter on a camping trip.

This must be from before the biker gang. He looks happy here, healthy.

I push off the door and start for the bed, smirking as I do. "Daddy dearest thinks I'm Adam." I tousle my hair. "Lucky for me we're both blonde."

She growls, gritting her teeth. "I don't need this, Slade. Leave."

This woman drives me nuts.

I like it when she's mad at me.

Leaning my fists on the bed, I stare at her with a cocked eyebrow. "Riggs is angry as shit. So, I'm not leaving until we know you're okay and that you're coming home."

She rolls her eyes, getting on her knees. "I'm not coming home. Not until this shit is over with."

"Yeah? So what're you gonna do, then? Hmm?"

She exhales slowly, raking her bottom lip. "I'm going to Richmond to find Dorian."

An exasperated laugh leaves me. "And you fucking think your men would let that happen?"

She pokes my forehead. "I can do what I want when I want. Those men do not own me."

"They're just dicks you use to get off, huh?" I snicker, poking her forehead back. "But they won't let you go knowing this Ghost fucker is trying to kill them. They shot at your house, Zay. You can't leave without a plan."

She licks those succulent lips again and I'm staring right at them, nibbling mine without realizing it. "And if the Donnelly brothers show up in Richmond and word gets around, Dorian and the baby are long gone. It's better if they don't come anywhere near that town."

I grumble, dropping my head between my shoulders and taking a few deep breaths.

I don't want to go against my president or VP. Let alone Adam who has been running this club when its leaders were too fucked to do it.

But fucking Christ, if this woman is stubborn.

Head hard as stone.

But she has a damn point.

"I'll come with you, then."

She laughs, shaking her head and grabbing the hair on the top of mine, lifting it. "You're fucked if you think you're coming."

I wink, adjusting my fists on the bed. "Not up to you, sweet thing. I have a loyalty to this club. And you, Zay, whether you like it or not are part of this club." She narrows her eyes, ready to spit something back. She's a little firecracker. "So if I have a loyalty to the Snakes, I have a loyalty to you. And I will not let you go on this suicide mission alone."

She angles her head up to face mine, gorgeous features that accentuate in the dim lighting, as if she knows which angles will make her look her best.

I can see why these men swoon over her.

Fuck, it's tight in these jeans all of a sudden.

"Tell me, Slade. What's in it for you? All of this, hmm? What's being loyal to the Snakes ever going to bring you?" she asks, eyebrows pinched together.

I widen my smile, leaning forward, and feel her pull in a sharp breath of air. Goddamn, this is why it always smells like coconuts when she's around.

She's paradise, I'm sure.

"A purpose."

Her tongue comes out of her mouth and sweeps her bottom lip, nodding slightly. "There's more to life than gangs and violence." She nudges my chin. "Find a better reason than it being your purpose. Everyone deserves to find their purpose, but this club should not be yours."

I lean lower again, face inches from hers. I can kiss her if I want, and she's so upset at these guys she'd probably let me just to spite them. But I won't do it, even if those lips look divine. "What's your purpose, Zay?"

A soft chuckle leaves her and she almost closes the gap between us, her lips feather mine and I inhale her minty breath. "My purpose died when I was shot in the chest because of this club."

With that, she pushes my face away and gets off the bed, opening her door and standing by it, as if I'm supposed to listen to her and leave.

But I'm gonna need a second.

I'm as stiff as a plank.

Her eyes are downcast, studying the white area rug. "Tell Adam I'll call him in the morning."

With a few more deep exhales, I push off her bed and nod, making my way to her. "Wanna trade phones?"

She smirks slightly, taking mine off her dresser. The bandage around her hand needs to be changed, but I'll let Riggs deal with that. I don't think he'd like me touching her even if I'm just helping.

She holds out my phone. "You're one sick fuck."

I laugh, tucking my phone away. "You shouldn't have snooped."

She tilts her head to the side and lifts a shoulder. "I'm curious by nature."

I scan her, stopping on her tits with a devious grin. "Leave me a pic of those?"

She rolls her eyes and crosses her arms, popping out a hip. "In your dreams." But the playful side of her leaves when I bring a hand to my mouth and wipe it. Her eyes catch the Snakes tattoo on my finger. "Don't tell Adam my plan, please. Or Riggs for that matter."

I tilt my head to the side, arching a brow. "Too late on gigantor. He's downstairs and very pissed off."

She growls through gritted teeth and charges out of her room. Little sassy pants is about to flip out.

I've seen her upset before, calling Peter and Riggs out on their shit. It's funny seeing someone who's 5'2" boss around men who are over a foot taller than her.

But they listen like little puppy dogs.

And holy crap do I get it.

I wonder when my turn's going to be.

Her stomps echo through the home and I chuckle, sitting on her bed and awaiting her return. There's no way I'm going out there with a stiffy.

"Riggs!" she belts. "Upstairs, now."

I look down at my crotch and see the outline of my dick in these jeans that were not designed for men with boners.

Shit, this is embarrassing.

She stalks her way back upstairs and Riggs's heavy footfalls are right on her tail.

A huff leaves her when we lock eyes and I smirk, sitting on the bed to try and hide this child-like erection I have over a girl who's fuming.

Why do I find it so damn hot when she's angry?

This woman will be the death of a lot of men, I can guarantee it.

Peter

Adam is feeding Carter as I'm pacing the dining room. She left. The woman fucking left and doesn't even give us the courtesy to tell us where she's going.

Now Riggs and Slade are out looking for her while Adam and I are stuck being housewives. I guess I can understand why Zay's fed up with this life. Sitting and waiting, wondering when the fuck they'll come home is eating away at me. I hate this. Hate it even more knowing this is what she's been going through all this time. It's nerve-wracking.

I grumble and drop onto the chair in front of Adam, scratching roughly at my chin. I'm not itchy but I'm itching for a fucking bump. But I promised. I fucking promised the woman who walked out on us I'd quit. "Why is your wife such a thorn in my side?"

He chuckles, spooning some chicken onto Carter's tray. "Because we love her and care about her."

I shriek and get up, tapping my home screen. "It's been two hours, can someone give me an update?" How are they *all* ignoring me?

Adam sighs, putting the spoon down. "Zay's been wanting out for a while, Peter. She hinted at leaving right after we bought this house. But she stayed for Carter, for his safety. After today, I don't think she can handle this type of pressure or stress or whatever the fuck it is in her head that she won't express. None of you know Zay like I do, and this right here, was her breaking point. She's not coming home until we walk away with her, or let her take Carter away from this life like she wants."

I thought she was happy.

I thought things were looking up.

But I was too lost in the drinking and cocaine to realize my Zaynab was silently crumbling still.

Scratching quickly at my chin again. I need a fucking fix, but *again* I promised. Fuck, I promised her.

"What the hell are we supposed to do, then?" I ask, trying to be serious but I wink at Carter when he wrinkles his nose at me. Kid has my heart, I'll give him that. Rosa does, too. And now that I know what she looks like, there's no stopping me from finding her.

Adam opens his mouth to answer when a call comes in from Zay. He scrambles for his phone and answers it. "Babe? Hey, where are you? Are you okay?"

I snatch it from him and put it on speaker. "Zay, come home."

"It's me," Riggs says, grunting as a bed squeaks behind him. "She ain't coming home. Not yet."

I wipe a hand down my face, scoffing. "What're we doing about this shit, Riggs? What about Carter? Hmm?"

"Where is she?" Adam asks, offering Carter his bottle of milk.

Riggs clears his throat, chain bracelets clanging together like he's scratching something. "She's at her house with her parents—"

"Can I talk to her?" Adam interrupts him.

"In a minute," he says, huffing. He's about to hit his breaking point, too. "Slade and I are going on a little trip to the charter up north. See if they know of anything that's going on with Rosa. Adam, hold down the fort. Peter, clean up and stay with Carter. When we get back, shit's changing."

I scoff, leaning closer to the phone. "So we're just supposed to sit and wait? What about Zay? She coming home? Who's going to protect her if those fucks go to her parents' house?"

"You don't gotta worry about that, I promise. Just clean up, kid." He sputters and groans. "I think it's time to throw in the towel once and for all. For the sake of our kids, of us, and for this woman that's driving me to fucking drink."

Adam chuckles, looking up at me. Zay is his wife, but we wouldn't be able to go on without her and he knows it. "Can I talk to her now?"

Whispering spreads through the receiver, Zay and Riggs having a silent argument before she blows a raspberry and takes the phone. "Adam?"

She may be our rock, but she knows which buttons to push. And she's pushing all of Riggs's buttons right now.

"I'm here, babe," Adam says, his lip quirking up as he stares at the phone. "You good?"

She hums, clicking her tongue. "Thank you for not barging into my parents' like this fucking guy."

He laughs, smiling at Carter. "Peter and I are on Daddy duty, so we couldn't leave even if we wanted. Boss's orders." He frowns a moment, tapping the phone. "You're coming home, though, yeah?"

She inhales a breath, releasing it rapidly. "I'll call you in the morning, okay? Take care of the baby."

"Zay?" He lifts the phone. "Hang on a second."

"You're coming home, Zay," I call out, making her grumble.

Adam sighs, taking in the silence that's filled with shallow breaths. "I love you," Adam adds, I'm sure to stop me from adding fuel to the fire. Her breathing calms, replaced with a sniff and click of her tongue. He wasn't lying when he said he knew her better than we did. As much as I want to know Zay inside and out, Adam is the only one that does.

That's why she chose him.

"Call me in the morning." He nods, pinching the bridge of his nose. "Please, babe, call me."

She hangs up without saying she loves him back.

She always says it back.

"Fuck," I mutter, dropping my head onto the table, forehead taking all of the blow. "Fuck."

"Something's wrong," he says, frowning at the phone. A picture of Zay and Cater lights up his home screen. She's so breathtaking with him. So natural, meant to be.

I haven't changed mine. It's still Zaynab staring at the poster. Even when Dorian and I were together, even when I loved that woman with everything I was able to give her. I couldn't change it out of guilt for what I put Zay through. She deserves happiness, and I'll give my life for her to achieve it.

Adam's right, though. Something's up and I don't like the rumbling feeling in my stomach.

The torment coming in to say hello.

The worry stopping by and bringing with it anxiety.

Something's going down and Riggs doesn't want me or Adam in on it.

Peter, clean up and stay with Carter. When we get back, shit's changing.

Zay leaving must've flicked a switch in his head. His eyes are open and he can finally see the fucking chaos our lives are becoming.

No more happy endings. It's time we sort this shit out once and for all.

Zay

Well, now that Riggs and Slade have barged into my parents' house, I have no choice but to entertain them since Riggs is being a pain in my fucking ass and refusing to leave. I can't blame him, though. I did barge out of the house and tell those men I was done with their bullshit.

Only because I *am* done with their bullshit.

They're the most annoying group of men I chose to live with and raise a baby with.

Maybe I'm the problem.

Maybe I'm the one with issues that can only be resolved if I surround myself with stupidity like these fucks.

No, I stay because I love my Adam, I love Carter, and by God, do I ever put up with Riggs and Peter. I won't deny that there are lingering feelings toward Riggs. Feelings I know I'll never fulfill, but they're alive and active and always aching for his attention.

Just not recently.

No, recently I want away from him and all the chaos he brings. I know if I give in and allow myself to let these feelings grow, my heart won't be able to handle it.

Slade is lounged on my bed, hands behind his head as he stares at me hanging up the phone. "All good, sweet thing?"

I swear, he's worse than Peter. A child walking around in an adult's body. At least Peter has a heart, I'm not sure Slade does. Even if I cut the one beating out of his chest, he'd still live on like the arrogant fuck he is. But I won't deny it, every now and then, I'll get a glimpse of Slade who's sweet and kind. Then the guy who acts like Peter comes in and I roll my eyes all over again.

Sometimes I think it's all an act to fit in.

I huff out a breath and toss my phone on the bed, looking at Riggs with his elbows on his knees. "Happy? Now, can you do me the favor and get the fuck out of my room?"

That laugh leaves Riggs. The same one that used to frighten the shit out of me when we first met. Now all it does is annoy me.

No, let's be real for a second. That laugh sends heaving throbs between my thighs and I have to cross one leg over the other to stop the wetness pooling in my underwear.

"Zay, I'm trying to be as calm as I fucking can, given that I don't want your parents to freak out or call the damn cops on me, but I ain't leaving you alone."

Growling, I shriek softly, and stomp into my walk-in closet, then slam the door. I'll sleep in here tonight, I don't give a shit. Just once, just fucking once, I'd like something to go my way. Just once it would be nice if these men would listen to me.

I tear off my clothes and sift through a closet I haven't gone through since Adam and I moved into our little bungalow. I miss that place sometimes. The large backyard, our blue-green walls, and the park that was across the street. Now, our house reminds me of the one I'm standing in and I can't remember a single happy memory in this house.

That's not true. Lillian was the only thing that made living here worth it. She was my neighbor, my best friend who'd risk getting in trouble to sneak out at night and watch the stars with me. Simpler times, much simpler.

I get into a pair of silk shorts, pulling a tank top over my head when the door opens and Riggs comes in, that sympathetic look on his face. "Riggs, please, I just want to be alone."

He puts a hand up, closes the door behind him, and steps closer to me. His chest is heaving, and I hate it when it does that. I hate when he's nervous around me because it makes me second-guess my love for Adam. And I should never question it. He stuck by me through everything. All my downfalls, all my faults, all my fuckery. He was there. He'll always be there. Even when he hid his bullshit from us, he never left.

"Why did you take this off?" he asks, taking his ring, my wedding rings, and the chain be bought me from his back pocket. "I gave you this for your birthday, sunshine."

I sniff, staring at the chain in his hand. "I was angry at you."

"Are you still angry at me?"

My eyes scroll up his body and stop at those blue eyes. "Yes."

He smirks, placing the jewelry on the shelf beside him. "This makes it so much better."

Confusion paints me before I realize what he means.

With a thundering step, he grabs my face and forces us into the clothing, tongue sliding against mine. I push against his chest, realizing I'm barely making a dent because of his monstrosity. But it's enough for him to pull away from my lips and look down at me hungrily.

"One more time, sunshine. That's all I ask for." He's breathless as he stares at my lips. "It ain't much, but a night with you can cure all my faults."

I press his chest harder, shaking my head. "No, Riggs," I whisper. "It won't."

"Baby, it will." His breath fans my face, cradling my head as his lips feather mine. I close my eyes, tears slipping free, and I try to imagine a life without him in it. Just Adam and I. Maybe with children, living in the cabin. Living a happy life.

But I can't. My life involves Riggs no matter how much I push him away, he'll never truly leave. He stole a piece of my heart at that cabin, a piece that will never heal. Adam must feel it, too. He never stops Riggs from holding me or sneaking kisses. "Riggs, I—"

The closet door opens, and Slade pokes his head in, smirking at us. "There's a knock at your door, Zay."

Moving past Riggs, his fingers graze mine. What was I thinking? Holy shit, I think I was just about to admit I loved him. Is that possible? Do I love Riggs? Is it possible to love more than one person?

No, shut up, stupid heart. We love Adam. Only Adam.

I open my door and my mother is standing there, fist up about to knock again. "Oh, hi, dear. Just wanted to make sure you're all set for the evening."

I nod, looking over my shoulder at Riggs and Slade. "We're fine."

"There are leftovers in the fridge if you'd like something to eat. It's a leftover Shepherd's pie." She gulps when Slade steps up behind me, sliding his arm around my shoulders. She was never a fan of tattoos and these two men in my room are covered, Slade more so than Riggs. I don't think she knows about the two tattoos I have. "Enough for your husband and his brother."

Slade smiles, leaving a kiss on my head. "Thank you, ma'am. We might take you up on that. I'm starving."

I smile, sliding my arm around his waist knowing this would drive Riggs crazy. He hates seeing Adam and I kiss, let alone someone else touching me. Whenever Peter hugs me, I feel Riggs's glare from across the room like the hot sun sizzling my skin.

I wonder what he thinks about Slade kissing my head again.

Why do I want him to get mad?

Maybe my sadistic mind wants Riggs to shove me into the wall and take me like he did the first time we had sex at the cabin against the fridge. Yeah, just one hot, quick release.

We could both use it.

"Have a good night, Mom, we'll be out of your hair in the morning," I say, slowly closing the door.

"Hey, what about the Shepherd's pie?" Slade whines, pouting as he looks down at me. "Come on, sweet thing." He leads us into the hallway as my mother steps back and hesitantly heads to her room while her daughter has two strange men in her room that are as tall as trees. Thank fuck I'm not a teenager anymore, I think she'd have heart failure if I brought them home. "Let's get some grub."

I glance back at Riggs as he sits on the bed, the linger of his tongue on my lips sends a chill through me. Oh, God, I don't think I'll be able to last the night without keeping my legs closed.

This will not go well. I can guarantee it.

***

Slade collapses on my bed after scarfing down two platefuls of Shepherd's pie, and fixes the pillow behind his head, groaning softly. "Man, this bed is comfortable."

"Nuh-uh." I waggle my finger at him. "If you think you're sleeping in my bed, you've been sadly mistaken, Mister. You and Riggs will take the guest room. I will be sleeping alone."

Slade chuckles, his tongue dragging across his bottom lip. "What is this? A California King? We can all fit on this, yeah? Plus, isn't this what you guys do at home?"

Folding my arms across my chest, I tilt my head with a sigh. "Adam and I sleep together, Riggs has his own room, and so does Peter. What do you think goes on at our house?"

Slade raises his eyebrows, glancing at Riggs who's sitting at my desk. "Aren't you all in some polygamous thing?"

Oh, God, is he for real? Okay, so maybe I've slept with the three men I live with, but that doesn't make us in a relationship. We simply live together and raise a baby together, but I'm married and sleep with one—I think about sleeping with the eldest one of them because I'm a freak—and holy shit, are we in a polygamous relationship?

Riggs laughs, hand on his stomach as he leans his head back. "That would be something, wouldn't it, sunshine?"

I roll my eyes and start for my bed. "I have enough of your bullshit to deal with, the last thing I need is to deal with your naggy and whiny selves when I don't fuck you enough."

A smirk spreads to Riggs's lips and he leans forward, gripping my wrist. "Hang on a moment, *wifey*. We gotta talk about your plan to go to Richmond without me."

I shoot daggers at Slade making his hands go up in defense. "Hey, I told you I have a loyalty to this club and Riggs is the president. There isn't anything I'd keep from him."

He has me there but I hoped he'd keep my secret until the morning so I'd be able to map out a better plan. What plan? Do I have a plan? No, it's not a solid plan. It's more like an idea.

Riggs clears his throat, pulling me closer to him. "What're you thinking, Zay? You'd walk in there by yourself and take the baby from Dorian without someone shooting at you?"

I frown, shaking my head. I don't know what my plan is, that's the problem. All I thought about was getting to Richmond and things would unfold as I arrived.

But this isn't the case.

"Um…i-if you guys come in there guns blazing, then they're going to up and leave and we'll be up shit's creek again trying to find Rosa. If I go in there and scope out the area around the post office, then there's a chance I'd be undetected. Peter can't go anywhere near Richmond, and neither can you. You'll stick out like a sore thumb." I take my wrist back and glance at Slade. "If Slade and I go to Richmond, there's less of a chance anyone would recognize us."

Riggs takes in my half-assed plan with a nod, and wipes his mouth, down his neck. All I'm thinking about doing is running my tongue along his neck, breathing him in. Kissing him, tasting him. Feeling him inside me again.

And by the tick in his smirk, I think he can read the horny right off my face.

With a glance at Slade, he pushes his lips together and grunts. "And how do you expect to approach her and the baby?"

I shake my head, jerking my shoulder. "I don't know. But I see the idea in my head." My eyes close naturally as I lift my head to the light. "Moms go to the park often with babies. Shit, I'm there at least four times a week with Carter." A nod moves my head, lowering it to look at Riggs. "I'll corner her at the park and take the baby. She can scream all she wants, but I'll scream louder. All Slade has to do is keep the car running and I'll clip the baby in and—shit, it's a bad idea, isn't it?"

Slade sits up, sitting cross-legged. "No, it's actually not half bad."

Riggs regards me with a once-over and glances back at Slade. "You up for a ride?"

He claps his hands and gets off the bed. "Let's get your niece, pres."

"I gotta make some calls," Riggs says and gets off the chair, taking my chin in his hands. "You did good, sunshine. Real good." Kidnapping a baby at a park is a little messy, but getting to Richmond and scoping out the post office is a start to something.

"I know," I whisper, smiling as his lips plant on mine and he retreats from my room, his heavy footfalls descending the stairs and leading out the front door.

Slade taps my back, nodding. "Shit's about to get messy. You ready for it?"

"Are you?"

He laughs, nodding. "I look forward to making you mad, Zay." He winks. "Of course, I'm ready."

I roll my eyes and head for my bed, getting under the covers for a sleep I know will not be a good one.

Peter

I've been staring at the pictures of my Rosa all night, waiting for Carter to stop wailing, but he's having a rough one without Zaynab around. She's his rock, much like she is ours.

Looking at this picture reminds me of the weekend I found out Dorian was pregnant. A weekend I thought was the best day of my life, turned out to be the start of my downfall. The moment I found out a part of me was growing inside Dorian, I knew I'd never be able to let her go. And yet, even though she destroyed me, I still fucking love her.

Before I found out Dorian was pregnant, we liked heading to the cabin to unwind a little. Especially her. Work stressed her out a lot and with her long hours, I didn't blame her for wanting an escape. Little did I know, her long hours included her plan to betray me.

We drove to the cabin early that morning, I remember there was a fog dancing slightly above the grass as we whipped by. Dorian gripped my hand as we followed Riggs up with Shyanne, Carter, Zay, and Adam in the same car. Riggs always made it a point to protect everyone, and with him at the wheel, in his mind, no damage would be done. Which is true, I'd trust him over anyone else at the wheel.

"Peter," Dorian asked, looking out the window as the sun crested the tops of the trees causing them to appear black in the lighting.

I brought our twined hands to my mouth, pressing my lips on top of her hand. "Yes, my love?"

A deep exhale left her, her gaze focused on the rising sun outside the window. A soft rose gold kissing the dark blue sky. "You love me, right? This is actually going somewhere and I'm not just some rebound to help ease your heart because of Zay."

Shooting her a glance, I tried to keep my eyes on hers and my focus on the road. My heart lept from my chest. I thought she was leaving me, that this weekend getaway was her reason to soften the blow because I'd have my family around to support me. "Baby, where'd that come from? I mean everything I ever say to you." I glanced at her quickly, my heart in my throat. "The first time you came to the club, did I not tell you we were meant to be? Matching scars, Dorian. Me and you." I kissed her hand again. "My feelings for Zay are nothing compared to my feelings for you."

It was true then, I loved Dorian with everything that I was. She opened my eyes and showed me that life didn't mean violence. Love didn't mean forcing someone under me. Love meant what we had. That rare spark caused my heart to speed up and slow down at the same time.

What we had was special.

I only experienced that type of special once before, floating high while watching the stars.

"What's wrong?" I asked, frowning as I followed Riggs into the next lane. We were two exits away from our cabin.

She let go of my hand and sniffed, opening the purse on her lap. "I wanted to wait until everyone was together, but I can't hold it in any longer."

She pulled an envelope from her purse and handed it to me. I tore it open, using my knee to steady the steering wheel. I'm the better driver of my brothers, Riggs has us beat on the bike, but give me anything with four wheels and I'll master it.

There it went again. My heart thumped like a jackhammer. My palms were sweaty and my vision blurred. But I was excited. So happy I barely remember if I laughed or started crying first.

"A baby?"

She laughed beside me, tears streaming down her face. "That's why I've been sick lately. It's not a stomach bug. It's our baby. We're having a baby."

I was crying and laughing, kissing her hand again as we took the exit. I don't think I've ever been that happy in all my days.

Not even when I came inside my first woman.

Or when Zay first smiled at me.

Or when Mama used to hold my head in her hands and tell me how perfect I was.

No, that moment trumped all of that.

I was going to be a daddy! And I'd be the best damn daddy this world had ever seen. I just wish I didn't find out while on the highway.

Riggs pulled into the little grocery store in town before we ventured out into the middle of nowhere. I was so happy he did, too. I was swerving like a motherfucker.

Quickly unclipping my belt, I grabbed Dorian's face and kissed her like the fucking world was ending. This was it. Our relationship started quickly and was blossoming even faster.

And I couldn't be happier. She was my forever.

I glanced at the photo, tears still rolling down my cheeks, and kissed those succulent lips again.

"You're sure you're okay with this given our five-year age difference?" She furrowed her brows, boring deeply into my eyes.

"I don't care about that, it's you, baby, always has been." I smiled, kissing her again as Zaynab knocked roughly on the window, making Dorian jump.

"C'mon on, let's get some food so we can get our drink on!" Zaynab rang out, knocking again with her tongue out, but stopped when she took notice of the tears. "Hey?" She jerked open the door and I stepped out, wiping my cheeks. "What's wrong?"

Riggs came up behind her, taking in the tears. "Hey?" His eyebrows raised, looking at Dorian and clenching his fists at his sides thinking I did something.

With my hands raised in defense, I started laughing, holding up the photo. "She's...we're having a baby."

Shock didn't even fill their eyes. It's like they expected it given Dorian's history with her ex-husband. But I did it. I gave her the gift she'd been craving for years.

Adam cheered, embracing me in a running hug, and Riggs wrapped his arms around the two of us. The last time we hugged like this, Mama bought us a slip n' slide. It was the best summer of our life. All we did was use it from the second we wove up until Daddy came home and told us to go inside or the mosquitos would get us. Being happy with my brothers was the highlight of my childhood.

"Holy shit, man," Adam said, clapping me on the back. "That's great news."

Zay and Dorian were in a laughing hug, ogling over the ultrasound picture when Shyanne came up to us confused as a two-week-old Carter started fussing in the car seat. "What's going on?"

Dorian held out the photo, sniffling. "Peter and I are expecting."

Shyanne giggled, kissing my cheek. "Welcome to the club, darling."

Riggs slung his arm around Zay's shoulders. "You're next, sunshine."

She snorted, rolling her eyes and punching his side. "You wish."

He did, and he still does.

I caught Zay's eye smiling as Dorian wrapped her arms around my waist. Those hazel eyes winked at me, giving me that relief I needed to know that my life had finally started to look up. Her eyes were the only ones that were able to calm me. *Promise me you'll move on and find someone so perfect for you it feels like your heart will explode.* I did and I'm so damn happy about it.

Zay led the way to the little store, wheeling a cart out to Shyanne. Zay wore this skimpy bikini under her white dress, hoping to run off the dock and dive into the water as soon as we got to the cabin. She loves swimming, one of the reasons she brought me to the water when we first met.

God, seeing Zay in that pink microkini when we picked them up made Riggs and I glance at each other with wide eyes. The damn thing didn't covered anything. But holy crap was it ever sexy. The small triangles barely covered her tits, giving them the perfect tight squeeze. And the bottoms were basically a thong, Adam was one lucky bastard. I wonder what happened to that thing?

Adam snickered, taking Zay's hand and leading us toward the snack aisle, grinning over his shoulder at me. "Daddy Peter, funny ring to it."

It did, but holy crap was I ever proud of myself. I wondered if this was how Daddy felt when Mama told him she was pregnant with Riggs. Did my father feel that pride of his seed carrying on the Donnelly name? Or was he just happy that he got to claim Mama as his own and make her into the loyal housewife she was?

Shyanne held a bottle for Carter as Riggs placed snacks in the cart. We never spoke about how he felt when he found out he became a father. Was his pride oozing? Was he scared? Was he proud to pass down the Donnelly name?

Knowing Riggs, he probably hated every second of it before he heard that baby's heartbeat. He never wanted children because of Daddy. He was scared they'd follow in his footsteps and want to be part of the club. I do not doubt, the second he heard that heartbeat, his entire being exploded with warmth.

He reached the top shelf, getting Zay a box of Oreo cookies, when another box tumbled, nearly hitting her in the face. "Jesus Christ," she shrieked.

Riggs caught it, chuckling at her, it was nice seeing my brother laugh without that malice seeping through. "Used to make you say that a lot," he teased sticking his tongue out at Zay.

She shoved him, frowning. "Shut the fuck up."

I held out my hand to Dorian, jerking my head to another aisle. Being here with her was the best day of my life. She made me whole, cured me, and helped me see the bad things I did weren't benefiting anyone but the club. Slowly, I was changing. I would become the man I should've been before my father tainted me.

I would become the man Zaynab saw the night we floated high.

I would be the best damn man for my kid.

Dorian kissed my cheek and smiled at me, ignoring the world around us for a moment as we found the soft drinks.

I couldn't hide my emotions. I lifted her and spun us in a circle.

"Peter!" she squealed.

I laughed, putting her down and kissing that precious face. "I love you, Dorian. So damn much it's driving me crazy."

And I did.

I did so badly that I thought our love was fake. I thought my feelings for her were out of guilt for what I brought her into. But then, one early morning a week prior, I looked over at her as the sun started to poke through the dark skies and I realized how blessed I was. How Mama brought me Zay when I needed her, and now, she gave me Dorian to love and cherish until the end of my days.

Dorian's smile slowly faded, that worry spreading to her face. "Promise me one thing."

I curled the wisps of her hair behind her ears. "Anything."

"Leave this club. Leave all the bullshit."

There was no denying how excited I was to be leading this club with Riggs at my side. He was my best friend, my leader, the man I looked up to my entire life.

But Dorian surpassed all of that. Especially with my baby growing in her belly.

Riggs would understand because Shyanne wanted the same thing. She hated seeing Riggs in his cut, hated when he spent late nights at the club when he should be home with their newborn. They argued about it, a lot. But they made up rather quickly when he'd wipe a hand down his face and apologize. She forgave everything. Ignored a lot. And accepted the bad times.

She was an angel, I'd give her that. But seeing them after everything went down with the club, I don't think they were happy.

I nodded quickly, kissing Dorian's hand. "For you, baby, I'd do anything."

She smoothed out my cheek and studied me for a second. Those gray eyes welling with tears. Happy tears as a smile spread to her face. "You're a good man, Peter. A very good one. I hope you become the best man you can be for our baby."

From that day on I opened my eyes. I saw the wrong. I saw the deception. I saw my faults and flaws.

From that day on, I vowed to change.

For our baby.

Smiling against her lips, I kissed her. "The old me died the moment I looked into your eyes."

She laughed when I licked her face, that dimple poking through. Gosh, she was perfect, wasn't she?

"Hey, lovebirds, stop sucking face and come join us," Zay called out at the end of the aisle, giving me the finger.

I flipped her right back, winking as Dorian placed a hand on my chest.

"You're a good man," she whispered, heading for Zaynab.

I believed her. I believed I achieved redemption through her.

Because of Dorian, I smiled again.

I loved again.

I healed.

Zay skipped to the ice cream section, scanning it for chocolate fudge, the only flavor she liked when we came to the cabin. She's cute when she wants to be, and when Zay scanned the ice cream aisle, she was the cutest.

Riggs noticed, too, his eyes eating her up while his wife and their newborn son were right behind him. No shame then as he has now. Shyanne noticed it, too. She noticed a lot when Zay was around, and she was around a lot. Many of Riggs's and Shyanne's arguments were caused by his infatuation with Zay.

Zay stole our hearts and brought them to life again, but I released her grip from mine and gave it to Dorian. She deserved all of my love because I loved her and vowed to love her until my dying day. But she betrayed me. The fucking bitch killed me and didn't even know it.

Zay bit her lower lip and placed the ice cream in the cart, waggling her eyebrows at me as Adam dropped cones on top of the pile of food.

We've come a long way, too, from all the torture I put her through. I was broken back then. Broken without a means to repair myself. And I took my depletion out on Zay.

I promised I'd change.

And she forgave me for it.

And I was changing. Little by little, the old me died and became the man Mama raised.

I'd be that man again.

For my unborn child.

⁕

That night, Riggs sat on the back porch, staring at the fire, then into the house. Doing the same double take for the past ten minutes. Adam and Zay had gone to bed a while ago, same with Shyanne and Dorian, but I wanted to sit with Riggs and hear what he had to say about what it's like to be a father.

I needed my brother more than ever.

Holding out a fresh beer for him, he guzzled down the one he was working on before taking mine. "What a day," I said, dropping into the chair beside him and widening my eyes.

I understood why he wanted to sit in this chair. The window in the guest room off the living room was open, giving us a full view of Zay and Adam having sex. She was on top, those tits bouncing on her chest as her head shot back in a silent moan.

"Well, now that's something to keep me up for a while," I commented, chuckling.

Riggs tilted his head to the side, bringing the beer to his lips. "Mmm," he grunted.

I watched for a moment—we both did—ogling the sexy woman we'd tasted time and time again. We watched until Adam sat up and turned her onto her back. Hiding her from us.

Riggs brought the bottle to his lips again and sighed, wiping a hand down his face. "You love her, don't you?" I asked him, still staring at the window even though Adam's back was all I could see.

"She's the mother to my kid, of course, I…love her," he said, whipping his head around.

I pointed at the window with the bottle. "I meant Zaynab."

Silence consumed us; the crickets and crackling of the fire were the only things moving through the yard. I struck a nerve, but I only spoke the truth. Part of me loved her, too. Shit, part of me would always love her. But when was enough, enough?

"I don't think," he paused, taking a breath. "I don't think I ever got over us." He glanced at the window again. "It's hard to explain what we had, but it was something. Shyanne helped me heal like Dorian is doing for you. But whenever Zay's around, my heart's confused."

His breathing wavered, and he looked into the fire. "Seeing Zay in that bikini today all smiles and laughter. I love that spunk she has, that sass." He drained the bottle of beer and placed it beside the other four empty ones at his feet.

Oh, I didn't think he was going to pour his heart out. I came out here to talk about my baby. But this was how most of our heart-to-hearts started, wasn't it? Over a couple of beers and some lonely, drunken nights.

"I sometimes wonder if maybe I shoulda tried harder to keep her, even when she chose Adam. I should've tried. Shit, I showed up at their wedding but couldn't bring myself to go in. I ain't that strong in the end because I knew if I walked in there and saw her in that dress, I woulda pummeled Adam just so she'd say *I do* to me." He sighed, leaning over to take the rum on the other chair.

I had no idea he came to her wedding. No idea he felt this way. If Zay had chosen him, she would have been safe without my stupidity. No one would have touched her. She'd be loved, happy.

So damn happy.

I wish I knew this.

He flicked off the cap and looked at the bottle. "Maybe I'd be here with Zay and our son instead—"

"Hey." I touched his arm, stopping the bottle of rum from making it to his lips. "Don't you ever say that. Shyanne is an amazing woman and I know you love her, Riggs. She gave you the most precious gift."

He grunted, finally bringing the bottle to his lips. "I know. I know." He sighed again. This was hitting him hard. If only there was a way to mend our broken hearts without Zaynab as our crutch. "Maybe I've had too much to drink."

I chuckled, taking his hand and forcing myself to change the subject and stop him from saying anything else he might regret out loud. "Maybe, brother. But hey, we're just a couple of Donnelly Daddies sitting by the fire. Nothing leaves this bubble."

He laughed, ripping his hand from mine to nudge my shoulder. "Can't believe you're gonna be a daddy, kid."

I scrunched my nose, leaning back and looking at the stars that were so clear and clustered here. I loved it. "And you thought she was too old for me."

"She's five years older than you, Peter. You're still a kid leaning to walk and she's already riding a bike without training wheels," he said, leaning forward with his elbows on his knees. "Shyanne likes her and she's a pretty good judge of character."

I started picking at the label on the beer bottle. "Do you like her?"

He smirked, rubbing his eye. "Yeah, she's all right. She's bringing me a niece or nephew." He nudged my arm again. "She's making you a better man, too. She's okay in my book."

Hearing those words leave Riggs's lips made me realize how special Dorian was.

How much I loved her.

Riggs offered me the bottle of rum and chuckled. "Remember when Mama got tipsy with us on some JD?"

I laughed, taking a sip. "God, I miss that woman."

"Yeah, she probably would've knocked you out for getting Dorian pregnant out of wedlock," he teased, looking up at the stars with me.

"She's probably watching us now." I nodded slowly, tears rolling down the sides of my face. "You think she'd be proud of me?"

"Well, Mama always said, for every wrong thing you do, God will punish you for it, but if you do something great for every wrong thing you've done, he'll accept you." Riggs let out a rush of air. "You did a lot of bad things to Zay, Peter. But I see the good you're trying to do, and yeah." He turned his head to look at me. "I think she'd be very proud of you."

That lit a fire in my belly, making a whimper leave my lips and Riggs reach over to take my hand. "I'm going to be a Daddy."

"Yeah, you are, kid," he said, tightening his grip.

As I gazed at the stars I knew Mama was watching us, smiling at her boys. Proud of her boys for making her a grandma. She'd have been the best damn grandma this world had ever seen.

I sniffed, wiping my eyes as my other hand still held onto Riggs's. "Look at us, a couple of tough guys crying while stargazing."

"Fuck off," he said, tossing my hand away. "I ain't crying."

We laughed a lot that night, reminiscing about Mama. About her love, her beauty.

Comparing our women to her and how much I knew Mama would love Dorian.

A good Christian girl.

As we ended a string of giggles, the back door slid open and Dorian smiled at us sleepily. "Hey, Peter, you coming to bed?"

"Yeah, baby," I said, tapping Riggs's leg. "Goodnight, my good man."

He smirked, saluting Dorian. "Take good care of this kid, he has the hots for you."

She laughed sleepily, covering her face. "I'll do my best."

I stumbled to her, kissed her quickly, and headed to the master bedroom at the end of the hallway where Zay was held captive. "I do love you, Dorian."

"And I love you, too, Peter. My drunk prince," she teased, chuckling. "Let's get you some sleep."

I grumbled as my head hit the pillow, muttering nonsense as she fixed the comforter on me. "Baby?"

She sighed softly, turning on her side to look at me. "Go to sleep, Peter."

I smiled, eyes fluttering shut. "If we have a girl, let's name her Rosa. That was my mama's name."

"I like it," she whispered, kissing the tip of my nose. "Goodnight."

"Soulmates," I slurred, placing a hand on her hip.

"Soulmates," she repeated before the entire spinning room turned black.

The more I think about that night, the more I realize she didn't tell me *I like it*, she said *I know*. She knew who my mother was, and knew everything about my life before I divulged it to her.

She knew and did nothing to stop the betrayal.

Dorian broke me and now, I'm going to break her.

Riggs

Zay fell asleep a few hours ago, curled up in the middle of her bed as Slade was sprawled out at the bottom. The bed is so big it eats up her tiny body.

Zay knew better than anyone that I'd refuse to stay in another room other than hers. The only problem is I can't even relish winning this argument by holding her sleeping body.

My mind won't shut off.

I keep seeing her getting shot at.

I keep hearing my son's screams.

The cuts on her flash through my mind.

Peter's words.

Adam's worries.

All of them piling on me.

I can't believe I wasn't there to protect my family. They could've gotten hurt.

Killed.

And I wasn't there.

I sniff, looking at Zay's pouty mouth as Slade's snores vibrate at her feet. She's cute when she sleeps. Her cutest when she's not mad at me.

Taking my phone out, I quietly clear my throat, and dial Peter's number. I need to know if this decision is a good one. I need to know we're not leaving any stones unturned.

I need to know he'll protect my son.

Almost four rings before his groggy voice answers. "Yeah?"

"You good?" I ask, keeping my voice low as I watch Zay.

He grunts on the other end, the bed squeaking. "Shouldn't I be asking you that, brother? It's almost three in the morning."

"Can't sleep."

He hums, yawning. "Neither could your son. Adam's co-sleeping with him tonight."

I chuckle softly, stirring Zay a little. "He misses her."

"Zay's the only mother Carter truly knows, y'know." He yawns, the bed squeaking again. "We tried to do her routine, but Carter wanted his mama."

I don't want to dwell on Carter needing his mother. Whenever I think about it, all I see is Shyanne and the bullet in her head. The sacrifice she made for this fucking club. Zay is his mother, no matter how much it hurts to think of Shyanne and how happy she was to have this baby, how her plans to have more kids when Carter was old enough went out the window.

All of that was thrown out the window that sunny afternoon at Daddy's grave.

The Ghost has a death wish and I can't fucking wait to grant it.

"Look—" I paused, pinching the bridge of my nose and going into the walk-in closet so I don't disturb Zay's sleep. "We're leaving in the morning to Richmond. Zay's idea. She didn't want to tell you but—"

"What time are you leaving?" The bed squeaks again and drawers can be heard opening through the receiver.

"You ain't coming with us."

He scoffs, raising his voice. "The hell I *ain't.*"

"If Dorian truly is in this town and spots you, she'll go into hiding and there's no telling if we'll ever be able to find her again. There's a huge risk with me going, but I ain't letting Zay do something alone with Slade. I still don't trust the guy, no matter how loyal he is."

That isn't true.

I trust Slade with my life, but I don't like the way he looks at Zay.

She wouldn't open her legs to him, I know that because she won't open her legs to me, but I want to be there to protect her at all costs.

Peter sniffles, the bed squeaking again. This fucker needs a new mattress.

"It's my daughter, Riggsy."

"I know, kid. I know."

"Did you talk to the club about this suicide mission?"

I chuckle, wiping a hand down my face. "No, and I'm not going to. Not until Adam's suspicions about Judas are cleared up."

"You think he had something to do with this?" Peter asks, clearing his throat.

I contemplate his question for a moment and nod. We've gotten into many arguments about the club. He's always hiding in the shadows when we clean up the mess the club has made. Now with Skeet, Lip, and Adam pointing out the flaws, I have to man up and fix the mess yet again. "I do. Until I know what the fuck is going on, there isn't anyone I can trust."

"Okay, brother," he says sighing softly. "Adam and I will hold down the fort. I'll give a call to the charter in Richmond in the morning, let 'em know you're coming."

"Don't, the less these people know of our whereabouts, the better." Sitting on the floor of the closet, I adjust the phone on my ear. "I want you to call the charter in Texas and tell them we're coming home."

Peter snaps his fingers. "Throw them off, huh?" He chuckles sleepily, groaning softly. The bed squeaks again, I assume he lied back down. "I like it."

"I also want you and Adam out of the house. Take Carter and hold up at the club, or talk to Lip, I'm sure he'll let you guys stay in my old apartment."

"Sounds good," he says, sniffling.

We don't say anything for a little bit, just basking in the sound of our breathing. We'd do this often as kids. He'd jump into my bed when he couldn't sleep and lay beside me with no words, no actions, just brothers needing each other. It continued when we were older, I'd lie in bed with him and watch the tablet.

When I moved out, sometimes Peter would show up at my apartment above the clubhouse, I'd set him up on the couch or in bed with me, and again, we'd just bask in the silence. It was nice not to think about anything other than sleep.

I inhale a breath, smirking at the thought of living above the club. "Remember when Mama came to visit me when I moved in upstairs?"

He laughs, yawning. "She brought you a lavender plant, didn't she?"

"Thing didn't go with the décor or anything, but I took damn good care of that plant until Daddy stole it and gave it to Natalia," I scoff, remembering how happy she was holding that plant. I wanted it back because it was Mama's gift to me, but I have a soft spot for a girl in her glory. And Natalia was in hers before Daddy destroyed her.

Fucker.

Peter sucks his teeth. "Was I the only one who had no idea she was making her rounds?"

"She wasn't Miss Innocent like Zay remembers," I comment, looking at the closed door of the closet. "She was passed around the club like a Snake Biter."

"Not like Zay's any better."

"Maybe, but who isn't nowadays," I say, always in defense of my girl. "And Zay's better than Natalia. She ain't some whore trying to fuck her way into the club."

Peter exhales slowly. "Yeah, I know. She's our girl, isn't she?"

I lean my head back, looking at the shelves before me. Some are empty, some still have loads of dainty colorful shoes I'd love to see Zay wear. She already has a lot of clothes, and this closet is still loaded to the nines with shit she didn't take home. As soon as all of this is resolved, she's taking her things. The house I bought her will be the only place she runs home to.

Grunting, I hang an arm off my knee as I thumb my wedding ring. "Slade thinks we're in a polygamous relationship."

Peter lets out a laugh, shushing himself as he does so as not to wake up my son. "Of course, he would. Fucking guy is hornier than a man released from prison."

"I wonder if Adam would allow it?"

Peter snorts. "You mean, you wonder if Zaynab would."

"She's already been with all of us, we live together, the only thing missing is sex," I say, hoping someone could be on my side with this. If being in a relationship with Zay and my brothers is the only way to be with her, by God,

I will do it.

I'd do anything.

"Yeah, no, I doubt she would."

I adjust the phone to my ear, sighing. "Yeah, you're probably right. But it's worth a shot."

He laughs softly. "I'd love to see you ask her."

"When we come home with your baby girl. I'll make us a family, you'll see, kid," I say, nibbling my lower lip. I'm still twirling the ring with my thumb.

I don't even think it over, I remove the ring, feeling lighter. Free. I set Shyanne free and let the heart I denied her to love the one person who gave me peace.

Like the devil heard my words, the closet door opens, and Zay's tired face comes into view. One eye shut from the light, and nipples so erect, it's like they're asking for it.

"Here she is."

Frowning, she shuts the door behind her and tiptoes to me. *Who is it?* she mouths.

"Tell her to be careful, and call me in the morning, brother," Peter says, sniffling again. "Love you."

"Love you, too, kid." I hang up and drop my arm, letting it dangle off my knee as I study this perfect woman before me. "I didn't wake you, did I?"

She shakes her head, wiping the sleep from the corners of her mouth, and folds her arms. "Um, i-is everything okay?"

I nod, tapping the spot between my legs. "Just called Peter about what's going down."

"He's okay with us going to Richmond?"

I chuckle nasally, loving how well she knows me. I couldn't keep this from Peter even if I tried. "No, but he wants his daughter back. So long as nothing happens to our girls, we'll be fine."

"Your girls, huh?"

Leaning forward, I take her hand and pull her down. "We're in a polygamous relationship, baby. Deal with it."

She laughs softly, adjusting herself between my legs and leaning her head back against my shoulder. "We're not in any relationship, Riggs. Remember that."

My arms naturally wrap around her, leaving a kiss on her temple. "You keep telling yourself that."

She taps my arm but stays in her rightful place.

"Soon, Zay. Everything will be so perfect."

She releases a breath, turning her forehead to my lips. "Let's hope so."

I hold her like this for a little while, basking in the calmness of her beating heart.

Someday soon she'll believe me.

Someday soon I'll show her that we're meant to be.

Someday soon happiness will be knocking at our door.

Slade

I remember when I first showed up at the clubhouse. Fuckers scared the shit outta me but I've wanted to be part of something for so long. I didn't have the best upbringing, I don't even have a family I can look back on and call on holidays.

I have no idea who my father is, and my mother was a junkie, just like Adam's. But I didn't have the luxury of Donnelly blood running through my veins to have a mother raise me like theirs did.

From the time I was three, I was in foster care until the ripe age of eighteen when I walked out of my foster parents' house at midnight. No one ever called to see if I was okay or how I was doing. Been working odd jobs for five years, couch surfing for most of those with random chicks I'd swoon. Until six months ago when I walked into *Judas's Hideout* looking for a bartending gig.

There was an ad in the local paper about security and/or bartending, and I headed over as soon as I had the means. I've wanted to be part of a motorcycle club since I was a kid watching shows we weren't allowed to watch after hours. I'd see the anarchy, the blood, and the ultimate brethren between men.

Craving that comradery. I never had brothers or best friends. I had foster siblings, people I hung out with when I was forced to go to school, and those who'd call me when they needed something. But I never had that closeness. Figured I'd show up at the bar and maybe work my way into the club. I'd prove my loyalty and devotion to the Snakes.

And seeing the burly men with tattoos smoking out front as I approached, I knew I was home.

I pushed the door open, immediately hit with the stench of stale liquor and cigarettes wafting my way. But I didn't show my disgust. I'm not a drinker or a smoker. But I sure do know how to make a stiff one. This bartending job was my in. If I showed skill and loyalty, maybe they'd ask me to join.

To be able to wear one of those leather vests and belong. It's a craving I need to feed. My purpose I'm aching to find.

This goddess looked over her shoulder at me, tight little shorts and a dress shirt tied in the front to show off some of her stomach. God, the legs on this chick had me from six to midnight in five seconds flat.

"We're closed," she said, nodding her head at the wall beside me. "Doors open at seven, come back then."

I shook my head, scanning her as many times as I could. I was certain this sex kitten belonged to someone. She had to. A girl this sexy wasn't available. But if she was, I'd have her screaming before nightfall.

"Yeah." I chuckled awkwardly, scratching the back of my head. "I'm actually looking for a job."

Those hazel eyes narrowed, and she placed a fist on her hip to reveal a baby on a high chair in the booth. "A job, he says."

Talk about a MILF.

She slowly licked those lips as I approached her, making me hold my backpack in front of me. I got laid three days ago, I shouldn't have been that excited over a girl I didn't know. But goddamn. "Do you know who owns this bar?"

Nodding quickly, I pulled my credentials from my backpack. "I do."

I handed her the paper, touching the soft skin on her finger. She felt like silk.

She scanned it, cocking a brow. "Slade Smith?"

I gave her a flirtatious smile. "That's my name, sweet thing."

The baby cooed behind her and she looked back at him, wrinkling her nose. "Just a sec, Carter."

Seeing a baby again brought back memories of the multiple group homes I grew up in. Rooms I had to share with babies, toddlers, and teenagers. Fuck, my sixteenth birthday I was up all night trying to calm a teething one-year-old because the foster parents were passed out from a drunken night out. For half of my teenage years, I was stuck babysitting instead of being a teenager.

I didn't get to live until I ran away.

Then, I lived, and have been for five years.

"He's cute," I told her, sitting down in the booth and sticking my tongue out. "He's what? Five, six months?"

She nodded, smoothing out his hair. "Looks just like his father."

I smiled, catching a ring on her finger, and looked up at her. I knew she was taken, the guy must've locked her down as soon as he laid eyes on her. Who the hell wouldn't? "You work here?"

She shook her head, putting my CV down. "No, his father is the president of this club. I just watch his kid while he's busy."

I cocked an eyebrow. "Watch his kid?"

"You think I'd risk getting stretch marks?" She laughed, shaking her head. "You're one foolish man, Mister Slade."

Man, she had a wicked smile.

A tall, brute man walked out of the double doors at the back of the bar, fixing his vest. There it was, a president patch etched on the breast. This guy was a beast. Big and thick with muscle. I didn't want to gush, but this guy became my idol. I wanted nothing more than to hold the power he exuded. Or at least stand by his side while he guided me.

He eyed me as I stuck my tongue out at Carter again, coming for us rather than the front door where he was headed. Guy's protective, I can smell the testosterone from here for this girl.

He frowned, nodding at the bombshell. "What's going on, Zay?"

Interesting name for an interesting woman.

She glanced over her shoulder, smirking at the president of the motorcycle club. "This is Slade. Says he's looking for a job," she said, tapping my CV. "Brought references and everything."

He brought a tattooed hand to his mouth, wiping the corners of it. He has a rose on it in black and grey, much like I have on mine. Except my rose morphs into the hair of a gnarly skull.

"You know what bar you walked into?" he asked, folding his arms across his broad chest. Fucker was scary looking, no wonder this club was well renowned.

I nodded at his leather vest. "Yes, boss, I do."

"Is it the bartending you're interested in?" He pointed at the 'help wanted' sign in the window. "Or is it something else?"

I puffed out my lip, shrugging. "Depends on what you're offering."

He glanced at Zay, and she shrugged, returning her attention to the baby. "We might have a few openings, but you gotta earn your keep."

I nodded, smiling like a damn teenager about to get his dick touched for the first time. "Whatever you need, boss, I'm all yours."

He looked at Zay again, whispering something in her ear that caused her to smile. "She's the boss, Slade. I just run this club." He put his hand out to me, mitts as big as mine. "I'm Riggs, this here is Zay."

I rose from the booth and cracked my thumb knuckles before shaking his hand. "Your wife?"

He cackled, slapping her ass, but the little minx shoved him.

"He wishes," she hissed.

"It's a long story," he said, looking over his shoulder. "A story she'll fill you in on I'm sure."

A blonde with long hair came out of the back room, followed by a bunch of other colorful men. All in leather vests. "Who's this tall motherfucker?" the blonde asked.

"Your newest prospect," Riggs called. "Give him hell, boys."

I laughed softly, looking at all these men and somehow I knew, this was home. "Slade." I saluted the men, looking at Zay with a grin.

Riggs introduced me to everyone, including his brothers Peter and Adam, whom I found out was her husband. She's into blondes, guess I still had a chance at ravishing this delicious piece.

Peter clapped me on the back, freckles decorated under his tired eyes. "How about we get you to clean the bathrooms, hey?"

So I did.

I scrubbed the toilets, mopped the floors, washed the mirrors, and took out the garbage. I wanted them to know I meant business, I wanted them to see I was a good man. A loyal man. I would devote my life to the club.

All my life all I craved was a purpose. A family. Something to call mine. I tried joining another club out east—the Sharks, they called themselves—but I didn't like the way they ran things. Slapping women, branding their men, and using torture as a way to get their way. That's not me.

I heard about the Snakes, heard about the fuckery of what happened to the OG founding father, and about what went down a few weeks ago at the cemetery.

Word on the street was that these men were changing the wicked ways of the club. And I wanted to be part of something life-changing. A purpose.

By the time I was finished cleaning, the sun started setting. I took out the last of the garbage and tossed my gloves away, spotting Zay watching me. She leaned a hip on the threshold, nodding her head at me as I wiped my brow.

"You know you didn't actually have to clean the toilets, right?" she said, shushing the baby strapped to her chest.

I smirked, clapping the sweat from my hands. "I know, but I'll do it because the boss told me to."

She scanned me, taking me in. All my colorful tattoos, all the self-inflicted scars on my arms. She'd tell me her story and I'd tell her mine if she wanted. "Why a motorcycle club?"

I sauntered toward her, looking at the baby. *A purpose.* That's what I wanted to say. Something to be proud of. But I didn't need to get all mushy-gushy for her. Heck, I walked into the bar looking for a different job, not to be part of a club right away.

Yet there I was, earning my keep.

"If there's anything you need, Zay, you let me know," I said, winking.

She chuckled, poking my shoulder. "Yeah, keep in your pants, tough guy. I'm called for."

Grinning, I tilted my head down. I was about to try my signature flirt with her when yells and crashes came from the bar.

She whipped around about to head for it, but I pushed past her, seeing Riggs and Judas wrestling on the ground. Riggs had him pinned down, hand around his neck, looking feral as ever.

"Knock it off!" Adam yelled, pulling on Riggs.

The big fucker didn't budge.

Peter stumbled out of the hallway that led to the bathrooms, pinching his nose and sniffling. Guy had to have been doing blow, it was still caked on his upper lip.

What did I get myself into?

Peter grabbed Riggs's other arm, looking at me to help. So I did. The three of us pulled the rabid dog off Judas and stumbled onto our asses.

"What the fuck is going on?" Zay yelled, bobbing the baby up and down.

Judas jumped to his feet, baring his teeth. "This fucker is useless as a president."

Well, that pissed Riggs off.

He got to his feet and thundered forward, but I stood in the way, eyebrows raised and ready to take a hit. "This is my daddy's club, and I warned all of you before my wife died that this place was changing. And it is!" He gritted his teeth at everyone, then shoved me, growling. "Don't you ever get in my way again, boy!"

I put my hands up, looking at Zay as she flicked Riggs's ear.

God, this girl was gutsy.

"Calm your fucking self," she snapped, still bobbing the baby.

He thundered toward her, Peter and Adam grabbing his arms. "Watch your fucking mouth—"

"Hey, why don't we go outside and take a chill pill, yeah?" I interrupted him, taking in the shocked faces of the guys.

I don't think I was supposed to do that.

Riggs flared his nostrils at Zay, but the little pistol whip stood her ground, standing taller even though he loomed over her by over a foot and a half. "Mmm," he grunted, swearing under his breath as he pushed the door open, causing it to slam on the side of the building.

Adam scoffed, looking at Zay. "When he's having one of his tantrums, you can't get in his face like that."

"I'm raising his fucking kid because of this club, I can do whatever I want," she said, narrowing her eyes at Peter who was halfway from passing out he was so out of it. "You got anything to say, too? You're the only Donnelly who didn't give me shit."

Peter stepped back, hands raised in defense. "I got nothing to say, sweetie."

She found my gaze again, jerking her head at Adam. "Come with me." She started for the back room, but none of us moved. Seeing her glare over her shoulder gave me another stiffy. "Now!"

Adam and Peter followed quickly, I wasn't sure if I had to follow, too, but I did anyway.

Zay took the baby out of the carrier and handed him to Adam as Peter stumbled into the back bedroom and sat on the bed with a crazed look in his eyes. The blow was hitting him hard. "Slade, I should catch you up on all the bullshit that's happening. And it's a lot of fucking soap opera drama, I hope you're ready for."

I nodded, looking at Adam making the baby a bottle, then returning my attention to this beauty.

She told me everything, and I mean *everything*. She told me what she did to Peter, what he made her do, what Daddy Donnelly did, what Roaden did, and what happened a few weeks ago at the cemetery. Dorian stole Peter's baby, Shyanne died, and now Peter was snorting cocaine like it was the 80s again, and Riggs was an angry pitbull that snapped so easily. Oh, and they both drank themselves stupid.

I sputtered, shaking my head, but so damn happy she trusted me enough to divulge this shit. "That's a lot to take in."

"Welcome to my world, baby, this shit is fucking fantastic," she said, taking Peter's chin as he swayed on the bed. "Are you high? *Again?*"

He smiled, eyes glazed. "It helps keep the pain away."

She growled, pinching the bridge of her nose. "We have a band coming to play tonight, Peter, we needed you."

I cleared my throat and stepped forward, scratching my chin. "I can help. It's what I'm here for."

Adam glanced at me, feeding the baby. "Take a shower, I got some clothes in the closet."

Smiling, I cracked my knuckles and pointed at Peter. "I don't mind keeping an eye on him, too. My foster brother was a junkie. I've sat through many nights of tweaking, and withdrawals with him."

She chuckled nasally, taping my arm and giving me that award-winning smile. "You'll fit right in, Slade. Welcome to the fucked-up family."

She made me feel like I had a purpose.

Then this club gave me hope. It gave me a family.

I may be a horny fuck that checks her out every chance I get, but I stare at her because of how nice she was to me. How thoughtful, and caring. She didn't know me from a hole in the wall, but she showed me there are kind people left in this world. People who help direct me toward my purpose.

***

Hearing Riggs pacing the bedroom all night and only getting into bed around four this morning, I decided to let him sleep in and I left early that morning, picking up some things from the club and getting bags from their house. Zay and Riggs were still asleep when I left, her tiny body disappearing in his thick arms. There's love there, a unique kind of love that I don't think they know how to explain, but it's there. Anyone with eyes can see their relationship is more than just her raising his baby. Don't know how Adam deals with it, either. He's one patient, trusting son of a bitch.

I've never been in a serious relationship before. Yeah, sure, I've been with a slew of women since I was fourteen years old, but none of them told me they loved me or looked at me the way Zay looks at her men for protection and security.

I'm sure I'll find it one day. I'll find the perfect girl with a nice rack and a bubbly personality. But for now, I'll continue picking up drunk chicks at the clubhouse, and staring at Zay like she's the winning lotto ticket just out of my grasp.

It's nearly seven when I walk into their house, Adam's in the kitchen leaning his head on his hand with a cup of coffee in front of him. By the looks of him, I think he's sleeping. "Adam? Hey, Adam."

He grunts, snorting softly and jolting when his head lolls forward. "Shit, hey, uh—" He wipes the drool at the corner of his mouth, gawking behind me. "Where's my wife?"

I drop the house keys on the island and rub my eye. "She's with Riggs, they were asleep when I left," I answer, taking his coffee and sniffing it. "What's in this?"

He taps the home screen on his phone. "It's a cappuccino, one sugar."

I gulp from it, looking over to see Carter attempting to take a few steps and falling on his butt. My foster sister was almost thirteen months old when I left, and she took her first steps the day before I split. Seeing her take her first steps made me second-guess my decision to leave that night, but I couldn't stay in that house any longer. I was a prisoner. No phone after dinner. No TV. Only homework or books. I've read my fair share of novels to know I prefer scrolling through Instagram aimlessly than picking up another Shakespeare. So I left, leaving her a letter to reach out to me when she's older. I doubt those foster parents will let her keep it, but I had to try.

Carter starts fussing, calling out for his mama. But Zay is fast asleep with no will to come home unless we have Peter's daughter with us. She's stubborn and will fight as hard as she needs to, to get her way. And she always gets her way with these men.

This trip is going to be an interesting one.

"Where's Peter?" I ask, finishing the rest of his coffee.

Adam pushes himself up, dragging his feet to the fridge for a bottle of milk. "Still sleeping. Was a rough one last night."

I smile, picking Carter up as he crawls past me. "Where do you think you're going?" He giggles, then fusses when he sees his bottle. "You guys have a whole system here, don't you?"

Adam shakes his head, plopping back down at the island. "Not really. All of this is because of Zay, without her, I think none of us would be okay. Riggs would be passed out somewhere or have gotten himself killed because of his drunken rage. Peter would've overdosed or choked on his own vomit after drinking himself to sleep. And as for me, I probably would be so busy cleaning up their mess with the Snakes that I'd forget about my wife and she'd be home raising the kids, praying for an escape."

I'm sure Zay already feels this way. The way she ran out of the house, leaving everything she loves behind goes to show she's had enough. She needs her out. And I think as soon as we find Rosa, these kids will be her out.

I wrinkle my nose at Carter, letting the air around Adam settle before I speak. "Give it one day at a time, boss. Things will look up."

He nods, reaching for Carter with a yawn. "Thanks, man." He points to the dining table behind me. "I packed Riggs and Zay a bag. Tell her to look in the inner pocket, I left her a little something in there."

I waggle my eyebrows. "Naked photos?"

"No, you perv."

Lifting a shoulder, I take the bags off the table. "Any chance to see your wife naked, I'm game."

"Why would I put naked pictures of her in there? It's something *for* her," he says, narrowing his eyes.

"Hey." I swing the bag on my shoulder. "Maybe she likes to touch herself to naked pictures of the two of you, I don't know."

Adam chuckles, shaking his head. "Just tell her to look in the pocket."

I nod, open the front door, and stop, looking over my shoulder at him. That grin slowly disappears, and his eyebrows furrow, gazing into the empty mug in front of him. He's hurting. Seeing his wife walk out like that must've been an eye-opener, the last nail in the coffin.

"It'll be okay, I promise."

He glances up at me and smiles, kissing the side of Carter's head. "Let's hope so."

This family is disjointed, but it's a family. A love wrapped in bubble wrap, slowly popping each bubble one day at a time.

Zay

Not even one ring goes by before Adam picks up, his groggy, tired voice filling my ear. "Zay?"

"Hey," I say, sitting on my bed.

Riggs steps out to take a phone call and I figure this is the perfect opportunity to call my husband and let him know what we're doing. I don't think Adam will like it, but I have to do this. I'm so done with this club and the danger it inflicts. I'm taking the kids and leaving this life. They'll be better off away from the madness. I just know it.

Was it smart to leave in the middle of a family meeting? Probably not.

Do I regret taking off my ring? Hell yes. And I seriously hope Adam didn't see that I did.

Is my plan good? Nope, but we're doing it anyway.

He sighs, and the sound of a door closing moves in the background. "Talk to me. What happened last night, Zay? What made you storm out when we were supposed to sit and talk about what we were going to do about everything."

"I was shot at, Adam. *Again!* You promised me new beginnings and instead of that, I'm living with your brothers, raising your nephew, and living the life of someone I didn't want to become. Yet here I am, a forced mother, a housewife, and a fucking servant to three men." I sniff, wiping the tears from my cheeks. "Where's my happy ending, Adam? What about me, huh?"

"Baby," he whispers.

"Don't *baby* me, I'm done. I've said it once, and I refuse to say it again," I growl, getting up from the bed and heading to the bathroom. "We're heading to Richmond, staying for a few days until we get Rosa. And when we do, you can choose to come with me and the kids, or you can stay and be loyal to a life you can't fucking stand. The ball is in your court, Adam. I fucking hope you choose wisely."

He's crying on the other end, soft muffled cries. "I told you yesterday I was coming with you and that hasn't changed. Don't leave me, babe. I can't do any of this without you."

I let out an exasperated laugh. "You can't wash your clothes or cook your meals or run a motorcycle club without me?"

He sniffs, whimpering. "No, I can't go on without you."

"In three days when we get back, me, you, and the kids will leave. Promise me we'll leave like you did in the shower. Promise me you'll be able to say goodbye to these people," I say, bracing a hand on the vanity in the bathroom. "Always and forever with me."

"Yes, babe. Forever and always."

"Say it."

He inhales a breath, sniffling again. "I'm with you. This club is nothing compared to a life without you in it. You're my forever, Zay. My forever."

"Okay," I whisper, nodding at my reflection.

"I love you."

Wet mascara runs down my cheek, getting lost at my chin. "Me, too."

"Come home to me."

I wince, sniffling. "When this is all done, we'll raise those kids the best way possible."

He chuckles. "Yes, we will. And we'll have a little bean of our own, too. A little spunky one just like you."

"Or a pain in my ass like you," I say, staring at my reflection in the mirror. My hazel eyes have more green in them this morning.

"I can't wait."

I let out a rush of air and sniff once more. "Keep Carter safe."

"You stay safe, too," he says, groaning. "Fuck, I don't like this. I should be there—"

"Riggs is here, he won't let anything happen to me," I interrupt him.

"That's the problem, I don't like him being there. His rage hasn't been in control since Shyanne died. He'll—if he does anything, babe, you tell me," Adam says, sniffling. "God, Zay. I really don't like this."

"I'm FaceTiming you." I remove the phone from my ear and switch our call over. His tired face comes into view, tears welling in his eyes. "Trust me, okay?"

He sniffs, pinching his eyes together. "I do, Zay. You know I do." He smiles softly, taking me in as I wipe under my eyes. Even in a moment of sadness, he always sees the brighter side of things. "How did I get so lucky?"

Tilting my head with a smirk. "I'm all kinds of damaged, baby. Am I really that lucky?"

He laughs, shaking his head. "You're perfect, my love."

Adam looks off-camera, frowning as Peter's Irish whisper spreads through the room: *Is that Zaynab?* "Just gimme a sec."

"Is everything okay with Carter?" Panic sets in that I wasn't there this morning. I wasn't there last night. And I won't be there for a few days until I bring his cousin home.

"Yeah, he's all right, sweetie. He just took a monster dump and it somehow made it to his elbows, I can't even explain that one," Peter calls off-screen.

A laugh leaves me, making Adam return his attention to his phone. "We'll be staying at the clubhouse, okay? Peter is planning on having someone come in and fix the place, too. Whatever it takes to make this feel like home again, Zay. Okay?"

I nod, inhaling. "Okay." I push my lips together, wondering if doing work is worth it. I've said it a million times, I'm done. I don't want this.

But no one listens.

Wiping my cheek as the last tear escapes my eye and rolls down my cheek, I expel a breath. "I'll call you later."

"I know, babe. I love you."

"I love you, too," I say, taking in his beautiful face before I hang up without another word.

I drop the phone on the vanity, releasing another slow breath. How am I going to do this? Survive this? How am I going to take a baby from a woman who used to be so kind to me, someone who isn't a bad person, either? Something changed her ways.

Or maybe it didn't. Maybe she was all an act.

I have an angel on one shoulder telling me to leave it alone. And the devil on the other telling me to do terrible things to her.

Groaning, I look at the reflection of the disturbed woman standing in front of me. I barely recognize myself anymore. Who the fuck have I become?

I clean myself up and walk into my closet. Immediately, I spot the necklace and rings that Riggs put on the shelf. The moment Adam bought me the engagement ring, I haven't taken it off. As ugly as it is, it's exactly what I wanted. His name is engraved inside it and everything.

And yet, guilt rides me as I stare at it. I'm only happy when I'm with Carter. When I'm with Adam I smile, there's nothing fake there, but I'm not happy in this life. The life we built is chaotic. Why can't anything be normal?

Taking a new gold chain from my jewelry I box, I place the small gold heart Riggs bought me onto it, then affix it around my neck. I touch it softly as it feels so foreign on my neck. Adam was upset when Riggs gave this to me. I didn't blame him for obvious reasons, but this necklace means so much to me that Adam wouldn't understand.

I may have chosen him, but this symbol hanging from my neck is proof that Riggs's heart belongs to me.

This is the life I chose, whether I like it or not, I have to fix things to smile again. And I will. I'll have my family and that happiness I've strived for.

I slide my rings on and notice a fourth ring in the bunch that isn't mine. It's a plain band, white gold with an engraving on the inside which reads, *Shyanne*—oh, shit. This is Riggs's wedding ring. Why would he take this off? *When* did he take this off?

I hope this doesn't mean what I think it does.

I put the ring back, turning it so Shyanne's name is front and center. He took this off for a reason, and if my gut is telling me the reason is me, then I'm not entirely sure I'm ready for it. Why is life always so complicated when he's around?

With one more deep breath, I head downstairs, spotting Riggs still on the phone pacing the driveway. My mother smiles at me as she sits in the den with a book in hand, while my father is probably in his office working as usual.

"Good morning, dear," she says, sipping her tea. "How did you sleep?"

"Just peachy." I look around the den, a room I haven't been in for at least four years.

It's weird being home again. Surreal in some ways. Chaotic in others. But it's my home. Always has been. Even when I hated it. It's like my safe haven.

My piano is still at the other end of the den, polished and tuned I'm sure.

I head for it and slide my hand along the piano keys, an instrument I haven't played since my senior year of high school. I was good at it, too. My parents wanted me to play the violin, but something about the sound of a piano spoke to me. It calmed me. On my toughest days, I'd play until my fingers cramped.

Lillian loved listening to me play, too. She'd smile as she watched me, mesmerized by the way I lost myself in the melodies.

I haven't had the itch to play in years, and yet, my fingers are getting that itch to press the keys again.

Riggs clears his throat, putting his hands in his pockets. My mother looks up and smiles, gesturing at the spot on the couch in front of her. "Thank you, ma'am."

I press a key, its sharp note ringing silently.

"Why don't you play something?" Riggs asks, hanging an ankle off his knee.

I shake my head slowly. "I haven't played anything since high school. I'm going to be so rusty."

He smirks, clasping his hands together on his lap. "Anything you play will be amazing, sunshine."

My heart speeds up, thumping wildly.

He makes me nervous all on his own, but having him watch me play piano, something Adam hasn't even seen is maddening.

My hands are already shaking and I haven't even sat down yet.

My mother closes her book as Slade comes into the house and wipes his shoes before taking them off, quietly sitting beside Riggs.

An audience, great.

I sit down, cracking my knuckles, and steadying my hands over the keys. I choose to play "Für Elise," the first song I learned to play, and to my surprise, my fingers move on their own. Muscle memory of a song I've played a million times over.

Getting lost in the melody is something I used to do to relax my scattered mind. And it's helping so much right now.

Note after note is hit and pressure is released from my shoulders.

Riggs has a smile on his face, nibbling his lower lip as he watches me. Mesmerized as usual. The way he's staring at me is like I'm playing a siren song. Ensnaring him. I keep my gaze held with his for a beat, wondering if the look he's giving me has anything to do with the wedding ring he took off. Is our second chance among us? Would I really do that to Adam?

Slade has his eyes closed, head tilted downward, listening to the music.

We need this, the calm before the storm. We know a war is about to wage. Something beyond our control.

Halfway through the song my stomach isn't in knots anymore. It releases, and I'm able to breathe for the first time in a long time. I was suffocating and didn't even know it.

When I play the last of the notes, trailing off on the final tune, a smile spreads on my lips.

Life will be better.

It has to.

Peter

Carter fell asleep in the car, so Adam sat outside with Lip and Skeet, watching our nephew snoring through the open windows. It's been one helluva crazy couple of days. I'm withdrawing like a motherfucker, aching for a drink, and all I want to do is sleep. While Adam's a zombie trying his hardest to keep his eyes open.

I'm sitting in a booth, head in my hands, and breathing through my cravings. I need Zay now more than ever. No, I fucking need Dorian. The woman I gave myself to through and through.

The woman who broke me yet I still fucking love her. I'll always love her.

But I can never be with her. Not after what she did to me.

If I can forgive Zay for stabbing me in the neck, I can forgive Dorian, can't I?

I don't know.

I really don't.

"Hey, brother, you look like crap," Judas says, dropping down in front of me.

I groan, leg tapping restlessly. "I feel like crap."

He reaches into his pocket, taking out a little baggy of cocaine. Asshole. "Here, this'll help you."

I shake my head, sniffling. I'm about to puke. I avoided it this morning. Woke up nauseous like you wouldn't believe. I couldn't even help Adam when Carter started fussing about breakfast.

Then when Slade showed up, fuck. I was doubled over the toilet praying to Mama for strength. But I didn't puke.

Now, however, I feel the bile rising in my throat.

Wiping the sweat from my forehead with a shaking hand. I push the stuff away and get up. "Just hitting the head, then we gotta talk, okay?"

Judas does a bump, making the demons in me scream for a sniff. "Yeah, brother."

I don't give in.

I buck it for the bathrooms and dry heave before the bile finally releases. Thick chunks, liquid, and saliva coat my mouth in three rounds until I drop back against the door, breathing heavily. Heart thumping rapidly.

One hit will make it go away.

"No," I growl through gritted teeth.

I'm stronger than this.

I'm a fucking Donnelly.

Leaning my head back, I close my eyes and breathe. I don't need Zaynab. I don't need Dorian. I need me. I have to get better for myself. And for my daughter.

She's the only person that matters.

My Rosa.

After another deep inhale, the nausea returns and sends me shooting forward for another round of vomit. Fucking disgusting.

I stagger out of the stall and turn on the tap, staring at it as more nausea hits me. I rub my stomach and rinse my face and mouth, bracing my hands on the counter as water drips off my nose.

"Mama, give me strength to survive this mess," I whisper, shaking my head. I drop it between my shoulders and exhale, spitting in the sink. As if she heard my prayers, my phone starts chiming, and beautiful Zaynab's name pops up on my screen.

I let out a rush of air, trying to calm my racing heart. They're probably in the car on the way to Richmond. Risking their lives for me when I'm the one who should be with them getting my daughter back.

Me.

Why the fuck am I not there? It's eating away at me. The words *pathetic, useless, a failure* are seeping through my thoughts.

Zay ran out of the house because I couldn't protect her and my nephew. She's broken again and it's my fault. Again.

Fuck.

ZAYNAB: *Hey.*

ME: *Hey, sweetie.*

ZAYNAB: *I'm sorry.*

ME: *There's nothing to be sorry for.*

ZAYNAB: *Yes, there is. I left and now we're going to Richmond to find Rosa and I don't know. I'm feeling uneasy about you not being here.*

Me? Not Adam?

Riggs is with her, too. She's the safest with him than she is with any of us. Maybe I'm looking too much into this but this is the first time in our friendship that she's ever shown any vulnerable emotions toward me. Usually, she calls me an ass, but right now, she wishes I was with her.

ME: *Riggs was right, I shouldn't be there. They won't be looking out for you, they'll be keeping their eyes peeled for me.*

ZAYNAB: *We're here for your daughter, though. Something about this doesn't feel right. I don't know. My tummy never lies about these things.*

ME: *Then come home and we'll sit down and plan it better. You guys are going out on a whim—a damn hunch. You don't even know if Dorian is there.*

ZAYNAB: *We're ten minutes away.*

ME: *Then stop for lunch, and come home.*

Three dots pop up, then disappear. I can't even stare at the screen anymore, my hands are shaking too much for that.

When Zay has a bad feeling, it sends me spiraling into the unknown thoughts that I try to keep at bay.

They're waiting for them, guns cocked and ready. Shoot to kill.

What if Dorian and Rosa aren't even in Richmond? The letter was a diversion.

Riggs, Zay, and Slade went there for nothing and will come home with nothing. Leaving me hopeful and broken.

Fucking Christ.

I close my eyes and breathe.

Mama, please protect our girls.

My phone vibrates and there Zay's name is. She probably nibbling on her thumbnail as she's waiting for my reply.

ZAYNAB: *I'm not coming home without your daughter. I'm bringing her home, Peter. It's a promise I'm going to keep no matter these bubbling feelings in my tummy. I'm bringing her home.*

Stubborn Zay can't even come home when her stomach is telling her this is a bad idea. Usually, she listens to her gut, this time, there's more on the line.

ME: *Call me?*

ZAYNAB: *Kiss Carter for me.*

ME: *Come home!*

ZAYNAB: *I'll be home in three days, Peter.*

ME: *Sweetie, listen to me. If you're not sure about all this, listen to yourself and get out. The last thing I want is for you to get hurt helping me. Haven't I hurt you enough over the years? Don't let me feel like even more of a failure, please.*

ZAYNAB: *You're far from that, Peter. A fuck-up, maybe, but not a failure.*

ZAYNAB: *Good men make sacrifices, and you've suffered enough pain. You keep losing the women you love, it's about time one of them comes home, no? Let me bring Rosa home.*

Tears skim my cheeks, reading over her messages. I have lost many women in my life. My mama, Lillian, Zay, Dorian, and now Rosa.

I've experienced so much loss, I didn't care who I hurt. And I hurt Zay a lot.

Redemption. I can use that about now.

ME: *Be safe.*

ZAYNAB: *Riggs is here, he won't let a fly get within three feet of me.*
ME: *Love you.*
ZAYNAB: *Yeah, yeah, love your stupid face.*
ME: *Call me when you're settled, please.*

She sends me a thumbs-up emoji and I lock my phone, taking another breath. Yep, my tummy is having rumbling feelings, too.

Cracking the bones in my neck, I leave the bathroom and find Judas leaning on the bartop, flirting with one of the barmaids we hired recently. She's not one of the whores like the other chicks, she needed a job to help pay for school and the more chicks we have walking around the bar and behind it, the faster the service is at night when it's packed.

"Judas," I call, waving him over. "We need to talk."

He taps the bartop, winking at her before joining me. Prick has a girlfriend, a three-year-old, and a one-year-old at home. But that doesn't stop him from getting his dick wet every chance he gets.

Seeing this makes me realize how much of an asshole I used to be. I've cheated, I've played, I've slept with two women at the same time. And I never felt bad about it.

And now that I've lost my love, it sickens me to see what I used to be. A goddamn lowlife who deserves everything that's happening to me.

Judas claps my shoulder, leaning on the wall beside me. "What's good, brother?"

I don't even beat around the bush. I come out with it. "What're you planning, Judas? You've been sketchy since Riggs took the mantle. Leaving in the middle of the day, hiding shit in shipments. Are you dealing without telling us?"

Judas smirks, wiping his mouth and looking over his shoulder as Skeet and Adam walk in. Carter's still asleep on Adam's shoulder, the little guy had a rough night, but we big guys have work to do.

"Yeah, sure, I'm still dealing," Judas answers. Crooked liar written all over his face. "Coke, the same stuff you sniff."

I have to play him, there's no doubt about that. He doesn't trust any of these fucks. Maybe he'll trust me. I lower my voice, stepping closer to him. "I'm getting off the stuff, but mind getting me in on your deals? Could use the extra cash to fix up the house."

He winks, squeezing my shoulder. "We'll talk soon, brother."

Adam starts our way, fixing the diaper bag that's wrapped around his wrist. "Hey, we have chapel in five."

Judas's annoyed face comes back and he saunters off, eye-rolling as he does. Dick.

Maybe I can get something out of him if I make him believe I'm screwing over my brothers. The good ole Donnelly way is keeping secrets and doing dirty.

Maybe, just maybe.

Adam looks back at Judas, then returns his attention to me. "You good?"

I nod, sniffling. "Just asking about Riggs," I say loud enough for him to hear.

Adam lowers his voice, raising his eyebrows. "What'd you tell him?"

I glance at the guys, lowering my head. "I told him I want in on whatever he's doing. If I make it look like I'm crossing you guys and joining his stupidity, maybe he'll trust me enough to tell me what's up," I whisper.

Adam lifts the diaper bag, handing it to me. "Pass it by Riggs, yeah?"

He continues to the back room to put Carter on the bed, poor little guy is involved in so much fuckery it's not good. Shyanne was right when she called us the devil's workers. Nothing's fucking changed, either. No matter how hard Riggs has gotten us out of the illegals, nothing will ever be enough.

I jerk my head at the new barmaid, giving her a sultry grin. "Hey, honey, wanna do me a favor?"

She smiles, still full of life. That won't last much longer. This club is great at sucking the life force from its victims. "Hi, Peter. Does the chapel need a restock?"

I shake my head and point a thumb behind me as Adam makes his way back. "Watch my nephew, yeah?"

She nods quickly, eager to do anything we ask her. If I wasn't so broken and so love-struck, I'd have her pinned against the bathroom wall praying to God I don't stop.

Adam places a monitor on the bartop beside me. "Keep an ear out for him."

"Sure thing," she says, pressing the volume button on the monitor and getting back to cleaning the bottles.

I follow Adam, glancing over my shoulder at her. A pretty face that's surrounded by a halo of bouncing curls. Maybe I'll give her a good dicking after this meeting. I could sure use it and she'd be hella lucky to be another etch in my bedpost.

Adam nudges my side, jerking his head at her. "She's cute."

"Lip hired her. Chick says she needs money for school," I say, taking a toothpick from the condiment caddy in the booth.

A smirk spreads to his lips. "You planning on having some fun while Zay's gone?"

I frown, moving the toothpick from one side of my mouth to the next. "Why do you say that?"

"The only way any of you fucks get off is if you're lucky enough to walk in on Zay naked or changing." He cocks an eyebrow, crossing his arms. "Need a release after what Dorian did, don't you?"

I glance over his shoulder at the barmaid, her curls bouncing on her shoulders as she washes the bartop. Those tiny tits aren't supported by a bra today. "Slade thinks we're all in a polygamous relationship," I spit out, trying to block my dick from growing any more than it is as I stare at her erect nipples grazing the shirt.

Adam laughs, shaking his head. "We're not."

"I mean, we all live together, raise a baby together—"

"None of you sleep with her anymore," he interrupts me, nodding his head at the barmaid. "Zay's off the market. Maybe Addy could be the next chick you obsess over."

He walks past me and steps into chapel, leaving me staring at Addy with a half-chub and wondering what Zay would think of me if I moved on.

Adam

The guys are riled up, they don't like the fact that we told them Riggs up and left for "Texas" without so much as a warning. But we have to cover for him. If word gets out that he actually went to Richmond, I'm sure The Ghost is going to be waiting in the shadows for the right moment to strike.

"He's doing business out there trying to prepare us for the possibility of a Panthers merger," Peter says, scoffing. "It's not like he's been doing much here, anyway. You gotta problem, bring it to me or Adam."

The guys rile up again; swearing, and throwing their hands up. Not one of these fucks will listen to me. So I make them. I bang the gavel on the table and everyone silences immediately. "You done?"

"Riggs is doing business we don't know about, kid. How're we supposed to trust him?" Mickey asks, spitting tobacco into his mason jar that I can smell from where I'm sitting.

Disgusting.

"Has he ever double-crossed any of you fucks?" I ask, looking around the table at a bunch of shaking heads. "He's changed this club to something Daddy didn't even think was possible. Yeah, we're not making as much as we were, but no one is getting killed over the business we're running. Riggs righted Daddy and Roaden's wrongs, yeah? We're standing in our president's corner because we trust him. Whatever business he has going on in Texas is something that will benefit us, right?"

I get grunts and nods, but their faces say otherwise. They're telling me to fuck off without spilling their truths from their lips.

Peter pushes himself into a standing position, leaning his fists on the table. "Look, we have someone on our ass for all the bullshit Daddy used to do. The trafficking that none of us knew about. Riggs is fixing things. And when he's not here, *we're* fixing things." He scoffs, shaking his head and dropping it slightly. "My house got shot at while his baby was home and Zay was there. She nearly died for this club, and almost got killed again. No, I will not sit by and let you fuckers speak ill of my brother when he's doing the best he can with what he got. He lost his wife and still sat at this table the day after it happened. His devotion to this club is something a lot of you lack and I hope you fuckers open your eyes and stand by my brother instead of choosing to walk away."

Silence.

Skeet looks at the men sitting around the table quietly drinking from their beer bottles and pushes himself up. "We're with you. We're with Riggs, through thick and thin, the Snakes will rise again."

"Hear, hear," Lip says, tossing his beer bottle at the door, glass shattering everywhere and sending the men into guttural cheers.

More glass is broken, and more whoops are yelled. These guys are a crazy bunch but Daddy and Riggs trust them. So we trust them, too. These men stand by us, all except for one.

Judas is staring at me, eyes narrowed as he drinks his beer. I don't trust him, and I think he knows that. I nod, tilting my beer to him and draining it. Fucking asshole dares to smirk and sit back in his chair, tapping the side of the bottle. He's going to throw it at me.

As if I saw it happening before it did, he tosses his bottle at me, missing my head by an inch. And the silence spreads through the room again.

"You ain't my president," Judas says to me, standing. "Neither is Riggs."

Skeet sucks his teeth, nudging Judas's arm. "Sit down, dickwad. Your ego still bruised when the patch was taken away from you."

"We ain't letting the fucking Panthers join our club. We killed their men last year. And for what? Family drama? Now these two fuckheads are running this club because the man you voted in as president is a lost cause. No, I ain't supporting this no more," Judas growls, hesitating before he takes off his cut.

Gasps spread through the room.

"What're you doing?" Peter asks, looking at the cut on the table.

"I'm out," Judas says, his voice cracking.

Dillion shakes his head, looking at me, then at Judas. "You quit, then you gotta remove your tattoo, man."

Judas growls again, looking at me with disgust and snapping at Skeet. "This fucker can black it out right now."

Peter steps over to Judas, putting his arm around him and whispering something. I can't hear a lick of it, I don't think anyone can. It can't be good, either. Peter is still on the cusp of sobriety and Judas was his supplier. If he leaves, there's no telling if Peter will follow or let him go.

He's been broken since Dorian left. And who could blame him, but I need my brother back. I've tried time and time again to get him to quit the drinking and the drugs, but nothing worked.

I'm hoping seeing pictures of his daughter gave him the incentive to get clean.

"Think about it," Peter says, turning away from Judas and nodding at me.

Judas picks up his vest and grumbles, storming out of the room. His heavy footfalls lead right out the door. Fucking Christ, this shitshow continues to just get worse, doesn't it?

"What did you say?" I ask Peter, grinding my damn teeth.

"Told him to think about this before making any rash decisions. That goes for all of you, okay? Think before you act. Because we don't give chances if you remove your ink." Peter takes his beer and gulps from it, belching quietly. "Anyone else have anything stupid to say?"

The men share glances, looking at one another before returning their attention to Peter and me. "Nope," Skeet says, lighting a cigarette. "Best we get started on making plans with Domino, hey?"

I inhale, nodding slowly. "Yeah, we'll set up a meeting in three days when Riggs comes back. Until then, we'll mellow out. Keep the club clean, stand guard during opening hours, and answer your phones when I call. We have a shipment going out tomorrow, parts for our brothers in Staten Island. Make sure everything is accounted for and ready to head out."

"Everything's in the shipping container out front," Mickey says, spitting his tobacco. "Loaded it two days ago."

I take the gavel and turn it in my hand. "Good, take the order list and double-check it. Make sure every bike has keys, every part is there, and make sure there's a few bottles of Jack packed away for Miller."

Mickey nods, hitting Dillion on the shoulder. "Let's go, big boy."

I bang the gavel and sit back, watching as the men scatter like flies. Doing whatever it is they have to do while their leader is fighting his own fight with my wife.

Lip is the last to leave and closes the door behind him, letting Peter and I bask in the afterglow of Judas. I knew something was up, and for him to want to leave is fishy. No one bats an eye when Riggs isn't here. He lost his damn wife because of this club's fuck up. And yet, Judas is the only one who doesn't cut him slack.

"Wanna tell me what you said to Judas?" I ask Peter as he leans his fists on the table with his head dropped between his shoulders.

He releases a slow breath, nausea probably still getting the better of him. "I told him we needed him. That if he left, he'd have no protection out there. But with the Snakes in his back pocket, he'll be protected with whatever he's involved in." Another slow release of air. "I have an idea. It's a long shot, but it's gonna work," he groans, rubbing his stomach. "I'm going to pretend I'm interested in whatever shit he's involved in. If your hunch is right, which I have a funny feeling it is, I'll figure it out. He trusts me, has since all this shit happened." He points at the scar on his neck and wipes the sweat from his forehead. "It's a thought I think will work."

I thumb the label on the beer bottle and narrow my eyes, wondering if it'll work. Judas doesn't trust any of us. Ever since Riggs took the patch, Judas has been off. He used to answer to Daddy, then he answered to Crew, then he became the law and made it a mockery. Now that Riggs is getting it back to the way it used to be, Judas is trying to jeopardize that.

"It's a thought." I look up, meeting his tired eyes. "Talk it over with Riggs before doing anything stupid."

He lets out one more rush of air and heads for the door. "That was the plan."

I shoot up from my seat. "You good?"

He gags, putting a hand on his mouth. "Fucking withdrawals, man." His running footfalls move through the bar, followed by the door to the bathroom slamming shut.

Plopping back down, I lean my head back and spin my chair to the Snake logo on the wall behind me; blood spatter stained on it. Daddy would be proud of us, and yet, none of us give a shit. All he wanted was to be the most powerful biker club in all of the United States. And he got just that. Our club branches out to different states. Different countries. There are so many charters we sometimes forget who's from where. But we're all brothers in the end. We all support and help each other. We all share the same snake tattoo…except for me.

Yet when I stare at the Snake logo that has become something so extraordinary, I feel nothing but disgust for it.

That logo brings with it destruction, harm, and betrayal.

I almost lost Zay because of that fucking Snake.

Now, I have no idea what's hiding around the corner waiting to strike. I hate every second of it. But look at me, sitting at the head of the table knowing I can do this until my dying day.

Slade

We checked into a motel just outside of town. Riggs wants to scope out the area before we let Zay do it. If anything happens to her, I'm pretty sure he'd never forgive himself for losing not one but both of his women. He said to me on one of his drunken nights that he already failed Shyanne. He loved her in many ways; loved how she saved him, how she bore him a son, but he never wanted to marry her. Never wanted that family life when the woman he lay his head beside at night wasn't the woman his heart belonged to. But he's as loyal as I am, and he stayed because of his responsibility to her and their son. He failed Shyanne. But now, she's gone and Zay isn't. She's raising his son, healing his heart. And if he fails Zay, too, I think this guy will be seeing red for a long time.

She sputters, sitting on one of the double beds and looking at the box TV on the dresser. "Classy place you got us."

I chuckle, dropping the suitcases on the other bed. "I wonder if the beds have a vibrate feature."

"Ooh, and for fun, we should take a black light to these sheets," she adds, giggling.

Riggs sucks his teeth, giving us the finger. "Fuck off."

She laughs again, still looking around as I open my suitcase for one of my hoodies. It's a lot colder here than it is back home.

She wrinkles her nose at the ceiling, pointing to a stain. "I wonder what that spot is."

I glance up at a brownish spot on the ceiling, something black is growing out of it. I'll admit, this place is a dump, but it's the closest motel to town.

And Riggs was adamant that we don't stay at a bed and breakfast. Something about the creepiness of people letting strangers sleep in their homes weirds him out. Also, he wanted to lay low. Cash deposit, rather than a credit card like he would've used at the Hilton fifteen minutes from here.

He waves a hand. "Learn to live with it. We're here for three days."

Springing up from the bed, she comes to me and digs into my back pocket for the car keys. "You're buying me clean sheets, then." She tosses the keys at him and opens the door. "And I mean now, Mister."

I chuckle to myself, looking over my shoulder at her as I get into the hoodie. "She's a little spitfire, isn't she?"

He wipes a hand down his face, already regretting bringing her along. "You can say that again."

He follows her outside, and so do I. But I keep my distance. The entire car ride over I could cut the sexual tension between them with a knife. She vaguely told me about their stint in the cabin together, but I don't know more than *he was keeping an eye on me until all the shit was dealt with.*

Zay looks back at Riggs, the warm sun shining down on her like beams of light. Radiant.

Succulent.

A goddess in all her forms. Woman has men on their knees, begging for her love, and she brushes them off like peasants. Yet they come back for more.

She must have one magical pussy.

"Hey, sunshine," Riggs starts, tilting her chin up. "I got some calls I gotta make, Slade will take you shopping." Without question, he hands her his wallet. "Get us some food, too."

I shouldn't be watching this, but seeing their interactions is a thing of beauty. Pure lust and forbidden love. It's breathtaking.

She winks. "And a tetanus shot."

A laugh leaves him, causing that gorgeous smile of hers to grow. He cradles her face and lowers his forehead to hers. "I promise you, sunshine, things will be different. I swear it on my life."

Her hand lays flat on his chest, feeling the beating of his heart. "Don't lie to me, Riggs."

"I won't." He leaves a soft kiss on her lips before I clear my throat. Interrupting a moment. Maybe she'll tell me her story and why she chooses to live with three men and raise a baby with them. It can't just because they're family, can it? No, there's a secret here I need to figure out.

Riggs opens the door for her. "Have her back in a couple of hours. And don't draw any attention."

"Yes, boss."

He jerks his head at me. "You packing?"

"Knife strapped to my ankle and gun in the back of my jeans," I answer, looking at Zay as she gets in the car. "Before you say it, I already know. Protect her with my life."

He nods and heads back into our room, leaving Zay and me alone for the first time in a while.

Every time we're alone, I can't help but stare at her. It's the only time I can study her without one of her men glaring at me. She has this uniqueness, this spunk that I'm sure adds more flavor to her aura. Her beauty helps, too.

But what is it about Zay that makes people fall head over heels?

Her voice is like a siren song, people are instantly attracted to it. In love with it.

In love with her.

Maybe it's her feistiness. She doesn't backdown...ever.

She opens the window and leans her elbow on the edge of it, looking out at the fields that have a few farms scattered about. "I wonder if we're going to get lucky and find her here."

I lift a shoulder, lowering the volume on the radio. "I think you will. Your family has suffered enough, I think it's time you guys find that peace again."

"Peace," she repeats, a smile forming on her face. Life has been tough for them and I hope that with my help, it can make it just a little bit better.

She raises the volume on the radio and bites her bottom lip. "Let's get some food first and look for a place that sells bedsheets we can burn once we're done with them."

"Don't get all flirty with me now, Zay," I tease, sticking my tongue out.

She shoves me, laughing. "Shut up."

We drive into the little town, muted storefronts surround a statue in the middle of it. I've been to towns like this before. There are loads of tiny communities with people who'd give you the shirt off their backs before learning your name. I've jumped from home to home growing up, slept in different beds throughout my life. And the more places I stayed, the more of our country I learned about. And small-town folk are the most wholesome. Something I love most about our little community, too.

I spot the post office at the other end, eyeing things nearby. There's a pub, a dry cleaners, a barber shop, a bakery, and a general store. Nothing seems out of the ordinary. The place is quiet. A few locals are walking around, but nothing sets me off. Although, this could be what they want us to believe. Silence until it's time to strike.

Zay gets out of the car first, pointing at the post office. "First thing tomorrow, we storm it."

I nod, still scanning the area. "Yes, ma'am."

She wiggles her finger at me. "Nope, don't call me *ma'am*, doofus."

"Boss lady?" I narrow my eyes and follow her to the market. "No, you're obviously not a Snake Biter like the rest of the chicks that hang out at the clubhouse."

"Zay is fine," she says, taking a basket and hanging it off her arm. "What about you? I highly doubt your parents gave you the name Slade Smith."

I smirk, taking a bottle of soda off the shelf as we pass. "My name means valley. My mom thought it fit since my last name is also Valley. *Slade Valley.*"

She chuckles quietly. "Valley Valley."

"But I go by Smith because I don't know my father and I haven't spoken to my mother since I was five years old. The Smiths were the first foster family to take me in and help me, but when they moved away, they weren't allowed to take me with them. So boom, back in the system after living with them for close to six years. But I was lucky enough to keep their last name."

She stops walking and raises her eyebrow. "You talk about your foster siblings a lot but I don't think I ever put two and two together until just now."

I shrug a shoulder, dropping some chips in the basket. "It's all good. My life isn't sunshine and rainbows. But it's my life and I gotta make the best of it."

A soft smile spreads to her lips, holding my gaze. "I like that."

"I don't look it, and even though I didn't graduate high school, I'm as smart as a whip. The last foster family I had before I was on my own, the dad was a professor at one of the universities and the mother was a doctor. Very serious about reading and writing. I was lucky to even get an hour of TV time per week." I've never admitted this to anyone. My cheeks burn up, and stammer on a couple of words before she taps my chest and giggles.

"Don't have to be shy around me. I may have gone to university, but I'm as dumb as a doorknob. Look at the men I'm with," she says, smirking before narrowing her eyes. *"What's thy fav'rite booketh?"* A laugh leaves her, wrinkling her nose.

"The Hobbit," I answer, knowing there are loads of other books I've read, but something about this one struck my creativity. Reading kept my mind away from the reality of my life. It kept me from hating myself, from wishing it all would end. I entered different worlds, fell in love with different characters, explored relationships, and chaos. I loved the chaos. "You?"

"Pet Sematary."

She turns on a dime, and that cute little bum sways side to side and grabs more snacks from the shelves. I understand what they like about her. She's easy to speak with; a gentle soul.

Nothing will ever sprout between us, but a true friendship has. She's the only person in the club that I can open up to without feeling embarrassed. And she listens. We talk often, even though her men don't like it. She asks me questions about my life, interested in my tattoos, my history. She wants to know me outside of the Snakes. Not many people want that. But she does.

Before turning at the end of the aisle, she freezes and steps back into me. Face pale and tears form in her eyes.

"What?" I ask, looking at her as my heart speeds up. Holy crap this pang of anxiety strikes me, pushing her into the shelves. "Zay? Speak to me."

Her lower lip quivers and she looks to the side, the tears finally escaping. "Dorian is right there," she whispers, her voice cracking. "Gosh, look at Rosa. She's...she's so beautiful."

Leaning in closer to hide her in case Dorian turns around and spots us, I see her ahead of us, reading the back of a cereal box. The baby is sitting on her own, a pacifier in her mouth. Those big blue-ish eyes are unmistakable. She's Peter's twin, all right.

I look down at Zay who grabs a fist of my hoodie, still staring at them. "We can't do anything now, Zay. You know we can't."

"They're right there. Rosa is right *there*," she whispers, choking on a sob at the end.

"I know," I whisper back, watching her as she stares at Rosa.

The green in Zay's eyes comes to life with tears in them, giving off this golden hue, too.

I wish I could make things better and disobey orders from my president. But I can't. I promised to keep her safe and that's exactly what I'm going to do.

Taking my phone, I snap a couple of pictures of Dorian and Rosa to send to Peter. We have proof. That's what we came here for. As much as I like Zay's original idea, it's dangerous, something that could get us arrested or killed.

I glance over my shoulder and Dorian has made it to the end of the aisle, heading for the cashes. Just like that, she's gone. But now we have proof that she's right where we need her to be. I swallow the lump in my throat, trying my hardest to conform Zay and ignore the fact that Dorian is right out of reach. I can't imagine that happening to me. How Peter still wakes up every morning with hope, shows how big of a man he can be. What he did to Zay aside, he's stronger than I'll ever be.

Zay leans her head back, dropping the basket and releasing a deep breath before pulling me closer to her and embracing me. I let her sob a little, the chaos that has been her life for the past three years is weighing down on her. Sooner or later, this pistol whip will snap. And it's coming very soon.

"She was right here," she repeats, releasing me and meeting my gaze.

I wipe under her eyes and hold her head in my hands. It looks so tiny in comparison. "We tell Riggs and plan this out accordingly, okay?"

She nods, another tear escaping as she studies my face this time. "It's not going to work, is it?"

"What do you mean?"

She sniffs, touching my hand. "This fucked up plan. We're never getting Rosa back. I have this funny feeling in my tummy."

I wipe another tear, letting my thumb graze her bottom lip. "Maybe you should tell your tummy to back off. We're getting Rosa back."

She chuckles, sniffling again. I release my hands and she looks over at the empty aisle. All the hope is uplifting, drifting away from her and getting lost in the heavens.

She doesn't believe it as much as I believe I'll see my birth parents again.

Our chances are slim to none. But I have to give her some faith. Without it, we're on a mission that will bring us straight to hell.

Peter

The music is booming tonight. Another local band is playing alternative music, filling up the bar. Adam has the baby upstairs, doubt he'll be able to get him to sleep but we can't stay at home. It's too dangerous.

But Carter usually sleeps with white noise, so muffled music might help. I hope it does. My head is already throbbing, the last thing I need is another sleepless night with a head stuffed with worry, a crying baby, and a bad case of cravings.

So, I've distracted myself and flirted with Addy all night. Craving a fix and figured might as well use pussy to cut some need for a line. It helped before when I needed someone to help me get over Lillian, then help me forgive Zay.

And it doesn't take me long to convince Addy to join me in the bathrooms. I have her pushed into the side of the stall, panties at her ankles, my jeans at my knees, pounding her from behind. It feels good to fuck something I have no attachment to. An empty hole I'm filling for a release.

I haven't worn a condom in years because of Zay, then Dorian. I fucking hate this feeling.

But Addy's loving it. Moaning and groaning as quietly as she can, nails trying to dig into the metal. "Oh, Peter!"

I grunt, squeezing my eyes shut. I don't want this. Every thrust I hear Zaynab's moans. And every moan reminds me of Dorian.

Fucking betraying bitch.

"Fuck," I mutter, pulling out of Addy as my dick goes limp.

All I see is Dorian being so ashamed of me for going back to my old ways.

I'm sorry, baby.

But fuck you.

"What's wrong?" Addy asks, looking back at me.

I pinch the condom off and toss it in the toilet. "Get out."

She turns around, shaking her head. "I can finish you off with my mouth—"

"I said, get out!" I yell through gritted teeth.

She jumps, pulling up her panties, and storming out of the stall. I'm a fucking wreck. Ruining another pretty face for my own selfish needs.

When am I ever going to learn?

When am I ever going to grow up?

I fix my jeans and sit on the toilet with my head in my hands, sighing softly as tears well in my eyes.

And it's like Mama came crashing down on me and hugged me herself.

My phone vibrates, once, twice, three times.

When I look at it, it's Slade sending me pictures from a grocery store. No, oh, fuck. My heart leaps up to my throat and I can't control the tears anymore. They're pictures of Dorian and Rosa. My beautiful baby girl has a big green bow on her head and she's sitting up in the shopping cart. Dorian looks as beautiful as ever, curvier than she was but I wouldn't have her any other way.

My girls are right there in the flesh.

It's not a dream. My baby girl is there.

My life was written out.

It was set in stone.

Then Dorian took it away from me. This beauty took my heart away and crushed it. Stealing my everything in the process.

I zoom in on Rosa's face, chuckling softly as more tears roll down my cheeks. She's so perfect. Beyond anything I could ever imagine.

My beautiful Rosa.

***

About eight months ago, Dorian and I were in the bath, bubbles covering most of us, but her big soapy breasts still breached the surface.

She hummed, leaning her head on my shoulder. "Are you happy?"

I chuckled, hands on her growing stomach. "So happy, baby. Why do you ask?"

She shrugged a shoulder, moving bubbles around. "It's a big change for both of us."

I kissed her temple, pressing my lips there as I spoke. "Are you happy?" She laughed, nodding quickly as movement hit my hand. "Is that?"

She sniffed, moving bubbles out of the way so we could see her belly. "It kicked."

"Woah," I said, keeping my hands steady as another kick sprang to life. "Hey, baby. It's Daddy."

"They can't hear you from all the way up here, silly." She cupped the side of my face as I looked over her shoulder at the mounds of breasts and stomach before me. "You have to be up close for that."

I nipped at her ear, licking softly at the spot behind it. "Yeah? Like when I'm worshipping that precious pussy?"

She shushed me. "No bedroom talk around our baby."

"Mmm, they're not born yet, I can talk as nasty as I want, my love. So long as you only scream for me." I turned her, adjusting those thick thighs around me. "Tell me, Dorian, tell me I'm yours."

The way she bit those plump lips always sent me overboard. "You're mine, Peter. And I'm yours."

I pulled her face to mine, claiming her mouth. "Marry me, don't think, just answer."

"Yes."

I eased into her with a smile on my face, taking my woman in a swarm of bubbles as our baby grew in her belly, and a ring would soon be slid onto her finger. "Soulmates," I whispered, kissing those lips I craved even when I was on them.

My happiest memory with her was that afternoon.

That beautiful afternoon I've grown to hate the more I replay it in my head.

But that's all it is. A memory of something fake.

Lying cunt.

***

My phone rings and I see Riggs's name pop up. I'm two seconds from tossing the phone. But I can't do that to my brother. I have to answer this if I know what's good for me.

"Yeah?" My voice is hoarse, shaky.

"Hey, man, you get the pictures?" he asks, hesitant to begin with.

I nod, clearing my throat. "Yeah, I got the pictures. What's the plan, then?"

He sighs, a door squeaking open, and Zaynab's giggles move through the speaker. Gosh, I never thought the sound of someone's laughter would give me butterflies. But with Zay, they've always been there. Even when I was with Dorian. She's my fucking soulmate and Zay still managed to overtake her love.

"We're thinking of something. Tomorrow the plan is for Zay and Slade to scope out the town, starting with the post office." He groans when he sits down. The man has the body of an old man and he's only in his late twenties. "Dorian's not in the city, it's this little town right outside of Richmond that looks an awful lot like the town Mama used to bring us to when she'd crave that cinnamon ice cream, you remember that?"

I chuckle softly, closing my eyes to better see Mama's smiling face when she licked that frozen treat for the first time while we devoured our ice cream. "Of course, I remember."

"Something about this place feels familiar, I just can't put my finger on it," he adds, sucking his teeth when Zay cackles again. He hates it when people are loud when he's on the phone. An attribute he got from our daddy dearest.

"You're seriously on Tinder right now?" Zay asks, her voice brightening my mood.

Slade laughs. "What the fuck else am I gonna do? Watch you and Riggs eye fuck each other all night?"

"He wishes," she says, snapping her fingers. "I'm taking a shower, if Adam calls, tell him I'll call him in the morning."

I raise my voice so Riggs can do it before she gets in the shower. "Tell Zay I want to talk to her."

Riggs scoffs. "Now?"

"Yes," I urge, my leg tapping restlessly.

He moves the phone away from his ear and whistles. "Hang on, sunshine.

Phone for you."

"I told you to tell Adam I'd call him back."

"It's Peter," he says before silence spreads through the receiver.

A door squeaks and shuts before the sound of the shower turns on. "Peter?" Zaynab asks, her voice low and worried. "You okay?"

Here they come. My sobs. My vulnerability. My heartache.

And she lets me cry into the receiver. Listening to me break all over again.

"I'd say it's going to be okay, but I have no damn idea," she says as my cries die down.

I sniff, groaning. "I fucked up. Bad."

"What did you do?"

I drop my head so far back it's hard to swallow. "I thought I'd turn to sex to stop the cravings. I've been sick all day from withdrawals." I shake my head, hating how disgusting I feel. "I thought I'd go to my old ways and fuck the new barmaid, Addy. I barely got into it before my dick went soft because all I saw was Dorian and all I heard was you. Now I'm having a fucking panic attack and I can't fucking breathe and my daughter is going to be so ashamed of me and all I want is a fucking drink or a bump or—fuck, Zay. I need you." I sob, my head in my hands. "I need you *here*."

"Peter," she says as my wails move through the receiver. "Peter, listen to me a sec, will you?" I sniff, whimpering softly. "Okay, just breathe. In and out. Easy as that. Okay? Breathe with me."

So I do. I take a breath in through my nose, and out through my mouth until I'm relaxed again. "Is that better?" she asks, still breathing with me.

"Yes." I rake my fingers through my hair, leg still tapping but I'm much more relaxed than I was. "Thank you."

"Hold down the fort for me, will you? I don't need you catching something from the Snake Biters, either." She giggles. "Didn't you hear we're in a polygamous relationship?"

I laugh, sniffling and wiping my nose on my hand. "Riggs told me. You think that's what everyone thinks of us?"

"Well, if they do, what do you think they're going to say if they find out you fucked the new girl?" She struggles in the background, voice muffled for a moment before it's clear again and the sound of the shower is clearer. "Fix this."

"I will. I'll talk to her and tell her to keep her mouth shut," I say, rubbing my eyes. "What're you doing?"

"Getting undressed. I want a shower before I sleep in this murder motel," she replies, fake gagging. "I swear, I'm catching a disease before I get home."

"But you're coming home to us, right?"

She inhales a deep breath and releases it through her nostrils. "I'm coming home, Peter, and I'm bringing your daughter with me. Gosh, you should have seen her. Pictures don't do her justice. She's gorgeous. So damn perfect. I can't wait to see your face when she smiles at you for the first time."

Her words have me laughing and crying, shaking my head as I rise off the toilet at the sound of the bathroom doors opening. "I can't wait for us to live in that cabin. All of us as a family. The kids playing in the sand, seeing snow, and learning to fish. It's not a fantasy, sweetie. I'm making this happen. I'm making you happy again. I promise. We all do."

"I know," she says quietly. "Now go get some sleep and kiss Carter for me."

I run my fingers through my hair again, smiling as I close my eyes. "All right, bye, sweetie."

"Hugs and kisses," she adds before hanging up.

I don't feel the greatest, but I feel a helluva lot better than I did before I got the call.

I'm not going back to my old ways. I slipped, I fucked up for the last time.

I open the pictures of Dorian and Rosa, smiling when I zoom in on that little button nose. She's got her Mama's nose, but everything else is me. My daughter is all mine.

I'm coming, my love. I promise, Daddy will be whole when you get home.

Riggs

Slade is scrolling through his phone, swiping left and right on women in the area. I hope he doesn't bring anyone here, the last thing I want is for someone to recognize me or Zay.

I release a breath, take the remote from the nightstand since Zay has my phone, and turn the TV on. A box TV I haven't seen since I was a kid.

News. Sports. Some cheesy Western movie. Or the weather.

Switching back to the sports channel, I curl an arm behind my head to watch some baseball game. I'm not big on sports, never was. Daddy said it was a bunch of Mama's Boys playing with balls for a living. And even though I love my mother to death, I wanted to be strong like Daddy as a kid. So, Peter and I never got into sports over something so stupid.

Bastard of a father.

I adjust my head again on these pillows that Zay insisted we have since this motel is not up to her standards.

I don't blame her. I'd give her the world if I could. But I've lived on the streets for a better part of my time before meeting Shyanne and learned to appreciate everything given to me.

One day, Zay will learn appreciation, too.

My little sunshine hasn't gotten spanked by me in a long time. Maybe I should show her who's still the boss. I'd love to see my handprints on her ass again.

Slade drops his phone on the nightstand, adjusting his head under these fluffy pillows. "You a Red Sox fan, too?"

I grunt a response, tapping my fingers on my stomach. "I don't watch sports."

"Says the guy watching a baseball game," Slade replies, chuckling.

"Fuck off."

He adjusts himself into a seated position and takes the chips from beside him. "I've seen them once when I was a kid. My foster dad was a huge fan and brought us to a game. It was wild. I ate my weight in hotdogs and popcorn. And I even caught the winning ball." He turns to me, crunching on a chip. "I should give the ball to your son. Would be a shame if no one ever got to play with it again."

I frown, looking over at him. He's always been loyal to the club. Kind to us and loving to my son. But people aren't nice like this without dark secrets in their pasts.

I've never met a genuine kind person before.

Everyone has always fucked me.

Why is this any different?

I smirk, shaking my head. "You don't gotta do that."

He bites down on a few chips, sending crumbs to his bare chest. I thought I was heavily tattooed, but this fucker takes the cake. There isn't a lick of bare flesh on his body other than his face and parts of his neck. "It's no bother. It's not like I'm having kids any time soon." He chuckles again. I think chuckling is a nervous tick of his, he does it all the time. Guys are starting to get annoyed when he does it during chapel. But again, his loyalty to my club and my family surpasses his little tick. "Gotta find me a pretty lady for that to happen."

"Yeah, they're not that hard to come by." I wink. "Got one in the room over there that refuses to have me."

"I will never understand your relationship." He chugs from the bottle of soda and belches. "You guys are fine with the fact that you're pining for a married woman?"

I shrug a shoulder, knowing how bad this must look. But I don't care. Zay was mine once upon a time. Why can't she be mine again? Having the chance to spend a lifetime with her, raising Carter, popping out more babies, and making love the dirty way we do. A happy ending for both of us.

As if the woman could hear my thoughts, her little voice moves through the closed bathroom door. "Slade? Riggs?" She calls out again, louder this time. "Hey?"

I jolt up from the bed and head for the door, opening it to her beautiful face poking out from behind the shower curtain. A face devoid of any makeup, just how I like her. "What's wrong, sunshine? Lonely in there?"

She sucks her teeth and wipes the water rolling into her eyes. "There aren't any towels."

I laugh, taking a step out into the room and grabbing fresh towels from one of the plastic bags. "Princess forgot to take her towel," I tell Slade.

He smirks, guzzling more soda. "Air dry that shit. I don't mind."

"No!" she yells, putting her hand out to me, but I step into the bathroom and close the door. With a roll of her eyes, she closes the curtain a little more. "Riggs, what're you doing?"

I shrug, pulling my t-shirt over my head. "I need a shower, too, sunshine."

"Didn't you get a good look at me the other night when I was in the shower with my husband?" she spits out as I whip the shower curtain open and reveal that beautiful ivory skin kissed so delicately in moisture. "And again tonight."

She steps out of the shower and I drop to my knees, staring at that perfect pussy bare before me. She got a small tattoo last year when we thought things were settled, a cherry blossom on her hip as a symbol of new beginnings. It's low enough on her hip for Adam's eyes only.

But not tonight.

I look up at her, meeting her gaze as her chest heaves and my hands meet her hips. "You're beautiful."

She rakes her fingers through my hair and my eyes close automatically, focusing on her movements. "Riggs, we can't do this."

I shake my head, eyes still closed. "Because you won't let it."

Her fingers leave my head, my hands drop from her hips, and she steps away, wrapping the towel around her. "I'm sorry," she whispers, looking at me over her shoulder.

I get on my feet with a grunt, undoing my pants. "Don't be, sunshine. Just know I'm waiting for you."

"You're going to wait for a while—"

Grabbing the back of her neck, I slam my lips on hers. Just one kiss. One more before I get into this shower. And by the light of God, she kisses back, letting her tongue swarm my mouth before pulling away.

"Mmph, God, you're trouble," she says, tapping my chest and leaving me with a raging hard-on. Her eyes trail to my package and she chuckles, pointing at the shower. "Enjoy."

Oh, fuck, will I ever.

She closes the door to the tiny bathroom that reeks of mildew and steam. She's not mine anymore and driving me mad with a mixture of pleasure and rage.

How could I have been so stupid and not fight for her?

How could I have walked away?

The scalding water pelts off my skin, hitting the tiles and curtain beside me. I don't even settle in the shower before my hand is wrapped around my cock and I'm stroking savagely through an orgasm that she helped produce.

The little tease has no idea what she does to me and what she won't let me do to her.

I feel her tongue on mine as I close my eyes, her perky breasts just out of sight.

I ride this orgasm home, balls clenching, stomach tingling, and I release. My hot seed leaks down my hand before being washed away.

Next time, I won't beat off alone. She'll be standing in front of me taking my cum on her tits or in that sassy little mouth.

The door to the bathroom opens as I wash my face and closes a second later. She brought me the towel. I wonder if Slade wasn't with us, would she let me devour her like she used to? Just the two of us alone in a strange place.

Wouldn't that be something?

Her giggles hit my ear as soon as the shower's off. Nope, don't like that.

She shouldn't be laughing with him.

She should be laughing with me.

But a friendship blooms, something I never noticed until I was alone with them.

She's sitting cross-legged on my bed facing Slade on his—who's still sitting in the same position I left him in—and she's munching on some candy. "You have a lot of trust in people."

Slade shakes his head, nodding at me. "I have this feeling when I first meet someone, and that feeling hasn't strayed me wrong yet."

"Still, I wouldn't let anyone ink my skin without seeing the design first," she adds, biting off the head of a gummy bear. "I have two tattoos and it took me four months to be okay with the design of my last one. And you know what my new tattoo is?" He shakes his head. "It's one cherry blossom two-quarters wide. That's it. And you let your friends tattoo you without knowing what the hell they're putting on your skin." She tosses a gummy bear at him. "Doofus, I'm telling you."

I run the towel through my hair, tossing it on the bed and purposely hitting Zay's side. She looks back at me as I get into a black pair of boxers, narrowing her eyes like she knew I tossed the towel at her on purpose so she'd get a good look at me naked. The first time she saw me naked had me spent. Her eyes scrolled over me with such intrigue—no, such awe.

"What about you, man?" Slade sits up, hanging his legs off the bed as I get in behind Zay. These double beds leave my feet hanging off the end. As much as I wouldn't want to sleep without Zay, Slade has the bed to himself and won't have to deal with his feet hanging off. "Who does all your tattoos?"

"Skeet," I tell them, grunting as I adjust my head on the pillow.

She turns with her back to the TV. "I didn't even know that."

"He used to be a tattoo artist before he joined the Snakes." I point a thumb at Slade. "This fucker got unlucky when he joined because Skeet messed up his hand last year." I drop my hand on her lap, my thumb grazing her calf.

Slade watches my hand, sucking chip residue from his teeth. "Why doesn't Adam have the Snakes' tattoo?"

She turns to me, bringing an orange gummy bear to her mouth. "Something about their father and how Adam's not a purebred or something."

"If my mama had it her way, none of us would have the damn tattoo," I add, my thumb moving in slow circles along her pebbling skin.

Slade finishes off his soda, taking the towel from beside Zay. "And what happens when you decide if the Panthers are joining us, will they have to get the Snakes' tatt, too?"

I shake my head, bending a knee. "I ain't sure what I'm doing with them… one thing at a time, boy."

"Whatever you decide, I'm right by your side, pres." He taps my knee and swings the towel over his shoulder, leaving Zay and me alone as he showers.

She waggles her eyebrows at me, tossing a gummy bear at my face. "How was your shower?"

I grip her calf, snaking my hand between her legs to separate them. "Woulda been better with you in it."

"Showers are always better with me in it," she teases, getting off the bed in nothing but my t-shirt and a pair of blue panties.

I grunt as I get up, taking her by the wrist. "Take those off before coming to bed."

She looks down at her outfit, then back up at me with an arched eyebrow. "I'm not sleeping naked with Slade in the room."

"Then he sleeps in the car," I say, getting on my knees on the bed and holding her face in my hand. "You always look so fucking sexy in my shirts. I like that you still wear them, even when Adam's around."

Removing my hands from her face, she settles them on her hips and wraps hers around my neck. "Regardless, I'm not sleeping naked."

I tap her ass, kneading her buns. "Just take this off. That's what I asked for anyway."

She pushes my face and chuckles, going to the sink outside the bathroom to brush her teeth.

There my dick goes again, growing at the thought of touching her. Letting my hand move along her smooth skin, inching her clothes off and revealing that precious body beneath it. Fuck, letting my tongue taste her like it was the first time—I take a deep breath to relax myself when those cheeky little panties hit the side of my head and drop on the bed. I sit back on my heels and look at her over my shoulder. Little tease is biting her lip, hert-shirt hanging off her shoulder.

Oh, this fucking tease is getting it tonight.

Just you fucking wait.

She tiptoes back to me, the little tease knows what she's doing. It's funny seeing her mood change. When we're away from stress and memories of heartache, she's happy. She's back to the woman I fell for.

Then when shit hits the fan, she's sad again. Those hazel eyes get big and wet and make me want to burn the world to a crisp just so she could smile.

"You're a fucking tease," I growl as she gets on the bed.

That smile hits me dead in the heart, making me take her and roll all over the bed until she's under me, giggling uncontrollably.

"Riggs, stop." She's still laughing as I'm nibbling her neck, fingers digging into her sides. "I will beat you! Stop!"

I lick up her neck, kissing the corner of her mouth. "How can I stop when that laugh is music to my ears?"

She rolls her eyes, putting her hands above her head. "You're a foolish man, Riggsy."

I prop myself up on my fists, looking down at this goddess under me. Scars decorate her wrist, her palm, and a fresh bandage is affixed to her right hand. Scarred but still so fucking sexy.

"And yet you continue to tease me just to get a rise outta me, huh?" I thrust into her, making her suck her teeth. "Wouldja look at that, can you see how much my cock missed you?"

Her tongue darts out, sending me overboard. But I don't show it. I want her to leap.

I want her to tell me she chooses me once and for all.

"I can't," she whispers, staring at my lips before meeting my eyes.

I lower myself on top of her, cupping the side of her face. "For years I beat myself up at the fact that I let you slip through my fingers. I beat myself up at the fact that on your wedding day, I sat outside the church and let you say *I do* to Adam instead of me." She frowns, flickering her gaze from one of my eyes to the other. "I regret it every single day that I walked out of the hospital after you were shot and didn't make you mine. What we share is beyond anything you have with my brothers. Admit it, you may be in love with your husband, but it's me you see your future with. Tell me, Zay, tell me I'm wrong. If you say it, then I'll stop. If you push me away, I'll leave. But if you don't. If you kiss me right now, I'll keep trying. I'll get on my knees right now and beg you. I'll worship you with everything that's inside me. I'll be yours. Raise our son together. Raise him right. Make you happy." I lower my head, my nose touching hers. "I'll keep that smile on your gorgeous face."

My heart's beating wildly, jumping all over the place as her breathing shakes. Her nerves getting the better of her. But I know Zay, she listens to her heart more than she does her head and I'll be right here waiting for her when she comes to the decisions of who to choose.

She'll choose me.

"If Shyanne were still alive, you wouldn't be like this and you know it." She sniffs, a tear slipping free. "If Shyanne were alive you'd be home with her right now, raising *your* son together. I wouldn't be a thought in your head, Riggs, so—"

"I loved Shyanne, I'll never take that away. But she wasn't you. I walked away thinking you'd be happier without my darkness. You weren't, and knowing I walked away and met an angel who healed me makes all of this so much worse. I beat myself up every single day for walking away from you. And she knew that. And then when you came back into my life, she knew my heart wouldn't be hers anymore because it always belonged to you." I don't realize it until she wipes the tip of my nose that I'm crying. Talking about Shyanne does that to me. I wasn't faithful to her if I look back on it. I never slept with anyone while we were together, but my head did. My head was with Zay. My heart was, too.

I sniff, groaning softly and staring into those eyes I thought I'd never see again. "When you came back into my life, Zay, she knew as well as I did that I'd want you back. The arguments Shyanne and I went through were what caused me to stay at the clubhouse most nights. I wasn't working or researching ways to stop the trafficking. No, I was staying there to get away from my wife because my heart wasn't in it anymore. And I fucking hate myself for it. She deserved happiness, but didn't get it because of me." My voice cracks and I roll off her, rubbing my eyes as I stare at the stained ceiling. "We were planning on getting a divorce once everyone settled into their homes in Texas. She had the paperwork written out, my signature on it, and everything. It was just a matter of when she'd sign it."

Zay shoots up, placing a hand on my chest. "What? Why didn't you say anything?"

I shake my head, inhaling sharply. "She died. I didn't think it was right to taint her like that. Shyanne was an amazing woman, but...when you're around, you're all I see, baby. You're all I ever see."

Zay lowers her mouth to mine, kissing me softly. "I don't know what to say," she whispers.

"Tell me you feel the same way."

I run my fingers through her damp hair, sliding my hand down her back to her ass. I barely have time to lift the shirt when there's a knock at the door and the knob starts to rattle.

She shoots a look behind her but I'm on my feet faster than she can react. "Riggs, what if—"

I grab my gun from the side table, put a finger on my mouth, and jerk my head at the bathroom. "Keep quiet and tell Slade to get his piece out."

Zay crawls off the bed and glances at me. I poured my heart out to her, something I never fucking do because my troubles with Shyanne were private. She'll always have a place in my heart, she gave me a son and saved me from the dark road I was traveling. Shyanne will never be forgotten, and I wish we settled things before she was taken from me. Before my son lost the woman who birthed him.

But that's not how this terrible world works.

Zay goes into the bathroom, steam dances around her before she closes the door. My heart beats slowly, waiting for my sunshine to be safe before I react and whip open this door.

And when I hear Slade shut the water, I creep closer to the door as the knob starts to jiggle again. "Hey!" I let out, banging a fist at the door. "You ain't got business here."

The knob jiggles again and laughter follows suit. "I was jus' lookin' for Marcie. Have y'a seen my Marcie?" the man slurs on the other end, making me ease back on the tension in my shoulders.

Slade comes out of the bathroom, towel loosely wrapped around his waist as a gun is cocked and loaded in his hand. "What's up?" he whispers loudly.

Zay's behind him, gripping his bicep as she nibbles her bottom lip. I hate when she's scared, hate when she gets that look in her eyes that I've failed her. She's the last person I need on my list of letdowns.

I hate it more that she's gripping onto him for safety.

I put a hand up to Slade and open the curtain. Some drunk, homeless man is holding a credit card at the door, a brown paper bag with a bottle in his other hand. "Marcie ain't here, old man. Keep on going."

The drunk man snorts, and staggers for a second before he continues to the next door. Something about that doesn't sit right with me, but none of us are leaving this room until I deem it safe.

Zay scoffs, still holding onto Slade. "I told you this place was a dump."

I let my eyes roam the parking lot for a second, scouring in the darkness. There's nothing here but fireflies and crickets. "Yeah, well, it's safer to be undetected, sunshine."

Slade makes his way to me, poking his head out the curtain with Zay still gripping his bicep.

I didn't like it five seconds ago, and I don't like it now.

I pry her hand off him, and give it a gentle squeeze, letting her know she's safe.

That same reassurance I gave her at the cabin.

That same reassurance I give her when she's on the bike with me without a helmet.

The same reassurance I give her whenever she's with me.

Slade fixes the curtains and tosses his gun on the bed as I bring Zay to ours, tucking her in it while I grunt, trying to lie beside her with my back to the wall. Zay likes sleeping on the left side. As much as I hate the fact that her side is closer to the door, Slade is right there to react in case something happens.

Fixing the fluffy pillow behind my head, I see her relax slightly as she sits up and crosses her legs. "I wonder who Marcie is." She narrows her eyes in thought. "I bet you Marcie gives good head."

Slade bursts out laughing with me, my arm draping across her legs. "What the fuck?" he says, taking clothes from his bag. "What would possibly make you say that?"

She lifts a shoulder, nibbling her thumbnail. "If some drunk guy is here asking about her, she must be this dump of a motel's regular prostitute, no?" She closes an eye in thought, looking at the stain on the ceiling again. "I bet she has some fishnet stockings or even those thigh-high boots. Oh—" She giggles to herself, making Slade start chuckling, too. "I bet she has no teeth, or like one little snaggly one, y'know?" Were in a fit of laughter listening to Zay being so rudely stereotypical. But I think it's helping ease her scattered brain. "Therefore, good head."

Slade snorts, wiping a tear from his eye. "How you come up with half the shit you say is astounding." He shakes his head. "One snaggly tooth," he adds under his breath.

She chuckles, looking down at me with a grin. Melting my heart one day at a time.

Her hand gently touches mine, dragging her nails in a calming fashion up and down my arm. She's staring at the TV, trying to drown out the chaos in her mind. I've seen her do this a thousand times over. Scrolling through her phone doesn't help, staring at the flashing images does.

When her eyes widen, I glance away from her and take notice of Slade standing there butt-ass naked, fixing his shorts. "You have a tattoo on your balls?" she blurts out.

He laughs as he jumps into his shorts, eyeing me before he answers. "Yep, my ex-girlfriend tattooed them."

"Oh, God, why?" She shakes her head, seemingly looking like she's disappointed in her curiosity but it's Zay, of course, she's not. She likes understanding people's quirks. "No, not why did she do that—why do I want to see them again?"

I can't help but laugh at her innocence sometimes. Getting to know her over the years, she's far from being a good Christian girl. She's wild, like me. But every now and then she'll let out something that makes me fall for her all over again.

Slade eyes me and I know he can read the *I'll fucking kill you if you do* from my face. "Don't worry about it, boss. I won't whip out my balls for your girl."

He snickers, getting in bed. "It's a little lawnmower with *DeezNuts* underneath it."

She hums, nodding her head. "You are one funny little man, Valley Valley."

He sticks his tongue out and gets comfortable on the bed beside us. "And you're one—" I lift my head leaning forward to glare at him, making him push his lips together in a smile. "And I will keep the comments to myself, Mrs. Donnelly."

She fixes the comforter on her legs. "It's Lovett, actually. I'm not a Donnelly."

"Yet." I nuzzle my head on her stomach, staring at the TV. "I'll make you a Donnelly soon enough."

She sucks her teeth, flicking my ear and hitting one of my many piercings. "You wish."

"You'll see, baby."

Slade shuts the lights off, keeping his gun on the pillow beside him. "I'll never understand your relationship, but I'm glad it keeps y'all happy."

She smiles at that, looking down at me again before getting comfortable beside me. "Mmm, goodnight, Slade."

He chuckles, turning on his side to face the door. "Don't let the bed bugs bite."

She hisses, taking candy from the bedside table and tossing it at him. "Don't say that, I'll sleep in the freaking car!"

A gruff laugh leaves me as I fix my arm under her head and tug her close to me, leaving a kiss on her cheek. "You're safest with me," I whisper.

Slade's chuckle moves through the quiet room as the flashing lights from the TV fill the rest. When she looks up at me and mouths *goodnight*, I know from this moment on, this is how I want my nights to end.

With her in my arms.

No more worries.

No more panic.

Just us, together.

What do she and Adam say? *Forever and always?*

Well, that's what I want with Zay.

She's my home.

My forever.
Always.

Zay

Slade has me pinned up against the wall, slamming his mouth on mine and shoving himself inside me. He holds still for a moment, letting me adjust to his size before he pulls out and thrusts back in, sending me into a spiral of euphoric bliss. My moans seep from my lips, filling the motel room as the setting sun pokes through the curtains.

He's rough, pounding me like he's mad at it. Biting my neck and groaning into the nape of it. "Fuck, Zay, you're so tight."

I let out a breathless moan when the bathroom door opens and Riggs steps out in a gust of steam, cocking an eyebrow at us. "Who said you could play without me?" his deep, throated voice says, sitting on the bed with that monstrosity between his legs glaring at me. "Come sit down and claim what belongs to you, sunshine."

Slade pulls out of me, making me whimper, and drops me on top of Riggs as he guides his dick inside me while I shriek. "She wet enough for you, boss?"

Riggs growls, spanking me. "She's always wet enough for me." He spanks me again. "Does it weep for me, sunshine?"

Fuck, my legs are like jelly when he enters me, capturing my slit with the dick I've craved for far too long. "Oh, God!"

He thrusts upward, moaning as he speaks. "Yeah, baby. Say my fucking name again."

Before the words leave my lips, the door bursts open, light blinding me as Peter walks in wearing nothing but a cowboy hat.

What the actual fuck is happening right now?

I'm riding Riggs, scratching down his chest as Slade licks up and down my neck, grabbing my breasts, then pinching my nipples. "You like it rough, sweet thing, don't you?" Slade says with a sultry grin.

Peter comes up behind me, forcing Slade to get on the bed and touch himself as he watches us. "Bend over, sweetie. It's about time you let me in that fucking ass."

Riggs separates my cheeks, as Peter gets on his knees and licks me until another shriek leaves my lips. Oh, fuck, I don't think I've felt an orgasm vibrate through me to the point of passing out. But it's coming. Oh, fucking shit, is it ever coming.

Before I know it, Peter spits on his hand, rubbing the head of his dripping cock at my puckered ass, and slides into me. Riggs thrusts upward, and Peter thrusts from behind. Filling my holes so we can come as one while Slade watches, groaning.

Peter and Riggs thrust together, jolting me forward as I scream, letting these men destroy me, and take me in ways I've denied them.

Adam walks into the motel room, the blue bow tie from our wedding around his neck. "Hey, babe. Don't come without me."

Slade moans, tilts my chin up, and opens my mouth with the head of his dick; his salty liquid spilling on my tongue. "That's a good girl. Swallow me, Mrs. Donnelly. Take it like a good girl."

Riggs is next, his deep moan throws his head back, filling me whole. "Fuck, sunshine. I can't wait to watch as I leak out of you for days."

Peter grunts, stilling as Adam shoves himself into my mouth next, pumping roughly and ignoring my gags. "Oh, sweetie, it's an honor to be the first to come in here," Peter adds, slapping my ass as Adam grips my hair.

"Watch me as they finish you off," Adam growls, thrusting deeply.

Tears are streaming down the sides of my face as I lap my tongue up and down his length.

I let him fuck my mouth.

I let them defile me.

Riggs moves out from under me and takes Slade's head, shoving it between my legs. Riggs watches me as Slade's tongue does wonders on my clit. "Make her scream, prospect. Make my woman fucking scream."

We're a mess of tongues on my body, moans, groans, and fluids mixed together.

Adam looks at the ceiling, spilling down my throat, and pulls my head off his dick with a pop. "Now, babe, I don't think you finished enough."

Slade lies back as Peter fixes me on his face, letting me ride his tongue until I scream again.

And I'm screaming bloody murder.

Peter captures my mouth, Adam has my tit in his, and Riggs has his fingers inside me as Slade's tongue finishes me off.

"Oh, God!" My voice is hoarse, cracking. "Oh, fucking Christ!"

"Say it again," Riggs growls, thrusting his fingers into me.

"Right there! Oh, God, I'm right there," I buck forward, creaming all over Slade's face when a car honks in the distance.

My euphoric high lightens, coming down from the most intense orgasm of my life.

Honk.

Honk.

Honk!

I jump, the black room coming to life. No, no, no, no! It was a fucking dream.

Goddammit.

It's just past two in the morning, Slade is passed out, snoring, facing the window and Riggs is holding me from behind, his heavy breathing tickling my ear.

Now that I'm awake, my bladder is throbbing and my pussy is aching. Goddamn stupid dream.

I groan, whipping off the covers. The honking car in the distance slowly decreases as it drives away. Stupid fucking car.

I tiptoe to the bathroom and plop on the toilet with my head in my hands. I'm a raging storm down there, dripping and soaking the space between my thighs. If I had on the underwear that Riggs insisted I remove, then those would be drenched.

What a dream it was, though. Perfect spank bank material when I'm home alone and bored.

But it got me thinking about what Slade mentioned to us. Are we really in a fucked up relationship? Would it be so wrong to be in one? To be the plaything for these men? It sure would be a less stressful living situation.

Yes, yes, it would be wrong. I'm a married woman. A happily married woman.

Riggs's muscular back faces me as I make my way back to the bed, his muscular arm curled onto my spot, and that gorgeous face so calming and angelic when he sleeps.

It would be wrong, but holy crap I could use a release right about now.

One more time, sunshine. That's all I ask for. It ain't much, but a night with you can cure all my faults.

My screaming thighs are clenched together when I get back in bed, trying not to move too much. Slade is still facing away from us. I think I'd be mortified if he were awake right now. Albeit, last night was the first time I saw him naked, which I'm sure doesn't do him justice, but still. The dream felt so fucking real.

As soon as my head hits the pillow, Riggs slides his arm around my waist, pulling me closer to him. As if the little shit meant to do it, my t-shirt lifts above my hips.

I try to move it down, but that just causes him to squeeze me tighter, thrusting into my backside. "Riggs," I whisper, turning my head.

And that's when he kisses me. Sending my common sense right out the window and bringing his participation in the dream back to life.

His tongue invades my mouth, dampening me even more.

Shit.

"Just say yes," he says so quietly, it's barely audible.

I can't help it. I truly can't. I need this. Oh, fuck, I need this.

I'm so fucking sorry, Adam.

I push my ass into Riggs's crotch, giving him my answer. It doesn't take him long to get out of his boxers and slide the head of his dick up and down my wetness. A guttural groan leaves him, squeezing my inner thigh and lifting it so he can slide right inside me.

I let out a soft squeal when he enters me, slapping my hand on my mouth. "You're so fucking tight," he says breathlessly into my ear. "That pussy hasn't had me in a while and forgot how big I am, didn't it?"

I nod quickly in response, letting him destroy me like he used to no matter how much it hurt. It's the best kind of hurt there is.

Slade is still asleep, thankfully, as Riggs pounds me, turning me onto my stomach and hiking me up on my knees so he can see what he's doing to me. He loved watching that dick of his enter me, how I screamed when he'd shove it in too quickly. I'm much too tiny for him, and I think that turns him on even more.

His balls slap against me, ready to explode soon. He squeezes my ass whenever he's close, and the way he's gripping it, separating my cheeks, and thumbing my asshole, I know he's close.

And holy fuck am I close, too.

He pulls out, turning me onto my back and sliding inside me again, making me see the fucking galaxy. His forearms rest on either side of my head, fingers tangled in my hair. "I love you, Zay. I don't care if you don't love me back, but you need to know how I feel," he whispers.

My eyes well with tears, hating how parts of my heart belong to him.

I don't respond. I can't. Adam is my husband. Adam owns my heart.

Yet what the hell am I doing?

I pull the t-shirt over my head, staring at Riggs as he watches my breasts bounce. He reaches between us, touching me until my eyes roll back, and slams his lips on mine to keep me as quiet as he can.

If Slade is awake, he's getting one helluva show.

But I don't expel a single sound. Only heavy panting as Riggs's tongue slides up my neck and a grunt leaves him, stilling on top of me. "Oh, baby," he whispers.

Our lips meet again, kissing intensely until he moves away from me, rolling onto his side. "Thank you," he says softly. "Let's get some sleep, sunshine."

I frown, raising an eyebrow. "That's it?"

"If I had it my way, I'd have my head between your legs making you scream, but we have company," he says into my ear. "I'll take you the way I want, tomorrow."

Touching his face, the moonlight making his eyes sparkle, I sigh. "What if this was a one-time thing?"

He smirks, kissing my lips. "I'll give you the world, baby. Just you wait."

He settles behind me, lifting the covers over us again and covering our naked bodies. His lips meet my cheek and he pulls me closer to him, a smile spread to his face.

I just slept with Riggs.

I just cheated on my husband, *again*.

What will Adam think of me after our conversation about starting our new life together?

What on earth have I done?

***

Slade is on the phone with Lip, being filled in on something at the club. Riggs is in the bathroom and I'm standing by my luggage still reeling from last night.

I'm thankful that Slade and I woke up more or less at the same time. I don't know if I could have handled facing Riggs alone after what happened.

Fucking shit I slept with him again my throbbing pussy hasn't let up since I woke up. This is really bad. Oh, why did I do that? Stupid fucking dream.

Pulling a blush pink dress from my luggage, I spot a piece of paper tucked into the inner pocket. As I slip the dress on, I pull the paper from the pocket and recognize Adam's handwriting.

Okay, so now I feel like utter crap.

I stuff my feet into my flats and step outside, sitting on the bench under the window, and unfold the letter.

My forever,

You left in such a hurry, I couldn't understand why.

Then, when I packed you a bag for this trip you insisted on going on with my brother and our prospect, I discovered the outburst.

I love you, baby. Always and forever.

It's you and I.

And our little family.
Come home to us.
Come home and I'll give you the new beginnings like you'll be giving me.
I'm out of the club the moment I see your face again.
To the cabin, right? Raising the kiddos in the snow.
Come home, Zay. Please, come home.
Yours until my dying day,
Adam.

I twist the wedding ring on my finger, wiping a tear from my cheek as I reread the letter and hate myself that much more for being with Riggs. But, God, did it ever feel fan-fucking-tastic to sleep with him again? I never realized how much of a drug he is. That itch I can't scratch.

My love for him never died, either.

God, what a fucked up chain of events I've created.

"Hey, sunshine," Riggs says, placing a hand on my shoulder.

Speak of the fucking devil and he shall appear.

I smile, blinking away the wetness of my eyes. "Morning."

He kisses me sweetly, sitting beside me with a sigh. "Last night was… interesting."

"Yeah, it was."

His arm moves behind me, fingers grazing my shoulder. "I meant what I said, Zay. All of it."

Swallowing thickly, I glance over at him with a deep, shaky breath. "As did I. It was a one-time thing."

That laugh seeps from his lips, deep and guttural as if he knows the sound of his voice is enough to ignite a storm. "Say that to your clenched legs right now." He nods his head at my lap, and wouldn't you know it, my legs have a mind of their own and betrayed me like my vagina did last night.

I suck my teeth, crossing one leg over the other. "Don't be so cocky."

He nips at my ear, kissing the bite mark he left on my neck, and lowers his voice. "Tell me, am I leaking out of you, baby?"

Glaring at him, heat climbs up my throat and parks at my cheeks. "Shut up."

"Make me."

I growl, opening my mouth to tell him where to shove it when he kisses me. Fucking shit, why does he do this? The lady-boners he gives me overpower any viable train of thought that will make my life simpler.

"Riggs," I whisper against his lips.

He kisses me once more, raking his teeth on his bottom lip, and sits back. "We'll talk about this later, we don't got time for how easy it is to make you squirm." He winks, then grows serious. "Lip says The Ghost sent them another letter."

I sit up straighter, staring at him with furrowed brows. "Carter?"

"Peter and Adam are taking him to the cabin. Lip and Skeet are creating decoys so they won't be followed." He smooths out my hair. "I ain't letting anything happen to him, sunshine. We're going home to our boy."

Placing a hand on my heart, I breathe deeply as I scan the fields across the street. *Our boy.* Oh, God, I'm royally fucked. "Do you think The Ghost knows we're here?"

"I don't know," he says, pinching my chin so I turn my head to face him. "But we're not waiting any longer. We're going in today. Scoping out the post office, the parks, and anywhere that will point us in the right direction." He leaves another soft kiss on my lips. "Don't worry, Zay, you're safest with me."

I take in some air, capturing his minty breath as I do, and nod. He said this to me the day we met. He says this to me every time I get on his bike. He says this to me when he leaves the house. He's saying it to me again when our lives have become one jumbled mess. "So I've been told."

Slade taps the doorframe, making me shiver. I wonder how much he heard of that and how much he heard last night. "Got a lead, by the way." Riggs nods his head at him to continue. "I called the post office before breakfast, and left them a voicemail about my 'missing sister'. Lo and behold, the description the woman gave me said that she's supposed to come in today to pick up a package."

"Then let's go," I say, pushing off the bench.

"If I don't like it, we're backing down," he says, looking up at Slade, then back at me. "If I think you're in danger, we back down, sunshine, go it?"

I nod quickly, tucking the piece of paper Adam wrote me into my pocket. "Aye, aye, Captain."

Slade stuffs his cell phone in his back pocket, clearing his throat. "There's one other thing."

Riggs leans forward, elbows on his knees, bracing for impact. "What it is?"

"Judas is MIA. He tried to quit the club the other night and now he's missing. Peter's been trying to get ahold of him, but no one knows where he went. Not even Mickey and they're attached at the hip lately," Slade says, fixing his hoodie. "I don't like this, boss. I think we should back down entirely. Go home and fix things before storming the beaches of Normandy."

Riggs taps the tips of his fingers together, elbows still fixed on his knees, and stares at the little ant hill in front of him. There's no telling what's going through his mind. There's no telling if he'll listen to Slade or say fuck it, we're going in.

I know my choice. Bring Rosa home.

I turn to Slade. "What did the letter say?"

He takes his phone out again and hands it to me with the picture Lip sent him this morning.

Whatever you're planning, think again.
My haunting will soon come to an end.
I have ears to the ground and eyes in the sky.
One more trick up your sleeve and all the Snakes will die.

I gulp, wondering what the hell we have to do with any of this. Daddy Donnelly and Roaden were the head honchos, not us. I don't care if Riggs and Peter have Daddy Donnelly's blood running through their veins, they're not like him. Neither is Adam.

Handing Slade his phone back, I nibble my bottom lip and bring my defense mechanism to the party when I don't know how to act when I'm scared. "The Ghost is a poet and didn't even know it."

Slade chuckles nasally, pushing his lips together when Riggs rises. Don't want to poke the bear when he's already on edge.

Riggs cracks the bones in his neck, takes the gun from the back of his jeans, and cocks in. "We go in."

I'm a cocktail of scared and turned on, it's not a good look for my underwear today.

But we're doing it. One way or another, we're getting Rosa back and fixing this chaos.

Slade

I have my feet on a bench in the middle of the town, ass perched on the top of it as Zay stands in front of me. She's nibbling her thumbnail, gawking at the post office, and trying her hardest to keep calm. I can see her nervous breathing with every deep inhale she takes.

Riggs is sitting at the coffee shop not too far, newspaper in front of him, sunglasses, and one of my baseball caps on. He has to stay hidden, but the giant sticks out like a sore thumb.

Shit, we both do.

I eye a bite mark on her neck and chuckle, causing her to look at me as I point at my neck. "Where'd that come from?"

She smirks, shaking her head. "Don't ask."

Leaning forward, I tap her elbow. "Oh, c'mon. You don't think I didn't notice you wake up naked this morning."

She covers her face and laughs. "I like sleeping naked, sue me."

Her face is a deep red, and now she's biting her bottom lip like she's hiding something.

They fucked, I'd put money on it.

"I did have a very wild dream last night." She widens her eyes and sputters her lips. "Like something that should be documented, it was that…intense."

"Oh, yeah? Do tell." My hands hang off my knees, elbows pressed into them as I study her face.

The blush comes back, her hands are probably sweaty because she keeps wiping them on her dress. Ah-ha, she had a sex dream last night. I bet you I'm in it.

"Well, let's just say, you have an extremely wild tongue." She bends her knees as she says this, making me laugh. "And I had no idea it was possible to fill all my holes at the same time."

I'm like a teenager around her. The zipper on my jeans better serve me right today because I have a massive boner just thinking about going down on her. I have yet to see her naked, but I did get the glory of seeing her ass last night as she got in bed.

Now I'm the one who's blushing.

"Have you ever had a threesome? No," she pauses, counting on her fingers, and widens her eyes. "A five-some."

I'm laughing again, taking in the look on her face as if she's never watched porn in her entire life. "I have not, but I have seen my fair share of dirty movies."

She puts her hands on her face. "You don't understand. Riggs was in my front, Peter in my back, you came all over my tongue, then Adam shoved himself in my mouth. How is something like that even possible? Like, how would I even move? Can I move? Jesus, it still makes me all throbby just thinking about it."

I put a hand on my stomach, leaning back as I cackle at her red face and how she's so shocked at something that has been done a million times over in porn.

It's cute. She's not innocent by any means given her track record, but seeing her right now reminds me of my first time. The poor girl took a good look at my dick and gasped, wondering how on earth that thing would fit inside her and not make her scream like I was killing her.

I made her scream all right, right up until she left me.

"You're a tiny little thing, too. That seems like a lot of men for you," I say, wiping the laughing tears from the corner of my eyes.

"Too much." She shakes her head, her wavy hair billowing in the breeze. "It's all this polygamy talk you shoved down my throat. It's making my horny mind all confused."

I smirk. "In that horny mind, I did get to shove something down your throat, didn't I?"

She pushes my face, rolling those golden eyes. "Oh, shut it." She smiles, looking at the ground. "In that dream, you have a tongue of the Gods, I'll tell you that much."

Oh, she has no idea what this tongue can do.

"And who says I don't actually have the tongue of the Gods, hmm?" I tease, winking at her.

She pouts, folding her arms. "It's too bad I'll never find out, now isn't it?"

I tap my head and wrinkle my nose. "You got enough spank material in that dream to last you a while. And seeing your ass was enough to last me the next couple of days."

"I do have a nice ass," she says, turning to me with a chuckle.

My chuckle barely leaves my mouth when a white van speeds our way. I see Riggs at the corner of my eye slowly stand up, which makes me do the same.

Zay stiffens, looking at the van, too, but we're too fucking stupid to look behind us. "Slade?"

"Zay, go back to—"

Something hits the side of my head, sending me barreling to the ground.

Bits and pieces of things come to me as my eyes flutter.

I hear Zay screaming. "Riggs! No—Riggs!"

Shuffling sounds around me, grunts and strains until the van speeds off.

I groan, unable to bring a hand to my wet, throbbing head. What the fuck just happened?

Before everything goes dark, pounding footfalls come my way and Riggs screams, a painful shriek that sends goosebumps through me, breaking my heart.

He drops to his knees beside me, tears rolling down his cheeks. "Zay," he whispers.

I reach a head out to him, but it collapses on the ground and that's when I give in to the darkness.

Peter

dam's driving one of the KIAs we have stashed at the clubhouse.
They're our getaway cars if anything goes sour.

And shit fucking went sour.

Whatever you're planning, think again.
My haunting will soon come to an end.
I have ears to the ground and eyes in the sky.
One more trick up your sleeve and all the Snakes will die.

I can't stop reading this letter that the damn Ghost sent us. I think he knows Riggs, Zay, and Slade went to find Dorian. And my guess is that he knows about it because of fucking Judas.

The bastard is missing and so is his bike. Girlfriend doesn't know jack shit and neither does Mickey.

All of this is my fault. Riggs and Slade are risking their lives for me. Zay is risking her life for me—someone she used to despise—and I fucking let her go on this trip to bring my daughter home when it's no one's responsibility but my own.

I've failed them.

I've failed.

Mama, give me strength.

We tried staying at the club, but it's too hard for Carter to get any sleep—even if Adam and I made an uncle sandwich, the kid still wouldn't sleep. We're fucking exhausted trying to power through the little sleep we got last night when the dashboard lights up with Riggs's name and I immediately hit answer, sniffling as I do. "Yeah?"

"They took her!" He sounds frazzled, panicking. "They fucking took her right in front of me. A goddamn decoy so they'd know where we'd be. Fuck!"

Something crashes in the background.

"Fuck!" he yells.

Adam and I share a glance, and both of us sit stiffer, frowning. "What're you talking about?" I ask, my stomach in knots.

What the hell happened? Is it Zaynab? Is it Dorian? My daughter?

The phone scrambles and Slade clears his throat. "We need you here ASAP. Three guys jumped me, knocked me the fuck out, and took Zay into a van." He groans, bed springs squeaking. "Fuck, man, I knew there was something off about this bullshit."

"What the fuck happened to my wife?" Adam raises his voice, gripping the steering wheel until his knuckles are white.

More crashes and bangs sound in the background. Riggs is tearing the motel apart, there's no doubt about that. He let down our woman. He didn't protect Zay.

He's the protector. He always has been.

Mama, please. Please guide us through this mess.

"Fuck." I punch their dashboard, then do it again and again until Carter starts crying.

But I don't care right now. Zay was kidnapped by someone we don't even know. She was taken to God only knows where.

And I wasn't there to help.

I wasn't fucking there and we don't fucking know where she is!

I scream, punching the dashboard again and again until Adam pulls over and wraps his arms around me. He's sobbing, trying to calm me as he shushes Carter.

"I don't know what to do," Slade's voice comes through the speakers.

My sobs commence next.

We lost her.

We actually lost her and there's nothing any of us can do but sit and wait for The Ghost to contact us with his demands.

Or worse, start sending her home in pieces.

"We're coming," Adam says, sniffling and turning to the dashboard. "I'll drop Carter off with Zay's parents and we'll get there as soon as we can."

Slade groans, coughing. "Yeah, okay. Just know that her parents think I'm her husband. Long story, it was a way for me to get into the house without them slamming the door on our faces."

I'm too angry to take in anything he's saying.

My hands are in fists on my lap, the betrayal I felt for Dorian has skyrocketed. As much as I love the bitch, she's a fucking dead woman if she dares touch Zay.

"Okay, yeah, okay." Adam pinches his eyes shut. "Fuck, stay put and calm his fucking ass down before someone calls the damn cops."

Slade sniffs, breathing heavily. "Bring cash. I think our motel bill is going to be a lot more than forty dollars a night."

I hang up and growl, gripping the handle. "Move the car, Adam, before I get out of it and walk head first into a fucking truck."

He swallows hard and drives, heading straight for Zay's parents' house. We don't have anyone we can trust with the baby. No one knows about them, either.

And I like it that way.

I'm not a fan of her parents, never have been, but they know me because of Lillian.

They're our only hope right now.

Mama, please, I need you.

***

Zay's mother opens the door with a confused smile on her face. "Peter, is that you? I haven't seen you since Lillian's funeral. What're you doing here?"

"Hey, um, yeah, it's been a minute." I scratch at the five o'clock shadow on my face. "I need a huge favor." I look at Adam, then Carter. She's going to say no. Why the hell would she say yes? She never seemed like she liked me. Never showed an interest in me when Lillian brought me around. Why the fuck would she care now? "Can you watch my nephew for a few hours?"

She lets out a laugh, immediately shutting up when I don't change my stoic expression. "Oh, dear, you're serious?"

Adam steps forward, clearing his throat. "Yes, ma'am we are. There's been a family emergency and we can't bring him along. Aside from us, we don't have anyone. Zay said you wouldn't mind doing us this solid."

She scans him, flickering her gaze to me. "You're also living with Zaynab and her husband? And that giant football player? What's his name? Riggs, was it?"

I frown, looking at Adam. I guess they lied a whole lot to them about who we are. "Y-yes, that football player is my brother, Riggs." There's hesitation on her face as she eyes Carter.

"You two look exhausted," she comments, folding her arms and popping out a hip. "Maybe living all together isn't the best, now is it?"

I chuckle wryly, rubbing my eye. "P-probably not, but look, I wouldn't ask if it wasn't out of desperation. But please, Zaynab needs us right now—f-for a project for school." I smile at Carter. "This kid keeps getting in the way of our schoolwork."

"Why isn't Zaynab with you? May I speak with her?" she asks, looking behind us.

I smile, arching a brow. "Of course, you can speak with her, but she's taking a nap. She was up all night with Carter. Woman is a damn champ, if you ask me."

There's skepticism in her gaze, eyeing Adam and me. I don't know her very well. Shit, I don't know her from a hole in the wall, but I have no one else to trust. Not a single person who isn't associated with the club.

A sigh leaves her and she grins at Carter. "If my husband were home, I do believe the answer would be no. But he's out of town for the next couple of days." She reaches out for Carter and Adam hesitates, but hands him over. "Since my Zaynab won't be giving me grandchildren, I'll take care of your nephew as much as you'd like, Peter."

Adam's face grows red, gulping as his hands shake. "Why do you say that?" He hands her the baby bag.

"She's been very adamant since she was a teenager to have her tubes tied so she wouldn't have to procreate and bring a spawn into this world. She always hated them." She laughs. "But I never allowed her to do the procedure. That poor husband of hers must have his hands full with my little devil."

He sure does.

Adam gulps loudly, stepping forward to leave a kiss on Carter's head. "We'll be home soon, buddy."

I put my hands together in a praying motion. "Thank you for this, truly."

She nods, scrunching her nose at Carter which makes her look like Zay. "Come, let's get you cleaned up."

The door closes as we step away and a piece of me feels like it's dying today.

Haven't I suffered enough?

Sniffing, I head back to the car and drop in the passenger's seat. I can't help it, I start crying, weeping like a damn child with my head in my hands.

"Hey," Adam says, his voice cracking as he slides a hand onto my back. "We'll find her. This is Zay we're talking about. She'll find a way to escape. You know she will. She's tougher than we give her credit for."

Looking up at his watery eyes, I whimper. "What if we're too late?"

"Don't say that," he whispers, unable to stop his lip from quivering.

I huff out a breath, watching as a tear rolls down his cheek. "It's all that's running through my mind. Dorian was my fiancée and I didn't know a thing about her or what she was capable of—"

"Fiancée?" he interrupts me, brows furrowing.

I brush it off, it's not important anymore. We kept it silent so that it would be something that was just ours. I have a feeling we kept it silent so she wouldn't feel so attached to me.

"Zay's already gone. That's all I can think about because it's the only reality I know. People leave me. Always have. It's like a fucked up pattern of my life like I'm being punished for all the wrong I did. I used women, cheated, and lied, so God took Mama from me. I killed people, so God made me kill Lillian. I hurt Zay, made her sleep with me for the fucking club, and what does it get me? God's ultimate punishment. He brings me my queen and rips her from me with my daughter in her belly." I sniff, wiping my nose. "And now, now that I've turned to drugs and alcohol, He takes Zay away from me for committing more sins. I deserve all of this. Every last fucking thing."

Mama instilled religion in us as kids. Made us go to church every Sunday. I never liked it, I don't think Riggs liked it, either. But we went and we learned and now, I'm reaping the consequences of hating Sunday school. Now God is striking me down for my sins.

We reap the consequences we can't predict.

Adam takes my hand and squeezes, wiping his cheek on his shoulder. "Redemption, brother. Seek redemption and you'll be forgiven."

Leaning my head back I sigh, staring at the empty road in front of us lined by mansions. "Let's hope so."

There's only one way out of this, and that's saving my girls. I can't lose anymore. I let everyone down. Every single woman I care for is gone. I don't know how much longer I'll be able to hold on.

Mama, save me from this life I paved for myself.

Save me before I hurt myself.

Please, Mama.

Please.

Riggs

Slade has his arm draped over my shoulder, instructing me to breathe the way Zay does when Peter's having an episode.

I don't get anxiety.

I don't panic.

I don't fucking cry.

But when they took her. When those fucking demon-masked men took hold of her and held a cloth on her mouth. All my will to live left with her.

I failed.

I fucking promised she was safest with me.

But she wasn't, was she? No, they took her right out from under me.

They took her just like they took Shyanne.

I could blame Slade all I want. Point fingers at the fuck for not protecting her, too.

But he was just as clueless as I was.

We were played. Fucking played.

There's a knock at the door, and Slade groans, looking at it. He was hit pretty hard, a local had an ambulance come to look at him. The paramedic said he might have a concussion, but he shrugged it off and told her *been there some that, I'll be fine.* Cops were called, too, they wrote a report but I doubt anything will happen. The second they search our names they'll know it's probably a biker thing they won't want to get their hands dirty for.

Slade staggers when he stands, and heads for the door, looking out the window. "It's your brothers." I nod for him to open it and stand, waiting to embrace Peter like I used to do when we were kids. He'd come running at me with his baby blues red and wet with tears, knowing he'd be safest with me.

I don't think that stands true anymore.

Peter storms in the second Slade opens the door, and sobs before he makes it into my arms. "What the fuck, Riggs? What do we do?"

Adam comes in next, eyebrows pinched together. He looks terrified. "Did anyone reach out?"

I shake my head, sniffling as I rub Peter's back. It's funny how the tables have turned. He did this to me not too long ago when Shyanne was killed.

Now, it might be Zay.

"What happened exactly?" he asks Slade, sitting on the bed.

Slade pokes his head outside, looking left and right, then closes the door and leans on it. "I, uh, I called the post office this morning. Asking if someone by Dorian's description had come by. The lady said she was coming in to get a package today. So we went to the town to stake it out. They fucking came out of nowhere. One second Zay and I are laughing, the next someone clocks me on the head, and she's screaming for him." He looks at me and drops his head. "I didn't fucking keep a good lookout. Fuck, I'm sorry, boss. I fucked-up."

"We couldn't have known. It ain't your fault. It ain't none of our faults. What we're gonna do is knock down every single door in this town until we find our girl, got it?" I flare my nostrils, looking at the men nodding around me. "How many guns you got on you?"

Slade takes the one from the back of his jeans, tossing it on the bed. "I have two clips for it, but that's it."

I take mine and toss it on the bed, going in my luggage to take the other two. "Also two clips each."

"Shotgun's in the truck of the KIA, but I have my nine and a clip for it," Adam says, hands clenching and unclenching in his lap. "Peter has his nine, too."

I wipe a hand down my face, my hand still smells like Zay. The dirty bastard in me didn't wash my hands this morning so I'd have her scent on me. Now I feel like it's the last time I'll smell anything of hers. That coconut spray isn't lingering in the room anymore, as if it knew she wouldn't come back.

Peter sits beside Adam, letting out a shaky breath as his leg taps restlessly. "Tell me she's okay. Someone say she's okay and we're not going to find her body. Please." He releases a shaky breath, having one of his anxiety attacks. "Please."

I crouch down in front of him, doing those damn breathing techniques. "In and out."

He breathes with me, shaking his head and dropping it between his shoulders. "Fuck."

"In and out," I repeat, tilting his chin up.

"She's okay, Peter. We'll bring her home, just like we'll bring your daughter home," Slade says, sniffling as he sits beside Adam, then forces out a chuckle. "She'd probably make some stupid joke right about now at what big pussies we are for crying."

Peter laughs on an exhale, shaking his head again. "Her stupid defense mechanism is her humor."

"That's my favorite thing about her," Adam says, spinning his wedding ring on his finger.

Peter meets my gaze, lip twitching slightly. "You'll bring her home, right?"

How can I tell him the truth when I don't even know it myself?

"Yeah, kid, we'll bring her home." I tap the side of his face, sniffling, and sit back on my heels. "But we have to be careful about this. We have to plan it out. As much as I wanna go in guns blazing, we don't have time for fuck ups. We gotta be smart about it."

Silence spills free, filling the room like water in a pool.

It's thick, suffocating, and I can't catch my breath even as I breathe with Peter.

I failed Zay. I can't believe I let it happen. I can't believe I couldn't do my job and shield her. I told her I loved her last night. I confessed it for the first time sober.

What if I didn't walk away? What if I told her how I felt sooner? What if we lived our lives away from this chaos? Leaving like she wanted, just us and the open road.

Where did we go wrong?

Maybe we were never meant to be. Always living in the what ifs.

Adam cracks the bones in his neck and sighs. "I'm telling you all this now because the second we find her, we're out. I don't care what any of you say." He glances at me. "We're taking Carter and leaving the club. Leaving anything to do with the business."

"I'm right with you, man," Peter says without skipping a beat. "I promised her the cabin. For once, I don't want to disappoint her. She deserves all the happiness she can get."

"She does." I nod, looking at the bed we destroyed last night. "Fuck, last night we…um…" I can't tell them what we did last night. I can't tell them because it would ruin Adam. But I have to.

Slade clears his throat, studying me like he knows my secret with Zay. "Before she was taken, she was telling me about this crazy dream she had." He let out a laugh, leaning his elbows on his knees and clasping his hands in front of him. "Let's just say, we were all involved and all her holes were plugged."

Adam scrunches his nose and laughs, listening to Slade describe her very exotic dream. Something I know would never happen. I'm not one to share. Zay is the exception. Until she declares her love for me, I have no choice but to let her be with Adam.

Soon, very soon she'll be mine again.

Peter falls back on the bed, ending a string of chuckles. "Why the hell was I wearing a cowboy hat? I don't even own one?"

"That's what you're focusing on? Not the fact that Dream Zay let you in her ass?" Adam says, looking back at him. "I'm her husband and I still can't get in there."

Slade looks at me. "Have you?"

"Always been off limits," I reply, tapping Peter's leg as I get to my feet.

She'd give it to me, she'd let me enter that ass if I asked nicely as my head was between her legs. She agrees to anything when I lick that sweet little pussy of hers.

Adam chuckles softly. "She does have a nice fucking ass."

"Pairs well with her nice fucking tits," Peter says, sticking his tongue out.

Slade licks his lips, wanting to add to the comments, but knows I'd rip his head off if I heard anything wicked coming off his tongue. "She's a beauty."

And we failed her.

Expelling a breath, I'm feeling antsy. I gotta be doing something. Sitting here and sulking will only make things worse.

"All right, boys, enough fantasizing about her ass. Let's knock down some doors and find our girl." I clap my hands and take my gun from the bed. "Shoot to kill only if Zay's in danger, and *only* by my orders. Got it?"

"Aye, aye, Captain," Slade says, smirking up at me.

This guy will be my right-hand man as soon as this shit is settled. He won't be a prospect much longer, I'll make damn sure of that.

Adam

Thirty-six doors were knocked at.

Thirty-six nos.

Thirty-six people telling us it's not a missing person until forty-eight hours.

Fuck.

Riggs is sitting in the driver's seat, staring straight ahead. He's not blinking and his breathing is so shallow, I'm scared if I say something he might crack.

But he has no idea what this feels like. My wife is missing because of him. My wife could be dead because of this club. When I broke up with her, it was for her own good. I thought if I left her and cut ties with her, then she would be safe from this life. No one would want to touch her.

But fuck, was I wrong. Crew got wind of her parents' wealth and a plan was set in stone.

Now, the Snakes have their teeth so sunk into her, I don't think she'll ever escape.

I fucking ruined her and there's nothing I can do about it. I've tried to remain as calm as I can until we have proof of what's happened to her.

Inside, I'm screaming, I'm punching things, breaking things, I'm fucking crying like a baby. Inside, I'm acting just like Riggs.

"Riggs?" I whisper.

He blinks once, sinking into the seat. "It was my job to protect her and I didn't."

"We couldn't have known," I say, my voice cracking.

But I should've. I should've said no. I should've protected her. I should've gotten her away from this life.

He shakes his head, eyes cast downward. "I knew this was a suicide mission and I let her come. This Ghost fucker is dangerous and I let her be out in the open like that. I did this. I fucking did this."

A tear rolls down his cheek, getting lost in his beard. I hate it when he's broken.

He was like this with Shyanne. Shut down. Sad all the time.

He turned to Zay for comfort and my wife is the best person to go to for advice. She gives it to you straight, making you laugh when you understand. She's good at making me laugh in awkward situations. Now I might not hear that laugh again.

A weight has been pressed on my chest since she left. I knew her secret and still, my selfish fucking ass let her leave. While packing her a bag for this trip, I found a pregnancy test. The digital screen was blank, but Zay wouldn't buy something like this without being certain.

That's why I wrote her a letter.

That's why she wanted out.

That's why I'm kicking myself in the ass for letting this bullshit happen.

For letting her go. I LET HER FUCKING GO!

"I think Zay's pregnant," I admit, shaking my head.

Riggs punches the steering wheel, huffing out a breath through his nostrils, then goes to town and attacks it like it's some scumbag the club was asked to beat up for money.

His knuckles break, but he doesn't stop. Instead, he turns to me and hits me in the face. "You knew she was pregnant and let her fucking come!"

I groan, warm liquid spilling from my nose into my mouth and down my neck. "I didn't let her do shit! I begged her not to do this. I fucking tried, but she's a stubborn fucking woman! You should know this. Wasn't it your idea to stake out the post office this morning? That's where she was taken! On your fucking watch—fuck!"

Bringing my t-shirt to my nose as the KIA pulls up beside us, Peter frowns, looking at the blood on my face and hands. "Don't you fucking put this on me. We're all responsible for not protecting her, jackass," I add before I get out of the car at the same time as Slade and he whistles, going into the glove compartment for baby wipes.

"The fuck happened here?" he asks, eyeing me, then Riggs.

"Apparently it's my fault Zay was taken," I say, spitting blood on the dirt road.

Peter glares at Riggs, who's still sitting in the fucking car and takes my face to inspect the damage. "It's not broken."

Doesn't make Riggs's way of dealing with his anger any better.

Slade bends over, looking into the car to check on Riggs. "You okay there, pres?'

"We gotta keep going," he says, clenching and unclenching his fist.

"It's gonna get dark soon," Peter says, nodding at a diner of the parking lot we're in. "Let's eat and we'll continue until people snap at us. Then we'll keep going until this entire town is torn apart to find her."

Riggs grunts, getting out of the car and slamming it shut. "They better have cold beer."

Slade chuckles, eyeing me and heading to the trunk. "Might want to change your shirt before we go in."

I remove it from my nose, blood still leaking from it, and eye Riggs as he stares at the sky. He and Peter tend to do that a lot when they're under stress. I think they're praying to Mama Rosa for strength, or praying in general. She was a stickler for praying.

Peter sits on the hood of the car, cracking his knuckles and scratching quickly at his chin. "What got you so fired up to hit him?"

Riggs shakes his head and looks back at me as I pull the dirty t-shirt over my head. Slade hands me a couple of baby wipes, helping me clean the blood from my face. "He says she might be pregnant."

Peter's eyes widen, whipping his head at me. "She's what?"

I sniff, pulling on a fresh t-shirt on. "Look, I don't even know if she is. I found one of those digital pregnancy tests in the garbage. The screen was blank. She might not even be—"

"That's why she stormed out of the house all huffy," Peter scoffs, cracking his thumb knuckles. "She wanted out of this in case she was."

Slade claps me on the back, grinning. "If she is, congrats, dude. We'll celebrate when we find her because we *will* find her."

"How can you be so sure of that?" Riggs asks, his voice low, scared.

Slade smiles, urging me forward. "I'm not but we gotta have faith."

Riggs is hesitant, but he steps forward as well, Peter right beside him, as the four of us goons head into the diner. Sadness swarms and joins us for a meal I don't think I can stomach.

We sit at the closest booth and stare at the table in silence. There's no telling what will happen, all I know is that I'll never forgive myself if I let Zay go like that knowing her secret. Knowing the danger.

I bang my fist on the table, gritting my teeth as tears slide down my cheeks. Slade puts his arm around my shoulders, letting me sob as quietly as I can. All the emotions pour out of me.

All my love.

All my sadness.

All my anger.

It's coming in waves.

Destroying me.

My love is gone and I'm the only one to blame.

***

The first time I met Zay, she crashed into me and sobbed uncontrollably onto my chest. I didn't know what to do so I held her. I let her sobs and worries leave. And something about her holding me, infiltrating me with her coconut smell, I knew I was a goner.

But I never saw her again. I never got her name or her number. I never got to hold her like I did before she walked out of my life looking all disheveled. I didn't find out until years later that the reason she looked so distraught and the reason her clothes were torn was because of Peter. He always did a bang-up job at hurting her.

The first time I saw her again, she was in front of me at Starbucks. We were in a long ass line and I was building up the courage to talk to her. It took fifteen customers before it was her turn and I still didn't say anything. I came to the understanding I wouldn't have the balls to jokingly ask her if she needed another hug.

Then, as if by some miracle, I found my opening.

"You're twenty-five cents short," the barista said, and I grew a pair at that moment, stepping forward with a grin.

"Add a cappuccino—one sugar to the order, it's on me." I took out some cash and handed it to the barista, smiling at her. "Hey."

She blushed, the redness growing from her cheeks to her neck. "You didn't have to do that."

"It's no bother." We moved to the side to wait for our orders. "We need all the caffeine we can get during finals."

She chuckled, moving her hair out of her face. She looked tired, bags under her eyes. But wow, I'd take her at her worst or her best. This woman was perfection. "I'm Zay."

"Adam," I said, taking our orders and looking for an empty table. "You busy right now?"

She shook her head and followed me to a table. There it was, that coconut scent wafting around and devouring me. She captured my soul that day and held onto it for dear life.

I smiled at her as she took the lid off her coffee and blew at it. I was a wreck of nerves, wondering what I was supposed to say let alone talk about with her. I never got nervous around women, but that's when I knew she was the one. She made me flustered, made my heart skip, and I've never felt so tongue-tied as I did that day. "Tell me something crazy about you."

She narrowed her eyes and chuckled, clearing her throat. "I'm secretly a furry." She laughed, covering her face. "I'm kidding. No, gosh, that's weird. Unless you're into that or something—" I shook my head, chuckling at her humor. "Um, something crazy about me, huh?"

I smiled. "Yeah, like would you believe me if I told you I knew how to ride a Harley?"

She widened her eyes, scanning me. "Mister Preppy over here can ride a motorcycle?"

I looked down at my outfit; dark-wash jeans, a pristine white shirt, and brand-new Jordans. "What's wrong with the way I'm dressed?"

"You're too clean-cut to be a biker," she said, sipping her coffee.

Arching an eyebrow, I scanned her cleavage for the first time that day. Holy fuck, it was perfect. I was standing behind her for a good twenty minutes, all I got to see was the way her ass looked in her jean shorts and the fact that I could see her red bra through her t-shirt. Seeing her up close, this woman was going to be my girlfriend by the end of the night.

"Not all bikers are rugged."

She shrugged a shoulder, licking the coffee from her lips. "Yes, but you're too pretty to be a biker."

I laughed, hand on my chest. "You think I'm pretty?"

She smiled, lifting her chin into the air. "Mmm, yes, darling, I think you're absolutely dashing."

We laughed, making the students around us stare and roll their eyes. I didn't care. I'd laugh into the sunset with her until my dying day. I found my better half and I was only nineteen.

"And I think you're stunning, Zay," I said, leaning forward on the table.

There it was again, a blush.

She didn't know it yet, but I would make her mine. All mine.

"What's your major?" she asked, crossing one leg over the other and letting her foot touch my shin. Oh, God, the goosebumps that spread through me at her touch were enough to know I was marrying this girl.

I was never the luckiest with women, that was more Peter's department. Girls swooned over him but spoke to me more because of my blonde hair. They liked that typical blue eyes blonde hair thing. But I never pushed it farther than a few drinks if I didn't see a future. Peter and Riggs liked having a revolving door of women. I was picky. I didn't need a hole to store my dick for a night like Peter did and I didn't need a whore to dominate the way Riggs did.

I liked the intimacy, the relationship. Call me a softie, but I ate that shit up.

I chose my women carefully, but there wasn't a single one of them that swooned me the way Zay did. She captured my heart with nothing more than a smile.

"I'm in graphic design," I told her, seeing her light up with excitement.

"Me, too." She leaned her elbow on the table and placed her chin on her hand. "Looks like I'll be seeing a lot more of you, won't I, Adam?"

"I'd like that," I said, winking at her.

She scrunched her nose and giggled. "Don't try too hard to impress me. Be yourself. I like it best when someone shows me their quirks and doesn't try to be someone they're not."

I smirked, tilting my head down as I turned my cup. "I'm very shy and a bit of a dork."

She bit her bottom lip, trying to suppress that smile. "You're perfect."

Grinning, I licked my lips. I knew right there and then that I wouldn't introduce her to the life that I grew up in. She was my ticket out of here.

My future.

We sat there for hours, talking but mostly laughing. I loved laughing at the beginning. Things were simpler then. Happier.

Easier.

Before we knew it, I was sitting beside her, arm on the back of her chair and she was leaning into me, staring at my lips and waiting for me to make the first move.

I didn't know how to make it. I didn't want to screw this up. I didn't want her to laugh if my kisses weren't good enough.

It had to be perfect.

She stared at my lips again when she turned to face me, tucking those brown wisps of hair behind her ear. "I have a final in the morning, think you can walk me home?"

My fingers grazed her arm, smiling at her. "Yeah, sure."

She smiled, biting her lip, and stood to take her things, those little jean shorts showing off her purple thong. It took everything in me not to take her to my dorm room, but I wanted our first time together to be special.

Everything about us had to be special.

We walked out into the cool evening, and she took my hand, interlocking our fingers. My heart skipped so many beats, thumping wildly in my ears. I hoped she didn't mind how sweaty my palms were.

She led us to the far side of campus. Our dorms weren't anywhere near each other but I'd walk miles to be able to kiss her goodnight.

"It's not out of your way, is it?" she asked, adjusting her fingers with mine.

I pulled her in, draping my arm across her shoulders. "Nothing's out of the way for you, Zay."

Another blush. I loved it when she blushed.

"You're a little charmer, aren't you?"

I shook my head. "No, I swear it, I'm the last person you'd have to worry about. I'm not a lady's man. I'm that dork in the corner who's always the third wheel."

She pouted, poking my side. "Awe, baby."

Instant boner.

Instant attraction.

Instantly in love.

No one had ever called me 'baby' before. Not a single girlfriend gave me a pet name or showed any affection to the point where I'd call her my love, my babe, my person.

But Zay? I hadn't even kissed her yet and I knew she was my ending.

I held the door for her when we got to her building, climbing the three flights of stairs. It was really hard not staring at her ass in those shorts.

Fuck, she was all ass and perfect perky tits.

I'd say it again, I was a goner.

She fished her keys from her bag and leaned against the door, smiling at me. The door was riddled with pictures and flyers and had a whiteboard with her name on it. "So, I'm going to kiss you, then you're going to give me your number, and take me out on a proper date."

I laughed, leaning a forearm above her head. "A proper date, huh? What's your favorite food?"

She narrowed her eyes, looking at the ceiling. "Pizza."

I slammed my lips in hers, catching her by surprise as a gasp caused her to inhale my breath. And when she kissed back, my knees went weak. The woman crawled inside me, invaded my heart, and buried herself deep within my soul. Nothing will satisfy me enough until I know this woman has become my everything.

Her tongue slid against mine and she hummed, placing her hands on my chest. "Mmm, goodnight, Adam."

I bit my lip, looking down at her. "Goodnight, Zay."

Taking the dry-erase marker, I bit the cap off, writing my number down beside her head. "I'm taking you to pizza, and when I do, you're going to become my girlfriend and kiss me a thousand times over as if the world is ending."

She giggled, pulling my t-shirt and planting another kiss on my lips. "I'll call you tomorrow, Adam. I promise you this."

With one last peck, she opened her door and winked at me, closing it between us.

I smiled, resting my head on her door knowing wholeheartedly that this woman was the love of my life.

And yet, that pang of guilt rode through me because of the call I would get in a few short days telling me Peter was in the hospital. A place she put him in.

Nothing was ever normal with us. Nothing was ever peaceful. Except for that night.

That night was *absolutely dashing*.

***

I chug the rest of my beer, sniffling with a wince as we sit in the booth in total silence. Riggs and Peter order a burger, Slade orders the chicken fingers, and I'm staring at the club sandwich. I'm too nauseated to eat. Too scared to think about myself.

I let my wife jump into a den of lions knowing she'd be eaten alive. And with the possibility of her being pregnant, I feel like an asshole without any way of fixing things.

As Peter said, for all we know, she could be dead.

A couple of cops step into the diner, fixing their belts as they do. To our dismay, they look our way and eye my bloody nose. Riggs growls in front of me, spotting them, too.

"Stay calm," Slade says, dipping a few fries in a ketchup and mayonnaise mix. "The less attention we bring to us, the easier it'll be to find Zay."

The shorter of the two cops comes our way, his slicked-back hair shines under the fluorescent lighting. "How you boys doing tonight?"

Peter smiles, nodding his head as he swallows the bite in his mouth. "Good, thanks for asking."

The cop eyes Slade, then me, staring at the dried blood in my nostrils. "You boys just passing through?"

"Yeah, we're on a road trip. Heading out to our cabin near the border," I say, smiling at them. Riggs keeps his head down, paying attention to his food rather than the cop. I'm sure if he looks up and the cop gives him one wrong look, we'll all be sitting in jail for the night.

He nods at Riggs, eyeing Slade. "You the men who were involved in what happened in town? The girl getting taken."

Riggs clenches his fists. *Oh, shit. Oh, shit. Oh, shit.* "No."

"Some folks are saying men are knocking at their doors asking about her, you wouldn't happen to know anything about that, now, wouldja?" the cop continues.

"No, sir," Peter answers. "We're just passing through, might stay the night at the motel. Nothing more."

The cop grunts, hooking his thumb into his belt loop, and nods at the other cop. "Well, just so you know, there's a curfew in this town. Anything past ten, folks around here can call us. We like our privacy and we respect other people's properties, okay?"

Slade smiles, licking the corner of his mouth. "Heard you loud and clear, big man."

He taps our table, and takes a step away, looking back at us as he sees me sink into my seat. I must have that defeated look on my face because he comes back. "I don't know if you heard of the farm around here that takes in abused women. Maybe try looking for that girl there. Could be worth a shot."

"Thank you, officer," I say, returning my attention to my uneaten food.

Peter glances over his shoulder, leaning his elbows on the table, and nods. "Well, guess where we're going in the morning."

"We should go there now," Riggs says sternly.

I shake my head. "It's almost nine-thirty, we don't even know where this place is and what we'd expect to walk into when we get there."

He sits back and wipes a hand down his face. "So we just leave Zay out there overnight? We ain't even gonna try to look some more?"

"Riggsy." Peter sighs. "What help would we be if we're locked up? We rest for a few hours, and at sun up, we go to this farm. Ask around and see if anyone has seen Zay or even Dorian. We have to try."

Slade drapes his arm on the back of the booth behind me. "He's right, boss. We gotta do this the right way."

Riggs sucks his teeth and takes the empty beer bottle, bringing it to his lips and growling when only a few drops spill out onto his tongue. "Tomorrow. Fuck, tomorrow we bring our girl home."

My girl.

Tomorrow I bring my girl home.

Zay

My head throbs waking me from a very chaotic sleep. All I dreamt of was Riggs screaming, Slade's frightened gaze, and those masks. They'll haunt me forever.

When my eyes flutter open, dizziness consumes me and nausea takes hold next.

The assaulting yellow room makes my eyes sting, and then, the reality of everything comes crashing in. Someone took me. Someone made me sniff chloroform. *Holy Fuck, Riggs!*

I jump from the bed and stagger, falling back instantly and nearly tumbling forward. Oh, man, I'm dizzy. It's like I've been drinking all night and finally decided to get up. "Ugh, stop," I grumble, bringing a hand to my head.

There's a water bottle beside me with a peanut butter and jelly sandwich. I ignore it for now and look at the basket of stuffed animals in the corner of the room as farm animal picture frames decorate the walls. I'm in a child's bedroom. *What the fuck?*

Pushing myself up again, I rub my stomach, heading for the window as the sun shines brightly in the sky. It can't be morning, can it? No, no, no, no. Oh, God, where the fuck am I? I was in town, it was nearly noon by the time we started scoping out the post office. Riggs, where the fuck is he?

I study the land; there are rows and rows of trees on one side of the garden, and loads of bushes and plants on the other. A few people are picking and placing fruits and vegetables in baskets. Children are playing in the treehouse in the distance, and a few men are building a chicken coop at the far end of the valley.

Did I fall into *Little House on the Prarie?*

I take a few deep breaths and look at the door. I have one of two choices, stay here or go and explore. The curious fucker inside me is telling me to rain hell on this house, but I don't even know what to expect on the other side of this door.

What if they're waiting for me on the other side of it with guns raised, ready to shoot?

My lower lip trembles, tears rolling down my cheeks as this aching feeling in my stomach takes hold. I can panic, I can kick and scream. But what good will it do?

I hold my breath and squeeze my eyes shut, whipping open the door. To my surprise, nothing but a gust of wind from the force of the door brushes my face. The hallway is nothing but beige walls, decorative accent furniture, and a staircase that seeps laughter.

Where the hell am I?

Creeping back into the room, I search for something I can use as a weapon. Of course, there's nothing. But the stainless steel candle holders will be good enough.

Most of the bedroom doors are open, unmade beds and more stuffed animals crowd the rooms. While neatly folded clothes and well-placed shoes crowd the rest.

Laughter hits my eardrum again and I stand at the top of the stairs, my heart beating like a jackrabbit.

Fuck, I don't know what to expect. I don't know what I'm about to walk into.

The hair on the back of my neck rises as I take the first step, gripping the candle holder until my nails dig into my palm.

Voices hit my ears, multiple women and children laughing as someone speaks.

A chill licks up my spine as the front door shoots open and two little boys run in, one running past me up the stairs, the other running to the kitchen.

I close my eyes, dizziness taking hold again, and glimpses of what happened to me flash through my mind. Slade and I were joking about my dream, then someone hit him on the head. A van showed up and someone in a devil mask grabbed me, placing chloroform on my mouth.

I called for Riggs until my voice cracked and then everything went black.

Ugh, fucking pricks.

Adjusting the candle holder in my hand, I round the corner at the bottom of the stairs and tiptoe as the floorboards crack under my shoes.

The kitchen is wild with people, cooking and placing jam into jars. No one notices me until the little boy who ran past tugs on an older woman's apron. "Look, that lady is up," he says, pointing at me.

The older woman turns, silencing the kitchen. Her dark salt and pepper hair is tied in two French braids, smile lines around her eyes are deeply grooved as freckles decorate her cheekbones. And when she smiles, I drop the candle holder and bring a hand to my mouth.

"Good morning, Zay," she says, wiping her hands. "How did you sleep, sweetie?"

My breathing is short, wavering. I grip the doorframe to steady myself as she steps forward. "You're…holy shit, you're their mother."

She smiles, studying my face, curling a lock of my hair around her finger and tucking it behind my ear. "I see why my boys are so fascinated by you. You truly are breathtaking."

I expel a breath, looking at the other women watching me. I feel it, that overwhelming sensation bursting through me. Dizziness takes hold, sweat beads glisten on my forehead, and a roaring bursts through my stomach. "You're supposed to be dead."

She touches my face, turning it so I'm looking at her. Gosh, those eyes. Peter has her eyes. "I had no choice but to make them believe that, sweetie. Until it's safe again, they mustn't know."

I place a hand on my stomach. "Oh, God, I think I'm gonna be sick."

One of the women grabs a pot from the rack behind them and holds it in front of me as I release the bile in my throat. Mama rubs my back, shushing me softly and humming. God, why is she humming? How is she not dead?

Am I dead?

Holy fuck, what the fuck is happening?

I groan, shaking my head. "No, no. You're dead. They told me you died—they told me...they—"

She smooths out my hair and smiles sweetly. "That's what they had to know."

I whimper, spitting in the pot. "But—"

"Come, sweetie, there's a lot we need to discuss. We'll talk over tea," Mama says, wiping my mouth with her apron and guiding me to the kitchen table. I sit down and pull in a rush of air, whimpering as I stare at her making us tea. "You've been asleep for nineteen hours, I think you could use something to eat, no?"

Their mother is here.

Their mother isn't dead.

They worship a woman who betrayed them, too. All of the shit they know about her is a lie. How is she so calm? Why is she so calm? Oh, God, I think I need that pot again.

I put my head in my hand and breathe, closing my eyes and imagining myself home in bed with Adam, laughing like we used to, innocent like we used to be back at university.

Back when things were normal. Safe.

I miss those days the most.

Mama sets down two cups, filling them with scalding water that smells like fresh flowers. "You must be wracking your brain with questions."

I chuckle awkwardly, looking around as the women continue to fill jars with fresh jam as more is cooking on the stove. "What is this place?"

She sits down, places a blueberry scone in front of me, and takes a breath. "I want to apologize for how my men approached you. That is not how I work. I got out of that life for a reason, but some of the men here are far too lost to escape it."

"Are you The Ghost?" I ask, hands shaking as I reach for the tea. I have a million questions. One is why she didn't contact her boys.

She shakes her head and chuckles. "No, sweetie. The Ghost is someone we lost very long ago. His men work for us, for protection, but I've been trying to put a stop to them. It's taking more time than I intended." She smiles when we lock eyes. All of Peter comes crashing in. His innocence, his thoughtful kindness. It's all right here. "Anyway, I want to apologize once again for that. Are you still a little dizzy?"

"I'm okay," I tell her, looking over as the backdoor swings open and more children come running through. "Is this like a group home?"

She takes my hand, squeezing it and smiling. "Let me show you around and I'll answer all your questions. My Peter loved telling stories, now it's time you heard mine."

I inhale through my nose and out through my mouth as she rises, taking her tea with her. It's like she's been waiting for me to wake up so she can speak. No, like she's been waiting to tell her story for years but had no one who knows her past life who would understand. "You have to tell them you're alive."

She pushes open the back door, blinding me with the sunlight as she steps off the porch and onto the grass. "In due time."

Sipping the tea, it's heat burns down my throat. Irritating the bile that coats it. Everyone seems so happy here. So free. They're picking vegetables, eating apples, and laughter seeps all around us. This sanctuary is heaven, it has to be. I've died, that's what happened. I've died and popped into a TV show—one of those Thursday night sitcoms.

She places a hand on my back, looking at the sky. "I first met Richard when I was seventeen. I snuck out of my parents' house and we met at the clubhouse. He was the most handsome man I've ever laid eyes on, but he was too much of a sinner for me to even question trying to give away my innocence. But I couldn't help myself. I smiled at him, even though I was saving myself like God wanted me to until I married a devoting man. Well, things didn't turn out that way."

She grins, sipping her tea as she side glances at me. We pass a row of people digging out carrots, bidding their good mornings at us. "Richard and I eloped when my parents kicked me out for smoking his cigarettes. He took me in and loved me without asking any questions. It's funny, we got married right there under the jacaranda tree." She nods at the tree. "I have a funny feeling he only married me so I would sleep with him." She laughs, shaking her head as she inhales. "But we did it. We married after knowing each other for a week and he swept me right off my feet. I was too naïve to know the truth of his doings, his past, *himself*. He loved me, though. He adored everything about me. But I was scared of him. As much as he stole my heart, his ways were wicked. And wicked men always get punished."

We step over to the jacaranda tree and she points at the carvings in it. Two Rs are in a circle as an RJ and P are etched right outside of it. "I did that when I was pregnant with Riggsy and that one when I had Peter. I brought them here whenever Richard left. He used to leave often, more often than I liked. Business in other states most of the time. And while all the other men cheated, he never did. Until I got pregnant with Peter. He did once during all our years together, and for some reason, it was my fault…but that was the way of a biker's wife. We're trained to shut up and take it. However, there was only so much taking I could allow."

She inhales a breath, smiling at the carving in the tree of her sons' initials. "I always told my boys that they'd burst into flames for having Donnelly blood running through their veins. And I tried to stop them from being like their daddy. I made them go to church and Sunday school, but Richard always got his way. My boys weren't allowed back in the church until they begged God for forgiveness. By that time, Richard had his hold on them and I was too late." She leans on the tree, raking her eyes over my body. "You got sucked into the wicked ways, too, didn't you?"

I'm tongue-tied, trying to wrap my brain around this fucking shitshow of a reveal. Peter would break down in tears, Riggs would hit something, and Adam would be speechless, just staring at the woman who raised him like she were a rare artifact at a museum.

"Not by choice," I say softly. "I married Adam, not the club…but my wicked ways came back to bite me in the ass, and marrying Adam came with a price."

She nods like she knows what I did to Peter. What he did to me. And what Riggs suffered for. "Richard tried to kill me many times, y'know. He's raped me, beat me for talking back, but I saw it in his eyes after he'd strike me, that forgiveness. It was the devil shooting through him that caused it. But deep down, he would always be that good-hearted man who loved and cherished me." She nods, sipping her tea. "One day, Zay, you'll be free."

That hits me hard. I can't help but sob as I stare at Riggs's initial. He's promised me freedom, happiness. Adam, too. But I don't believe them. How can I? Everything surrounding them ends in ruin. Who's to say if they come to save me, this rescue won't end in ruin, too?

I stare at her radiating beauty; a face I've stared at for years. So reminiscent of the men I cherish. I wonder why she never left sooner. Why she allowed the suffering to go on for so long? Our similarities are uncanny, it's frightening.

"Why did you wait so long to free yourself from his clutches?"

Her shoulder slowly rises, looking into her tea cup. "Not all of God's fallen angels can rid themselves of the devil."

That hits hard.

Sinking my heart.

I feel her pain, I see it in her eyes. She was at a crossroads, loving the man who hurt her. Devoting her life to him and raising his babies. In some ways, I see myself in her. I stay because I love these men. I stay because I devoted so many years to them, to helping and loving them.

I, too, am a fallen angel trying to escape the clutches of the devils who lured me in.

She smiles at a young couple walking by, the girls are holding hands and giggling. This place is freeing. Allowing these poor people to live as they please after being taken against their will. She saved them. Every single one.

"I planned on leaving Richard the day after Peter's eighteenth birthday. I told my boys I'd be away for a while and that I'd come find them when it was safe. But I never had the chance to leave. Richard found out about my plan, he thought I was a rat. He thought I didn't love him anymore. That I wanted him dead. All because he caught me with my brother delivering him a list of names of the girls he had to save." She sniffs, shaking her head. "Richard shot me in the stomach for betraying him, then immediately rushed me to the hospital. But he didn't know I survived. My boys didn't know, either. I wanted to keep it that way because if my boys knew, they'd come looking for me. And if they came looking for me, they'd end up hurt or killed because of my dealings with ending the trafficking.

"Richard was money hungry and when Roaden dropped this in his lap, he couldn't say no. He knew it was wrong. But money speaks volumes, sweetie. And if my boys found out about the trafficking, I feared they would get involved. Richard brainwashed them to their core with his wickedness." She inhales, looking up at the tree. "All this here, these are all the women I've saved and continue to save. All the children and men, too. I'm doing good for this wild world. Something my boys should be proud of."

Scanning the area, I do see the tranquility of this place. The peace it brings. That peace that Riggs always sought was right out of reach. If only he knew, things would be so different. He may have followed in his father's footsteps, but Riggs is a good man. He wouldn't let this happen.

"This was my parents' house, they gave it to me when Peter was born but I never told Richard. I thought this could be my haven when I was finally able to leave with my boys, but that day never happened. Richard brainwashed both of them into being a Snake. And, well, we all do things we regret in life. Mine happens to be lying to my boys and never being able to see them become men," she finishes, tilting my chin up as a tear rolls down my cheek. A soft grin spreads to her lips as if she can read all the words I'm unable to say by the look on my face. "I never got to see them live or be happy."

I'm at a loss for words. Here I am complaining about my life and how shitty it's been when it's nothing in comparison to this woman before me.

This truly angelic woman only wanted the best for her family.

Much like me.

"Your boys may have taken the wrong path, but they're good men. Strong men who would do anything for each other," I say, nodding softly. "They saved me in so many ways."

She chuckles, moving hair off my shoulder. "And would do anything for you, it seems."

I nod, sniffling. "I'm pretty sure they will. But how do you know that?"

"You wouldn't still be standing here if they didn't," she says, putting her arm out to me.

Another sentence that hits me hard.

Because she's right. Riggs manhandled me a lot the first time we met, but there was a soft side I brewed out of him. A love that grew and shaped him into the person he's become.

Peter has always been wicked, I don't think it'll ever truly leave him; but again, his love for me continues to grow triumphantly. And he's learned from his mistakes.

And then there's my Adam, a man who has always been a softy with me until shit hit the fan and he became powerful, domineering.

Sometimes I don't even recognize him.

But he will always be the love of my life.

Through and through.

I hook my arm with Mama's, feeling at peace with her. Feeling like we've connected on a deeper level only we can truly understand. She taps my hand, a smile spreading to her lips, and leads me to the apple trees. "If you're wondering how I know so much about my boys, your answer is right there." She points to one of the apple trees, and my heart sinks again.

Dorian has Rosa strapped to her chest, picking apples and dropping them in a basket. I always admired what Peter saw in her. She's absolutely beautiful. The way her dark hair falls in subtle waves, her round cheeks, and her plump lips shape her face into the perfect woman. Someone he needs.

But she betrayed him, much like Mama did to her husband and her sons. Peter sought refuge in her, someone who was just like his mother.

Dorian kisses the top of Rosa's head, and glances in our direction, face pale and sweat sparkling on her brow. "Zay?" She steps off the ladder and glances at Mama, keeping a protective hand on the baby. "Y-you're awake?"

I put my hand on my mouth as Rosa turns her head and smiles when we lock eyes, making me whimper. "Oh, God."

Mama rubs my back, smiling at the baby. "She's a mini version of my Peter."

She takes my teacup and places both of ours on a tree stump, smiling at us. There's that pride oozing out of her I see when Riggs looks at Carter. Their reason to be on this Godforsaken earth. Placing a hand on my heart, my eyebrows raise when Dorian wipes a tear from her cheek. I should be screaming, charging at her. But there's a reason she left. There's a reason she came here.

There's always an explanation.

"C-can I hold her?" I ask, my voice cracking.

A smile crests her face as she unwraps the baby from her chest and kisses her cheek before handing her over. I'm a mess of dizziness, fatigue, laughter, and tears. But it's all worth it to see my niece's little smiling face.

"Are they here?" Dorian asks, fidgeting with her fingers.

I nod quickly, bringing Rosa's head to my lips and inhaling that baby smell Carter lost a long time ago. "Why did you do it?"

She glances at Mama and chokes on a sob. The old me would feel bad for her. The old me would cheer her on for getting out of this life. But she has no idea what she put my family through. No fucking idea. "I had no choice. If I didn't leave, they were going to kill him."

I swallow thickly, gritting my teeth. "Who was?"

"The Ghost," she says as Mama places a hand on her shoulder. "My brother, Wilde, he's…his girlfriend at the time was taken and sold into sex trafficking. Daddy and Roaden were the two that helped lead to her kidnapping. Wilde hasn't forgiven them. I don't think he ever will."

I bob Rosa slightly. "The guys in the demon masks?"

"They work for Wilde." Mama steps in. "They help find the girls and bring them to me, but they don't go about things in the right manner."

"Like shooting up my house with my son inside it, and kidnapping me?" I spit out, huffing. "You know Peter and Riggs had nothing to do with your brother's girlfriend."

Dorian nods, wiping her cheek. "I tried to explain it to him, but my brother is so stubborn. He doesn't care. He's planning on destroying the club and anyone affiliated with it."

I wince, letting Rosa grip my finger. "I had nothing to do with it. Carter has nothing to do with it, Adam, neither. This is insanity, Dorian. You have to get him to stop or at least have a sit down with them."

She looks at Mama, shaking her head. "I don't know how."

Mama smooths out my hair, smiling at Rosa. "I'm going to fix everything, my sweeties. I'm going to right all the wrongs I did."

Dorian scoffs, furrowing her brows. "We can't."

"We will."

"I'm not ready."

Mama kisses Rosa's cheek and chuckles. "I think it's about time I see my boys, don't you?"

My heart is hammering violently, looking at Mama as she curls another lock of hair behind my ear. Her story is maddening. Her life is a soap opera. But this reality is coming to a close. The finish line is just out of reach yet something is telling me none of us will be able to cross it, not until we end things. Not until we satisfy everyone's revenge.

And that's the biggest problem, isn't it?

Zay

We've been standing by the apple tree for a few minutes, basking in the beauty of the farm. Other houses are on the property aside from the main house. Loads of little shacks span the far end of the property by the corn fields. Every couple has a tiny house, every person has a safe place. It's a great thing Mama is doing. I wish she told her boys about it. They would have helped her the right way. No killing, no lies, no pain, only safety in a new life.

Dorian and Mama have filled up two baskets of apples as I get to have my moment with Rosa. Getting to know my beautiful niece who is so happy and protected here, unlike Carter. He's trapped in the web like me, burning with the venom from the Snakes. He'll be free soon. I'll make sure of it. Even if we come here, he'll be rid of this life.

I kiss Rosa's nose and she giggles, making Mama smile at me as we continue walking through the garden. It's absolute paradise out here. Birds chirping in the trees, goats roaming the land, and pigs and chickens have their respectable areas, too.

A butterfly glides by as I look at the clear blue sky and a smile touches my face. For over three years I was a slave to this club, someone who suffered by its hand. Albeit, I deserved it for what I tried to do to Peter—I paid my dues with a bullet to the chest. I suffered enough.

One day, you'll be free.

One day, I will. And when that day comes, I will not regret saying goodbye to anything this club is associated with.

Dorian cracks her knuckles, glancing at me. She's uncomfortable, as she should be. The last time we saw each other she ran away from us with Rosa in her belly. Leaving Peter a destroyed mess. I wonder how much of what she told us was the truth and how much she spilled was just lies conjured up so she can fulfill this fucked up plan.

I look in front of me at the blue butterfly again, landing on a sunflower in the distance. That anger boils to the surface, churning an ache in my belly that needs to erupt before I scream. "Why did you do it?" I ask again. "Do you know what you put Peter through? All the nights he kept me up weeping. Snorting cocaine and drinking himself into a metaphorical coma. You fucked him, Dorian. Broke a man into a million pieces when he was finally healed. And all you do is send him a single letter four months after his daughter is born. That's fucked up. Even for someone like you."

She's sobbing, nodding her head in understanding. But I don't care. I don't want to comfort her. I don't want to tell her it'll be okay. I don't want anything other than my niece home with me. "I'm sorry," she whimpers. "I truly did have no choice."

I growl, flaring my nostrils when Mama puts her hand on my shoulder, and then smooths out my hair. Why do I find this oddly calming? The same way Riggs can relax me with a stare, or stroke of my cheek.

Mama takes Dorian's hand and squeezes, inhaling a breath. "Wilde came to my brother, Liam, many years ago when his girlfriend Lenora was taken. I happened to be there giving my brother intel when Wilde arrived." She taps Dorian's hand, furrowing her brows. "We planned this together. Built this sanctuary for the women we saved from trafficking. Unfortunately, we couldn't save Lenora. No matter how hard I tried and how many times I risked my life for those women, we couldn't save her." She looks at the sky and closes her eyes for a moment. "Wilde is vengeful. He won't stop until he kills everyone involved. I left to save my boys. If they knew I was alive, Richard would hurt them just to spite me. Dorian did the same thing. She left to save them."

Scoffing, I shake my head. "And what about Shyanne, huh? What the fuck was that for?"

Mama moves a flyaway hair behind my ear. "A life for a life."

I look away, blinking rapidly to hide my tears. *A life for a life.* She died for the sins of her father-in-law. Something Riggs didn't know about. She died for no fucking reason. "She didn't deserve that. If Wilde is trying to save these women from being sold into sex trafficking, then he wouldn't go by that motto. He wouldn't kill someone who was nothing but a saint. Shyanne didn't deserve that." I glare at Dorian. "And you fucking know she didn't."

"He was aiming for Riggs, but he missed," Dorian sobs. "Shyanne died because of Wilde's shitty shot."

"And Dorian left so no one else had to die," Mama adds, wiping a tear from my cheek.

I move my head away, sniffling. "Your brother's shitty shot left Carter without a mother."

"I'm sorry," Dorian whispers.

Looking away, the fear and anger take hold, and I sob with Rosa bobbing in my arms. They have no idea what life has been like for me. They have no idea what I've suffered—no, they do. Mama nearly died for this club and faked her death to escape it. Dorian gave up a life with Peter and their daughter to save him.

They know exactly what I'm going through. If I'm being honest, I'm the only one who doesn't know true pain. I haven't lost anyone. I haven't given up anyone.

We're one and the same.

Before I turn back to them, I spot Judas talking to one of the guys. He isn't wearing his leather vest but he's handing them papers. A stack of them, pointing at something, and the other guy is nodding. Is he the rat Adam was talking about? Judas is doing what Mama did all those years ago.

"Why is Judas here?" I ask, frowning.

"He's giving us information from the club. Panthers want to join forces with the Snakes, and Riggs is considering it last I heard, but it's not the smartest idea." Mama stares at Judas, pushing her lips together. "The Panthers still help in taking women. Judas saved his girlfriend from the horrors of what could happen. And has made it his priority to avoid anything to do with the Panthers."

I glance at Judas again, shock filling my veins. "Why didn't he say anything to Riggs?"

There's so much we don't know. So much that was kept in the dark from us.

"He thought Wilde would be able to stop the Panthers before the merger." Dorian steps forward, wiping drool from Rosa's mouth. "But Riggs hasn't had a sit down with anyone yet."

I scoff, letting a growl seep through my lips. "He's been in mourning as I'm home raising the baby, of course, he has no fucking time." I narrow my eyes, looking away from Judas. "I think Riggs needs to have a sit down with your brother, not the Panthers."

Mama bops Rosa on the nose as we continue walking. "I do, too, sweetie."

What am I doing here?

Why did I involve myself with these men and their wicked ways?

Why do I stay?

A tear rolls down my cheek as Mama places her hand on my lower back, turning us toward the chicken coop. "Rosa loves chickens," Mama says, laughing. Her laugh is comforting. The perfect way to help change the godawful subject. "She giggles the most when we walk in he—"

A siren blares, sending everyone into a panic. The siren is loud, booming—the rapture. Whatever everyone's doing is dropped, and they run to the large light blue warehouse at the far left of the property. All the women, children, and teenagers head that way. Even the people in the house are scrambling to get out. Men scramble to help the children, carrying some, and taking the hands of others. Anything to get to the warehouse.

What on earth is happening?

My eyes widen, looking at Mama. "What the fuck is this?"

"Someone's trying to get in—"

Guns go off near the house, and men helping the others, pull guns from their pants and dart for the sound. This is supposed to be a sanctuary for trafficked people. Why do these men have guns as if they're ready to attack at any given moment?

Dorian ushers us toward the warehouse, looking back at the main house with furrowed brows. The gunshots get louder, causing Rosa to start to whimper and cry in my arms.

But there's no time to stop.

No time to comfort her as bullets head our way and hit the trees around us. Holy shit, what the fuck is happening.

Dorian yelps as more gunshots go off and she pummels to the ground. "Fuck!"

More bullets rain on us, grazing my leg and upper arm. Fear licks up my neck as I look down at Rosa, her cheek sprayed in my blood.

She's screaming, but she's okay.

Thank fuck, she's okay. She'll be okay. She'll be safest with me. I have the protection of those fallen angels that call me their girl looming over me.

Mama drops to her knees beside Dorian as I hide behind a tree with Rosa, shushing her and soothing her the best I can. "They hit your leg."

"Keep going, I'll be fine," Dorian groans, gripping her leg as blood squirts from it. "Just get Rosa out of here, please."

Tears well in my eyes, glancing back at the house. "We're not leaving you behind!"

"Get her out of here!" she yells, covering her head as more bullets surround us. "Mama Rosa, please. Get my daughter out of here."

Mama looks at me and nods, putting her arm around Dorian. "I'm getting you to the house." She secures her arm around her waist. "We can make it, okay?"

Dorian winces, crying softly as we make our way to the warehouse, praying we don't get hit. For a sanctuary, this is extremely psychotic. But the men who take these women happen to be dangerous. Men that wouldn't bat an eye knowing how many women and children live in this house. They'll rain bullets on this place to get the diamond they want.

A few of the teenage boys come our way, sliding their arms around me and Dorian, helping us get there faster. "Four men stormed the gates, our guards just started shooting," the one whose arm's around me says.

Mama looks over her shoulder and growls, urging us forward. "Is there a walkie inside?"

The boy helping Mama nods, glancing back at the house with a worried wrinkle on her forehead.

Two more young women hold the doors for us, slamming it shut as soon as we're inside. Rosa's cries surround us and I don't know what to do. I don't know how to calm her.

She doesn't know me. All she knows is this house.

This sanctuary.

She doesn't need me. She needs her mother. She needs a family.

Dorian collapses on a chair, whimpering as she pulls herself into a seated position, and tucks her hand under the cushion of the chair beside her, pulling out a snub nose like the one Riggs taught me how to shoot. "Where's Karen? Fuck, where is she?"

Mama takes the gun and tosses it aside as a woman with a pink hijab comes our way, white metal case in hand. "What happened, Mama Rosa? What's going on?"

"I'll find out, Karen." Mama looks at me. "This isn't supposed to happen here."

The boy who shielded me touches my arm. "You're hit."

"It's okay," I say through a cry. "Can you get her something? A pacifier? A bottle?" I wince as I look down at her again. "A cloth to clean this blood from her face?"

He nods, taking the bandana from his back pocket and wrapping it around my arm. Everyone is packed in here like sardines, but this seems routine to them. Normal.

"Does this happen often?" I ask the girl closest to me.

Shakes her head, looking down at the ground. "We do drills, though, in case it ever does."

"The men we rescue everyone from are cruel, sick bastards. There's no denying something like this would happen eventually," Mama says, stepping past us and going deeper into the warehouse.

The sirens stop abruptly as Dorian sucks in her teeth. Karen is tending to her bullet wound, inspecting and poking the hole. "I have to get the bullet out to see the damage, okay?"

The teenage boy comes back and places his hand on my upper back, holding a bottle for Rosa. "She's probably hungry," he says, lifting the bottle as he bites down on his lip ring. "I'm Sebastian."

I frown, wondering where I've heard that name before. Why is it ringing bells?

He has scars on his neck, matching ones on his wrists, as if he were in restraints. Wherever he was taken, whoever had taken him, I'm sure forced him to do things. Used him as a pet.

All of these people have nightmare stories as to where they were before they got here.

Horror stories that are every person's worst nightmare.

Mama is going good here, saving all these people. Helping them heal.

My heart sinks when I see children with matching scars on their wrists and ankles. Such a fucked up and disgusting world we live in.

Dorian groans, whimpering when someone wraps a towel around her leg. "Zay?" Dorian says, looking up at me. "At the back of this warehouse, there's a door that leads to the far side of the property. Take the blue Volkswagen, keys are in the ignition and there's a diaper bag in the trunk."

"I can't just leave, what about all these people?" I panic, covering Rosa's head with my hand as she drinks the milk. "This place is supposed to be a safe place is it not?"

Mama returns with a bucket of water and towels on her shoulder. She is as calm as ever, fixing her scarf around her shoulders. "I told you, the men who help us find the women are not men to trust. This is exactly why I'm trying to fix things. But sometimes, shit hits the fan."

"Shit really hit the fan today," one of the teenage boys says, crouching down beside Dorian.

Mama is handed a walkie-talkie as worried and panicked faces stare at us. "Things will be okay. Please relax everyone."

She smiles, pulling in a breath as she presses the button on the walkie-talkie, calling whoever is listening. "Hold your fire! We have babies in here!"

Static.

She presses the button again and car alarms go off in the distance. "Hold your fire!"

"Zay, please, go," Dorian pleads, sobbing as Karen digs into her leg. "Fuck!

A few more shots go off before they're silenced and all we can hear are the car alarms before those are silenced, too. Who's here? Which one of these women do these monsters need back so desperately?

"Zay!" Dorian yells. "Please, get her out of here now!"

Mama grumbles, gritting her teeth the way Riggs does when he's pissed off. She presses the side of the walkie-talkie again, growling into it. "Whoever the fuck is shooting at us, better stop! We have injured people here. Again, children and babies! Hold your fire so we can get them help."

Static.

I look at Dorian's wet gray eyes and see the pleading desperation in them. Her lower lip quivers as she stares at her daughter. "Zay, please. If anything happens to me, you keep her away from this life. You keep her away from this club—"

"Nothing is going to happen to you Dorian, okay?" I interrupt her, weeping softly.

Karen inhales, wrapping the towel around Dorian's leg. "I need to get her to the operating table, Mama Rosa."

Mama exhales slowly, closing her eyes for a moment. Peter gets his beauty from his mother. Those high cheekbones, long lashes, freckles, and the little pout on her lips. Riggs and Peter don't have many similarities aside from their height, the shape of their eyes, and their striking blue irises. But seeing Mama in front of me, her boys get all their soft features from her.

"Okay," she says, opening her eyes. "Karen, Donnie, Mitchel. You will take Dorian to the first aid hut and get her fixed as fast as you can. I will greet our unwelcomed guests and settle this intrusion."

No one talks back. They move quickly, Donnie and Mitchel lift Dorian and head to the back of the warehouse with Karen following suit.

I don't move. I stare at Mama as she lifts the walkie-talkie to her lips and parts them to speak. "Someone answer me."

The walkie-talkie statics, a deep voice coming through. "We need you out front. They promised they won't shoot anymore, but they wanna talk to the person in charge."

My stomach sinks.

My heart racing wildly.

"I'm coming with you," I spit out as Mama holds the walkie-talkie to her mouth.

"No," she replies, pressing the button on the walkie-talkie. "I'm coming out." She tosses the walkie-talkie on the chair and lets out a breath as she faces the panicked gazes of everyone in the warehouse. "Everyone stay in here until I return. I promise this is all a misunderstanding."

She goes for the main door, and one of the older women unlocks the deadbolt.

Fear licks up my spine, but there's no time for me to think. I have to get out there and see what this is. My tummy telling me it's my saving grace.

Mama steps out into the sun and I charge after her with Rosa in my arms, acting like a fucking idiot and risking our lives for a hunch that Riggs and Slade are the ones who are out there looking for me.

"What're you doing?" Mama asks, glaring at me the way Peter does when I don't listen. "I don't know if it's safe—"

"It could be Riggs, and if it is, he'll need me more than ever seeing you again," I interrupt her, tears rolling down my cheeks.

Her gaze flickers from one of my eyes to the other, tears welling in them as well. She completely understands and doesn't say anything else. Allowing me to stand by her side as we face whoever it may be at the gates.

My tummy is telling me Riggs fought tooth and nail to find me. Burning down the town to make sure he sees me again.

And he will.

He'll get everything he could ever want in a few short minutes. All the happiness he could ever ask for.

Today, we'll be free.

Peter

Riggs barely slept a wink last night. I heard him roaming the room, taking a shower, then sitting outside for a bit. Adam was with him, too. They sat outside for a good two hours just staring at the stars without saying a single word. Zay would love them here at night. The stars were so clear and sparkled so brightly. We'd float for hours just watching them.

The only words Adam spoke were when he pushed up off the bench and looked back at Riggs, *you should get some sleep.*

Riggs grunted his response, as usual, *I'll sleep when she's home.*

Adam cried most of the night, trying his hardest not to wake Slade up. But I think Slade can sleep through anything. I've seen him passed out during one of the punk rock shows at the bar, as if it was his goddamn white noise.

"Hey," I whispered around three in the morning, reaching my hand out to Adam.

He sat at the edge of the bed and sniffed, wiping his nose. "Go to sleep, Peter. I'll be fine."

"We'll bring her home, okay?" I sat up, too, swinging my legs off the bed. Adam placed a hand on his face, shaking his head. "Hey, look at me."

"Why is she even with me? All I ever do is disappoint her. Fuck, I dragged her into this mess. I got her shot, and look at us now. She's missing and it's all my fault. I couldn't protect my wife because I was too busy being part of something she hates more than anything in this world." Adam wiped his eyes as Slade stirred a little, turning over to face us with half-glazed eyes. "I promised her a lifetime of happiness and all I gave her was an ending. Pure fucking hell."

Riggs came in, looking at me and closing the door behind him, eyebrows pinched together. He seemed more worried and sad now than he did when Shyanne died.

"What if she's dead?" Adam whispered as a whimper escaped his lips. "And what if she is pregnant? My sad excuse as her husband couldn't even protect her. I let her go—"

"We all let her go knowing the risks," Riggs interrupted him.

I take Adam's hand, holding it the way he did when Zay put me in the hospital. "She did this for me. To bring my daughter home."

Slade rubbed an eye, turning onto his back as his groggy voice filled the room. "I was right next to her and didn't pay attention."

Riggs stepped forward, getting onto the bed behind me. "We're all to blame. If she's fucking dead, that's a weight we have to carry for the rest of our sad excuse of a life."

Riggs turned over, grunting and mumbling to himself before silence consumed us.

We were a bunch of sad grumpy fucks who just want our saving grace back.

We didn't get much more sleep after that. Riggs woke us up at the crack of dawn eager to find the place the cop spoke about. I wondered why he mentioned it to us. What is this place and why would her kidnappers bring her there? If she's there. Is it a trap?

I'm standing in front of the dresser, stretching out my back as Adam comes out of the bathroom. We're a bunch of comfortable guys because he's naked, and so am I.

I never noticed before but he has a tattoo. Adam's the only one of us without a Snake tattoo, shit, I just got mine three years ago. But it's the only tattoo I have.

Adam has a Z on his hip bone, something small and private for the two of them. "You look the place up?"

I nod, getting into a pair of boxers. "Yeah, it's about twenty-five minutes north of here. The place is called Maddison's Gardens."

Slade narrows his eyes, sitting upright after tying his shoes. "Maddison's

Gardens? The safe house for abused women?"

I take my phone from the dresser, slide it open, and find the website. I scroll through the website but nothing on it tells me anything other than what fresh produce we can purchase from the local market. "It seems like a regular farm."

Slade shakes his head, glancing at me, then Riggs sitting behind him on his phone. "No, I don't think it is. It's like a front or something."

"How do you know?" Adam asks, putting his jeans on.

"One of the chicks I used to fool around with from the group home said her sister was at this place. It's for women who were saved from all walks of life," Slade replies, scratching the back of his head. "If it's true, then we have to be prepared. These fucks are protected like a fortress."

Riggs puts his phone down, narrowing his eyes. "You been?"

Slade shakes his head again. "The chick told me stories of the guys who saved her. Fuckers were armed to the nines. They kept her there for a few months until it was safe enough for her to re-enter the world without the fear that she'd be kidnapped and sold again. But I don't think these people will like a bunch of bikers showing up asking questions."

"We're going to see if Zay's there. Ain't our fault they're paranoid fucks," Riggs scoffs. "If they're armed, then we will be, too."

Adam's frowning, deep in thought, but he isn't saying anything. He's staring at the carpet in front of him, chest rising and falling. He sighs, pinching the bridge of his nose before dropping his hand. "We ready?"

Something isn't sitting right with me.

And I have a huge fucking feeling it has everything to do with this farm we're about to go to. Like Zay says, she can feel it in her tummy. And mine is rumbling like a motherfucker right now.

***

About a year ago, three months into making Zay see me every Tuesday afternoon, I sat at the bar, making her a whiskey drink and waiting for her to arrive. Judas and Mickey were talking by the pool table, but I don't think they noticed me there.

Judas sucked his teeth, breaking the pool balls. "MG is running smoothly, we got six more in this week."

Mickey nodded, eyeing the balls and finding the right angle. "Got the guys out getting three more today."

"Fuckin' A," Judas said, chalking his pool cue.

"Think we should get out there soon, tell her what's going down with those fucks out west," Mickey said, still talking in some sort of code so none of what they said made sense. "MG is going to save so many lives."

MG, what the fuck was that?

I frowned, looking at them and getting off the bar stool. "What're you guys talking about?"

Judas eyed me, hitting a few balls into one of the holes. "Don't worry yourself none."

Mickey cleared his throat. "It's just a movie we're talking about."

"A movie? What movie?" I lean my forearms on the bartop.

"Last time I checked, I'm your president, VP. Stay in your lane," Judas said, taking his beer and draining it.

I stepped forward, gritting my teeth about ready to tear them a new asshole when the door opened and Zay walked in.

Zaynab nodded at Judas and Mickey, their eyes raking over her. "Hey, guys."

Judas swallowed hard eyeing me at the bar, turning a brighter shade of red. He smiled at Zay. "Have fun."

I stared at them, feeling their lies spewing from their glare. I should've gone forward, beat the answers out of them. But Zay was in a short black dress that had me wilding.

The whore behind the bar gave me two whiskey sours and a beer, grinning at Zay as she eyed me and continued to my room. She looked extra pissed today, something about it had me going, but something about it also had me confused. She was never happy to be here, yet her being here felt wrong. For the first time since things started, it felt wrong.

I neglected the club when she was around. I neglected *a lot* when she was around, and something kept telling me to forget about Zay for a minute and talk to Judas about what *MG* was.

But my dick had other plans for me. Angry Zay made me hard in five seconds flat.

I took the drinks and jerked my head at Mickey and Judas. "Gimme half an hour, we need to talk."

Heading to my room, that guilt for not prying the truth from their lips ate away at me. But when I rounded the corner and approached my open door, I found Zay standing there in nothing but a black thong. *Oh, holy fuck.* "Hey, I-I got you something to drink."

She took it and gulped half the drink before setting it down. Those perfect tits bounced as she moved. I watched her, mesmerized by her movements. Always in a trance around her. "What're you doing? We only have an hour."

I smirked, tilting my head down. "I take it you're coming around to the idea of us?"

She scoffed with a chuckle. "No, *us* will never happen, Peter. But if you must know." She popped a hip out and crossed her arms. "Adam refuses to have sex with me lately. The last time we had sex was three weeks ago, so these Tuesday sessions are the only thing getting me off." She kicked off her heels and snapped her fingers. "Now, if you don't mind. I have a review in class today that I'd like to get to."

I put my drink down and stopped her, turning her around so her back pressed against my chest. "Mmm, so for once you actually want to do this, huh?"

My hand trailed up her sternum, rounding her breasts and playing with her nipples.

A moan slipped free, making me bite her neck. "Tell me, sweetie, tell me how badly you need my cock," I growled, pushing myself into her.

She bit her lip as my hand traveled lower, past her belly button, and into that thong I still have tucked away in my underwear drawer. "It's not your cock I need, baby. It's an orgasm."

I chuckled in her ear, lowering my voice. "You're telling me my cock can't give you one, huh? My cock can give you multiple, sweetie. Just lie on that fucking bed and spread your legs."

She turned around, tits grazing my t-shirt. "Lock the door."

For once, she wanted me. I didn't care that it was because of Adam. She wanted *me.*

My priorities were fucked. I should've focused on the club. I should've paid attention.

I wasn't.

Instead, I pulled the t-shirt over my head as she opened her legs, that black thong teasing me. I lowered on top of her, dick confined in my jeans that made me ache. Fuck, my balls were throbbing at the thought of being with Zay when she wanted it.

I kissed her chest, tongue licking her nipple and biting them, then my nose trailed down her body. She smelled like heaven, always did. Coconuts.

I bit down on her thong, I pulled it off with my teeth as she propped herself up on her elbows and looked down at me, biting her lip. "Want me to touch myself for you?"

Shaking my head, I inhaled her as I tucked her thong in my pocket before I got out of my jeans. I smirked, sliding my finger over her slit. "You're already so wet."

I looked at that beautiful clean-shaven pussy in front of me, dripping and I wasn't even touching her yet. I was going to make her scream. For once, Zay was going to beg me to fuck her. Ache for me while her legs twitched around my head.

I licked my lips, sliding my tongue up and down her slit as she watched me. I loved it when she watched me.

My tongue dipped inside her, feeling her clench and tighten. "Tell me how badly you want me to lick that clit of yours."

"If you don't lick it in two seconds, I'll get myself off," she said breathlessly.

I growled, forcing two fingers inside her and lifting myself so we were face to face. She tilted her head, feathering her lips with mine. "Touch yourself, then."

She slid her hand between us, parting her lips as a gasp escaped. I fucked her with my fingers, panting on top of her as she started writhing under me. Just where I wanted her to be. I slammed my lips on hers and bit down, lowering myself again and tasting that sweet pussy as she ground it on my face, letting me ride her home.

Her moans filled my ears, sweet nectar squirting all over my face and mouth. Soaking the bed under us. "Fuck, Zaynab. Fuck, you're so sexy," I growled out.

I lapped my tongue once more, before removing my fingers, seeing them glisten as I brought them to my lips. "You taste the fucking best, sweetie."

She growled, gripping the hair on top of my head. "Fuck me, Peter."

So I did.

I fucking rode her all the way around the world, hitting that cervix, then flipping her onto her stomach, and creaming all over that sexy fucking ass.

I loved coming on her. Marking my property even when she refused to be mine.

I cleaned myself, tossing her my t-shirt, and sighing as I watched her wipe my cum from her ass. "God, Zay, you're so fucking sexy."

She dropped the t-shirt and quickly dressed, looking for her thong she wouldn't find because it was in my pocket. "Thanks. See you next week."

She headed for the door, ripping me off like a Band-Aid. But I stopped her, turning her around. "That's it? C'mon, sweetie, at least kiss me goodbye, cuddle me, or finish the drink I made you."

She inhaled sharply, staring at my lips, and kissed me quickly. "I'll see you next week, Peter."

I pouted, cupping her chin to lift her face to mine and opening her mouth with my thumb. "Bye, sweetie."

I kissed her, forcing my tongue into her mouth and moaning softly.

She rolled her eyes, opening the door as I smiled, listening to her footfalls echoing through the bar before the music took over and she was gone.

As I started getting dressed, Lip's laughter hit my ears, bringing me back to reality for a second. Zay wrapped me in her cloud of lust and derailed me, sending me away from the task at hand.

I stuffed my feet into my shoes and pulled a fresh t-shirt over my head as I briskly walked out of my room, looking for Judas. But it was only Lip and the whore who made me drinks at the pool table. "Hey," I said, looking around. "Where's Judas?"

Lip nodded at the door. "Said he had to run an errand. Wouldn't be back until tomorrow."

I flared my nostrils, knowing I should've asked more questions, and made Zay wait for me.

But my infatuation with her took over my common sense.

I wiped a hand down my face and turned to head back to my room, but stopped turning to Lip. "Can I ask you something?" He nodded at me, bringing the beer to his lips. "What's *MG*? I overheard Judas talking to Mickey about it. Something about getting six in and three more today."

Lip shrugged a shoulder. "Maybe a coke shipment?"

I frowned, taking my phone from my pocket. "Yeah, yeah, maybe."

Calling Judas three times that afternoon without so much as a reply.

I tried looking up *MG*, but nothing showed up aside from an automotive marque and the fact that mg stands for milligrams. There wasn't anything that would make sense.

Maybe Judas was getting into cars.

Maybe it was our new side business.

Whatever it was, I fucked my chance at asking him face-to-face what *MG* could be.

Because back then, I didn't care about anything other than Zay.

I let Judas do what he wanted, and when we had chapel, the guys looked up to me but I had nothing to give them without the right guidance.

I fucked up my chances of finding out the truth.

***

We pull up to the farm, but metal gates block us from entering. This place looks like Slade described, a fortress armed to the nines. There are cameras at the gate, shrubs lining the property, and guards standing not too far from the entrance talking with guns tucked into their pants.

"This is a home for abused women?" Adam asks, leaning forward to get a better look. "Those guys have machine guns."

"You sure this ain't some drug lord's house?" Riggs slows the car down, gripping the steering wheel. "We ain't about to walk in here and get shot at for asking questions, are we?"

Slade lifts a shoulder, gripping the back of Adam's chair to lean in. "Look I don't know any more than you do about the place. We can pull up and ask if they've seen Zay, worse comes to worse, we leave and keep scoping out the area. Fuck, maybe there are cameras in town we can look at. Find the license plate or something."

There's something about this house that's making my tummy rumble. There's a huge chance that this could be The Ghost's house. There's an even bigger chance we're about to walk into some place we shouldn't.

As if Mama is blessing us from above, the damn van that Zay was taken in pulls up to the house, a masked man sitting in the front seat.

"Don't have to." I point at the van as Riggs slams on the gas.

None of us stop him, either. We want in this place as badly as he does to find Zay.

Fuck, to find my daughter and if we're lucky, the woman who ripped my heart out.

But charging in here will cause some fucking trouble.

The gates open and the van rolls in, not taking notice of us hot on their tail. Riggs cuts off the van and gets out, his gun tucked into the front of his jeans. "Hey!"

We all pile out of the car, looking at the house in front of us that seems to be flashing through my mind like I've been here before.

Why do I know this house?

The two guards with machine guns raise them and start shouting, sounding an alarm as they do. They're showering us in bullets and we haven't done a damn thing but pull onto their property. We didn't pull our guns out or shoot. We fucking drive in and they're shooting at us like we're in a fucking war.

Shit.

Fucking cunt sucking assholes got me in the fucking arm. "Argh!"

Slade skids to a stop beside me, Adam ducking behind the car after that. "Fucking shit, VP."

I grip my shoulder, looking at Riggs as he pokes his head out the side and fires a couple of shots. "Looks like we're gonna have matching scars, Riggsy."

I grit my teeth as Adam gets into position, too, shooting on the other side of the car.

The alarm blares louder, and screaming women and children echo in the distance.

"Hey!" I yell at Riggs and Adam. "Don't shoot, don't shoot! There are kids here!"

Riggs growls, getting on his knees and poking his head out beside the car again, bullets raining all around us.

This is not a safe place for abused women, it's so much worse than that.

Slade takes off his flannel shirt, tying it around my shoulder and fixing it into a makeshift sling. I let out a yell, moaning from pain. "Sorry," he says, keeping pressure on my wound as he ties the shirt.

I grit my teeth growling as beads of sweat form on my head. "It's fine."

Being shot is not at all as easy as Riggs makes it. The fucker can go on about his day like it's nothing. Shot four times and got up to keep fighting after each one.

He taps my face, taking in the sweat pouring into my eyes. "Walk it off, kid. It's part of the job description."

I grumble, sucking my teeth as I moan from the blinding pain again. But he's right. I'm a fucking Donnelly, I can move past this. I walk it off like the fucking man that I am.

The alarm stops, and seconds later so do the bullets. These guys shot first without question, we definitely do not want to meet their maker.

Riggs puts his hands up, slowly lifting his head above the car. "Guns are tossed, we just wanna ask some questions."

One of the guards steps forward, gun raised. "Who's asking?"

Static moves around us, walkie-talkie interference. Probably the leader telling them to blow our fucking brains out for stepping into their drugs operation.

Because what safe house has this many armed guards?

"Our girl was taken yesterday in town by three guys in a van just like this one and masks just like the one that fucker has on," Riggs shouts. "Just tell us where you took her and we'll leave."

Shuffling moves around us, and I push myself up, looking through the windows of the car as Slade and Adam do the same. "You're the ones who shot at us, y'know," Riggs adds, lifting his shoulders.

"You're the fucks who drove onto our property, *y'know*," one of the guys mocks, machine gun still in hand.

The first guy puts his hands up, snapping his fingers at his buddies to drop the guns, then points at the van. "We have two women and three kids in the van, I'm gonna open the door and bring them inside, is that okay?"

Riggs nods, slowly standing tall. "I have my brothers here, there's four of us. We ain't gonna shoot if you ain't gonna shoot. Can we come in and get our girl?"

There's a guy in a tower, sliding down the ladder and hopping off it with a gun strapped to his back. "She's coming to see what the mess is about," he says to everyone.

The man in the van nods, turning back to us. "You can talk to the woman who runs this place, she'll give you all the answers you want so long as you ain't here to take something that doesn't belong to you."

"You're the one who took something that doesn't belong to you," Adam growls.

Slade looks up at the house, a pretty yellow and white home with so many flowers, it looks like something out of The Secret Garden. "What is this place?"

The guy gets into the van and starts the engine. "A sanctuary for trafficked people."

With that, he pulls the van up to the side of the house, killing the engine again as another man opens the back door.

He wasn't lying; two women step out. One is battered and bruised wearing nothing but chains under the blanket she has draped on her shoulders. The other is wearing a red dress that shows off her ass.

Three kids come out in nightgowns, eyes wide and filled with terror. Children? Fucking children are taken and sold, too! Jesus Christ, this is insanity. Is this the same fucking shit that Daddy was involved in?

"What the fuck?" I let out, seeing the woman in chains pick up the little boy and help him into the house. "Roaden and Daddy were involved in shit like that?"

Riggs grunts, fists clenched at his sides. "Not anymore. Those fucks are rotting in hell for everything they did." He spits at the ground, knowing full well he's spitting at Daddy.

The guy approaches us again, putting his gun down on the ground and raising his hands. "Weapons stay outside, please."

Adam nods, dropping his gun at his feet and lifting his hands. "No problem with that, we just want to see if my wife is inside."

As soon as our weapons are at our feet, Riggs takes the first step and follows the guy inside. Going someplace unknown is normal to us. We've raided homes, entered warehouses, and gone into places blind. Being on unfamiliar grounds is part of the job. But this place isn't unfamiliar. No, I've been here before.

Familiarity infiltrates me as we enter the home, I think Riggs feels it, too, because he exhales slowly, eyes bouncing around the home. The white floral wallpaper on the walls by the stairs sends chills down my spine, the way the floorboards creak under our feet brings a twinkle to my eyes. This house. We've been inside this house before.

Riggs frowns, stopping at the kitchen and stepping into it. Fresh fruits are boiling on the stove, and jars of fresh jam are sitting on a long wooden island. A couple of jars are broken on the floor from having to charge out of there, I'm guessing. I can see the field out back, rows and rows of vegetation, trees, and other homes sit on the property.

Trying to shake the sudden familiarity from myself, I spot a ceramic rooster perched on the windowsill looking at the acres of land. Riggs points at the rooster, face still scrunched up. "Why do I know that thing?"

I shake my head, looking back at Adam who frowns as well. He recognizes this place, too.

"Why don't you join us in the dining room," the guy says, poking his head into the kitchen. "She'll be here any second to answer your questions."

We follow, looking around the place and trying to remember how I know it. Even the familiar scent of dried flowers tickles a distant memory I can't quite get to.

"A cop told us to check out this house," Slade begins, looking at the large material couches. "Are they involved in this, too?"

The guy shakes his head, putting his hands in his pockets. "Local sheriff is seeing the owner of this place. Anytime someone is reported missing, they come here to see if we've heard anything. He's supposed to come by sometime today to ask about that girl that was taken in town."

Riggs puffs out his chest, gritting his teeth. "So you know her? She's here?"

The guy sighs, then nods. "That wasn't my doing. We have some… questionable people who believe in our cause but aren't so clean about their execution. They said there was a woman held against her will—but when she came in yesterday, she was unconscious and the guys had smiles on their faces like they obeyed an order. I'm sorry about that." He jerks his head toward the hallway. "And those fucks opening fire at you without seeing who you are happen to be part of those people."

I scoff, groaning as I adjust the flannel on my shoulder. "Yeah, thanks for that."

He nods at my shoulder, eyeing the blood soaking into my t-shirt. "Want me to take a look at that? We have a doctor on site."

"Yeah, sure," I say, wincing as I try to move my shoulder but the pain searing through me feels like someone is sticking their finger in the hole and toying with it.

The backdoor opens and slams shut, whispering moves through the home and the four of us turn to look at the voices that come our way while the guy eyeing my shoulder stands taller, placing his hands behind his back like someone in the goddamn military.

My heart is beating out of my chest, nerves crawl up my spine and settle that lump in my throat. Why am I so fucking anxious right now?"

Riggs tenses, hands fisting at his sides as he stares at the hallway, preparing himself for whatever is coming.

Then Zay steps forward, blood leaking down her arm and leg. She sniffs, shaking her head. She's here and she's holding a baby.

She's holding *my* baby.

Oh, my fucking God.

"Is that Rosa?" I gasp, coming forward and whimpering when her precious blue eyes find mine. "Oh, my God."

Zay's crying, nodding quickly. She eyes my shoulder, eyebrows pinching together. "Did you shoot up the place looking for me?"

"These fuckers shot at us first, we just returned the favor a little," Slade says.

Zay stares at my shoulder, eyes bouncing from Riggs to Adam, then back to me. But I can't take my eyes off my daughter. She's perfect, beautiful. She's mine.

"I'm okay," I whisper, my shaking hand reaches up to touch that gorgeous little face suckling on a bottle of milk. "Can I hold her?"

She kisses Rosa's head, then hands the baby over, helping adjust her with my good arm.

Fucking shit, I'm holding my daughter. I finally have her in my arms.

My baby girl.

Holy shit. I'm a fucking Daddy!

Riggs steps forward, kissing Zay's head. "She's beautiful," he says to me, placing a hand on her head as the bottle releases from her mouth.

She smiles.

My daughter.

I have my daughter in my arms.

I inhale her and sob, kissing her head as many times as I can. "Hi, baby girl."

Adam places his hand on Zay's back, rubbing it up and down as she wipes her eyes. Adam pulls her in, kisses her, and whispers sweet things only she needs to hear.

But Zay isn't registering anything.

She's watching me hold the baby. She's smiling and sniffling. "Guys, I need you to sit down."

Riggs steps forward, taking her hand and kissing it. "We know about the pregnancy."

She shakes her head quickly, more tears welling and falling. "I'm not pregnant," she whispers. "It was just stress-related."

Adam releases a breath, pulling her into another hug as Riggs leaves a kiss on her head. "You will be. We'll have our forever, baby. Me and you and this fucked up family we have," Adam says into her hair.

"I promise, sunshine," Riggs adds as his lips meet her temple.

She giggles, nodding against Adam's shoulder. "Please sit down."

I kiss my daughter's cheek again, sitting in the armchair behind me as Adam and Riggs pull Zay between them, and Slade leans on the chair behind me, the loyal fuck protecting us if we need it.

"Dorian is here," she says, taking a breath. "The Ghost is part of this. He's seeking revenge for girlfriend that Daddy and Roaden took." She sniffs, looking at the hallway, then back at me. "Panthers are still involved in the sex slavery. They want to join forces with the Snakes so that they'll have more protection if shit ever goes south."

Riggs squeezes her hand, locking their fingers. "How do you know this?"

"Well, for one, Judas is here telling the guys about the Panthers merger and letting them know pick-ups and whatnot." She takes a shaky breath, looking at the hallway again as a sob choked her. "And second because..." she groans, tears sipping free. "Because she told me everything."

The floorboard creaks as a woman walks in. I don't register at first, but when Riggs shoots up, face as pale as I've ever seen it, I look over and see the most heart-wrenching moment of my entire life.

"Mama?" Riggs whimpers. "What the...fuck?"

Adam gasps, slapping a hand on his mouth as tears roll down his cheeks.

But nothing and I mean nothing can compare to the utter shock flowing through my veins. I held this woman as she took her last breath. How the fuck is she standing here?

My breathing shakes, verging on gasping as I watch her smile at us with eyes welling with tears. "My boys."

Riggs's legs are wobbly, gripping the side of the couch before he falls onto it, breathing quickly and ragged, too. "Mama?" he whispers, looking at me.

"Please listen to what she has to say," Zay says, kissing Riggs's shoulder.

His head drops between them, sobs leaving him as our Mama comes to me, getting on her knees and hesitantly touching my knee. "Hi, sweetie." She touches Rosa's head, looking between the two of us. "She's just like you were when you were a baby."

Panic thrums and I shoot up, shaking my head. I let my anger take over the happiest feeling exploding inside me. My mama and my baby are here. I should be smiling, defying all the odds that this can possibly be, but I'm fuming. I'm fucking fuming.

"No, no!" I step away from her, going for the window. "No, you don't get to just say hi like we saw you for fucking lunch last week. No, you can't act like this is okay. You don't get to pretend we didn't fucking lose you," my voice cracks, tears streaming down my face as Rosa starts to cry. "You died in my fucking arms, Mama. You were dead, you—"

Zay stands, putting her hands out to take the baby. But I don't let her. I turn and bob Rosa kissing her head and shushing her. "She had no choice, Peter," Zay states, tears welling in her eyes.

"Your Daddy was doing bad things, sweetie. He's gotten so many women hurt and killed. I wasn't standing for it anymore," Mama says, going to Riggs. "If I told you guys I was alive, your Daddy would've hurt you just so I'd come home and he'd finish the damn job he failed to do."

Riggs lifts his head, looking up at her. "All this time you were alive?"

She nods, wiping a tear from his cheek. "Yes, sweetie. But I have done so much good in this world. I have saved so many lives."

Riggs grits his teeth, standing again. "Mama, those men out there shot at my house where my woman and my kid sleep. What good have you done?"

She puts her hands up, placing them on his chest and his tense shoulders instantly relax. Mama's always been good at taming the beast. "That was not my doing, Riggsy. I save these people, but the man I work with goes about things the wrong way."

"It's Dorian's brother, Wilde. He's The Ghost," Zay adds, rubbing a hand up and down Riggs's back. "He wants revenge for what happened to his girlfriend. And that means hurting all of us in the process." She looks at Mama. "A life for a life."

Mama smiles at Adam, who hasn't moved from his seated position, and puts her hand out to him. "Come here, sweetie." She places a hand on Riggs's shoulder and looks at me. "My boys, come here, please."

I step forward, sobbing like a fucking child, and drop my head on Mama's shoulder. "Mama," I weep, feeling her arm wrap around me with Rosa between us.

"I'm here, sweetie. I've never left," Mama says, kissing my cheek. "I would never leave my boys unless it was unsafe." Riggs drops his head on the other side of her, shoulders hunched and shaking, too. "I love you, boys. And I'm sorry for this. I truly had no other choice. Your Daddy was a wicked man who deserves to rot in hell. But at least," she pauses, moving her arm so Adam can join us. "At least he gave me the most precious gift of all. My boys." She sniffs. "My beautiful boys."

Zaynab wipes her cheeks, looking at us with a smile. "You should meet your grandson, just as handsome as his father."

Mama laughs, sniffling again. "I'm sure that he is."

She leaves a kiss on all our cheeks and we step away, baffled by this.

I'm dreaming, aren't I?

The fucks shot me dead.

I have my daughter in my arms.

My Mama standing in front of me.

All I need is Dorian and my life is complete.

"Where's Dorian?" I ask, looking at Zay.

Mama urges me to sit, taking the baby from me to help calm her fuss. Without my daughter in my arms, it's like the knife in my back has managed to wedge its way into my heart. There's no way in hell I'm ever letting her go. "The bullets you boys let loose on us managed to hit Dorian's leg. She's being tended to. Much like you should be, sweetie."

Riggs grunts, sitting down and taking Zay's hand. "He'll live."

One of the men gets Mama a chair, helping her sit into it as she shushes Rosa. "Why don't I tell you boys a story, hmm? Wouldn't that be fun?"

She adjusts Rosa on her lap, my daughter biting on her hand as she looks at me and scrunches her nose. I can't take my eyes off her. I helped make that. I helped create the most perfect little lady this world will ever see.

"Can I have her back?" My voice is scratchy as a sob starts to crawl to the surface.

Mama smiles, kissing the top of her head. "In a minute."

Adam kisses Zay's shoulder, gripping her hand so tightly his knuckles are turning white. "M-Mama Rosa, this is Slade. He's a member of the Snakes, too."

She smiles, studying him with those kind, tired eyes. "I know, sweetie. I know a lot about what has been happening. Just like I knew what happened the day you went to Daddy's grave." She puts her hand on Riggs's knee, leaving it there. "You didn't deserve that—"

"All the wrong I did in life, Mama, I deserve a lot worse," Riggs interrupts her, sniffling.

She takes a breath, letting a tear escape, and looks at me. "This place was my home before I met your daddy. I brought you boys here every time Daddy went on one of his trips with the club. You broke your arm trying to climb that tree, Peter. Do you remember?"

I furrow my brows as I look out the window, trying to remember memories that don't seem to exist in my mind. Did Daddy brainwash us so much that I pushed out happy memories from my childhood? Memories of a life Mama tried to build for us.

Riggs, on the other hand, releases a breath and nods. "You used to bring us here for that cinnamon ice cream."

Mama nods, letting a giggle seep through. "It was like torture watching you eat ice cream. You hated every second of it."

Zay sniffs, chuckling. "He still hates anything sweet."

Riggs smirks, looking over at her. "I don't hate you."

She sucks her teeth, shoving his face away. That chuckle in my ears sends the slightest pressure to release from my chest. Reality is coming in full swing and for once in my life, I think I can take it.

Mama laughs, kissing Rosa's head, then grows serious. "Wilde is seeking revenge on my boys for the wicked ways of their daddy. I tried to reason with him, I tried to stop him, but Wilde is dead set on hurting you to heal his pain." She shakes her head. "The men in masks are his men, but they're good guys. They help bring me hundreds of women, children, and men. They bring them to me after saving them from being sold or tortured. They're doing good for this world, my loves. But he's a bad man that doesn't care about the people that hurt him." She sniffs, tilting her head to the side to reveal a fresh cut on the side of it. "He did this to my throat when I told him he wasn't allowed anywhere near you boys. Not even three days later, I heard about what happened at your home. Judas just arrived last night and filled me in on all of it."

Riggs cracks the bones in his neck. "Is he involved with The Ghost?"

She shakes her head. "No, he's helping us. Giving us intel from the Panthers."

I frown, looking out the window, when it hits me. He always said he saved his woman, but he never said how he saved her. Judas saved his woman from slavery. He saved her like Mama saved everyone pouring out of a warehouse at the end of the property.

I look at my daughter, blood smeared on her face probably from Zay. She has a bandana wrapped around her upper arm. But my daughter is beyond beauty. I'm so fucking blessed. Everything about her is perfect and I can't wait to get to know her.

Now, all I have to do is find Dorian and find out why she broke me before I rip my daughter from her and slap custody papers in her face so she understands true pain.

My eyes shift to Mama, and to my surprise, she's already staring at me. A smile touches her face and she wipes the tears from her cheeks. She always had a softer spot for me than Riggs or Adam because of my ears. I was also the rowdy one out of us three. But in the end, we're three lost boys in search of salvation. "Why don't I show you boys around, hmm? You sure did cause a ruckus this morning."

"Just tell me one thing," Riggs says, looking up at her. "Why didn't you ever try to get in contact with us? After all these years, why didn't you try?"

Tears roll down her cheeks as she studies him, adjusting Rosa on her lap. "Your Daddy is why. If he got wind of me being alive, he would have killed me. Or worse, hurt one of you because of me." She cups the side of his face, smiling softly. "I'd do anything for my boys. And leaving to save you and open up this place to save hundreds of people—I hurt you, Riggsy, I know. But look at the bigger picture. Look at all the good I did—"

"Were you ever going to talk to us again?" Adam interrupts her, slowly standing. "If it wasn't for Zay being here, would you have reached out?"

Mama inhales, rising from her seat. "One day, yes, I would have. But when Dorian was brought to me and told me her story, I knew that day was coming up. I wanted to make sure none of you were in harm's way before I did."

"And are we?" Zay asks, sniffling.

Mama looks at me again, nodding at the man behind me. "Tend to his shoulder, will you?"

"I'm fine, Mama," I let out, eyeing Rosa again.

But it's not like I have a choice.

The guy comes up to me, taking the flannel off my shoulder to inspect my wound. I wince, the feeling is as if my sockets are grinding together, sending jolts of pain through my body. Like I keep knicking my shoulder against the corner of a table with every move I make.

He cleans it and prepares to stitch me up without anesthetic. Not like Zay would let me, anyway. She asked me to quit drinking and the drugs, so I'm going to stand by that. For my little girl, I will stand by it.

The second the needle penetrates my skin and he starts stitching me up, I suck my teeth. It fucking kills. But I stare at Zay and she breathes with me; in through her nose and out through her mouth. I mimic, wincing and sucking my teeth again as he pulls the stitches through.

Beads of sweat roll down my temples, getting lost in my greasy, wet hair. But I'll pull through for those big blue eyes staring at me as she gnaws her little fist. *For you, my baby girl, I'll do anything.*

I expel another breath, holding Zay's gaze as she has Adam's hand locked in one of hers, and Riggs's interlocked with the other. Her men holding and protecting her. How it will always be.

A soft smile spreads to her lips and she inhales another breath with me, eyeing my shoulder. *You got this*, she mouths.

Fuck, I mouth back, wondering if I'll ever have my shit together.

I drop my head back and groan through clenched teeth as Riggs chuckles at me. "Don't be such a baby," Riggs teases.

I narrow my eyes at him, wiping sweat from my brow. "I'd like to see you do this without anesthetic, fucker."

When the guy's done, he wraps it and helps me into a sling. "Bullet went straight through. You'll be fine," he says, looking at Mama as he rises to his feet, then returns his attention to me. "Keep it dry as best as you can. Don't lift anything heavy or you'll rip your stitches open."

I groan, adjusting my arm. "Believe me, I don't want you closing me up again, man, thanks."

Mama kisses Rosa's cheek, handing her back to me, and fixes her scarf on her shoulders. "Come, I want to show you something."

My heart is hammering, thumbing against my ribcage as I stare at this woman. I don't know if I should be happy to see her. Thankful that she's not dead. Or angry at her for leaving us and lying all these years.

Mama left us.

She lied to us.

She betrayed us.

But then again, how is Mama any different than me?

I lied. I betrayed. I cheated and fucked around.

I took what wasn't mine.

Inhaling a shaky breath, I stare at Rosa in my arms. I feel like I'm drowning, staring at the surface before me, unable to kick my legs and breach the surface. This too shall pass, right? I'll be able to breathe again. Live my life again.

I'll be able to say goodbye to the club and never look back.

It pains me to say it, but Mama is no better than me.

Riggs

Mama is alive.

After all this time, the woman we thought our father killed is living and breathing.

I'm at a loss for words.

I'm a basket of nerves.

I'm about to blow a fuse.

Zay is holding my hand, calming me just as Mama did when she placed her hands on my chest. She used to do that every time Daddy and I got into an argument. She'd soothe me with her humming and place her hands over my heart.

Peter is in heaven right now, holding his daughter and staring at her in this mesmerizing kind of way. Just like I did the first time I laid eyes on my son. That pride coming out of me, that instant connection and urge to protect him from anything evil.

And I'll get that look again as soon as Zay and I talk about what happened the other night. As soon as everything is settled, I'll pop a baby in her and leave the club. I don't care if Adam joins us, I'll share her with him so long as she's mine.

We all deserve happy endings, don't we?

Mama wants to lead us out of the house to the garden where so many people roam the grounds, the laughter and screams of the children from outside float in through the windows. She did good at least. Left her boys behind but saved all these people.

Yet why do I feel like all of this is too good to be true?

Zay stands, tugging me and Adam with her. But I can't move. I can't fucking face the reality that my mother is alive and my entire life for the past five years has been a lie.

A chaotic fucking lie.

"I just…need a minute," I say through a breath.

Peter grunts as he stands, his face pale and sweaty still. But he's in all his glory holding his daughter right now to care about the blistering pain in his shoulder. He's lucky it went right through and didn't hit bone like it did mine. My shoulder still aches. "Where are you taking us, Mama?"

She grins, reaching out for Adam's hand. "The treehouse your granddaddy built when you were babies."

I chuckle, dropping my head between my shoulders again. I remember that damn thing.

Bits and pieces come back to me. I must've been no older than six or seven the last time we came here. Mama let us paint the treehouse ourselves. I painted my half black while Peter and Adam painted their side a highlighter yellow or maybe it was orange. I don't remember my granddaddy all that much, but I remember how he used to talk to people. *Always look them in the eye*, he'd say. *They'll respect you more*. And I always do. Mama used to tell us she'd save us from Daddy one day. She'd bring us to church and tell us that God would guide our path. But I didn't listen because I thought Daddy was God. I worshiped him for so long. Knowing how wrong it was. He was the devil in disguise and deserves everything ever given to him as he burns in hell.

Zay sits back down, putting her hand on my back. "We'll be out in a second," she says, smiling at everyone.

Adam lowers, kissing her lips softly, and eyeing me. "Okay, babe."

Mama nods, placing her hand on Peter's back, then taking Adam's hand and leading them out of the room. Slade waits a minute before Zay shoos him away and he joins everyone, leaving us alone. I appreciate his loyalty—not only to the club but to my family. To me. To Zay. I owe him my life and he doesn't even realize it.

Mama acts like everything is fine.

Like everything is normal.

She knew about what we did with our lives all these years, but we didn't know anything about hers. We thought she was dead—now she's living and breathing and smiling like everything is fucking fine.

It's not.

I've lived with a weight on my chest for far too long. A failure loomed over me that started when she died. It grew even more when Zay was shot, took over when Shyanne died, and now it's a permanent resident inside me. This weight presses down harder on my chest, sending me into a silent panic.

I release a breath when I hear the backdoor slapping shut behind them. I don't need her here for this. I'm about to lose it and the last thing she needs is to witness my downfall. "Zay, you don't have to stay."

She presses her lips on my shoulder, looking at me. "I'll always stay, Riggs. You know that."

Staring at her, my eyes getting lost in hers for a moment before they trail to her lips. This is a better time than any. She never said it back. I need to hear those words leave her lips and be directed at me. Everything will be better when she says it. "You'll let me give you the world?"

She frowns slightly, a tear rolls down her cheek, and she looks away. "I'm married."

I take her chin, turning her head to face me. "You love me, baby. Admit it. Tell me you love me, too, and we'll figure this thing out."

She sniffs, wipes the tear away, and inhales. "Riggs—"

"Why did you sleep with me, then? Huh? You hated Peter for making you sleep with him because you didn't want to cheat on Adam—"

"—now's not the time for this—"

"Tell me, Zay. Why do it if you ain't gonna be with me?" I growl, shaking my head. "Did you fucking use me?"

She gets on her knees beside me with a wince, hands on my knee. "I would never do that to you."

I grit and bare my teeth. "Then tell me."

She inhales again, more tears falling as I glare down at her, those perfect lips parting slightly. "Because I don't know what to do."

"Say it," I whisper.

She shakes her head. "I'm married."

"Say. It."

Her forehead rests on my knee, hands gripping the fabric of my jeans around my shins. "I love you, Riggs. I chose Adam because he's home, but you." She lifts her head, eyes leaking. "You're my eternity."

I grab her face and slam my lips on hers, inhaling her breath and taking her whimpers down my throat. "You're my eternity, too, sunshine."

She groans, wincing. "But we can never be," she whispers. "I'm sorry."

She'd have been better off shooting me in the fucking chest and taking my soul with her.

Then, she rises, as if this moment couldn't get any worse, and sobs as she heads to the kitchen and leaves me to soak in the morning from hell. I may have found Shyanne; my angel, birth mother to my son, but no one—nothing compares to Zay. No one has stolen my heart like Zay has. The first girl to make me want out of this life. The first girl to show me what it's like to want more out of life itself. The only girl who showed me peace.

My heart is bleeding from my chest, flopping onto the ground and watching me as it takes its final beat.

***

I'm quiet the entire time Mama shows us the grounds. There's this giddiness in her that used to be there when we were kids. Seeing her talk about the farm and the animals. Seeing her show us the land and introduce us to people. Pride is shining from her. For the first time I see a new side to Mama I wish I saw when we were kids.

She used to smile all the time, even when we were teenagers, that smile was always there. But when I moved out, that smile faltered and I never saw the signs. She hid it from me the best she could. And I was in too deep with the Snakes at the time to notice it disappear.

Mama hid it so well from us, that Peter, her pride and joy, didn't see it leave, either.

If I had known how badly she needed out, my brainwashed mind would've saved her from that life. Maybe Zay would want me then. A good man like

Adam.

Zay glances at me over her shoulder as her brows come together and a fresh tear rolls down her cheek.

I smile softly, tucking my hands in my pockets. She doesn't know it, but the woman still holds my heart even though her words broke me.

It wasn't the time to talk about us.

It was the wrong moment.

That's all it was.

I'll get her alone and we'll talk about this when all the shock isn't suffocating us. We'll talk and she'll see it's us. It will always be us.

You're my eternity. But we can never be.

Mama smiles at me, watching as I stare at Zay, and places her hand on her shoulder. "Why don't we get cleaned up and have some lunch? I'm sure I can dig up a bottle of whiskey to share with my boys."

Peter chuckles, looking at Rosa in his arms. She's breathtaking. The perfect little one to add to our ever-growing family. Wherever Dorian is, she better stay hidden. I am in no mood to deal with her fuckery or sad excuse as to why she did what she did. The girl hurt my brother and took his daughter from him, it'll take a lot for me to get over that.

"My baby girl is sleeping anyway," he says, smiling so much his cheeks must be killing him. The last time I saw him this happy was the time he got his first blowjob. Have to say, I can damn near guarantee you this trumps that.

Zay giggles, touching the baby's back delicately. "Isn't she the most precious thing?"

He kisses Rosa's head, inhaling. "You have no idea."

Adam chuckles, clapping Peter gently on the back and following Slade and Mama inside, reaching his hand back for Zay. "Come, babe. Let's get the blood cleaned up."

I get to her first and pull her toward me. I need one chance. I know I can convince her. I have to. "Just need a second of your time, sunshine."

She glances at Adam and nods, leading me to the apple trees as everyone heads back to the house. There are a few of the women walking around us, heading to the bushes on the other side of the apple trees, leaving Zay and me alone. I like this place. It's calming. I can't understand why I ever let it slip from my memories. Why would I give this up for a life of crime? A life of death.

"Riggs, what're you doing?"

"I just—" I'm overdone by emotion and shake my head, dropping it in my hands as a sob seeps through.

I don't cry.

I'm no fucking pussy.

But here I am letting everything out.

Shyanne. Mama. Carter. Zay.

All my loves have lost in so many ways and I can't do it anymore.

I can't keep this weight on my shoulders.

I failed Shyanne by getting her killed.

I failed Mama by not protecting her and making her fake her death to get away from the life she was given.

I failed Carter by not being there when he needed me most.

And Zay, my sweet sunshine, I've failed her by not keeping her heart when I should've.

"Riggs?" She touches my shoulder, sliding her hand to my bicep. "Hey, look at me?"

I shake my head again, whimpering as she takes my head, pulls it to her chest, and holds me, kissing the side of it. "I'm right here," she whispers.

"I can't—" I weep, letting her see how destroyed I've been. Holding in my fears.

Keeping in my breakdown.

Falling apart at the seams and she's the only one who can repair me.

"Riggs, on what planet will this work? How will we be able to love freely when I'm with Adam," she says, forcing my hands away from my face. "Don't you see that I'll never leave him?"

"But you love me." I sniff, exhaling deeply.

She wipes my cheeks, holding my face. "Why don't we deal with one thing at a time, okay? Your mom is alive, Peter has Rosa, you found me—"

"But we can never be, right?"

I remove her hands from my face, wanting a simple answer from her.

I wish she'd stop fighting us and just let it happen.

Let us be like we were last night.

I squeeze her hands and let them go. I let them go as I did at the hospital.

I walk away.

"Riggs, please, wait," she pleads, sniffling. "Riggs?" She whimpers, but I keep walking.

I continue even as I hear her sobs move through the apple trees.

I keep walking until I get to the porch where Slade is leaning, resting his forearms on the railings. I don't care that I'm crying. I don't care how red my face is. I'm so conflicted this morning, I just want to go home. No, I just want to get on my bike and ride down the open road.

He glances at Zay, making me follow his gaze. Her fingers are interlocked behind her head and she's looking down at the floor. Her shoulders are shaking. She's crying and I'm ignoring it. She has no idea how much it's killing me. "All good, boss?"

I sniff, turning back to him. "No, but who the fuck cares anymore?"

Whipping open the backdoor, I head to the dining room when I get a whiff of cinnamon. A memory shoots through my head from that smell; the taste of apple pie. I remember laughter with it, too. And Peter gobbled up a piece of pie as I gagged trying to prove I could eat sweets like a normal kid. But I hated sweets, still do. And it's a memory worth retelling—but then I find Mama sitting with Adam and Peter. They're laughing, as if our pain from her death doesn't matter anymore.

But it fucking mattered.

We mourned for years, we're still fucking mourning.

Now that she's here, everything feels like a lie. All this fucking time the woman who raised us and tried to take us away from this only pushed us farther into the darkness.

Peter looks up at me, kid all smiles like a kid on Christmas morning. "Hey, come sit. Mama's telling us about the time she brought us to the petty zoo, you remember that?"

I nod, forcing a grin, and sit at the table beside Mama, her hand finding mine. But I snatch it away. I don't want to hold her hand, not yet anyway. I'm still sour. Still hurt. Fuck, I need Zay now more than ever. But she won't have me.

Mama tells us the story of when Peter got trampled by a herd of sheep at the petting zoo for his sixth birthday. Daddy was with us, which was unusual for him. He never joined us for outings. Most of my birthdays involved Mama preparing for a party with the kids from our class while Daddy came home after it was finished and gave us a gift. But he came to this one and Peter was happy he did, kept calling me to come see the animals, and kept yelling at Adam to stop snorting like a pig all while Daddy watched his sons smiling with pride. It was our first family moment. The only one I can remember.

Peter had two handfuls of feed, dropping it at his feet for the pigs to eat. Adam and I took his time, giving them little nibbles so our handfuls could last. But Peter didn't care. He thought it was funny how they followed him around for feed, and Daddy made sure we were the only ones at the petting zoo so no other kid would dare get in the way of his sons.

Well, Peter decided to stuff feed into his pockets until they leaked while he held some out to the chickens. What he didn't expect were the goats to nibble at his pockets, trying their hardest to get into them. Three goats charged at him, nearly ripping his shorts off to get the feed.

Daddy, Adam, and I were laughing our asses off as Mama was swatting the goats away, emptying Peter's pockets so they'd leave him alone. Peter remembers that day as a happy one, something Mama brought her boys to. But all I remember is the death glare Mama gave Daddy for laughing and not helping. When she ushered us into the car, Daddy slit the throat of one of the goats and thanked the man for his time.

Adam and Peter spoke about the animals all the way home, where I only saw the blood leaking from the throat of that goat. I didn't see the happy day we had, all I saw was death.

Mama was lucky Daddy didn't punish her that night. No, he spared her and celebrated Peter's birthday with cake, balloons, and Nerf guns. I want to smile and laugh with everyone as they reminisce, but I can't. How can I smile when every memory is painful?

Mama laughs, covering her mouth as she places a hand out to Adam. She laughs but she knows the truth. She knows the hatred that was our life.

That still is.

Mama is here and pretends nothing ever happened. She moved on, didn't she?

I should be happy she's alive. Jumping for joy.

But I'm not.

Everything is fucking incomplete.

This isn't the ending, no, it's merely the beginning of more fucking bullshit.

Slade

I look back as Riggs heads inside. The air is still heavy, but I think Adam and Peter are happier than pigs in shit to see their Mama again. Riggs, I'm not so sure about. He's a hard one to read. One second he's all smiles, the next he growls and grinds his teeth. Shit, he's a ticking timebomb ready to go off.

Mama risked her life to save all these women and saved so many children and young men, too. I praise her for it. She has a good thing going here, something so many people are proud of. I see how Peter looks around in awe, how Adam asks a bunch of questions, how interested he is in farming, and then, there's Riggs.

He's angrier than I've ever seen him. Hating every second that we're here.

Truthfully, this entire morning is just a shitshow, but he should be happy. His mother is alive. He should be like Peter, thrilled that his whole life has come together. He has his family back. But Riggs is even more distraught than he was when we left on this trip. And it's probably because of Zay.

No, I think it's because even though we're one step closer to finding The Ghost, it feels like we're miles away from finding who the hell is behind taking all these women.

I doubt we'll ever find the culprit, but we can at least find the fucker who gives the names and locations to the Panthers. If we can find their source, then maybe we can end the disgusting fucks who own these women.

Zay wipes her eyes and looks at the sky as she exhales a deep breath, finally making her way to the house. I jerk my head at her, straightening up as she climbs the steps. "All good?"

She shakes her head, wiping her nose with her hand. "Don't think it ever will be. But it doesn't matter, right? Peter has his daughter. That's what matters."

I take her wrist, stopping her from going inside. "Why don't we leave them alone for a sec to bond with their mother they thought was dead for, what? Five years?"

She sniffs, plopping down on the top step and hugging her knees.

Sitting beside her, the quietness take over. It's truly beautiful here. A perfect place to heal after such a fucked up situation. The chick I used to fool around with told me her sister was kidnapped and reached out to her months after she was taken. She told her about this place, how beautiful it was, how freeing, and happy she'd become.

I bump my shoulder into Zay grinning as I do. "Tell me, what's going through that crazy head of yours?" I want to make her laugh, seems like we can all use a good chuckle today instead of more tears. "Any more sex dreams I should know about? I hope my dick was to size, I'd be pissed if dream me had a raisin dick."

She arches an eyebrow, side glances at me. "Your dick was fine, not as big as Riggs's but kinda like Adam's, at least dream yours is."

"I've seen him naked, I'm okay with that."

She chuckles weakly, looking up as a bird flies by, then releases a sigh. "I feel like I'm dreaming and this entire place is just purgatory." She huffs out a breath. "It's too good to be true, don't you think?"

Shaking my head, I crack my thumb knuckles. "Nothing is ever too good to be true. Mama Rosa was meant to open up this place. We were meant to find it with you and Rosa here, and her sons were meant to find her again." I smile as she flickers her gaze to me. I lower the neck of my t-shirt and show her the tattoo across my collarbones. "*Not all those who wander are lost.* And it's true. You may have wandered off your path, sweet thing, but you're not lost. You're finding your way home. And I think this trip will help you do that."

Her tongue moves along her upper lip and she rises, stepping off the porch with folded arms. "So this trip will help me live a life with a man I've loved since I met him, while married to another man who also stole my heart?"

Riggs and Adam are not going to like sharing this one.

"What's your heart telling you?" I ask her, squinting from the sun in my eyes.

She meets my gaze, lifting a shoulder. "It's telling me to leave and never look back."

"And your brain?"

She plops down beside me again and leans her head on my shoulder. Even all bloody and sweaty, she still smells like the tropics. "To find a way to make this work."

"Then do that," I whisper, leaving a soft kiss on her head.

"I don't know how."

The backdoor squeaks open, and Adam steps out. "Babe?"

"I'll be in, in a second, Adam," she says, sniffling.

I look back at him and he's tonguing his cheek, looking into the house. "Why don't we go inside now, hmm? I'm kinda hungry anyway." I tap her knee, smiling weakly at the sadness in her eyes.

She groans, pushing off the step, and looks up at him. "Guess I'm coming in now."

She walks past him, going into the house and leaving this sour taste in my mouth. She's always had it hard, life has yet to give her a break. And I don't think it'll give her something any time soon. But I really hope it does.

Adam wipes a hand down his face, looking at me with a sigh. "You coming in?"

I nod, jerking my head at the house. "Things just got so complicated."

"You're telling me."

"What're you guys going to do?"

Adam pushes the door open more so I can go inside and join them. "Family meeting, c'mon."

This is the first family meeting I've been invited to, the first time I feel wanted.

Life for me was much like Zay. I never caught a break. Always given the shit end of the stick.

But ever since I joined the Snakes, I'm needed. Since meeting Zay, she has included me in things. Fills me into the family drama. She cares. And Adam has become one of my closest friends.

I used to cut myself growing up, thinking feeling physical pain would make the mental pain go away. And when it didn't work, I'd cut deeper, more often. Until the scars on my wrist continued up my forearms. And when that wasn't enough, then I'd cut my thighs, starting from my knees. And when that wasn't enough, I fucked my feelings away. But again, that wasn't enough. So I sought out help.

But help was still not enough.

Then I found this. I found the Snakes and I finally belong.

I finally found my family.

When I enter the dining room, the air is intense; filled with happiness and grudges. Not a good mix.

Drinks are being poured and Zay swirls the amber whiskey in her glass, sitting opposite Riggs, then gulps it back. It's hard to breathe in here. The air is heavy, and thick with unspoken regrets and resentment. But no one says anything.

Mama Rosa smiles, as I sit down next to Riggs, smiling at Peter sitting at the head of the table with his daughter sleeping on his chest. "I wanted to invite all of you to stay with me for as long as you need to. I would surely love my boys with me, have my grandbabies raised here, and my daughters-in-law, too."

Peter leaves a gentle kiss on Rosa's head, looking around the table. "It's something we can talk abo—"

"No," Riggs says, shaking his head. "We have a whole life out there, Mama. Something we built. Responsibilities and houses we own. We ain't gonna up and leave because you chose to come back from the dead. No. We're not doing it."

"Riggs," Adam scoffs, frowning. "This is our ticket out of the Snakes."

"I don't want my daughter anywhere near the club," Peter adds, resting his cheek on his daughter's head as she sleeps on his shoulder.

Zay doesn't say anything, but she and Riggs are looking at each other. I know they fooled around the other night. A fucking deaf person could have heard her moans and his nuts slapping against her. I wanted to turn and watch them. Fuck, to see her naked would have been heaven. All I got was side boob yesterday morning and her ass in that thong.

But something changed since the other night. I think reality hit them like a brick wall.

Zay's eyebrows raise and tears shimmer in her eyes. Riggs, on the other hand, clenches a fist on his lap and huffs. "Well, I ain't got a choice. I'm the damn president of the club. My son has no one but me—"

"He has me," Zay steps in. "We had a plan, Riggs. You promised—"

"Yeah, well, plans change, don't they, Zay. They can never be," he growls out, rolling his eyes. And looking at Peter. "When things are settled, I'll leave, for now, I ain't got a choice."

Adam taps his index finger on the table, looking between Riggs and Peter. "We gotta set up a meeting with the Panthers, find out why they're still helping the trafficking when they know we've been trying to erase all of it from our hands."

Peter nibbles his bottom lip, nodding slowly, deep in thought. "Mama, you think you can get in contact with The Ghost? Set up a meeting with him."

Mama downs her whiskey, nodding. "I can try."

"Good," I say, leaning forward. "The faster we fix this mess, the better, right, boss?"

Riggs grunts his answer, taking the bottle of whiskey and filling his glass.

Zay does the same, maintaining eye contact with him as they shoot back the liquid. Christ, it's no wonder they're meant to be. There's this unspoken connection they share, a lust that's tamed behind closed doors and an aching anger that spews in the wild. It's even more tense in the room now that these two are about to brawl.

A young man clears his throat, blood decorating his shirt. "Mama Rosa, Dorian's here."

Mama shoots up from her chair, smiling. "Oh, how is she doing?"

He nods, holding the hem of his shirt. "She's okay. Karen patched her up and gave her some pain medicine."

Mama smiles, looking at Peter, then Zay. "Would you bring her in, sweetie?

We're having a family meeting I don't think she should miss."

Peter stiffens, jaw clenching as he looks at the table. I've seen him angry before. I've seen him on the verge of killing someone while high off his ass. But I've never seen this before. Distraught, broken, and upset without a way to cope.

He's seeing the woman who destroyed him for the first time in months. I'd be on the verge of a mental breakdown if I were him.

The sound of someone walking in crutches comes our way, followed by a whimper when Dorian appears down the hallway. The young man moves out of the way, nodding at her as he heads for the kitchen.

I wasn't expecting a bigger girl, didn't seem like Peter's type. But I see the appeal. Dorian is just as gorgeous as Zay. Long dark hair pulled up into a messy ponytail, big gray eyes that are red and crying, and huge lips I'm sure Peter loved having wrapped around his dick.

Time and place, Slade.

Blood is all over her shorts, splattered on her other leg, much like the blood on Zay's arm and neck. These girls need to clean the blood off their bodies before lunch.

Mama's smiling. I don't think she stopped since she saw her kids. "Come, sweetie."

"I can't," Dorian whispers, her eyes shifting around the room, catching Zay's gaze, Adam's, wincing when she looks at Riggs whose eyes are locked on Zay, and Dorian's brows furrow when they spot me. She hasn't looked at Peter yet, I don't blame her, either. If he weren't in his right mind or if his daughter wasn't in his arms, he'd be reacting before thinking logically.

Peter grunts, slowly rising from his seat with the baby still asleep on his chest. He doesn't turn to face her, but the way his chest is heaving and his lower lip is quivering, there are a lot of emotions that need to be expressed.

One is forgiveness.

"I'm sorry," Dorian says as Mama guides her forward. But Dorian can't move.

Mama helps her take a couple of steps, urging her closer to Peter and the baby.

Slowly, Peter turns, taking Dorian in as if it's the first time he's laid eyes on her. Tears escape, streaming down his face. All that anger uplifts and he weeps, pressing his lips on his daughter's forehead. "She's beautiful."

Dorian nods, letting out a sob as Mama helps her forward some more. "She is."

He stares at her, studying her face before he drops his head back and breathes, looking at the ceiling. "Why did you do it?"

Dorian sniffs, releasing a breath. "Riggs was the target that day, not Shyanne. If I didn't leave, he would have killed all of you."

Riggs scoffs, finally looking at her. "So instead you killed my wife?"

"It wasn't my idea, I was just trying to save you," she weeps, shaking her head. "I'm so sorry, Riggs. I promise I never wanted any of this."

He stands, shoulders back, eyebrow cocked. "What was the end goal here, Dorian? Huh? We know your brother lost his girl because of this fucking club. So what, you push yourself into our lives by my fuckhead of a brother so that you can find our secrets? So you can get him to impregnate you and fuck off with his kid? What the fuck were you planning? Because it sure as shit ain't something any of us saw coming."

She shakes her head frantically, limping forward. "I swear it, Riggs. I didn't plan anything until Wilde came home for my ex-husband's funeral. My sister told him who I was dating and that's when plans were set in motion." Tears skim her round cheeks. "I was already pregnant by then. I couldn't leave."

Riggs grits his teeth, cracking the bones in his neck. "Would've been better if you did so he wouldn't know anything about the baby."

"Riggs," Zay says softly.

He shoots a glare at her, grinding his teeth and leaning those mitts in fists on the table. "Zay."

"Why didn't you just reach out to me?" Peter adjusts the baby in his arms and steps closer to her. "I would've protected you."

She weeps, lowering her head and shaking it. "I'm so sorry, Peter. He threatened to kill you, threatened to take the baby away if I didn't go along with his plan—"

"And this is the guy you work with?" Adam interrupts her, scoffing as he looks at Mama. "He tried to have your son killed and you still work with him?"

Mama adjusts her scarf, staring at Adam until she slowly blinks. "He helps save these people. He's not a good man. I never once said he was. But he gives me the resources I need to bring these people here."

"And where is he?" Riggs asks, fists still on the table staring down at Zay.

The little kitten hasn't backed down, either. She holds his stare for as long as she needs to. Zay doesn't like to lose, and neither does Riggs.

Oh, to be a fly on the wall when they hash this shit out.

Mama folds her arms and shakes her head. "Last I heard from him was three days ago."

"When he shot up our house," Peter says, pressing his lips to the baby's head as Dorian watches in utter amazement and regret.

She fucked-up and there's only one way to fix this. Sorry isn't going to cut it, either.

"He told me he would leave you alone if I left," Dorian adds. "Then when he brought in a van of young girls last week, he lost it and everything's been a shit show since."

"What made him snap?" Zay asks, her eyes flickering between those big balls of blue on Riggs's face.

Mama places her hand on Riggs's shoulder, sensing the tension and aggravation emanating from him. "He found out that Snakes and Panthers are considering a merger. And the Panthers are the ones who still aid in taking these innocent people and bringing them to auctions." She slides her hand to his back. "You can't do this merger, Riggsy."

He grumbles, finally looking away from Zay. Her face grows red, and she exhales a breath glancing at me before looking down at her hands under the table. "I ain't doing shit."

Zay gets up and sniffs, looking at Mama. "Just gotta use the bathroom." Adam eyes her, then Riggs, and gets up to follow.

"Sit, sweetie." Mama urges Dorian forward. "I'll make us some lunch and you can clean up afterward."

Riggs huffs, looking down the hallway where Zay and Adam disappeared.

He's going in, isn't he? He starts heading that way, making me audibly groan. Yep, he's going in.

I don't want to third-wheel this reunion with Dorian and Peter so I escape to the kitchen to help Mama. This kitchen reminds me of the last group home I was in.

The place was pure chaos. Ten children of different ages running around. A mess of clothes and shoes scattered the rooms. The foster parents didn't care, they just collected their checks as we kids ransacked their house and raised ourselves. But it was home, and I'll never forget the first steps of my foster sister before I left and was dumped on with new family. The chaos brought me my first look at happiness.

"Slade, is it?" Mama says as I'm looking around. The white and yellow kitchen has one too many chicken decorations in it. But I like it. This place feels like home to me and I've only been here a couple of hours. "Why don't you come help me, sweetie."

I nod, taking the plates from the cupboard. "You have a good thing going, Miss Donnelly. But those men who work for you, they're not good men."

She touches my cheek, smoothing it out as she smiles at me. "I know, and I'm trying to change things. And please, call me Mama Rosa."

I clear my throat, having just thought of it now. "If it's protection you need, I'm sure Riggs and I can find a few of the bikers from the other charters who would be willing to help and work for you instead of this Wilde guy. People who don't stand by Roaden or Daddy Donnelly's choice of business. People like us."

She opens the fridge and takes out some sandwich meats. "I would like that, Slade. I truly would." She takes a couple of tomatoes and hands them to me. "I stand by my offer. I would love it if all of you lived here. It would be good for the kids, for my boys," she pauses, touching the self-inflicted scars on my arms. "For you."

"Those are from a long time ago," I say, washing the tomatoes with my cheeks heating up.

She lifts her shirt, revealing a bullet wound and burn scars on her stomach. "This was from a long time ago, too. But we all need that leap of faith to help us heal."

A smile spreads to my lips and I look out the window, watching as the women, boys, and children roam freely. Living their life without the fear of being taken again.

A curvy girl that's no older than me gets on her knees in the hot sun. Her orange hair is twisted into a knot on her head, freckles kiss her shoulders, arms, and scatter on her neck. She's collecting carrots and placing them in the basket beside her. There isn't a lick of emotion on her face. No residue of fright of the bullets or the raid.

She's desensitized from all of this because of her experience. But her life here will start anew. And maybe, just maybe, mine will, too.

Peter

As soon as Slade leaves, lean on the edge of the table, staring at Dorian. This perfect fucking woman who hurt me is right here in front of me and I can't even stay mad at her.

I can't hate her, look at this baby she gave me. This precious little gem I'm already so in love with.

"I'm sorry," Dorian says again, covering her face as she sobs.

Something dark sparks in my chest. Something that knows I could end her right here right now. It's cruel, evil like the fucking demons making my father suffer in hell. I have my gun tucked in my jeans, one bullet right between those gray eyes, and a fucking smile will touch my face for what she did to me.

But as soon as she drops her hands and flashes me those doe eyes, I can't break her like she broke me. I love this fucking woman with every fiber of my being. One way or another, we will try to be a family.

Forcing my arm out of the sling, I wince in blinding pain as I reach out for her. "Baby, come here."

"No, I hurt you—"

"Are you telling me the truth?" I interrupt her. "You breaking me was to save my life and the life of my brother?"

She nods quickly, adjusting the crutches. "I didn't want to lose you even if I had to leave you."

I stand tall, holding Rosa on my shoulder with my good hand. "Tell me again, Dorian. I need to hear you say it. I need to know this is real."

Her breath hitches, her chest rising and falling quickly. God, she looks fucking fantastic. Seeing her again, all round and juicy, it's like my love for her never died.

I don't think it ever did. I was mad. I was angry.

I wanted to fucking kill her at one point.

But seeing her again, all that disappeared. The happiness blooms forward, surpassing any anger I had toward her. I set it free.

"We're soulmates, Peter," she whispers, a fresh tear rolling down her cheek. That does it.

I step forward, slamming my lips on hers and tasting this woman again.

I devour her, inhaling her air and invading her mouth.

She takes it, all of it and drops one of the crutches to fist my shirt. "I love you so much, Peter."

I sob, leaning my head on hers. "Don't hurt me again, baby, you have no idea how broken you made me."

She cups the side of my face, smiling as Rosa coos. "I wouldn't dream of it so long as we can live here. Leave that life behind and start fresh. You should see her with the animals, Peter. It's so beautiful. This place makes her happy. It makes her happy. This place will be good for you, too."

I laugh softly, sliding my finger down her nose before lowering my mouth to hers. "I'd run to the ends of time with you, Dorian. Wherever you want to live, I'm right there with you."

"I need to hear you say you're done with the club," she whispers, wiping a tear rolling down my nose.

"I'm done with the club, baby. As soon as your damn brother backs off, I am done." I sniff, kissing her lips delicately. "I'm going to marry you like we planned. I'm going to fill you up with as many babies as you can push out. But it'll be us soon, my love. Our little family."

Those deceiving gray eyes smile, oozing out her forgiveness and regret for everything she did. "I wish I could take it all back."

"You should've told me, that's all you should've done."

She leans her forehead on my chest, pulling in a shaky breath. "I didn't know how."

"Why here?" I sniff, letting my anger take hold for a moment. "Why didn't you reach out to me and let me help you?" She shakes her head, unable to fathom an answer for me.

Looking back, I knew something was off. She'd randomly get quiet sometimes. She'd work later when she didn't have to. She'd be home but her mind would be elsewhere. There were issues but my stupid selfish fucking brain kept thinking it was just me. She had to get used to the idea of being with me. I thought she was ashamed of me and my wicked ways and my devotion to a club I grew to hate. It wasn't that at all. Knowing Dorian, she was looking for ways to fix the mess without having to break me.

"Tell me, how was her birth?"

She giggles, looking up at me. "Your mother helped deliver her." Pride oozes from me. My mama got to deliver my daughter, her namesake. "She was six pounds and refused to shoot right out of me. There's a doctor here, Karen, she had to cut me a little because our little angel has her daddy's head."

I laugh, stirring Rosa awake. "Shit, sorry."

Dorian chuckles, adjusting herself to sit on the chair with a wince, and reaching for her as our daughter starts to cry. "She's probably hungry."

Dorian's leg is wrapped, dried blood still caked on her other leg. Sexy thick thighs I can't wait to have wrapped around my head. She has this motherly look about her. This newness I find utterly attractive. I made this woman a mother and she's even more breathtaking because of it.

She cradles the baby and lifts her shirt, taking one of her breasts out so the baby can drink. Her tits are wild; so much bigger than I remember.

"I didn't know you wanted to breastfeed," I say, watching as Rosa suckles.

Dorian smiles at her as she brushes pieces of hair away from the baby's face. "I wasn't planning on it, but your mother convinced me. But I do both. Especially for nighttime. She's a night owl."

I groan, adjusting my arm in the sling before I drop to my knees and kiss Dorian's thigh. "I'll do night shifts."

She sniffs, choking on a sob. "I hate that I took this away from you."

I shake my head. "You didn't, baby. You didn't. Because I'm here and I'm going full-on Daddy mode. There's nothing my baby girl will go without and there's nothing her Mama has to do unless I'm not around."

Rosa unlatches, sneezing softly and looking up at Dorian with a milk-drunk grin. She places the baby on her shoulder and taps her back, leaving herself exposed to me.

I smirk, staring at Dorian's breast as milk still leaks from it. I can't help it, I lean forward and suckle, tasting that sweet milk. "Mmm, and I get to have snacks whenever I want."

Dorian gasps, covering herself as her cheeks grow a deep red. "Peter!"

I laugh, licking the residue from my mouth. "A lot sweeter than I expected."

She laughs, still burping the baby as she does. I join her, and in seconds we're in a fit of laughter that tears start to fall from our eyes.

We did it. We made it to our happy ending.

An ending I know will only shine brighter the longer we bask in it.

Zay

I shut the door behind me, releasing a breath. How am I going to do this?

Why the hell did I open my legs to Riggs?

No, why the fuck did I admit my feelings? Nothing good ever comes from that.

I'm about to splash water on my face when a knock strikes the door. "Babe? Open up, will you?" Adam says, knocking again.

Great.

I unlock the door and it immediately opens. Adam comes in and holds me, squeezing me against his chest. "God, Zay. I was so scared. So damn terrified that something happened to you." He releases me, holding me by the shoulders. "No more. Anything to do with this club is finished."

I wipe an escaping tear, looking up at him. "Promise?"

He nods, planting a soft kiss on my lips. "You and me, babe. We'll live in the woods."

How do I tell him this?

Will he accept?

Will he let us be more than just…us?

"Carter, too," I whisper.

He smooths out my hair, kissing the tip of my nose. "Yes, Carter, too. And our babies. Lots and lots of our babies."

I giggle, placing my hands on his chest. "I have to tell you something."

As if the fucking goon heard my thoughts, Riggs opens the door and forces himself inside it. This bathroom is barely big enough for two people, and with his size, this is just ridiculous.

"Riggs, I'm speaking with my wife—"

"I can see that, but I think I need to be part of this conversation, too," he states, leaning against the door. "Don't I, sunshine?"

Oh, God.

My heart is thumping wildly.

My hands are clammy.

There's this prickle of dread crawling up my spine.

A clog in my throat.

And a fucking raging storm down below.

Yeah, my brain's all sorts of twisted.

Adam scoffs. "No, you don't."

I let out a shaky breath, meeting Riggs's eyes. "Yes, he does."

Adam whips his head at me, frowning. "Why does he?"

I grip his t-shirt, wincing as I open my mouth. I have to tell him. He has to know that I was with Riggs yesterday. That he finished inside me.

He has to know my heart belongs to two men.

It has since this fiasco with the club started.

My heart isn't confused, it's been the most knowing thing this entire time.

"I love you, baby, you're my forever," I say to Adam, then look at Riggs. Oh, God. I don't want to break his heart, but I know I will in some way. "But he is, too."

Adam scoffs, a puzzled look on his face. "What?"

"I told you she'll always be my girl, too," Riggs says, leaning a hip on the vanity.

Adam growls, pushing my hands away from his chest. "You're leaving me?"

"I would never leave you," I plead, taking his head in my hands, which he removes immediately. "Adam?"

He shakes his head, tongues his cheek, and closes his eyes. "What is this, Zay? Hmm?"

He knows what I'm going to say. They both know. I can choose one of them. I can live my life with Adam and love him until the world ends, but then that wouldn't be fair to Riggs. My heart wouldn't be fully in it. Like it's always been.

Something was missing. From the moment I chose Adam, my first true love, there was a piece of the puzzle that didn't fit right.

And Riggs was that missing piece.

Adam looks over at Riggs, who's staring at me, watching as tears fall from my eyes as I wait for Adam to speak. "Wait…both of us?"

I lift a shoulder slowly, glancing at Riggs. "I don't know how to do this."

Riggs tilts my chin up, kissing me delicately, and smiles. "One day at a time, sunshine."

Looking at Adam, my brows pulled together. "Can we?"

There's contemplation on his face. The wonderment and betrayal eating away at him. There was a reason he stayed with me after knowing I was with both his brothers. There was a reason he didn't bat an eye when Peter slept with me.

There was a reason he allowed Riggs to hold me and kiss me the way he did.

Adam doesn't get jealous. Territorial, maybe. But not jealous.

And a little part of him liked the fact that other men wanted me. Would swoon over me.

He's a cuckold. And I'm fine with that.

"I don't know what to say," Adam whispers, watching the tears well in my eyes.

They're happy tears for once.

I swallow thickly, looking at Riggs who's smirking at me. He's won and he likes that power. He enjoys the thrill it gives him when people do what he wants.

But will Adam do what I want?

Pulling Adam's face to mine, I kiss him, letting my tongue slide against his. And that's all it takes because he moans against my lips, lifting me onto the vanity.

"You're mine, babe." He looks at Riggs. "She'll *always* be mine, yeah?"

Riggs nods, breathing quickly. "She'll be our little plaything."

Adam returns to my lips, kissing me in ways we only do when we're about to mess up our sheets. "You're going to watch me take her right now because, in the end, she belongs to *me.*"

Riggs chuckles roughly, that deep sound that's gotten me hot since we met. "Whatever you wanna tell yourself, so long as she comes home to me."

"*Us,*" Adam corrects, undoing his pants. "She's going to love both of us, right? This is what you want, babe? Riggs and I to come home to."

I squeal when Adam yanks my thong to the side, forcing himself inside me as Riggs watches. "Yes, this is what I want," I moan softly.

Adam pounds me, taking me as rough as he can while I keep my eyes locked on Riggs's.

Slowly, he unties his belt, releasing the button on his jeans and inching the fly lower. I can see the outline of his dick in his boxers, aching to be released.

I moan, biting Adam's shoulder as Riggs takes it out and strokes himself.

He grips the vanity as his strokes increase, sending me overboard. Oh, God, this is what our life will be like from now on. Insanity, but the best kind.

My head falls back in a silent moan as Adam grips my hips, looking down at where we're connected. "Come for me, baby."

Riggs grunts, watching like Adam is as I release, waiting for my men to do the same.

Adam growls, thrusting harder and filling me with his seed.

I'm smiling, for once, I'm smiling and it's pure.

Riggs breathes heavier, stepping forward and releasing all over my thigh, dripping down to where Adam and I are still connected. "This is going to be a wild ride, ain't it, sunshine?"

I'm out of breath, biting my lip as I glance between my men. "The best one yet."

Adam kisses me and Riggs drags his tongue up my neck.

This is my happy ending.

Pure, orgasmic, happiness.

Adam

We stumble out of the bathroom, cheeks red and giggles floating around us. Riggs slaps her ass, biting his lip as he watches her walk ahead of us, glancing over her shoulder.

"You sure about this?" I ask him, stopping by the stairs as she continues to the dining room.

Riggs scratches under his chin, nodding. "I've wanted her since I walked outta that hospital room. I wanted her when I was inside other women. Fucking Christ, I wanted her when I was with Shyanne. It's always been Zay, no matter how we gotta do this. We're doing this."

I inhale, nodding, and take a step forward but stop, spotting Judas outside talking to the guy who led us into the house earlier. "Judas is here."

This bizarre newfound relationship we started can wait. There's unfinished business with the club that's taking precedence at the moment. Riggs whips his head around, jaw clicking, and pushes open the front door. "Hey!"

Judas freezes, eyes wide with fear. "R-Riggs. Adam."

"Why the fuck didn't you tell me about this, huh?" Riggs takes him by the sweater, pulling him to his tiptoes. "My mama was alive and you didn't say shit? I could disband you for this. Strip you of the Snakes title. I could fucking end you."

Judas puts his hands up in surrender, glancing at me. "Your mama asked me to keep my mouth shut."

"Then why didn't you tell me about the women, huh?" Riggs goes on, still holding him by the sweater. Judas is struggling to stand, feet barely touching the ground. "You know I've been trying to stop this shit. Get the Snakes away from this life. Why the fuck didn't you tell me about the Panthers? About The Ghost?"

Judas struggles to breathe, it's quick, ragged. "Look, my girl was part of this. She was taken because of the Panthers and I saved her. I ain't about to let no more girls get taken because of them. I thought I could do it on my own. I thought if I didn't involve you, then they'd trust me more."

Riggs bares his teeth. "You thought fucking wrong."

It's been haunting us since we found out. Eating at the back of our minds that someone is out there giving names to the Panthers of innocent people to kidnap and trade-off. They probably make a pretty penny off of it, too. That's why Daddy did it. But Riggs has washed our hands of it.

All of it.

The source must be someone leading the Panthers.

"Who's in charge of the names they have?" I ask, folding my arms across my chest.

"No one knows. It's just an envelope that arrives at their clubhouse and the names are distributed to whoever wants the assignment," Judas answers, swallowing thickly. "My girl still talks to the whores there. That's how we get the names. But I don't know who runs it." He winces as Riggs lifts him higher, choking sounds cast through the warm breeze. "I swear it, Riggs."

He grunts, releasing Judas who stumbles back on his ass with a shaky breath. "I want a sit down with the Panthers. I want it done *now*."

Judas nods quickly, pushing himself up and dusting his hands. "Course, Riggs."

"This shit is ending. Whoever is involved in the club will suffer consequences. That goes double for any of my Snakes." Riggs has his finger pointed at Judas, scolding him like a child. "Do I make myself clear?"

Judas nods, taking his phone out. "I'll set it up now. We can probably swing by the Richmond charter, use their chapel."

"Have everyone there in two hours." Riggs grunts, turning back to the house. "Adam, inside, *now*."

I'm still staring at Judas, frowning and trying to understand how things continue to unravel.

Can't we catch a fucking break?

I groan internally and follow Riggs. He roams the house to find Slade in the kitchen, helping Mama Rosa make lunch. "Make yours to-go. We got chapel in two hours. Peter ain't coming, I can assume that, but we gotta be there." Riggs reaches back and taps my stomach. "Adam will be my VP, you'll be my sergeant at arms. We got shit we need to deal with before changes are made. Soon, we ain't gonna be part of this no more. I need all hands on deck—"

"No need to ask me twice, boss." Slade smiles. "I'll be right by your side 'til the end."

Riggs nods, stepping back as Mama smiles at him. "We'll be gone for a little, Mama. Don't bother making me a plate."

"Be careful, please, Riggsy," she says, placing a gentle hand on Slade's bicep.

Riggs inhales sharply, heading for the dining room, and wiping the sweat from his brow. While I'm still trying to wrap my head around what the fuck happened in the bathroom. Are we doing this?

Are we seriously going to be one of those weirdo throuples who galavants everywhere and fucks all the time?

I know Zay loves me, there's no question about that. Everything she put up with just to be with me proves it. But she's always had a soft spot for Riggs since she met him. I was jealous for a time when he returned, hated that they shared longing glances from across the room, as if no words needed to be said for an *I love you* to brew. Their bond is strong, like ours. And now our bond will be united. All of us.

Oof, this is going to have to take some getting used to.

"You all right, man?" Slade asks, taking a savage bite out of a sandwich.

I nod, wiping a hand down my face as Mama turns her back to us to make some iced tea. "I think I'm in a throuple."

He snorts, chuckling softly. "Anyone coulda told you that."

I hum. "Mmm, with my brother, though."

"Not like you have to fuck him, you're both sleeping with Zay, right?"

I nod, taking a step back. He's right, but I don't know how quickly this newness will sink in and be normal and less complicated. I inhale sharply, pushing it aside for when the time is right to sit and talk it through, and head to the dining room where Peter is already standing and scoffing at Riggs. Just want we needed, more arguing.

"Just like that? You're gonna walk out now? Mama is alive, Riggs, we should be here and leave the club bullshit for another time." Peter places a hand on his shoulder, wincing. "That shit can wait."

Riggs glances at Zay who is bent over the table, making silly faces at Rosa. "You got your family back, I'm just getting mine. I want this settled before we move on. Only way to do that is to deal with it now before it festers. I ain't waiting. And you're not coming."

Peter scoffs, looking back at Dorian whose mouth is set in a hard line. "Adam and Slade going?" Riggs nods, crossing his arms. "Everyone going?" He nods again. "Fuck, okay." Peter sighs, dropping his head. "Okay."

"Nothing you gotta worry about, kid. Be with your girl and your baby," Riggs says, squeezing Dorian's shoulder and heading for the door without another word.

"Riggs?" Zay says, staring at me. He glances over his shoulder, eyes on the ground. "Be careful."

He grunts and continues down the hall with Slade hot on his tail.

Zay smiles, coming to me and placing her hands on my chest as she rises on her toes to kiss me. "Come home to me."

I smirk, kissing the tip of her nose. "Always and forever, babe."

With a hesitant sigh, I follow Riggs and Slade into the hot sun, grumbling under my breath. From this day forth, we're burying all our faults and banishing the bullshit the club is involved in. I don't want to see that frightful look on my wife's face again. I want to stay home with her. Be with her. *I'll come home, babe. Forever and Always.*

This day is one for the world records, what more shit can explode in our faces that haven't already?

Riggs

Tapping my thumb on the steering wheel, I stare at the clubhouse in Richmond I've been to before with Daddy. He and Gunner go way back. They started the Snakes together, but Gunner stepped down and became a nomad when Daddy and Roaden went dirty.

I don't know how Gunner will react to seeing us again.

Seeing me. The last time we spoke I defended Roaden for something I didn't know was all his fault. He was my uncle, my only thought was family is family. I always gotta defend them. I only found out the truth later. He killed a hooker because she bit his dick. That hooker happened to be Gunner's VP's sidepiece. War broke out that Daddy ended, stating we separate the club. We stay in San Jose and Gunner stays in Richmond.

Well, now we're here and I gotta face reality eventually.

Slade wipes his mouth, tonguing his cheek from the two sandwiches Mama made him. Shit, Mama. It's going to be interesting saying her name again. Seeing her face and calling her when I need her. Today has been both bitter and sweet. "All good, boss?"

I grunt, looking in the rearview at Adam. "Gunner—their president—and I had a falling out because of Roaden. Don't know if he's still pissed about that."

Adam sputters, shaking his head as he looks out the window. "It's been ten years, Riggs. I'm sure he's over it."

Gunner steps out of their clubhouse, handlebar mustache completely white with a cigarette dangling from his mouth, and stands at the entrance, arms crossed over his chest. Nope, he's still pissed.

"After this meeting, we're gonna call Peter, fill him in," I tell them, killing the engine and getting out of the KIA that has bullet holes on the right side of it.

I have mixed feelings about being here. We didn't end on good terms the last time we spoke, I can only imagine what today will bring. But I gotta turn over all stones, lay this club to rest once and for all. And that means making amends.

Gunner's clubhouse is far different than ours. His is a warehouse they turned into an autobody shop where they fix cars for cash, have their meetings, and have bedrooms at the back for their security. Everything is beige and black, unlike the reds our clubhouse bleeds.

Adam lifts his jeans, standing by my side as Slade does the same. "Hey, man," Adam says, waving at Gunner.

He grunts, pulling the cigarette and flicking it aside. "What did I tell you, boy? You ain't allowed here no more."

I grumble and step forward, putting my hands up in surrender. "I ain't Daddy and I ain't Roaden. I didn't know what went down before I defended that dickhead. They paid their dues—"

"I know, we had a party for your loss," Gunner interrupts me.

I take another step closer, seeing Gunner puff out his chest like this is some dogfight he needs to be prepared for. "They're taking women, Gunner. I wanna put a stop to this. Mama wanted a stop to this—"

He smirks, interrupting me again. "I know, I have dinner with her every Sunday after church."

Another person who knew Mama was alive and didn't say shit to me.

I'm about to light up this place in a second.

But I breathe like Zay does with Peter. She doesn't like me when I'm mad.

The less angry of a man I am, the better I'll be for her.

"Think we can sit down with you and fill you in before the Panthers get here?" I ask, releasing another breath.

Gunner narrows his eyes, looking from me to Adam, then Slade. "You didn't know your mama was alive?"

Adam and I shake our heads as I inhale another slow breath. "Daddy and

Roaden kept us in the dark about a lot of shit," I scoff, frowning. How much did Daddy keep in the dark? Did *he* know Mama was alive?

Judas pulls up to my left with Lip, Skeet, Dillon, and Mickey. I nod at them as they get off their bikes, taking in the situation. "All good?" Lip asks, eyeing Gunner and nodding his head at him.

I jerk my head at Gunner. "All good?"

He claps his hands, fanning them to either side of him. "Let's get some whiskey in us and call this chapel what it is, a reunion to the death of the fucks who're rotting in hell."

I chuckle, following suit and heading inside the clubhouse.

But I don't think we'll have time to fill them in, the Panthers are pulling up, too.

Fuckers.

Still, I keep walking inside and my men follow me, heading to the back of the warehouse where a long table sits with an assortment of chairs around it. Not as nice as our clubhouse, either. This one is dirty and filled with boxes and containers. The damn table is just two folding tables placed together with graffiti of the Snakes' logo.

But that's Gunner for you. He cares more about paying his men than fixing up their clubhouse.

Gunner sits at the head of the table with his crew around him. I take the other side, Adam to my right, Slade to my left, and wait until everyone is in before I bang my fist on the table. "Now, Riggs, I think we should take a moment before going all hostile."

I shake my head and Gunner sits back, about to enjoy a show.

Grabbing Domino by the hair, I slam his head on the table. His crew doesn't move, they eye each other about to go for their guns but I think they know better.

Judas must've informed them of what this meeting was going to be about.

"Domino, last time my VP saw you, you came to him scared shitless because The Ghost sent you a letter. Why don't you tell my brothers-in-arms here, why he sent you a letter," I grit out, pushing his head into the table as blood seeps from the cut on his brow.

He whimpers, looking at me from the corner of his eye. "Look, Riggs, it ain't me. I don't want this shit. This is all—"

I lift and slam his head down again, more blood decorating the tip of the Snakes' tail. "I don't want excuses, I want answers."

Domino's crew does nothing. All little puppy dogs that know they did wrong, waiting to get fucking beat. "We don't know where they come from. We just get letters in the mail with pictures, names, and places. Sometimes there's more than one name, sometimes there's just a location and a picture. At the bottom of every letter, there's a different address, mostly warehouses, but it's never the same place. We take the girls and bring them to the location. We don't meet anyone, we don't trade them over. We leave them drugged, tied up, and then money shows up at our doorstep the next day. I don't know who is part of this, all I know is what I told you. Liam tried stopping it. He burned every letter that came to us and told Mama Rosa where to send her goons to pick up the girls. He'd save them before being taken—"

"And now you just let them get taken like a fucking disgraceful bastard," Slade spits out, raising his voice. "There are kids, too, man! Do you take the fucking kids, too?"

I grind my teeth, staring at the shameful faces of a few of the Panthers.

Motherfucking assholes.

Every last one of them will suffer an excruciating death. I'll make sure of it.

Do it my-damn-self.

Domino whimpers, saliva, tears, and his blood seep onto the table, sending that thrill racing through my heart. I fucking missed this.

Oh, Zay will be in for a wild ride when I leave the club. I'll only be able to get this thrill when I slap her ass around a little. Don't think she'll mind some ropes, blindfolds, or wear my handprint proudly on her ass and my bite marks on her thighs and tits.

Now I'm fucking hard, but I can't do anything about it until these fuckers pay.

I grunt, lifting Domino's head and slamming it down a third time. His head is probably throbbing, stars and spots clouding his vision.

"What's the endgame here, Riggs?" Gunner asks, nostril-flaring at the

Panthers around us with their heads down. Ashamed fuckers. "This shit is the reason I ain't part of your charter no more."

I don't know what to do.

These fuckers don't know anything.

Things are dropped off.

Empty warehouses for the girls.

Not a single one of them tries to find out the truth.

"Cameras," Slade steps in, looking at me. "You guys gotta have cameras around your club, no?"

Domino groans, trying to get up but I push him down harder. "Our clubhouse got busted last year, we installed double the cameras but…"

Adam growls, pushing up from the table. "But lemme guess, they don't work whenever the fucker drops off the names or the cash."

Domino nods and whimpers when he looks at Skeet adjusting the brass knuckles. "I can give you all the footage. Anything you want. We don't know nothing other than the color of his car. Black Mercedes. No plates. That's all we know."

Judas arches a brow, joining his hands on the table. "And how do you know that?"

His VP, Miguel, releases a breath, and his shaking hands hold out his cell phone. "Last week when they dropped off cash, we got footage of their car and someone dressed in black."

I snatch the phone, watching the video with Adam over my shoulder. A black Mercedes pulls up, but we can only see half the car through the falling water, the front half.

They came by that stormy night last week. I remember it because it was the night I walked in on Adam and Zay in the shower. I stayed in the shadows watching as he took her from behind. Her tits pressed up against the glass.

The video shows someone getting out of the car, clothes black and baggy from head to toe. They run to the front door, drop off a duffel bag, and leave.

The video glitches when they drive away and resumes to the empty parking lot as the rain showers down on the asphalt.

"Nothing else?" I ask, dropping the phone on the table. It hits Domino's face, making Slade chuckle.

Domino shakes his head. "Nothing."

"Any new *shipments* come in?" Lip asks, leaning on the table with a hardened jaw.

Miguel looks at his crew as silence fills the room. Gunner growls, getting up from the table and taking Miguel by the ponytail, dragging him to where he's sitting. "You ain't gonna talk, spick? Fine. Then you won't be needing this no more."

He opens Miguel's mouth, holding his tongue out with a smile. Miguel screams, thrashing and falling back with a thud. Gunner's about to cut his fucking tongue out.

Gunner's VP lifts Miguel, holding his arms back as another Snakes member holds Miguel's head still. "Ready?" Gunner chuckles, sliding his blade from his ankle holster.

Oh, fuck.

Gunner slices Miguel's tongue off in one quick slice. Blood shoots from his mouth, splattering on Gunner's face as he lowers himself. "Now, there are six of you men here. I don't mind doing this to every single one of you. After I'm done with your tongues, I'll start on your fingers, then your toes. And when I'm done with those, I'll cut off your dicks, then your nuts. And Hey, if I'm feeling generous, I'll let you keep one of them. God gave us two for a reason, no?"

Adam and I share a glance, finding Judas's gaze, then Slade's.

This fucking guy is just as crazy as Daddy.

Domino is crying on the table as he watches Miguel hold onto his bleeding mouth, man is so shocked he isn't even screaming. "We have three scheduled."

"When?" I growl out, lifting his right arm to his back, and twisting it as far as I can without snapping it.

Domino whimpers, sucking his teeth. "Check my back pocket."

I lift off him, tucking my hand in his pockets, and find the paper. There's a long list of names on it. "There's ten fucking names on this list."

Domino sobs, snot, and saliva leaking from him. "It's a big payout. Our last one of the year. He promised. He fucking promised."

Gunner laughs, taking another one of the Panthers, kicking him to his knees. "Ten names, you say?" he asks me. I look back at the list and count, answering him with a nod. "Ten names, six guys, that's two body parts each if math serves me right." He laughs gripping the hair on Miguel's head. It doesn't, but no one says anything. "See I ain't too good in school, that's why I dropped out. But the way my VP is counting on his fingers, that's two body parts per person."

Dillion cracks the bones in his neck, rubbing his hands together. "Tell me what you want me to do, Riggs."

"I ain't a disturbed fuck like that." I eye Gunner. "I prefer it if they end up six feet underground. I don't mess with body parts."

Gunner laughs roughly, the tip of his blade pointed at Miguel's eye. "Lucky for you, I do."

His VP snickers, gripping Miguel's arms again. "I'll take care of this one, Riggs. Consider it absolution from all the shit your daddy did."

Something doesn't feel right, but we don't have answers.

Not a goddamn answer.

I wasn't expecting anything, either. This guy in the Mercedes is probably not even the one running things. He's a messenger, I'd bet my tongue and nuts on it.

This will never end.

No matter how hard we try. No matter how hard we fight, we ain't never gonna find the leader of the trafficking.

I'm out. As soon as I hand over the reins, I'm leaving the club. But I'll be there when they need me. I'll keep trying to find the culprit. I'll search until my fingers bleed.

Not a single girl will be taken because of a motorcycle club.

Not another one sold or beaten.

No more will be raped.

We are ending this.

One day at a time.

Gunner gets to work, cutting Miguel's fucking eye out as the rest of Gunner's crew grab onto the Panthers, preparing them for the torture they're about to endure.

Every single one of them deserves it.

I lean down, gritting my teeth as I bring my mouth to Domino's ear. "If I find out you're still involved in this shit after he's finished with you, then it will be me who knocks at your door and you're going to wish it's just body parts you're losing. I will make your life a living hell. Do you understand me?"

Domino nods and I release him, letting him slide off the table onto the floor.

Slade grimaces, watching Gunner and his VP laugh as Miguel screams bloody murder, eye popping out of its socket. "Fucking nasty." He rubs his stomach, looking at me a little green.

I inhale sharply, jerking my head at Gunner. "Hey, man. All settled?"

He smiles over his shoulder, blood coating his face. "See you at church on Sunday, brother."

This feels wrong.

But I have no choice. I want to see my woman. I want my son.

I want to start our life the way it should have been and leave all of his behind us.

Soon, we'll find the bastard.

Soon, we'll kill the fucker who's in charge.

Today, I got the satisfaction of getting my woman but I didn't get the satisfaction of finding the fucker who hurts these women.

One day we will.

One day, all of the innocent women will be free.

For now, I will love freely in this newfound relationship Zay, Adam, and I will build.

We'll fill our house with babies, mine and his.

We'll fill the house with moans.

Laughter.

Happiness.

We'll live freely like God wanted for us.

Maybe I will go to church on Sunday. Show Mama I'm still the good

Christian boy she raised. Maybe, just maybe, things will be so much better. Because I finally found my peace.

Adam

After that shitshow, we're finally back at Maddison Gardens. The first thing I do is kiss Zay like I just got back from war, and well, so does Riggs. They stare at us, but I don't care. We chose this and I'm actually coming around to the idea. Any chance to see Zay's eyes roll to the back of her head and toes curl is fine with me.

We're free. At least it feels this way. Sooner or later, the trafficking will fade. Sooner or later, the problems we had with the club will be no longer. Sooner or later, we will be free.

The sun is setting as we sit outside after dinner, enjoying the serenity of this day. Heartache brought us together. It destroyed us, too. But look at the family we have. It's chaotic and wild, but it's ours.

Riggs has his arm draped over Zay's shoulders, but her lips are on mine, kissing me as whiskey invades our mouths. We've had one too many tonight, but we needed it. All of us did.

After the knife that felt like she stabbed into my heart, I realized that maybe living wildly is what we need. We're not the stale, typical family who wakes up, goes to work, comes home, tends to the kids, and fucks on a schedule.

Zay and I have always been different.

What's more different than this?

Slade lets out a laugh as Mama fills his glass, telling us stories the way she always did as kids. Stories about her life, about us, about the farm. Mama tells us stories until our bellies hurt from laughing.

It was a shock to see her again. Another knife to the heart. But Mama did so much good for this world. "Good" we all silently agreed we're going to help with.

Panthers are ending their aid in trafficking. Gunner's making sure of that by dismembering them slowly but surely. I didn't know the fucker was that deranged.

But even though we're out of the club, we'll still have one foot in. I don't want to ignore the fact that we don't know who is the ring leader for the trafficking. We have to for now. For now, my wife is more important. And she'll understand that we need to stay and help end this bullshit.

As for The Ghost, well, we're going to end him before he hurts any more of my family. He's done enough damage over the years. Enough is enough. We'll get through to him sooner or later, right? Dorian is his sister after all. He can't stay mad at us forever over something we never caused. We'll have a sit down as soon as someone finds the fucker.

Peter and Dorian sit in front of us, baby suckling on her breast as Peter's good arm is wrapped around her shoulders watching. I've seen Riggs melt from pride when he looks at Carter, but the way Peter is staring at his girls. It's utter bliss.

Beauty in all its forms.

It's happiness.

Zay drapes her legs on my lap, biting her lip to hide her smile. She's always been my forever. My love.

We're embarking on a new journey away from this club. And for once, I'm going to do what I promised her. I'm going to quit this life. I'm going to give her babies. Give her the house she deserves.

We both are.

She's mine, but I don't mind sharing now and then, as long as I get to watch.

I kiss her knee, tracing circles around her calves. *I love you*, I mouth.

Forever and always, she mouths back.

This right here, sitting around the table, is pure happiness.

Epilogue - Zay

I'm looking out the window, watching as the gentle snowflakes fall onto the ground, coating it in fresh fluffy snow. The windshield wipers scrape against the glass as Riggs keeps a protective hand on my leg while gripping the steering wheel with the other.

The roads up here aren't too bad, but sometimes, black ice is hiding under the fresh snow and could derail any car into a ditch or the trees surrounding us. But with me and Carter in the truck, Riggs drives so damn slow, it would be faster to walk home at this point.

Life has been so crazy the past three years. I'm still blinded by all the chaos we went through to end up here. Happy. Finally fucking happy. I thank God every damn day for my happiness. Something I strived for, for so long, and now that it's here, I can't thank Him enough.

About a year after Maddison Gardens, Riggs, Adam, and Peter were rid of the club. They wiped their hands clean of it and handed it to the men who continued to stand by their sides no matter the mess it brought. Every now and then, Riggs and Adam will check in, still in search of the ring leader for the trafficking. They've captured and sent many assholes to Gunner for some torture over the years, but the guy who runs the entire shitshow is still a mystery. Something they expected. They don't think they'll ever find this guy, but they're hopeful, and that's all we can ask for.

Slade is the only one who stayed a member, but he works for Mama Rosa now. Changing up the way things are run at the sanctuary. Lip and Judas work for her, too, helping bring so many people to safety. No more masked men. Just honest tough guys who needed a purpose. Slade finally found his purpose.

And Maddison Gardens is truly a magical place.

Peter and Dorian have popped out two more children—Sara and Mina—filling the little home he purchased for them that's just outside of Maddison Gardens. Seeing him with his girls is the most precious thing I could ever ask for. He finally has that sparkle in his eyes. No more mischief, no more heartache. Just beauty. He's never been this thankful to God in all of his days. Peter got his redemption. He got his ticket out of here. And I hope his smile never goes away.

They go to church again—something we do, too. Every Sunday like clockwork we sit in the pews and listen to the pastor recite his sermon. Meanwhile, Riggs tries his hardest to be that good Christian boy his mama raised, but I won't lie and say we didn't have sex in the confessionals at least twice. Adam joined the second time.

It's been interesting, to say the least, with Adam, Riggs, and I. But we manage.

We love hard, fuck hard, and laugh so much my face hurts.

Last I heard, things with the club have been running smoothly. They haven't returned to guns or drugs. There aren't any more drive-bys or shoot-outs. There's peace like Riggs wanted.

The Ghost has been MIA since he ordered the hit on us. Riggs installed security systems at everyone's homes, keeping all of us armed as well. The last thing he wants is for an unwanted guest to come back from God knows where to seek revenge once again.

Mama has tried reaching out to Wilde, she's tried to make amends, but The Ghost remains hidden. Evaporated into nothingness.

It's a lingering fear that licks up my spine when I'm alone, wondering when he'll show up or when he'll decide to hurt us. Riggs constantly reminds me that he's here, that he won't let anything happen to me. It has been three years. I keep telling myself that The Ghost is history. And eventually, I'll believe it.

I groan, adjusting myself on the seat. "Ugh, I gotta pee again."

Riggs laughs, looking in the rearview mirror as Carter makes engine noises with his toy cars. "Baby giving you a hard time?"

I move my hands over my belly of seven months and chuckle. "My boys are always giving me a hard time."

Riggs laughs again, squeezing my thigh as he does. "Almost at the finish line, sunshine."

I growl, leaning my head back against the headrest. "I can't fucking wait. I don't understand how Dorian has done this three times. She's crazy."

"You would've been just as many babies deep if you stopped taking your birth control, y'know." Riggs waggles his eyebrows and sticks his tongue out. "Just wait, after this one, I'm popping another in you."

I arch an eyebrow, my pulse beating with excitement at the thought of taking it raw from him. "Such a cocky bastard to think this baby's yours," I tease, giggling as he bites his bottom lip and squeezes my thigh. I don't have the heart to tell him I think Adam won their little game at who would get me pregnant first.

Another growl moves its way to his lips. "You're gonna pay for that later, baby." He glances in the rearview and grunts. "If he wasn't in the back seat, I'd force your face on my c-o-c-k."

I hum, leaning over and kissing his shoulder. "Do go on."

He sucks his teeth and pulls onto the road that leads to the cabin we've been living in for the better part of two years. Carter loves the snow, he says it's his favorite because he can eat it and make snowmen with it. Riggs hates it when he eats the snow, but Adam and I don't say anything, we're right there with our tongues hanging out as the fresh snow coats it.

"I'm hungry," Carter whines, dropping his toy car as we pull up to the cabin.

I smile over my shoulder, unclipping my belt. "Then let's get something to eat. And maybe we can have hot cocoa for dessert with extra marshmallows, would you like that?"

He smiles, looking just like his father, and tries to unclip himself from the car seat.

Riggs kills the engine and pulls me in for a kiss. "Love you, sunshine."

I chuckle softly. "Yeah, yeah, love you, too, you big galoot." I get out of the truck and stretch out my back before I unclip Carter. "Hurry up, big guy, Mama's gotta pee."

He giggles, jumps out of the car into the slush on the ground, and runs to Riggs's side of the truck, going headfirst into a pile of snow. "Carter!" Riggs scolds. "Go inside."

I haven't stopped smiling for three years.

And I don't think I'll ever stop.

Adam stayed behind today when we went into town for groceries, he's doing the laundry and the dishes. He doesn't like going out in public as a family all the time. He says people stare too much for his liking. I don't blame him, not many people choose to be in this type of relationship, but for us, it works.

For us, I wouldn't have it any other way.

I look back as Riggs lifts Carter over his shoulder and falls back with him in the snow bank, emitting so many giggles from his son it makes my smile grow. Gosh, we do have something beautiful here, don't we?

Pulling open the screen door, I reach for the knob on the front door only to notice it's broken. Why is it broken? Fear licks its way up my spine, sending an unnerving shiver through me.

I bring a hand onto my stomach and gulp, pushing the door open with my foot. Adam's muffled screams move through the home as I see him on his knees, blood leaking down his face as his long blonde hair sticks to his sweaty temples. His mouth is covered in duct tape, hands bound behind his back. "Oh, God," I cry, taking a step back.

The man in a green devil mask sits at the table, holding Adam up by his hair as a knife twirls in his hand. "Well, well, well. Seems like you bunch are a lot harder to find than I thought."

I whimper, keeping the screen door open with my shoulder and I protect my unborn child with my hands. This is a dream, right? That prickle on my skin isn't from the sight of my husband bleeding and bound. It's from a nightmare I'm about to wake up from.

No.

No.

No.

"Zay?" Riggs asks out of breath. "Zay, what's wrong?"

I turn my head slightly enough for him to see the fear on my face and tears as they fall.

He takes off running, tossing Carter into the truck, and coming toward me as slush splashes under his feet.

"There's no use in running anymore, is there?" The masked man laughs. "The Ghost has come to haunt this home and all who live in it."

He stands, gripping Adam's hair harder and dragging him toward me. My poor husband thrashes, screams, and cries as he's manhandled like a ragdoll.

While I'm frozen in disbelief. The Ghost came out of hiding to destroy us like he planned.

Destroy us over something we had nothing to do with.

Feeling myself unravel, I take a sharp breath in and watch this demon come to life, hurting my husband while I can't even move a muscle to help.

Fear rushes over me like a dark suffocating wave. This is it, isn't it?

We're paying for our sins.

The Ghost stops in front of me, gripping Adam's hair tighter and forcing him back onto his knees. That demonic mask isn't removed. It stays in place, tilting to the side as it stares deep into my soul. The devil has come home to drag us to hell.

I hear Riggs's heavy footfalls coming closer, but it's not close enough.

A cry leaves me as The Ghost brings the blade up, laughing as he does, and changing everything that ever truly made me smile.

Everything flips.

Everything we built is gone.

My screams aren't enough to wake the dead.

Adam's cries aren't enough to protect us.

Riggs's yells aren't enough to save us.

Once your fate is sealed, it never truly leaves you, does it?

IV

Slade

Slade

The Stowaway Series - Part Four

SLADE

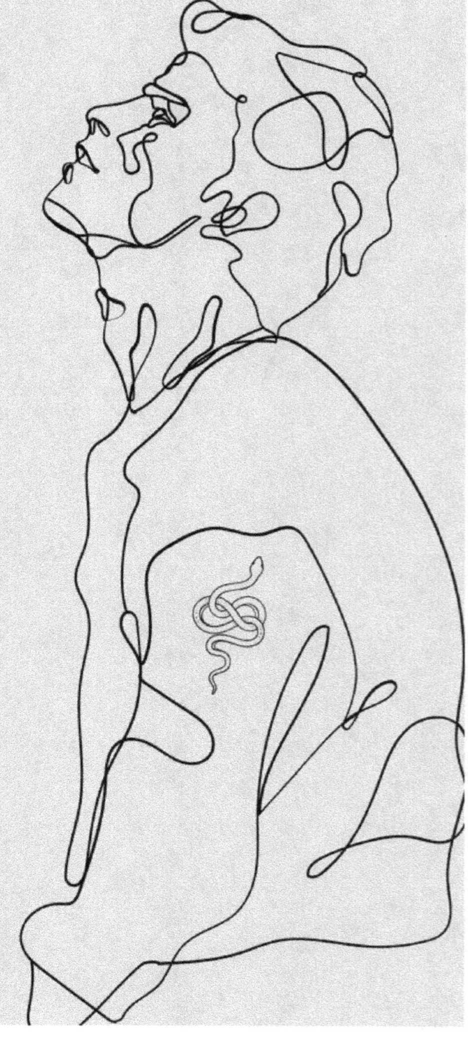

Award-Winning Author
Alyssa Milani

One man's hope for freedom turns into one woman's fight for survival.

Riding never felt so freeing. Getting lost on the open road, just me and the bike. No one telling me what to do, no one to stop me from making stupid decisions.

Only freedom.

I'm pulled over, taking a much-needed piss break. I left Mama Rosa's not too long ago, heading to San Jose to see Lip about some Snakes' problem at the bar. I'm the go-to guy when Riggs and Adam aren't free. It's been an interesting few years, to say the least.

As soon as I release the piss onto the snowbank, my phone vibrates in my pocket. It's probably Palmer, my strawberry-blonde queen from Maddison Gardens. She's helped me through many lonely nights and I'm aching to get back to her, but duty calls with the Snakes, and my loyalty will stay with them for as long as I'm needed. Or until I make her my wife. When she'll accept us for more than what we are, I'll cut my ties to the MC altogether. Take a page out of the Donnelly boys' book.

Looking down, a private number lights up the screen on my phone—it's probably from the cabin. Riggs makes sure to keep their phone numbers hidden, exiling them from the world. He's the protector, always will be. And now that they're growing their family, staying hidden is high on his list.

Mama Rosa makes sure all her boys are present and proper every Sunday at mass. And I'm happy to announce that I'm included. She makes sure to make me feel welcome—they all do. For once in my life, I finally found a family worth staying with.

I glance at my phone again, frowning. *Why would they call me?* I just saw Zay and Riggs this morning when they picked up Carter. They never call me, the only time they do is if there's an emergency. Not liking this panic settling in my belly.

"Yellow?"

Silence spreads through the line.

"Riggs? Adam?"

Nothing.

"Zay?"

A soft breath moves through the speaker and I frown, leaning the phone on my shoulder to tuck myself away. "Hey? Everything all right?"

A sniff, too soft to be the guys', and too innocent to be Zay's. "Hello?"

"Uncle Slade?" Carter's voice sends a sharp tug at my insides, and all my senses heighten.

Why the fuck is he calling me on the private phone?

"Hey, bud, what's up? Is everything okay?"

He sniffs again, whimpering. "I'm scared," he whispers with chattering teeth.

Nope, don't like that.

I'm gunning it to the bike, switching the phone to my AirPods, and shoving my helmet on.

Kicking it into high gear.

I'm forty-five minutes out. If I speed, I'll make it there in thirty. It's mid-March, but snow still sticks to the ground, fresh slush coating the open road. It's a death trap for a motorbike, but I don't give a shit. I'll ride until they take the damn thing away from me.

There's a fucking rock lodged in my throat, an urge to protect this four-year-old takes hold and he isn't even mine.

But I'm here, I'll do whatever he needs, he just has to ask. "What're you scared of?" I try to gulp this lump down, but nothing is working. The fear that boils inside me is maddening. "Where's Mommy? Or your Daddies?"

He sniffs again and it sends me into a fucking panic. This kid is so strong. So damn smart to think to call me. He's gone through hell the first year of his life and is living in his glory with Zay, Adam, and Riggs as his parents. He doesn't need more heartache.

He doesn't fucking need it.

The pit of my stomach flutters. That same feeling Zay gets when something bad is about to happen. I don't like this one fucking bit.

"Carter? You still there, bud?" I raise my voice a little, speeding through the cars like I have the cops on my ass. "Talk to me."

He whimpers softly, lowering his voice. "Daddy put me in the truck and said to hide. I don't know where my mommy is." He sniffs again. "I want my mommy, Uncle Slade."

Tears well in my eyes, blurring my vision. If something happened to her, all hell would break loose. These men will burn this fucking planet down to figure out what happened, not only to her, but to the baby in her belly, too.

I clear my throat, exhaling slowly to calm my racing heart. "What do you see? Do you hear anything, Carter? I need you to be my eyes until I get there, okay?" I grit my teeth, switching onto the shoulder of the highway and gunning it. "Did you call Uncle Peter or Auntie Dorian?"

"He won't pick up the phone."

I nod even though he can't see me. "Okay, can you tell me what you see? Don't get out of the truck, stay low, okay, bud?"

The *swish-swish* of his jacket moves through my ears, and so do his sniffs.

The two agonizing minutes make me audibly growl, punching the space between the handles of my bike. I've called his name seven times, but he doesn't answer. Fuck, why did I tell him to move? Why did I say to be my eyes? He should have fucking remained where he was. Stayed hidden until I got there. If something happens, I'll never fucking forgive myself.

A pressure settles on my chest, making it hard for me to breathe. "God-dammit, Carter!"

He starts crying, his jacket *swishing* again. "I'm sorry."

I sigh, the pressure easing up a little as I take notice of the exit up ahead. "No, no. I'm sorry, bud. I shouldn't have yelled. But you have to answer me when I say your name, okay?"

"Okay."

I'm still on the shoulder, brushing past people as they yell and blare their horns at me. "Tell me, what do you see?"

"I'm hiding behind Daddy's chair."

I sniff, taking the exit and slamming on the brakes at the light at the end of the turn. "Okay, good. Good. But what do you see around you? Outside?"

"The front door is broken and Mommy is painting."

I release a shallow breath. "What do you mean? What is she painting?"

"Something red."

My heart's in my throat as I inch forward, trying to see a way through the parked cars at the red light. "Okay, okay."

"Daddy was yelling after he put me in the truck. Maybe he didn't like the color Mommy picked."

I wince, finding my opening and taking it. This kid doesn't need more blood in his life.

He doesn't need death.

He needs that happiness that his family gave him.

That peace.

"Okay, bud, I'm coming. I'm a few minutes away. Do not move."

My bike skids on the road, slipping and sliding all over the damn place. There's a reason we're not allowed bikes in the middle of March. I don't give a shit, though. None of us do.

But I make it. I'm on the road to their cabin.

"I hear a motorcycle, Uncle Slade. Is that you?"

I grit my teeth, seeing Riggs's truck just a few feet away. "It's me. I'm right here. But stay in the truck, okay? Stay in it until I come get you."

I stop my bike, too fucking scared to look at the house but I have to. By God, I have to help *my* family.

My phone dings and I see an incoming call from Peter. A call I'm too fucking scared to answer. But again, I have to answer.

"Carter? I'm going to hang up now, okay? But don't be scared. I'm calling Uncle Peter. Remember, I'm right outside the truck, okay?" I reassure him the best way I can. "I'm right here."

But I don't know what to fucking do.

"Okay, Uncle Slade."

With hesitation, I hang up and slide my thumb over the screen, answering Peter's call and building the courage to look up at Zay. "Jesus, fuck," I gasp.

Everything is in shambles.

The door is broken, the screen billowing in the breeze. There's so much fucking blood. And Zay is just sitting there, blood decorating her torso; her hands shaking on her lap.

"Slade? Everything good? Riggs called but he's not answering—"

"Something happened!" I yell, storming to Zay. "Zay? Hey. Hey, look at me. Hey? Zay, what happened?" I wince, looking at the blood on her, and glance back at the truck. "Zay, who's blood is this?" She doesn't answer. Fuck, she doesn't even move more than the shaky breaths she's taking. "Zay?"

"What?" Peter shouts. "What happened? Slade? What the fuck happened?"

"I don't know," I whisper, moving strands of bloodied hair from in front of her face. "Zay? Hey, talk to me."

"Where are you?" Peter demands.

"The cabin—"

"I'm coming! Don't you fucking move, you hear me? I'm coming!" Peter says angrily, growling as he shouts something inaudible.

"Zay?" I tilt her chin up, looking into the house as a trail of blood leads to the back door.

There's so much blood on the front porch, even more soaking in the snow.

What the fuck happened here?

"Zay? Hey, can you look at me?"

She sniffs, eyes staring off at nothing as blood covers her. The paint Carter was talking about. Her breathing hitches as her hazel eyes slowly meet mine.

That desensitized look so many of the women have back home is written all over her face.

She's not scared. She's not sad or angry.

She's finished.

"Zay?"

Tears rise and slip free, moving through the blood on her cheeks. "The Ghost…he's back."

Peter

I run a hand frantically through my wet hair, slicking it back. I've kept it a medium length over the years for Dorian. She likes grabbing hold of it when my face is between her legs.

She fixes her bra strap, looking at our second born daughter, Sara, running to the living room. "Peter, what's wrong? You're scaring me."

I'm pacing the kitchen, gripping my hair when I stop by the island. "Zay… she's…I don't know. Fuck, I don't know."

Dorian swallows slowly, glancing back at our girls having breakfast by the television. "Peter?" she whispers.

I take my phone from the floor where I dropped it and call Riggs's phone. Not even one ring goes by before it's picked up.

"Riggs? What the fuck is going on, brother? Slade said Zay's—"

"Uncle Peter," Carter's shaky voice moves through the speaker.

I whimper, taking the phone from my ear and putting it on speaker. "Hey, big guy. Where's your Daddy?"

Carter sniffs, lowering his voice. "I don't know. Uncle Slade said not to move."

Dorian gets up from her seat and comes forward, moving the phone to her. "Carter, sweetheart? Can you explain what happened?"

He sniffs, making my heart break. My nephew has gone through enough. Anyone can see it. Everyone knows it.

My hands clench into fists and I punch the fridge, leaving a lovely dent in it.

"I want my mommy," he cries quietly, gasping next when the door to the truck opens.

"Carter? Carter! Who opened the door?" I yell, panic taking over my ability to breathe.

The Ghost...he's back.

"Hey, bud, it's just me. C'mere," Slade says, making my violently hammering heart calm slightly. Carter sniffs, voices muffled before I growl and bang my fist on the island.

"I'm sorry, baby, but I'm going." I snag the keys off the hook by the front door and stuff my feet into my boots.

"Peter—"

"Hello?" Slade's voice moves through the speaker.

"Hey," Dorian says, looking at our girls as they glance back at us. "What's going on?"

Slade sighs, shushing Carter. "How far out is Peter?"

"I'm leaving now," I call out, getting my jacket on and kissing my girls one by one before I plant a juicy one on my wife and take my phone. "I'll keep you posted, baby. In the meantime, get them ready and head to Mama's until I figure out what's going on."

She nods, wiping an escaping tear as I drag a finger down her slender nose. She has no idea how hard it is for me to be calm right now. My mind is panicking, my body is shaking, and I'm nauseous beyond words.

I haven't had a panic attack like this in ages.

Breathing slowly through it; in through my nose and out through my mouth, before I get into the car and the phone switches over to Bluetooth. "Slade?"

"I'm here."

"Is everyone...alive?" I ask the dreaded question and lean my head back, squeezing my eyes shut.

"There's a lot of blood. Zay's just—" he grumbles, grunts, and sniffs. "How long will you be?"

I reverse out of the long driveway, speeding down the slushy roads and heading to the cabin. "Twenty tops."

He releases a breath, shushing my nephew again. "I'm gonna get Zay in the truck and look around—"

"No, wait for me. I *have* to be there," I growl out. "Tell her I'm coming, okay? Fuck, tell her she's safe. Please."

He sniffs, his gruff voice moving through the speakers. "She's safe with me, Peter. I'll protect them with my life."

Releasing a breath, I hang up. I don't bother saying bye, I'm having a fucking panic attack. The first one I've had since my Sara was born.

Three years. Three goddamn years we were safe, protected. Now? Fuck, now I have no idea what's going to happen.

***

The first family meeting we had was the day after my wedding. A year after I got my girls back, and just months before Sara was born.

We sat at the table in the cabin; Riggs, Adam, Slade, Zaynab, and Dorian. My family.

Riggs sat at the head of the table with Zay to his left and Adam beside her.

They had a weird thing going, but I couldn't see it any other way. They matched. And Zay was the happiest I'd ever seen her.

Slade sat to Riggs's right, leaning his forearms on the table, waiting for Riggs to tell us what to do.

As for me, I was at the sink, gripping it as I watched Carter and Rosa play in the guest room that had now become his room. They were my reason to live. They always would be. They were my reason to protect this family. The way Riggs always wanted to protect me. I understood it and I wanted to do it, too.

"Kids are settled?" Riggs asked, clasping his hands in front of him.

I nodded without looking at him, keeping my eyes on the way Carter was helping Rosa build a tower with blocks.

He was just like his father, the protector, the teacher, and the one we always looked up to.

The way Rosa was staring at Carter as he held the tower in place; her big blue-gray eyes smiling at him with such admiration, they were going to be close all their lives. The best of friends.

"What're we gonna do about The Ghost? It's been over a year since all that shit went down. You think he's done?" Slade asked, looking at Dorian. "Has he reached out?"

She shakes her head, glancing at me. "I've tried reaching out to Gray, too. But nothing."

"Was she in on it?" Zay spoke up, folding her arms across her chest.

Dorian lifted her shoulder, making me crack the bones in my neck. I had a funny fucking feeling that Dorian's sister, Gray, and her girlfriend, Bells, had a hand in helping The Ghost; their half-brother, Wilde. But Dorian wouldn't let me bring it up during any family meeting. It would set everyone off and I loved Dorian with my entire being. I didn't want my family hating on her.

Plus, the last time we saw Gray and Bells was at our wedding, they'd been MIA ever since.

"We've got extra security at Judas's Hideout," I said, taking the non-alcoholic beer from in front of me and draining half of it.

"None of Mama Rosa's guys have heard anything from him, either," Adam added, draping an arm behind Zay's chair.

Riggs glanced around, nodding and listening to us. He had a plan but wanted to hear us out before he said his piece.

Slade tapped a finger in the table, shaking his head. "So we're just supposed to wait around like sitting ducks before this fucker comes back and kills one or all of us?"

"Seems so," Zay said, pushing herself up and heading to the fridge behind me, opening it.

Riggs leaned back in his chair, nodding slowly. "Well, I ain't gonna be the one to come out and say it, but what the hell else are we supposed to do other than sit around and wait? Dorian isn't in contact with anyone in her family, Mama lost one of her contacts, and I've tried pulling some strings, but I can't find anyone willing to get dirty and find out where this Ghost fucker is."

Zay cracked open a can of soda and sipped it, standing beside me. "So we're sitting ducks like Slade said."

Riggs dragged a hand down his face, his jaw twitching. "Yes, baby. There's nothing any of us can do but keep our eyes open for anything suspicious."

She scoffed, pushing the can aside and walking down the hallway to the bedroom—this cabin had become their home, something they turned their unconventional family into.

Riggs growled, pushing up and out of his chair to follow her, but I went to stop him. "Move before I move you," he said through gritted teeth.

"She needs a minute to relax," I said, tapping his brute chest.

Adam rose from his seat and sauntered over, clapping Riggs on the shoulder, then tilting his chin at me. "I'll talk my wife down."

Riggs growled again and I pressed my hands onto his chest again. "All she needs to know is that we'll keep her safe, we'll keep my wife safe, and most importantly, we'll keep the kids safe," I explained.

"I want to talk to her," Riggs huffed as Adam made his way down the hallway.

Looking back at him, I tugged Riggs's arm and sighed. "Can we talk?"

He grunted, glancing down the hallway as Adam knocked on the door, and flung his arm from my grasp. "Two minutes."

Riggs stormed outside, rounding the front of the house and sitting on the hood of my car. He's always been an intimidating fuck, but something about being in front of him when he looked at me with anger and fear in his eyes, made my insides turn to mush.

"Riggs, we can't just sit around and do nothing," I said, taking a cigarette from my pocket. Dorian let me smoke when I was stressed, and I was stressed out a lot back then. "I have kids, man. A wife. I can't be looking over my damn shoulder every day of my life."

Riggs unfolded his arms and scoffed, standing upright. "The fuck am I supposed to do? I've been looking. The guys have been looking. Judas has been looking at his hookups, and still, nothing. The Ghost just vanished—"

"Someone doesn't just vanish—"

"He ain't someone, he's a goddamn monster and you're married to his fucking sister," he shouted, looming over me like Daddy used to do when I did something wrong. "Now, I'm not gonna sit here and explain myself. There's nothing I can do but sit and wait for him to reappear. I got people all over the place keeping their eyes peeled. We gotta keep them peeled, too."

I knew he was right, but I also knew there had to be something else we could do. Something more. But as I saw things, I hated it because there wasn't anything we could do but wait...

The front door opened, Slade stepped out and leaned on the doorframe. "All good here, brothers?"

Staring at Riggs, my heart leaped from my chest. I didn't know if we were good. I had no idea what to feel other than remorse toward this whole situation.

A situation I knew would come back and teach us a lesson.

Slade

I'm holding Carter to my chest to keep him warm. I'm too scared to start the truck in case it's rigged with explosives. Too scared to go into the house and grab a blanket. I'll stay right here until Peter comes. Right fucking here while my arms are wrapped around this little guy and my eyes are glued on Zay.

The rumble of an engine echoes, coming down the driveway. My entire body stiffens; one arm remains holding Carter, while the other goes to the gun tucked into my jeans.

Tendrils of relief sweep through me when a black Audi comes into view and I spot the colorful beaded bracelets hanging from the rearview mirror that Rosa made for all of us—I still wear mine with pride.

Lifting Carter, I kiss his cheek. "Uncle Peter is here, bud. I told you we'd keep you and Mommy safe."

Peter shoots out of the car and charges for Zay, skidding to a stop in front of her. "Zay? Zaynab, hey." He touches her bloodied face and turns her attention to him. "What happened?"

Tears well in her eyes, spilling over but she doesn't speak. Instead, she frowns, swallowing thickly and going back to staring at the forest.

"Zay?" He tries to turn her chin, but her gaze doesn't shift.

He tucks some of her matted hair behind her ear, staring at the dried blood splattered onto her. Either Riggs or Adam is dead or on the verge of it. There is way too much blood here.

"Zaynab, can you look at me, sweetie?" Peter says soothingly, trying to get her attention.

Still, her hazel eyes don't waver—or blink—as she stares at the forest. Has she been staring at it the entire time?

Peter follows her gaze, glancing up at me. "I'm going to get her in the car, then I'm going to check on whatever the fuck she's staring at."

I didn't even think to look that way. I didn't even notice she was staring off into nothing. She seemed shocked, frightened by the entire situation.

I never notice the little things like this. All my life I was slapped with the oblivious card because of my ADHD; the kid who will amount to nothing, who doesn't pay attention, who can't sit still. For years I never let their words get to me, I *never* let anything get to me.

Except right now. When it mattered most of all, I didn't even notice that Zay had been staring in the same fucking spot for the last thirty minutes.

Peter whimpers when he looks into the house and sees all the blood splattered on the hardwood floors. It's a goddamn bloodbath and I have no idea what the fuck happened because the one person who can tell us is mute.

He lifts her, holding her close to his chest and whispering sweet nothings in her ear that I can't make out. But it's enough for her to sniff and nod when he places her in the front seat.

Touching her pregnant belly, he sighs, closing the door and glancing at me. "I'm going to check out the—"

"I'm coming," I blurt out, opening the back door and placing Carter inside. "All right, bud. Can you be a strong boy for Mommy? She's upset about the paint, too. So why don't we sit right here and I'll be right back with Uncle Peter."

He nods quickly, glancing at Peter smiling softly. "Please hurry, I'm scared, Uncle Slade."

I kiss his forehead and touch Zay's shoulder. "Mommy's right here, okay? Nothing will ever happen to either of you. I promise."

Closing the door, I lift my jeans, take the gun and cock it. I don't know what to expect to find in the bushes. Don't know if we'll see Adam or Riggs bleeding out.

Fuck, if they're dead, it's going to kill Zay and scar Carter. I know what it's like to grow up without parents, the last thing he needs is to lose his.

Peter looks at the cabin and glances over his shoulder every ten seconds, keeping that protective eye on them. "What the fuck happened?" he finally says, glancing over his shoulder once more when I grab his jacket and yank him to a stop.

Blood decorates the snow, leading deeper into the trees all the way to the lake. Peter puts a hand on his mouth, muffling a sob as he crouches down and stares at the blood that could belong to any one of his brothers.

"Jesus Christ," he whispers.

There's no time to sit and mope, we have to figure out what happened.

Taking the first step, I raise my gun and slowly inch closer to the bushes. Peter stays crouched, staring at the blood and he keeps a fist on his mouth. We're all feeling the pain. We're all wondering what the fuck we have to do with any of this. It wasn't our decision. It wasn't our cause. The men who started this have paid their dues and are buried six feet under in an unmarked grave.

But this, no, this isn't right. Something isn't fucking right.

Keeping my eyes peeled as I search the bushes, droplets of blood in the snow taper off until they disappear altogether and snowmobile tracks replace it.

Lowering my gun, I spot cigarette butts in the snow, protein bar wrappers, and empty water bottles. Whoever struck, has been sitting here stalking them for a least a day or two.

I tuck the gun back in my pants and stand. "They were being watched," I call out to Peter, pointing at the ground. "Cigarette butts and food."

He sniffs, standing tall. "Let's get them out of here. Pocket what you can. I'll have Lip call in a favor with the Captain."

I nod, stretching my sleeve down so my fingerprints don't get on the butts and pocket a few.

Peter strides back to the car and I jog up behind him, smiling at Carter sitting in the middle seat. "Follow us back to Mama's, okay?"

Jerking my head at Zay as her eyes are downcast, staring at her hands. "If she doesn't open up to you, gimme a chance with her. She's my friend and she might need me more than family right now."

Peter claps my shoulder, squeezing softly. "You are family, brother."

In all this chaos, those words make me smile. "Thanks, man." I glance at Zay, then Carter again. "Told him that Zay was painting and Daddies didn't like the color."

Peter nods quickly, sniffling again. "Fuck," he says, punching his eyes shut. "This is not fucking good."

Pulling him into a hug, I clap his back. "Let's not panic until we have to, okay? We don't know what happened. And until we do, we stay positive."

He sniffs, nods against my shoulder, and pushes off me, heading to the car with tears shimmering in his eyes.

This easiness was just that, too easy. Life was running smoothly and not a single one of us was worried about The Ghost anymore. We moved on and started living our lives. But now, now everything is so fucked up, and the chaos has only just begun.

Peter

Carter is staring out the window, watching the trees whip by. The radio isn't playing, no one is talking. The silence is deafening. I try to reach for Zaynab's hand a couple of times, but she's as stiff as a board. Barely breathing, barely coherent.

I need answers to find my fucking brothers.

Slade whips ahead of me and waves at the guys standing guard at the gate to Maddison Gardens. We've upped security here and forgot about ourselves. We wanted to protect these men, women, and children from abuse and forgot about our families. If someone was on watch at the cabin, none of this would have happened.

Mama is on her way out with a yellow folder in her hands, frowning when she sees Slade toss his helmet as he gets off his bike. "Slade?" Her eyes find mine as I pull up beside Slade. "Peter?"

Dragging a hand down my face, I shake my head when her face grows pale, spotting Zaynab beside me covered in blood. The pure terror bleeding from my mama's eyes is enough to know this is not fucking good.

Getting out of the car, I close the door, releasing a breath. "The Ghost, Mama. He took Riggs and Adam."

Her eyes well with tears and she nods quickly, then shakes her head. A thought crosses her mind, but she doesn't share it. Not yet. "Bring her to my room, we'll get her washed up. Slade, bring Carter to the other kids in the barn. There's story time going on."

Slade sniffs, opening the back door with a smile. "Hey, bud. Come with me a sec, okay? We're going to sit with Palmer and read some stories."

"What about Mommy?" Carter asks, holding onto Slade.

"She's covered in paint, she needs a bath before she hears some stories, don't you think?" He eyes me, then Mama, and walks through the snow to the barn at the back.

Mama places a hand on my cheek, causing a wince to escape me. "Tell me what you know."

I look over my shoulder at Zaynab, she's still staring at her hands shaking on her lap. "Slade got a call from Carter saying he was hiding in Riggs's truck. Slade called me and I headed right over." I exhale, finding my mother's gaze. "There was blood everywhere, Mama. We even tracked it to the lake where Slade found cigarette butts."

Her eyebrows pinch together, studying Zaynab. Concern written all over her face.

Fuck, I'm just as scared because if The Ghost can kidnap the toughest guy out there, then he's a helluva lot more dangerous than any of us let on.

"I'm going to call my people. Get her inside, Peter. I want all that blood off her and I'll call our doctor to come check her out." She places a soft kiss on my cheek and takes her phone from her pocket, that yellow folded clutched close to her chest.

I don't know who she's going to call, but I sure as shit know it's someone she promised she'd never bring into her life again.

A couple of the security guards stare at me as I round the car and hesitantly open the door. I don't know what to expect; I don't know if Zaynab is drugged and that's why she's so calm.

I hate when Zay is calm in stressful situations.

But she's always so calm lately.

I crouch beside her, placing a hand on her thigh. "Zay? Sweetie, I'm going to bring you into Mama's room, okay? Get this…blood off you."

She sniffs, staring at her shaking hands, and closes them into fists.

She doesn't talk.

She doesn't move.

Her breathing hitches.

I unclip her seatbelt and ignore the ringing phone in my pocket. I bet it's

Dorian worried sick about me. About our family. But I don't have time for her right now.

Zay is heavy in my arms, heavier than she's ever been. And it's not because she's pregnant. Her body is deadweight. Regardless, I'd use the last of my strength to carry this woman and my own if need be.

The house is warm and alive with people; the smell of stew wafts from the kitchen. It always smells like home here. A reminder of growing up with my brothers as Mama raised us to be the best men we could be—but Daddy's tainted seed soiled us before she had the chance to right us.

Smiling at a couple of young women walking down the hallway to the kitchen, they completely ignore the distraught woman in my arms. It's easy to ignore the harsh realities of the world here. It's easy to forget that life is hell and this sanctuary is the only heaven ever brought to these women.

Kicking my boots off, I climb the stairs, adjusting Zaynab in my arms. I press a soft kiss into her hair, smelling the rich copper that's mixed into it as her raspy breaths cloud around me.

I just spoke with them this morning when they picked up Carter. Zay was joking around about how panicked Riggs gets whenever they talk about her due date. How Adam needs a haircut because his blonde mane is getting too long. And how Carter won't stop calling her huge belly a balloon.

We were laughing over the phone. Fucking *laughing*. Now, this.

I sit her down on the toilet and start the bath, feeling the water before I whip off my jacket. Zay is frowning, staring at the tiles under her feet. She looks defeated. The same look she had when this club used her to pay back Lillian's debts.

This club has done nothing but bring misery to her life. Ruined her for almost seven years. Taken her life from her. Her dreams. Her ambitions. Her happiness and sass. This club ruins everything it touches. But we fixed what broke—we tried, at least. Yet it's still ruining her.

I don't say anything and take her arm, sliding it out of her jacket. I do the same to the other and unravel her scarf. When I get on one knee and start untying her boots, she looks up at me with teary eyes.

"Peter," she whispers.

I take her face in my hands, smiling as our eyes anchor together. "It's me, Zaynab. I'm right here, all right?"

Tears spill free and she nods quickly, looking back at the tiles on the floor. Broken, just like before.

"Talk to me, sweetie. What happened?"

Silence. She's back to that zombie state where she stops blinking, her eyes widen and her focus is on nothing. They've done her in. *This* has finally done her in.

I undress her, scanning her body for any cuts or bruising, but there doesn't seem to be anything of the sort. They wouldn't drug a pregnant woman, would they? Shit, they've probably done worse. This madness is only the tip of the iceberg. I have a feeling the bloodbath at the cabin was only to send us a message.

As soon as I remove her pants, I lift her naked body and help her in the bath.

She's shivering.

Lower lip quivering.

She's still mute.

I've redeemed myself over the years. With Dorian by my side, I've become a better man than I could ever imagine. And doing right by Zay has always been something I never felt I'd done enough. I brought her to hell and didn't bother to offer her salvation. She deserves so much more than she's given.

As I drop water on her shoulders, there's a knock on the door before it opens, and there my wife is, beautiful as ever. Her short hair is pin straight, gray sweater is tight on that curvaceous body with gray jeans to match. "Jesus Christ," Dorian gasps, closing the door behind her and staring at the pinkish hue in the water. "Zay, what happened?"

Zay sniffs, looking up at Dorian with glassy eyes. All she does is sniff again and put her head back down. But Dorian doesn't stop analyzing her, taking in every single inch of her skin. The disbelief has worn off almost as quickly as it came when Dorian's eyes find mine and she frowns. "What—"

"She's in shock," I interrupt her. "You would be, too, if you saw the likes of that fucking house."

Dorian moves some of Zay's hair off her shoulder and stiffens up; her eyes grow darker as she stares at her neck, brushing more hair back. "Zay, honey, what did they give you?"

I move the cloth across Zay's chest and tilt her head to face me so I can see what Dorian is staring at. There's a small scabbed prick on her neck, a couple of inches under her ear. How could I have missed that? How could I have been so blind? Dorian noticed because she cares. She knew to look because of this fucking place…

I grab Zay's face and make her look at me, the pupils of her eyes are large. Zay is here, but she's not here. She sees me but doesn't. It's that same stare I used to give her when Dorian ran away. The same state I used to be in before my babies came around. That out-of-body experience. That haze.

"Zaynab, you alright, sweetie?" My gaze flickers from one of her hazel eyes to the other, but she isn't there. She's on that plane far away from here. No fucking wonder she won't talk to me.

How can I be such a fucking oblivious idiot?

"The doctor is downstairs, should I tell her to come up?" Dorian asks, eyebrows furrowed and filled with worry.

I nod, sniffling. "Yeah, yeah. Just let me clean her up. She has…just…a lot of my broth—blood on her."

Dorion touches my hand as I move the washcloth along Zay's chest again. "Peter, we'll find them. We *will* find them."

Dorian leans over the tub and kisses my forehead, retreating from the bathroom. There's a heavy cloud filling the washroom, something that is going to take a long fucking time to clear out if we don't find my brothers soon.

The longer we wait, the harder it'll be to find them.

The harder it'll be for things to just be fucking normal.

My father's dead and he's still fucking us bareback.

✳✳✳

Emptying the tub twice until the water running off Zay is clear, I wash her twice, making sure every bit of blood is rid of her body.

I now have her in a towel, ashamed to admit seeing her naked again gives

848

me butterflies. And seeing her naked again while pregnant is something I never knew my stomach would scream for—my dick would get hard for.

But here it is, mentally cheating on my wife because Zay will always have a place in my heart. No, I need a fucking drink and someone to knock some sense into me.

When I open the door of the washroom, Slade is standing with the doctor, biting his thumbnail. "She okay?" he asks and follows us into Mama's room.

"She's out of it and not because she's shocked." I sit her on the bed and Zay sways slowly. "They injected her with something." I move her wet hair out of the way to show Slade the injection site we both missed. I will forever kick myself in the ass for missing it, too.

What the hell else did I miss at the cabin?

He wipes a hand down his face as the doctor smiles sweetly, placing her hand on Zay's shoulder.

"Hi, dear. Do you remember me?" Karen asks, pulling on a pair of rubber gloves.

Zay is staring off again so I stand in front of her and help her settle on the bed, her wet hair splayed on the pillow.

"Zay, the doctor is going to run some tests, okay?" I turn her face to look at me, but there's nothing in her gaze. "Should I bring her to the hospital room in the barn?"

Karen checks her pulse, flashing a light in Zay's eyes. "I think that would be best. I can't do all the tests here. And I want to do a few without you boys in the room. One is an ultrasound to check the baby's vitals, and the other is—"

A growl rumbles through me at the thoughts of someone like The Ghost raping her to prove a fucking point. "I want to be there for that," I state, glaring at Karen who nods.

Slade snags my mama's house coat from the back of the door. "Get your boots and jacket on, I'll bring her and you can meet us there," he says to me.

It feels like a dream, everything happening around me and I'm just standing there, watching as my family is slowly being torn apart.

What the fuck am I supposed to do to help?

How am I supposed to help?

I fucked the club up once before; I've fucked up a lot before.

Yet it seems like everything always falls in my lap.

And here it is again, weighing me down like a ton of bricks slowly sinking me deeper underground.

Slade

Karen, the doctor, is doing an ultrasound on Zay as we speak. She's done blood tests, which I helped with by holding Zay's arm and making sure to keep her awake. Her body is unresponsive at the moment. I know bringing her to the hospital is the right thing to do, but we have no idea what type of danger we're in.

Karen asked Peter and me to step out of the exam room so she could look at Zay in private—my mind keeps going to the darkest of places at what this sick fuck could do to this poor woman. So we hope and pray that she's okay. Zay has to be okay.

I don't like this waiting game. This wondering and overthinking.

Reminds me of the time I was just about to get transferred to another foster home. It would be my seventh one so far. I sat in the group home waiting for my name to be called. One by one my friends were all placed with families, and I sat there, waiting for my turn. I skipped lunch, and snack time. I even held in my pee because I knew my turn was coming.

But my turn never came.

And I have a feeling Zay's freedom will never be granted.

Karen comes out of the back room and takes off her gloves, Peter and I shoot up from our seats. The air is already thick with fright, and waiting for Karen to tell us what's going on with Zay is making all of us anxious.

"What's the verdict, doc?" I ask as Dorian grips mine and Peter's hands.

Karen doesn't look us in the eyes, she keeps her gaze on the floor, a twitch in her jaw before her eyes travel to ours. "I sent her blood work to the lab, so as soon as I get it back, I'll know for sure what they injected her with. She's sleeping now—fell asleep while I was doing an ultrasound—"

"The baby?" Peter blurts out.

Karen releases a slow breath, tossing her gloves in the trash bin nearby. "The heartbeat is stable, he's growing at a good rate—baby's a big one—but he isn't moving as much as I'd like him to—"

Dorian winces, letting go of my hand and gripping Pete's arm. "Did she say anything to you? Anything at all?"

Peter steps forward, eyebrows pinched together. "Mumble something? Even something incoherent?"

The doctor shakes her head, grinning softly. "Let her rest, boys. I have security coming to stand guard so I can get to the hospital in time for her results."

Peter doesn't seem happy with that response. His shoulders tense and his back hunches as he watches Karen leave, gritting his teeth in frustration. "Fucking shit."

Folding my arms across my chest, I widen my stance. "Judas is on his way with Lip and Dillon."

Peter hasn't been active with the club in almost three years, keeping his promise to his wife. But I have a funny feeling in my gut that he's going to be back. And having him back means shit is about to hit the fan.

"Good. Meeting in the dining room as soon as they're here." Peter lets go of Dorian's hand and shoves the door to Zay's room open, closing it behind him with a soft growl coming from the other side.

Dorian hasn't changed much over the years; her hair is shorter but she's still that curvy girl she's always been. And hating this club is still cinched in her mind, brainwashed from before she knew who the fuck we were. And something is telling me that bringing us down is still at the top of her list. I wonder how she feels about her husband being part of this club again.

She sighs, zipping her jacket up. "Make sure he doesn't do anything stupid, will you?"

"Cross my heart."

My phone goes off in my pocket, and the last time I got a phone call was this morning when Carter called me. That worry in his tone still sends shivers down my spine.

Dorian follows me out of the warehouse, heading for the barn where the children are having their lunch. Mama Rosa makes sure the children stick to a routine; school in the morning, story time before lunch, school after lunch, and then free play until dinner.

Palmer—my sexy little redhead—is one of the teachers for the younger kids. She's been here almost four years, and I was graced with her presence three years ago when Mama Rosa walked back into her sons' lives.

I've never had the itch before, but seeing Palmer with the children always sends me over the edge. I'm going to pump her full of babies one day when the time is right. And I think the time is going to be soon. Palmer is my life, she's my heart, my eternity.

"Yeah?" I answer Lip's phone call, holding the phone to my ear as I step out into the cold.

"We're fifteen minutes out," Lip says, exhaling a breath. "Got some men from Gunner's charter."

Palmer laughs as a few of the children are making snow forts in front of the barn with the little snow that's left on the ground.

My little ginger sunshine looks up and spots me, curling a lock of hair behind her ear and blowing me a kiss. A smile shouldn't touch my face in a time like this but it does because she is heaven and I've walked the planes of hell just to find her.

"Good. Good," I say to Lip, running a hand through my hair. "Peter said we'll have a meeting in Mama Rosa's dining room."

The revving of the bikes hits my ear, the way he zooms in and out of cars with the rest of the gang. Loyal brothers coming to help us because we're all like family.

"All right, man. See you soon."

He hangs up and I stare at Palmer again. Her eyes are still on me, staring with worry even though there's a playful gleam painting her freckled face.

My duty is with this club, but I know in my heart I have to soothe that worry first. My feet march in the snow, grinning at the screaming children before I stop in front of my beauty.

"Is everything okay?" she asks, her voice low as her hands slide up my chest and one of them touches my cheek.

I place my hand over hers and close my eyes. She's not my wife yet, but she knows how much I love her. Our late nights together over the years and the truths we shared are enough to prove I'm in this for the long haul.

"It's just a fucked-up situation."

She takes my hand and leads me to the barn, pulling me behind the door. "What happened to Carter? He's not talking or laughing like he usually does. Hell, I just saw him this morning and he was happier than a pig in shit—"

"The Ghost was waiting for them at the cabin. I don't know how they missed the signs, but the fucker was watching them. Waiting for the right moment, and that was this morning when Adam was alone." I exhale a shaky breath and lean my head on hers. "When I got there, there was so much fucking blood. And Zay—they pricked her with something. She's out of it. And the baby—"

"Oh, God, Slade, no!"

I press a kiss on her pillowy, freckled lips. "Hold your worries, darling. Hold them tight for now." I brush a tear from her cheek. "Doctor says the baby is fine, just not as active as he usually is."

She sniffs, shaking her head. "Did they hurt her...like they *hurt* the women here?"

I exhale, closing my eyes to a flash of the look on the doctor's face. There was something she wasn't telling us. Something she didn't want to share. "I don't know."

"I need to see Zay. Where is she?"

Palmer always asks to see the newcomers at Maddison Gardens. To talk to them and prove that life may be shit now, but they're saved and they can be happy again. Palmer has burned through her torture, coming out on the other side shinier than a goddamn diamond.

Cradling her head in mine, I kiss her delicately. "She's resting. As soon as she wakes up, you can see her."

Palmer nods quickly, sniffling again when a bell rings and the screaming children make their way into the barn.

A smile tugs my lips and I pull her in once more, kissing my darling with everything that I have. "Snakes are having a meeting in a few and I wanted to tell you now, I might have to leave for a couple of nights. A week, tops, until we figure this out."

Palmer nods again, tapping my chest. "Just come home to me, okay?"

"You're my home, darling. The only place I ever want to be."

A smile graces that freckled face before she steps away and joins the ruckus of children running around to find their table. Carter is mixed in with the children, as are Peter's kids, but the little guy is off.

Truthfully, I don't blame him. The last thing he needs is more loss.

I tousle his hair and grin. "Hey, bud. Why don't you go play, hmm? Rosa is here with Sara, too."

He looks up at me with eyes so blue they're practically glowing. A mini-Riggs only with hair as blonde as Shyanne's. "Where's Mommy?"

I don't know what to tell him. The poor kid is only four years old. He doesn't need this much chaos going on around him.

So I lie. Like all my foster families did to me.

"Mommy's resting, okay?" I help him out of his jacket. "She also had a lot of paint on her, Uncle Peter is cleaning her up. Y'know, red is not a good color on her."

Carter shakes his head, taking my hand. "Can you play with me, Uncle Slade?"

My heart aches, tightening at the innocence in his tone. "Right after I have a sit down with Daddy's club."

He releases my hand and runs off, joining the rest of the children.

I don't want to leave him.

I don't want any of this shit to be happening.

But it fucking is and we knew this day was coming. We fucking knew and did nothing.

Slade

Two years ago, my ginger queen first spoke to me. I'd been keeping tabs on Maddison Gardens, helping when they needed me. But my devotion was to the Snakes. Riggs showed me the way, guided me so that he wouldn't have to deal with mundane crap. He's still our president, but he isn't present unless shit hits the fan.

When I approached Maddison Gardens, I lit a cigarette as soon as I got off my bike and exhaled the smoke, watching it trickle and evaporate. It's been a long week of nothing but being security at the bar for a few local bands. I've been getting close to three hours of sleep per night, living in the back room at Judas's Hideout. I loved it, nonetheless, but I needed a break.

"Hey, you one of the bikers who keeps tossing your cigarette butts on the ground?" Palmer said, hands in fits on her hips. "I've picked up enough of your garbage for one lifetime."

My heart skipped too many beats, sending me into a coughing fit. The second I laid my eyes on her, I knew one way or another, this woman would lie with me. This woman would love me. This woman would become me.

Her hand came up and tapped my back, a sultry grin spread across her freckled lips. "You okay there, Slade?"

Blood pounded in my ears, a steady beat making a symphony in my head to the beauty of what she did to me. "You know my name?"

Her hand moved to my upper arm, sending me into a world of panic. This woman was a dream. A goddamn goddess. The warmth of her hand seeped through my shirt, kissing my skin with the want for her.

That lust I knew I wouldn't be able to fulfill. She was there for a reason; she was *one of the saved. A life with me would never be.*

She chuckled, crossing her arms as a cool spring breeze rolled in. "Of course, I know you. You're one of the bikers who works for Mama Rosa. It's a real good thing she's doing around here."

The safety that washed over her when she glanced around made me appreciate everything I continued to do to make sure this place stayed protected. To make sure the club stayed straight.

She felt pain. Endured it and lived through the horrors.

This place brought her safety. Haven.

This place brought us the light.

I nodded slowly. "Yeah, it really is."

She brushed a few strands of hair from her mouth and the sleeve of her shirt lifted, showing scars on her wrist.

Scars from her taker. The man who paid to use her. Enslave her. The man who needed to rot in fucking hell.

She pulled her sleeve down quickly to hide her scars from me but I reached out, taking her hand and slowly lifting her sleeve. Her breathing hitched; shaky and nervous.

"Don't hide your scars. They tell our stories; good or bad. They prove we were strong enough to move past the things that could've ruined us," I said, brushing a thumb on the inner part of her wrist.

Tears shimmered in her eyes. "How would you know? Your life didn't get dragged through hell for three years."

I was unable to clear the gravel from my throat, it was lodged there, sinking deeper with the will to choke me because of her past demons.

I released her wrist and lifted my sleeves, showing the self-harm I had done over the years. "I don't know what you went through, but I know scars. I know how I wanted my life to end. I know that with every cut I made, I tried to go that much deeper until no one would save me. But I didn't because I knew my upbringing wouldn't ruin me. My upbringing wouldn't define me. My scars would prove I saved myself. I didn't need anyone but myself."

Her delicate fingers traced the lines on my arms, turning over to trace the tattoos that barely cover them. "Do these help forget? Your tattoos?"

I lifted a shoulder, bringing the cigarette to my lips. "They help from people staring at them. Now people stare at my arms to see the designs, not the scars."

She looked down at her wrists, fixing her sleeves as if she could feel my stare. Those long unpainted lashes batted twice before her eyes met mine. The long whisps of her hair tickled her cheek, making her brush it back again. That beautiful face was surrounded by a halo of orange curls. This woman stole my breath away.

"Slade?" Lip called, parking his bike nearby.

I was so entangled in her web, I didn't even hear him pull up.

Stammering on a couple of words, I looked back at him, wincing when the cigarette burned my fingers. So entranced I didn't realize this thing was between my fingers. I never waste a cigarette.

The front door squeaked open and Palmer headed inside, the sleeves of her shirt bunched up in her hands. "Hey—"

Her big eyes looked back at me, smiling softly. "I'll be around," she said, letting the screen snap shut between us.

The air sucked from my lungs the moment her orange hair was out of sight. A beauty in such horror, a light to shine in my darkness, and a woman to finally call my own.

Lip clapped my back, chuckling as he dropped his cigarette and stomped his boot on it. "She's a pretty little thing."

I smirked, looking down at the two cigarette butts we just left for her to clean up. "Yeah, she is."

Dillon punched my arm, chuckling as he stepped onto the porch. "About time you found yours, big fella."

And he was right. There were only so many nights I could find a decent Snake Biter to bag before that became old. Only so many nights I could fuck the bartenders or the customers. Only so many nights I could lie awake and wonder when my pretty little thing would be sleeping beside me.

I got off my bike and picked up the cigarette butts, tossing them in the tin can by the front door. We'd come to Mama Rosa's twice a month to help her when it came time for protection. She'd find where girls were being held and when she sent out the cavalry to fetch them, we'd escort the van back to Maddison Gardens.

No one messed with Mama Rosa if they knew what was good for them.

We got seven charters backing us up—all thanks to Riggs making amends with Gunner and his crew.

The number of body parts that fucker had sawed off still made my stomach turn. But the fuckers who took these innocent women deserved it. And by God, Gunner was not someone you want to double cross, either.

We made our way into the house that always had some baked goods smell to it. No matter the time of day, if Mama Rosa wasn't cooking a meal in the kitchen, the home smelled like freshly baked cookies.

Mama Rosa was seated at the dining room table, a pair of reading glasses at the tip of her nose. At this angle, the similarities with Peter were unmistakable. The way she frowned, puckered her lips, and studied the materials in front of her. Peter may have his daddy's colors, but those freckles and her features have passed onto Peter and his daughter, Rosa.

Mama Rosa looked up with a smile, closing the folder in front of her. A yellow folder compared to the purple ones she always used. "Boys, welcome."

"Whatcha got for us, Rosa?" Lip asked, plopping down at the corner of the table.

She sucked her teeth and rose, flicking his neck. "You'll have manners in my house and use a chair, heathen."

I chuckled, sliding into one of the chairs.

Dillon sat beside me, leaning over. "You think she's single?" he asked quietly.

"Riggs and Peter will kill you if you ever try anything," I whispered, raising my eyebrows.

He didn't care, to be honest. His eyes roamed along Mama Rosa's body like she was the crown jewel. And she was a beautiful woman, but I knew my place. I devoted my life to her sons, the last thing I needed was for them to catch my eyes wandering. But Christ, if given the chance, any of us would lay our life on the line for a night with her.

She placed the yellow folder on the chair behind her and leaned forward. "Okay, boys. This is an easy pick up. Two teenagers and three adults. The van should be here any minute and once it arrives, you'll follow it to make sure everything runs smoothly."

Dillon looked around, baffled. "There's only three of us. Want us to call in more guys?"

She shook her head. "I told you, this is an easy one. Gunner already has the bitch running the house tied up in his warehouse. All I need is you boys to meet his men there and load up the van."

"There's enough room here for five more people?" Lip jerked his head at the window behind her and all the people roaming the grounds. "You're getting a little overcrowded here, Rosa."

She nodded, and slowly licked her lips. "Don't you worry about that, sweetie. Now go on and get. You should be back in time for dinner. I'm making a chicken pot pie."

Lip rubbed his hands together as Mama Rosa left the room with the yellow folder clutched to her chest. There was something in that yellow folder that was important.

How important?

We would soon find out.

***

The pick up was easy, five people came out of the building, and then Gunner's men torched the place. We followed the van back to Maddison Gardens, but it was nearly nine o'clock when we arrived and supper had been served and packed away. All the leftovers were given to the women who were picked up, and none of us could blame them. They were so thin, I could count the ribs on the little girl.

I cleared my throat and stood on the back porch, staring at the night sky. The stars were wild out here, clear and shimmering in so many different colors.

My hands were in my pockets as I watched the stars, thinking of all the good we were doing. How the reason I wanted to join this motorcycle club was to make a difference. And we finally were.

"Hey," Palmer's voice startled me, making her way from the side of the house with a basket of laundry resting on her hip.

I looked at her and smiled, heat rising in my cheeks. "Hey."

She stopped walking and stared at the sky as well before turning her attention to me. "Bringing some clothes to the girls you helped escort here."

I nodded, kicking at the porch. "That's good, that's good. Are they okay? Settling in?"

She glanced at the warehouse where the doctor had her office set up. "They're getting checked by Karen now. A couple of us are bunking with each other so the girls can have their own beds tonight. Mama Rosa has to add some more huts if she plans on keeping all of us here."

"Heard her say she's working on something."

A gentle smile spread across her face. "That's good."

I watched as she kept her gaze on the open area, the way the branches danced in the soft breeze, slowly growing their leaves back from the harsh winter we went through.

"You staying the night?" She broke the silence, glancing at me.

Lifting my shoulder, I shook my head. "I wanted to, but there isn't anywhere for us to crash. So we're heading to Gunner's as soon as Lip gets some food in him—he gets angry when he's hungry—and we'll crash on a few couches in the clubhouse."

The moon shined a silvery glow onto her pale, freckled skin. But that didn't stop me from staring at her gorgeous face. No, I could stare at her for hours. The contours of her face were always a mystery to me. Every glance at her, something even more beautiful than before appeared.

A slow nod moved her head, but our gazes locked and my entire body shifted. If I could run over and kiss her until the sky started falling, I would. But this wasn't the type of place you found a woman to love. This was the type of place you saved women from falling into the wrong hands.

I scratched the back of my head and looked away from her, releasing a shaky breath. "I'll, uh, see you around, Palmer."

Her cheeks grew a darker shade of red as she tried to hide her smile. "I'm sure you will, Slade." She continued on the path to the warehouse, stopping once more to look back at me. "Don't be a stranger."

The smile that spread to my face was unlike any I ever conjured. A smile that gave me hope. Hope in new beginnings.

Slade

Leaving Carter, then Palmer in the barn the way I did, didn't sit well with me. I'm sure there will come a time when I give up this club for good and live my life with my ginger queen somewhere with our toes in the sand where no one knows our names.

But for now, I gotta do what I gotta do.

Sitting at the dining room table, I clasp my hands in front of me and grin at the tattoo of the letter P Skeet inked onto my hand a couple of weeks ago. Palmer slapped the side of my head playfully and told me I was an idiot to do that when we weren't labeled boyfriend or girlfriend yet. But when I told her, "my world belonged to you", those big eyes brightened and she kissed me in a way that felt like forever.

Mama Rosa prepared sandwiches for us, and the guys are attacking them, leaving two for me. But my stomach is still in knots after what I witnessed this morning. All that blood, all that heartache.

"Slade, why don't you fill us in since you're now promoted to stand in president until Peter gets his head outta his ass," Lip says with his mouth full. Slowly turning my head in a death glare, he put his hand up in apology. "Sorry, until Peter finishes with…Zay."

I gulp back the nerves bubbling in my belly and slide my sweaty hands on the table. I don't know how to be a president. I don't know how to lead. I don't fucking know.

But these men trust me.

Riggs trusted me from the moment we met. He told me I'd go far if I kept my head up and focused.

And look at me now.

"Well," I start, sighing. "I was heading to the clubhouse this morning when I got a call from the private number Riggs set up at the cabin. Carter was on the line and the poor kid was scared shitless." My heart still aches for him and his soft little voice coming through the phone.

What I wouldn't do for any of the Donnelly kids.

"Anyway, when I got there, it was a fucking bloodbath. Zay was covered in blood, the cabin was soaked in it. And there's a trail of it leading to the water. Someone was staked out in the snow, watching them for God knows how long. But—"

"Did you catch anyone?" Judas interrupts, wiping his mouth on the back of his hand.

I shake my head. "It was a ghost town."

Pun intended.

"Is she hurt?" Skeet asks, leaning forward.

I lift a shoulder. "Hard to tell. The fuckers drugged her."

Lip gasps, banging a fist on the table. "She's pregnant! It's one thing to attack us members, but it's a whole other game to hurt our old ladies and the babies."

Nodding quickly, I sniffle. "She said The Ghost is back, but that's about all we've gotten out of her."

"Let her rest, we'll reach out to other charters and tell them to keep a lookout for Riggs and Adam—"

"And what if there's nothing to look for?" Dillion interrupts Judas. "We should be seeking out the fuckers who are connected to this Ghost prick. Doesn't Mama Rosa have their contact info?"

"And we will," I say, pushing up from the table to loom over these men. "We're going to seek out *all* the contacts who find these women for Mama Rosa, see if they heard any whispering about where The Ghost might be. It's not much, but it's a start."

The men start to argue, yelling at one another that they weren't careful enough. Weren't protective enough. Weren't on the lookout for our president and his family.

But none of us are to blame. We can only act without dwelling on the past.

The future is what counts and making sure our president and VP are safe is our top priority. Riggs and Adam will come home.

Banging my fist on the table, the men quiet down as soon as my fist hits the table a second time. This title, this position holds way too much power for my liking. "They got Riggs and Adam. The only thing we have to do is keep our ears on the ground, and reach out to as many of our brothers as we can. The faster we find this fucker, the faster we'll get them home."

Lip nods, glancing at Skeet, then Dillon, and coming back to me. "Your call, brother. Whatever you choose to do, we'll follow."

That's the problem, isn't it? I don't know what to do.

As I open my mouth to speak, Dorian charges in looking pale and shocked, like that time she accidentally walked in on Skeet getting a blowjob from one of the Snake Biters at Riggs's 30th birthday party. She shrieked, Peter laughed, she huffed, and he had to leave because of her hissy fit. I don't think she'll ever recover from that. And I don't blame her, either. Skeet is one ugly motherfucker.

"Dorian, this is a Snakes meeting. No old ladies allowed," Lip says, sitting back in his chair.

Her eyes find mine and her shaking hand holds out Riggs's cell phone. "Slade, it's—"

A distorted voice cackles through the speaker, humming softly when the room falls silent. "I assume I'm on speakerphone with the members of the Snakes?"

Everyone nods as silence and panic take over the energy of the room.

Dorian takes a couple of wobbly steps, placing the phone in front of me. Her big gray eyes are riddled with unfallen tears, but now's not the time for comfort. We have to act fast; smart, but fast.

"Who is this?" I ask, deepening my voice for intimidation.

The distorted voice cackles again. "Slade, I presume? Mmm, you're Palmer's man. Sexy curvy ginger, isn't she?"

My entire body burns hot, stiffening. But I can't lose control. I have to remain calm if I know what's good for me.

"What do you want?" I ask, putting my hand up to the men at the table gritting and baring their teeth.

The distorted voice sighs, chains clanking in the background. "Well, I have a decision to make and I'll only be able to make this decision if you cooperate with me."

It's safe to assume the decision is which one of the Donnelly men to kill. Riggs or Adam.

"Now," the voice continues. "You took something of mine, mangled it, and returned her to me far more damaged than she was when she was taken—"

"We don't take girls, Ghost. We help save them from the fucktards who kidnap and rape them!" Dillon yells, his face a deep red.

The distorted voice laughs, sending a chill through the room. "It's not about taking the whores, it's about a certain woman listening in right now. A certain sister, someone who has crossed you once and wouldn't think twice about doing it again."

My gaze shoots to Dorian, as does everyone else in the group. She puts her hands up, tears slipping free, and she shakes her head frantically. It's easy to point fingers at her. She had betrayed us before. She's also related to The fucking Ghost. But something about the fear on her face proves this guy is lying.

"I'm listening," I say, keeping my eyes anchored with hers.

Metal chains clank once again, it's sound is piercing and repetitive like someone is tugging on them.

Then, the silence becomes deafening and the room stands completely still.

Riggs's growls and groans move through the quiet, and Adam's whimpers follow suit.

"You hear that? If I don't get my demands met in the next three hours, I'll start sending home pieces of them. As promised, let Mama Rosa know her boys will be coming home," the voice says with a grunt.

Mama Rosa has been standing by the doorway, listening in on the meeting. But when her name is spoken, that angered and frustrated look is washed away and replaced with something I've never seen grace her face before. It's fear.

"Why don't we set up a meeting? Just me and you. Choose the place and location, my men will keep their distance and we can discuss your needs face to face." A shaky breath escapes me, but it's not enough to settle the nerves leaking into my words.

It's quiet for a beat, chains clanking as Riggs's growls and muffled words fill the void.

The distorted voice exhales sharply. "I'll send my first demand in an hour."

The line goes dead.

All of us are staring at the phone; rattled breaths take over the words we're too afraid to speak.

"They're alive," Dorian whispers.

Placing my fists on the table, I rise to a standing position. "Skeet, get Gunner here ASAP. Clue him in on what's happening. Judas, call your girl and tell her to reach out to her people and see if anyone knows anything. Offer cash and protection for those who are too scared to speak. And Dillon; you, me, Peter, and Lip will head to the cabin to check the tapes, see if we can find anything out there. A clue. Something."

Dragging a hand down my face, I sigh. "And someone go fucking get me Peter."

I slap the cell phone away, growling as I lock my hands behind my head and walk toward the window. The beauty of this sanctuary is tainted with all the horrors of what these women, children, and teenagers endured.

But the true horror lies within these men behind me. Within the lies some of them spew. Within the things some of them don't say. We used to have a rat, and I think we still do. Only this time, the rat is out for revenge.

Peter

I haven't moved from Zaynab's side for the past hour, locking the door and refusing to let anyone come in. Not even Dorian. Fuck, not even the doctor. I missed a Snakes meeting on top of it.

I don't care if this is against my vows to my wife; Zay will always hold a place in my heart. She suffered by my hand, went through hell, and came out a strong, badass angel we all look up to. She stepped up to the plate when all of us were crumbling. We owe her our lives.

And now that she's lying here in a drug-induced sleep with my brother's baby in her belly and my nephew worried sick, the only thing I can think of is sit with her and hope she wakes up soon.

My priority should be to sit in on the meeting with the club, but I just can't. I fucking can't go back there. *I can't.*

My forehead is resting on our clasped hands, leg tapping restlessly. The club is in the dining room, they're planning and plotting what the fuck to do. But I promised my love that I wouldn't partake in any club business anymore. For her and our girls. I promise Dorian, and here I am on the verge of a fucking panic attack because I need answers and I won't be able to get them.

Because I fucking promised.

As I release a deep shaky breath, Zaynab squeezes my hand, groaning as she turns her head. "Fuck," she draws out, rubbing her temple.

I shoot up and bring our clasped to my chest. "Hey, sweetie. Don't move too quickly, all right—"

She winces, trying to push herself up, but I place a hand on her chest. "Relax, Zay—"

"Where's my son!?" she shouts, eyes wide with fright.

"He's with my kids." Sitting on the bed, I flash her a soft smile even though my heart is beating out of my chest. "We're at Maddison Gardens—"

"Yeah, I-I know," she interrupts me, placing a hand on her belly. "God, my head," she groans, rubbing her forehead.

She needs rest, but I need answers, some form of information to help point us in the right direction.

I need to save my brothers.

"Zay, I need you to tell me whatever you know. Anything at all." I tuck a strand of her wavy hair behind her ear. Goosebumps rise on her neck, causing my eyes to follow as they spread to her chest and disappear behind the towel still wrapped around her. "When I came to you—there was so much blood, Zay. What happened?"

Tears rise in her eyes, but before words leave those succulent lips, she gags and shoots up from the bed. I grab the trash bin for her and hold it out. She pukes as I hold her hair back. The goddamn drugs are leaving her system.

She pukes a second time, bringing back memories of how she rubbed my back when I thought my life was over, when Dorian took Rosa from me. Zay was there to comfort me. She was there when I was at my lowest, and by God, I will be there whenever she needs me.

Shushing her as her sobs break free, I crouch behind her and press my lips to her back. "It's okay, sweetie."

She shakes her head, spitting in the trash. "You have no idea, Peter. It's not okay. It's not *fucking* okay."

I wrap my arms around her neck. "I'm here. I'm right here, Zay. You just have to tell me what's going on so I can fix things."

She sniffs, leaning into me. "I can't," she whispers.

Turning her, I grip her shoulders and raise my eyebrows. "You can tell me anything."

"You don't understand," she whispers. "If I talk, they'll kill one of them."

"Zay—"

"No." She whimpers, dropping her head on my chest and sobbing as someone strikes the door.

If she talks, someone will kill them.

But how would they know?

The rapping continues until I lift Zay and unlock the door, cradling her close to my chest. Slade pokes his head in, eyes widening when he sees her in my arms.

"Hey, she okay?"

I nod quickly. "She won't talk."

She sniffs against my chest and I set her down on the bed, fixing the towel before it falls right off her. "I can't talk," her gravelly voice says.

Slade pinches her chin and moves her face to meet his gaze. "We need something, Zay. Something to save your men."

A tear spills over, rolling down her cheek and dripping off her chin. "There's as good as dead already."

Slade sighs, shrugging out of his jacket and draping it on her shoulders. "Why don't you rest up a little more? Carter is anxious to see you."

She sniffs, wiping her cheek. "Just get me out of this room."

I go to lift her but Slade places a hand on my shoulder. "You need to speak with the club, brother. With Riggs gone, Adam gone, you're next in line for pres."

"Dorian won't let me do that," I scoff, wrapping a blanket around Zaynab's legs.

Slade lifts her and grunts, jerking his head at the door. "Things are changing, brother. And your family needs you now more than ever."

With that, he leaves, letting this heavy cloud loom over me and I have no fucking idea what to do other than turn to the bottle like I used to.

But I can't.

Not for my girls.

And I can't go back to a life with the club.

This is fucked.

I tug on my jacket and head outside. It's awfully quiet on the grounds compared to before. Deserted. Barren. What happened to everyone?

The screen door slaps shut at the house, alerting me to keep following Slade, but this silence is so deafening, it's making my skin crawl.

A warmth blooms in the house as soon as I step in, kicking off my boots beside Slade's. Fucker has big ass feet. And I thought Riggs's size fourteen foot was insane. Slade's takes the cake.

Mama is in the kitchen making a bit of tea and smiles at me over her shoulder. "Hi, sweetie. Here," she says, pouring me a cup. "Drink this. It'll relieve some of your stress."

I look at the murky water in the dainty tea cup I've used many times playing tea parties with Rosa and Sara, but I don't want fucking tea right now. I want a goddam shot of vodka and I'll chase it down with a line or two of cocaine.

"Thanks, Mama."

She fixes more cups onto a tray and nods her head at the doorway. "Boys have been waiting for you. Think it's time you join their meeting."

"I don't know if I can, Mama. I promised my wife I wouldn't for our kids's sake." I set the cup on the island, looking out the window above the sink. "Dorian wants us as far away from this bullshit as we can get."

"And I wanted that for my babies, too. But look where that got me. When push comes to shove, we put our shit aside and do what's right for our families." She lifts the tray, sighing. "You were born and bread a Donnelly, Peter. If she can't accept that, then what the hell did she sign up for? When your brothers need you, you're always there. Now when they need you the most, you want to back away?"

"That's not what I meant, Mama—"

"They could die, Peter. They could already *be* dead," she raises her voice, tray shaking in her hands. "I will not let The Ghost kill my babies without revenge, do you understand me?"

Nodding quickly, I'm like a lost puppy dog getting scolded for running away.

I don't even know where my wife is to let her know that I'm not with Zaynab anymore. I don't even know if she's still here with my kids. I don't know fucking shit and it's killing me.

Stepping into the dining room, I take in the men I'd lay my life on the line for. The goddamn Snakes.

"Peter, my boy," Skeet says, smiling at Mama as she hands him a cup of tea.

"Sit, we have loads to discuss."

Discuss is not something I want to do. My mind is in a panic, jumping around the room from one face to the next, wondering if we have a rat in the house again. It's happened more times than we like to admit, and as much as I want to believe The Ghost is back for revenge, that anxious little boy inside me is jumping to one conclusion after another.

"How's Zay?" Lip asks. "Baby okay?"

I lift a shoulder, easing into a chair at the head of the table. "Haven't spoken to the doctor yet—more, I mean. Haven't seen her test results or anything. Zay's been resting."

Dillion wipes a hand down his face, expelling a breath. "Sit back, VP. You're not gonna wanna hear this."

The walls close in, my heart stalling for a beat. "My brothers, are they dead?"

"We're waiting for demands—"

"Are they dead?" I interrupt Lip.

He shakes his head no. "But they will be if we don't act fast."

"He called Riggs's phone saying some interesting things," Skeet says, folding his arms. "You ready to hear it, brother?"

I pinch my eyes shut, shaking my head, then nodding. I don't want to hear it, but I have to. I have to put my foot back into the club until my brothers are safe.

My eyes bounce around the table; one familiar face to the next, but no one speaks. As if they're too scared to reveal what's going on. "Will someone spit it out already?"

Lip sputters and places his hands in front of him. "Well, The Ghost warned us that if we don't follow his demands, he'll start sending Riggs and Adam home piece by piece."

Nodding quickly, I lean my elbows on the table and sigh. "Okay, so we'll follow his demands."

Lip looks at Skeet and shakes his head. "Ghost also said that...a certain sister wouldn't think twice about double-crossing the club."

Frowning, I glance around the table and all of the men look guilty of something. "What sister?"

"Dorian," Lip says without skipping a beat. "And what if he's right, brother? What if your wife is—"

Acting before thinking, my fist meets Lips's face as a growl booms from me. "You shut your fucking mouth!"

Skeet stands, coming forward in case a fight breaks loose, but all I'm seeing is red. He's coming for me, isn't he?

My hand shoots up and wraps around his throat, hissing at him. "She is my fucking wife! The mother to my daughters! Not a single one of you will think she's a rat until we have proof."

Skeet's chokes and gurgles move through the deafening silence in the room.

"Do I make myself fucking clear?" I growl out, releasing him and gritting my teeth. No one says a word. "I said, do I make myself clear?!"

Everyone nods, sitting properly at the table as I take a breath and collapse in the seat behind me.

And just like that, the happy life of a suburban dad with a smoking hot, curvy wife, has now become a living nightmare.

Slade

Carrying Zay to Mama Rosa's room, I sit her down at the end of the bed. I don't know how Zay does it, but after having all that blood on her, she still smells like coconuts. "You doing okay?"

She sniffs, shaking her head. "Why the fuck does bad shit always follow me?"

Placing a hand on her shoulder, I squeeze gently. "You're not the only one, sweetheart."

There have been nights that Zay and I would stay up texting. Palmer knows all about it, Riggs and Adam do, too. Zay and I do nothing but talk about our feelings and our lives. A connection that bonded us since we met. She knows all about my faults, all the reasons why I have scars up and down my arms. She knows about my love for Palmer and has been encouraging me to light a fire under my ass to slap a ring on her finger.

And I know all about Zay's life before the club, her love for her best friend, her piano recitals, her popularity in high school, and her excitement toward graphic design. Most importantly, she divulges all the nasty-ass things Riggs and Adam do with her. It's hot as fuck. Their love is unique and something to live by.

Zay is my best friend through and through.

Dropping my hand from her shoulder, all of me wants to stay and comfort her into believing that everything will be okay. But who are we kidding, I don't even believe it. I turn on my heels and head for the door to give her some privacy. She's still loopy from the drugs they gave her. When she is ready to talk, then she'll talk. She's not the type to force her feelings out.

Several reasons why she and Riggs always argued before they became a couple. They're almost the same emotionally damaged individuals.

I take the doorknob, nodding softly as the thought of Palmer flashes through my head. My heart is waiting for me in the barn and I want to make sure she's okay before we leave Maddison Gardens and seek out our brothers. Someday soon, I promise, I'll make an honest woman out of her.

"Slade?" Zay asks, her voice cracking.

Stopping, I stare back at her. "What's up?"

"Can you help me get dressed?" Her voice is weak, quiet. That vulnerability seeping through. Zay isn't one to ask for help. She isn't one to show weakness. She's the farthest from that. She's strong like these women in this sanctuary. A survivor.

Closing the door behind me, I saunter over to her and grin. "You don't even have to ask."

She shrugs out of my jacket, sniffling again. Her wavy hair falls in front of her face, poorly hiding the tears rolling down her cheeks. I don't want to push, but I gotta. I need to know what happened before I got there. I just don't know how to ask.

Grabbing a pair of floral leggings from Mama Rosa's closet, I scratch my head at what else Zay can put on. She has a big belly, and I doubt Mama Rosa has any maternity clothes. Smiling meekly over my shoulder, she holds the towel loosely against her chest.

"A tank top should be fine," she says, a drowsiness to her tone.

Taking what I can find from the dresser, I get on my knees by the bed and clear my throat. She lifts her feet one at a time and I help her ease them into the leggings. Then, I swear, it's like my mind shuts off. Zay drops the towel and uses my shoulders to stand up.

I won't lie about it, I've had a hard-on for Zay since I met her. Anyone would. The woman is gorgeous; naturally highlighted brown hair, hazel eyes that get greener when the sun shines on them, plump lips, and a smile that brightens up anyone's day. But her personality is her most attractive quality. That sass we all crave on our darkest days.

My gawking isn't right. This woman has gone through enough, and here I am checking her out like she's some piece of meat that may or may not lose her husband today.

I squeeze my eyes shut, her cherry blossom tattoo on her hipbone printed behind my eyelids. "S-sorry, I didn't mean to look."

She chuckles weakly. "It's not something you haven't seen before."

"I assure you, seeing a pregnant woman naked is *not* something I've seen before."

Seeing Zay naked is something I *have* seen before, however. About a year ago, right before she got pregnant, we crashed at their cabin and I remember waking up in the middle of the night. The cabin was quiet, soft snores from Adam and Peter moved through the closed doors. I couldn't sleep—that normally happens when I'm sleeping in a bed that isn't mine—and Palmer passed out from the rum she and Zay were throwing back. I roamed the house, tiptoeing my way to the kitchen when I noticed the crackling fire still going in the firepit outside. Inching closer, my eyes shot to Zay riding Riggs's dick reverse cowgirl. Her soft moans seeped through the crack in the door, her tits bounced against her ribcage, and Riggs's tattooed fingers rubbed her clit until she tossed her head back. Like a pervert, I watched them, studying her tiny body as his large hands roamed and groped. I never said anything, I don't think I ever will, but that night flashes through my head more than I'd like—especially when I see the two of them together.

Keeping my eyes closed, I wait for her to tell me what she needs help with next, but when the squeak of the bed rings in my ears, I wink one eye open and see that she's getting my jacket back on.

"You're not going to knock Palmer up any time soon?" she asks, arching an eyebrow.

"Eventually." But this isn't something I want to talk about. Not while Zay has dark bags under her eyes and a glazed look still beaming. "You wanna tell me what happened?"

She winces, looking down at the pair of ankle socks on her lap. "I can't, Slade," she whispers. "They'll kill them if I speak."

"But how would they know?"

She sniffs, her gaze unfaltering. "I can't."

No, I have to know. Fuck it. I said I wouldn't push, but we're on a time limit. The Ghost could call us back at any given moment, send us demands we're unprepared for. I need to know what happened. I have to fucking know.

I slide my phone from my back pocket and open up the Notes application.

Zay, you don't have to speak, just tell me what happened. Write it all down so I can save them.

I hand her the phone, and she reads it over, nodding quickly. "Can you check on Carter for me?"

Helping her feet into the socks, I kiss her head and inhale that coconut smell that seems to calm all of us. "I'll be back in a few, okay?"

She remains seated on the bed with my phone in hand, her thumbs hovering over the keyboard. When she's ready, that page will be filled with the truth.

Until then, my heart is calling me.

My Palmer, the one person I'd protect the most in this world.

***

I came to Maddison Gardens a lot when the life of a Snake—post-Daddy Donnelly showdown started to settle. Things were changing for the better. We were less into drugs and guns and more into helping these girls, doing rides for charities, offering protection to bars and clubs, and opening Judas's Hideout to bands.

It's the life of a biker I craved.

And being at Maddison Gardens guaranteed me a glimpse of that ginger beauty with the freckles.

There's a small slope at the back of the property—a far distance from the house, but close enough to call for help if needed. I was leaning on a tree staring at the starry night that seemed so awe-inducing here. No city lights or noise drowned out the beauty. It was pure chaos trapped in serenity.

That spot was the only place that eased the noise in my head. I suffered from ADHD, diagnosed at thirteen. My foster family at the time tried to force me to take pills for it, but I didn't want to change who I was because they couldn't handle me. I admit, I was hard to handle at times, but when your mind runs a mile a minute, everything around you is always in slow motion. I tapped my leg a lot, fidgeted, and constantly needed to do something. As an adult, I learned remedies to help ease the rave in my head. And watching the night sky was one of the techniques.

"Stars got you hooked, too?" That sultry voice that brought me to my knees startled me. Palmer grinned, her beauty cast in the silvery glow.

I smiled, scratching the back of my head, and looked at the stars. "Y-yeah, they're something else out here."

She sat in the grass and stretched out her legs. "This is my spot, y'know. I don't take kindly to handsome men filling my bubble."

My heart tripped on its valves at her words. Everything she did always made me swoon. Her stride, the way she tied her hair in this ball of mess that only I craved to untangle. How she'd nibble her bottom lip when something was unnerving. She was heaven in a world that was nothing but hell.

I chuckled, hesitantly walking over to her and sitting down; leaving two feet between us. "I was here first, green eyes."

She looked at me and the corner of her lip quirked up, but by the crinkle in her brow, she wasn't in a playful mood. Something was on her mind.

Untying her ginger curls, she tucked it all back into a messy knot and lay back, exhaling sharply. "The new girl that you guys brought in today, she...Christ, she was missing pieces of her skin."

I squeezed my eyes shut, shaking my head. "Perks of this job is the family I've always wanted. The downfall? The people we rescue who don't deserve the heartache and torture given to them."

She released a breath, whimpering softly. And when I glanced over my shoulder to look at her, tears slipped free. The way her eyebrows pinched together, the way she swallowed, and how her lower lip quivered—the woman who came in brought back the ghost of her past, didn't she?

Putting my hand out to her, she smiled softly, waving her pain away. "I'm fine, but you're right. I couldn't have said it better myself."

I lay back, adjusting my arm under my head. "Don't hold in your scars. Scream them out to the world. I promise you'll feel better."

She cleared the gravel from her throat and sighed. "If I was able to voice the noise in my head, I would. Mama Rosa encourages us to talk to one of the on-call therapists. But I can't do it. I don't think I will ever be able to talk about what happened to me."

I turned my head to stare at her; her long lashes blinked slowly, watching the stars as I watched her in awe. Her beauty is undeniable. Indescribable. Perfection. "I'm here when you're ready, Palmer."

She chuckled softly, turning her head. Those green eyes were almost black in this lighting. Doll-like and filled with so much hatred, there wasn't a doubt in my mind this woman would kill the man who tortured her if given the chance. And I'd be right at her side handing her the goddamn weapon.

"I like you, Palmer. Your beauty and mystery fascinate me."

Even in the dark, I could take in the blush coating her cheeks.

But what killed me next was the self-doubt that removed the redness and replaced it with a pale glow.

"You shouldn't, Slade." Her voice cracked, wavering. "I'm disgusting," she said so quietly, but the words were louder than a gunshot.

I rolled over, cupping the side of her face as half my giant body was on top of her frail, yet curvy frame. "You're farthest from disgusting. You are perfection wrapped in a pretty pink bow that's been scorched but survived. Beautiful as ever."

More tears spilled over and I caught every one of them with my thumbs. Her breath was hot against my face, a hint of cinnamon wafting off it.

"C-can I kiss you?"

She sniffed, shaking her head. "If you knew what happened to me, you wouldn't want to kiss me," she whispered.

I didn't want to know. But that sick fuck in my head had to know and wanted to absorb all her pain to help make it go away. "Tell me."

Her glassy eyes blinked rapidly, but those tears still spilled over. "It's not something I like talking about, Slade."

"I don't think any of the people here like talking about what happened to them. But Mama Rosa always says get the heartache off your chest to help you heal." Brushing my fingertips along the side of her face, I smiled. "Don't tell me. But know that I'm here, Palmer. We've only hung out no more than half an hour every couple of days for the past year, but you've done something to me and I don't know how to get away from it."

Her hot breath fanned my face, wavering and hesitant. But that look in those beautiful eyes blinking slowly told me something different. "You've done something to me, too, Slade. But you don't want this—"

"I do. All of it. Mind, body, soul, and everything else you'll give me." I pressed a kiss to her forehead, leaning mine on it. "I'm so happy you fell into my life, so happy that you were saved. So happy that you look at me with happiness and not with the thought that I'm a lowlife like everyone else sees. You see me, darling. Like I see you."

Like pulling my heart from my chest, I knew I had to give her space and let her come to me. With women like her, victims who had no other choice, showing my feelings with words was better than actions.

I lay back down, closer to her this time. My fingers grazed her hip. I'd wanted that off my chest for weeks. Wanted to tell her every time I saw her walking along the property that no matter how long. I was hers. I'd wait. I'd be celibate. I didn't care. I wanted her.

Our breaths mixed in with the trills of the night; the insects, the birds. But it was the beating of my heart that took hold of everything else and savored this moment. Loved this moment. Craved moments like these when shit was wild.

She sat up suddenly and moved quickly, planting a kiss on my lips and pulling away. She seemed shocked, relieved, but happy. A face filled with emotions staring back at me like a confession she didn't know how to voice boomed deeply, all the way to my soul.

I ran my fingers through her hair and grinned, pulling her face back to mine to give her the kiss she deserved as our first kiss.

Her tongue slipped through the seam of my lips, exploring my mouth in a way that was desperate, longing. Something we've held back for far too long.

Turning her over, I fixed her legs to either side of me and deepened the kiss. She kissed like an angel. Pillowy lips, a succulent tongue, and she tasted like the cinnamon cookies that were served after dinner.

I rock gently against her, our clothes the only thing separating me from being inside this angel. But fuck, I couldn't do anything unless she welcomed it. Being a victim of sex trafficking came with its consequences, and having sex for pleasure was something that wouldn't come easy for her anymore.

Pressing her hand against my chest, she pulled away from me with a gasp. "Slade,

I can't—"

I captured her lips once more and lifted my head to stare into her watery eyes. "I know. I won't do anything until you tell me to."

She smiled, nodding. "Thank you for seeing me."

I pressed a soft kiss on her lips before I got off her, adjusting her head on my shoulder. "This is where you belong," I whispered. "Right here in my arms."

She nuzzled her head onto me, inhaling. "Why didn't you ever tell me how you felt?"

Shame flowed through me, and it shouldn't have, but every time I wanted to say something, all I thought about was the look on her face when she remembered what happened. Guilt would ride me at the thought of all the things I wanted to do to her...and then I'd hate myself because of all the dirty things I did to the whores at the clubhouse because I couldn't do them to Palmer.

"I didn't think someone as beautiful as you would like a mutt like me."

She giggled, propping herself up on her elbow. "You're the beautiful one, Slade. The way you hold your head high, no matter what happened in your life. You're happy, free." She inhaled softly, closing her eyes as my fingertips traced down her nose. "I wish I could be free. Rid of all the darkness in my past—the same darkness that consumes me, day in and day out."

Pulling her face to mine, I kissed her sweetly. "Darkness does not consume you, darling. It does not define you." Grinning, I raked my teeth on my bottom lip. "The first time I saw you, I knew I'd make you mine and all you were doing was picking tomatoes."

Shaking her head, she lay back down, arm sliding up my chest that sent my entire body into a chokehold. "I remember that day. You guys came in here on a mission to find Zay—"

"And I ended up finding you."

She laughed, tapping my chest. I didn't know what was so funny, but I loved her little quirks. Whenever she got shy, she'd laugh. Her laughter was like a symphony. "We're two messed up souls, aren't we?"

"United in perfect harmony."

We lay there for another couple of hours, silence consuming us as we watched the stars.

And we watched them until my eyes got heavy and she nudged me to get some sleep. And sleep is what I got with her in my arms. From that night on, my new home was at Maddison Gardens in a tiny ass bed with my Palmer.

Riggs

The creaking of metal takes hold of the quiet.

Filling.

Invading.

Becoming.

We've been hanging in this damn room that smells of rot and mildew for hours.

Adam is hanging in front of me, his long blonde hair in shambles. His head is hanging low, saliva and blood leaking from his lips. Every now and then he'll let out a cough, but he's bleeding out and if I don't get him outta here, he'll die and my girl will never recover.

They ambushed us.

Shot me with a tranquilizer before I made it to her. And my body hit the slush faster than I could yell out her name.

The last thing I saw before my eyes shut was her perfect fucking face crying, screaming, calling out my name before they injected her.

I don't even know if she's safe.

I don't even know if my son is safe.

I failed at protecting them.

I failed and I might lose my brother, my woman, and my kids in the process.

Groaning, I drop my head back with a wince. Every time I move, my wrists chafe. Blood is leaking down my arms, my bare chest, and soaking into my waistband.

My shoulder is dislocated.

My head is pounding.

The chain keeps digging into my wrists and my screams are doing nothing to help.

Nothing at all.

The tips of my boots barely touch the floor, but it's enough to give me some slack when I need relief on my shoulder.

Adam wheezes, coughing softly. "Riggs?" he whispers, his matted blonde hair tangled with sweat and blood, hiding his face. "Tell Zay I love her. Reminder her that she's my forever and always." He wheezes, body slumping more than it already has. "Tell her, Riggs, please promise me you'll tell her."

I grit my teeth and yank my arms, screaming as I writhe in pain. "No, Adam, no. You'll tell her your damn self," I growl, yanking again.

He lifts his blue eyes to meet mine; they're glassy, heavy, riddled with tears. I've never seen him so sweaty and pale before. Not even when we'd do things with Zay he was uncomfortable with. This isn't Adam staring back at me. It's his ghost. He's not going to fucking make it.

His wheezes fill me.

Devour me.

Until they stop.

Slade

Lip and I step into the cabin, guns raised as the smell of blood soaks into us. Peter is walking the grounds with Dillon and Gunner's crew, scoping it out for any traces or signs of something that can help.

The Ghost said he'd call us with his demand, but we haven't gotten a call yet. Skeet and Lip say we should let Dorian meet up with him to see what he wants. He did ask for her during the call, but Peter was not having it. He had Skeet by the throat with the intent to do damage. And when they pulled him off, he clocked Lip on the mouth with the rage to keep going. Peter was fuming, teeth bared and gritted, face red and his breaths were ragged.

I don't think he's ever been that angry before. What I learned today when push comes to shove, Peter is exactly like Riggs.

Lip whistles softly, jerking his head at me to follow him down the hallway. There aren't any signs of breaking in aside from the busted front door, but multiple boot prints dirty the ground. A mix of mud, wetness, and smeared blood.

The Ghost has many men in his back pocket, Mama Rosa used to be one of them before The Ghost disappeared completely and he learned we were cleaning out her pockets of any unwanted vermin; making Maddison Gardens a wholesome place for the victims.

But of course, he found our weak spot and is now filling it with cement. Soon, we'll sink to the bottom of the ocean and be forgotten.

Lip and I walk quietly down the hallway of the cabin. Every single door is shut except the door to the cellar that's used as storage. This door is never open. Adam is scared Carter might get down there and hurt himself so Zay made Riggs bolt it shut. Yet it's open now like someone used the key to unlock it.

Lip crouches to step into the opening; the cellar door is half the size of the regular one. And I practically fold in half to get down here. I helped Riggs last summer unpack the patio set from here since the shed is filled with his bikes. Carter's crib and some baby things are also stacked down here, along with a lot of Shyanne's things that Riggs didn't know what to do with and didn't have the heart to throw out. This cellar is nothing but junk.

Lip gags, slapping a hand on his mouth as the gun shakes in his other hand. "The fuck is that?"

I try to turn the light on but the switch is fucked. Have Adam and Riggs been down here the whole time?

I pull my phone from my pocket and open the flashlight app. Boxes and junk piled high, cobwebs moving softly, and dried blood. More fucking blood.

Lip gags again from the rotten smell. But I pull through. I've smelled worse and experienced worse things growing up. I was homeless for a good part of my life, appreciating a warm meal and a shower far more than a bed to sleep in. When I ran away at eighteen, I found myself broke and there were only so many couches I could crash on before the women I fucked caught on that I was using them. This smell is nothing compared to the men and women I bunked with under bridges and in alleyways.

Lip keeps the gun steady as I inch forward, letting my nose find the culprit.

The rot is increasing.

The splatters of dried blood are like my breadcrumbs.

"Riggs? Adam?" Lip whispers, checking behind the staircase.

My heart is thudding loudly, pulsating in my ears at what the fuck we're about to find.

I take a step around the boxes and that's when I see it, flies buzzing around a body. Maggots rolling around on the floor, twitching and feasting. Whoever the fuck this is has been dead for more than a week.

"It's not them," I call out, staring at the corpse dressed in black from head to toe; their face is hidden from view, but their slim, short body gives me the answer.

Lip gags again, shaking his head. "I gotta get outta here, brother. It stinks so bad."

I nod but don't look at him. "Yeah, just a sec."

With the butt of my gun, I poke the corpse. It shakes and a wave of living maggots moves under their skin, leaking out from under their mask. I'm going to have to remove it to know who the fuck this is.

The smell is burning my eyes, turning my stomach, yet all I do is bring my forearm to my nose and groan when I lean down to push the mask off with my gun.

Slowly, the face filled with decay looks back at me. The betrayal The Ghost was talking about. The backstabber who wasn't scared to backstab again.

Gray's hollow eyes stare ahead at nothing as one sole maggot dangles in the corner of her eye.

"Slade?" Lip calls, but I can't look away.

What in the fuck did Peter get himself involved with?

I stand tall and step back, shaking my head as my gaze remains on her.

To say I'm shocked is an understatement. To say she didn't deserve it makes me feel like I should rot in hell.

But holy fucking shit, I know The Ghost is Wilde—Dorian and Gray's half-brother. Yet the last I heard, Gray went to Florida with Bells. Then disappeared completely from Dorian's life.

Now she's lying on her belly in the basement, rotting away.

Following Lip as he coughs, we make our way back upstairs, heading right out the front door. He barely makes it outside, puking in the bushes beside the front step.

"Dude, the fuck?" Dillon says, stepping back and glancing at the house.

I'm on autopilot. Walking slowly, calculated. It isn't until I see Peter running his fingers through his hair that I huff out a breath and find his gaze. "It's Gray."

"What?" Peter shakes his head, glancing at Lip, then back at me.

Lip spits, groaning. "Smells like death down there."

"It's Gray," I say again, staring at Peter until his eyes widen and he darts into the house.

"Cellar," I call out to him, my shaking hand going for the cigarettes in my pocket.

I manage to light the cigarette at my lips and Peter lets out a yell before I even inhale. "Whatever this fucker is after, he's made it more than personal and I think we better figure this shit out before he starts killing more than just Adam or Riggs," I say on an exhale.

"What do you mean?" Dillon asks, glancing up as Peter stumbles out of the house, looking as green as Lip.

"Ghost said he wants Dorian, but it's her sister lying in that cellar rotting—"

"What did they inject Zay with?" Lip interrupts me, wide-eyed.

"Doctor hasn't gotten back to us yet," Peter answers, staring at me.

Then it dawns on me. Half of the girls that are saved have an implant removed from their body before they join the sanctuary.

Half of them are stoned out of their minds.

Zay was out of it.

Zay was injected.

Zay was *implanted*.

I gasp, thinking of nothing other than my darling. "Maddison Gardens. Mama Rosa is very strict about who knows that location. I'm sure as shit The Ghost doesn't know. The fucker is trying to find the sanctuary—"

"How can you be sure?" Dillon asks, getting his helmet from the hood of the Audi.

"Daddy Donnelly and Roaden started this fucking bullshit, taking Wilde's girlfriend in the process. Now she's gone and he wants revenge. What better way than to expose the goddam sanctuary that failed to save his girl, and destroy every one of us who uses it to protect our fucking family."

Peter grabs me by the arm and shoves me at my bike. "You better fucking hope you're wrong. My wife and fucking kids are there. Carter and Zay—"

"Then why the fuck are we fucking around here? Let's go!" I shout, getting on the bike and whipping out of the driveway to the place that holds my heart.

Slade

This morning, Palmer's pussy was clenched around my cock as she came apart, screaming my name into oblivion. And I was right behind her, riding into the sea of destruction.

The tingle started at the top of my head, rolling down my spine as my balls tightened and I released, filling that magical pussy. Pushing as deep as she could take me, I milked every last drop of my cum. "You, darling, are my life, my home, my eternity."

Buried inside her is the only home I ever want to know...

***

I come to a shrieking halt and get off my bike; Dillon, Lip, and Gunner's VP chasing after me. Mama Rosa is in the dining room, that yellow folder tucked under her arm.

"Boys?" she calls out, but I'm heading for the barn.

For my darling.

The kids.

Zay.

"Zay's upstairs," I say to Peter who's hot on my tail before I cut through the kitchen. "In Mama Rosa's room."

"Get everybody to the shelters, Mama," Peter yells.

He charges upstairs. Zay is the bomb we're all too afraid to touch, but Peter would do anything for her. That guilt is ingrained in his skin.

I buck it across the yard, shoving the barn door open with a grunt.

Palmer gasps when I charge into her classroom, the kids jumping from their seats. "Slade, what's—" Some of the kids look terrified. I would too if a six-foot-eight-inch-tall tattooed man barged into their classroom unannounced. But Palmer smiles, putting her hands up and tapping their heads as she walks toward me. "Hey, it's okay guys. It's just Slade, he's the best guy. I promise."

I swallow thickly, smiling the best I can. "Palmer, we have to talk a sec."

"Okay, okay," she says quietly, smiling again at the kids again. "Why don't we have some free play? I'll be back in a second."

Taking her hand as soon as the kids are up and playing, I bring her into the hallway. "Darling, I need you to take everyone to the panic room. Lock it up and—"

"What's going on?"

Exhaling slowly, my heart beats out of my chest and my anxiety is in full force. I kiss her hand and sigh. "I think they implanted Zay."

Palmer's gaze flickers from one of my eyes to the other before her eyebrows furrow. "They implanted me months before they took me."

I squeeze her head to mine, my breathing quick and jagged. "Where's Dorian and the kids?"

She sniffs, touching my chest. "She took the girls and Carter to Mama's room for a nap—"

"When?"

My distrust in Dorian is still alive and well. But I hide it. We all do. She betrayed the club before, there's no telling if she'd do it again.

"Like fifteen minutes ago—Slade, tell me what's goi—"

A bang sounds, vibrating the area.

An explosion.

Windows blowout.

Screams penetrate.

My heart stops, grabbing onto Palmer and pushing her into the wall, using my body as a shield, protecting her from the glass.

Siren blares.

Shouts and yells come from outside.

Pure insanity rolling in.

There's a ringing in my ears causing everything around me to silence. The steady high-pitched hum takes over the chaos. Everything blurs. My skin crawls as if little ants march along every pore.

Palmer panics, pushing off me and bringing me back to life. "The kids! Slade, the kids!"

I yank open the door to the classroom, wails and screams come from the children. No windows in here, thankfully. Not a single one of them is hurt.

"I'm scared, Miss Palmer," a little girl says, her wet brown eyes looking at Palmer, and her little arms wrap around her waist.

Palmer nods, waving her arms. "Guys, let's go. Remember how we practiced? Quickly now."

I take my gun and hand it to Palmer, pressing a kiss to her forehead. "Stay low and out of sight."

"Slade, please, don't leave—"

"Darling, I have to make sure no one is hurt—" I stop myself, sighing and nodding quickly. "Okay, okay."

She sniffs, looking back as the kids follow us through the barn to a door at the back that leads to a bunker underground which Mama Rosa calls "the panic room." The place she tells us to run to if things ever go bad. The warehouse used to be the go-to, but Riggs didn't think it was safe enough. He used his connections and had eighteen large bunkers built into Maddison Gardens.

Let's hope it's enough to keep us protected.

Palmer's shaking hand punches in the code and the children pile in.

As her hand is in mine, my eyes are roaming the grounds. Searching. Scanning. Hunting.

Then an ear-rendering shriek from someone causes me to shove Palmer into the bunker with one final kiss.

"I love you!" I shout, slamming the door shut and ignoring her pleading on the other end.

My devotion is to the club until this shit is settled.

When it is, there will be no hesitating or searching. My loyalty will remain with her.

Peter

I bang on the door of Mama's room, jiggling the knob. "Zay? Zay, open up!"

Silence.

I growl, taking a step back so I can shoulder my way in when my mother comes up the stairs. "Mama, I told you to get everyone out of here."

"What's going on, Peter?" she huffs, shifting her gaze from the locked door to me. "Zay isn't in there. She left with Dorian and the kids about twenty minutes ago."

"Where did they go?"

"Your house."

I charge past her, but she follows after me, holding a yellow folder close to her chest. She's been clutching that folder for months, and every time I ask about it, I never get a clear answer. There's something important in there, something that might help us…but my fucking brain isn't prioritizing the importance of *why* this is happening. All I'm prioritizing is helping my family.

Stopping dead in my tracks when I reach the door, I turn around when my mother bumps into me. "Get everyone to the bunkers, sound the alarm. I think they implanted Zaynab with a tracker like they do to all these girls. No one figured it out until we brought her here and we led them right to these people we spent years saving. Slade believes The Ghost is coming to fuck shit up. We can't risk anyone getting hurt. And if Zaynab went to my house with my kids, my wife, and my nephew, I have to get to them before *he* does."

Mama groans, looking back with a deep inhale. I don't know what's going through her head. I rarely do. She never talks about the business side of things when we're all together as a family. It's just that, family stuff—church, dinners, seeing her grandbabies. Never business.

But we're all about talking business now.

"I'm coming with you. I've spoken to him before. Maybe I can push him in the right direction and show him that even though we couldn't save Lenora, that doesn't mean he has to destroy our cause. The men who helped in her captivity are…" She shakes her head. "There doesn't need to be any more dead bodies on our hands." Taking the walkie-talkie hanging on a hook by the door, she pressed the button. "I'll tell everyone to take cover."

I whip my phone from my pocket as I step outside. I'm in no mood to argue. My house is twenty minutes from Maddison Gardens, which means I'm twenty minutes away from saving my girls.

Lip and Dillon round the corner of the house, out of breath and sweaty. "Everyone is getting into the bunkers as we speak."

Mama opens the passenger door, tucking the folder under the seat. "You boys stand guard. I have six guards posted everywhere, but the more eyes the better."

Lip nods, taking a cigarette from his pocket. "Yes, ma'am."

Dropping into the seat of my Audi, my mother joins me as I press the button to start the engine and reverse, when everything fucking changes.

The ground rattles, vibrating and erupting.

The windshield blows up, making me twist the car into one of the vans. My ears are ringing. Lip is screaming. The rippling effects of the explosion still booms in my chest. When I open my eyes, blood coats my lashes, but it's not enough to hide Mama's house up in flames; broken into a million pieces scattered everywhere.

The memories.

The laughter.

The happiness that the home held is now bleeding all over the frozen ground.

I wipe the blood from my eyes, wincing loudly at the cuts that decorate my face. "Mama? Mama, are you okay?"

She's sobbing beside me, just as shocked and hurt as I am. Her soft features bear scratches from the glass that will turn into scars as time goes on. She's staring at her house, the glow of the fire reflecting in her eyes. "Peter, we have to get to your house, *now!*"

I return my attention to the house, Dillon is face-first in the snow, Lip screaming beside him…The Ghost planned this. A total wipeout.

But he has no idea who the fuck he's messing with.

No idea what an angry Donnelly will do to protect what's his.

No idea at all.

***

I wipe my face with one of Sara's blankets, the fluffy pink one she slept with last night. Blood covers the blanket, taking away the innocence of something that belongs to my daughter.

Mama takes the blanket from me and wipes at my neck, sniffling. "He'll pay for what he did to my safe haven."

"I don't understand why the fuck he'd do this knowing Maddison Gardens is a place for people who have been saved. It doesn't make fucking sense." I grit my teeth, hissing softly as she holds my face and picks a piece of glass from my cheek. "Fuck, Mama."

Wincing again, I wipe more blood from my face while keeping my eyes on the road, focusing on everything around us. On the lookout for anything suspicious.

"Just drive, Peter. I don't know how many people we lost, but I sure as heck know I will not lose my grandbabies or my daughters in the process."

Her daughters, my women. *Dorian.* The only woman I'd ever lay my life on the line for. *Zaynab.* There will never be a time in my life that I wouldn't help her. My wife doesn't like how close we still are, but I will forever be in her debt. Until the day I die, Zay will know I redeemed myself for hurting her.

I take a sharp left, speeding down the open road toward my house at the end of it.

There's an uneasiness settling in my belly. I don't know what is waiting for us at the house and I don't know why the fuck I didn't help my brothers after the explosion. The men who stand before me and are loyal as fuck.

And all I did was drive away, leaving Slade to deal with this shit without me. But he'll understand. He'll know I left for my family.

Side-glancing at Mama as we approach the long driveway, I squeeze my eyes shut, forcing the blood from my eyes. There must be cuts all over my damn face. "Mama?"

"It'll be okay, sweetie."

I grunt, shaking my head. "What's in that yellow folder you keep with you all the time?"

Redness crawls its way up her neck, disappearing in her mascara-stained cheeks. "Now is not the time."

"What is it?"

I come to an abrupt stop, her gasp filling the tension. My front door is open, Dorian's car is still on, and there's a man in a devil mask that shines in the sunlight standing at the door; a blade stained in blood gripped in his hand.

I don't even have to question it.

This is The Ghost.

Slade

Screams envelop me as I make a run for the home that's in shambles. Pieces of it are stabbed into the ground.

Doors are hanging from apple trees.

Walls have flattened the gardens.

Furniture is unrecognizable.

The house is nothing but brick and mortar, as if it's been unused for years.

Coughing, I wave my hand through the smoke, trying to walk over debris toward the front of the house. The fire is still roaring from where the bomb went off. Still swallowing everything in its path. What the hell was The Ghost thinking? He helped save these people. Why would he put them at risk?

Let's hope no one was in the house. Let's hope everyone got out alive.

Lip's calling out for help, dragging his body toward Dillon, and calling out to Peter as the Audi revs out of the driveway. Where the fuck is he going?

We need him here!

I cough again and tap Lip's shoulder. "Hey. Hey, man. Hey, c'mon, let me help."

He looks back at me with gritted teeth. A sharp yelp escapes as I lift him, but he doesn't cry. Snakes don't show weakness.

"What happened, brother?" Lip asks, his voice cracking.

I sniff, helping him lean against the side of a van. "Don't know. But I hate the fact that I was fucking right."

I check on Dillon next, he's face-first in the snow, blood pooling around him. "Dillon? Hey, man—" I turn him over and he gasps, coughing uncontrollably. "Take a breath, it's all right. Take a breath."

He groans, wincing when he tries to lift his arm. A piece of glass from the blown-out windows is lodged into his bicep, blood squirting out of it. "What the fuck, dude?"

The house is practically nonexistent. The warm kitchen with home-cooked meals isn't standing. The dining room has half a table and missing chairs. The stairs that go to the bedrooms are there, without an upper floor.

"Was there anyone in the house when it happened?"

Lip lifts a shoulder, holding his jaw. "Mama Rosa scrambled to get everyone out when you guys stormed the place."

I gasp, looking at the nonexistent upper floor. "Zay?"

"I don't know, brother," Lip says softly.

I go for my phone, then stop and look at the debris. I left it with Zay.

Lip sucks his teeth when I search his pockets for his cell phone and call Peter.

One ring.

Two rings.

On the third ring, he picks up but doesn't say anything. It's a faded conversation, voices in the distance until I hear Peter say something that sends me over the edge.

"You come into my fucking house and hide my children from me?!"

Dillion sucks his teeth, getting on his knees. "What's going on?"

Putting myself on mute, I keep the phone to my ear, glancing around at the bikes blown over in the explosion. "Peter is on the phone, I think they're at his place…he answered the call so we could listen in."

"Call Gunner, tell him what's going on," Lip groans, holding his side. "Fuck, I think I smashed a rib or two."

"Call some doctors. Who knows how many of us are fucked," Dillon scoffs, applying pressure to his arm.

Lifting my bike with a yelp, I switch the call over to my AirPods and get on it. As soon as I'm close, if Zay is still alive, I'll track her with my Find My Phone app. She's smart, she'd have turned it on and kept the phone hidden with her if someone had taken her before this explosion happened.

"You can't go there alone, Slade. Wait for backup. Gunner's crew will be right over—"

"Dillon, we don't have fucking time to wait. They're at Peter's house where his fucking kids are!" I interrupt him, barring my teeth. "Go help whoever needs help. Do what you can—"

"I'll tell backup to head for Peter's," Dillion interrupts me this time, getting his phone from his pocket.

Calling backup could fuck us—who knows how many people are in on this. But my brain is too clouded to see straight.

Lip holds his gun out to me, gripping his side. "It's fully loaded."

I tuck it into the back of my jeans and start the bike. "Make sure my woman is safe."

Lip nods, gritting his teeth when he tries to move.

I'm lucky I have nothing but scratches on me from the windows being blown out.

Bucking it down the driveway, I skid on the road before I regain traction. I'm twenty minutes out. I can make it in ten to fifteen. I have to fucking make it.

The voices are even more muffled now that I'm driving like a madman through the streets. Cop cars are wailing in the distance, but the muffled cries coming from Mama Rosa take over everything. I can barely make out what they're saying, barely hearing anything over the wind hitting my face and shaking the AirPods.

I'm five minutes out, I can already see my turn up ahead. But something is telling me to slow down. Something is screaming at me to stop.

I bring the bike to a slower pace, staring at my turn when I see it. Two men crouching in the bushes with black masks on, guns in hand. If I turned, they would've ambushed me. Jesus, fuck. What the hell is going on?

Turning at the next corner, I ditch my bike in the trees. I'll do the rest on foot.

I take the gun from my pocket and remove an AirPod, forcing my ears to listen. Yet there's nothing but silence. Silence that's too fucking suspicious. It's making my skin crawl.

Everything is still, except the soft gust of wind moving branches above me and shaking loose a small dusting of snow. I don't like silence. I never fucking have. Growing up, my foster families kept a TV on in our rooms, letting us fall asleep on whatever the hell we wanted. Half the time, us boys watched porn until our eyes were in the same socket. Most of the time, I'd turn on documentaries. They were the easiest to fall asleep on. Until I switched foster homes again and books became my escape, those were the things that filled the silence.

Taking careful, calculated steps, I walk through the wooded area, seeing Peter's house come into view. The white brick and dark blue shutters are muted in the dreary winter. This home is lively and inviting in the summer. But right now, it's something out of a horror movie. That waiting, intensity of a jump scare about to happen.

The front door is open and Peter's car parked out front; the windshield missing.

Dorian's car is running, all the doors open, but no one is inside.

Flashes of blood blur my vision but hearing Peter's voice ensures me that no one is dead. At least not yet. He'd be raining havoc on those who hurt his girls. That includes Zay.

My heart is beating in my throat as my raspy breath clouds around me. I wish I was more prepared. Ready for what to expect. Hell, we all wish we knew what to expect when bad things happen. But that's the point of it being bad, isn't it? Something that doesn't go our way…

The muffled voices grow louder as I approach the house, but I stay hidden in the shrubs surrounding the property. I'm good at being quiet. The Snakes use me a lot for stealthy deals. I'm a giant but light on my feet.

"Where are they?" Peter says, his voice the clearest of them all.

"They're at home," a distorted voice says, someone I can assume is The Ghost.

"And Zay? Where is she?" Mama Rosa demands.

The Ghost laughs, that distorted box making it more sinister. "*Home*, how many times do I have to repeat myself?"

Home?

What does he mean "home"?

They aren't at the cabin.

They can't be at Maddison Gardens.

They aren't at the clubhouse.

They're—*oh, fuck.*

Retracing my steps, an idea buzzes through my head to go back to the place where this all started. Back to where we were first introduced to the men who led us to The Ghost. Back to a home that was shot up three years ago.

Back *home.*

Their *home.*

The sanctuary they created when shit hit the fucking fan the first time around.

How could we not have seen it?

I get on my bike that I stashed in the bushes and end the call with Peter so I can call Dillon. One ring before he answers. "Gunner's men are right there, Slade—"

"They're keeping Riggs and Adam at their old house in San Jose. Do you remember the house Riggs bought for Zay?" I shout, seeing the bikes come down the road. I wave them down and shake a hand at my throat. Hopefully, they understand what I mean. "The Ghost is hiding them there."

"What about Peter's house?" Dillion asks as Gunner's crew pulls over to join me.

"The Ghost is talking to him now. I'll keep you updated when I can. Your job is to stay at Maddison Gardens, understood?" When Dillon grunts a response, I hang up, nodding my head at Gunner.

"What's going on, boy? We were given orders—"

"There's two men with guns at the end of Peter's driveway, hiding in the shrubs. Take the driveway next door and head in that way," I interrupt Gunner.

"You look like you're about to pass out," Gunner adds, clapping my shoulder.

"Today has been a fucking shit show." I wipe my brow and shake my head. "I'm heading to San Jose. I think I know where Riggs and Adam are."

Gunner whistles, flagging three men. "Allistair, Byron, and Luthor will follow you."

Allistair salutes me; his bright pink mohawk is mussed from the helmet he removes. Byron adjusts the silver rings on his fingers, cracking the bones in his neck; his dark, round face is always so angered. And Luthor's frail hand brings a cigarette to his lips, exhaling the smoke as he pulls the bandana from his head.

"Just let us know what you need us to do, brother," Allistair says, his multiple lip rings stopping him from opening his mouth all the way.

"Stay close, stay quiet, keep your fucking eyes peeled." Wiping my nose with the back of my hand, I crack my thumb knuckles and tap my pocket. "I have Lip's phone if you need me."

"Stay safe, boy," Gunner says, snapping his fingers at his men as they start up their bikes again.

I nod, pulling back onto the street with Allistair, Byron, and Luthor beside me, and praying I'm right and they're at the house. Praying I can save my family. Praying I get out of this alive to start my own.

Peter

Trying to steady my hands, but they're shaking like crazy at my sides. Much like they were when I got sober. Sobriety is about to meet its maker when this is over.

And it will be over. I'll make sure to stab that fucking blade The Ghost is holding into his jugular.

"I'm not asking again, prick. Where the fuck are my kids?" I yell, staring at the two other masked men in my kitchen. My face stings from the cuts; warm from the blood still trickling down my cheek.

The Ghost laughs, that godawful distorted voice is like an irritating tick. "I wouldn't hurt children, *prick*. Your daughters and nephew are safe." He folds his arm and taps the chin of the mask. "Your wife, however, that's a whole other story."

Dorian's muffled screams move through the house. A third masked man comes in holding her by the hair. Duct tape covers her mouth and binds her hands. Those gray eyes stare at me with such horror. For the first time in my life, I'm powerless.

"You see, Peter, seeking revenge is simple, really. Someone does something to hurt you and you want nothing more than to make them suffer and would do anything to see it happen—"

"We had nothing to do with what happened to your girlfriend!" I interrupt him, the chords in my neck bulging. My focus is on Dorian as she sobs behind the tape. "My father and his brother are dead. What more revenge do you need when the men who started this are gone?"

The Ghost laughs again, coming closer to us. I shoot a protective arm out in front of my mother, puffing out my chest. "Why don't you explain why I'm not letting this go, Mama Rosa, hmm? The most notorious woman who saved so many sex-trafficked men, women, and children. Why don't you explain to your son why the fuck his brothers won't make it through the night?"

Mama whimpers, shaking her head quickly. "It's not my fault."

The Ghost growls, grabbing Mama's face before I can step in to stop him. And when I do, there's a gun pressed to the side of my head; the masked man who brought my wife in is shaking his head at me.

"All this time I thought my girl died because Mama Rosa couldn't save her. But that isn't true, isn't it? No, my fucking Lenora is someone's pet. Tied to a goddam bed and fucked until she bleeds, but who cares, right? She's not fucking family. She's just some girl Mama Rosa couldn't save."

The Ghost lets go of her face and shoves her back a step, folding his arms across his chest. "But she could be saved, can't she? She could've *been* saved years ago, but Mama Rosa is seeking more than just one girl. No, she wants to save hurdles of them. So she ignores my pleading woman and saves others, leaving her to rot in that hell."

I glance at my mother, tears streaming down her cheeks. "The fuck is he talking about?"

She shakes her head, sniffling, and keeps her eyes locked on The Ghost as he roams the kitchen, tapping the chin of his mask in thought.

"I thought I found her location, thought I was able to save her, turns out, a biker gang had raided the joint and she was moved to another location. Someplace only one person knew but your brother put a bullet in his goddamn head, so I was never able to find her. And now I don't know if I ever will. The trail has gone cold." He outstretches his arms. "So tell me, Mama Rosa, has the trail gone cold or do you know where she is?"

Clenching my hands into fists, I glare at my mother. "Is this true? People have fucking died and all you had to do was give him a fucking *location*! The house blew up, my children were taken, my brothers could be dead, and God only knows what they're going to do to Zaynab as payback. This is my fucking life, Mama. A life you walked out on when I was a teenager. And for what? Huh? So you can save these people only for us to end up as fucked up as them?"

"You don't understand—"

"No, I *fucking* don't." I grit my teeth at The Ghost, pointing at my wife. "Let her fucking go and I'll make this sad excuse of a mother of mine give you the location."

Dorian screams, shaking her head when the masked man lifts her by the hair and chuckles.

"If only it were that easy, Peter," The Ghost says, turning his blade in the sunlight. "Do you ever wonder what sort of screams would leave your wife if a blade slid into her belly?"

I swallow thickly, staring as she thrashes in the masked man's arms. "She has nothing to do with this!"

"She has *everything* to do with this!"

Dorian knows I'd take a bullet for her. I'd lay my life on the line for her. But I have to make sure the kids are safe before I sacrifice myself for my woman.

"Gray is dead," I blurt out. "She's rotting away in the basement of the cabin."

Dorian wails, her knees giving out on her. I wanted to tell her in a different setting, to ease her scattered mind about where her sister is. But all this time she was right under our noses.

The Ghost appears confused, baffled. His arms drop to his sides and he looks back at one of the men standing guard. He had no idea.

"Was she working for you?"

"Did you kill her?" he interrupts me; yanking me by the shirt toward him. "Did you fucking kill my sister?"

I shake my head, raising my hands in surrender. "I've done nothing. We found her like that."

He lets go of me and shoves me back. "Did you know?" He points a finger at Dorian. "Did you fucking know she was *here*?"

He yanks the duct tape off her mouth, those plump lips cracked and bleeding.

Dorian shakes her head frantically, pleading. "No, Wilde. I had no idea. Last I heard she was in Florida with Bells—"

"And yet she's rotting in a goddamn basement!"

One of the masked men steps forward, lifting a hand. "We found a body this morning, didn't know it was Gray."

The Ghost doesn't hesitate, he takes his blade and stabs the man in the jugular; gurgles taking over the silence.

I've met crazed people before.

I've killed crazed people before.

But I've never felt a tension like there is in here. This heavy fog envelops us. Suffocating.

The Ghost tilts his head at Mama now, yanking the blade from the guy's throat and sauntering toward her. "You see how easy it is for me to kill someone loyal to me? How do you think I would feel killing someone like you? Hmm? Now, you either give me what I want to know or I will make your grandchildren orphans."

Dorian whimpers, a sob breaking free. "Mama, please."

Mama straightens out her shoulders, a soft smile cresting her lips. There's this evil look about her, something sinister that I've never seen before.

And I don't think this is going to end well for any of us.

"Tell me, *Ghost*. What would you do if I gave you something far grander than a silly address to save your girl?"

He shakes his head, lifting the blade to her chin. "Where is she?"

A laugh seeps from Mama's lips, causing the man holding the gun to my head to ease back a little.

This isn't my mother beside me.

This is the evil my daddy bestowed onto her.

An evil she's kept hidden for years and it's finally broken free.

Riggs

The chaffed skin and blood are making it easier to move my wrist around. The pain is intense, making me see stars, but with one more tug, I'll be able to get my wrist loose.

I grunt, wincing as I grit my teeth and pull. I have to get to Adam. I gotta know if he's okay. He hasn't said a word in almost an hour—I think. It's so damn dark down here. The only source of light is from a dirty window covered in newspaper clippings in the corner.

No one has come to see us.

No one has tried to save us.

I gotta do what I failed to do and protect my goddamn family.

Giving my wrist a break, more blood leaks down my arm. The scar I'll bear won't be enough to remind me of this horrible day. My Zay could be dead. My fucking son—

I close my eyes and tug my wrist again, thinking of Zay, thinking of how beautiful she is. Of how she consumed me from the moment we met, of how much I've loved her even when inside someone else.

Tugging at my wrist, the pain is blinding. Nearly sending me over the edge. But her face; that gorgeous angular face with almond-shaped hazel eyes and suck me lips…I think of Zay and my favorite memory of her comes to life. It was at my 30th birthday party at *Judas's Hideout*. Her smile helps me through this pain…

Zay had been dancing all night, swaying those fucking hips to the beat like a goddamned tease. She knew what she was doing, too. Wearing that skintight red dress.

Nipples hard.

Ass fit.

No underwear, either.

Woman was killing me.

Peter nudged my side, smirking. "All eyes are on her tonight."

Waggling my eyebrows, I chuckled. "I know, and she's all fucking mine."

"Almost," Dorian chimed in, smiling coyly. "She's still Adam's wife, y'know."

Rolling my eyes, I focused back on Zay as she pulled Palmer away from Slade to dance, making him laugh and sit closer to me.

The way Zay's hips moved to the beat, there wasn't a doubt in my mind if I had seen her before all this madness began when she was an innocent university student, I would have fallen to my knees and begged her to marry me on the spot. This life tainted her, but that wild, happy girl is back tonight. Laughing, drinking, dancing—the life of the party. It didn't bother me that she stole my night. She deserved it. All my birthdays would forever praise her. My sunshine. My goddess. My goddamn lifeline.

Flipping her hair over her shoulder, Palmer hugged her and ran off in the direction of the bar. Zay bit her bottom lip and shimmied her shoulders toward Adam, sipping his drink. She kissed him softly, laughing as he winked at her before she headed to the bar to join Palmer, those hips still bobbing to the beat.

A growl rumbled through me, knowing this woman was mine for the keep.

I shared Zay, sure. But deep down, I owned her in every form. Mind, body, and soul.

Slade jabbed me in the ribs, nodding at Zay. "You got that look in your eyes, brother. She's your trophy, isn't she?"

"My goddamn heart."

Adam pulled his hair into a knot on his head. He'd been growing his hair out since we became a unit—the two of us messing around with Zay. I've had threesomes before—with two girls—but never how we did it. No, Adam and I with Zay was something special. It was paradise. And one night, while I was in that tight pussy, she finally let him in that ass. The three of us fucked into oblivion and we knew it was forever. It would always be forever with her.

I licked my lips and got up, striding toward my goddess. The scent of her coconut perfume hit me before I even got to her.

Woman was driving me mad.

I hooked an arm around her waist and tugged her to my chest. That giggle, it was one in a million. "Dancing like that on purpose, baby?"

She ground that ass against me, sending me into overdrive. "It's your birthday after all. It's not like I can give you a striptease in front of all those people."

I nipped at her ear and lifted her, walking like I was on fire to the hallway that led to the back bedroom. But I wouldn't bring her there. No, I liked treating Zay like my whore. My trophy. My goddamn queen.

She bit her lip when I turned her around, lifted her and pinned her against the wall. "Are you going to fuck me out in the open, Riggsy?"

She opened her legs wide around me, letting me see that glistening pussy. And it was mine, all fucking mine.

Unzipping my jeans, I pulled myself out. My cock was hard and ready for her like it had been all night, painfully constricted in my jeans. "Scream for me, baby, will you?"

Easing into her entrance was my favorite thing on earth. I could die, as long as I was inside her, I'd go to heaven because she was my heaven.

I thumped hard and rough, feeling her high heels bounce against my ass. "I'm gonna put a baby inside you, Zay. You hear me? I'm gonna fill you up with babies and marry you one day."

She moaned, pulling the hair on the back of my neck. "I think that's illegal."

I thumped harder, making her squeal. "Does it look like I've done anything legal in my life?" I licked her neck, tasting that sweat coating her skin. "Marry me, baby. Fucking marry me before I come undone."

She threw her head back, calling my name as we rolled over the edge together.

Her tight pussy milked every last drop of my cum.

"Yes!" she exclaimed, smiling.

A smirk graced my lips. "Yes, what, sunshine?"

"I'll illegally marry your fine ass."

And she kissed me, bringing with her my happiness. My love. My home...

I tug on my wrist once more when a door opens and heavy footfalls make the trek downstairs to Adam and me. My heart is already hammering violently; sweat dripping from my face. I don't look like I've been passed out this whole time but I act like I've been doing nothing and let my head fall forward like Adam's, pretending I'm still passed out even though sweat from the pain trickles down my nose.

There's a grunt, some shuffling, and the heavy footfalls leave.

But I don't open my eyes yet.

I listen.

There's a soft whimper, sniffling, and a heavy breath I'd recognize anywhere.

My eyes shoot open and I rattle the chains to look around. And there she is. My sunshine.

Tears simmer in my eyes, blurting my vision. "Zay!" Her eyes are covered with a black cloth, hands bound behind her back. "Baby, hey. Hey, you okay?"

She leans forward and sobs, shaking her head quickly. Her entire body tremors, pulling at my heartstrings that I'm not holding her right now. That I can't take her pain away.

I'd do anything to see that breathtaking smirk on her succulent mouth.

"Riggs?" she cries, lifting her head in my direction. "Oh, God. He blew up Mama's house. He blew it up and I don't know who was left inside," she sobs, leaning forward again as much as she can with her belly. "What the fuck is going on?"

Tugging on my wrist with an ear-rendering shriek, my skin tears, and blood spews, dripping down my arm…but my right hand is free.

I don't dare look at it, but the skin is lifted, muscle exposed. The pain is excruciating, I'm about to pass out. But I can't. I'll pull through until she's safe.

The chain slips right off the beam, pooling onto the floor. It takes me a second to gain my traction but once I'm steady on my feet, I whip the chains off my left arm and I'm free.

My head spins, making the dark room appear warped, crooked. But I need to make it to her. With a wobbly step toward Zay, I lift a shaking hand out and drop to my knees with a wince. She's still sobbing, still shaking. But when I lean my head on hers she stops, walking on her knees closer to me.

"Riggsy, where's Adam? Where is he?" she asks, sniffling.

With my good hand, I lift her blindfold pulling her face to mine and kissing her. "Keep your eyes on me, baby. Just keep your eyes on me."

But it's Zay, she never fucking listens.

Her eyes wander, looking around the room, then behind me, and her eyebrows furrow. She's staring right at him hanging here. Tears line her lash line, slowly spilling free. Her lips part and a soft whimper escapes before she closes her eyes, inhaling the deepest breath.

On an exhale, those large hazel eyes meet mine. "Are you okay? You're covered in blood."

My right arm is held against my abdomen; my shoulder a throbbing mess, and my wrist mangled. "I'm okay." I lean over and snap the duct tape off her wrists. "Where's Carter?"

She whimpers, shaking her head. "Dorian came to get me with the kids. We were heading to her house to put them down for a nap when The Ghost ambushed us and made us watch the house explode. Someone blindfolded me, he took her, and someone else took the kids."

A fire burns inside me. An anger that makes me clench my teeth. The kids. My son and my nieces. My family.

"I'm gonna fucking kill him."

She removes the blindfold from around her head and takes my wrist, wincing when she sees the likes of it. It's mutilated, bleeding profusely. Skin is pulled back, flapping about. But she touches it anyway, wrapping it in the blindfold and tying it tightly before leaving a gentle kiss on top of it.

"Let's get you outta here, okay? I'll come back for Adam later." Helping her stand, I grit my teeth as more sweat rolls down my temples. My body feels like it's been dragged through hell. I have no idea what they did to me after I fell face-first into the snow, but they did enough to dislocate my shoulder and rough up my body. The fuckers probably pushed me down the goddamn stairs and that's how I dislocated my shoulder.

She stares at it now, touching the area softly. "What happened? Is it dislocated?"

I keep my right arm against my stomach, limiting its mobility. "I'm fine, sunshine."

"Riggs—"

"Please, now's not the time to worry about me. I need to get you somewhere safe," I interrupt her, wiping my brow.

She sniffs, nodding quickly and glancing at Adam, then back at me. "Okay."

Shrugging out of her jacket, she helps me in it, wiping her cheek on her shoulder. She's not in her clothes, that much I can tell. Zay doesn't own anything this floral. Her leggings have sunflowers down the sides of them, the black tank top is tight on her belly, and the cardigan is something I've seen my mama wear a time or two.

"Slade gave me his jacket along with his cell phone." Zay opens a hidden compartment in the jacket, taking his phone out.

I take it from her and glance at Adam, he's still hanging there, his feet barely touching the concrete floor, looking like a piece of meat hanging in a freezer.

Her hand comes to her stomach, rubbing circles on it. "What if he doesn't make it to meet his son?" she whispers.

I hate when she says the baby is *his*.

The baby is *mine*.

I don't give a shit about our situation.

I don't give a shit that there's a chance it's probably his because the goddam math adds up.

This baby *is* mine.

But she's right, the way he was wheezing and then stopped. There isn't a chance in hell he'll walk out of this mess.

She doesn't go to Adam, as if she's scared to confirm her fears.

A little out of sight, out of mind.

I'm ashamed to say I haven't checked, either.

And I won't until I get her someplace safe.

"Don't worry about him right now. I gotta get you and *my* son out of here," I say through gritted teeth.

I nudge her toward the stairs, but she resists, tears spilling free as she stares at Adam hanging there. Just hanging like he's not a person anymore. His soul is gone, I know it. The air in this basement is different. If he were alive, there wouldn't be this impending doom looming over us.

"He's not breathing," she whispers on a sob.

"Let's go," I urge, forcing the tears back.

I don't care how fucked up our relationship is, he's still my brother. The kid I razzed all my life. Half-pint. Shaky hands. He's the reason I met Zay.

A wince seeps through her lips, but she follows me, one hand holding her stomach and the other wrapped around my bicep. Everything screams at me to comfort her, hold her, and kiss her, but how can I when I'm too frail to protect her? I'll save our kisses for later.

My arms are weak, shaking slightly but I have to pull through. I'll fall to the ground and rest when I know my woman is somewhere The Ghost can't find her. But I'm so damn weak. So much so that my grip on the phone loosens and I drop it on the landing.

The entire area is spinning, yet I shake it off, forcing myself to focus. With a grunt, I bend over and pick it up right as an incoming call from Lip lights up the screen.

This anger bubbles inside me, waiting for the chance to escape and rain hell on the men who couldn't keep my family safe when I was taken. I trusted these men, and right now, all I can think of is *for what?*

With a wince, I hold the phone to my ear; my arms shaking from being chained for God knows how many hours. "Who is it?"

Slade gasps on the other end. "Riggs? The fuck? Where's Zay? Is she okay? Where are *you?*"

I groan as she climbs the stairs behind me, my arm straining to keep the phone at my ear. "Fuckers brought her to us. Don't know where we are."

"Brother, I think you're at your house—your old house," he says, the sound of his bike's engine turning off.

I stop halfway up the stairs, Zay bumping into me. We didn't have our old house for long. Maybe a year, if that.

And the basement was one place we never went.

And I mean *never.*

We had no reason to. All the shit we had was in our rooms. Shit, we barely had any furniture to begin with. But I couldn't let go of the house. It was Carter's home. It was the home I felt so much pain in, the home Peter was lost in, the home I bought for Zay to stay. It was a house that brought us so much agony and I needed it as a reminder of how far we'd come.

Glancing back, I look at Zay, then at whatever I can see of Adam at this angle. "Shit."

"Don't move, brother. I'm right outside."

Slade has always been one loyal fuck. From the moment he walked into the clubhouse, I knew he'd have my back. And he has, that's why I made him sergeant at arms. And when shit got bad and I wasn't around, he'd be the stand-in VP or president. Whatever was needed.

Zay grips my bicep, stepping up beside me. "What's going on?"

I press a kiss to her forehead, inhaling a sharp breath. "I need you to be my eyes, Slade."

"You got it, boss."

I put my finger to my lips and bring the phone back to my ear, inching up the stairs slowly.

As time went on, I learned it was okay to depend on people. I've always been a leader, the one people looked up to until Natalia fucked me over.

Then I faltered.

But I came back, guns-a-blazing, and took the mantel.

People bow down to me.

Worship me.

Then my Zay brought me back to life.

Now I have people who stand by me and rule with me.

To be a leader, your men need to trust you. Love you. Respect you.

And that's exactly what I got.

My men respect the shit outta me that they lay their lives on the line for my family.

And let's hope they're up for this fucking challenge this time because so far, they've failed.

Slade

About a year ago, Palmer and I were at the cabin having dinner with Riggs, Zay, and Adam. Something about the evening felt off. There was this silent tension in the air that no one seemed to notice. Laughter pooled through the area, drinks were flowing, and the food that Zay cooked was impeccable.

But even behind the festivities, a darkness lingered and I couldn't put my finger on it.

Adam stepped outside for a toke, and I joined him, leaving a kiss on Palmer's forehead as I walked past. "Be back in a sec, darling."

As soon as I stepped outside, the air was heavier. Suffocating with words unsaid. But what fucking words? It ate away at me.

Then again, maybe it was just me. Maybe I was looking too much into everything because I was scared something was hiding around the corner that would take my newfound family away. I didn't have much growing up, didn't have people who loved me. Sure, I had that one foster family who cared for me and let me keep their last name. Yet they left when they could have fought to keep me. They left like everyone else.

These people I met in a biker bar cared about me. And I didn't want to lose them. Yet something in the air tonight told me I might.

"You good, man?" Adam asked, tucking a lock of hair behind his ear before he lit the joint.

I plopped down on the patio chair, taking the joint he offered. "Think I just woke up on the wrong side of the bed. I've had anxiety on and off all damn day."

Holding onto the smoke, I exhaled slowly through my nostrils as I glanced inside at Palmer scrunching her nose at Zay. My darling was gorgeous, those freckles, that *ass, her fucking mouth. I found my forever.*

Adam chuckled softly, hanging an ankle off his knee. "Think we're all anxious just sitting around and waiting for something to happen. The Ghost disappeared and left us wondering when the hell he'd strike again." He sucked in a toke, coughing slightly before handing it over to me. "There isn't anything you have to worry about aside from that curly-haired ginger in there."

I smiled, bringing the joint to my lips. "She's a dream, man. Unlike anyone I've ever been with."

"Much like my Zay."

I nodded, glancing back at Palmer again. From the moment I met Adam, I knew I could trust him. We'd been inseparable whenever the Snakes called. He and Zay were like my therapists. They listened to my blabbering when they didn't have to and gave me unsolicited advice, and I welcomed all of it.

"Palmer and I have been unofficially together for a year now and I still don't know what happened to her. She never wants to talk about it. Which I get, it's a fucked-up situation, but it makes me feel like she doesn't trust me."

Adam flicked the ashes, relighting the joint, and exhaled slowly while leaning his head back. "Mmm, she spoke with Zay about it if you want to know anything."

Arching an eyebrow, I sat up straighter. "Did Zay tell you?"

"She tells me everything," he said, rolling his head on the chair to grin at me. "They're friends, y'know."

I nodded, glancing back as movement caught my eye. The neighbor's cat tended to roam around at night. Riggs had a security light installed and the cat set it off ten times one night. The lights didn't last very long, but security cameras were installed. And that cat, it was as if he only liked to roam around there at night.

"It's not your place to repeat what happened, either. Zay shouldn't have told you." With a scoff, I shook my head, a little ashamed of Zay for opening her mouth when it wasn't her place to. But a part of me kind of understood her. Depending on the story, it must've been a lot to shoulder.

Adam's grin grew, bringing the joint to his lips. "I'm the best at keeping secrets. I've kept secrets not even my wife knows about."

"Yeah? Like what?"

He laughed, fixing the hem of his jeans, and sighed. But he didn't tell me. It was easy to keep secrets because of the club. Easy to find something out and be threatened to take it to your grave.

But the thickness that was suffocating rose even more. He had secrets that could fuck us all. It was the uneasiness in my belly that knew.

My leg tapped restlessly, staring at the forest in front of me as the hooting of an owl filled the quiet. Adam and Riggs fixed up the area a lot over the years. There was clear access to the lake now, a sand pit for the kids to play in, and a large workshop for Riggs's bikes at the far end of the property. It was also a place he kept an extra bed so he could fuck Zay silly and loud without waking up anyone in the house—his words, not mine.

Blinking slowly, my eyes fell on the joint between my fingers. I didn't want to know anything about what happened to Palmer. I wanted her to trust me enough to open up. But she hadn't. I didn't think she ever would. I knew her inside and out, and if I knew the darkest part of her life, she'd think I'd view her differently. But I wouldn't. I'd love her just the same. Worship her just the same. Be hers just the same.

Adam cleared his throat, flicking the ashes once again. "You ever going to ask her to be your wife?"

I squeezed my eyes shut, shaking my head but not at his question. At myself for the words that left my mouth that I couldn't stop. "What happened to her?"

Adam looked at me with narrowed eyes, holding the joint. "You're sure?"

"No," I whispered. But he told me anyway.

With his head leaned back and his gaze on the starry night, he licked his lips and broke me in ways I could never repair. "She was nineteen when they took her. The poor girl was at some frat party when a van pulled up, taking her and a friend. The usual shit happened like it does to these girls. They were raped and forced to do things they didn't want to do. Palmer was a virgin when it happened. Some lowlife with a crack addiction kept coming back to her for more, knowing she was the cleanest of the women in the house. After about a year or so of that, some rich fuck bought her out. Used her as his arm candy. The sick fuck had a knack for cutting her while he fucked her—"

"Stop," I interrupted him, fisting my eyes. Her scars flashed behind my eyelids, the white lines along her body, the cuts on her wrists, the slits on her inner thighs,

and the fucking bite mark on her cunt.

But Adam didn't stop. I didn't think he could. The anger seeping through his words kept coming until his voice cracked. "He cut her real bad one time and had to bring to her a hospital. That's where she escaped and walked into the charter outside of town. They called Gunner and he brought her to Mama Rosa's. Palmer suffered at the hands of the same man that now—" he paused, shaking his head. "No one seems to be able to find the guy that did this. But she's lucky as hell to get out of there alive. Many of his victims end up dead when he gets tired of them. He slits their throats and bathes in their blood. At least that's what Skeet told me. Who knows if it's true—"

"Stop," I growl out, pushing up from the chair. "This is—fuck."

Adam brought the joint to his mouth. "I told you, you probably wouldn't want to hear it."

Wiping a hand down my face, I looked into the house as Palmer sipped her drink; there were over twenty bracelets on each wrist to hide the scars she bore. She suffered for three goddamn years with that nitwit. Three years of torture for her to end up in a sanctuary for women just like her. A place of healing. And then she met me. A man with a dark past as well. What can I give her but even more torture? My job wasn't safe.

Nothing that I did was safe.

But I'd make sure to protect her.

Make sure nothing happened to her ever again.

Just like Riggs protected his family.

Just like Adam tried his best to do what was right.

Just like I knew I'd have to do when my time came. And by the slight smirk spread on Adam's lips, that time was coming sooner rather than later.

***

Allistair and Byron are walking around the house toward the back, guns in hand. Luthor is nearby keeping watch. While I'm crouched out front, looking into the windows and scoping out the area. There was a car that drove off about five minutes ago, heading in the opposite direction from where we were coming. The windows were tinted, yet the car slowed down before peeling away.

Keeping the gun firm in my hand, I inch closer to the front door, peering inside. "I don't see anything, pres. I think the coast is clear," I say to Riggs; his raspy breathing moving through my ear.

"No movement inside?" Riggs asks, his voice weak and drained.

I jiggle the knob, testing to see if it's open. "Nothing, front door is locked. But I got two of Gunner's men checking the back door. Another keeping watch."

Zay sniffles in the background, her soft whimpers oozing her fear and worries. I failed to keep her safe, failed to protect Carter. I've failed and there's nothing I can do but ask for forgiveness.

"I'm gonna break a window to unlock the door, yeah?" I say, scouring the area again.

"Keep your eyes peeled, brother," Riggs says, grunting softly.

I elbow the corner of the glass door, shattering it immediately. But before I unlock the door, I wait, listening for anything. Any sign of movement. Anyone hiding in the shadows.

But there's nothing.

Sliding my hand through the hole, I nick it on a shard of glass and suck my teeth. "Fuck."

"What?" Riggs's panicked voice comes through the AirPods.

"Just cut myself. It's nothing, pres."

Riggs grunts again, the squeak of a door moves through the house and the phone. I hold my gun up, walking quietly through the house. I don't even know where the hell the basement is. I don't think any of us do. It's never been used. Half the house hasn't been used. There's an inground pool in the backyard that has water so rotten in it that frogs and snakes have made it their home.

Gunner's men are at the back door; Allistair waves at me and Byron runs back around the house to the front, gun held in front of him.

"Slade?" Zay's voice hits me, all my senses come forward.

I whip my head around and see her holding onto Riggs's arm looking frightened and distraught. She's paler than usual, eyes feral and riddled with tears.

My gaze falls on Riggs, and *holy fuck*. He looks like he's moments from death. His sweaty, pale, exposed neck and chest are covered in blood. His right hand is held tight against him; hand and wrist wrapped in a black cloth, dripping blood.

I charge forward, bringing Zay into a hug and holding her shoulders out in front of me when I pull away. "Fuck, Zay. I'm so sorry. I had no idea. I only figured it out when we scoped out the cabin. If I'd have known—"

"It's okay. I'm fine, I'm fine," she interrupts me, looking at Riggs. "Adam is downstairs, can you get him?" Her lower lip quivers. "Please."

"Is he okay?" I ask the dreaded question, meeting Riggs's eyes.

They don't say anything, but the tears shimmering in her eyes are enough to make my mind wander to dark places. And one of them is having to plan a funeral for one of my closest friends.

Riggs groans softly, leaning against the wall. "Make it quick, brother." He leans his head back and exhales roughly. "I'm just gonna—" He slides down the wall with a yelp, gritting his teeth.

"Riggs," Zay gasps, her voice cracking.

He forces his eyes open as I lean down about to lift him. "No…I'm just gonna rest my eyes, baby. Just…just a little bit."

"Slade, we have to get him out of here." Her panicked voice makes me shoot to my feet and snap my fingers at Gunner's men coming into the house.

"Get him to the clubhouse, keep her with me—"

"No," Riggs says through a heavy breath.

"She has a tracker in her neck, boss. She's safest with me. When I get it out, I'll bring her to you," I say, looking at Allistair and Byron again. "One of you come with me to get Adam, you'll bring him with you, too."

Zay whimpers, touching Riggs's cheek. "Riggsy, open your eyes," she whispers.

He grunts, straining to move but doesn't budge an inch. "I'm okay, baby. I'm okay. Just gonna rest my eyes a bit. I promise. I'm just gonna rest." His breathy words prove how weak he is. Proves we have to get him help.

"Get him to one of the cars in the garage. Allistair, stash your bike in here. And Luthor, you'll follow the car with your bike," I instruct Gunner's men.

"Byron, let's go get Adam…Zay, just stay with them until I get back."

She nods, sniffing and holding onto her belly with a shaky exhale as Allistair and Luthor lift Riggs with a deep grunt. The fucker is a big boy. Still as ripped as he was the day I met him.

Riggs doesn't wince, doesn't complain. He's hurt.

Breaths shaky.

He fought enough. Now that we're here, he can finally give in to the weakness.

I head toward the only open door that leads to the basement, the stench of blood, sweat, and urine fills my nostrils.

There are chains on the floor where Riggs was hanging; blood pooled beneath.

There's a second set of chains on the floor, another puddle of blood with droplets leading away to the darker, wetter, part of the basement.

"Adam?" I call out, looking back at Byron with his gun aimed high.

Nothing.

"Adam?"

Silence.

I hold my gun high, too, inching closer to the other end of the basement to find stairs that lead outside. A gust of coldness envelops the area, blood droplets lead toward the exit.

Someone took Adam.

"Someone knows we're here," Byron whispers.

"Fuck."

Byron is already running toward everyone else, taking the steps two at a time. I'm hot on his tail, skidding on the marble floors when we get to the garage to find Riggs seated in the backseat with his head back and Zay standing by the door holding his good hand.

"Did you find him?" she asks. "He's okay, right? Please, tell me he's okay."

I wipe a hand down my sweaty face and expel a breath. "Adam isn't downstairs."

Riggs shoots his heavy eyes open and finds my gaze. "Get her out of here."

Nodding quickly, I snag a helmet from the shelf in the garage. "I'll protect her with my life, pres. I won't fail you this time."

She kisses Riggs, whispering something, and closes the door. There's no denying the love they share, no denying they're meant to be. But something is telling me this unit is about to crumble.

Slade

Renting out a room at a "pay-by-the-hour motel," I stopped at a pharmacy first for supplies and some electrolytes for Zay. She appears weak, tired. My worries for the baby are on overdrive. I need to get her energy up before I call Karen for her results.

A call I'm sure she's too damn busy to answer.

I should get Zay to a hospital. Fuck, we should get *Riggs* to a hospital, but nurses and doctors ask questions, and we're still waiting on the Captain for a callback with the DNA results for the cigarette butts. The last thing we need is to head to the hospital and they start asking questions. Knowing we're part of a motorcycle gang, they'll instantly arrest us and put us into holding until we speak to the Captain. And we cannot have that with our lives on the line.

Zay sits at the end of the squeaky bed, scratching her shoulder. "Is everyone at the house okay?"

I unzip my sweater and toss it on the bed. "No idea. I made sure Palmer and the kids were in the bunker before I bucked it outta there to come find you."

A thick tear rolls down her cheek when I take the bag from the pharmacy and set it down, exhaling slowly. "Where'd they inject you?" I ask, wanting to console her but knowing I have to act fast before they find us.

She opens the bag and takes an elastic from the pack, twisting her hair into a bun. She doesn't have to point it out, either. I can see the injection spot on her neck, a couple of inches under her ear. The poor girl has scars all over her body from the club. A scar from a bullet to her chest, another from a bullet that nicked her neck when they shot up her house, and scars on the back of her legs from the shootout when we first arrived at Maddison Gardens.

She doesn't deserve more scars, but I have no choice but to give her another one. Scars are beautiful. They tell stories. But her scars are not stories worth repeating.

"This is gonna hurt," I tell her, turning her chin to look at me. A sob breaks free and she covers her face with her hands. "Hey, now."

"Why is this happening, Slade? Everything was perfect. Our lives were perfect. And now…" she pauses, huffing out a shaky breath. "What if he dies?"

"Riggs won't die, Zay."

She shakes her head, removing her hands from her face. "And Adam? Where was he? How could he not be there? I just saw him hanging—he didn't look like he was breathing."

If I had the answers to ease her mind, I'd give them to her. But I have nothing.

There isn't anything I can give her that will put a grin on her face. Not even some reassurance that'll come off as horse shit. Because I don't know.

I rip open the alcohol swabs and clean her neck. Sitting on the bed with a bent knee so I can face her. "Take a breath, Zay."

She doesn't move, just sniffs and stares at her shaking hands on her lap.

I know what it feels like to lose everything. To be alone, to feel alone. I had nothing growing up. I had nothing until I found the Snakes. They made me feel welcomed, like family.

The sadness and pain I held toward my parents abandoning me and every foster family giving me up because I was different, took its toll on me. It still does. There are times I'll stare at my scars and wonder if doing them was a call for attention. No one seemed to notice when I cut myself. The social workers wrapped my fresh cuts and sent me on my way. It's like they were used to that type of stuff.

Truthfully, I think I cut myself to feel something other than abandonment.

Zay had everything she could ever want growing up. A lavish lifestyle, friends, people who loved her. Family.

Now, she has to look over her shoulder wherever she goes. She has men crawling on their hands and knees for her, but if it was for the Donnelly men, she'd have no one. She has no friends aside from Palmer and Dorian. Even then, Zay spends most of her time with Carter. She won't admit it, but I see it because I've lived it. She's lonely. So loved but so alone.

I take my switchblade from my pocket and find the rubbing alcohol, splashing some on it. Her lower lip is quivering, making her entire body shiver with fear. I've never done anything like this before. I was the one who helped the other foster kids when they got hurt and whatnot with Band-Aids and shit. But never this.

I use my lighter as an extra precaution just to be safe; the tip of the blade goes up in flames before it settles.

Zay closes her eyes and exhales slowly; her plump parted lips are dry. "Do it quickly, please?"

I'm not squeamish, never have been. I've seen my foster brother snap his ankle jumping off a roof with his skateboard onto a ramp; the bone poked out, and I was the only one who could stomach putting pressure on his ankle until the ambulance came.

Shit, even when I started with the Snakes. A few of the Snake Biters taught me how to do stitches. And I've stitched up many of the guys—Riggs included. I'm honored my brothers trust me enough to patch them up. But hurting the president's old lady is on another level.

The tip of the blade punctures Zay's skin and a small droplet of blood rolls down to the nape of the neck. She's wincing and whimpering, softly sobbing, but I can't stop.

I have about a two-inch cut before I dig my finger into her neck. I can feel the tiny device. All I have to do is get it out of her.

She cries out when I hook my finger, grabbing onto my wrist. "Slade, stop!"

I grit my teeth, ignore her nails digging into my skin, and sigh with relief when the tiny device is between my forefinger and thumb. "I got it, sweetheart. I got it."

She's crying, staring at the device between my blood-dripping fingers. "What the fuck?!"

Holding gauze to her neck, I stare at her lips as her tongue darts out and wets them. "It'll be okay, Zay. It'll be okay." I press a kiss to her temple and rise. "Let's clean you up and get out of here."

My heart is pounding violently. I've never done anything like this. Never hurt someone to save them. I've hurt people to prove points, to get my way. But never to help them.

Applying pressure to her neck, she pushes off the bed and holds onto her stomach. A thought crosses my mind that if Adam or Riggs die, she'll be completely alone with two kids. Although, Peter would never let it happen, and truthfully, neither would I. Palmer and I would be with her, help raise those boys. Zay will never be without for as long as she lives.

Grabbing anything blood has touched, I head to the bathroom. Zay follows me with the first aid kit and cleans her neck. She knows what she's doing, too, and winces when she places butterfly stitches on it. I'm in too much shock to help her. Who wouldn't be? She was drugged, kidnapped, implanted, and the sanctuary blew up. The Donnelly brothers who are our protectors are dropping like flies, and their kids are missing. *What's fucking next?* This entire day has been one big shit show and it's only two o'clock.

Blood coats the stained sink, swirling around the drain. I don't notice my hands are shaking until the device slips from my fingertips and rolls right down the dark hole. Nausea rolls in, hitting my belly like a fog on a lake as I watch the water turn pink.

Zay clears the gravel from her throat, finds my gaze in the mirror, and inhales slowly. "Slade, promise me you're not going to hurt me."

I frown, drying my hands quickly and staining the towel pink. "Zay, you're one of my best friends. Why the hell would I do that?"

She whimpers, her lower lip quivering. "Because the man I've loved since university has ruined everything."

I take a step back, shocked. "Adam?"

She doesn't say anything. She holds my stare, another tear rolls down her cheek.

Everything is crumbling.

Everything feels like an illusion.

We're supposed to be a unit, fighting the enemy together. But instead, the man I thought was a friend, is probably nothing but a betraying fuck like the rest of them.

I wipe a tear from her cheek, smearing blood on her face. "Zay? What happened at the cabin?"

She huffs out a breath. "Pure insanity."

I stare at her tears with furrowed brows. I don't know what to do. I don't know what the fuck to do. No, what do I believe? Where do we go? Who the hell do we trust?

We're all just fucked, aren't we?

Riggs

About a year and a half into this relationship the three of us started, Zay came into the cabin wearing a beige trench coat. She wasn't holding Carter, only a small pink gift bag.

"Hey, sunshine." I brought a beer to my lips, stirring food at the stove. "Where's the baby?"

She scrunched her nose at Adam as he chopped vegetables for dinner. "With your mom."

He waggled his eyebrows. "Date night for my birthday?"

Her shoulders shimmed as she walked over to the dining room table, leaning on it. "Something like that."

"It's hot as sin outside, what're you wearing a coat for?" Draining the beer, I set it on the island, bracing it as I watched her.

Fuck, she was always so gorgeous. So perfectly captured in any light.

A beautiful disaster.

There was a playful gleam in her expression as she untied her coat and let it fall to the floor; revealing black lace lingerie I didn't know she owned.

"Well, isn't that a surprise?" Adam said, pushing the tip of the knife into the cutting board.

I nodded my head at the bag. "And what's in there?"

Our sex life was wild, to say the least. We'd have threesomes almost every night, rarely getting a chance to have her to ourselves without the other. But I had a bed in the garage I'd pull her to in the middle of the night. Having my way with her without him around was something I craved. Don't get me wrong, this unit we had was beautiful, too. But Zay and I would forever be bound deeply. We didn't need

Adam to fulfill that.

She opened the bag and pulled out something that set me off. I rounded the island and bent her over the dining table. A bright pink butt plug and some lube rolled out of the bag and onto the table; the type of plug that stretches and would ready her fucking ass for me.

"The panties are crotchless," she said with a giggle.

I pulled myself out of my shorts and spread her legs, easing into her tight pussy with a groan. "Fuck," I drew out.

She giggled, shaking her ass against me. "Do you like my new outfit and accessories?"

Adam pranced over, taking her wrists and yanking her gently across the table so her face was against his crotch. "What did you have in mind, babe?"

She giggled again when he got down to her level, kissing her lips as I fucked her slowly. "You've been begging enough, and since it's your birthday and all. I figured my baby deserves the best gift of all—"

She yelped when I slapped her ass, a pink handprint slowly forming on her cheek.

"You're letting him in there before me?" I asked through a moan.

She moaned this time, digging her fingers into the table. "You're far too big for my pussy let alone my ass, Riggsy."

I growled, taking the lube from the table and squirting some of it on her ass, watching the liquid as it rolled to where we connected. "Tell me, then. If I'm not allowed in here, then what am I going to do, hmm? Watch him fuck this ass while you blow me?"

Adam took the butt plug out of the box, smirking as he lowered again and spat on it. "I'm a lot bigger than this."

She bit her bottom lip, moaning. "I can take you."

Growling again, I slapped her ass a second time, loving how fucking naughty she gets when she needs to be. Zay is my fucking whore. My gorgeous sex kitten.

Squirting more lube on her ass again, Adam handed me the butt plug, and I eased it into her, inch by inch. She winced, squeezing her eyes shut, but Adam kissed her. Distracting her from the pressure.

He pulled himself out and grabbed a wad of her hair, lifting her head so her mouth wrapped around his cock.

He fucked her face.

I fucked her pussy.

And the bright pink toy slowly fucked her ass, getting her used to the feeling.

"Touch yourself, baby. It'll help you stop clenching," I said, slowly removing the toy out and inching in back in.

Her hand traveled between her legs and she moaned, rubbing that clit as we fucked her.

I wasn't going to come. Not yet. But the way she gagged and moaned, made me exhale sharply. The thought of her touching herself was nearing me to the edge.

As soon as the toy was all the way in, I pulled out and tossed her over my shoulder. Adam growled, hating how much I took charge in the bedroom. These two had no idea what they were in store for when we agreed to this.

No fucking idea.

Zay knew I liked it rough; she knew how dominant I could be. Adam didn't, and hated when I bossed him around on how to fuck our woman. But I didn't fucking care. She was mine to play with how I fucking pleased.

I tossed Zay on the bed, pulling my t-shirt off. "You're gonna come for us, and then we're gonna come in you."

She opened her legs for us, licking her middle finger and touching that sweet, dripping clit. "I want you inside me when Adam is."

Both of us bound to her for all eternity.

Adam smiled, getting on his knees in front of her and tugging her closer to his face. "Time to feast."

He licked her slit, dipping his tongue inside her before biting down on her clit. Zay threw her head back, holding onto his head as he ate the best-tasting pussy I've ever had.

Fucking sweet.

Fucking succulent.

Fucking mine.

It didn't take her long until her legs were squeezing his head and she bucked forward, moaning like a cat in heat.

Her tits were falling out of the corset she had on, her nipples hard and ready.

I got on the bed and gripped her hair when Adam pulled away, licking his lips.

"Sit on your throne, baby."

She didn't deny, she did as she was told. Crawling to me, biting that fucking lip.

My fucking Zay.

I eased back into her; that pussy still clenching and throbbing.

She rode me fast, scratched down my chest as she threw her head back. "Fuck, Riggs. You're always too big for me."

I chuckled, looking over her shoulder as Adam got on the bed between my legs. But my focus was back on her. "Come here." Capturing her lips, I forced her to lie on me, trusting upward as I did. "You ready for us, baby?"

He grabbed her ass and slowly pulled the toy out—something I knew should be in a bit longer, but how the fuck did she expect us to wait when she walked into our home wearing that outfit?

"Take a breath in," I told her, forcing my tongue in her mouth.

She moaned softly, squeezing her eyes shut. She didn't have to say anything for me to know he was making his way in. I could feel him.

"Adam," she breathed, reaching back and squeezing his wrist.

His hands were on her ass cheeks, opening her wider. "I'm almost all in, babe." He moaned, grunting softly. "Fuck, Zay. You're tight. So fucking tight."

I knew this was wrong, feeling him inside her. But this unit we created. This love. This bond.

It worked.

It was ours. No one's but ours.

He started thrusting slowly, moaning quietly as I thrust upward, holding Zay close to me. "I got you, baby, just relax." Kissing her jawline, I nipped at her ear. "Eyes on me."

She bit down on my neck, suckling and moaning, her body shaking between us.

She was coming.

She was screaming.

She knew this wild ride wouldn't be the last.

"Oh, God, I love you!"

I licked the side of her neck, my balls clenching and ready to burst. "Until the end of my fucking life, baby."

Adam leaned forward, holding onto her hips as his head rested against hers.

"Forever and always, Zay. Forever and fucking always."

He busted before I did, releasing into that ass I knew I'd get a round on one day.

We cherished her that night. Made her come again, then watched as my cum leaked from her pussy and his cum leaked from her ass.

It was fucking beautiful.

She was fucking beautiful.

My Zay.

My fucking queen...

I'm in a fever dream.

Coming in and out of consciousness.

But it feels real. Everything feels so real.

I try to lift my hand but it's heavy.

I try to open my eyes but I can't. A firework of colors are all clustered together in the dark.

There are voices.

So many voices.

It's cold, then hot.

I'm sitting, then I'm lying down.

I smell smoke and stale beer.

There's yelling, and frantic orders being tossed around.

Until everything goes out again and my Zay comes back to me.

Slade

Zay and I head to the clubhouse, her legs draped over my lap and her head resting on my shoulder. She's still shivering, even with my sweater. I think she's withdrawing and definitely in shock. But I keep her close, telling her it'll be okay when I don't know if I can believe it.

Riding with the cool air on my skin makes me realize that even though the Snakes are my family, sometimes walking away from family is the right thing to do. And if my Palmer knows what a loyal fuck I am, she'll see I just want the best for her and me.

I'll walk away when this bullshit is settled with her hand clasped in mine.

The two of us out in the big bad world away from anything that will break us.

I keep repeating it because I mean it. I think I'm done.

Getting off the bike first so I can help Zay off it; her body tenses as soon as she looks up at *Judas's Hideout*. "It's okay, Zay. Let's get you inside and warmed up—"

"I want my son," she snaps, turning to me with watery eyes.

"I'm meeting up with Gunner as soon as I know you're safe." I hold her shoulder, forcing a reassuring grin. "I'll bring the big guy home, I promise you."

"I hate this." She sniffs, glaring at the clubhouse before she takes a step toward it, hugging herself in my sweater.

I hate this, too. But there's nothing I can do about it.

A few of the guys turn around when the doors open, eyes wide when they see Zay tucked under my arm.

Skeet comes our way, shrugging out of his parka, and drapes it on us. "Riggs is unconscious. We were gonna bring him to the hospital, but Dillon said to wait until you got here, boss."

I nod quickly, glancing around. "Where is he?"

Skeet jerks his head at the back room where a couple of waitresses walk out with towels covered in blood. "Dillon is with him. Boys just got back a few minutes ago."

I lead Zay to the back room, a room she despises because of Peter.

Riggs is lying shirtless on the far side of the bed; the blood on his body is poorly cleaned off, and a bandage is wrapped around his wrist.

Zay whimpers, releasing me, and goes right to him. She crawls on the bed and touches his face delicately. "Riggsy?" she whispers, kissing his head. He shifts, grunting, but doesn't open his eyes. "Hey, baby, I'm here. I'm right here," she says, kissing his cheek.

I close the door behind me once Skeet and Dillon walk out. She'll be safe here. Safe enough from the chaos walking around at Maddison Gardens. Once I find the kids, I'm taking my Palmer away from this life. I'll bring Zay and the kids along, too. I'm sure Riggs is sick of living like this.

Dillon wipes a hand down his face, shaking his head. "What the fuck, dude?"

"I know."

"That's bad," he goes on, looking at Skeet.

"I know," I huff out.

"The fuck do we do?" Dillon asks, nervousness in his tone as he adjusts the sling on his arm.

"I don't know."

Skeet scoffs, dropping his hands at his sides. "The fuck you mean you don't know? Riggs appointed you to stand in for a reason. Be the fucking reason, Slade."

I pinch my eyes shut, shaking my head. There's too much going on. Too much noise, too much pressure. *Too fucking much.*

"I just…" I groan as my phone vibrates in my pocket. "Fuck, I need a minute. Just one goddamn minute."

I storm past them and head out the back door through the kitchen, slamming the door behind me. My breathing wavers, my chest tightens. I haven't had a goddamn panic attack in ages.

Today is not a good fucking day for this.

I was seven when I had my first panic attack. The family I thought was my forever family, left me and I was back in the system. Bouncing around from home to home until I was settled with the nastiest fucking family. They hurt us. Burned us. Abused us.

After being whipped and slapped for not finishing my dinner—known as wasting food in the house—I was shoved into a closet. It was dark, cold, quiet. So fucking quiet. To this day, I'm still terrified of the dark. And it started that night. I couldn't breathe. The walls kept closing in. Everything vibrated, and my mind kept wandering. Escaping to the darkest places. I let the voice in my head take control, screaming and grabbing hold of my innocence.

It was the worst night of my life.

And from that day on, anything overwhelming brings on anxiety.

Today is no different.

My phone starts vibrating again, another incoming call; and I answer it without looking. "What?"

"Slade?" Palmer's scared, little voice comes through the speakers, sending my heart into overdrive.

I whimper, sliding down the wall until my knees are bent. Short, quick breaths spurt out of me. My throat closes in on itself. My chest tightens like a heavy weight pressing down. "Oh, fuck, darling. It's a fucking day. A bad fucking day. I need you. I just want to get out of this fucking life and spend my days holding you. Just you."

She's sobbing on the other end, shushing crying and panicked children. "I love you, Slade. So much." Silence passes us as we listen to each other sob and sniff until she expels a breath. "Please, promise me one thing."

"Anything, darling, anything."

"You'll come back for me when all this is over. You won't get yourself killed trying to save people who got you into this disaster," she says, sniffling. "Come home to me."

She's right, but they're family. I want out but I can't turn my back on the

Snakes after everything they've done for me. Yet she's my goddamn world. My life.

I'm torn.

How can I be two people? A loyal member of this club and a devoted man to my woman.

Ignoring her question because I can't fathom a response, I exhale and close my eyes. Her beautiful face pasted in the dark. "You still in the bunker?"

She clears her throat and sniffs, causing me to open my eyes. "Lip got on the walkie-talkie and told us to hold tight. Karen is doing rounds to see who's hurt and who isn't. So far only Dillon and Lip are the injured ones from what he told me. But Dillon left when she patched him up."

"And you? You're okay?"

A heavy sigh leaves her, a sound that pierces straight into my soul. "I'm scared, Slade. I'm so scared something's gonna happen or someone's going to take these girls again—or take *me*."

I grit my teeth, rising to my feet. "No one will ever take you again, do you hear me? You're safe with me. I promise with all my heart."

She chuckles softly. "Then answer me. Promise me this, Slade. Promise me you'll come home to me."

Running a hand through my hair, I smirk. "Darling, I'll be home with you until the end of life on this godforsaken planet."

She sniffs again, and the way her tongue clicks, I know she's smiling all kinds. "I love you."

"I love me, too."

She laughs, saying something to one of the kids in the background. "Finish this, okay? Finish this and come home to us."

"I will."

Her sniff moves through my ear once more before she hangs up.

I know I have to man up. I'm in charge right now. *Me*, for fuck's sake.

I'm running this game until their leaders are well enough to take the reins again. And I'll make sure not to let the stress take hold.

I can't have another panic attack. I need to grow a fucking pair and be the kid who got out of that closet stronger. Who got out and was able to defend himself. I'll be the man who stopped waking up every day wishing it were my last. No, I'll be the man who grew the fuck up and became a dependable human being. The man who can stop this.

My darling helps me heal, but I'm the only one who has the guts to lay my own path and discover my destiny.

I have to be strong, for Riggs, for Peter, and for Zay. For the kids.

Pulling the backdoor open, I make my way through the kitchen to chapel where everyone is already seated with shots of whiskey ready and waiting.

Skeet jerks his head at one of the Snake Biters. She pulls out the chair at the head of the table for me and taps the top of it.

Jesus, fuck. I am not ready for this.

Exhaling slowly, I go to the chair and sit down, feeling that power take hold of me.

I am not a Donnelly.

I have not been part of this club from the start. Yet here I am, sitting in the chair at the head of the table while the men sit around me and wait for my instructions.

Looking at the gavel beside me, I slide my hands on the table, drumming my fingers. I have so much to say but can't formulate any words. My head is like a spinning top; one image after another until I find the beauty in all the chaos. My freckled ginger smiling and telling me it'll be okay.

Our prospect, Sammy, clears his throat, looking at the guys before he speaks. "Slade, what the fuck's going on?"

I exhale sharply, sitting back in the chair. I only explained what happened to a few of the guys; Skeet, Judas, Dillon, and Lip. The rest of our men and two of Gunner's men need to hear this. "This morning, Riggs and Adam were ambushed by the guy who calls himself The Ghost. Place was full of blood—"

"It was a massacre," Dillon interrupts, grunting softly and holding onto his arm in a sling.

Dude is one tough little shit.

I nod, my leg tapping restlessly. "They drugged Zay and implanted her with a tracker, which led them to Maddison Gardens and…they exploded Mama Rosa's house."

Gasps commence, spreading through the room. There's no time to dwell, we have to act, fast. And coming up with a plan is a must.

"I spoke to my girl, she said no one's badly hurt aside from Dillon and Lip. Everyone managed to get away before the explosion happened—" I pause, frowning.

How would people know to get away when we just got there to warn them?

"Uh—um, The Ghost is at Peter's house. Gunner and the guys should be with him." I wipe a hand down my face, rubbing my palm on my chin. "I had a hunch that Riggs was at his old house, and I was right. Found him and Zay there. He was hanging in the basement with Adam, but—"

"Adam wasn't there," Byron interrupts me, tonguing his cheek.

"No, he wasn't. He's missing, Riggs's son and Peter's girls are missing. Dorian's sister is dead, Mama Rosa isn't answering her phone—"

"And Peter drove off while the fucking house exploded without helping us. You forgot to add that," Dillon scoffs, sucking his teeth when he tries to move his arm.

"Who's double-crossing who?" Skeet puts out there, making everyone look at me for answers when I don't have a single one.

"We need to come up with a plan. Something that'll show The Ghost we're not who he thinks we still are." I inhale sharply. "We need to set up a meeting with him and I think we're going to have to get a little messy doing it."

"Then let's fucking go," Dillon barks, howling.

The men bang their fists on the table, shaking it and spilling the shot glasses.

My plan is shit. A meeting won't help when he already has Peter and the kids. The fucking Ghost wanted to give us demands but failed at that and hurt our men in the process.

A meeting will do nothing but allow The Ghost to laugh in our faces like he's been doing all these years.

Peter

Flaring my nostrils, I stare at my mother, and then the fucker with his mask still on. "Listen, d'you hear that?" The rumble of engines soars through the silence. "Those are my fucking men. Either you cut the fucking bullshit and let my kids go, or they will rain on your asshole until you plead for us to stop."

The Ghost tips his head from side to side and rolls his shoulders back. "If you tell your men to fuck off, I'll let your wife and kids go. But I'm keeping you and your *mama*."

"Done."

Mama shoots me a glare, fists clenched at her sides. "They'll kill you, Peter."

"So long as my wife and babies are safe—my nephew, Zaynab, and brothers, too, fuckface—then I don't give a shit what happens to me."

Dorian is screaming, and thrashing as one of the men grabs her and escorts her out of the house. I try to stay strong and bite down without looking at her, but I can't help myself.

I glance back and catch sight of Dorian; her gray eyes riddled with tears. *I love you*, I mouth, before her sob breaks free and silences behind the front door.

The Ghost steps forward again, holding the dripping blade to Mama's throat. "Tell me where my Lenora is, *now*."

Mama's devious glare doesn't falter. She holds it and blinks slowly. "As soon as I know my grandbabies are safe, I will."

The Ghost lowers the blade and takes his phone from his back pocket; blood smearing on the screen. He pulls up a feed that shows Carter and Rosa playing with action figures and Sara is wearing a crown. Mina is asleep in her car seat, but where they are is still a mystery.

Then I see it. The damned pale blue wallpaper with the clouds that Zaynab made me put up three years ago when my heart broke into a million pieces. They're at the goddamn house Riggs bought for Zay so she'd stay with us. The place that's remained baren for three years.

How could I have been so stupid not to check *home*?

"They're safe. I'm not some psycho who would hurt kids, Mama Rosa." The Ghost locks his phone and tucks it away, folding his arms across his chest. "Now, speak."

She glances at one of the masked men and raises her eyebrows. "In the car, there's a yellow folder under the seat on the passenger's side. Be a dear and get it for me."

"Mama, the fuck is going on?" I ask, frowning as I watch the man wait for The Ghost to give him the okay to move.

The rumble of engines comes to a stop, The Ghost's phone vibrates in his pocket. He scratches his chest with a growl, taking his phone out again. "What?"

Nodding to whoever is on the phone, he wipes the blade on his thigh; the blood smearing on the light-wash jeans.

I can't hear a lick of what is being said on the other end, but if I know my crew, they're not going to go down without a fight.

The Ghost shoves the phone at my chest, lifting his mask to reveal a gnarly fucking scar on his face that has mangled his left eye. No wonder this ugly fucker wears a mask. He is nothing like my Dorian. Not a single feature connects them as half-siblings.

He smiles, straight teeth that stretch out the scar down his face. "Not what you expected, was it?"

"What happened to you?" Mama asks, her eyebrows pinched together.

The Ghost lowers his shoulders, pushing the phone to my chest again. "The fucker who took my Lenora did this when I tried to save her the first time."

I take the phone, staring at his white eye as it blinks. Scars never grossed me out. I have plenty of them; my brothers, too. But this one hits home and turns my fucking stomach.

Bringing the phone to my ear, I clear my throat. "Who is it?"

"It's Gunner. Some fucker is stopping me from coming in and said I had to speak to the man in charge. This Ghost fucker best let us pass if he knows what's good for him."

I smirk, nodding slowly. "Where's everyone?"

"Clubhouse."

"Get them to my house. The big one we had no reason to own—the boys know the one. My babies are there."

"Slade is on his way there—"

The Ghost yanks the phone from my ear, pulling some of my hair in the process and making me hiss. "Just give me what I fucking need and stop messing up my goddamn plans!"

"Plans? What fucking plans? We don't know anything and you come into our lives after being silent for so goddamn long, only to take my brothers, then my wife and kids? You fucking think I'm going to comply with anything you fucking do when you're this fucked in the head!?" I'm screaming, the veins in my neck bulging.

"You disappeared for three years, Wilde. After being in contact with me and giving me the names and locations of people—you disappear because of everything that happened. Why are you back now? Why after all these years?" Mama asks, her voice calm and collected.

"Because I found out that you know where she is," he says, kicking out a stool and sitting at the island. "Now, can we stop fucking around so I can go get her and we can get back to our lives?"

Arguing and shouting come from outside. It's Gunner and his crew vs The Ghost's masked men. But seeing how these fuckers act, the Snakes are goners.

I head that way, shooting the door open. "Hey! No fucking shootout is happening here. Let's deal with this without a fucking bloody show." I exhale sharply, licking my dry lips. "Look, I want you to go to the house I owned with Riggs. Leave me two men, the rest of you head out. Slade's in charge, clue him in when you get there."

Gunner nods, narrowing his eyes as he tries to see past me. "Aye, aye. But I reckon you should check your phone, brother. Slade's been trying to get a hold of you."

"I'm a little busy—"

Gunner steps forward with his hands up, coming up the stairs and lowering his voice. "They found Zay and Riggs in the basement of your old house. Adam disappeared and no one knows where this fucker brought him—"

"All right, already. Get back in here, Peter," The Ghost yells. "I don't have time for the sappy soap opera drama you call your family."

I growl, clenching my hands into fists. "Go, Gunner. I'll be fine."

One of the masked men comes back toward the house, holding the yellow folder Mama hasn't let go of for months. The fuck is inside that that will cause The Ghost to forget about his love?

Making my way to the kitchen, Mama is at the fridge collecting things to make some sandwiches. "Set the folder on the table, would you?"

Heading to the table, I yank the folder from the masked man as he chuckles and stands by the backdoor with crossed arms. My hands are shaking when I sit at the head of the table, facing the fucker with the gnarly scar who is slowly ruining our lives.

Opening the folder to papers with Mama's scribbles all over it: dates, times, and locations. There are pick ups we went on that have been crossed out, the ones that haven't are highlighted in yellow.

Pick ups that we never went on, women that were never saved. And for what?

"Damien Glass" is the name I keep seeing. Every date that's highlighted has his name beside it. Who the fuck is this guy?

I flip six pages of dates, times, and locations with multiple yellow stripes before I stop at the last page. A photo of a woman with long brown hair and big brown eyes stares back at me. She looks sad in the photo, thin and sickly.

"Lenora Thrills," I say, lifting the photo and turning it to The Ghost. "This your girl?"

He rises, sauntering over the me and snatching the picture. "When was this taken?"

"Three days ago," Mama answers, licking mustard from her thumb.

I bare my teeth and rise, resting my fists on the table. "What the fuck are you into, Mama? You're supposed to be saving these women, not letting the ones highlighted keep getting tortured—"

"They're not getting tortured, Peter," she interrupts me with a raised voice. "Not…exactly."

"Then what the fuck?" I scoff, flipping the pages again, and stop, looking at the last page in the folder. Everything around me vibrates, shaking and feeling like water filling my ears. "Why is Adam's name on this?"

Mama smirks, cutting sandwiches in half and putting them on plates. There's this cloud above her, a cloud that reminds me of my daddy. An evilness she never bestowed, until now.

She places a plate in front of each of us and sits at the other side of the table, sighing as she picks up half a sandwich. "C'mon, eat up boys. I have some things you might not want to hear."

Shoving the sandwich out of the way, The Ghost bares his teeth. "Speak."

But all she does is take a bite of her sandwich, chuckling at him like she isn't frightened in the slightest. And I think that's what makes this whole situation that much more terrifying.

Slade

I lost my virginity at fourteen years old to someone I don't remember. How fucked up is that? One of the most important moments in a girl's life, I forgot about because I shoved my dick into so much pussy, my first is officially forgettable.

I used women growing up. A lot of the time it was for a bed to sleep in, for food in my belly, and for someone to get the noise in my head to quiet down. I fucked my emotions away until I grew tired of them or they woke up and realized I was nothing but a mooch.

Every face of every girl is morphed; the blondes become brunettes, and the brunettes become the gingers. The color of their skin is all the same to me; a pussy to slide my dick into.

Until I met Palmer.

Our first time together was anything but forgettable. I think I was more nervous than she was.

After our first kiss, we spent every single night together cuddling until I had to head back to the clubhouse. Most nights I didn't want to go, but I had a duty to my brothers. A duty that included working for the club to earn my keep. Earn all the money for our future.

The day we first united was my day off and I knew I was going to spend my entire evening with Palmer. But when I arrived at Maddison Gardens, I couldn't find her anywhere.

Searching her room, the barn, and the warehouse—I went as far as searching the bunkers. But my darling wasn't there.

When I stepped back into the house, Mama Rosa was in the kitchen cutting up strawberries with a grin. "She just went to the store, she'll be back soon. You look like a lost puppy dog searching for a home."

Chuckling and running a hand through my hair. She was right, Palmer was my home and I didn't know what to do with myself without her. "I care for her, Mama Rosa. A great deal."

She smiled, dropping the strawberries in a bowl and brought one to her lips. "I see that. You're here more than my own damn kids."

I laughed, scratching my stomach. "I don't like being without her. And living at the club is tough because there's always someone knocking at the door trying to get me to do something."

"Joys of the lifestyle," she said, placing the fruits on the tray with a bunch of juice boxes and crackers. "It's never too late to get out. I have more than enough room for you here. You can help with the girls and—"

The front door opened and something clattered, causing a gasp to leave Palmer. "Shit," she growled under her breath.

Mama Rosa scrunched her nose at me, reminiscent of Peter's features, and headed out the back door to the screaming kids in the play structure Peter, Adam, and I put together last month.

My feet moved on their own to Palmer on her hands and knees wearing a floral sundress that was much shorter than anything she owned. Something Dorian lent her; I remember seeing her wear it at Sara's birthday party three weeks prior.

"Palmer?" I said, startling her as she picked up her things from the floor. "You all right?"

She nodded, sitting back on her heels and blowing a lock of hair from her face. "My purse broke. The handle just full-on ripped off."

Picking up the mess of things she kept in her purse; bills, tubes of lipstick I'd never seen her wear, a hairbrush, an obscene amount of hair elastics, tampons, granola bars, and a switchblade that made me stop.

"Darling, why do you have this?"

She snatched it from me, holding it to her chest. "I don't like going anywhere alone without it."

Touching her hand and lowering the weapon. "Then don't. You call me next time and I'll come with you."

Tears brimmed her lashes before she blinked them away. "I can't always depend on you."

"You can and you will." I leaned forward and kissed those plump, freckled lips. "I will always be here for you."

She smiled against my lips. "This was the one thing I had to do without you."

I didn't like the sound of that. What was she hiding? What could she be hiding? Her whole life was confined to these walls.

"Why?"

"I went to see Dorian." Palmer looked down at her dress, smoothing it out. "She lent me this dress and some other things."

Curling a lock of her hair around my finger and smiling. "Darlin, I love you, and it's not because of how you dress. I love you just the way you are. You don't have to impress me with skimpy dresses that Zay gets everyone to wear."

Palmer's eyes went wide, her mouth dropping open. "You love me?"

I didn't realize I said it until the redness climbed her neck and settled in her cheeks. I thought about it for a while and told her I loved her in my head without the words slipping from my lips.

I smiled, and relief swept through me that I said it out loud. "I do. A lot."

She laughed, covering her face. "Oh, Slade. I love you, too."

Kissing her, I swirled my tongue in that beautiful mouth. It bothered me a little that we'd been making out for months and nothing came of it. But I knew with someone like Palmer and her history, I had to take my time. Let her come to me when she was ready. She'd never had a boyfriend before or someone who made love to her. Palmer was a victim of sex trafficking; she didn't know what having sex with someone you loved felt like.

To her, sex was a chore. It was forced, disturbing, and disgusting.

When she was ready, I'd show her what having sex was like with someone who cares.

Holding her head in my hands, I smiled. For the first time in years, my heart felt alive again. "Come, let's get something to eat and fix your purse."

She chuckled, dusting off her knees when she rose. "You can fix this?"

Kissing her temple and draping an arm across her shoulders. "Darling, I'm a jack of all trades. I can do anything."

We headed out of the house and made our way through the garden and apple orchard toward her little hut at the back that had nothing more than some furniture and a bathroom. Palmer had truly made it her own with pink splattered all over the place, fresh flowers in a vase on her nightstand, and a Taylor Swift poster above the dresser. Although her bed was a twin and her windows didn't open, this was our home. It also gave me a glimpse into our future; we'd be living in a hut by the sea with nothing but the ocean breeze blowing through our windows.

Palmer set her purse on the dresser as I kicked my shoes off and plopped on her bed, leaning back on my hands to stare at her.

"Christ, you're beautiful," I said, watching as she carefully took everything out of her purse and placed them beside it.

The way her long ginger curls lay a mess on her but was always so prim and proper. How her curvy physique was radiant in anything she wore.

And this dress. Fuck, I'd never seen her in anything this form-fitting or short before. And we sleep beside each other every night—of course, she's always in pj pants and one of my t-shirts, covering the beauty that is her.

She bit her lip and looked over her shoulder. "Dorian said I could keep the dress." She smoothed her hands over it. "I feel like it's too much."

I wanted to tell her I didn't care what she had on; she could wear a garbage bag and I'd still stare at her over everything. But I didn't, because all I wanted was her mouth on mine and for our hearts to beat as one.

"Then take it off."

Her freckled cheeks reddened; her fingers playing with the hem of the dress. "But...um—"

"I'll get naked, too. It'll be a hoot." I winked, chuckling to try and ease up her nerves. But it didn't help. The roll of her throat showed the fear she still had. "I'm kidding, darling. You look beautiful in anything you have on. I like you best in my clothes, but I'm just being biased."

Worrying her bottom lip with her perfectly straight teeth, a smile spread to her face that sent a jolt to my heart. Fuck, this woman was amazing. I don't care about her history, just like she shouldn't care about mine. Because this woman was my endgame.

Her breathing shuddered as she walked slow, careful steps toward me, stopping between my legs. "I think...I might be ready," she whispered, vulnerability painting her words.

Sitting up, my hands slid to the back of her legs, inching their way to her hips and settling there. "We don't have to rush into anything."

"We're not rushing." The words flowed out of her as if they were rehearsed. She shook beneath my fingers, her nerves getting the better of her.

And who would blame her? With the history and fuckery she went through, I wouldn't mind going celibate for her. Not even a question.

Her delicate fingers gripped the hem of her dress and she slowly lifted it off of her, revealing a succulent body with dips and curves. Perfection wasn't even the right word. Angelic. Goddess. Pure and utter beauty.

I kept my hands on her hips, staring at her attentively. Imbalance oozed from her gaze, from her shaking hands, the roll of her throat, and the rattle in her breaths. I didn't want her to do anything she didn't feel comfortable doing. And something told me she didn't feel comfortable about having sex. Ever.

"Don't do this because you think this is what I want." I kiss her stomach, looking up at her. "I just want you, darling. Your beauty, your laughter, your little snores—"

She laughed, covering her face. It's when she uncovered it, the wetness in her eyes caused me to jump to my feet and cradle her head. "I love you, Palmer. You, okay? Let's not do this. I don't...your nerves are making me hate myself for wanting you."

She sniffed, chuckling as her cold fingers touched my face. "I'm nervous because I've never had this experience before. This one on one with someone I have feelings for. This...truthfully, it's going to be the only memory I want to keep as my first time."

I didn't like it, but my heart still did a double take. She trusted me enough with this, enough to give herself to me after what she'd been through.

She trusted me.

She loved me.

She wanted me.

I was never wanted before, never looked at like I mattered. She made me feel mattered.

My heart climbed my throat, beating so loud in my ears they started ringing. I don't remember much of my first time; I don't remember much of any of the women I'd been with. Names and faces tend to blend together after a while.

But Palmer's would be my last, the only clear face I ever want to see under me again.

Our breaths were equally shaky and ragged, especially when she slid her hands to my chest and gripped my shirt.

"I'm ready, Slade. I want to be with you in every way I can that isn't just giving you my heart."

Capturing her lips, I sat back on the bed and let her take the lead. Still fearful that I'd take it too far and the last thing I wanted was to make her uncomfortable.

Palmer straddled me, keeping our lips locked as her nails dug into my chest. "C-can I take off your shirt?"

I yanked it over my head and came back to those lips, such beautiful pillowy lips. She was by far the best kisser I've ever had, the way she suckled my bottom lip, biting it playfully every time we made out. Dark thoughts of how she learned that always crept at the back of my mind, but that was her history. It was part of her and we could never erase it, only move on from it.

Pulling away from me, her eyes bounced around my face to my chest, studying the tattoos she had seen a million times over.

Her hands dropped and reached behind her, unhooking her red lace bra that sent a shiver through me.

My eyes scanned her, taking in her luscious curves. She told me about the scars on her body; always hiding the ones on her wrist from me. But now that I saw her—all of her—she was even more breathtaking. Her scars were my favorite part of her. They showed that even the most precious things could break, but with time, beauty would always unfold and become anew.

"You're so beautiful."

Tucking a lock of hair behind her ear, her cheeks reddened, touching my nipple ring. "You don't care that I'm not a size zero like all the women you used to date?"

Laughing, I turned her onto the bed and adjusted her legs around me. "I didn't date any of those women. They meant nothing to me. A bump in my very rocky road."

Kissing down her neck, I could feel the rapid beating of her heart against my lips causing me to kiss harder; suckling and nibbling her neck until she sucked in a breath.

"I used to be like that—skinny—but ever since I was rescued, I never stopped myself from the things I craved. The things they wouldn't allow me to have," she murmured as my kisses trailed down her chest, stopping at her tits.

There was a scar between her breasts. A thin pink scar that looked like a stab wound. I didn't need to know, but deep down, I had an urgency to hear everything that happened to her. Yet I couldn't push or force it, she'd tell me everything I didn't know when she was ready.

"I love you, Palmer. You, not the size on the tag of your dress. You and all your fucking curves," I growled, gripping her hips. "I fucking love these."

She giggled, covering her face as her ginger mane of hair spilled like a halo around her before her bottom lip quivered. "And my scars?" she whispered.

Rising on my knees, I got off the bed and stood, helping myself out of my pants as her hands slowly peeled away from her face. My clothes left my body pretty quickly, my nerves and erection didn't help the point I was trying to prove, but being vulnerable around Palmer would make her feel better.

Standing before her naked as the day I was born. All tattoos, piercings, and bad decisions. "This is me, darling. I have scars, too. Plenty of them. I'm not as muscular as my brothers. I'm tall as shit but skinny as hell. And I can't grow a decent beard for the life of me."

Her eyes wandered, taking me in as those big balls of green bounced from my face, my chest, my dick, my legs, and back again. Having her eyes on me made my stomach do backflips, my heart palpitate, and my dick to leak pre-cum.

Crawling back onto the bed, I hovered over her on my fists, smirking. "If you'll have me, darling, I'd love to be your first true love. In this life and the next."

She nodded with tears spilling free. "I want you to be my first—even though it's not real, I want it to be."

"If you say it is, then it shall be."

Being her first everything made my heart swell.

I helped her out of her red lace underwear I know for a fact she went and bought with Zay, I came crashing down on Palmer and kissed those lips like they were my lifeline.

Even with the pearls of pre-cum dripping out of me, I wanted this moment to last. But my dick was painfully hard, having been untouched for far too long.

Kissing down her neck, I found her nipples—hard and tender. A moan slipped free from those pouty lips as I suckled her breast, leaving hickies and bite marks. No one owned her. No one would dare scar her again. But I marked her because she was mine for the keep.

As I made my way down her stomach, kissing along her tiny scars, she stopped me and lifted my head to hers. "I don't want that," her trembling voice sent stabs to my heart.

"I want to taste you, to swallow you as you come undone."

Her lips met mine and she reached between us, stroking me a couple of times. "Just sex for now, okay?"

Grinding into her, she was dripping for me. Wetter than I'd felt in a while. But why wouldn't she let me down on her? I wanted to taste her sweet pussy.

"Can I ask why?"

She brushed her fingers through my hair, kissing my chin. "He...it was his favorite," her voice cracked at the confession, tears followed suit and I kissed her, swallowing all her pain.

"No, don't think about him. Don't let it happen. You're safe, darling. I'm here. I'm right here."

"I know," she whispered, taking my bottom lip between her teeth and pulling back. "Make love to me, Slade. Show me I'm your girl."

"You are my girl," I purred adjusting myself so that the head of my cock was at her entrance. "No one's but mine."

I hesitated, holding my cock in place; her wetness coating my head. I've never gotten to know someone before having sex with them. I've always fucked them, then gotten to know them and realized that fucking them was so much better. It shut them up. Everything was different with Palmer. It was better, calmer, perfect.

She licked her lips, nibbling the bottom one right after. And it threw me over the edge.

Easing into her tight pussy, I groaned, growled, and cursed until her back arched and a moan slipped from those beautiful fucking lips. She was so tight, so wet. All fucking mine.

"Jesus, Slade. Either I'm too small for you or you're too big for me." Her fingers dug into my arms, making me smirk as I looked down at her breasts.

"Darling, I'm not even all the way in yet."

A sound escaped her.

A melodic note that emitted a moan from me and I slammed the rest of the way in. She screamed, head rolling back, but I waited before thrusting. I wanted to feel her pussy throbbing for me. To feel the way she molded to my size.

To know what making love felt like.

And I started rocking gently, kissing her neck and bathing her chest with licks. "Do you like me inside you? Tell me, Palmer. Tell me I'm the only dick allowed in your fortress."

Her moans grew louder, nails digging deeper. "You're the only one, Slade. The only one."

My tongue flicked her nipple, making her shudder. Fuck, I loved making her quiver.

So I did it again and again until my balls tightened and I gripped her thighs, bending her knees until they practically reached her ears.

"I'm gonna come inside you, so deep—ugh, fuck, so fucking deep." A growl climbed my throat as I thrust, feeling the walls of her pussy pulsate. "Are you gonna come for me? Please, finish with me."

She threw her head back, mewling. "Forever with you!"

And I released, locking eyes with my curly-headed beauty.

Tears rose and fell, but I couldn't break eye contact, not until every last drop was milked from me. "I love you so much, darling," I said, lowering on top of her as we caught our breaths.

"You brought me back home," she whispered, pressing a kiss to my cheek.

I didn't know what it meant, but it was enough for me to kiss her and know that this was the life I knew I'd be living for the rest of my days.

Just her and I.

Slade

Seated on the floor with my back to the dresser, I'm watching Zay and Riggs sleep. Her back is against the headboard, head tilted to the side as one hand is on her stomach, and the other on Riggs's chest. Somewhere between my panic attack outside and chapel, she changed into something more her style—jeans and one of my hoodies.

I always found their relationship unique yet forbidden. Everything around them forced their love apart, but they always found their way back to each other. No matter if she was married. No matter if his wife just died. No matter if Carter wasn't hers. Zay and Riggs found a way to be together.

And now is no different.

My arms drape off my knees, fingers fidgeting as I debate whether or not to wake them up. I need more answers, something Zay can give me. A face. A name. *Something.*

I have nothing stopping me, yet when I look at them and see how peaceful and beautiful they look, I don't want to ruin this moment. But *everything* is ruining this moment.

Taking my phone from the floor between my legs, it lights up with a picture of Palmer's smiling face. She's my world. My heaven. My hell. My lifeline. There isn't a thing in the world I wouldn't do for her and yet here I am trying to figure out what this bullshit my family is suffering from when my life is frightened and crying in a bunker.

Unlocking my phone, I find myself closing all the apps I left open and stopping on my Notes application. I never use the damn thing. Half the apps I have on here are useless. I'm not on social media anymore, my Tinder has been deleted, and the bubble-popping game is for Carter.

Scrolling to the top of the page, my name is the first thing that catches my eye. Zay wrote this when she had my phone at Maddison Gardens before it exploded. She spilled her truth about what happened and I've had it with me all this time. How could I let this slip my mind?

Slade,

I don't even know where to begin. But things are fucked. My Adam is involved. How deep? I don't know, but when The Ghost came to us, Adam pretended to be scared. The Ghost cut him and Adam screamed...but then he laughed soon as they shot Riggs. I don't know if he's dead or alive. After everything we've been through, he fucking <u>laughed</u>! But it didn't stop there, no, it didn't fucking stop until he grabbed my face and kissed me.

"This is merely the beginning, my love," he said with that stupid fucking grin on his face.

The Ghost pricked me with something and I was in a daze, barely paying any attention as they dragged someone out of the house and into the woods. I don't know who it was, their face was covered but they wore a Snakes vest.

Then Adam took Riggs and left like I never mattered to him. What if I never did? He set me up all those years ago; locking me in the cabin with Riggs over something my best friend did. <u>Not me.</u>

Adam spoke about some man called "the boss." He's the one who runs the trafficking. He's the one who finds the girls. He's the one who Daddy Donnelly and Roaden dealt with. He's the fucking one who brainwashed my husband into becoming everyone he always hated.

Save us, Slade.

Please.

Z.

Re-reading the note three fucking times to try and understand what the hell is going on. I knew that Daddy Donnelly brainwashed Adam into becoming a Panther to get intel on their rat, but I thought that's where it ended. Adam suffered a bullet to his kneecap for it and begged for forgiveness. We gave him that forgiveness for fuck's sake. Now he's back like he never fucking left and I'm sitting here trying to put the puzzle pieces together. And I hate fucking puzzles.

First "The Ghost."

Now "The Boss."

My head hurts and we've barely scratched the surface of this fiasco. Things will unravel when we least expect it and still, our questions won't be answered.

Riggs groans, turning his head and wincing as he tries to lift his arm. The guy looks worse for wear, but bringing him to the hospital wasn't the best idea until we spoke with the Captain so he'd cover any questions, but we can't seem to get a hold of him.

Riggs grunts, looking up at Zay with a sigh before he quietly winces to keep from waking her, and he sits up.

"Hey," I say softly.

Shooting his attention to me with feral eyes, he calms slightly, shoulders slouching. "Hey, brother."

Dragging a hand down my face, I exhale and lean my head back. "How you feeling?"

"Like I need something to numb this pain." He sniffs, wincing again when he looks back at Zay. "How's she?"

Shaking my head, I close my eyes and breathe. "She's fine. She's fine…she'll be fine."

He pushes himself to his feet and staggers slightly before he settles and finds one of my hoodies. "Wanna tell me what you know?" Gripping his shoulder, he massages it slightly and looks at the work that the guys did to pop it back in place. Don't know if they did a good job or not, but he tries to roll it and sucks his teeth.

"That's the problem. I don't know shit. Every time I figure something out it's like it's too late," I scoff, sniffling and exhaling again. "Three steps forward and ten back."

This goddamn panic attack just won't let up.

My chest is tight.

My palms are sweaty.

Everything is spinning and closing in and widening. I can't breathe.

Dropping my head in my hands, I try to breathe in through my nose and out through my mouth, wheezing as I do. Riggs grunts, tapping my head. "You're doing great. Better than any of us." His boot touches mine, causing me to meet his gaze with watery eyes. "Love you, brother."

Sniffling, I nod and exhale again. "Yeah, love you, too."

The approval I never knew I needed.

With my heart still lodged in my throat, I jump to my feet and take the hoodie from him as he attempts to put it on. "I got you, brother."

Holding it open and helping him into it, he winces, strains, and growls, but we manage to zip it shut. "Fuck," he hisses as he adjusts the sleeve around the bandage on his wrist.

"They got you good, didn't they?"

He rubs his neck and sucks his teeth as he rolls his shoulders. "Fuckers came outta nowhere."

"Zay says Adam's in on it," I reveal, making Riggs's jaw twitch.

"Mmm, wouldn't surprise me."

Taking my phone from my pocket, I open the Notes app and hold it out to him. It doesn't take him long to frown and read over what she wrote. Takes him even less time to growl out curses and drag a hand down his sweaty face. "Something kept telling me he wasn't done, but I didn't listen."

"Too caught up in your little sex cloud to notice." He shoots me a glare, causing me to raise my hands in surrender. "Didn't mean anything by it, pres."

Grunting again, he clicks his tongue and sighs. "You ready for what's to come? All this shit is going to end in bloodshed."

Nodding quickly, I exhale the shakiest breath and steady my voice. "We do what we gotta do, boss."

Violent knocks strike the door, sending my heart leaping out of my chest. Riggs winces, heading for the bed. He gently touches Zay's shoulder, shaking it. She jolts, but her hooded eyes find Riggs and immediately calm.

"Get behind me, baby," he whispers, keeping his sore arm against his chest. She crawls on the bed toward him, holding onto her stomach.

The gun is gripped in my hand and I hold it up as I go for the knob. But whoever is on the other side of the door, whips it open causing me to stumble back.

Gunner storms in right before I nearly pull the damn trigger. His face is red and sweaty, teeth bared. "Slade—"

"Jesus, fucking fuck, dude. I could've shot you!" I yell, dropping my hand. "The fuck are you doing here?"

Gunner stares at Riggs, jerking his head. "Ghost has your brother and your mama hostage. Peter is gonna put an end to this, but we didn't stay—his orders—we had to get your kids first."

Riggs looks back at Zay, taking her hand. "Where's our son?"

"Snake biters have the kids in chapel. Getting them something to eat," Gunner says, then eyes me. "We need to move, Slade. They're honing in and we need to get to Peter before The Ghost loses it."

Pinching my eyes shut, I nod quickly, exhaling again. "Yeah, yeah. On it."

A hand slides up my back, the nails brushing against my sweater. "Just breathe," Zay's voice moves through me. "You're all we have, Slade. You can do this."

No pressure, right?

Nodding quickly, I look at those hazel eyes and force a meek grin. "Take care of Palmer in case something happens to me."

"Don't say that—"

"*Please.*"

Zay places a hand on my cheek and nods, pulling me into a hug. "If you see Adam, put a bullet in his skull," she whispers, kissing my neck before releasing me and walking out of the room.

Riggs pulls guns from the top drawer of the dresser, tucking a couple into his jeans. "I want three people with my family—the rest of you, we're heading to Peter's."

Stepping in front of him, I'm no match for Riggs, but I'm not letting him leave this place in his condition. "You're gonna stay here, pres. You're fucked if you think otherwise."

Gunner guffaws, folding his tattooed arms across his chest. "Sit this one out, Riggsy. Keep your woman safe and that boy, too." He jerks his head behind him, his VP, Allistair leaning on the doorframe. "Peter's girls are here, too."

Riggs grunts, taking a gun out and pushing it against my chest. "Make sure one of these ends up between my half-pint of a brother's eyes."

With another grunt, he steps out of the room; his heavy clunky footfalls taking over the rock and roll music playing softly in the bar. They're pissed at Adam, I understand that but he's my best friend. I refused to believe he'd be the culprit in this without proof—even though everything makes sense. Everything points at him. I fucking refuse.

Tucking the gun into my ankle holster, a sigh escapes me when I meet Gunner's angered expression. "Back to Peter's, then?"

"Can't go in guns a blazing, but we can go in there and demand answers," he tells me, snapping his fingers at Allistair. "Call other charters. I want all hands on deck."

As soon as I step out of the room and enter the bar, Dorian is sitting on a bar stool with ice on her lip as one of the Snake Biters is tending to a gash on her cheek.

Dorian stares at me with furrowed brows, guilty in all of this, unlike the rest of us. Her fucking brother is The Ghost and she sits here acting like she knows nothing.

For all we know, this is all an act and she's in on all of it like Adam could be. "Slade?" she calls.

"No," I growl out, staring at her over my shoulder with gritted teeth. The fright on her face makes me feel bad but I will not let those big gray eyes swoon me over.

Stepping out into the late afternoon, I breathe in the cool March air and know that today has barely fucking begun.

Riggs

I should be in a hospital bed attached to an IV filled with painkillers and antibiotics. But instead, I'm limping to chapel to see my woman and our son.

The pain I'm experiencing is blinding.

Destroying me.

Weakening me.

But I have to be strong for her. Always for her.

Zay sits at the head of the table, Carter has his arms wrapped around her bandaged neck and two of my nieces are spinning on the chairs. I didn't want this for Zay or our son. This is not something she deserves. This isn't something our son should grow up witnessing.

This is the life, though. This is all I remember growing up when danger was amok; sitting with Peter and Mama in chapel with the other kids and wives.

Staring at my Zay, I see exactly that. The life I wanted out of, the life I thought we had under control. Everything is out of whack and look at what I did. Look at what happened. They aren't safe. I couldn't keep them safe.

Zay's face lights up when she sees me, kissing Carter's cheek once more. "Daddy's here, baby."

But Carter doesn't let go of her, he squeezes tighter like he's scared. Why would he be scared of me?

With a pained grunt, I make my way to the VP chair and stop it from spinning. Rosa looks up at me and smiles, looking just like my brother. "Hey, baby girl."

"I'm hungry," she says, right as Sara hugs my leg.

I can't stretch out my arm to touch her head, but those big blue-gray eyes smile at me anyway. "Food's coming, okay? We'll have—" My mind draws a blank on the Snake Biters' names. Probably a good thing. I used to use these women for a fuck many nights before I met Zay. "Someone will bring you food and set you up in Slade's room for a movie."

Carter wiggles free from Zay once hearing my voice and comes running. "Daddy, Daddy."

With all the strength I have left, I groan and grunt until I'm on my knees with his arms around my neck. "I'm here, okay? I ain't going anywhere."

He's not frightened of me…he's scared of his other "daddy."

He's frightened of Adam.

"I'm scared," he whispers, sniffling.

"I'll protect you. I'll protect Mommy. Nothing's gonna happen to my family." My gaze doesn't shift from Zay's as I speak, meaning every word of it. Her hazel eyes well with tears, but she blinks them away and breathes, rubbing her stomach. The baby must be kicking up a storm from all this stress. I need her to see Karen again. Get an ultrasound to make sure *my* baby is okay.

"What about Dad? He—" Carter pauses, releasing my neck and looking back at Zay. "Are they done painting now?"

"Painting?" Frowning, I shake my head and open my mouth to speak, but Dorian comes in holding a bag of ice on her lip.

"Hey," she says, her voice hoarse.

Zay pushes up from the chair, hand on her belly, and peeks at Mina in the car seat. "I think we need to talk about what's going on. Because this shit—you have a lot of explaining to do, Dorian."

She scoffs, dropping the ice. "Explain what? I'm going through this shit just as much as you are."

Zay's cheeks redden and she takes a thundering step forward, but I grab her hand, stopping her. "Riggs—"

"Not in front of the kids." Holding her poignant stare, she huffs, continuing out of chapel and calling out to one of the Snake Biters—Addy.

Dorian smiles at her daughters, staring at me with raised eyebrows. "I swear it, Riggs. I have no idea what's going on."

"I don't wanna hear it, Dorian." With a wince, I stand tall, towering over her by a foot. "We'll talk when the kids are in the back room."

Dropping the bag of ice on the table, she takes the car seat while smiling sweetly at the sleeping baby and takes Sara's hand, walking out of the room. Rosa is still spinning in the chair and Carter has a death grip on my leg.

I don't want to leave my son more than I already have, but I have to know what's going on. I'm the goddamn president of this motorcycle club and I'm as much in the dark as the fucking Snake Biters.

Skeet and Lip walk into chapel; Skeet smiles and claps his hands when he sees the kids. He dresses up as Santa every year since Carter was born, saying we need more joy in this chaotic lifestyle. The kids love it and they haven't figured it out yet. I hope they never do.

"Come with me, kiddos. We got some chicken nuggets cooking with French fries and veggies. And there might be some chocolate ice cream for dessert if you eat your greens."

Rosa takes Carter's hand. "Let's go eat."

Running my hand through his blonde hair, he squeezes my leg once more before following Skeet to the back room. "See you soon, bud."

Lip releases a breath, dropping onto one of the chairs and waits until the kids are gone. "Dude, the fuck?"

I grunt, sitting in the chair in front of me and exhaling sharply. My wrist is throbbing, stinging, and aching. My entire body wants to shut down, but I won't let it—at least not yet. My dislocated shoulder isn't put back correctly; a stabbing sensation pierces through it, shooting daggers up and down my arm. "I don't remember shit about what went down. Everything is in pieces. It's...fuck. Zay says that Adam is the reason. That Adam set this shit up, but the fucker was hanging in that basement with me, bleeding and wheezing. I don't fucking understand what the hell is going on."

Pinching my eyes shut, I sense her before she even enters the room and I snap my head at the door. Zay is holding a glass of water and a bottle of painkillers, kissing my forehead as she passes.

"Take these. Skeet said he'd take you to the hospital as soon as we hear back from the Captain." She holds the pills at my lips, urging them into my mouth. "But something tells me we're not going to hear back from him anytime soon."

"Why do you say that?" Lip asks.

Zay inhales sharply, helping me drink water. "Adam."

"Being a little vague, sweetheart," Lip says, tilting his head to the side. "Slade's running around trying to help everyone and figure this out and all you're telling him is *Adam*, nothing else."

She scoffs, slamming the glass of water on the table and spilling some of its contents. "I don't know any more than all of you. I just know Adam is involved, he…fuck, he let them inject me with drugs, he laughed when they shot Riggs with a tranquilizer, and he killed someone with a Snake's vest on—that's whose blood was all over me—then they implanted me with a fucking tracker—" She points at the bandage on her neck. "All the while you're here trying to figure out what happened and pointing fingers at me when I don't know jack shit."

Attempting to sit up straighter at her confession, my shoulder seizes, causing a wince to leave my lips. "What did you say, baby?"

"Snake's vest?" Lip gives me a quizzical stare, doing what I'm doing and counting off the men around us still alive. "Who the fuck could it be?"

"Call all charters, we got a fucking rat in the house," I growl out, pushing myself into a standing position. "I want the kids out of here, too. Take them anywhere—"

"My parents," Zay interrupts me. "They'll welcome us no issue."

Nodding as Dorian comes back into the room with a blanket over her shoulder, shielding the baby from suckling on her breast. "You and Dorian will go with them—"

"Riggs—"

"Baby." Lifting my throbbing arm, I cup Zay's chin. "If anything happens to you or Carter again—I didn't protect you and—"

"Riggsy, we're fine. Okay? Plus we need you to come with us—"

"I'm going to a hospital, with or without the Captain's okay. I'm hanging on by a thread here, sunshine. If I don't get help, I ain't gonna make it."

Resting my forehead on hers, I breathe staring at the tears rolling down her cheeks. "I'll come home to you when I'm better. You, me, and our boys." Kissing her lips. "Just you and me and blueberry pancakes. How it shoulda always been."

She nods, wrapping her arms around me and deepening the kiss, her tongue sliding with mine. "Promise me one thing," she whispers.

"Anything."

"I want confirmation from someone—*anyone* that Adam is dead." The anger in her words sends a chill up my spine. She's always been the one to defend Adam, to side with him. But seeing the hurt and betrayal in her hazel eyes, my woman has finally seen the light. "I need to know we're not sitting ducks anymore."

Kissing her forehead, I nod, then touch her stomach. "Our new beginnings are just getting started."

Lip places a hand on her shoulder, leading her and Dorian out of the room. "I'll stay with the kids until we get a couple of guys ready for transport," he says standing at the door.

Zay glances back at me, a single, fat tear skimming her cheek. What am I doing? Leaving my woman to sit in a hospital bed to nurse my wounds. I'm not like that. I'm the tough one. The one who walked for three fucking miles with two bullets in his side.

Now I'm weakened, crumbling from pain.

I've grown soft.

So fucking weak.

All for those hazel eyes scowling at me.

All for her.

Lip dips his chin at me as I lean against the table. "You look like hell, brother."

"I'm living it."

He nods again, coming back in and leaning right beside me with crossed arms. "You're leaving your woman to go to the hospital?"

"As much as it sounds like I'm lying, I ain't. I don't know how I'm walking normal right now. Everything hurts like they fucking dragged me on the back of their car before chaining me in the basement."

Lip exhales sharply, sucking his teeth. "You believe Adam is involved?"

"I do."

He scoffs with a chuckle. "Fucker can't even shoot straight."

"Something tells me everything that half-pint does is a lie. Daddy's been grooming him, training him and we didn't even know it. He chose Adam to be the rat for the Panthers, he chose Adam to take the fall for my fuck-up so we'd get money for the club. He trusts Adam because Adam isn't one of us. He's a bastard child seeking attention from Daddy. And that's exactly what he got. He'd do anything to be accepted, and I have a feeling that means taking over the trafficking that Daddy and Roaden started."

Scoffing and shaking my head, I touch my shoulder with a wince. "Right under our fucking noses and we never saw it."

"How can you be so sure?"

My gaze finds Lip's holding it with nothing surer in my life. "How things have played out is exactly what Adam predicted, don't you remember?"

Lip frowns, holding my stare as the memory tugs at us. "The BBQ at your mama's place when Zay announced her pregnancy?"

I grunt, slouching as I stare at the open door and think back on the day I could have avoided.

On a day I could have saved my family.

On a day I should have killed him.

Riggs

lmost seven months ago, Zay was unusually quiet. But she'd get that way from time to time when we'd drive up to Mama's house. Said it reminded her of the time she almost lost me.

Little did she know, I'd never go anywhere.

She sat in the backseat of my pickup truck with Carter; her eyes closed and head leaning back. She wasn't feeling well last night—throwing up almost all damn night. But pregnancy was the last thing running through my mind because we said we'd discuss it before jumping in. Adam could argue it all he wanted—get red in the face for all I cared—I would be the father if we decided to have kids. But again, we didn't discuss shit, and we said we would if we wanted more kids.

Adam tapped my arm, glancing back at Zay. "You think she has the flu or something? She puked last night and said she's nauseous this morning."

Glancing back at her, she exhaled slowly, lifting her head as Carter whined for his toy on the floor. "Rosa was sick last week. Maybe it's that."

Adam nodded, looking back at her again with a smile. "How you doing, babe? You up for a barbecue?"

She groaned, picking up the toy. "No, but I can manage."

"I can turn around, sunshine. We already missed church. It's just a barbecue. There's always next weekend," I suggested, reaching my hand back and placing it on her knee. "You should rest."

She smiled, taking my hand. "I'm okay, Riggsy."

My stomach did backflips, letting the butterflies loose. I loved when she called me that. Much more than when she called me babe or baby. This woman was my dream, and as crazy as our life had been, there was always a part of me that wondered if I stayed after she got shot how our life would've turned out. I wouldn't have Carter, I know that. I wouldn't have met Shyanne, but as much as she meant to me, I was never in love *with her. I loved her, she saved me and gave me a son. But my heart remained with Zay since we met at the cabin.*

It's still hers and will forever be.

But I wondered where we would've been now if things played out differently. Where would we live? Who would be at the head of the table? How would our lives be connected to the Snakes if we vowed to leave it? Would Peter have found his salvation? Would Adam still be betraying us?

The guards at Maddison Gardens opened the gate, letting us in without question. Peter sat out front with Mina asleep on his chest, rocking on the porch swing. It was funny seeing my brother as a father. Seeing him care for someone other than himself. And he cared for his girls. He changed drastically for them, became the man our mother wanted. Gave up the drugs, the alcohol, the late nights of fucking his life away. He grew the hell up since shit went down and I was so proud of him for it. He smiled more, and that's all I could ever ask for.

Adam saluted him, hopping out of the truck. "Hey, where's Dorian and the girls?"

Peter placed a finger on his lips, jerking his head to the side. "With Mama. They're helping make some food platters."

Glancing back at Zay, she exhaled slowly again, staring out the window. "Baby, lemme drop Carter off and we'll go home, okay?" I said, placing my hand on her soft knee again.

She shook her head, flashing me a meek grin. "I'm okay, I promise. Let's go see my nieces, yeah?"

She hopped out of the truck, waving at Peter as he got up from the porch swing to kiss her on the cheek. "How's the baby?" she asked, touching her head.

"Gave Dorian a hard time last night, so she's taking it easy today while I'm on dad duty." Peter smirked, placing a hand on Zay's shoulder. He won't admit it, but my brother still had the hots for her. Who could blame him? Zay was beautiful, funny, smart when she needed to be, and made sure to always keep us in our place.

Of course, our relationship situation was a bit messy, but it didn't bother me. I had her, that's all that mattered.

Placing a kiss on Carter's cheek, I lifted him out of his car seat and he wiggled out of my arms, running straight inside to his grandma and the girls. It was nice to have this. A family life.

A life outside the chaos. Outside the club.

It was ours and no one could take it away from us.

Adam clapped Peter on the back and walked along the porch to where Slade and Palmer were talking under one of the trees. He'd gotten close with Slade when I was going through a bender after Shyanne died. And Slade stepped it up, showing he's man enough to run this club if I ever stepped down.

And I was thinking about it a lot. Especially when Zay played with Carter. The way her face lit up around him, the love that oozed from her...they were my family, my everything.

If I left, it guaranteed their protection.

Running my fingers through Zay's hair, I tugged it slightly moving her head back, and she grinned. "Hey, baby." Planting a sloppy kiss on her lips—something I liked doing in front of people to show that this sex kitten was all mine.

"Mmm," she hummed, tapping my chest.

Peter chuckled, bobbing the baby in his arms. "Looking a little pale, Zaynab. You good?"

She rolled her eyes, opening the screen door. "You Donnelly boys worry too much."

The screen door slapped shut behind her, leaving my brother and me in its wake. But he was right. Adam, too. Zay didn't look well and it bothered me that I didn't know why or how to fix whatever was wrong. Was there something wrong?

I hated being helpless.

"Hopefully she didn't get what Rosa had," Peter grunted, sitting back on the porch swing and tapping the spot beside him.

My soul was with Zay, but my body sat down, resting an arm on the back of the swing. Enjoying the rare alone time with my brother. Sometimes pressing Zay for answers was worse than giving her space. "How're the girls?"

He snorted, gently kissing the top of Mina's head. "They're fucking wild, man. Dorian is so calm and quiet, and the one thing my kids get from me is my hyper-ness. How is that fair?"

Laughter spilled from me, looking over at him. "Payback for all those times you drove Mama mad."

"Hopefully this one is calm," he said, kissing Mina's head again. "She likes me the most, but I don't have tits to breastfeed, and Dorian is very adamant about doing it."

Smirking, I brush my knuckles along Mina's chubby cheek and grin. "Zay was the one who did the feedings at night—"

"You mean Shyanne."

Shaking my head and cracking the bones in my neck. "Shyanne was in his life for only a few months before Zay became his mother."

"Shyanne's still the woman you made him with."

Grunting, I fixed the stainless-steel bracelets around my wrist. "Why are you trying to get under my skin right now? You don't think I know that? Shit, Adam says it all the time and urges us to tell Carter who his birth mother is, but I ain't ready for that because—as much as Shyanne meant to me at one point, Zay always meant more. Zay was there when Carter was born, remember? I was late because of the club. She was the first to hold him before Shyanne or me. And when Shyanne died, no one asked her to take over. But Zay did. She's been more of a parent to my son than his own parents. That's why I consider her his mother. No other reason than that. So fuck off with your bullshit."

Peter laughed, shushing himself before waking Mina. "I'm just saying, eventually, Carter's going to want to know the truth."

"And what's so wrong with him not knowing?"

He took a deep inhale, resting his head back against my arm and staring at the clear blue sky. "I see that look on your face every time Carter calls Adam his dad. Now imagine if Shyanne were alive. How would she feel having Carter calling Zay his mom?"

Anger built up inside me, bubbling in my belly and ready to erupt if he kept on. I did hate it every time my son called Adam his dad, but we signed up for it, and let's face it, as much as Carter looked like me, his hair was so blonde that people thought he wasn't my kid.

But where Peter was wrong was that Shyanne wasn't alive. She lost her life for the fucking club. And I honor her by raising our son without the knowledge of how fucked up his father is.

"Zay is his mother, Peter. End of fucking story."

He chuckled, glancing over at me. His freckles were darker today, standing out against his pale skin and those blue eyes as sparkling as mine. "Sir, yes, sir."

Opening my mouth to speak, Mama's voice moved through the quiet. A cheer that startled Peter and me. Dorian's laughter moved through the next, and Zay's quiet chuckles hit my ear last. "What's going on?"

Peter sat up, jerking his head at the door. "Let's go find out, brother."

Adam's whoop followed suit, making me quicken my pace and step in front of Peter as we entered the kitchen. Adam had Zay in a hug, her legs wrapped around his waist as he kissed her neck repeatedly. Slade and Palmer hugged Mama, congratulating her.

"What's going on?"

Mama wiped her cheek, picking Carter up. "I'm going to be a grandma again."

Widening my eyes at Dorian. "You just popped this one out," I said, glancing back at Peter.

She laughed, touching Mina's back. "Not me, silly. You or Adam—Zay's pregnant."

My heart did a double beat, shooting my gaze to my sunshine. Thundering forward, I ripped Zay from Adam's arms and cradled her in mine. "Is it true, baby?"

She wiped her cheeks of fresh tears, chuckling. "I wanted it to be a surprise for later when we got home, but your mom can read right through me."

As everyone was hugging and congratulating Adam around us, a smile so big spread to my face and I gripped her tighter, holding my woman as close to me as I could. "You're my world, sunshine. You have no idea how happy you make me. How you brought me back from a dark place. How you have become my home," I whispered for her ears only.

"I love you," Zay said, kissing me softly before everyone wrapped their arms around us for a giant hug.

Slade cheered again, tousling my hair. "Congrats, brother."

Chuckling, I adjusted Zay in my arms so her legs wrapped around my waist. "Thanks."

Mama whistled loudly, shooing everyone out of the kitchen. "Boys get out and man the grill while the ladies start talking gender reveals and baby showers."

Zay laughed into the nap of my neck, kissing it softly. "Maybe I should've taken you up on that offer to go home."

"It's not too late," I whispered.

"We can't leave," she said for my ears only.

"Says who?"

With a deep inhale, she tapped my chest and I set her down, getting more claps on my back from my brothers. She raked her bottom lip and lifted a shoulder. "Go man the grill, my love."

Peter handed the baby over to Zay and pulled me in for a hug, keeping his arm draped over my shoulders as we ventured outside. I was going to be a father again, but why didn't I have that pride oozing from me like it did when I found out Shyanne was pregnant? What a day that was. She was desperate to keep me home and did anything to get me to stay, and when accidents happen, sometimes they happen for good reason. And Carter was the only good reason I would ever have married her.

But with Zay, I'd give her the fucking world to bear my last name. And she'll own it soon.

Before we have this baby, I'm going to marry her. I don't care if it's illegal, I've never done anything legal in my fucking life. The one thing I will do that's legit is give Zay the life she deserves.

Slade and Adam held trays of burgers and hotdogs, bringing them to the grill all while my heart was still beating wildly, looking back at Zay smiling as Palmer leaned her head on her shoulder.

Zay never wanted kids, she made that known every time one of us finished inside her, and yet, here she was with our son and a baby in her belly. Utter perfection, utter bliss.

My whole world was coming together.

Judas, Lip, and Dillion were sitting around the patio table, talking to a few of the women who lived at the sanctuary. They were respectful toward them, compared to the women at the club. Most of the conversations between the bikers and the women we saved were for information on whatever they knew. And half of the girls knew more than they thought. We saved countless other victims because of these talks.

Lip saluted me, taking the raw burgers from Slade and heading for the grill. "Hey, pres. We got a lead—"

"We ain't doing that today," I interrupted Lip. "Today is not for work, it's for

family."

Adam laughed, clapping my back. "Just found out I'm going to be a father."

Snapping my head, I glared at Adam, but who was I to correct him? For all we knew, he could be right. But I knew deep in my heart, that baby was mine. No matter fucking what, that baby had Donnelly blood running through his or her veins.

Lip smiled over his shoulder. "Congrats, brother."

Grinding my teeth, Slade took notice and squeezed my shoulder. "Let's hope it's not a girl as hot as Zay. You'll be in so much trouble."

My eyes found his, and his gentle smile eased my aggravation. I hated it whenever Adam became possessive over Zay. He'd do it often, too. Always reminding me that she was his wife, she loved him first, and she slept with me out of spite.

But my Zay loves me more than she'd ever love that half-pint.

Now was no different.

Adam pulled his long hair into a knot on his head and jerked his head at Slade and me. "Got a sec?"

"We gotta man the grill," Slade said, pointing a thumb behind him.

"Lip's got it, right?" Adam called out.

Lip shot us finger guns and chuckled, tossing hotdogs on the grill. "On it, brother."

Adam placed his arm around my shoulders, shaking slightly. "We're going to be dads."

There was no smile spread to my face when it should've been. This moment was supposed to be this joyous time, yet jealousy soured through me at the thought of raising more kids in this relationship. This was what we chose, I knew that. I wanted Zay to myself, but she loved her husband. How could I ask her to choose? More importantly, how could I keep my family safe and still be part of this club?

Slade pulled out a joint, lit it, and passed it to Adam as we walked between the apple trees.

Adam would bring us here often to talk, I never understood why, but he'd come up with plans and ideas for the club, sharing them with us.

Glancing back at the house, Zay walked onto the porch, holding Mina to her chest with a tray of veggies in her other hand. My sunshine still looked pale, bags under her eyes from being up most of the night last night, but the way the sun beamed down on her.

She was radiant.

Beautiful.

My fucking woman was pregnant with my baby.

What a beautifully disastrous family we created.

"What did you wanna talk about? Thought we said no club talks today?" Slade asked, holding in the smoke before handing the joint to Adam.

After two puffs, he held it out to me and released the smoke from his nostrils. I wasn't much of a smoker, but I needed one toke to get me through this sudden burst of annoyance coursing through me. Jealousy wasn't a good look on me.

"It's almost three years and we haven't heard from The Ghost," he said, leaning against a tree.

Choking on the smoke, I brought a fist to my mouth and tried to control the fit. But nothing worked, not even Slade's taps on my back. "Fuck."

Slade laughed, sucking on the joint. "Shows you don't smoke much, pres."

"Kinda hard to focus when this fucker brings up The Ghost like he's an everyday topic," I scoffed, shaking my head and clearing my throat. "The fuck you bringing him up for now?"

Adam lifted a shoulder, bringing the joint to his lips. "I think we should be ready in case he decides to come back with a vengeance. Y'know, like what if he just shows up randomly, fucks up our day with secrets and lies we had no idea were right there in front of us."

"Where's this coming from?" Slade asked, eyeing me with a frown.

Adam lifted a shoulder smiling at Zay as she sat in the hammock with my nieces and our son. "It's been bothering me for a while. Someone as powerful as him doesn't just fall off the face of the earth. No, he plans and prepares to take down the people he believes fucked him."

Something about the way Adam's mouth curled up at the corner when he spoke, as if he knew something we didn't. As if he was more than just worried about The Ghost coming back, he knew he would knock on our door soon enough.

Folding my arms across my brute chest. "And how do you figure?"

Adam licked his lips, taking the joint from Slade. "Put it this way. If something happened to Zay, you wouldn't sit back and wait, would you? No, you'd plot and plan and strike at the right fucking moment. And I think The Ghost is doing just that. Watching us when we're not looking, studying us and our family. He'll slowly pick us off one by one until we get him what he wants."

Slade side-glanced at me with a worried look in his gaze. The same look I shot back at him. Adam was onto something, yet the way he spoke made it sound like he knew more than he was guessing. "What're you talking about, brother?" Slade asked, inhaling the joint.

Peter jogged over, whiskey bottle in hand. His smile brightened up when he approached, draping an arm over my tense shoulders. "Donnelly family is growing, hey?"

"That it is," Adam said, taking the bottle and staring right at me. "To new beginnings."

But these weren't new beginnings. His ramblings made something tick inside me.

A bomb counting down and about to go off.

Adam knew something we didn't.

He was hiding.

Betraying.

He was still a fucking rat and I didn't even notice until it was too late.

"Yeah, new beginnings," I said, my gaze shifting to Zay. Her eyes were closed, the baby asleep on her chest and Carter resting his head beside hers.

Everything was calm.

Tranquil.

Until it wasn't.

Slade

Growing up in group homes, I've learned that the people you're closest to aren't always the ones who become the most trusting. I've had friends I've looked at like brothers, other I knew from the start they were backstabbing assholes. And yet, the ones who I judged were the ones who had my back. And the ones I trusted were the ones that fucked me.

Adam is one brother I trusted.

I'm pulled over three blocks from Peter's house. Gunner and his men went ahead, I just needed a moment to think of what to do. *I don't know what to fucking do.* There's a cold sweat leaking down my back, sending a rippling agony in my belly. This panic attack has become a part of me, this nausea becoming me and I don't know if it'll ever go away.

The sky is hazy today, the smell of snow in the air. The sun hasn't breached through the clouds once, and it feels like my skin is scorching; blistering from its heat yet freezing like I've been standing in zero-degree weather. I promised my brothers I'd lead this fuckery. I promised my woman I'd protect her. I promised Zay, too.

I promised Carter nothing would happen to him, all the while I have no idea what the fuck is waiting for me around every corner.

But one thing I do know is none of my found family will suffer.

Not a single one.

Glancing at my phone, I told Gunner I'd be over in ten minutes, it's shy of eight now. But before I can settle onto my bike, the phone rings and Adam's name pops up on the screen.

An ache burns in my chest, hot and unexpecting as fear sizzles in my veins. What on earth could he want?

Sending a quick text to Gunner to let him know I'll be a little longer—I answer Adam's call.

Adam pops gum on the other end of the call, chewing abnormally loudly. "Slade?"

"The fuck is going on, man? You're in on this? You risked your wife's life, the life of your brothers, your nieces—your fucking unborn son for some fucker in a mask—"

He laughs, guttural and demonic. "No. No, no, no. I wouldn't risk their lives over some fucker in a mask, Slade. It's so much more than that. You'll see."

My throat closes in, lifting the visor on my mask to scour the area in case the asshole is here, watching me. And truthfully, I wouldn't put it past him. Adam was always a step ahead of us when it came to club shit. Like Daddy Donnelly was feeding him intel from the grave. Like he knew what to do and when to do it.

Like the asshole is still alive and running this crap through his bastard son.

A black Cadillac Lyriq zooms past me, the passenger window is open, and long blond hair billows out the window. Adam's chewing increases and he chuckles again.

"What the hell are you doing, Adam? What the fucking hell are you doing?"

He pops a bubble, spitting the gum out the window when the SUV stops and takes the turn onto Peter's street. "Come on over, Slade. We'll talk this out and I'll explain everything."

With that, the line goes dead and I'm left staring at an empty street, my breath clouds in front of me, and the only thing I'm able to think about is Palmer and if I'll ever see her again.

Please, God, let me see her again.

Slapping the visor shut on my helmet, I speed off after the Caddy, zooming through the streets until I come to a halt at the end of the driveway where the rest of the Snakes are held at gunpoint. Gunner's still sitting on his bike, hands raised, and a few of our men are on their knees in the muck and slush, the barrel of a gun pressed to their temples and under their chins.

The passenger door of the Cadillac Lyriq opens and Adam jumps out, running five fingers through his hair. "Boys," he says with a smug grin.

Continuing until I come to a stop behind Gunner, I toss my helmet off and swing a leg over my bike. "Adam," I yell, causing him to turn around, his damp blonde hair lying flat on his shoulders. "You're not going in there without me."

He rubs his hands together, nodding slightly as one of the masked men walks up to me with the gun pointed at my face. "Leave your guns here."

Reaching for the gun in my holster—the one Riggs gave me—I drop it in the snow, kicking it aside and raising my hands. "Promise me one thing, Adam." He jerks his head at me and one of the masked men pats me down. "Nothing happens to my family."

A rough laugh seeps from his lips as he saunters over to me, pressing his chest into mine. He's eight inches shorter than me, and he still stares at me without a hint of intimidation. "*Your* family? Last I checked, you have no family, Slade. No mother, no father. No brothers or sisters. You're as alone as a goddamn stray cat. So don't you dare come to me talking about *family*."

A stabbing ache moves its way from my chest, settling in the middle of my forehead. "I may not have any blood relatives, but the family you're betraying is the closest thing to a family I got. And they mean a whole lot to me. If they meant *anything* to you, you wouldn't be doing this fucking shit—"

He grabs my face, yanking me down to his level. "Watch what you say next, *brother*."

"Then show how much you care for your fucking family, *brother*, and call your wife. She's worried sick—" I pause, shaking my head out of his grasp. He doesn't need to know how pissed Zay is or what she said to me before I left. All he needs is to think about his family so that whatever bullshit he has planned, might fuck up. "You had your pregnant wife drugged—"

"She was pricked with morphine, she's fine."

I scoff, stepping forward before a gun is lifted to my head. "You drugged her! Your fucking wife and your kid—"

"Who says it's my fucking kid? Huh?" he screams, the chords in his neck bulging. "When Zay conjured up this fucking stupid idea, I went along with it because I loved her. But you've seen Riggs with her. If I'm not there, it's like I don't fucking exist. And if that's what they fucking want, then so be it. They can fucking have each other. Just like Peter. He says he's my best friend, but I was always the outcast with my brothers. Always the black sheep of the family because I was a goddamn bastard—and yet, Daddy chose *me*. He trusted me with everything. So don't come to me about her and my family. I have no fucking family. I never did."

My face reddens, staring at Adam as tears brim his lash line and a blush forms on his cheeks. Their relationship is a bizarre one to begin with, but I never judged them. I've been in open relationships, I've had threesomes. But what they have is deeper. Children are involved. And now that Zay is pregnant, their bond is breaking.

And after all this time, Adam never left the bullshit he started behind. He became Daddy Donnelly's pet—he drank the Kool-Aid and let it ruin him.

"If you're done being a fucking tool, can we go inside so I can end this?"

Shaking my head, my jaw clicks before I speak. "You're not walking out of this one alive," I growl out.

His face grew serious as I swallowed over a rock in my throat. I've never seen Adam on the cusp of regret and fury. "Who says I want to?"

Nearly knocking me to my knees like thunder clapping through me at his words. There's something he's not telling me. Something so powerful that would allow him to give up the life he has, the woman he loves, the baby that could be his…the family he has.

Could he be so filled with guilt that he doesn't care if he lives or dies?

Adam steps back, heading to Peter's house as he pulls his hair into a messy bun on top of his head. Gunner curses under his breath as Adam passes, causing a chuckle to seep out of him. But he doesn't stop, he continues up the long driveway, saluting a few of the masked men out front.

I'm shoved forward, gun aimed at the back of my head as I follow, nodding gently at Gunner. I don't have a plan aside from getting inside and scoping out the situation. I'll call Gunner and do what Peter did, leave the phone on in hopes he'll hear what the fuck is going on.

When I walk in, Mama Rosa is seated at the head of the dining room table, Peter at the opposite end with a yellow folder open in front of him. The same folder Mama Rosa has been carrying around for as long as I can remember.

Is Mama Rosa in on this, too?

How fucked up is—

"Adam? Slade?" Peter gasps, shaking his head as he sits on the table. "No, I told you I didn't want anyone in my family involved. You said you'd leave them out of this if I stayed—"

Adam makes his way to him, gripping his shoulders with that same smug smirk as he leans down, pressing his lips to Peter's temple. "I'm the one you should be worried about, Peter. Not any of these fucks and their petty nicknames, *me*."

Peter slowly turns, glaring at Adam. There's a twitch pulsating in his neck. His eyes become large and glassy. The pieces have come together. "Are you fucking kidding me? You drugged Zaynab! Killed my wife's sister! Hurt our brother—"

"That's beyond the fucking point!" Adam screams, releasing him and kicking out a chair beside him. "Slade, sit." He huffs, flattening his palms on the table when he looks from Peter to me, then Mama Rosa. "Am I going to be the bad guy and explain this shit? Or are you man enough to do it?"

She laughs softly, rising from her seat and pulling the folder to her, clearing her throat. "I'm more of a man than my husband. I can reveal the truth to my boys, Adam."

He tilts his head, looking at The Ghost who is standing next to Mama Rosa. "You going to sit down?"

The Ghost's arms are folded across his chest, his stare shifts around the room. I wasn't expecting to see this fucker without a mask on. There's a scar down the side of his face, through his eye. I don't know what happened, but it's enough to know this guy is scared of no one and nothing will get in his way.

Mama Rosa smiles, tapping her finger on the table. "This, Peter, is something your father was trying to start. When I got word of it—of the nightmare he was doing with Roaden—I had to put a stop to it. Damien Glass is a man you know rather well. Someone who you've met before, shared meals with, share the love for someone with."

Peter frowns, pushing his fingers into his eye sockets. "I'm so tired of the fucking tricks and games. Can someone just tell me what the fuck she's talking about?"

"Damien Glass is my father," The Ghost lets out, exhaling a shaky breath as he steps closer to the table and picks up a picture of a woman with long, curly brown hair, and deep brown eyes that match her skin. "Now, you need to explain why the fuck my father is the man involved with the kidnapping of my girl and the underground sex trafficking bullshit you were supposed to *stop*."

Mama Rosa's eyes turn to me with a grin. "Damien is the one who approached Daddy; he's the one who convinced Roaden to start tracking and kidnapping girls before you boys put an end to it. Then, he came to me. And Damien is one of the most powerful men this world has ever seen. If he's told no, then consequences are given—" Mama Rosa stands, lifting her shirt to reveal the burn scars I always thought Daddy Donnelly gave her. "So I stayed and I did what I was told, but I will have you know, none of these women who are highlighted in here were sold as sex workers. The women who are highlighted, are taken to safe houses." She looks at Peter, inhaling a breath. "Much like your wife was."

Peter frowns, shaking his head. "Fuck you. She isn't a goddamn victim."

Mama Rosa sits down, placing her hands on the table and riffling through the papers. When she finds what she's looking for, she slides the paper over to Peter and his face pales. "I told you, Peter. Not everything Dorian has told you has been the truth. Somethings are better left unsaid."

I take the paper from Peter, seeing Dorian's name and Gray's name highlighted on a long list of other people's names, dates, and locations. Some of them have price tags beside them.

When I set the paper down, I take notice of the other papers sitting in front of Mama Rosa with a similar list of names, dates, locations, and prices—some highlighted, most not.

Swallowing thickly, I realize I should have kept driving. I should have gone to get my girl and left this fucking club. But now I'm stuck, locked down until we discover more secrets, more betrayal, more goddamn bullshit none of us can make any sense of.

Until everything is over, we're all simply fucked.

Peter

Pinching my eyes shut, I'm still trying to wrap my head around what the fuck is going on. Mama hasn't lied to me yet about anything that's been going on with the club and with the people she deals with. But Adam…he's shown us betrayal before by abiding by Daddy's stupidity and becoming a Panther to help sniff out the rat.

And something tells me my father is still feeding him orders from the grave.

"Why is your name on this folder, Adam? My wife's name…Gray's…Wilde's girl?" Glaring at my half-brother, I point out the names, stopping on Lenora's before curling my hands into fists. "We were out, brother. We were out of this nonsense, starting our family away from the nightmares we went through. This shit…what you did to your wife and Riggs, that's not something you do to the people you love."

Adam's wolfish grin darkens, lowering his face to mine. "I lost my wife the second you conjured up the bullshit with the club. I lost her when you forced her to fuck you every Tuesday afternoon. I lost her when Riggs came back…I became non-existent when Shyanne died and Zay couldn't bear leaving Carter without a mother." Inhaling a sharp breath, his nostrils flare. "I lost my Zay a long fucking time ago and was too blind to see it."

"What changed?" Slade spits out, glaring at The Ghost, then Adam. "What fucking changed for you to decide to fuck things up now?"

Adam inhales again, looking over at The Ghost before he cracks the bones in his neck and groans. "The Boss is getting impatient. He's been in contact with Daddy and Roaden for years until three years ago."

"Daddy never stopped the trafficking?"

Adam shakes his head at me, turning to Mama and tapping the list of names. "But Mama Rosa knew all about that. Which is why she set up Maddison Gardens, isn't it? The sanctuary to save the ones she doesn't ignore."

I frown, looking at Slade before staring at the papers. *The ones she doesn't ignore…* "The highlighted names…"

"The highlighted names are the ones Mama turns a blind eye to so The Boss can keep his auctioning business alive." Adam snickers, plopping onto the chair beside me. "How do you think the club makes its money? The Boss sends Mama a price per highlighted name and we get a cut of that."

Swallowing over the rock in my throat, his confession feels like a stab to my heart. Something my own mother was hiding from us. Something she swore was over. Something she lied to our faces about and covered with love and comfort. These women aren't brought to safe houses, they're sold right under our noses.

And here I am staring right at her and wondering who the fuck this woman is.

She sacrificed herself to save these women, and now she's letting them slip through her fingers for fucking money.

"Mama?" I whisper. "Is this true?"

She sniffs, lifting a shoulder and reaching her hand out. "Peter, it's all part of my plan—"

"Your plan? Risking the lives of your children—your grandchildren—that's all part of your plan? For what? Fucking money? We have money. A fuckton of it that hasn't been given to us from bullshit deals you've conjured up with the devil—"

"Your father-in-law," Adam interrupts me in a sing-songy voice.

"Shut the fuck up!"

The Ghost slams his hand on the table, his serrated blade held in one hand as the other clutches a photo of a Lenora. "Why the fuck does this fucker have my girl?" His angered expression returns to Mama and he clenches his teeth. "And why the fuck have you kept this from me after all these years."

Mama sits back in her chair, that same look painting her face. This man doesn't scare her, Adam doesn't frighten her or cause her suspicion. Mama is in control and she knows it. "I have a plan. It's something I'm working on and once it's running smoothly, only then will all of this be over."

The Ghost grabs a wad of Mama's hair and yanks her head back so she looks at him while he speaks instead of mocking him with her devious grin. I show no remorse. Not a single movement to stop him. "All of this should've been over! We've been working tooth and nail to save these women—I have sacrificed enough to save my girl and you're telling me I have to fucking *wait?*"

Mama chuckles, tapping his arm to release her but that only causes him to grip tighter. "Damien is a powerful man, much more powerful than anyone you've ever crossed. He runs all the auctions, and the trafficking, all the deals…I want to be on his good side, be with his good graces so that I can gain access to his clientele, his power, and everything he knows. I'm so close, Wilde. So close to ending this all. And once I do, I'll put a stop to the trafficking as we know it."

I'm speechless.

Flabbergasted that Mama would allow such a thing.

She has an endgame, I see it, I understand it. She wants to take over Damien Glass's empire so she can stop it. But what's she's allowing beforehand is madness.

"What does my wife have to do with this? Why is her name here? Why is Gray dead?"

Adam leans forward, smiling at me with determination and pride. "Gray found out about this operation…I was given instructions to kill her. I did and left her in the basement of the cabin until I had a chance to dispose of her body—but living with Riggs and Zay, I never have a moment alone. And when I do, I'm too busy playing daddy to fix anything."

Tears blur my vision, rising and falling until I meet his blue eyes. "And who gave you these instructions?"

A deep laugh leaves him, placing his hand on my shoulder with a light squeeze. "Your wife."

Everything vibrates, zooming in and out of focus as my gaze stays locked on Adam's. There's a buzzing in my ear, a ringing that keeps growing louder by the minute. My Dorian is not a monster. She's the mother to my children, my girls. She would never be involved in something like this.

"You're a fucking liar."

He shakes his head, tapping the papers in front of us. "She's also the one who finds us the women."

The Ghost drags a hand down his face, shaking his head slightly. "You're fucked in the head if you think my sister is capable of this."

"Oh, but she is."

Staring down at the papers, Dorian's name catches my eye. My wife. My innocent curvy beauty is the cause for all of this. The reason our lives have been nerve-wracking for over three years. The reason my brother is losing his mind and my other brother is barely hanging on.

My wife is the devil incarnate and I fell for all her fucking tricks.

Riggs

A wave of cold meets me as I sit up, clutching my arm to my chest. "Easy there, Mr. Donnelly. You need to be on bed rest for at least twenty-four to forty-eight hours before doing anything remotely—"

"Thanks, Doc, but I got a family to take care of. And my girl is pregnant. There is no way I'm gonna sit on my ass while she runs around with our other kid," I interrupt him, my body is light from the top-notch painkillers running through my bloodstream.

When the storm passes and my body is healed, only then will I let myself lay back with my heart beating softly and exhausted. I'll bring my Zay and our babies away from this madness, move us far from California, and to bigger and better things. There's an abandoned safe house out in Canada that I'm sure she'll love. A safe house Roaden used when I was a prospect. Back when the Canadian charter worked with us. Now, the members of that charter have hung their vests for the safety of their families because of Daddy and his vile dealings.

Much like I should have done all those years ago when Zay and I were nothing but strangers.

Blueberry pancakes are my favorite.

I'll make you blueberry pancakes every morning until the day I die.

Will you, really?

Under different circumstances, I'd give you the world, Zay.

It was true then as it is now. Times are changing, I'm giving her everything I never did.

The doctor writes me a prescription, peels it off the pad, and hands it to me. "You'll have enough here for a long while, Mr. Donnelly. Be sure to use it sparingly."

Grunting my response, he helps me into the black hoodie that Slade lent me, then adjusts a sling around me. "Keep it in this for a month, apply ice a few times a day for—"

"It ain't the first time I dislocated my shoulder, Doc. The fucker just doesn't like being attached to my body," I joke, cracking the bones in my neck.

"Luckily you're lefthanded, then."

Nodding, I adjust the hood on my head. "I'll have the Captain call you—"

"He already did. You're fine." He chuckles, tapping my knee. "I've stitched your father a time or two."

Grumbling under my breath, I could bark back at him for bringing up the man who ruined my life—and seems to continue to do so from the grave—but I bite my tongue because that's what Zay would want me to do.

Be a better person, Riggsy. Someone your son could look up to.

Tucking the prescription in my pocket, he helps me off the bed and shakes my good hand. "Keep yourself on call, Doc. We may need you sooner than you think."

"Noted, Mr. Donnelly." Clicking his pen, he tucks it away and pulls the curtain open, heading to the next person in the emergency room while I'm still leaning against the bed and breathing deeply.

I don't know what to expect once I leave the hospital.

Death?

Vengeance?

More betrayal?

My family gone?

Groaning softly, I close my eyes and lean my head back. There's only one way to find out.

Grunting as I push off the bed, I start for the exit. The murmuring of cries, moans, groans, and pleading fills the waiting room. There are so many people sitting like zombies, bags under their eyes, annoyance painting their faces from waiting for hours on end. All it took was for me to flash my face to the security guard and I was bumped up to first in line.

My heart pulsates angrily when I spot a woman holding her infant no older than Carter was when Shyanne died. We abuse our power when we need it. And yet, this woman holding her baby has been waiting while the doctor fixed my shoulder.

Stopping before I get to the exit, I turn and head to the front desk, slamming my hand down and startling the nurse. "That baby right there, she's next."

The nurse fixes the large glasses on her chubby face and glances behind me. "Sir, we have a priority list that we abide by—"

"I said she's next." Gnashing my teeth, I pull the hood back, enough for her to see my face still caked in dried blood. "Do I gotta flash my goddamn cut for you to know who I am?"

Another nurse behind her steps forward, placing a gentle hand on her shoulder. "She's next, sir. Promise."

Grunting again, I look back at the woman whose face is red and riddled with dried tears. "Thank you," she cries, bobbing her baby in her arms. "Thank you."

With a small nod, I continue in my wake toward the exit, taking a turn when I stop dead in my tracks. Adrenaline burns in my veins. My Zay is waddling through the doors with Lip two paces behind her tugging on her arm.

"Zay, he'll have my goddamn head for this if he—" Lip looks up and finds me standing there, like a shadow lurking in the darkness. "And now I'm a dead man. Thanks, Zay."

Her hazel eyes find me and tendrils of relief ease from her gaze as she quickens her steps toward me. "Riggsy, I—"

"You're supposed to be at your parents'—"

"I don't fucking trust anyone. And that includes Dorian." She side-glances at Lip, then returns her attention to me. "After you left, Dorian asked me to watch the kids and call her when we head to my parents'—but my parents aren't home, remember? They're in Europe."

"Someone picked Dorian up from the clubhouse in a limo, brother. Some rich white fuck was in the back with her," Lip adds.

A cold dread begins to crawl up my spine, a realization like no other.

The fucking cunt never left the business.

"What do you mean?"

Zay shakes her head, placing a hand on her stomach with a slow exhale. "Slade isn't answering his phone, Gunner, either."

Lip points a thumb behind him as I study her, conflicted about what to do. My heart is with her, staying and raising our babies together. But my head is with the Snakes. "We got the kids in the van outside. Where to, boss?"

Knowing the babies are safe is what helps me make this hardest decision of my life.

Pinching the bridge of my nose, I shake my head and pull Zay to my chest. "You take my girl and the kids to Sanction Falls. Remember the place?"

Lip nods quickly, dragging a hand down his face. "How're we supposed to get them across the border?"

"Talk to Sammy. His girlfriend works border patrol. She owes us." Pressing a kiss to Zay's head as she kisses my wounded shoulder. I could lose my life, risking it for a club I've despised forever. I'm the president of this division; I have to put an end to what has started.

Even if it means hurting my love in the process.

Grunting, I nod at Lip. "You take care of them. Protect those kids with your life."

"Peter isn't gonna like this," Lip says, inhaling sharply as he steps out of the way for someone to pass.

"That ain't my problem. We protect our own, and those girls are better off away from Dorian and her conniving fucking bullshit." Gritting my teeth, I keep my good hand on Zay's stomach. "I knew I didn't trust that cunt the moment I met her."

"We don't know if she's in on any of it. I just have a funny feeling in my belly," Zay says, placing her hand on mine. "And I couldn't leave without making you come with me."

Kissing those succulent lips, I cup the side of her face. "Baby, you know I can't. I gotta end this the only way I know how."

She scoffs. "War?"

My stomach spins at her molten gaze, but still, I don't release her stare and run my fingers through her wavy hair. "I'll come home to you, baby. I'll always come home to you."

"Just stay," she whispers.

"I'm gonna get Peter and meet you at Sanction Falls. Lip will fill you in on the way." Kissing her again. "It'll be our home. Me and you, baby. Our love will flourish, our life will change but it'll finally be complete. You, me, and our kids." Tears rise and fall from her eyes, spilling down her cheeks and dripping off onto my hand. "I love you, baby."

She sniffs, nodding. "Yeah, I love you, too."

Her soft lips explore mine with a growing urgency as I lose myself in her essence.

Lip touches my shoulder, getting a seething growl out of me for pulling me away from Zay. "Sorry, brother. But I think we gotta make you come with us. There's no way of telling what the hell is waiting for us on the other side of this. And if anything happens to those kids on my watch, I'll never forgive myself."

"And if I can't stop these fucks from getting to you, then I'll be to blame and I refuse to have that hanging on my shoulders. I gotta be with Peter and Slade," I tell him, gripping Zay's hand. "Who's with you?"

"Skeet. Everyone else is heading to Peter's," Zay says, fixing the zipper on the hoodie right to the top. "Come with me, babe. Please," she whispers.

I want to.

But I can't.

"Have I ever broken a promise to you?"

She hits my chest, making me wince and suck my teeth. "Stop trying to be Mr. Fix It. You're breaking. Falling apart at the seams and all you want to do is fix the nightmare we're living. But you don't have to do that. You don't have to fix everything when you have people who need you. Be the family man you've been the past three years. Where is *he* all of a sudden?"

"He's left at the cabin trying to put the pieces together on why the fuck we were attacked!"

She huffs, breathing quickly as more tears shimmer in her eyes. "Come with me, Riggsy. Come with your sons."

Those words stab me, lodging a knife right through my heart. But I have to go. When this is all over, she'll understand.

Looking at Lip, I nod my head slightly, hoping he'll get the message.

Kissing her one last time before pushing her to Lip, I watch as she screams, wailing at me to go with her. I freeze, unable to will my body to go to her. My loyalty to this club stops me. Holds me back like the devil has a hand on my shoulder.

Lip doesn't budge this time. He lifts her through her slaps and punches, carrying her out of the hospital to wherever the van is parked. Her screams don't quiet down even when the doors shut.

While I'm left standing here wondering if the decision to save my brother was the right decision. Or if I should have said fuck it and protected my woman and sons.

I want to put an end to this, no matter where my heart is. I need to put an end to this madness before it consumes us all.

Some day soon all of this will be a horrid memory we look back on and see how far we've come.

All of this will be nothing but a nightmare we finally awoke from.

But for now, we're living in this, witnessing our loving family falling apart.

And I'm clueless about how to put the pieces back together.

Slade

The first time I cut myself was the first time anxiety coursed through me. It took over and became me. I just wanted it to stop. So I sliced my wrist and it felt better. I wasn't abandoned anymore; my soul was freeing my body as blood dripped from me.

I continued to cut myself for years after that. A cry for attention sometimes, other times it was to focus my anxiety on something other than my overthinking and racing mind.

And right now, I can feel my switchblade in my back pocket just aching to be freed so it can slice through my skin for the first time in over ten years.

Peter's been quiet for the past fifteen minutes as Adam is on the phone with someone. Mama Rosa sits there staring at him in the hopes he'll look up from the papers in front of him. But he doesn't. His focus is on his wife's name and the words that still hang in the air like a thick fog choking us all. *Oh, but she is.*

I lean forward with the intent to comfort Peter when The Ghost looks up at me with thinned eyes. "Don't you think of doing anything stupid."

I put my hands up in surrender, only wanting to place a hand on Peter's shoulder to comfort him. "Wasn't gonna."

Before Adam has the chance to hang up the phone, I hear it, just on the edge of my perception. The roar of an engine I know all too well.

Kicking Peter's foot under the table, he blinks his blue eyes at me; tears brimming his lashes. "Listen," I whisper.

His eyes shift again to the door, hearing that sound that snatches our breaths, leaving us hopeful. He sits up straighter, wiping his nose on his sleeve. "Adam, if you don't leave right fucking now, you're a dead man."

The way Adam's eyes widen for a moment before he says something quietly—I think that's when Adam hears it, too. The roar of the engine grows louder. He snaps his fingers at the masked men, waving his hand flippantly. "Go check it out, will you?"

"Adam—" The Ghost is cut off when shots fire.

Mama Rosa gasps, lifting her arms to protect herself. "God save us all."

One.

Two.

Three shots before blood-curdling screams blast through the area. *War wages on.*

The Ghost stiffens, reaching for his gun tucked into his jeans. "Adam, you're the fucker who came up with this plan, but that doesn't mean I gotta follow it. Now you better end whatever games you're playing because—"

The front door is kicked open and Riggs walks in with blood splattered on his face and exposed chest. He does not look fucking happy.

Peter jolts from his seat, eyebrows furrowed. "Riggs! Oh, my God! I thought you were dead."

"I'm good, kid. I'm good."

Riggs's right arm is in a sling holding a gun, the other has a fist full of Dorian's hair, dragging her through the hallway to us with a gleam of terror shooting from her gaze. "Cunt," he grumbles as he tugs her forward.

Gunner and his men walk in after him, guns raised high. They yell at the masked men around us, threatening to shoot if they don't surrender. The power Riggs yields, the brute strength to come in here guns blazing, while all of us surrendered in fear of what The Ghost would do. This is why Riggs is our president. This is why we listen when he speaks, why we agree with his authority.

This is why I stay.

The Ghost drops his weapons, raises his hands, and gulps when he sees Riggs like he's the goddamn chosen one to save us all.

Riggs tosses Dorian on the ground and takes the gun from his hand in the sling. "Now, before I start killing more people, why don't we get down to what the fuck is going on, hmm?"

Adam puffs out his chest, hands raised at his sides. "What's there to discuss, brother?"

"A lot," Peter hisses, looking at his wife crying softly on her hands and knees. "For starters, why the fuck this bitch of a wife of mine has been lying to me for over three goddamn years?!"

Dorian sobs, hands pressed to the hardwood floors. "I'm sorry."

"Shove it up your fucking ass," Peter growls, looking over at Allistair holding a gun out to Peter, then to me.

Adam chuckles, folding his arms across his chest. "Where's *my wife*, Riggs?"

A sinister expression devoid of any sympathy spreads to Riggs's face. "Safe."

"Think we need to discuss why the fuck you blew up my home, then tried to kill my son, Adam," Mama Rosa says. "This wasn't part of the deal—"

"You knew?" Riggs bellows, holding the gun steady and aimed at Dorian.

I rise, stepping back to stand beside Riggs and keep my eyes peeled on the men on their knees with their hands locked behind their heads—dumb ass masks still covering their faces. "Think you also need to explain why Zay said she saw you dragging someone with a Snakes cut out of the cabin."

Adam flares his nostrils, glaring back at The Ghost. "You guys have too many people watching your back. They spotted us coming a mile away and I had to change plans before we orchestrated today's—"

"Who was it?" Riggs interrupts The Ghost, still keeping his gaze locked on Adam's.

Adam lifts a shoulder, shaking his head. "New prospect. The dude who started last week. Wasn't part of the plan. I swear it."

"What was the plan, Adam? Hmm? 'Cause how I see it, you tried to kill Riggs and your pregnant wife, then blew up the one place all the women we spent years saving lived—and for what? Huh? So you can show us that you're top dog? That Daddy trusted you out of all of his sons? Daddy's fucking dead. We're supposed to be ending his bullshit and stopping the trafficking, but here you are trying to run it?" The veins in Peter's neck bulge, spittle forming at the corner of his mouth. "Tell me one fucking thing, why now? Of all the times you could have done this, why the fuck *now*?"

Adam's eyebrows furrow, pulling the chair out and slouching into it. "Because The Boss said if I didn't act now and expose the truth, then he'd take Zay as his pet. He didn't care if she was pregnant. He'd use her like he used all the girls coming in and out of his dungeon. I couldn't fucking have that."

"So instead of coming to us with this bullshit, you tried to take it into your own hands and destroy this family?" Riggs yells, face a burning red.

"Yes," Adam says through clenched teeth.

The tension in this room is thick enough to touch. There is so much unraveling, so much for me to take in. My mind recoils in horror as I realize this plan was set in motion before anyone ever knew about Dorion or The Ghost. Daddy Donnelly's plan to take over the trafficking business started years ago, and now, his plan is still in motion from his minions who took the bait.

Peter drags a hand down his face, wiping the spittle from his mouth before he looks down at his wife. "And you? What fucking role did you have in all this aside from fucking me over *again?*"

Dorian doesn't answer right away, she sniffs, whimpering before Riggs pushes the nozzle of the gun onto the back of her head. "He asked you a question, be a fucking doll and answer it, wouldja?" Riggs growls.

Dorian lifts her head slowly, looking up at Peter as the gun shakes in his hand. He wouldn't kill her, I know him well enough that even when he's upset or betrayed about something, he wouldn't stoop that low. They have children, a marriage. Dorian screwed him three days to Sunday, but she's still the love of his life.

"M-my father has been using Gray and I for his business since we were eighteen. We'd meet girls or guys and lure them to an apartment in the city, drug them, and let my father's men do whatever they did…I got out when I graduated from law school and met Erin—"

"Yet here you are," Peter interrupts her, wiping the falling tear from his cheek.

She whimpers again, looking down at the ground. "When everything happened three years ago, it was supposed to be the end of it. I was supposed to stay away from you and hope that things would settle down. But I got pregnant and things changed. My punishment for messing with the son of the man he's been trying to escape was to get back into the business."

I scoff, looking down at her as rage churns in my stomach. "So all these years of pretending you wanted to save these women, men, and fucking children, Dorian, was a lie? You fucking let them slip through your fingers and let these people get tortured, mutilated, raped! My fucking girlfriend was one of these women, you fucking cunt!"

She sobs, shaking her head as Peter gives her an eerie motionless glare, as if he has no idea who this woman is anymore. "You don't understand the power my father has."

"I met the fucking guy, he had a hissy fit over the way his fucking steak was cooked. You're telling me, *that* guy is the one running the show? The one that my daddy worked alongside with my uncle?" Peter snaps, nostrils flaring.

"Yes," she whispers.

Thousands of bugs are crawling beneath my skin, filling my skull with the buzzing. Everything is unraveling. Everything is happening.

And yet. No one is doing anything.

She's just talking, right?

Everything spewing from her plump lips are just words that have no meaning to them.

Yet everything she's saying means too much for my stomach to take.

Peter looks at Mama Rosa right when the doorbell rings for no reason since the door is wide open. Feet slap toward us, but I'm too frightened to turn around. Too manic to know what the fuck is about to happen.

But Riggs does with a slight tilt of his head. And that's when I meet Dorian's father for the first time. "Evening, everyone. Seems like we have a lot to discuss."

Riggs keeps the gun pointed at Dorian's head, smirking. "You got two seconds to speak before I put a bullet in your daughter's head."

Damien Glass laughs, unbuttoning his suit jacket, and takes a seat at the table next to Mama Rosa. "You don't even offer the man a drink before spilling your threats. Mmm, you're just like your father."

"I'm nothing like my daddy," Riggs curses, pushing the gun to Dorian's head.

Damien lifts a hand, nodding as he takes in the room. "All right, all right. No jokes."

Riggs and I are standing side by side, Gunner and his men are spread out around us, guns held tightly in their hands as the masked men remain on their knees before them. Adam, Mama Rosa, and Damien sit at the table as The Ghost still stands, baffled, by the island.

The atmosphere is heavy with unspoken words.

Secrets.

Lies.

Betrayal.

And the only thing we can do is stand here and wait until it all unravels and we're left vulnerable to the truth.

Zay

What a shitshow of a fucking day today turned out to be.

Last night, Adam kissed me sweetly, showered with me, and told me he would burn down the world if anyone tried to hurt me.

This morning, after I kissed him goodbye, Riggs held my hand to the truck and something told me to look back at Adam. When I did, he gripped the door frame with a wolfish grin, watching us with that long blonde hair and a pair of sweatpants low on his hips. He watched us knowing what was to come.

Knowing the happiness I finally achieved, would be for naught.

My hands are clenched in fists on my lap as I stare out the window. Trees whip by, fresh snow beginning to coat the naked branches. Riggs should be with me, holding my hand and reassuring our son and nieces that everything is going to be okay.

But he isn't here and it won't be okay.

I have a shitty fucking feeling about how today is going to play out and the longer I let my mind wander, the more I know it won't turn out the way I want it to.

Another tear rolls down my cheek right as Lip sighs softly, reaching back to tap my knee from the driver's seat. "It'll be okay, Zay. Riggs'll end this bullshit and come home, you'll see."

That's what Skeet said when Lip forced me into the van at the hospital.

But that uneasy, funny buzzing in my belly just won't go away.

Glancing back, Carter and the girls are all asleep; mouths ajar, head lolled forward. Peace in a time of chaos.

"I want to call Adam."

Skeet shoots his gaze back at me from the passenger's seat while Lip finds my gaze in the rearview mirror. "After what that fucker's done, you want to talk to him?"

"Yes," I say softly, letting tears spill over. "Just give me my phone, Lip. You already pulled me away from Riggs, the least you can do is let me talk to my husband and find out why he's ruining our lives."

Lip and Skeet share a look before Skeet tilts his head and puts his hand out to Lip. The way my stomach is aching like thunder rolling in before a storm, this phone call won't be a good one.

And frankly, this entire day hasn't been a good one.

I was drugged.

I witnessed my husband tear our family apart.

I could lose the one man I never thought I'd need most in my life.

And the sad part is, I don't know how to do this without them.

With curses and grumbles, Lip digs in his pocket for the cell phone and hands it to me. "No funny business, Zay. Promise me that."

"What funny business would I possibly do, huh? I'm not in on this like that bitch, Dorian. I love my family and want nothing more than for all of us to get out of this nightmare and back to a time when we didn't have to look over our shoulders. Haven't we suffered enough?"

Skeet nods, tapping Lip's arm. "We don't got anything more to lose than we've already lost. We joined this club to better ourselves and those we love. Instead, we got lost along the way." He turns to look back at me. "That kid is the son of our president and you're his old lady—those girls belong to the VP of this club. There ain't nothing we wouldn't do to protect you. We took an oath as Snakes members to keep our brothers and their kin safe. And that's exactly what we're gonna do, Miss Zay. So call Adam, call Riggs, call whoever you need to. We'll always be here for you."

Skeet is the only one who was always nice to me. Even when I was first introduced to the Snakes, he always made sure to remind me nothing would happen to me. Even when things were fucked, even now when they're beyond salvageable, he reassures.

"Do you think we can stop somewhere? I gotta pee," I say, clutching my phone in hand.

Lip nods, looking in his blind spot before taking the next exit.

We're in the middle of nowhere with barely any cars on the road and pull up to an empty gas station that appears abandoned from the outside. But I need a minute to breathe without people around me.

He kills the engine, inhaling softly. "I'll go in with you, okay?"

Turning back, the kids are still asleep looking so sound and totally oblivious to the mayhem around them. "Yeah, I won't be more than a minute."

My feet move faster than I can register and I'm smiling at the cashier asking for the bathroom key before everything shoots into focus. Lip comes in behind me, taking some snacks and drinks from the shelves, looking over at me as I make my way to the bathroom at the back.

I don't actually have to pee, I just wanted to be alone when I made the call.

Unlocking my phone, I'm about to find Adam's name on my favorite list, but my thumb hovers over the app, staring at the smiling picture of the three of us from last summer. Riggs has his arm around my neck, licking my cheek, and Adam is kissing my head. It's us, beautiful, sexual…happy. A picture that we have framed and sits on our mantle in the living room. It's us forever, unforgiving.

Just us.

Now, where the hell do we lie? Adam is a conniving asshole who broke us without warning. Riggs might end up dead because of all of this. And me? I'm about to give birth to a baby I don't even know who fathered it. All the while raising my son and maybe my nieces because who the fuck knows what'll happen to Peter. I warned Dorian when Rosa was born that if she ever fucked us, then I would take her daughter away from the life. And I'm doing one better now, I'm taking her *daughters* away to live a life in peace without being surrounded by danger.

Tapping Adam's name, the phone trills, leaving me more anxious than I was to tell them about the pregnancy. We said we'd discuss it before it happened, but it did and I was petrified at what they would say. I knew Riggs would be happy, he wanted to fill me with babies for a while. But Adam was the loose canon. He wasn't keen on our setup, but he loved me and that's what mattered. But having a baby in all of it...

My stomach churns, my head throbs, and my fucking hands are shaking.

Adam answers the call with a heavy breath.

"Adam?" I say quietly, looking at my reflection in the mirror as tears instantly brim my lashes.

"Hi," he says, groaning softly.

Silence consumes the entirety of this call, but I sniff and that's when I hear the grunt that throws me into overdrive. *Riggs.*

"What the fuck is going on?" I ask, turning away from the mirror. "What did you get us into, Adam?"

He sucks his teeth, growling softly. "I'd be able to tell you if a fucking gun wasn't pressed into my goddamn neck."

"It's either that or your fucking dick," Riggs barks, causing Adam to groan again. He must be pressing the gun down harder.

"I have a fucking plan that wasn't supposed to go down this way, but shit hit the fan this morning when you guys went to pick up Carter and I had no fucking choice, babe. I swear it. It was either I do this or—"

"Bullshit!" Peter yells in the distance.

Adam groans again, coughing slightly. "It's not."

Peter shrieks. "You put our brother in the hospital, drugged Zaynab, and put all those kids at risk—"

"That...fuck, can I please get two fucking seconds on the phone with my wife?" Adam shouts before Riggs growls in the background. "She is still my wife, Riggs. No matter what bullshit possessiveness you have on her—"

"Not for fucking long, I promise you that," Riggs says before the phone clatters, and Adam strains and argues for him to let go of him.

I turn back around and wipe the tears from my eyes, trying to picture them and where they could be. Are they at the clubhouse? At Peter's?

Where's Slade?

Who else is in the room with them?

"Baby?" Riggs' husky voice comes through the speaker and a smile instantly spreads to my face. "You okay?"

Sniffing, I nod, adjusting the phone to the other ear as I exhale slowly and hold onto my stomach. "Yeah…talk to me."

"Fuck," Adam grumbles in the background, the sound of water turning on fills the quiet. "You didn't have to break my fucking nose, asshole."

"Would you rather I break your jaw instead?" Riggs says sarcastically. "You're in the mood to play games today, huh?"

"Fuck off," Adam mumbles, wincing.

"Can someone fucking talk to me, please?" The door to the bathroom jolts, Lip opens it slightly to peer inside. *I'm okay*, I mouth, and he keeps it ajar, standing guard.

"I'll explain everything to you soon, sunshine. Once this shit is settled, I'll tell you everything." Riggs cocks the gun again when the water shuts off, clearing his throat. "As of right now, I don't know fuck all. Keep your phone off so no one traces it. I'll call you every hour on the hour. If it's not me, it'll be Slade. But you'll hear from me, baby. And I'll come home to you. I promise."

Everyone is making promises to me today and half of them mean jack shit.

"Can I talk to my wife alone for a minute?" Adam asks—he calls me *his wife* to Riggs as a power move. Something he holds over him because it's something Riggs doesn't have.

A sinister laugh leaves Riggs, a laugh Adam knows all too well because he whimpers, pleading with him. "Please, Riggs. *Please.* You guys can leave— you, Peter, and Slade—you can go wherever you're taking Zay. I love her to fucking death, but if me having a minute to talk to her alone means giving her up so she can be safe, then I will. I'll give her to you and know she'll be protected from this chaos. But please, just give me one more minute. Just one."

Riggs grunts softly, clicking his tongue. "You'd give her up for this fucker?"

"I don't have a choice," Adam whispers, sniffling.

"Everyone has a choice." My face reddens, and dizziness comes over me. I haven't taken it easy since this morning, and this baby is taking all my energy. If I don't relax, I might pass out and wake up in a hospital bed.

"I didn't, Zay. I *really* didn't."

Sobs leave me as I keep a hand on my belly and try to steady myself on my feet. Lip comes in but I wave him off, shaking my head. "I'm fine," I whisper.

"You're swaying and you look pale, Zay—"

"I said I'm fine," I growl out.

Riggs sighs, grumbling softly. "One fucking minute. And I'm outside this door."

A door slams, making Adam wince again before he breathes softly into the receiver. "Babe?"

This weight pushes down on my shoulders, as a tumble of nausea storms through me. "Adam, why did you agree to this?"

A beat passes before the sink turns on again and he whimpers softly. "This was set in motion for years. The man I work for—he's the man who Daddy was in contact with. The man who promised him he'd give us protection and let Daddy take over. But things took a turn when Lillian fucked with the club and Daddy was put in prison—"

"Why now, then? Why break us apart now?"

He sighs, sniffs, and clears his throat. "Because…every girl we don't save is a percentage given to the club. Riggs tried to get us out of this life and fuck, it was hard to hide this from everyone. But this is how the club makes what it makes. Every month an anonymous donation is made to the club for our contribution. And our contribution is turning a blind eye on a few of the women. Dorian…she helps find the girls. Gray and Bells have tried to get her out. They tried to infiltrate two months ago, but I stopped it. I fucking had to, babe. I wish I didn't, but if I left then shit would fucking explode and…I will not let anything happen to you."

Everything closes in, and I gasp, choking back a sob. The man I've been married to for almost six years has been running this disgusting business right in front of me and I didn't notice. He's been the devil, not Riggs. Not the man who opened my eyes during our first stay at the cabin.

No, the devil has blue eyes and blonde fucking hair.

"You're a monster."

"No, babe, no. I'm not. I work for a fucking monster and I'm in too fucking deep to get out of it," he huffs, sniffing with a wince. "I'm sorry, okay? I love you so fucking much. From the moment you smiled at me, I knew you'd be mine. Even when Peter fucked you, you were mine. Even when we agreed to this thing with Riggs, you still belong to me. Even when—"

He pauses, expelling a breath when a door creaks open. "Babe, if I didn't do this. If I didn't make it look like we were taken—drugging you—the fucker I work for was going to take *you*. That was the endgame. That's why I did this now. That's why I killed Gray and one of the prospects. She knew too much and threatened to out us—but we've been outed already. The Ghost wanted nothing more than to get his girlfriend back and he knew Mama Rosa had something to do with it. He blew up the sanctuary, he orchestrated this plan…I just went along with it." He sobs softly, lowering his voice. "You're my fucking life, Zay. I couldn't let him take you and sell you on the black market."

Lip has his eyes locked on mine, studying me as I listen to the words leaving a man I trusted wholeheartedly.

And now I don't know what to believe anymore.

Would someone have taken a pregnant woman to fuck over the club? Or is Adam so fucked he'll say anything to look like the victim?

"What about all those other girls you let that happen to? You don't think they have someone at home who loves them as much as you say you love me?"

Silence spreads, making my skin crawl.

I glance over at Lip and he lifts a shoulder, a sympathetic look on his bearded face. "Tell me, Adam. If I meant so much to you, why didn't you tell me so we'd be prepared? So we'd get the kids to a safe place, away from this life."

"If I told you and prepared, they'd know. They listen to everything. They'd kill you the second you tried to escape."

They know what the ins and outs of the club are. They know the moves before they do them…all this time the Snakes thought they were safe, but they were a target waiting to be hit.

They listen to everything.

"Adam," I whisper, crying. "You broke us."

"I know."

"You broke us for power and money."

"I know."

Wiping my tears, I find my face in the reflection of the mirror. "You chose this life and in turn lost everything. But I choose to move on, away from this life. You'll never see Carter or your nieces again. And you'll never meet your unborn son. You, Adam, are nothing to me."

He's sobbing, wincing after every sniff. But it's deserved. Fuck, so much more is deserved but taking the knife he shoved into my back and stabbing him with it feels just a little bit better. "Daddy would kill me if I stopped."

"How I see things, you're already dead."

I hang up the phone and growl, punching the mirror in front of me. Pieces of it flake off, scattering the sink below it. Cracks spread out like vines, distorting my reflection.

The last thing I remember before turning to Lip and marching out of the bathroom is the relief that spreads through me. The life I once knew has now come undone.

Slade

Adam and Riggs left for the washroom about fifteen minutes ago. The sound of arguing spreads through the house, making an unease rise even higher in me. This doom lingers in the shadows, waiting for the right moment to strike, but it seems like everyone at this table is mute, speechless to this so-called "cause" they're after.

Dorian sniffles, sitting back on her heels but keeping her gaze locked on the floor. I've known Peter to be ruthless, to have had a bad streak, and close to walking in the same footsteps as his father. Witnessing his wife betray him like this, the gun shaking in his hand, I do not doubt in my mind I might have to talk him over the edge before he does something he'll regret.

"This is fucking bullshit," he grumbles, looking at Mama Rosa. "When will this bullshit end?"

Mama Rosa smiles, folding her arms as she sits back in her seat. "That's what I was trying to do, but Mr. Glass has other plans."

"It's a multimillion-dollar business, why would I transfer it over to you so you can put an end to it?" Damien laughs, taking a cigar from his inside pocket.

"That's why this whole thing is happening so that you would transfer it over, Damien—"

"Change of plans, Rosa," he chides, looking at Dorian on the floor. "A plan my daughter came up with, actually."

Peter growls softly, scowling down at her. "Look at me." She doesn't move. "I said *look at me!*" Dorian's attention lifts, finding Peter's wet, blue eyes. "You are no longer under my protection—"

She cries. "Peter, I'm sorry. I—"

"Don't you fucking interrupt me!" he shouts, crouching down and holding the gun to her chin. "If you weren't the mother to my fucking kids I wouldn't think twice about putting a bullet between your fucking eyes."

"I wouldn't do that if I were you," Damien interrupts in a sing-songy way. Peter glares over his shoulder at him, huffing. "I have someone watching your kids, someone in deep with me but pretending to be one of you."

My attention shoots to Peter and I immediately take my phone, calling Zay.

Lifting the gun to Damien, I grit my teeth. "Who is it?"

"Someone who's in with Daddy Donnelly, someone who's been deep since the start."

Peter and I share a look right as Riggs and Adam come back into the kitchen; the gun in Riggs's hand trained on the back of Adam's head. Adam's nose is broken, blood still trickling out of it.

I can't think of anyone who was in deep before Daddy Donnelly was arrested. Lip and Judas were in when Crew was president, but when Riggs took the mantle and started changing shit, their loyalty never swerved from him.

As if on the same wavelength, Peter and I shoot each other a look. "Skeet," Peter and I say at the same time. He's the only one who was in deep and around since Daddy Donelly. How could I have missed that?

Riggs and I share a stare before Zay's sweet voice comes through the speaker. "Slade? Everything okay?"

"Where are you guys?" I demand, out of breath and frantic. "Are you with Skeet?"

"We stopped for gas. Lip and I are in the store—"

"Skeet's one of them, Zay. Get the kids and get the hell outta there!" I nearly shout into the receiver as Riggs snatches the phone from me, holding it to his ear.

"What? Slade, what the actual fuck is—"

"Baby, where's Lip?" Riggs asks, softening his voice for her as he always does.

The volume on my phone is loud enough that I can hear her as she sniffs, clearing her throat. "We're in line buying the kids some snacks and formula for Mina."

"Give him the phone," Riggs says, huffing as he shoves Adam into the seat I was in.

Shuffling spreads and then Lip's loud chewing comes on the speaker. "What's up?"

"Tell Skeet to use the washroom before taking off again, then haul ass somewhere and lay low until you hear from me—"

"Call Dutchess? They're a state over and always looking to help," Gunner calls out, gun still trained on the masked men on their knees.

Riggs nods, switching his gaze from Peter to the back of Adam's head, then Dorian on the floor. "Call Dutchess," he repeats, then looks at me. "I'm sending Slade to meet you. If anything happens, you call him. Understood?"

"Nothing will happen to those kiddos—or your old lady, pres. You have my word," Lip says, then hangs up.

Rolling my shoulders back, I nod even though he didn't give me orders and hold my gun out to Peter. "I have one on my bike. Take it and end this."

"With pleasure," Peter says, barring his teeth at Dorian.

Riggs dips his chin, pressing the barrel of the gun to Adam's head and huffs. "Where were we?"

Without waiting to see how this fucking craziness unfolds, I charge out the front door. My duty is to those kids, but first I need to swing home to get my woman.

If I'm taking them anywhere safe, she has to be there, too. Because godforbid anything were to happen to her, I'd never forgive myself. And I don't think I'd be able to stop cutting until all the life was drained from me.

Peter

My head is spinning, making me nauseous but I have to keep it together.

How could I have been so blind to the bullshit my wife was spewing right in front of me?

Riggs told me he didn't trust her—even after I got Rosa back, even after we got pregnant again with Sara…even recently when we had Mina. It's like my brother knew.

That sixth sense Zaynab has; that rumble in her belly.

Why didn't I ever see it?

"Care to share with me *your plan?*" My heart pulses angrily, glancing down at Adam as he sits there with a slight smugness to him, but sadness coats any of the cocky attitude he once had.

Talking to Zaynab will do that. She'll pull at your heartstrings and show you how horrible you can be. Believe me, I know it firsthand.

Damien smiles, leaning his elbows on the table as he clips and lights the cigar. "The plan was to blow up Maddison Gardens and have all the women transferred to a new facility—one of the vans would get lost, so to speak, and those women would be a major payout for us. Am I right, Rosa? I believe you hand-picked some of the women to be chosen, didn't you?"

"Are you fucked in the head, Mama?" Riggs snaps, still holding the gun to Adam's head like it's something he's been waiting to do for a long fucking time. "The hours on end we spent searching, risking our lives for these girls—and you were going to give it up like that?"

"I knew where the women were going, Riggs. I had it all all set up—look at the paperwork. The names are all on there. The van would be taken, yes, but the women would be saved before they were *taken*, so to speak. I just needed Damien to believe he won so that the business would be handed over to me and I could save the rest of the women he has locked in his dungeon."

I scoff, dropping onto the chair as I drag a hand down my face. "And this was all your idea, Dorian?"

"Yes," she says quietly, her head still downward facing.

"Why didn't you tell me?"

She sniffs, unable to look at me. "I couldn't."

"And why the fuck not?" Riggs growls, shoving the gun to the back of her head. "If you haven't noticed, your little stunt nearly killed me and drugged my pregnant woman—"

"Scarring our fucking kids!" I continue, glaring down at her. But she still doesn't move. "Show me some fucking respect and look at me while I'm talking to you, you fucking cunt!"

Her gray eyes lift, red and riddled with unfallen tears. "There's a reason I couldn't tell you. The same reason why my father isn't handing the business over to your mother anymore."

"Yeah? Why's that?" Gunner asks, just as intrigued as all of us are about this fucked-up day. "How I see things, there ain't nothing you can throw at us that we won't be able to handle."

She sniffs, looking at Damien, then Mama, and Adam, before meeting my eyes again. "Your father, Peter…he's the reason."

"And what could my daddy's reason for not ending this bullshit be? The bastard is dead," I say, gun trained on her again. She tenses up, unsure if I'll shoot her or not.

Part of me wants to. It would feel so fucking good to show her how much she hurt me.

But that other part of me that loves the living shit out of her, can't. She's the mother to my girls, my wife, and the only woman I've ever loved.

"He's…not," Mama says softly, inhaling sharply. "The devil doesn't die, Peter. He doesn't die."

Riggs and I shoot each other a look as the walls start to close in. Our daddy isn't dead but I held him while he took his last breath. We buried him and visited his grave before Dorian ripped my daughter away from me and Shyanne died. My daddy is dead and it was the only time I felt like I could breathe easily.

"You're lying," Riggs grits out, pushing the gun into Adam's head.

Adam grunts, wiping his nose with his hand. "She's not. Fucker can't die, it seems."

Daddy is alive.

If he's alive...we're all fucking...fucked.

***

Right before Dorian got pregnant with Mina, we went up to the cabin for the weekend to spend some time with my brothers, nephew, and Zaynab. The cabin had always been my favorite place. It was the house I recovered in after Zay tried to kill me, the place I escaped to a lot growing up. Mama never liked it up here because it reminded her of all the times Daddy forced her into hiding when shit hit the fan at the club. Yet when we were here, she asked constantly to move us to this place and away from the club. It never happened because it wasn't allowed.

I always loved nature, much more than Riggs ever had. The big fucker still had trouble getting in the lake without grimacing. He's a princess but refused to admit it.

Rosa ran toward the cabin, Sara waddling behind her and screaming—because that was what she did when she was excited. Rosa was the calm one, the lover of books and Barbies. Sara was the wild girl with dirt on her knees and a mane of hair always in disarray. She may be the mix of the two of us, but Sara was my personality twin whereas Rosa just looked like me with her mother's calm personality. And I liked it like that. My girls, taking the best pieces of me.

Riggs was out back swinging the axe down on some firewood. Sweat trickled down his scratched chest—something I knew Zaynab did. She was a stickler for using her claws. A shiver ran down my spine at the thought of when she did that to me.

I understood how wrong it was to force her to do the things we did and I appreciate her so much for her forgiveness. I was in a bad spot back then...shit, there are times I'm still in a bad spot...but Zaynab never judged me. She forgave me because she's a saint this world didn't deserve.

Zaynab walked out of the cabin with a beer in her hand; jean shorts that showed half of her ass and those long, beautiful legs. For a woman who's five foot two inches, her legs always looked like they went on for miles. The pink bikini top barely covered her breasts, hiding only her pebbled nipples from the chilled air.

Riggs wiped his brow and smiled, then shifted his attention to my girls running toward them. "Hey!" Taking a swig of beer, he set down the axe and crouched with a grunt, opening his arms to them.

Growing up, I never saw this life with my brother. He was the angry, stubborn biker who was destined to run this club while I was his right-hand man, fucking my way through the slew of Snake Biters like my father before me. I never expected to be where we ended up, with him and Adam, raising our kids with our women.

Yet there we were. Happy. So damn happy.

Zaynab smiled at me, twisting her hair into a knot on her head, and made her way over, wrapping her arms around my neck. "I thought you guys weren't coming anymore."

Dorian lifted a shoulder, dropping the baby bag on the Adirondack chair as I wheeled the luggage beside it. "I managed to get my work done in time to have a couple of days off. I might have to work on Sunday, but at least I'll have two full days of silence."

Zaynab squealed, taking Dorian's hand. "Good, I'm in the mood to drink." She pulled my wife into the house, leaving me and my brother alone with my girls.

Yanking off my t-shirt, I tucked it into the back of my jeans and took the axe from the tree stump. "How's it going up here?"

Riggs scrunched his nose at my girls, kissing their cheeks and pointing at the house. "Carter's in his room, go scare him."

Rosa giggled and Sara screamed again, charging for the house with her arms wide open, making me chuckle.

Riggs stood up straighter, grunting again as he straightened out his back. The guy was barely thirty-two and broken beyond repair. "It's going. Adam went into town for some groceries about an hour ago."

"How're you three doing?" I teased, smirking as I swung the axe down on the firewood, chopping it in half. "There are scratches all over you."

He laughed, smoothing out his chest with Zaynab's name tattooed on his left pectoral. "Zay and I went at it while Carter napped and Adam wasn't around. Nice to have her to myself once in a while."

"Must be something to get used to, huh? Living in a porno." I snickered, swinging the axe down on a new piece of wood. "I've had my fair share of threesomes, but never something like this."

Riggs dropped onto a chair and sipped his beer. "It's something, that's for sure."

Picking up on the annoyance in his gaze, the want to have Zaynab to himself ate away at him but there was an understanding that she loved her husband and couldn't leave him even if she loved Riggs, too. They agreed to this beautiful madness.

That love, however, wasn't enough.

He wanted it to be enough.

"You guys ever talk about the chance of shit happening?"

He spared me a glance before looking into the house at the commotion. "What do you mean?"

"What if you grow tired of this life and leave? What if Adam does? What if Zay falls pregnant and you have to deal with who the father might be?" Bringing the axe down, it snagged on the wood and I used my foot to hold it, pulling the axe out before he gave me an answer.

"We've talked about kids," he started, belching quietly. "But Zay doesn't want any—not now anyway. She loves Carter to bits. But Adam wants kids and tries to get her to stop taking her birth control all the time. Well...Zay is one stubborn woman."

"Don't I know it." I laughed, placing a new log on the stump. "Think we need to settle things with the clubhouse and all the danger our family could be in if some fucker tries to come back after we save the women. Once that shit is square, bringing more kids into this life is something to think about."

"We have eyes and ears everywhere. Before they can attack, we'd see them coming a mile away—" He stopped and smiled as Zay opened the door holding a tray with the kids running around her to get outside before she could. "Hey, baby."

The love they shared was something that grew during their time in the cabin. Something I watched on the cameras. How they'd look at each other when the other wasn't paying attention. How they'd steal glances and hesitate to go into each other's *rooms before they started fucking.*

But when the fucking happened, it happened everywhere. I shamefully loved watching the love story grow before my very eyes.

"We're gonna go swimming," she said, shimmying her shoulders as she leaned down to plant a kiss on his lips.

There are times I think of my afternoons with Zaynab. The times I forced her to have sex with me for the debt she owed to the club—the debt that wasn't hers, to begin with. I hate myself for it. Hate what I put her through, what I thought she deserved.

Zay was the only strong one out of everyone when life took a turn and nearly ended. She deserved all the praise anyone gave her. The praise of my burly big brother, and the praise my half-brother gave no matter what she did.

Taking my attention away from her, the sound of an engine moved through the silence. Riggs's truck pulled up, Adam smiling in the driver's seat. Sara loved him the most, always called him her prince. If only she could see him now.

He hopped out and grabbed the bags from the bed of the truck, carrying them over to us. "Hey," he said, nodding his head at Zay. "I got you cream soda. Took me three stores to find the stuff."

Zay squealed, clapping her hands before she took his face in her hands and kissed him. "Thank you, thank you, thank you."

Riggs laughed, picking Carter up and holding him tightly. "Ready to go swimming, tough guy?"

"Mommy says I don't have to wear a floaty if I stay in the sand." Carter had a bit of a lisp, but it was something I had when I was younger, too. Something Riggs will only poke fun at when I'm ossified drunk.

"Did she now?" Riggs arched an eyebrow, glancing at Zay.

"If he stays in the shallow end, yeah." She scrunched her nose and reached out for Carter. "C'mon, let's show these fuckers how it's done."

I laughed, loving how she never censored herself around the kids telling us that even though they shouldn't swear, keeping foul language away from them won't stop them from swearing, either. "Hey, my kids still need floaties!"

"In the shed," she yelled, running to the water with Carter cackling beside her.

They ran onto the dock, Zay saying something to Carter as she let go of his hand

and dropped her shorts, sprinting to the end of the dock and diving into the water. Carter squealed, clapping his hands, and waited until she surfaced, then took a running start and leaped into her arms.

Seeing her with my nephew was like seeing a mother with her son. It didn't matter if she didn't give birth to Carter, she looked at him as if he were her own. I just wonder if they were ever going to tell him the truth. Not that it mattered, Riggs was still there, and in the end, Zaynab would always be the woman who raised him. But Carter deserved to know his birth mother, didn't he?

Riggs grunted, pushing off of the chair as Adam retreated into the house and Dorian sat down to get the bathing suits on our girls. "Leave the wood a sec, I need you down at the water. Adam's hands started shaking again last week and he can't stop them. I need you to help me fix a plank on the dock."

"Is he okay?" Dorian asked, spraying sunscreen on Rosa, then Sara.

"Doctor's appointment is next week." Riggs shrugged, leaving his empty beer bottle on the floor by the fire pit, and jerked his head at me. "Get some trunks on, we'll be in the water."

He jogged out after Zaynab and Carter, his taut muscular back glistening with sweat in the afternoon sun. Carter's name in cursive letters resided on his lower back with birds surrounding it. It only occurred to me that he never got something for Shyanne, and Riggs was covered in tattoos dedicated to the people he loved. There's a swallow on his ribcage for me because I was obsessed with birds when I was a kid—much like his son. Riggs took me to a sanctuary, stealing Mama's car at fourteen just so I could see the exotic birds Daddy wouldn't bring us to. He had brass knuckles for Adam because of his shaking hands. Adam used to threaten us with them whenever we made fun of him. We still did.

Adam walked out of the cabin with a cooler filled with ice; beer bottles, Zay's cream soda, and juice were also buried in it. "Helping him with the dock?"

I nodded, dropping my jeans as Dorian tossed my bathing suit at me. "Says your hands are shaking again."

Adam shrugged, groaning as he carried the cooler to the dock. "I'm fine. Stress causes the shakes."

But something told me it wasn't just the stress. I just didn't know what yet.

Rosa and Sara ran after Adam, making him laugh. Sara grabbed onto the lanyard hanging from his shorts' pocket that held his keys and walked with him. Dorian chuckled at the sight, making a smile spread to my lips. I was gifted with the most perfect girls, the most beautiful wife, the funniest sister-in-law, and brothers I could trust with everything I had to give.

"She wouldn't shut up about Adam all morning," Dorian said, leaning back in the chair.

Tossing my boxers at her, she laughed softly, folding them in her lap as I got into my bathing suit. "Our girls love their family, baby. It sucks we don't see them enough."

Dorian chortled, pushing off the chair and tying her hair in a high ponytail. "We see them every weekend."

"I'm used to seeing my brothers every day, remember?"

She nodded, smiling. "Well, why don't we take the girls out of daycare and you guys can run your own daycare while I'm at work." She waggled her eyebrows, fixing her delicate red summer dress. "Wouldn't that be something? Tough bikers having a tea party."

I laughed, slapping her ass. "I don't need an excuse for a tea party—matter of fact, we'll have one right here by the fire after dinner."

"Oh, yeah?" We started for the water, our hands naturally threading by our sides. "You're telling me Riggs will be up for that?" She shook her head, coming down from a laugh. "This I'd love to see."

Adam set the cooler down by the chairs at the end of the dock and Dorian smiled at me, kissing my cheek before she headed for him and took a seat. He tapped her shoulder, saying something to her that made her smile falter, but she shook it away and whispered something in his ear. They weren't close by any means. Dorian wasn't close with anyone aside from Zay, Palmer, and her sister who was MIA. She tried with Riggs, but he was still cold toward her because of what happened two years ago.

But this was my family. People I'd do anything for.

With a cackle, I ran and dove off the dock, swinging my hair out of my face when I came up for air. Zay was swimming with Carter, instructing him to kick his legs as she held only his hands.

Coming here had always been relaxing. But Daddy loved the club more than he loved us, and we never stayed longer than we had to unless we were in trouble.

Riggs whistled at me and I swam over, winking at Zay as she stuck her tongue out at me. We've become friends again like at university. The laughing friends who found everything hilarious. We'd annoy everyone on April Fools Day with pranks we pulled at school. There was one time, she got Riggs so bad, I didn't think I'd ever recover from the punch to the gut. Dead fish in his pillow was not something he found funny—even though we did. But being with Zay without the incessant need to take my anger out on her by fucking her, was freeing. I missed who I was and didn't even know it.

When my feet touched the sand, I walked up the slope and got on my knees as Riggs jumped into the water, nails between his teeth. "This board here is loose. Figured we'd check the rest since we're at it."

My daughters were at the water's edge, dipping their toes in and giggling, when I'd glance over at them. My most precious gems. "Don't come in too deep, okay? No higher than your waist, babes."

"Yes, Daddy," Sara said in her growly voice that made her sound like the kid from The Shining.

Riggs chuckled, holding the nail in place as he hammered it in. "Kid's more and more like you every day."

"I didn't sound like that—"

"I have a video somewhere at the club of you at your third birthday party talking like Dracula," Riggs interrupted me, causing Zaynab to laugh.

"Oh, my God! I need that video, Riggsy," she said; the crinkle around her eyes made me smile. She aged so beautifully in the past nine years since we first met.

Shaking my head, I focused on helping my brother add as many nails as needed to the dock. Adam joined my girls when I was deep enough to get off my knees and walk. Then Riggs took over holding the panels as I hammered since I couldn't touch the ground anymore.

I hammered the last of the nails and looked around at the calm lake. "No one's up this summer, huh?"

He shook his head, lying on his stomach on the dock and folding his arms under his chin. "Clayton and his wife sold the place next door earlier this year. Gunner's charter bought it for their safehouse. Figured it would be best to be close to me in case I was needed."

Made sense at the time. Gunner became close with us since the shit at Mama's sanctuary. And I'm happy about it. Gunner is the only person aside from my brother I trusted with my life.

Jerking my head at the only other house on the lake. "And that one?"

Riggs adjusted his head on his arm and wrinkled his chin. "Think it's empty. Haven't seen a soul live there in at least ten years."

"Daddy!" Carter called, making Riggs grunt and pushing himself up off the dock. Carter kicked his legs, laughing as Zay held onto his belly. "I'm kicking!"

Riggs smiled, jumping in beside him and taking his son from Zay. "What do you say we swim deeper? Think we can still swim to Mommy when I can't touch the bottom?"

"Be careful, please," Zay said, swimming up to Adam and climbing onto his back.

Riggs winked, turning Carter so his little arms wrapped around his neck. "Let's go deep, yeah?"

As my family swam around me, my focus was on the seemingly abandoned house. The dusty windows; some covered in drapes, others boarded up from the winter. The grass around the property was overgrown, taking over the dock and the back porch.

But then I saw it. A light blinked on in one of the upstairs windows for a split second.

A face appeared. A shadow of a man that spread chills through me.

I thought I was seeing things.

Thought I was losing my mind.

The shape looked like my father. The man who died in my arms.

But it couldn't be him. It wouldn't be.

Yet there I was staring at the house, waiting for something to happen.

Nothing else did.

I wish I knew then what I knew now. That even the dead come back to life when you least expected it.

Slade

Pulling up to Maddison Gardens, the place is swarmed with ambulances, cops, and local TV stations trying to get the top story. Some of the motorcycle crews in the surrounding area we worked with when saving the people at the sanctuary are here, too.

Then I spot the vans Damien Glass spoke about parked nearby. *The plan was to blow up Maddison Gardens and have all the women transferred to a new facility—one of the vans would get lost, so to speak, and those women would be a major payout for us.* Fucking asshole.

I bring the bike to a stop the moment I spot Palmer talking to a cop. She looks distraught, sad. The same look she had when I first met her. Before I like to believe I brought life into those freckled cheeks.

She's nodding and answering questions as I approach, a couple of the other cops come up to me at the same time.

"This is a crime scene, sir. We have to ask you to leave—"

"My girl is right there. I'm not leaving until she's with me." I point her out and her whole demeanor shifts, brightening up when she sees me and finally lets the tears fall. "Darling! Come here!"

The cops turn around, hands hovering over their guns. I don't blame them. I'm tall as a tree, tattooed, wearing a cut, gun tucked in my jeans—I'm intimidating as fuck. The last thing they need is something to break loose.

This isn't the first time a cop would have pulled a gun out at me, either. One Friday afternoon when I was sixteen, my buddies decided to rob the liquor store because they wanted to get drunk after school. I was down, it had been a while since I stole from the stash at the group home. I got three bottles into my backpack before my buddy yelled *five-o*, and darted out of the store. There I was, caught red-handed holding the bottle as my backpack rested open at my feet. The young cop lifted his weapon, pointing it at me with shaking hands. Back then, I didn't care about life. I had nothing to lose so I tucked the bottle into the backpack and slung it over my shoulder, walking up to him. He looked petrified. Shit, I would've been, too. I wasn't as tatted up as I am now, but back then, I still had half a sleeve and the peace sign tattooed on my neck.

So seeing these cops in front of me holding onto their holsters is almost laughable.

Palmer jogs over, wiping her cheeks. "Slade." She ducks under the yellow tape and lunges at me, her chilled cheek pressing into mine. "I was so worried. Don't you leave me again! Don't you ever do that!" She hits my chest, keeping her body molded to mine. "Don't do that," she whispers.

Inhaling that perfect smell of roses and pine that only belongs to her, my grip around her tightens. "I'm here, darling. Right here, okay?"

Her sniffs sink my stomach. When she needed me the most, I was out fixing things I'm not entirely sure can be fixed anymore without blood being shed.

People have to die for this fuckery to get resolved.

"We have to go. I'll explain on the way." Kissing into her hair, I turn to a couple of bikers from the other gang nearby and step away from the cops.

"We were asking her questions—"

Standing upright, I glare at the cops. "And my girlfriend has answered enough. We have family at home who need us more right now. If you have any more questions, we'd be more than happy to answer them at the precinct."

The cop switches his gaze from me to Palmer, then his partner, and nods. "We have your information."

"Good." Taking Palmer's hand, I start marching toward my bike and stop, looking back at the bikers and waving them over.

"Slade—"

"Go to my bike, okay? I'll be there in a sec."

Three of the burly men nearly as huge as Riggs make their way over with arms as thick as my thighs, beards as long as a horse's tail, and one of them has blackout tattoos for sleeves.

The one in the middle folds his muscular arms in his leather jacket and jerks his head at me. "You're from which charter?"

"San Jose…but we deal with Richmond and here, too." Putting my hand out. "Slade, stand-in president while ours is injured."

The man looks at my hand, squeezing it slightly as he shakes it. "Tito. You got a firm grip there, Slade."

Cool, but I don't have time for niceties.

"Look, shit's going down and I was warned—can't say by who until I know for sure what the fuck is going on—but you can't let any of these girls leave the sanctuary, okay? My intel says one of the vans is gonna get hijacked and the girls will be sold into auction again. We *cannot* have that happen." My intense stare shifts from Tito to the other two men, feeling small for the first time in all my life. "Can I trust you?"

Tito nods, saying something to his men in Spanish, and claps my shoulder. "Riggs taught you well."

A burst of pride fills me, nodding as they break away, going under the yellow tape toward the vans. Cops shout orders, others try to stand in their way. But nothing is stopping this crew.

I don't have time to waste, I jog to my bike and grab a wad of Palmer's hair, tugging her head back so I could kiss her. Her cold lips warm against mine, her tongue easing into my mouth first. "You're safest with me, darling. I promise you."

She nods, stepping back from my bike so I can swing my leg over. Handing her my helmet, she puts an earbud in her ear before she puts it on. "Call me and explain, please?"

Finding my loose earbuds in my jean pocket, I stuff it in my ear and hit call on my phone before tucking it away. Not even one ring goes by before that glorious voice comes through. "Slade, what's going on?"

Revving the engine, I glance at what's left of Maddison Gardens; the broken building still smoking, yellow caution tape surrounding it, ambulances tending to those who were affected by the blast…the place is a ruin now. I wonder if it'll ever be saved.

Speeding down the road, I head north. It's all I know what to do right now. "Shit's fucked, Palmer. Dorian is in on this, her father, too. Goddamn Daddy Donnelly might still be alive and fucking Riggs put me in charge as president of this fucking club. Now we gotta find Zay and the kids because Skeet is involved in this, too."

Her heavy breaths fill my ears, soft whimpers come next. "Dorian's father?"

I nod, touching her arms that are wrapped around my stomach. "He orchestrated the explosion so that when they evacuated, everyone would get piled into vans and he'd take them…fuck, Adam is involved in this, too. He works for this goddamn asshole. This Damien Glass prick who's The Ghost's father, too."

She gasps behind me, her hold on me tightening as she chokes on a sob. "Did you say Damien Glass?"

"Dorian's father—"

"No," Palmer sobs, her head hitting my shoulders as her entire body shakes.

My mind is exploding with a million questions, but there's only one answer I can think of. An answer I need to hear from her lips before I slit his fucking throat. He's the man who took her. The man who raped her. The man who nearly killed her, isn't he?

Pulling over, I slide out from in front of her and toss her helmet off. "Tell me, darling. Tell me it's not true."

Her eyes glisten with tears, her mascara smudged under her eyes. "He's the man who took me, tortured me, and swore if he ever found me, he'd be sure everyone I loved would suffer until I bowed down and became his again."

Clenching my teeth, I growl and release her face, looking out at the snowy patches of wetness in the field before us. There is no way in hell Damien will ever touch her again. If he so much as looks her in direction, I'll take a page out of Gunner's books and remove his eyes with a rusted spoon.

"Do you trust me?"

She nods, swings her leg off the bike, and wraps her arms around my waist. "With everything that I am."

Kissing the crown of her head. "Good, because as of right now, Damien Glass just went to the top of my kill list. And I'm about to do things you will not be proud of, but darling, promise me you will always love me."

"I've heard and seen the things you've done, Slade. You're my person. No matter what gets in our way, my heart will always belong to you." Her eyes find mine in a faint smile. "I love you to death."

"The second this is over, I'm pumping you with babies and marrying you in the sand on a beach somewhere away from the snow and this life. This, I promise you." Kissing her lips, I take out my phone and call Zay, knowing we're going to have to meet somewhere secluded where no cameras or people can spot us.

Somewhere where not even The Ghost would know where to look, and I think I know the fucking place.

Slade

Palmer and I pull up to a motel a state over in the middle of nowhere. It's a motel I lived at for about a year until I turned nineteen where I found a pussy to fuck and a bed to keep me warm at night. But this place was cheap and with the job I had, it was all I could afford.

Palmer stays behind me as we approach a white van parked out front of room nine. Taking my gun from my pocket, I hold it steady as I knock and listen to the sounds of cheerful laughter from the kids. Tendrils of relief sweep through me. I don't know what I would've done with myself if something happened to them. Seeing Carter so scared this morning nearly broke me. But with the girls added to the mix, I'd be history.

The door creaks open and Lip sighs, opening it wider. "Hey, brother."

Tucking my gun away, I reach back for Palmer's hand and dip my chin at him. "Everyone good?"

He sighs, looking over his shoulder, and steps aside to let us in. "Things are fucked. I don't know what to do or who to trust. Goddamn Skeet, man. What the hell? I trusted that fucker with my life and he—fuck."

Palmer gets on her knees, opening her arms to the kids as they pile into her embrace. "Where's Zay?"

He drags a hand down his face and shakes his head. My body seizes, about to collapse when the bathroom door opens and she walks out, hands holding onto the wall for support. "Taking a piss. All this stress, brother, it can't be good for the baby."

I go for her, helping her to the bed. She's pale, sweat beads formed on her temples, but she forces her feelings as deep as she'll put them with a smile.

"You feeling okay?"

"I'm okay," is all she says before she sits with her back to the headboard and closes her eyes in a deep breath.

My gaze finds Palmer's and we're both concerned for her well-being and the baby's. We can't let anything bad come out of this day. Nothing scarring that will change our lives forever …we can't lose that baby.

"What now?" Lip asks as I take my phone from my back pocket and find Peter's number.

"I'm calling Peter and speaking with Riggs," I say, exhaling as my mind is bouncing everywhere. I need it to shut off for a sec. *Just for a second.*

Nodding quickly, I gaze at the beds and want so badly to rest my scattered head for a little. But when I hear Zay groan, I know I have to do what Riggs would do. Protect his family.

Sitting on the bed beside her, I touch her hand that's on her stomach and take notice of how her body shifts and her face scrunches. "Zay?"

Palmer is at my side, touching her stomach as well. "Zay, your stomach is hard. Are you…are you having contractions?"

Zay shakes her head quickly, opening her tear-ridden eyes and finding mine, then Palmer's. "I don't know," she whispers, tears spilling over. "I'm almost thirty-one weeks, this can't be good, right? The baby—it's too soon. What if—"

"Hey." Keeping my hand on hers, her body trembles under my touch. "It'll be okay."

Palmer and I share another glance, a concerned one. "It's probably Braxton hicks," Palmer suggests.

Frowning, I nod again and hit Peter's name in my contacts, waiting for him to answer.

Zay gets up from the bed, pacing the room as she breathes slowly, putting every nerve ending in my body on high alert. If she's in labor, there isn't a decent hospital for miles. And I'm not equipped to deliver a baby—let alone a premature one.

"Slade?" Peter answers, sniffling. "You get to them?"

"We're here now," I say, my eyes glued on Zay. "What are the next steps?"

"Meet with Dutchess. She lives by the border and will give you fake passports. One for each of you. You and Zay will be my girls' parents. Palmer and Lip, Carter's."

Makes sense. Palmer has bright orange hair, Lip has blonde, whereas Zay has milk chocolate colored hair in contrast with my dark blonde. The way I look, too, there's no denying people would stereotype me as a fuckboy with three kids and one on the way.

"What about…everything else?"

Peter sighs and Riggs grumbles in the background. "We're handling it. Turn off your phone from here on out. In an hour, turn it on and call me. If I don't answer, turn it back off and wait another hour to call back. If I don't answer again…then, tell my girls I love them."

With that, Peter hangs up, leaving the air too thick to breathe. But I have to. These children are my responsibility. My family. My woman and Zay will have my protection. And Lip, my brother helping me through this.

"And?" Zay asks. "Are they coming?"

Shaking my head, I lock my phone and flash her a reassuring grin. "Not yet. We're going to eat something, freshen up, then we're heading to Dutchess's house for passports."

Lip nods. "I'll head to the store across the street. Pick up some clothes and more diapers. Maybe get the kids some toys. Order us some pizza."

Palmer smiles, clapping her hands. "Hey guys, why don't we take a bath? Where do we stand on bubbles?"

"I love them!" Carter cheers.

"Bubbles!" Rosa giggles.

Sara screams, jumping in place. "Yay!"

I chuckle, lying back on the bed. My tense body slowly relaxes. It's been a fucking day. A shitty fucking day and it's only five in the afternoon. Palmer takes the kids into the bathroom, lifts the baby carrier with her, and shuts the door. Leaving me a second to breathe and Zay in a room with less stress than she already has. My woman is thoughtful like that.

Closing my eyes, I dig my palms into my sockets and breathe. Slowly, deeply. I breathe, releasing all the toxic chaos that fell into our laps today. I'm still uncertain how Peter and Riggs will handle their family crumbling before them; their mother, their half-brother, their father, Peter's wife! Everything is pure chaos.

And if things couldn't get any worse, Zay groans, gripping the corner of the dresser and winces. "Fuck," she mumbles, then gasps. "Oh, fuck!"

My eyes shoot open and I dart my gaze at her. She's looking down at her jeans; the crotch is soaked and her legs wobble. Her hazel eyes darken, staring at me with so much fear, my temples start to perspire, and my heart thumps in my throat. "Slade," she whimpers.

Everything happens in slow motion, the way the wetness pools at her feet, the grip she has on the edge of the dresser, and the way she lets out gasps…a shiver seeps through me, chilling my skin even though it's scorching like the desert sun.

I shoot out of bed and go for her, helping her sit in the desk chair. "Here." I hand her my phone. "Call Lip, tell him we're heading to the hospital, okay?"

"Slade, we can't have records—"

"I know the woman who works at the hospital in town—she used to be my foster mom," I interrupt her, smiling. "Let me tell Palmer."

My voice is calm, trying my hardest to ease the fear seeping from Zay's hazel eyes. "It'll be okay."

Knocking on the bathroom door, I open it to the kids splashing in the bath, making Palmer chuckle in a time of desperation and anxiety. She smiles, showing the kids not to live in fear. "Darling, we…um. Zay's water just broke."

Her eyes widen and her lips part, but nothing comes out. "Oh, my God."

"Lip will be back soon." Placing my gun on the sink. "You don't let anyone but him in, you understand me?"

She nods, her eyebrows pinched together.

"Where're you going, Uncle Slade?" Carter asks, wiping the suds from his chin.

"Just getting Mommy something to drink. We'll be back soon, okay?"

He nods, chuckling as Rosa makes a bubble beard on Sara's face.

Placing a kiss on Palmer's lips, I inhale her, savoring every bit of her essence.

"I love you."

"Slade," Palmer whispers, getting to her feet. "You stay with Zay, okay? Whatever it takes. Don't you let anything happen to her or that baby."

Kissing her once more, I nod, wanting to remember this moment before everything goes to shit.

***

I'm running with Zay in my arms through the emergency room, finding a nurse in the hallway. "She's—her water broke. She's not due for nine weeks."

The nurse stammers, nodding quickly and taking off running with me hot on her tail.

"Slade," Zay cries, burying her face in my neck. "I'm going to lose this baby. It's happening. And if I do, please don't tell Riggs or Peter until everything is settled. They don't need this stress on their conscience."

"You're not losing this fucking baby, Zay," I almost shout, stopping when the nurse does as she spits what I told her to the doctor—the one that was my foster mother for a few years.

The same woman I fucked in the dead of night before running away and never looking back. Angela's pale, aged face looks up, still as beautiful as the day she took me in, and when she spots me, the wrinkles in her brow crease. "Slade?"

My breathing wavers, ragged and gruff. But I hold Zay close to me. "My… wife is in labor. She's only thirty-one weeks—"

"I'll be thirty-one weeks on Friday." Zay sniffs, her arms tightening around my neck as she groans through another contraction.

"How far apart are her contractions?" Angela asks, speed walking to a room and opening the door, her dark brown hair billowing behind her.

I set Zay down and take off her coat. "I'm not sure. Not far off. Close like every three, four minutes."

"Okay, what's your name?" Angela asks, opening her chart.

"Samantha," Zay lies, sucking her teeth as she holds under her stomach. "Fucking Christ."

"Get her into a gown and I'll be back to check your cervix," she says to Zay, eyes darting to me before she steps out.

"Angela, wait—" I call out and she stops, looking over her shoulder. "We need this off the books...please."

With a heavy sigh, she nods her head once and closes the door for privacy. She was the only person I ever trusted, even though they ran a tight ship at the house, speaking with her was like entering a whole new world. They didn't let us watch a lot of TV or have cell phones. In her house, we read and learned. I liked learning late at night with her. We started by accident, too. Late one night while I was getting something to drink, she was in the kitchen, home from a night shift, and didn't know anyone was awake when she stepped out of the kitchen in nothing but her underwear. I didn't hesitate and fucked her raw on the island. Our little secret. Until it became our nightly ritual at three in the morning like clockwork bent on the island with me buried deep inside her.

Helping Zay out of her clothes, her stomach dropped significantly from this morning when I helped her get dressed. It's crazy how the tables have turned. How things have changed. How this day wants nothing more than to fuck us into submission.

She breathes again, taking my hand as she stands before me naked and rests her forehead on my chest. "Don't leave, please don't leave me to do this alone."

Kissing her hair, I hesitantly wrap my arms around her. "I won't, Zay. I'm right here, okay?"

As soon as she's in the hospital gown, my phone vibrates, reminding me that I didn't turn it off like I was told to do. Peter's name is on the screen. It hasn't been an hour, has it?

"Hello?"

Riggs's heavy breathing hits my ear and I squeeze my eyes shut. "Is she okay?"

"How did you—"

"Lip called." Riggs grunts. "Is she okay?"

"We're at the hospital—"

"No trace—"

"Don't worry, I have it covered," I interrupt him, sighing softly as Zay squirms on the bed, legs shooting open as another contraction hits. "She'll be okay. The baby will be okay. *Things* will be okay."

Riggs grumbles, sniffing. "You take care of my family, Slade. Raise them as your own."

"Riggs—"

"Things are ending today. I will goddamn guarantee it, but I don't know what will happen to me. I don't want my girl to hate me, but I want her to know I love her. Tell her that."

"She's right here—"

"No, just tell her." He hangs up, leaving me filled with more questions than answers.

Zay exhales slowly, looking up at me. She knows as well as I do. This day is just about to get that much worse.

Riggs

Placing the phone down, my heart hammers in my throat.

Zay is in labor.

My woman is suffering because of my family.

My woman has to be on the run because of my father.

My woman is alone because of *me*.

"What're we doing here, huh? Sitting around a table none of us wants to be at while my fucking girl is about to give birth to my son when she's—" I growl, catching Mama's eyes filling with tears. "This little fucking game you decided to play," I pause, nudging Adam's head. "Might make her lose the fucking baby who is far from ready to be born!"

Adam whimpers, crying softly. He's never been fit for this life. Never been able to rule with the big dogs. He'd do anything for Daddy's acceptance, but now, he's taken it too far.

"Riggs, sweetheart—"

"Shut the fuck up, Mama!" Peter screams. "You couldn't just put this shit to rest, huh? You couldn't just continue saving the people we were saving without thinking about money?" He huffs, roughly wiping his eyes. "So fucking selfish."

"It's not about the money," she says quietly. "If I didn't work with Damien—" Her face turns sour and she closes her eyes, I know hating herself for everything she's done behind our backs. "—they would've taken Zaynab. Her name is on the list."

She points to the papers in front of Adam and I shove his head aside so I can snatch them. Nothing makes sense. They're just names and numbers.

Some are highlighted, but most are not.

Adam reaches up, taking the papers from me, and sifting through them for the one with Zay's name, highlighted a different color than everyone else. "If I didn't jump on it now, Daddy would have taken her and sold her to people overseas. They pay extra for pregnant women."

Bile rises in my throat at the thought of something happening. My poor beautiful Zay who doesn't deserve anything I've ever given her.

My gaze shifts to Damien. "You're a disgusting prick."

He chuckles, puffing on his cigar. "A very rich one I might add."

Peter grips the top of Dorian's head and yanks it up. She yelps, trying to get to her feet. "Did you know about this?" A whimper escapes her and all it does is cause Peter to bring the gun under her chin. "Did. You. Know?"

She nods, a sob breaking free. "I told Gray and that's why she came to try and stop it."

"But he killed her," he says, keeping his gaze on Dorian as she looks at Adam.

"I had no choice." Adam glares at her. "It was your sister or my fucking wife."

Gunner clears his throat, letting the tension in the room fall silent. "Then where the fuck is Daddy Donnelly?"

Damien rises, fixing his blazer with a grin around the cigar. "He'll come when I call."

"Then fucking call," I growl out, lifting the gun from Adam's head to his face.

He chuckles. "As soon as I speak with my children—alone—I will."

Allistair steps forward, jerking his head at the back door. "Outside. And I'm coming with you."

Dorian sniffs, Peter's grip still in her hair. "I'm sorry, Peter. I am—"

"You're as good as dead to me. Don't you dare say my name or my daughters' names again. Do you understand me?" Peter says through barred teeth.

She's hysterical, thrashing in his grip to try and get loose. "You can't take them away from me! They're my children! Mina is still a baby, she needs me."

"They will *never* need you," he whisper-growls, shoving her toward the back door.

Her sobs are the last thing we hear before the door is shut and she collapses in The Ghost's arms. Peter tries to be strong, but when he looks at me, his lower lip wobbles, tears spilling over.

"Be strong, kid," I say, lowering the gun.

"Yeah," he says through a cry, dropping into the chair. "Fuck." He covers his face and sobs softly, his shoulders shaking.

Glaring at Mama as she sits there watching Peter sob as if she isn't partially to blame. "You happy now, Mama? You keep ruining this family."

"I'm sorry, Peter. I should have told you. But Damien…I couldn't let something happen to Zay." Mama gets up, rounds the table, and sits in front of Adam, putting her hand on Peter's arm. "Sweetie, look at me, okay?"

"Get your fucking hand off me," Peter says so calmly, goosebumps rise on my skin.

Mama sighs, looking at Adam. "Before you get mad at him. I told him to stay quiet. I told him to play along with everything because I didn't want Daddy to know how much Adam was on my side, trying to end this."

"When did you know he was alive?" I growl out, gripping the gun in my hand.

"Last year, right before Zay announced her pregnancy," Mama says, wiping her cheek. "Daddy had his eye on her since everything happened and you came home to me, but he stayed hidden."

"Who else knew?" Peter asks, sniffing.

Mama shakes her head, inhaling softly before Adam clears his throat. "Skeet and Judas."

Judas?

That two-timing bastard.

I growl, lowering the gun and heading to the backdoor. Fuckers think they can get away with a secret conversation, they have another thing coming.

"Dad, I warned you this would happen. I told you nothing gets past this club—"

"Shut up, Dorian!" Damien says through gritted teeth. "If you would have done what I asked three years ago and got in with the Snakes for intel, then got out we wouldn't be here playing these games. But we are and there's nothing I can do but let things play out. Once Daddy gets here, he can explain to his sons why they need to join us."

The Ghost scoffs, shoving his father. "You knew all I wanted was Lenora. You fucking knew I would burn this city down to find her. And you told me that Daddy Donnelly was the one who knew where she was, but when he died, all ties died with him. The only reason I worked with Mama Rosa was because I thought helping her would lead me to my girl. And all the fucking time she's been your pet? All this fucking time!"

A deep belly laugh leaves Damien, causing him to take a step back and shake his head. "I wasn't using her like you're thinking, Wilde."

"Then why the fuck haven't you told me!"

Damien inhales a sharp breath as I turn back to see Peter with his head still in his hands. I don't know how all of this will play out but I do know that my brother will be wifeless.

Adam, on the other hand, is staring right at me with furrowed brows. All this time he's been hiding this from us. Pretending to love us when he's been slowly inching a knife into our backs.

And as for myself, the pain is slowly returning. My shoulder throbs at the same beat as my pulse, and my wrist is stinging, aching for some more painkillers. But I need to be level-headed right now. Because I have no fucking idea what's around the corner anymore.

"I told him not to."

The Ghost shoots his attention to Dorian, his eyes wide with rage. "Why?"

With a sniff, Dorian curls her hair behind her ears and straightens her shoulders. "She brings in the most women, makes the most cash, and knows how to persuade the buyers. Lenora is our most valuable whore. I didn't think it was right to let her go when we needed her."

The Ghost doesn't hesitate, slapping Dorian across the face; its sound cascading and causing Peter to lift his head.

She holds her cheeks, eyes wet with tears when she looks up at him. "With that attitude, you'll never see her again."

"I swear to Christ, Dorian. You think your husband is upset? I wouldn't think twice about putting a bullet in you." He shoves her, grabbing her face.

"The only question is, which one of us will be the first to pull the fucking trigger?"

Damien laughs again like he's proud of his children. Proud of the chaos he created.

The sick fuck doesn't care about anything but himself.

"Daddy Donnelly will be here soon. Are we still good with the original plan?"

Dorian lifts a shoulder, keeping her eyes on The Ghost. "Ask Adam. He's going soft now that his brothers know about his involvement and that Zay is still on the list." She slaps her brother's hand away wiping the blood from her lip. "How far out is the van for pick up?"

"They found three hospitals in the vicinity of the gas station Skeet was picked up from," Damien says, looking down at his phone. "She'll be at the auction by this time tomorrow."

My blood boils, heating up my face and making my heart beat out of my chest, flopping out onto the floor. Like fuck they're taking my woman.

I act before my brain can register what I'm doing.

Shoving the back door open, I pull my gun out and shoot at Damien; the bullet skimming the side of his neck. Peter runs out behind me, gun held high. Adam stands at my side, face pale as blood leaks from between Damien's fingers pressed to his neck.

"What the fuck?" Dorian yells, looking back at me.

"You're fucking next, cunt!" I scream.

Damien sits up, bending one knee. "Take it you missed on purpose?" His voice is hoarse, trembling.

I cock the gun again, grunting as I crouch in front of him and press it to his sweaty temple. "Tell me which hospitals your men are going to. *Now.*"

Peter holds the gun to The Ghost, eyeing Dorian as blood is smeared on her chin. "You would let them do that to Zaynab? After everything, Dorian?"

Her eyes are downcast, ashamed of herself in the eyes of her husband. *Fucking bitch.*

"Judas picked up Skeet an hour ago. They went their separate ways. Call them and you'll get your answer," Damien says, his phone vibrating in his pocket.

Waving my gun at Allistair, he comes over, flicking his cigarette, and gets the phone from Damien's pocket. "Speak of the devil and he shall appear, huh?"

Daddy's name is on the screen.

A goddamn devil, alright.

Sliding my finger on the screen, I adjust it on my shoulder and flare my nostrils as his fucking voice comes to life. "Damien, my good man. Tell me, is it time yet?"

"Think it's about time you explain yourself a bit more, you goddamn bastard," I growl out, pressing the gun to Damien's head again. "And I want the truth, 'cause if you don't give me the truth in ten seconds, your boy, Damien, here, will get a bullet right between his fucking eyes."

Daddy laughs, *tsking* on the other end. "My Riggs, always the tough guy but never the smart one. Surprised my Petey didn't see this one coming a mile away…oh, that's right. Flash a little pussy at him and his brains go to mush."

"Where are you?" I ask, grunting as I rise into a standing position.

Then I hear it, the sound of the front door opening and footsteps hitting the hardwood floors in Peter's house. "Right behind you, son."

Lifting my head from my shoulder, the phone falls to the ground with a crack. I glance back and see Daddy smiling; a thick beard covers his face, hair is shaved to skin. Mama puts her hands on her mouth, elbows resting on the table, and stares at the man she's been trying to run from for over ten years.

And yet, here he is.

The whole family is back together for the last time.

Slade

Zay sobs, throwing her head back in a yell. "I can't do it! I can't! I want Riggs! Just please get me Riggs."

I have one of her legs lifted, while a nurse has the other. "You can do this, sweetheart. You're one of the strongest women I know. You can do this, okay? Push, c'mon, Zay. Push."

Angela glances up at me, hands between Zay's legs as her groans commence again and she pushes. I didn't mean to let her name slip, but I don't give two fucks right now. I'll answer questions later. If I know Angela, she'll want a reason as to why I want to cover up this delivery.

Angela takes a couple of her tools, keeping her focus between Zay's legs. "That's it. That's it. Keep pushing, keep pushing."

Zay screams, exhaling sharply, and stops pushing. "He's not ready to be born," she cries, leaning her head on my shoulder. "What if he doesn't make it? I can't lose him and Riggs. Haven't I suffered enough?"

A disturbing knot twists my insides, breaking me down piece by piece at every groan, moan, and sound that leaves Zay. She's right on every level. She didn't deserve this. Just like she didn't deserve anything life brought her.

But she's here and she's pulled through every single disaster that's ever been brought her way.

This is no different.

"You won't. This baby has a giant for a father. He'll come out stronger than you think."

She closes her eyes and lets air slip from her parted lips. "Okay. Okay."

Pressing a kiss to her sweaty forehead, I do the one thing I've been trying to avoid since she started pushing, and that is looking down.

But as Zay grips the bars on the side of the bed and braces herself for another big push, I look at her clean-shaven pussy filled with blood, and I smile.

"Zay, I see a head! Oh, my God!" I exclaim, adjusting her leg in my hands. "He's coming, keep pushing. Keep pushing."

As the baby comes out of her, I think of Palmer and how I'll be doing this with her one day. We'll be doing this as many times as my woman can handle it. And I can't fucking wait.

Emotions hit me like a Mack truck. I left her twice today when she needed me the most. I left her and vowed I never would. Vowed I'd protect her and I fucking left her alone. *Twice.*

But she knows, she always knows how much I adore her. How much I love her.

She knows.

With one more big push, the baby slides out of Zay, and Angela immediately gets to work. They wrap the baby and clean his mouth, tapping his back to get him to cry. Zay sits up, sniffling as she watches Angela tap the baby's back again.

No gasps. No breaths. No fucking movement.

Angela taps the baby's back harder, holding his head up. The baby's skin appears white, face devoid of expression. My heart is hammering, lodged in my throat and tears simmer in my eyes.

The walls close in as we watch and wait, painfully.

There's no telling what can happen.

There's no telling if he'll survive.

There's only hope...

Only. Hope.

With one more hard tap on his back, he gasps for a breath, causing Zay and I to sigh in relief. But she doesn't get to hold her baby yet.

Another doctor is on standby, preparing the incubator. Tubes and wires are being attached to the baby. Everything is happening so fast, my head spins. My breathing is erratic, but I have to keep it together. I can't lose it now.

I'll be strong, there will come a time when I can lose it and now is not that time.

It's the mantra of the day, isn't it?

Zay's cries breaks free and she grips the front of my shirt, pulling me to her. It snaps me out of my trance and my arms wrap around her. "He doesn't look real," she whispers.

Pressing a kiss to her neck, I smooth out her hair. "He's in the best hands. Angela's a great doctor."

"He's not going to make it." Zay sniffs, shaking her head. "I had a bad feeling in my belly about today when I woke up this morning. A bad fucking feeling."

Those words eat at me. Tear me apart in ways that nothing should. Zay's bad feelings always come true.

"Samantha? Slade?" Angela clears her throat, sitting in the chair between Zay's legs again.

Zay holds me tighter, her body trembling. I turn my head slightly, flashing Angela a meek grin. "No," Zay whispers.

"It's okay," I whisper back, nodding at Angela.

"The baby is attached to a breather and we've placed a feeding tube in him as well. I'm going to run some tests as soon as I finish stitching you up. I'll have more answers on how he's doing and how long we'll be here." She places a hand on Zay's knee. "You're lucky he's a big boy. Nearly five pounds. If he weren't, there might've been a different outcome today."

Tendrils of relief climb up my spine, sagging my body into Zay. "He'll be okay, see? He'll be okay, sweetheart."

Zay releases me slowly, looking at the other doctor as he and a nurse begin to move the baby out of the room. "Wait, where are you taking him?"

"He'll be in the NICU. Your husband is more than welcome to come with us." The nurse grins, moving the incubator out the door.

Glancing down at Zay, her eyes stay focused on them as they leave; tears streaming down her face. "I didn't even get to hold him," she says, lower lip quivering. Taking her hand, I kiss the back of it and she squeezes, wiping her cheeks. "Go with them!" she scoffs. "Don't worry about me. Stay with the baby."

"Zay—"

"Go!"

With a heavy sigh, I don't fight her on this. I know Zay will be on her feet as soon as the doctor is finished stitching her up. I made a promise to the Donnellys that I would protect them and their children. Yet, this stabbing ache is telling me to remain with Zay that leaving her might put her in danger. Nothing about today has been smooth sailing.

Opening the door, I look back and Zay is lying down, her hands covering her eyes as Angela stitches her up. There's no telling what the future holds, but I know one thing's for sure, I will dedicate my life to making sure Zay remains happy for the rest of her days.

Walking down the hallway, I reach for my phone and find Riggs's number, tapping it before I come to my senses and realize I'm adding more stress on his shoulders than he already has.

After two rings, he answers, huffing. "I told you we'd call—"

"It's a boy," I spit out, choking back a sob.

He groans, cursing under his breath. "Is she okay?"

"She's a champion. Pushed him out in four pushes." I sniff, stopping and dropping onto a chair. "He…he's so little. But the doctor said he's lucky he's a big boy. If not he wouldn't have…"

Riggs sniffs, remaining silent on the other end as shouts commence in the distance. I know he has to deal with whatever the fuck he's dealing with, but I think hearing about his woman and their baby is what matters most.

"I'm staying here with her, Riggs. Don't know how long the baby will be in an incubator. Could be a week, could be a month. I, uh, did some research while we waited for the doctor and—"

"Protect them with your life, you hear me? Raise him as your own. Make sure Zay never goes without."

He speaks like he's not coming back. Like this is the end of the line. I know there's so much to unravel, so much bullshit to square up, but he can't give up on his woman or his sons.

"Tell me, pres. Tell me this isn't goodbye."

He sniffs again, the shouting getting louder as if he's approaching them.

"Tell her I love her. I always have."

He hangs up, leaving the air around me so thick, I start gasping and claw at my neck for a decent breath of air.

A nurse comes to me, instructing me to relax, asking me what's wrong.

But that's the problem, isn't it? Everything is fucking wrong and this day can go fuck itself.

Peter

Riggs comes back to us, tears shimmering in his eyes as he holds the phone to his ear. I've never seen him so pale and distraught before. He doesn't want to be here doing this bullshit. He wants home, with his family. We both do. But we have a duty to our club. To the Snakes who we've dedicated our lives to before our families.

Yet our heart isn't in it anymore. I don't think we've been in it for a long time. Since our babies were born, I'm sure of it.

"Tell her I love her. I always have." He hangs up the phone and sniffs, tucking it into his pocket. "Can we get this fucking shit over with?"

"Who was that?" I ask, rising to my feet.

He flares his nostrils, shaking his head as he takes the gun from inside his sling. "Everything's good, kid. Everything fan-*fucking*-tastic."

"Was it Slade? Did Zaynab have the baby?" I press, eyebrows pinched together.

Adam leans forward, shaking his head with a sob. "Is the baby okay?"

Riggs ignores all of us and glares at Daddy as our father sits next to Mama, checking her out like he used to do growing up. How he'd eat her up no matter what time of day, no matter what outfit she had on, no matter how she felt. She had no choice but to succumb to his wicked ways.

"New plan," Riggs announces. "You let Peter walk outta here and we deal with whatever fucking crap you have going on. But he will *not* be part of it."

Stepping forward, I tug his arm "What? I'm not leaving you, Riggs."

His big blue eyes find mine; red and wet with welling tears. "You can and you will. You have a family to take care of."

Daddy laughs, sitting back in the chair with a groan. "This shithead can't even keep a fish alive, let alone children. Please—"

"I've done a pretty good fucking job the past three years, haven't I? Unlike you have our entire fucking lives!" I shout, staring down at the scum that decided to come back into our lives after all this fucking time.

"Me?" He places a hand on his heart, chuckling again. "I get the backlash when your mama is the one who walked out on you boys. Didn't you, my darling?" He runs his knuckles across her cheek, causing her to scour at him from under her lashes.

"And yet you did the same fucking thing, didn't you?"

He smiles at her, moving hair behind her ear. "Learn from the best, *mi amor*."

Damien sucks his teeth as he changes the hand towel on his neck to a fresh one—Riggs missed on purpose, but the graze is bleeding like a motherfucker. "Fine, Peter, you can leave. Then we'll get down to finishing this business."

"Damn, right we will," Gunner says, cracking open a fresh beer.

"I'm not leaving," I growl out, looking at Riggs, then back at Gunner. "I'm the fucking VP of this club, you can't make—"

"You're a goddamn father first and an uncle to my kids. Understood. They need you—"

"They need you, too, Riggs." I tilt my head to the side and sigh. "There's no fucking winning this game unless everyone is fucking dead."

He pulls me into a one-armed hug and lowers his voice. "That's the fucking plan." Pressing a kiss to my ear. "Go find Dutchess, send Lip to seek out Judas and Skeet. Stay with the kids and Palmer until Slade calls you with news."

"I can't leave," I whisper, my eyes bouncing from Mama to Daddy, and stopping on Adam. He stares at me with such pain like everything he's done wasn't what he wanted. And if I know Adam, it wasn't. But he's a follower. Always has been.

"You can," Riggs says, releasing me.

My being is frozen in place, watching as Riggs takes the keys from his pocket and hands them to me, clapping Allistair on the back and whispering something in his ear. Everything is in slow motion, the way Mama brushes

Daddy's hand away. How Wilde runs five fingers through his hair. Adam looking at me with tears streaming down his cheeks, and my wife—my cunt of a wife watching me with this look of betrayal in her gaze like all of this is my fucking fault.

But I meant every word of what I said, she'll never see our daughters again.

Riggs takes my chin and turns my head to his, snapping me out of the slow motion around me. "Allistair will ride behind you, got it?"

Words are at the tip of my tongue, but I can't speak. I can't voice the madness going on in my head.

But I see it. I'm screaming at my brother, telling him to tie everyone up and call the fucking cops to let them deal with these fuckers while we hightail it out of here.

But I don't move.

"Peter!" Riggs shouts, shoving me slightly. "Get on with it. Now."

Tears blur my vision as I stare at him and I know deep in my belly that this is the last time I'm ever going to see anyone in this room ever again. "Riggsy, I can't."

He grabs the back of my head, pressing his forehead to mine, and growls. "You're the only fucking one I trust, kid. The only one who can raise my babies right, take care of my Zay, and protect your girls."

"Riggs—"

"One for the road, brother." He knocks his forehead on mine with a forced grin. "Go on, now. You have a long drive ahead of you."

The ache builds, pressing hard on my chest as I stare at my big brother, knowing the ending is closer than he wants me to realize. But I see it. He'll be lying face-first in a pool of his own blood come nightfall.

My eyes find Dorian again and she looks away, tears rolling down her cheek. There isn't an ounce of regret yet about leaving her. But I know once I walk away, it'll have time to simmer and I'll need a fucking drink.

"Riggs," I whisper, the tears finally spilling over.

With one more clap on my shoulder, Allistair tugs my arms, pulling me away from him and everything in me is on fire. I'm walking away not because I want to but because it's what's expected of me. It's my turn to take the mantle and prove I'm man enough to take care of my family like Riggs has been doing my entire life.

"Riggsy?" I say when we get to the front door.

He smiles over his shoulder, the gun steady in his hand. "I'll see you on the flip side, kid."

And that's enough to break me.

Allistair closes the door between us, forcing me away from the house.

My cries break out.

My body shaking.

My mind spinning as I look at the place I called home for three years. The place I raised my girls in. The place I fucked my wife in the shower just this morning.

The last place I'll ever see my brothers alive.

***

I'm numb.

Going through the motions of driving because that goodbye wasn't what I expected.

Riggs and I were supposed to finish this together; Donnelly brothers side by side. Yet he's there, already on the edge between life and death. And I'm here, sitting outside of Dutchess's house on the border to Canada, waiting for Lip to pull me out of the car because I can't move.

I can't fucking move.

My phone rings and I glance down at it in the cupholder, Slade's name pops up. It's three times he's called now. Twice that I've ignored it. But I don't this time, I need to hear Zay's voice. The only thing that will help me pull through this downer. This panic. This fucking...*feeling.*

I answer, sniffling. My arms are too weak to hold the phone to my ear. I put Slade on speaker and rest my forehead on the steering wheel, staring as the seconds go by on the screen. "Yeah?"

"Jesus, fuck. I was worried sick! Riggs's phone is off, you weren't answering, and Palmer's phone is dead—"

"Where's Zay?" I interrupt him.

He sighs, yawning. "She's resting. I'm in the NICU with the baby."

"How is she?"

"Tired. Scared. Frustrated."

Chuckling softly, I wipe my nose with my fingers. "Sounds like a regular Tuesday for her."

Slade laughs, groaning. "It was hit or miss for a second, brother."

Exhaling slowly, I try my best to hold off from crying again. But this day has been one shitty fucking day and if one more thing comes my way that isn't good news, I might break. "How's he? The baby?"

Slade chuckles softly, tapping something in the background. "He's a trooper, Peter. He's over five pounds, and that's really good for a preemie. You should see him compared to some of the other babies, he's nearly twice the size of the one beside him. But…as much as he looks like a little alien, he has Zay's eyes and lips. And some long ass legs."

I'm laughing, imagining my nephew as this giant in the incubator compared to the other babies around him. That's pure Donnelly blood for you. My nephew is as strong as an ox. "I can't wait to meet him."

"I'm gonna talk with the doctor as soon as I can. See when's the safest time we can get out of here and out to Sanction Falls—"

"Where?" I frown, vaguely remembering the name. "Why does that sound so familiar?"

"No idea, it's the place Riggs told us we're going. Some abandoned house you guys used to have or something."

Lifting my head from the steering wheel, I stare at Dutchess's house and tongue my molars. "Sanction Falls," I whisper, a flash of the place comes to mind. A large black house with glass windows and a porch that wraps around the bottom. It's in the middle of the forest, I remember running through the trees as a kid—but that's the cabin. It's always been the cabin, hasn't it?

No, no. There were many safehouses Mama brought us to when we were babies. Her hopes for a new life for us away from the darkness. We spent many birthdays away from San Jose. I remember Daddy trying to teach Riggs how to hunt…I remember the time Adam almost drowned in the lake…I remember the petty zoo massacre…I remember so much that doesn't belong to just the cabin.

But why was Sanction Falls abandoned? Why didn't we ever use it?

Lip comes out of the house, nodding at me as he brings a cigarette to his lips. It's time to man the fuck up and be the person I promise my brother I'd be. The fucking man who will protect his family.

"I'm about to meet Dutchess. After I do, I'll send Lip to the hospital with your passports. One for the baby, too. Next phone call, though, I want to talk to Zaynab. Okay?"

"Yeah." He sniffs. "Yeah."

"Thank you, Slade. For everything."

He chuckles, sniffling once again before he hangs up and leaves me in deafening silence.

One more step before we're out of this. One more goddamn step before I kiss this life goodbye.

Lip approaches the car, knocking on the window with his index finger. "You ready to come in, brother?"

Shaking my head, I sniff and shove the door open. "I can't fucking—"

"The kids are asleep. Dutchess put them in her room," he interrupts me, pulling on the cigarette.

Fuck, I remember the feeling. That light-headedness of it. The way I instantly relaxed whenever the smoke trickled out of my mouth. It has been three years since I put a stick between my lips. I quit for that cunt, Dorian, because she hated the taste of it on my tongue.

"Slade said we're going to Sanction Falls." I lean against the side of the car, crossing my arms. "How do you know no one will find us there?"

Lip lifts a shoulder, flicking the cigarette aside. "We don't, but Riggs is certain it's the safest place. These children are the last people he wants to get hurt. And going to someplace that's off the radar is the best option. Plus, half these fucks can't cross the border."

"Why was it abandoned?"

Taking a drag of the cigarette, the smoke trickles from his nostrils. "What I just said, brother. They can't cross the border and Dutchess won't make anyone passports who is tied to Daddy. She hates him for what he's done. Half the Canadian clubs walked away when Daddy came out with his shit.

Place is abandoned because no one wants any connection to that fuck."

I nod, scratching the back of my head. "Riggs said he wants you to find Skeet and Judas. Apparently, he picked Skeet up at the gas station you left him at this afternoon. Daddy said he's involved in this as much as Skeet."

"Wait, what? Daddy Donnelly's…alive?" Lip pauses, scoffing with a laugh, and wipes his mouth. "Fucking guy, I swear it."

"The whole goddamned thing never ended. Daddy pulled a page outta Mama's book and faked his death so he could continue his bullshit behind our backs." Frowning, I uncross my arms and tuck my hands into the back of my jeans. "All this time, the women we were saving weren't even half of them. The fucking club is making money off of the ones we don't save. Y'know the anonymous donations we think we're getting for helping the charities and whatnot? Well, Adam rigged it so it would be the fucking bullshit they're dealing. All the auctions and trade-offs are what keep the power on at the bar."

Lip's mouth lies agape, staring at me as if I told him the Queen is still alive. "You're for real?"

"Believe me, I'm just as stunned as you. My fucking wife is involved in all this bullshit. Her father is the one controlling everything." Dragging a hand down my face. "Adam knew about everything and kept his fucking mouth shut because he's Daddy's pet. This shit is pure fucking chaos."

Lip takes another cigarette out and lights it, offering it to me but I refuse, pushing off the car and stepping toward the house. "What am I supposed to do when I get Skeet and Judas? I can't very well kill the fuckers."

Inhaling sharply, I shake my head. "I have an idea. It goes against everything we stand for as bikers, but it's the only thing that makes sense to me. The only thing that keeps my family safe and makes sure those fuckers rot in hell."

Lip spins the keys around his finger, pulling on the cigarette. "What's that?"

With my hand on the doorknob about to enter Dutchess's house, I blow out a breath and drop my head back. "Call the Captain. Tell him what Daddy has been doing, tell him what *everyone* has been doing. Record the call and use it as blackmail if he doesn't send the five-o to my house and arrest everyone. Including Skeet and Judas. Dutchess made you a passport, right? So ditch your cut and hightail it out of here as soon as everyone is arrested."

He exhales sharply, widening his eyes. "Your brothers are there."

"Riggs said to do whatever it takes to keep my family safe, and the last thing I want is for him dead. And the way things are going, it was going to be a fucking shootout. This way is best. No one *fucking* dies."

I'll find a way to get my brother out of jail. Whatever it fucking takes, he'll be there to raise his sons. He'll be with Zay and I. I'll guarantee it.

Peter

The sun is starting to rise. I don't know what's happened to Riggs. I don't know if it's over. I don't know how Zaynab is. I don't know where the fuck to go. I don't fucking know.

With a sniff, I wipe my nose with my fingers and get off the armchair in the bedroom, leaving the kids to continue sleeping. I've sat in that chair for the past three hours watching them. Palmer is asleep on the couch in the living room, Dutchess is in her office down the hallway, and I've been like a ghost roaming this house I've only ever been to once before.

When Lillian ratted on the club, Daddy got me sent here for a couple of days, but Crew insisted I stay close in case I was needed. Little did I know, I would be needed and used to seek revenge for what she did to my club. But as luck would have it, Zay had other plans and history unfolded itself. Now here we are again.

Palmer sits in the middle of the couch with her knees to her chest wearing one of Dutchess's shirts and fuzzy pink socks, staring blankly at the TV. It's still turned off, remote gripped in her hand. She's numb, much like we all are.

Our lives were good—*too* good. And that was the problem. We forgot about the problems at hand and lived. But if a problem is stowed away, then how will it ever get fixed? The Ghost haunted us, slowly waiting to possess the only good we've ever had. At the time, he posed no threat. He was just some guy who roamed around silently until yesterday when he came back with a vengeance and narrowly destroyed our happy little life.

Now everything is changing. Everything will never be the fucking same.

"Hey," I whisper loudly, making Palmer jump.

"Peter…hey," she says, tapping the couch and moving over an inch. "Can't sleep?"

Shaking my head, I drop on the cushion beside her and lean my head back. "My mind won't shut off because I don't know what's fucking happening with…anything."

"Slade isn't answering me."

Lifting my feet onto the coffee table, I cross them at the ankles and sigh. "I spoke to him a few hours ago. He was with the baby in the NICU."

"He's so little," she whispers, leaning her chin on her knee.

Rubbing my eyes, I groan as I sink into the couch a little more. "We need one good thing from today. And knowing he'll be okay has got to be that thing."

Palmer holds her ankles, staring at the glass coffee table where her empty coffee mug sits beside my feet as a single, fat tear rolls down her cheek. "Did you know that your father-in-law was the man who took me? The man who raped me for three years?"

My eyes widen and the sensation of needles prickling my skin filters through my body. "Palmer, I swear, I had no fucking idea about *any* of this."

"She's your wife."

Watching as the tears leave Palmer's green eyes, my heart bends, tearing in two at the bullshit she had to go through because of my wife's father. If only I knew…if only. "My wife kept a lot from me—too much that I don't know who she is anymore. Had three kids with the broad and she's as foreign to me as the outcome of this day."

Palmer wipes her cheeks and leans her chin on her knees again with a sigh. "If it wasn't for Damien's fascination with blood play, I'd still be locked in his dungeon like the other girls."

Palmer never talks about what happened. None of us know aside from Slade, and he only found out because Adam doesn't know how to keep his fucking mouth shut. I still remember the day Zay came over after having a spa day with Palmer. She appeared broken, in shock. Like she wasn't sure what to think. Palmer opened up about her experiences, told Zay every detail about her capture. Zay's easy to talk to like that. This aura of calmness oozes out of her. Something I wish I had with me right now.

"H-how did you get out?" I ask Palmer, turning my head slightly to look at her.

Sitting back, she pulls the front of her shirt down and shows me a stab wound in the middle of her chest. "He asked me to be his number one—his secret wife—and I wouldn't be passed around to his businessmen whenever they came around. I spat in his face and told him I'd rather die than be with him. He then stabbed me and brought me to the hospital. I snuck out and ended up finding Mama Rosa's sanctuary."

Dragging a hand down my face, I drop it on my lap and sputter. "I'm so fucking sorry, Palmer. Christ, I don't even know what to say."

"It's okay," she whispers. "Damien will get what's coming to him."

Nodding with a smirk because karma's a fucking bitch, I nudge her leg. "Yeah, he will."

Opening my mouth to speak, the floorboard creaks down the hallway and I grab the gun tucked into my jeans, shooting up from the couch.

"It's just me, Peter," Dutchess says, chuckling. Her dark skin is hard to make out against the bright orange headdress she's wearing with a moo-moo to match, and fluffy pink slippers. "I just need to know names and I'll have the passports printed in an hour."

Palmer yawns, dropping her legs off the couch. "I'll make some coffee."

Dutchess jerks her head to follow Palmer to the kitchen and sits at her long wooden table with a notepad and pen. "Now, who would you like to be?"

I lift a shoulder. "No matter."

She chuckles, looking up at me with big brown eyes as crinkles groove her dark skin. "Child, just give me a name to make my life easier."

Palmer clears her throat, pulling a chair out beside me. "*Charlie*. I'll be *Amelia*. The kids can keep their names so there's less confusion. Slade will be *Alex* and Zay—"

"Samantha," I interject, nodding at her. "I know it's the name she most probably used at the hospital, too."

"Why *Samantha*?"

From a time when everything was simple when the club didn't rule my life.

When Zay was smiling, happy. When her sparkle wasn't burnt out. It was a time when everything was easier.

"It was her best friend's middle name. She meant a lot to Zay…she's the reason everything happened to her in the first place…it's…all of this is my fault. From the beginning. I should have never sought her out. I should have kept my distance and let Zay live her life without all of us tainting it."

Tears brim my lash line and Palmer notices, placing a hand on my forearm. "Things happen for a reason, Peter. Whether good or bad, the reason is there and we can't do anything but let them play out."

Swallowing the stone in my throat, she's right. Palmer has always been the voice of reason when Slade wasn't himself. The panicked child comes out from time to time and she's always there to soothe his anxiety. The perfect woman for him and the perfect person to help me through this.

A smile graces my lips and I nod, looking up as Dutchess scribbles on her notepad. We haven't needed Dutchess in a long time. But my father used to keep her in our lives if shit ever hit the fan. Her husband was a member of our crew, a founding member like Daddy and Roaden.

But he died. Much like all the men who want to keep this club straight. Her husband didn't agree with how my father ran things, then one day, the brakes on his bike stopped working and he ran off the road into an oncoming truck. No one stepped forward or confessed his death, but we all knew either Daddy or Roaden cut his break line. Cockroaches invading our lives.

"Do yourselves a favor and get some rest, will you? I need you outta my house as soon as possible. I don't want any of you bikers destroying my life again," Dutchess says, pushing herself up from the chair and quietly making her way back to her office.

I lean my elbows on the table and drop my head in my hands. "New beginnings," I whisper. "New fucking beginnings."

Palmer's hand touches my back and she rubs it slightly. "I know you're losing your wife in all this but think of all the good you're doing by eliminating Damien from existence. All the people who won't be wondering when death will come to them because death is better than being forced to do ungodly things with disgusting people. Think of your children and how safe they'll be away from people like that in their lives. Think of the good, Peter. It's the only thing getting me by. The only thing that *got* me by."

Looking over at her, I close my eyes and release a breath. "I'm trying. I'm trying."

She smiles sweetly, getting to her feet. "I'll check on the kids. Why don't you lie on the couch for a little? Try to get at least an hour of sleep before Dutchess is done and we have to leave."

Sniffling, I tap her hand on my shoulder and sigh. "Yeah, yeah. Sleep…I'll get some sleep."

As she walks away and turns off the coffee maker, my heart starts to thump quickly as I spot a bottle of vodka and tequila just sitting on the counter. It would be so easy to down them, to escape to a place I know all too well. To go back to the life of pitying myself and hating my existence.

But I can't do that…right?

My heart does a double beat, causing me to grip my chest at the thought of leaving the only life I know behind. How the hell am I supposed to do this? Take care of my children alone? Take care of my nephew? Of Palmer?

How can I leave Zaynab and my newest nephew behind in the hands of Slade?

No, how the fuck can I trust anyone anymore?

Am I up for the task or am I just a millisecond away from completely losing it to the bottle once again?

Slade

No word from anyone yet and the sun is starting to rise; the sky is a rose gold with hints of blues and purples. I've sat in this chair for three hours now, waiting for someone to update me on Zay. But they've sure been checking on the baby every twenty minutes or so to make sure he's still breathing, he's fed, and the incubator is warm enough for him. He's a tough little man and I have no doubt in my mind he'll pull through.

But I need to hear from someone soon before I fucking lose it.

I've ignored the notifications on my phone for hours, keeping it on silent as I did research on the survival rate for a preemie. The outcome varies, but knowing this baby is two ponds bigger than the average preemie gives me hope.

Staring at my home screen, Palmer's gorgeous face lights up and makes me hate myself for ignoring her calls earlier. But it was hit or miss with the baby, and I wanted to be alert and ready in case I was needed. Now, it's too early to call her back.

It's too late to tell her goodbye for the time being.

This entire fucking day has been a shitshow and she's all I wanted, and I barely had her since we made love this morning. She's my rock, my queen, my goddamned life.

What I'm doing is good. *I'm protecting my family*, reminding myself of this every damn second of this entire fucking day.

Looking out the window again, the array of colors reminds me of a painting I used to stare at a lot. It was hung above my bed in the last foster home I lived in before I ran away. I'd rest my feet on my pillow and stare at it for hours.

There was no telling whether it was an abstract painting or a rendition of what I'm looking at right now. Nature's way of showing how beautiful it can be. That painting brought me calm when I needed it before Angela became the beacon for my anxiety and I used her for relief.

Leaning forward, I open the new texts from Lip, hoping he has some news for me about what's going on.

LIP: *Just left Dutchess's. Peter is there and told me his plan. I called the cops and sent them to his house. Don't know what's going to happen to Riggs or Gunner and his men, but those fuckers are all getting arrested. It's time we put an end to all of this bullshit.*

Reading over what he sent from a few hours ago, I run a hand down my face and nod. Calling the cops is the right thing to do. The only thing that will guarantee the assholes don't get away with anything anymore.

ME: *Send them away for good.*
LIP: *I'm trying to get in touch with the Captain, see what he can do about Gunner and Riggs.*
ME: *Keep me posted. Stay safe.*
LIP: *You, too.*
LIP: *How's the baby?*
ME: *He's cute, a Heffer.*
LIP: *Zay?*
ME: *Still cute, a champion.*
LIP: *Keep them cuties safe, brother.*

Rigg's will know what to do. He'll find his way home. He has to.

That's all anyone tells me to do. Be the person I've been trying to be my whole life. The person people look up to, rely on. Cherish. Be the man Riggs has become.

Protect them with your life, you hear me? Raise him as your own.

With the weight of the day weighing on my chest, I find Palmer's name and let my thumb hover over it. I need to hear her voice and know that she's okay. But before I can tap her name, someone clears their throat and startles me.

Angela flashes me a tired grin, looking at the baby before she takes the empty chair beside me and sighs, holding a clipboard to her chest. "Slade, I need to ask you some questions before I erase the birth of this child from the records of this hospital."

Chuckling softly, I lean my head back and stare at the fluorescent lights that are dimmed compared to the rest of the hospital. "I don't even know where to start."

"Well, you can start with why she says her name's 'Samantha' yet you called her 'Zay." Angela arches an eyebrow, looking over at me. Her bloodshot eyes are the same beautiful brown they were the last time I saw them. "Are you in trouble?"

"No, I'm not in trouble. It's trouble that's after us."

"What does that mean?" she asks, placing the clipboard on her lap.

"The less you know, the better. I don't want to involve you in any of this...I just ask you to do me this one favor and hide the fact that we were here. If word gets out, then we're as good as dead."

Leaning forward on my elbows, I drop my head and breathe slowly. This panic attack hasn't subsided in almost fifteen hours. Usually, when I have a bad one like this, I turn to pot or booze. Rough sex with Palmer sometimes helps. But I can't do that now. I need to be level-headed.

Angela rubs my back softly, tapping twice. "Is she even your wife?"

And the less Angela knows, the better. I'll keep up with as many lies as I can so she doesn't get mixed into this tangled web. "Yes, Zay's my wife."

Angela inhales slowly, dropping her hand and nodding. "I could lose my job for this."

"I know."

"People will start asking questions since you're going to be here for a while." She opens her clipboard and hands me some papers. "Write up some fake names. I'll do what I can with losing the paperwork, but the hospital needs something before I misplace it, if you know what I mean."

"Thanks."

She rises, stepping closer to the incubator, and clears her throat again. There's a cloud of regret hanging in the air, an awkwardness the pair of us are too afraid to speak.

She became my crutch and I became her escape. I left her house because there was too much pressure on us to succeed, to be someone we weren't. She was married, too, to a man who didn't love her and only lived off of her and the money from fostering all of us.

I could have lived a good life with Angela if I stayed, but I wanted more out of life. Freedom, love, experience. And I found that in Palmer. My freedom and love are her.

Angela sniffs, visibly forcing herself not to look at me. "Don't leave without saying goodbye this time, hmm?"

"It's not like I didn't want to say goodbye, it's just—"

"I don't need an explanation."

Blinking rapidly, I frown, reaching out for her hand. "And I'm not here to give you one. Just know that I never meant to hurt you. I wanted more and you…what we did was wrong, but it doesn't mean I didn't feel something for you, Angela. I did. A lot. But the past is in the past, right?"

She smiles sweetly, squeezing my hand. "I know it is, Slade. Believe me, I've moved on. But I'll never forget our nights together. Not a single one."

"Neither will I."

And that's the truth. A big part of my intelligence comes from living with her and I will never take that away. It's what Palmer likes most about me, the way I talk to her about books and all the ones I like. She loves when I read to her at night; more so than watching TV.

The door opens and a nurse wheels Zay in, her hazel eyes are bloodshot and puffy. It's good to see her up and at 'em. Even better to have her here with the baby.

"I didn't think you wanted me to stay," I add, staring at Angela as her jaw twitches.

She turns to me with fatigue bleeding from her gaze and sighs. "I did, Slade. I would have left him for you." Waving her hand at me as my expression drops. "But it's too late to dwell on the past. I'm heading home for a few hours of shut-eye. Don't leave this hospital. This will become your home for the better part of a month." With a squeeze to my shoulder, she steps away and does the same to Zay's shoulder. I never thought seeing Angela again would bring back nostalgia. There was a strong sense of safety in her house. Something that came back to me when I met Palmer. The home I always wanted.

Zay smiles at me, looking back at Angela as the nurse follows after her. "Old flame?"

Laughing softly, I drag a hand down my face and lean my head back. "Before I ran away, she was the foster mom who took care of a bunch of us."

Zay nods, looking back again. That's one thing about our friendship that I admire, we don't have to say anything to know what the other is thinking. We have a deep understanding of our history, our tragedies, and our lives outside this club. "You're one of the only men I know who doesn't put his dick in crazy."

"There have been a few. Remember that chick who kept coming to *Judas's Hideout*? Always asking for me until Lip kicked her out." I grimace, shaking off a shiver. "I don't do repeats unless I'm sure she won't hold a knife to my throat in the middle of the fucking night."

Zay chuckles softly, looking at the incubator. Even in a time like this, she always has to make sure there's a smile on everyone's face. The selfless person inside her needs to take a backseat and let us be the ones to help her.

She grips the arms of the wheelchair and pushes herself up. "He's so small," she whispers, her voice cracking. A single tear rolls down her cheek, dripping off the tip of her nose onto the top of the incubator. "It's funny, we had a plan for this day. Dorian and Peter were going to have Carter sleep over while Riggs and Adam stayed with me at the hospital." She scrunches her nose and waves her hand around. "Mama Rosa wanted me to have the baby in a bath at the sanctuary, but I needed all the drugs they could give me. I didn't want to feel any pain—"

"And yet you still had the baby without an epidural," I point out, smirking.

Rolling her eyes, she licks her lips and wipes her cheek. "We had a plan for his birth. We had a plan for our lives, and now it's like…what was the fucking use?"

"Nothing ever goes to plan, Zay. You should know that better than anyone." Reaching out, I take her hand and smile at her. "But we'll start a new plan, right? As soon as we're able to bring this little guy home, we'll meet Peter and Palmer in Canada and raise all those babies the right way. Far from the club, far from the fuckery. They'll never know what it means to have a panic room or a safe house. They'll just know...peace."

Squeezing my hand, she wipes a few more tears. "I really like the sound of that."

My phone vibrates on my lap, startling me slightly. Peter's name is on the screen and Zay snatches the phone, answering it with a quivering lip. "Peter?"

Taking the phone from her ear, I put it on speaker and lean forward with the phone held between us. "Hey, man, everything okay?"

"Feel like I'm having a fucking heart attack." Peter groans, sniffling. "Nothing is quieting down, everything is shaking. My fucking blood feels like it's on fire but frozen solid. I need a fucking drink or a bump or—"

"Hey," Zay interrupts him. "Remember what I always say? Take a breath. Just breathe, you'll be okay."

He sniffs again and exhales a wavering breath. I know anxiety all too well. I never turned to alcohol to cope. I used weed, sex, and cutting myself to help numb that fault. But Peter's been sober for three years. He can't go back now.

"Hey, man. Why don't you FaceTime us? You can see the baby," I suggest and Zay smiles, nodding quickly. "He's a cutie."

The call ends and a FaceTime call comes in, Peter's sleepy face coming into view. "You look like fucking shit," I say, teasingly.

Flipping me off, he runs his fingers through his hair and lies back on the couch. "I haven't slept yet."

Zay sits beside me and leans her head on my shoulder. "Did you hear anything? Where's Riggs?"

Peter closes his eyes and inhales a deep breath, exhaling it from his parted lips. "He let me go. Told me to come here and protect the kids. I know fuck all right now."

Zay whimpers, turning away from the camera, but I slide my arm around her shoulders and pull her back to me. "He didn't even give me a proper goodbye."

Peter's blue eyes get darker as tears rise and fall, siding to his ears. But he closes them again and squeezes his lips shut, shaking his head. I don't know what went down after I left. For all I know, Peter could be spewing lies and everyone is dead, he just doesn't want Zay to suffer any more than she already has.

Pressing a kiss to the back of her head, I inhale that faint coconut smell that's being taken over by a hint of her sweat. "Why don't we show Peter his nephew? We still have to name him, too, y'know."

Zay sniffs, smiling slightly. "I always liked the name Bryce, but Riggs said it was too much of a pussy name."

Peter laughs, tucking his arm under his head. "And the backup name?"

"Why? Do you agree with him?" she scoffs, narrowing her eyes at him.

"Yes."

She sucks her teeth, folding her arms across her chest and sighs. "Adam and Riggs liked Jasper the most. It matches Carter."

With a nod, I wrinkle my chin. "Jasper Donnelly. I like it."

Zay licks her lips, looking at the incubator as it hisses, keeping the little man on a breathing machine until he's capable of breathing on his own. There's a spark in her eye, an ounce of happiness for the first time today.

Peter smiles, eyebrows pinched together as he stares at Zay. "Can I meet Jasper now?"

Getting to my feet, I switch the camera to the other side and show Peter his nephew. There's a small laugh that leaves him, then a soft moan. We're all worried about Jasper, worried that he may not make it out of here. But I trust Angela. And if she believes he'll get out of here like many other preemies, then he will.

"Fuck, he has long legs," Peter finally says. "And Zay's lips. But that Donnelly brow is all us, isn't it?"

She sniffs, tapping the glass. "I wish I could hold him."

"He could probably fit in Riggs's palm," I joke, switching the screen around so it faces Zay and me. "Doctor thinks his size is what's going to save him. He's nearly two pounds bigger than other babies at thirty-one weeks."

"He's got Donnelly blood running through his veins; the kid's a champ. He'll pull through and join us when he's ready." Peter rubs his left eye, frowning before pinching them shut. "Fuck, this entire day is one for the fucking books, isn't it?"

"How're the kids?" she asks, leaning her chin on the incubator, watching Jasper as he stretches out his legs and curls them up again.

"They were asleep when I got here. But Palmer told them we were going to our new house in the forest. And she said they were excited to roast marshmallows." He sniffs, wiping his nose with his fingers. "They don't understand how fucking cold Canada is in the winter."

"Have you been?" I ask, placing a hand on Zay's back.

He shakes his head. "I don't remember a lot from our childhood, but apparently, this was an old safe house. The club doesn't use it anymore because the Canadian charter exiled themselves from Daddy's wrongdoings."

Another thing Daddy Donnelly fucked up. Whatever he touches burns.

"We used to go skiing in Vancouver when I was a teenager. It's beautiful, even in the winter. I didn't mind the cold so much. Riggs will hate it—if he gets a chance to." Fresh tears well in her eyes before she blinks them away. "We can't leave the hospital for at least a month. How are we doing this?"

Peter inhales sharply, sitting up on the couch with his elbows on his knees. "Palmer and I are heading to the border later this morning. Sammy's girlfriend changed her shift so she'll be at the post to greet us when we get there. We have passports and Lip picked up some clothes for the kids…Palmer and I get the place ready for you—"

"How're we supposed to get across the border?" I interrupt him, confused by this entire fucking plan. There's no way any of this will work. Especially if Zay and I try to bring her son across the border when it's time. They'll get one look at me and ask us to pull over. "If you called the cops like you said, who's to say our faces aren't on any wanted lists?"

"Lip spoke with the Captain—if me, you, Riggs, or any of the guys helping us whose name wasn't brought up by Damien or Daddy, they'll be safe."

Zay looks at the screen, eyebrow arched in confusion. "Daddy?"

"Surprise. The fucker didn't die. He's been in hiding working with Adam who's working with Dorian, whose fucking father is the mastermind behind the trafficking. It's like a freaking soap opera." He growls, wiping his mouth. "I swear to fuck, if I could've put a bullet in all of them, I would've."

Zay glances at me with fresh tears in her eyes and closes them, dropping her head back. "Fuck this day."

"You can say that again."

Looking over his shoulder, a woman with an orange headscarf waves her hand and jerks her head to follow her. "Gimme a sec," he says, turning back to us. "That's Dutchess. She's ruthless but thoughtful—and scares the shit outta me."

Zay laughs, clicking her tongue. "I like her already."

"Lip will call you when shit gets settled. He'll meet you and give you the passports. Sammy's girlfriend will help you get across. I'll text you her info and keep her in the loop for when the time is right." Peter runs his fingers through his hair. "We'll be safe, Zay. I promise you and the kids will be my *only* priority." He glances at me, rolling his eyes at how thin they are. "Palmer, too, until you get here, fuckface."

"Who'd have thought you and I would be raising kids together, Peter? Definitely not me," she says with amusement in her tone.

He chuckles weakly, sniffling. "We'll be floating once again."

I don't know what that means but seeing the smirk on their faces makes my body lighter, as if there is a light at the end of the dark tunnel. Slowly, we'll get there.

"Hey, Peter?" she says, leaning her head on me. His watery eyes meet hers with a nod. "I'll see you on the flip side."

A laugh seeps out of him before more tears spill free. "Yeah, yeah." He winces, looking down as tears drip from his eyes. "I'll, uh, call you soon, okay? Love you both."

"Love you, too, brother."

He hangs up, leaving a cloud hanging over us. But Zay inhales and looks up at me. "It's going to be okay." A smile spreads to her lips. "I can feel it in my belly. This time around, it's telling the truth"

Pressing a kiss to her head, I embrace her and watch Jasper shift again.

"We're in this together, Zay. No matter what, family sticks together."

She squeezes me tighter, nodding against my chest.

This day will get better.

Our lives will change.

There will be no more hurt or fear. Only brightness.

We'll be headed to Canada where I'll be able to finally hold my curly-hair queen and life will be whole once again.

Riggs

Mama and Daddy are yelling at each other, much like they constantly did growing up. There wasn't a time I don't remember them at each other's throats.

"You're a snake," she hisses, yanking her arm from his grasp.

The devilish smile spreads to his lips as he grabs her face and roughly kisses her. "And yet I'm your first phone call every night, ain't I, *mi amour?*"

"Fuck you."

Damien chuckles, still holding the cloth to his throat, and stares up at me. "Let me convince you, Riggs. Give me five minutes and you'll put that gun down and take a seat at the table with us."

I scoff, pressing the gun to the back of Adam's head. "You can try, but this is not the life I want to raise my children in."

Adam sniffs, pressing his palms on the table. "Exactly why my mother went to Daddy for help."

"What do you mean?" Gunner asks, standing off to the side with a gun in each hand aimed at two of The Ghost's men.

Daddy smiles and tugs on Mama's hair playfully before he cracks open a can of soda. "I've been in this business for many years—way before you were born, Riggs. And when Damien showed me his pets, Adam's mother was the one who stood out the most. Little did I know, the bitch would end up pregnant. But I did good. Got her an apartment, stocked her fridge with food. I gave her a life and introduced her to the man Adam thought was his daddy before she turned to drugs and neglected *my* son. That's when Mama started raising him. Adam didn't need any part in that life—"

"And yet here he is, in this life with a goddamn monster controlling him like a puppet." Wiping my mouth with the back of my hand, I drop it and tap the gun against my thigh. "What was the whole point of luring him in like this? Getting him on your good side because your other sons can't fucking stand you? You have grandchildren—three of them are girls. What if they were kidnapped and sold as sex slaves? You'd be able to live with yourself knowing you played a part in the trafficking that runs through this town?" Glaring at Dorian, I shove her head. "And *you*! You're allowing this shit to happen? Letting these women you've become friends with almost get taken again?"

"It was them or me, Riggs. I'm sorry if I was selfish and chose to save myself for my daughters!" she screams, gritting her teeth.

Leaning forward, I smirk, baring my teeth at her. "Yeah, and look at you now. Lost your husband, lost your daughters, and pretty soon, you'll have a bullet between those pretty gray eyes."

She spits in my face, licking her plump lips as her saliva leaks down my cheek. "Fuck you."

"I don't put my dick in crazy," I growl out, pressing the gun to her head.

"Hang on a minute," Gunner speaks up.

Glaring at him over my shoulder, he puts a hand up in surrender. "You about to announce that you were in on this, too, brother?"

He shakes his head, pointing the gun back at one of the masked men. "No. But I want to remind you that she is the mother to your nieces. Your brother's wife."

Smiling, I stand upright and cock the gun, keeping my gaze on Gunner. No second thoughts or regret is filling me as my finger eases onto the trigger and releases the bullet from the chamber. Dorian's body flies back, silencing the room.

"I ain't playing anymore. I'm tired of the lies and the fucking bullshit! I have eight rounds left. That's enough for you." I point the gun at Damien, then Daddy. "You." Then Mama and The Ghost. "You, and you." Tapping the top of Adam's head, he lifts it to look up at me. "And you...no one is walking out of this house alive if I have anything to do with it. Now, that's one fucking down, who's next."

Damien's face is pale as he looks down at his daughter, sweat trickling down his forehead. "I was going to offer you money, Riggs. A lot of fucking money to turn a blind eye and take care of your family." He whimpers, tears running down his cheeks. "She didn't deserve that!"

I have no sympathy for this fuck.

Not a single ounce of remorse.

He deserves everything coming to him.

"I don't want your money." I raise the gun and fire twice, hitting him in the chest. "I want this over with. You cost me my life, so I'm taking yours."

"Wait!" The Ghost steps forward, hands raised. "I just want my fucking girl back. That's all I wanted. I played no part in the kidnapping of women. I helped fucking save them!"

Sad thing is, I believe him.

Even though he's the one who started this game today, I won't kill him. The tiny part of me that's wrapped in Zay's embrace, sprinkled in good is stepping forward.

Instead, I jerk my head at him. "If I let you go, you give me your word that I will never see your ugly face again."

He glances at Adam, then at me, and takes his serrated blade from his back pocket, dropping it on the floor. "Ask Mama Rosa. I started all of this to get my girl back. If I would have known my father was keeping her as his fucking pet, I would have gutted him myself."

Mama sniffs, hand on her mouth as she looks at me like I'm a monster. But I don't care anymore. Something deep inside me knew not to trust Mama. Someone who loves her children wouldn't leave like she did, no matter the fear and fright, she'd beg for our help to get her out of the mess she was in. And yet, our mama left like we meant nothing. For ten years we lived with the thought of her as an angel when all along, she was alive and working with the devil. All this time she knew he was alive and did nothing but continue to fuck Daddy and let him get away with his wicked ways.

"Riggs, sweetie, please rethink this idea that killing us will solve anything—"

"Mama, I don't need you filling my head with lies anymore. You've done nothing but lie and lie and lie since we came back into your life. You knew Daddy was alive and you said *nothing*. You knew about the bullshit Damien was doing and you said *nothing*. You fucking *knew* about Adam and that dead fucking cunt and did *nothing!*" Huffing, I crack the bones in my neck and growl at the throb shooting through my shoulder. The painkillers have completely worn off, no longer targeting the damning pain, and I'm hanging on by a thread. But this has gone on for far too long. "Tell me, Mama. How long would you continue to do nothing? Until Peter was dead? Me? Zay? Your grandbabies? How fucking long?"

She rises, hands clenched at her sides. "All I needed was Damien to sign the fucking papers and I would have taken over his company. I would have put an end to every game he played. Did I turn my head to some of the girls? Yes, I admit it. I let a lot of girls continue to suffer so I'd keep Damien in my good graces. But the endgame was right there, Riggs. Until Wilde showed up and ruined the fucking plans."

"All you had to do was tell us, Rosa. We would have helped to speed up the process so no women would have continued to suffer," Gunner says, spitting on the ground. "Now, you deserve to suffer just like the rest of the women you ignored."

"Fuck you, Gunner." Daddy rises, leaning his fists on the table. "Now that my dimwit of a son just killed the guy running things, it's ours to keep—"

"It's not anyone's, Daddy. It's over," I interrupt him. "You're not here to save women like Mama. You're here for the money. It's always about fucking money."

"Money makes the world go 'round, boy."

Sirens blare in the distance, making all of us freeze and dart our attention to the front door.

Someone called the fucking cops.

One of the neighbors?

One of the girls at Maddison Gardens?

"Told you not to shoot up the place," Adam says, shaking his head.

Daddy takes a step back, heading for the back door and it's almost laughable if he thinks he's getting away from me; dead or alive.

Lifting my gun, I keep it aimed at Daddy and smile. "You ain't going anywhere, old man."

"The cops are here, Riggs. If they catch me, there's no way in hell I'm ever getting outta prison. I got a warrant on me and—"

"Don't worry. You won't make it to prison this time around," I jeer, grinning and I step around the table raising the gun to his forehead. "Everyone else, get fucking lost."

"Riggs?" Adam says, slowly rising. "You'll get arrested if they catch you."

"Don't worry," I say again. "They'll catch you, too."

"What about Zay? The kids? You can't walk away from them—"

"I'm protecting them!"

Adam scoffs, stepping back a foot, looking over his shoulder at the front door. "Like fuck you are!"

There's no way in hell he's getting away with this. No matter the unity we shared with Zay, he can join our father in hell for all I care.

I jerk my head at Gunner and he shoots Adam's kneecap—the same one that I shattered four years ago.

Adam yells out, crying in agony. "Fuck!"

A chuckle leaves me, glancing over my shoulder. "You can try to run now, Adam. Won't get very far, though."

"What're you stupid, Riggs? You're going to kill everyone and let my fucking wife be exposed and a suspect in this!" Adam shouts, crying out and gritting his teeth as he holds onto his knee.

Rolling my eyes, I scoff, keeping my focus on him like a goddamn rookie. "She ain't a suspect, Adam, and you know it. I wouldn't leave her without knowing she's fucking safe and—"

The cold metal of a gun presses under my chin. I turned away from the man I had a gun to. Something Daddy taught me never to do. *Lesson fucking learned.*

"Well, well, well." Daddy's guttural chuckle fills me with rage. "Looks like we're both fucked, ain't we?"

Flaring my nostrils, I look at him and hiss. "I won't think twice about pulling the trigger. Question is, will you be man enough to kill your first born son?"

He laughs, tossing his head back before gripping my shoulder. Pain shoots through me, taking hold of my entire being and nearly bringing me to my knees. But I have to stay strong for my family. I've come this far, now it's time to make sure this asshole stays dead.

The sirens are closer, much too close for anyone to drive out of here.

The captain always goes down with the ship, looks like everyone is sinking with me.

Mama places her hand on Daddy's, easing his squeeze. "It doesn't have to come to this."

"What does it have to come to, Mama? As far as I see it, this entire operation you conjured up just ended your family. So either you run out the backdoor with The Ghost and the rest of the bikers, or you stay with your son and your husband and watch as blood sheds on our hands for the last fucking time," I hiss at her, keeping my focus on my father.

She whimpers, looking back at The Ghost and sighing. "I have a getaway car parked on the other side of the forest. Make sure I get to it and I'll bring you to Lenora."

Scoffing, I knew she'd take the typical way out. Save herself over her goddamn son. "If I ever see you again, Mama, you better make sure there isn't a gun in my hand."

Daddy presses his gun harder into my chin, growling. "If I know your mama, she'll hide herself away for another ten years."

Sirens blare out front, cops calling for us to stand down and slowly come out of the house with our hands up. But I'm not moving.

Adam's whimpers blend in with the madness.

Gunner's heavy breathing does, too.

But Daddy and I? We're staring each other down knowing we're not getting out of this alive.

"Any last words, Riggsy?" Daddy says, lifting the gun to my forehead.

Staring at it, I smile like a goddamn kid on Christmas morning. Fucker didn't think to check the safety, did he? "See you in hell."

The cops are hitting the front door, trying to get in.

Shouts.

Screams.

Amongst all this chaos, I'm smiling and thinking of Zay. Her gorgeous smile and contagious laugh. The way she holds me and calls me "Riggsy" when she's vulnerable.

My Zay.

My boys.

My family.

The front door bursts open right as shots fire, and everything around me is finally at peace.

Peter

I didn't get a wink of sleep after hanging up with Zay and Slade. Dutchess showed me the passports and told me she was going to bed and not to bother her until noon, but I think we'll be gone by then.

Making my way up the stairs to the bedroom with the kids, their laughter already leaks from behind the door, bringing a smile to my face. They're my saving grace, my only hope.

And as luck would have it, as soon as I open the door, my heart bleeds with relief that this day will come of something good. Rosa is jumping on the king-sized bed with Carter and Palmer stands by the bed, feeding Mina with a laugh.

"Daddy!" Sara squeals, sitting with her back on the headboard as she holds the remote in her hands.

I flash the best smile I can create and drop on the bed beside her, my eyes finally getting heavy. "Hey, baby girl."

Rosa lands on me, emitting a grunt from my lips. But she holds me and rests her head on my shoulder. Carter sits with Sara, taking the remote from her and putting on some cartoons for them to watch.

Palmer comes to the bed next, lying beside Carter as she adjusts Mina between them and holds the bottle to her lips. "They woke up half an hour ago filled with so much energy." She chuckles, looking over at me. "Where do they store it all?"

I smile, my eyes finding hers in the mess of pillows, blankets, and children. "Perfect start to a day, isn't it?"

Palmer smiles, looking down at Mina. "We'll take it one day at a time, and soon, every day will feel like a brand-new day. We'll find our peace."

Peace.

I like the sound of that.

"Daddy, where'd Mommy go?" Rosa asks, poking my cheek.

Closing my eyes to hide the tears from my girl, I have to come up with something. Telling them the truth will scar them because there's no telling how far my tongue will let loose.

Turning onto my back, I smile at Rosa and brush her hair back. "Remember when Mommy goes on those trips for work? She went on one right now. A really long one so we're going to hang out with Palmer and Auntie Zay when she comes home."

"Where is my mom, Uncle Peter?" Carter asks, making his way to my side and cuddling up to me.

I kiss his forehead and inhale that hint of coconut that soaks into everything Zaynab touches. "She's at the hospital getting ready to bring the baby home." Running my fingers through his blonde hair, I tousle it and pull him closer. "You're a big brother now, Carter. Did you know that?"

Carter gasps, sitting up beside Rosa. "Can I see him?"

"Not yet. But you'll be able to see him really soon. I promise." Glancing over at Palmer, she places Mina on her shoulder to burp her. "His name is Jasper and he looks just like Mommy."

"How's he doing?" Palmer asks, kissing Mina's cheek.

Lifting a shoulder, I rub my eyes and yawn. "He's doing. Nothing much happening since he's in an incubator and attached to feeding tubes and wires. But Slade said the doctor is hopeful."

"That's good."

Rosa jumps on me again, resting her head on my chest, as if listening to my racing heart. I can't seem to calm it, even knowing we'll be safe and that it's almost over.

The unknown is eating away at me.

Clearing my throat, my hand rests on Rosa's back pulling Sara closer to me and holding Carter's hand. "We're going on a trip with Palmer. It's a little far from here, but it's going to be our new home. All of us will live together in the forest and there's going to be a buttload more snow in the wintertime."

The kids squeal in excitement, loving every second of the snow. Yet there's this ache still pressing on my chest. Weighing me down because of the unknown.

"We'll be happy there," I whisper, looking at the black ceiling.

"Free," Palmer whispers back, lying down beside us with Mina on her chest.

Nodding, I look over at her. "Free," I repeat with a grin. "He'll come home, Palmer. He loves you. He'll come home."

"Zay will come home, too," she says, meeting my gaze.

My hand reaches out and finds her, squeezing as we lie there while the kids jump on the bed in excitement, completely oblivious to the horrors of the past twenty-four hours.

Completely blind to the outcome of what our lives will soon become.

Four Months Later

Watching from my binoculars, I smile. Zay is breastfeeding a baby boy with light brown hair. He must be almost four months by now.

So beautiful.

So perfect.

Slade is sitting in the grass with Palmer leaning her head back against his chest, laughing, as Mina crawls around them, a smile on her little chubby face so reminiscent of her mother.

Peter is running around with the girls and Carter, taking over the fatherly role. He picks up Sara, tossing her over his shoulder before doing the same thing to Carter.

That handsome boy looks so much like his father.

Zay smiles down at the baby, brushing her fingertips delicately over the side of his face. There's that happiness oozing from her, the spark that was gone for so long. It's back, alive and well. And when she looks up at Peter as he growls holding the kids in his arms, she laughs tapping his stomach.

They're happy.

Everyone has found the peace we've craved for far too long.

No more looking over their shoulders. No more fear. No more heartache. Just smiles.

So many smiles.

Wiping the tears from my cheeks, I keep the binoculars on them, smiling when they smile, laughing when they laugh.

Watching them is my serenity.

Watching them makes me realize what I did was right. Justice was served and all the bullshit we endured is over.

It's finally over.

Zay places the baby on her shoulder and taps his back. He's so beautiful. His bright blue eyes look around the area, taking in the tall trees and vast greenery that spans out for miles. The home behind him is dark with wood panelling and black shutters. Peter and Slade have kept it proper for the past few months, making it a home for all of them.

A perfect family.

My beautiful family.

Peter puts Sara and Carter down and they run off to Rosa playing in the sandbox.

Peter smiles at Zay, pulling her head to his lips. She doesn't show the affection he's giving. Her eyes are on Carter, scrunching her nose at him.

But Peter doesn't let up, draping his arm across her shoulders and whispering something in her ear. She rolls her eyes and shoves him away, looking down at the baby.

It wouldn't surprise me if he tried to take this opportunity and make them a family. Fill her with his seed and pop out more minis.

But Zay knows better.

She loves me.

Loves us.

She wouldn't let him touch her again. Not after everything.

When she tucks her breast away and hands him the baby, she twists her hair into a knot on her head and stretches out her back. She's as beautiful as the first time I saw her. So pure. So sweet. Her figure is extra curvaceous.

All mine.

Going home is not the right thing to do. Leaving was. Staying away was.

But seeing my family again, home is the only place I want to be.

Dropping the binoculars, I grunt with a limp and make my way through the trees, shoving bushes and shrubbery out of the way. It's a long trek to them, but it's a trek worth taking.

When I get closer, I close my eyes and listen to the laughter and screams of the children. The conversations of my family fill the air.

The sounds of home.

"…oh, fuck off!" Slade cackles. "You will not."

Peter snorts, sitting on the lounge chair beside them. "I will so, dickhead. Watch, I'll prove it tonight. I'll stay up and do all the feedings. Zay will sleep like a baby."

Palmer chuckles. "Are we placing bets?"

"A hundred bucks says he doesn't make it past eleven," Zay calls out, picking up a ball and throwing it at Sara.

"I'll match that." Slade laughs, snapping his fingers. "Even better. If he doesn't let you get sleep tonight, then he's on laundry for a week."

Zay laughs, taking the water bottle from beside Peter, then stops, shooting her head to the forest as she hears the crunch of leaves under my boots. I didn't mean to make noise. I didn't want them to see me.

I just wanted to listen, to hear them one more time.

She freezes, scanning the area. But I'm still out of sight, in case I change my mind.

Because I might.

I don't want to show my face again and have her hate me.

It'll break me if she hates me for what I did.

"Zaynab, what is it, sweetie?" Peter asks, handing the baby to Palmer.

Slade gets to his feet, picking up Mina and snapping his fingers at Rosa, Sara, and Carter. "Code red, guys. Inside, now."

They practiced for this.

Even though it's over, the fear still lingers in the air.

But I can't take the fear seeping from Zay's gaze. I can't take the pressure that's building up behind my eyes.

My family.

My love.

My life.

My sunshine.

Stepping forward, I push the bushes out of the way, and Zay gasps, dropping the water bottle. It clatters and spills its contents on the cement ground.

"Brother?" Peter says, tucking the gun back into his waistband.

Zay takes off running, wincing when her bare feet hit the gravel. But I can't run to her, not after the hell I was dragged through.

She slams her body into mine, causing me to wince, grunt, and step back. But that coconut smell wafts around me, enveloping my air.

Her arms squeeze around my neck, sobs commencing once again. "Oh, my God! You're here. You're here! Please tell me it's really you and I'm not dreaming. Please, oh, God."

"I'm here, baby. I'm right here."

My arms wrap around her waist as my family smiles, coming over, too. The baby. Carter.

My heart has never swelled so suddenly before. But it's paradise.

This moment here trumps every fuck-up, every heartache, every goddamned thing that has ever caused us harm.

"I love you," Zay cries, tightening her grip. "I love you so much."

Chuckling, my fingers get lost in her hair, pressing a kiss to the nape of her neck. "Forever and always, baby. Just me and you."

And that's how it will always be.

And yet, even as my family envelopes me with hugs and our happy ending has finally arrived, the tragedy always follows us. Always lurks in the shadows.

The weight of something happening will forever linger. Even as Zay kisses me, even as Carter hugs my leg and Peter pulls my forehead to his. The ache that this isn't over will forever simmer and I don't think I'll ever be free.

Epilogue - Zay

The sand is cool beneath my toes, the ocean breeze billowing wisps of my hair. Such a beautiful evening for festivities.

It took us a while, but our family was finally happy. We didn't live in fear. We didn't dwell. We didn't look anywhere but right here.

"You nervous?" I ask Palmer as we hold hands, walking behind the girls and my sons.

Palmer breathes, placing a hand on her stomach; the white lace clinging to her body. "Extremely."

Chuckling, I glance up as Slade wipes sweat from his brow at the end of the aisle wearing a gray suit and a white shirt beaded with sweat. Peter and Riggs stand behind him, both in white shirts and matching gray pants. "Y'know, when I married Adam, I had the worst panic attack ever. I swear, it felt like my heart was beating so hard it would've flopped out of my chest. But when I saw him smiling at me, I knew it would be okay."

Guffawing, she looks over at me as we slowly walk toward the altar, Slade's entire face lighting up by her presence. "You don't even know what happened to him, how could you say everything would be okay when he's the reason for everything that happened two years ago."

Lifting a shoulder, I swallow sharply, squeezing her hand. "Because I knew deep in my heart that he would always love me. Yeah, sure, shit got meddled and fucked, but his smile still kept me grounded. It probably doesn't ring true anymore. We lost ourselves because of the club. And I found myself again with Riggs." Flashing her a meek grin. "There are times I wonder if we never got mixed in with this crap—those feelings on my wedding day, seeing him in a tux at the altar, the way he shifted nervously like Slade is…" Drifting off, I inhale sharply and nudge her side. "Sunshine and rainbows came from that moment of my life and I wouldn't change it for anything. But you, Palmer, have a good egg. Slade is nothing but an amazing man."

She exhales again, smiling at me. "He is."

The way he cared for me and Jasper at the hospital, how he put our needs first before his. I owe him so much more than this life we're living. So much more.

"Now put that gorgeous smile on your face and let's get you hitched."

Giggling, we quicken our pace and stop in front of Slade. "Wow," he says, looking Palmer up and down.

"Banging, right." Waggling my eyebrows at her, I kiss her cheek and take her bouquet of roses.

Rosa giggles, holding Mina and Sara's hands as we stand behind Palmer, eagerly waiting for the nuptials.

It's been two years since Riggs walked back into my life. My heart shattered when we didn't hear from him. Peter called the Captain and all we got as an answer was, "he wasn't at the scene." I didn't know what to believe, and yet, the only thing that crossed my mind was death.

I don't know where Adam is. There haven't been clues or signs that he knows where we are. But I'd be lying if I said I didn't want him to come home. I've loved him since I was twenty years old. Gave him my everything. He shattered it, crushed it like it never meant anything. But I know Adam, he had no choice. If he did, he wouldn't have hurt us.

Riggs winks at me, keeping his gaze locked on mine as Slade and Palmer say their vows. He's been wanting to marry me for years—asking me to be his wife on his thirtieth birthday. But with all the chaos going on, we never had the chance to do it.

I love you, he mouths as Jasper tugs on his hand.

Scrunching my nose, my gaze finds Peter smiling at his girls. He's changed drastically over the years. Became the man he always had the potential to become if it weren't for the Snakes tainting him.

He is kind, loyal, and cares more for these children than he cares for himself.

"Do you, Palmer, take this man to be your lawfully wedded husband. To have and to hold until death parts you?"

Palmer smiles when Sara squeals, wiping an escaping tear. "I do."

"Do you, Slade, take this woman to be your—"

"Yes, I do," Slade interrupts the officiant, eyes bouncing all over his new wife's beauty.

The officiant laughs, nods and closes his book. "Well, what are you waiting for? Kiss your bride."

Slade's big mitts cradle Palmer's face, kissing her fervently and dipping her as we clap. Peter whistles, making the kids cheer and scream.

All the while, Riggs finds my teary-eyed gaze again and smiles largely.

I wouldn't put it past him to ambush this wedding and make it a two-for-one, but this isn't our day. Someday soon, maybe. To be called his wife would mean the world to me, raising our kids the right way in the eyes of God.

But things happen for a reason.

Peter chuckles, rounding up the kids. "C'mon, I think I hear a pool with your names on it. What do you say?"

Rosa and Carter cheer, running up the sand toward the beach house we rented a couple of months ago. Being in Sanction Falls was beautiful and all—they know how much I love the snow— but I missed the warmth of California with my toes in the sand. I missed home.

Riggs and Peter found us a rental in Mexico and we traveled under the radar all the way here. And truthfully, I don't think I ever want to leave.

Slade lifts Palmer, making her laugh. "We'll be MIA for a few hours," he says, jogging through the sand with her in his arms.

"Minutes," she calls out, cackling as they head toward the house.

"Let's go swimming," I say, rubbing my hands together. "Then we'll head to that yummy restaurant for dinner."

Riggs takes my hand as I follow Peter to our pool, tugging me back. "We'll meet up in a sec."

Peter winks, taking Jasper from Riggs and lifting him onto his shoulders, following the rest of the kids up the path. I'm ashamed to admit that during the four months of seclusion, Peter came into my room a time or two when the baby woke up. Half the time, he'd stay in bed with me as I breastfed. He tried to help the best he could and pulled a couple of all-nighters so I could sleep. But two months in, after remaining in my room, his fingers found their way between my legs and I let him finger-fuck me until I saw stars. I never told Riggs, I don't think I ever will.

Riggs lifts me and my legs naturally wrap around his waist. "Think it's about time I make you my wife, isn't it?"

Capturing his lips before the words can register, I pause, pulling my head back. "What?"

"You think I would propose to you and not make you mine?"

Holding his face. "I'm already yours, Riggsy."

He brushes his nose against mine, biting at the air. "You're not *my wife*. Your only title."

He sets me down and threads his fingers through mine. Those butterflies I had while walking down the aisle toward Adam is incomparable to this. I loved him for as long as I can remember, but truthfully, I wasn't *in love* with him the way I am with Riggs. I understand that now. I see it. If Adam was my soulmate, I would have fought harder to stay away from Peter. I would have fought harder to ignore my feelings for Riggs. If I loved Adam, I wouldn't be happily crying like a baby about to marry this giant tattooed man.

"You don't want witnesses? It's something you have—"

"No, I want it just my woman and me. Just us," Riggs interrupts the officiant, smiling down at me. "You okay with that, sunshine?"

Nodding, he wipes the tears from my cheeks and smiles, a twinkle in his eyes. "Let's do this," I say, bobbing with excitement.

Barely registering anything being said, my cheeks hurt from smiling, looking up at this man I wholeheartedly hated when we first met. How he manhandled me onto his bike and barked his orders at me.

But he's changed, so much.

He's a father.

A lover.

My best friend.

He's the man I sought out and didn't even know it.

"I do," he says, kissing my knuckles. "I'll always."

"By the power vested in me, I now pronounce you husband and wife. You may kiss your bride," the officiant says, nodding his head with a smile. "Enjoy your lives. Live in the moment, for you never know what could be waiting at the end of the path."

Riggs grabs my face and kisses me, sweeping his tongue in my mouth. A moment I should be screaming in excitement about has me in shock.

What did he mean?

Why did he say that?

The officiant walks off, leaving Riggs and me alone on the beach; the sound of the waves crashing onto shore taking hold of me as our lips part and those big blue eyes riddled with happy tears look down at me.

"I love you, baby," he says, tracing my lips with his thumb.

"What—why would he say that?" My voice cracks, looking behind me as the officiant shrinks in the distance.

"It's part of the vows." Riggs grunts, lifting me in his arms and walking us toward the water. "Get out of your head."

"How can I not be stuck there after everything—"

"Baby." He sets me down, kissing me softly. "We're safe, right? We just got freaking married. No dwelling. Remember what we said, Mrs. Donnelly? We won't dwell on the past. We'll only move forward. No more Ghost, no more Daddy, no more fucking Dorian or Adam. Just us, remember?"

The words wrap around me like one of his warm hugs, holding me tightly in safety.

"I remember."

His lips press on my forehead, inhaling me slightly. "Then get outta your head."

Closing my eyes, my palms press against his exposed chest, the fabric of the cotton button-down wet to the touch from sweat.

I've been on edge for over two years.

Waiting.

Watching.

Wondering when the hell the end will come.

But I think it's over.

It's finally over and I'm still thinking about the impending doom…on my wedding day.

My love surprised me with the most romantic setting. The wedding I wanted in the first place. Just me and my husband with our toes in the sand.

He gave me everything and I'm thinking of the bad.

Shaking off the worry, a smile crests my lips. "Mrs. Donnelly, huh?"

He beams, a deep gruff chuckle seeping from his delicious mouth. "Liked the sound of that. Finally claiming what's been mine for almost ten years."

"Ten years? Has it been that long?"

Lifting me, he marches through the sand to the water's edge as his lips bathe my neck in licks and kisses. "You have no idea how long I've wanted to call you my wife. My everything. My fucking person."

He nips my neck, growling softly. "I fucked-up with you, leaving you to the wrath of my brothers. But not anymore. No, baby. I should've taken you away from this life when we met. Just you and me and blueberry pancakes."

Groaning, I drop my head back. "I am so tired of blueberry pancakes."

Laughing, he pulls me tight to him, bringing me to a large rock poking out of the water. I know exactly what we're about to do, exactly what we've done time and time again for some louder sex.

I grind my pussy into him, feeling his erection grow by the second. "Are you going to make me scream, husband?"

He growls, biting down on my neck and leaving his mark as he walks through the water, waves splashing into us. He stops when he gets waist-deep and places me on the rock. "I'm going to fuck my wife out in the open. Me and you showing the world what fallen angels do."

His tongue drags up my neck, swooping down again before I tug his face to mine and dip my tongue in his mouth, savoring his sweetness.

He climbs onto the rock, adjusting me under him as I rip open his shirt, revealing that beastly form. Curves and edges, rippling muscles. Beauty.

My nails dig into his back, making him growl. "Fuck, sunshine. You really want me to punish you, don't you?"

Giggling, I take his bottom lip between my teeth and tug. "I love it when you hurt me."

Yelping when he turns me onto my stomach, lifting me onto my hands and knees, that purr escapes him. "Tell me, baby. How badly do you want it?"

Moaning as the waves crash onto the rock and spray us in mist. "I'm dripping, Riggsy."

His fingers tug my panties to the side, easing his fingers inside me and pumping quickly. "I'm gonna fill you with my cum. As deep as I can go."

Moaning loudly, I throw my head back and cry out.

"You miss it, don't you?" he says in my ear, sliding his fingers out of me and licking them clean. "Fuck, you taste so fucking good."

"Yes, yes, I miss it."

He chuckles, releasing that monster from its confines; the head of his cock teasing my entrance. "You miss my cum, baby?"

"Yes."

Slowly, the head of his cock dips in and my entire body vibrates in response. "If I come inside you, I'm going to make you pregnant."

"Do it." I moan, my fingers gripping the rock. "Oh, baby, give me all of it. Give it to me forever and always."

His moans and grunts bounce off the horizon, thumping quickly and roughly. He slaps my ass, slowly easing out of me and ramming back in making me squeal. "Mine. My fucking wife."

He roars, his chest flattening against my back. "Baby, oh, fuck."

My body tingles like a heatwave coursing through me, sizzling the surface of my skin. My orgasm plummets, soaring from the top of my head to the tips of my toes, crying out his name.

Over.

And over.

He stills, pumping me with his cum, thrusting until I milk every last drop. "My wife," his hoarse, husky voice drawls.

Our heavy breaths mix with crashing waves, bodies slick with sweat.

"I can't believe you surprised me with an impromptu wedding," I say as he kisses my neck, licking up to my mouth and slipping his tongue inside.

"It was Peter's idea."

Chuckling, he pulls out of me and sits back on his heels, slapping my ass once more before I turn over and lean back on my hands.

"Y'know, I wouldn't have cared if you married me or not. You already gave me your heart, I think that's enough."

Yanking me onto his lap, he kissed my jaw, sighing. "Baby, I've given you my soul and it's still not enough. I owe you a better life than the one we're living. Making you my wife is just the tip of the iceberg."

"Oh, really? What else did you have in mind?" My arms wrap around him as he lifts us, and jumps into the water, moving us deeper.

My giggles echo across the horizon, soaking into the setting sun. His lips mark my neck, suckling until they meet my lips and dive deep, kissing me like hell is freezing over.

"This is our home. Our babies with their little toes in the sand. You, sun-kissed and breathtaking. Our family together. Us, baby. Just us."

My hazel eyes bounce around his face, taking in the words leaving his succulent lips. *This is our home.* "What do you mean? This…"

"Peter, Slade, and I had a long talk the other night about the next steps. And we think the next steps are staying as far away from anything that reminds us of the Snakes. Our only reminders are the scars and ink in our skin." He's up to his shoulders, the water calmer this deep. "Our sons don't need a reminder of that life. Our nieces don't need the reminder that I killed their mother. All those kids need is *this.*"

He fans his arms out and spins us, making me laugh again. "This clear water, this life of living off the grid. Love. All the love we can give, baby."

He's right.

I hate it when he's right because all I want to do is sit on his face until the angels call me home.

"Paradise."

A smile graces his face. "New beginnings."

Our lips meet again and he floats back with me beside him, hand in hand. Our new beginning is better than the last, and this time I know for certain there are only smiles at the end of the rainbow.

Tugging Riggs closer, he goes under and surfaces beside me with the flip of his hair. "I love you."

"Forever," I whisper.

Wrapping my arms around his neck as we watch the sunset, my head leaning on his. The orange and pink hues cast such beauty around us, such warmth and promise. "Riggsy?"

"Mmm?"

Squeezing him tighter, I smile. "It's the flip side, isn't it?"

"Yeah, baby. We finally made it."

And that we did.

Adam

The *thunk-drag* of the cane fills the cabin as I walk to the patio door. With a grunt, I lean against the doorframe and stare out at the water. It's still, like a mirror reflecting the setting sun. This used to be home. All the smiles, laughter. All the love of my family. My brothers. My son. My Zay.

Now it's empty.

A quiet hell.

For two years, I've locked myself in here, hidden from the reality of the world, until I explode.

I put this on myself. I ruined everything because I was tired of being the runt of the litter. Proved all of them wrong. But at what cost?

I lost my wife, my kids.

I lost everything.

Hissing at the throbbing in my knee, I walk toward the kitchen and throw the fridge door open. Fridge is full of food that's rotting away.

I don't want to eat. I just want to die.

Every day, I wish Riggs would have killed me after he put a bullet in Daddy's head.

Why didn't he fucking kill me?

Taking a beer, I uncap it with my teeth and spit the cap out, draining half the beer before I close my eyes and drop my head back.

Regret has fueled me every waking hour of every single day over the years. I ruined the best thing that ever happened to me. I brought her into this life, let my brothers ruin her, and let her believe she was worthless, all because of the power.

I fucking *loved* the power.

The taste of it.

The smell.

The feeling it gave me.

I loved it and look at me now. Alone and broken.

So fucking broken.

Guzzling the beer, I drop the bottle with the rest in the sink and grunt as I make my way back to the couch. Eventually, death will come to me and I can't fucking wait. I look worse for wear. Bags under my eyes, ribs poking out, and hair that hasn't been cut in five years.

With a yelp, I sit down, lifting my leg onto the coffee table, and stare at the family portrait above the mantle. The four of us laughing by the water. My beauty is smiling at me.

I wish I could have kissed her one last time before everything happened. One more kiss and she'd know how much she means to me.

One more kiss to tell her I'm sorry.

The front door opens, and a sigh leaves the only person who checks up on me anymore.

Lip drops his keys on the dining table and makes his way over, holding a takeout bag to me. "Evening, brother," he says. That sourness in his tone makes me close my eyes.

"You don't have to keep coming here. I'm fine."

"You're one day away from offing yourself, Adam. As much as everyone hates you, I can't have that on my conscience. Now eat." He pushes the bag to my chest as a second set of footfalls comes into the cabin.

Judas slowly sits on the opposite side of the couch, sniffling as he lights a cigarette. "You got what was coming to you, brother. But living like this isn't right."

"Why not?" I scoff, pushing the bag away from me and hissing as I move my leg off the table. "I listened to Daddy thinking it would do me good, and look at what it gave me? I ruined my family, men want to kill me, and the birth of my son—"

Lip shakes his head, dropping the food on the coffee table, and leaves, slamming the door behind him. He hates what I did more so than everyone. Judas understands, Skeet agrees, and Dillon doesn't know what to say.

But Lip hates seeing the only people he knows as family gone.

Judas looks behind him, leaning forward. "Adam, I know where they are."

Laughing, I lean my head back and run five fingers through my long hair. "Sanction Falls, I know."

He shakes his head, scooting closer. "They abandoned that place a few months back. They're out in Mexico." He takes his phone out, showing me a picture of Zay and my sons. Her hair is so much lighter, her smile so much brighter, and her body so curvy, my eyes well with tears. She's happy, so happy.

Zooming in, I laugh softly at the baby running in front of her, Carter not too far behind. The baby is perfect, my son. My boy. God, he looks so much like Zay. Down to her smile.

"How? Who took this?"

Judas takes his phone back. "Daddy Donnelly made a lot of enemies and they want revenge. This picture was their warning to the club."

My heart seizes, breath lodges with it. "What the fuck does that mean?"

Judas rises, pointing at the food. "It means it's time for you to seek salvation for all the wrong you did. Maybe then, your family will give you the redemption you seek."

With that, he leaves, the sound of the bikes coming to life and ringing in my ears.

My family is in danger.

My kids. My Zaynab. My brothers.

How in the fuck will they ever trust me to save them?

Better yet, how the hell am I going to find them and beg them to believe me?

About the Author

Alyssa Milani is a multi-award-winning Canadian author who studied at Concordia University obtaining a Major in Creative Writing and a Minor in English Literature. She independently published her first novel in 2014 of all the works that she wrote during her years at university. She now has twenty-four independently published novels under her belt, with many more to come. She lives with her husband and their children on the outskirts of Montreal.

If you'd like to learn more about Alyssa Milani and all her endeavors, follow her on Instagram @alyssamilani

You can connect with me on:

🌐 https://alyssamilaniwrites.etsy.com

f https://www.facebook.com/Alyssa21Milani

🔗 https://www.instagram.com/alyssamilani

Subscribe to my newsletter:

✉ https://authoralyssamilani.substack.com

Also by Alyssa Milani

What Is and What Once Was (an anthology)
Lylie
A Truth Be Told Arcane
The Decision (novella)
Jayme
Asylum Of Diction (an anthology)
Dire Road
Him & I (parts 1 – 3)
Was This The End? (A.M. Pickford)
Labeled: Miss Popular
Breaking Through To You (duet)
Horrorscope Volume 4 (anthology) (short story contribution)
Tell Me You Do (novella)
The Stowaway Series (Forbidden, Salvation, Redemption)
As Far As We Knew (novella)
Meeting You
Until Adleigh
Strangest Fiction Volume 2 (anthology) (short story contribution)
Deception
Seeking Me Through You